BLOOD IN THE DUST

BLOOD IN THE DUST

A HUNTER BUCHANON BLACK HILLS WESTERN

WILLIAM W.
JOHNSTONE
AND J.A. JOHNSTONE

PINNACLE BOOKS
Kensington Publishing Corp.

www.kensingtonbooks.com

PINNACLE BOOKS are published by

Kensington Publishing Corp.
119 West 40th Street
New York, NY 10018

PUBLISHER'S NOTE
Following the death of William W. Johnstone, the Johnstone family is working with a carefully selected writer to organize and complete Mr. Johnstone's outlines and many unfinished manuscripts to create additional novels in all of his series like The Last Gunfighter, Mountain Man, and Eagles, among others. This novel was inspired by Mr. Johnstone's superb storytelling.

ISBN-13: 978-0-7860-4723-9
ISBN-10: 0-7860-4723-2

First Pinnacle paperback printing: January 2021

10 9 8 7 6 5 4 3 2 1

Printed in the United States of America

Electronic edition:

ISBN-13: 978-0-7860-4724-6 (e-book)
ISBN-10: 0-7860-4724-0 (e-book)

CHAPTER 1

"That coyote makes me nervous," said shotgun messenger Charley Anders.

"You mean Bobby Lee?" asked Hunter Buchanon as he handled the reins of the rocking and clattering Cheyenne & Black Hills Stage, sitting on the hard, wooden seat to Anders's left.

He spoke through the neckerchief he'd drawn up over his nose and mouth to keep out at least some of the infernal dust kicked up by the six-horse hitch.

"Yeah, yeah—Bobby Lee. He's the only coyote aboard this heap and that there is a thing I never thought I'd hear myself utter if I lived to be a hundred years old!"

Anders slapped his thigh and roared through his own pulled-up neckerchief.

"No need to be nervous, Charley," Hunter said. "Bobby Lee ain't dangerous. In fact, he's right polite." Buchanon leaned close to the old shotgun messenger beside him and said with feigned menace, "As long as you're polite to Bobby Lee, that is."

He grinned and nudged the shotgun man with his elbow.

"If you mean by 'polite' give him a chunk of jerky every

time he demands one, he can go to hell!" Anders glanced uneasily over his left shoulder at Bobby Lee sitting on the coach roof just above and between him and Buchanon. "Hell, he demands jerky all the damn time! If you don't give him some, he shows you his teeth!"

As if the fawn-gray coyote had understood the conversation, Bobby Lee lowered his head and pressed his cold snout to Anders's left ear, nudging up the man's cream sombrero.

"See there?" Anders cried. Leaning forward in his seat and regarding the coyote dubiously, the shotgun messenger said, "I ain't givin' you no more jerky, Bobby Lee, an' that's that! If I give you any more jerky, I won't have none left for my ownself an' we still got another half hour's ride into Tigerville! I gotta keep somethin' in my stomach or I get the fantods!"

Hunter chuckled as he glanced over his right shoulder at Bobby Lee pointing his long snout in the general direction of the shirt pocket in which he knew Anders kept his jerky. The coyote's triangle ears were pricked straight up.

Hunter gave the coyote a quick pat on the head. "Bobby Lee understands—don't you, Bobby Lee? He thinks you're bein' right selfish—not to mention womanish about your *fantods*—but he understands."

Hunter chuckled and turned his head forward to gaze out over the horses' bobbing heads.

As he did, Bobby Lee subtly raised his bristling lips to show the ends of his fine, white teeth to Anders.

"See there? He just did it again!" Charley cried, pointing at Bobby Lee.

When Hunter turned to the coyote he'd raised from a pup, after the little tyke's mother had been killed by hunters, Bobby Lee quickly closed his lips over his teeth. He turned to his master and fashioned a cock-headed, doe-eyed look of innocence, as though he had no idea why this cork-headed fool was slandering him so unjustly.

"Ah, hell, you're imagining things, Charley," Hunter scolded the man. "You an' your fantods an' makin' things up. You should be ashamed of yourself!"

"He did—I swear!"

A woman's sonorous, somewhat sarcastic voice cut through Anders's complaint. "Excuse me, gentlemen! Excuse me! Do you mind if I interrupt your eminently important and impressively articulate conversation?"

The plea had come from below and on Buchanon's side of the stage. He glanced over his left shoulder to see one of his and Anders's two passengers poking her head out of the coach's left-side window. Blinking against the billowing dust, Miss Laura Meyers gazed beseechingly up toward the driver's box. "I'd like to request a nature stop if you would, please?"

Hunter and Charley Anders shared a weary look. Miss Meyers, who'd boarded the stage in Cheyenne a few days ago, was from the East by way of Denver. Now, Hunter had known plenty of Eastern folks who were not royal pains in the backside. Miss Meyers was not one of them.

She was grossly ill-prepared for travel in the West. She'd not only not realized that the trip between Cheyenne and Tigerville in the Dakota Territory took a few days, she'd not realized that stagecoach travel was a far cry from the more comfortable-style coach and buggy and train travel to which she'd become accustomed back east of the Mississippi.

Here there was dust. And heat. The stench of male

sweat and said male's "infernal and ubiquitous tobacco use." (Hunter didn't know what "ubiquitous" meant but he'd been able to tell by the woman's tone that it wasn't complimentary. At least, not in the way she had used it.)

Also, the trail up from Cheyenne into the Black Hills was not as comfortable as, say, a ride in an open chaise across a grassy Eastern meadow on a balmy Sunday afternoon in May. Out here, there were steep hills, narrow canyons, perilous river crossings, the heavy alkali mire along Indian Creek, and, once you were in the Hills themselves, twisting, winding trails with enough chuck holes and washouts to keep the Concord rocking on its leather thoroughbraces until you thought you must have eaten flying fish for breakfast.

Several times over the past two days, Miss Meyers had heralded the need for Hunter to stop the coach so she could bound out of it in a swirl of skirts and petticoats and hurl herself into the bushes to air her paunch.

So far, they hadn't been accosted by owlhoots. They'd even made it through the dangerous country around the Robbers' Roost Relay Station without having a single bullet hurled at them from one of the many haystack bluffs in that area. Nor an arrow, for that matter.

Indians—primarily Red Cloud's Sioux, understandably miffed by the treaty the government had broken to allow gold-seeking settlers into the Black Hills—had been a problem on nearly every run Hunter had been on in the past year. He'd started driving for the stage company after his family's ranch had been burned by a rival rancher and the man's business partner, his two brothers murdered, his father, old Angus, seriously wounded.

He wanted to say as much to the lady—a pretty one, at that—staring up at him now from the coach's left-side window, but he knew she'd have none of it. She was a fish out of water here, and in dire straits. He could see it in her eyes. She was not only road-weary but world-weary, as well.

Though they'd left the Ten Mile Ranch Station only twenty minutes ago, after a fifteen-minute break, and would arrive in Tigerville after only another ten miles, she needed to stop.

"Hold on, ma'am—I'll pull these cayuses to a stop at the bottom of the next hill!"

She blinked in disgust and pulled her head back into the coach.

"Thank you, Mister Buchanon!" Charley Anders called with an ironic mix of mockery and chiding.

"Now, Charley," Hunter admonished his partner as the six horses pulled the coach up and over a low pass and then started down the other side, sun-dappled lodgepole pines jutting close along both sides of the trail. "She's new to these parts. I reckon you'd have a helluva time back East your ownself. Hell, even in the newly citified Denver!"

"Yeah, well, I wouldn't go back East. Not after seein' the kind of haughty folks they make back thataway!" Charley drew his neckerchief down, turned to Hunter, and grinned, showing a more-or-less complete set of tobacco-rimmed teeth ensconced in a grizzled, gray-brown beard damp with sweat. "She's hard to listen to, but she is easy on the eyes, ain't she?"

They'd gained the bottom of the hill now, and Hunter was hauling back on the ribbons. "I wouldn't know, Charley. I only look at one woman. You know that."

"Pshaw! You can't tell me you ain't admired how that purty eastern princess fills out her natty travelin' frocks! You wouldn't be a man if you didn't!"

"I got eyes for only one woman, Charley," Hunter insisted. Now that the mules had stopped, the dust swirling over them as it caught up to the coach from behind, Hunter set the brake. "You know that."

"Yeah, well, sounds to me like it's time for you to start lookin' around for another gal. Sounds to me like you an' Annabelle Ludlow are kaput. Through. End-of-story." Charley narrowed one eye in cold castigation at his younger friend. "And you got only one man to blame for that—yourself!"

Gritting his teeth, Charley removed his dusty sombrero and smacked it several times across Hunter's stout right shoulder. "Gall-blamed, lame-brained, cork-headed fool! How could you let her get away?"

Hunter had asked himself that question many times over the past few months, but he didn't want to think about it now. Thinking about Annabelle made him feel frustrated as all get-out, and he had to keep his head clear. You didn't drive a six-horse hitch through rugged terrain haunted by desperadoes and Sioux warriors with a brain gummed up by lovelorn goo.

He climbed down from the driver's boot and saw that Miss Meyers was trying to open the Concord's left-side door from inside. She was grunting with the effort, her fine jaws set hard beneath the brim of her stylish but somewhat outlandish eastern-style velvet picture hat trimmed with faux flowers and berries.

"I'll help you there, ma'am."

She looked at him through the window in the door—

a despondent look if he had ever seen one. She was, however, a looker. He couldn't deny that even if he had denied noticing to Charley. He felt a sharp pang of guilt every time he looked at this woman and felt . . . well, like a man shouldn't feel when he was in love with another gal.

"It's stuck," she said, her voice toneless with exhaustion.

"I apologize." Hunter plucked a small pine stick from the crack between the door and the stagecoach wall. "A twig got stuck in it somehow, fouled the latch. I do apologize, ma'am. How you doing? Not so well, I reckon . . ."

As Hunter opened the door, she made a face and waved her gloved hand at the billowing dust and tobacco smoke. "The smoke and dust are absolutely atrocious. Not to mention the wretched smell of my unwashed fellow traveler and his who-hit-John, as he so colorfully calls the poison he consumes as though it were water!"

Hunter helped the woman out. He glanced into the carriage to see the grinning countenance of his only other passenger—the Chicago farm implement drummer, Wilfred Farley. The diminutive, craggy-faced man with one broken front tooth and clad in a cheap checked suit— which seemed the requisite uniform of all raggedy-heeled traveling salesmen everywhere—raised an unlabeled, flat, clear bottle half-filled with a milky brown liquid in salute to his destaging fellow passenger's derriere, and took a pull.

Hunter gave the man a reproving look, then turned to the woman, removing his hat and holding it over his broad chest. "Ma'am, let me apolo—"

"Will you please stop apologizing, Mister Buchanon?

I'm sorry to say your apologies are beginning to ring a little hollow at this late date. My God, what a torturous contraption!" She looked at the coach's rear wheel and for a second, Hunter thought she was going to give it a kick with one of her delicate, gold-buckled, high-heeled ankle boots.

She thought about it for a couple of seconds, then satisfied herself with a chortling wail of raw anger and tipped her head back to stare up at the tall, blond-haired, blue-eyed jehu hulking before her. "And must you continue to call me ma'am?"

"Uh . . . uh . . ."

"How old are you?"

"Twenty-seven, ma'a . . . er, I mean, Miss Meyers." At least, he hoped that was the moniker she'd been looking for. If not, he might end up with a swift kick to one of his shins, and in her state of mind, even being such a light albeit curvy little thing, he didn't doubt she could do some damage.

"Now, see—I'm younger than you are. Not by much, maybe, but I am young enough that you can feel free to call me Miss. *Miss Meyers.* Not ma'am. For God's sake, don't add insult to injury, Mister Buchanon!"

"I'm sorry, Miss Meyers, it's just that you seemed older . . . somehow." *Wrong thing to say, you cork-headed fool!* Backing water frantically, Hunter said, "I just meant you *acted* older! You know—more mature! I didn't mean you *looked* older!"

He'd said those wheedling words to her slender back as, fists tightly balled at her sides, she went stomping off into the brush and rocks that littered the base of the ridge wall on the west side of the stage road.

"Don't wander too far, ma'am . . . I mean, Miss Meyers!" he called. "It's easy to get turned around out here!"

But she was already gone.

CHAPTER 2

Hunter stared after the pretty, angry woman.

Something nudged his right arm. He looked down to see Wilfred Farley offering his bottle to him, and grinning, his thin, chapped upper lip peeled back from that crooked, broken tooth.

"No, thanks. If that's the stuff you bought at the Robbers' Roost Station, it'll blind both of us."

"Pshaw!" Farley took another deep pull. "Damn good stuff, and I see just fine."

"That's how Hoyle Gullickson lost his top knot." Charley Anders was climbing heavily down from the driver's boot, his sawed-off, double-barrel shotgun hanging from a lanyard down his back.

"What?" Farley asked. "Drinkin' his own skull pop?"

"No—brewin' it." Anders stepped off the front wheel and turned to face Hunter and the pie-eyed Chicago drummer. "He sold it to the Sioux. Several went blind, and the others came back and scalped him."

Farley looked at the bottle in his hand as though it

had suddenly transformed into a rattlesnake. "You don't say . . . ?"

Hunter snorted softly. He knew the story wasn't true. Hoyle Gullickson had lost his top knot when he'd been out cutting wood one winter and was set upon by four braves who'd wanted whiskey.

Gullickson had refused to sell to them because he'd already done time in the federal pen for selling his rotgut to Indians, and he wasn't about to risk returning to that wretched place. Incensed, the braves scalped him, so now he wore the awful knotted scars in a broad, grisly swath over the top of his head, making any and all around him wince whenever he removed his hat, which he loved to do just to gauge the reactions and turn stomachs.

Charley Anders, however, preferred his tall-tale version, which he related often and usually at night around some stage station's potbellied stove to wide-eyed pilgrims in his and Hunter's charge.

Hunter glared at the drummer. "I thought I told you not to smoke around that woman, Farley. And to stay halfways sober."

"Kills the time," Farley said with a shrug, raising a loosely rolled, wheat-paper quirley to his mouth and leveling a defiant stare at Buchanon. "I offered to share my panther juice with her, but she turned her nose up. That offended me. So I got the makings out and rolled a smoke."

He pointed his bottle toward where the woman had disappeared in the rocks and brush. "That pretty little bitch can go straight to hell."

"He's got a point, pard," Charley said, reaching through

the stage window. "Give me a pull off that, Farley. I could use a little somethin' to cut the dust."

"I thought you said it'd blind a fella!" Farley objected sarcastically.

Anders jerked the bottle out of the drummer's hand and swiped the lip across his grimy hickory shirt. "I been drinkin' the rotgut so long I'm immune to blindness by now." He stepped back and started to take a pull from the bottle. As he did, a rabbit poked its head out from between two shrubs roughly ten feet off the trail.

Hunter, who'd been looking around cautiously, wary of a holdup and also starting to get a little worried about the woman, had just seen the gray cottontail pull its head back into the shrubs. Bobby Lee gave a mewling yip of coyote excitement, leaped from the roof of the coach onto Charley Anders's right shoulder to the ground.

Charley jerked back with a startled grunt, dropping the bottle.

Bobby Lee plunged into the shrubs between two boulders, then shot up the ridge, hot on the heels of the streaking rabbit, the rabbit and the coyote darting around the columnar pines.

"Damn that vermin!" Charley wailed, clutching his right shoulder with his left hand. "He like to have dislocated my arm! What gall—using me as his damn stepping stool! Has he no respect?"

Hunter snorted a laugh. "That's what you get for being so tight with your jerky, Charley."

"The bottle! The bottle!" wailed Wilfred Farley, pointing at the bottle lying on the ground between Anders and Buchanon. "Good Lord, you're spillin' good whiskey!"

Hunter crouched to pick up the bottle. There was still an inch or two of rotgut remaining. Not for long.

Grinning at Farley, Hunter turned the bottle upside down. The whiskey dribbled out of the mouth to which dirt and pine needles clung. The liquid plopped hollowly onto the ground.

Farley was flabbergasted. "Good lord, man! Are you *mad*?"

"Jehu's rules, Farley." Hunter tossed the bottle high over the coach and into the trees and rocks on the other side. "No drinkin' aboard the coach."

"You're sweet on that gal!" Farley shook his head in disbelief. "You must like a gal who runs you into the ground with every look and word. Me—I got some self-respect. No purty skirt's gonna push Wilfred Farley around!"

"Speakin' of purty skirts," Anders said, staring off toward where the woman had disappeared. "What in the hell's she doin' out there—knittin' an afghan?"

Hunter glanced around, making sure no would-be highwaymen were near. He didn't like standing still here on the trail like this, making easy targets. It was always best to keep moving between relay stations, as a moving target was always harder to attack than one standing still in the middle of the trail with good cover all around for would-be attackers.

Hunter stepped forward and called, "Miss Meyers? You all right?"

No response.

"We'd best get movin', Miss Meyers!"

Hunter took another couple of steps forward, then stopped again, concern growing in him. "Miss Meyers?"

He didn't want to call too loudly and risk alerting anyone in the area to their position. He and Anders were carrying only two passengers, but aboard the stage they had ten thousand dollars in payroll money, which they were hauling to one of the many mines above Tigerville.

Hunter glanced back at Anders, scowling his frustration. Anders shrugged and shook his head.

"I best look for her," Hunter said. "Charley, stay with the stage. Keep a sharp eye out. I don't like sitting out here like a Thanksgiving turkey on the dining room table."

"You an' me both, pard," Charley said behind Buchanon, as Hunter stepped off the trail and walked into the rocks and brush littering the base of the western ridge.

Hunter pushed through the brush, wended his way around rocks. "Miss Meyers? Time to hit the road, Miss Meyers!"

He saw a deer path carved through the brush. It rose up a low shoulder of the ridge. Hunter followed it, frowning down at the ground, noting the sharp indentations of the heels of a lady's ankle boots.

As the path turned around a large fir tree, the indentations of the lady's heels became scuffed and scraped. Amidst the scuff marks was a faint print of a man's boot.

Instantly, Buchanon's hand closed around the pearl grips of the silver-chased LeMat secured high on his right hip in a gray buckskin holster worn to the texture of doeskin. He clicked the hammer of the main, .44-caliber barrel back and, his heartbeat increasing, the skin under his shirt collar prickling, he continued following the scuffed trail.

The prints led up and over the rise then down the other side, through tree shadows and sunlight. Somewhere ahead and to Hunter's right, a squirrel was chittering angrily. That was the only sound.

Hunter continued forward for another fifty feet before he stopped suddenly.

Ahead, a man crouched between two aspens. He seemed to be moving in place, making jerking movements. He was also talking in a heated but hushed tone.

Hunter could see a second man—or part of a second man—on his knees on the other side of one of the aspens. Hunter could see only the man's boot soles and the thick forward curve of his back clad in a blue wool shirt. This man, too, was making quick jerking movements.

He seemed to be holding something down.

Hunter stepped to his right, putting the left-most aspen between himself and the crouching man. He moved slowly forward, both aspens concealing his approach from both men before him. As he moved closer to their position, muffled cries blazed into the air around him.

Muffled female cries.

Hunter stepped behind a tree. He peered around its left side. From here, he had a clearer view of the two men and of Miss Meyers on the ground between them, partly obscured by tree roots humping up out of the forest duff.

The man on the right knelt by the woman's head, leaning down, holding her head against the ground with both of his hands pressed across her mouth. Miss Meyers was kicking her legs out wildly and flailing helplessly with her arms, making her skirts flop and exposing her pantaloon- and stocking-clad legs.

Thumping sounds rose as did the crackle of pine needles and dead leaves as she thrashed so desperately, her cries muffled by one of her assailant's hands. The kneeling man laughed through his teeth as he held the woman down, his brown-mustached face swollen and red.

The other man, tall and skinny with long black sideburns and a bushy black mustache, had pulled his pants down around his boots and was opening the fly of his longhandles, grinning down at the struggling woman.

"Hold her still, Bill. Hold her still. I'll be hanged if she ain't as fine a piece o' female flesh as I—"

Leaning forward, exposing the evidence of his craven lust, he grabbed Miss Meyers's ankles and thrust them down against the ground. Leaning farther forward, he slid his hands up her legs from inside her dress, a lusty grin blooming broadly across his long, ugly face with close-set, dark eyes set deep beneath shaggy, black brows.

The man clamped her legs down with his own and reached for her swinging arms, grabbing them, stopping them as he lowered his hips toward the woman's. He stopped abruptly, turning his head sharply to see Buchanon striding toward him.

The man's eyes widened in shock. "What the . . . *hey!*"

Hunter had returned the big LeMat to its holster and picked up a stout aspen branch roughly five feet long and about as big around as one of his muscular forearms—as broad as a cedar fencepost.

It made a solid thumping, cracking sound as he smashed it with all the force in his big hands and arms against the black-haired man's forehead. The branch broke roughly a foot and a half from the end. As the would-be rapist's head snapped sharply back, his eyes rolling up in their sockets, the end of the branch dropped with the man into the deep, narrow ravine behind him.

The other man cursed and leaped to his feet, his amber eyes as round as saucers and bright with fear.

"No!" he cried as he saw the stout branch swing toward him.

He tipped his head to one side, raising his arms as if to shield his face. Buchanon grunted as he thrust the branch down through the man's open hands to slam it against the man's left ear, blood instantly spewing from the smashed appendage.

"Ohhh!" the man cried as he hit the ground.

Buchanon stepped forward, raising the club again, rage a wild stallion inside him. Only the lowest of the lowest gut wagon dog did such a thing to a woman. This man would pay dearly—and he did as Hunter, straddling the man's flailing legs, smashed the club again and again against the man's head. After the third or fourth blow from the powerful arms and shoulders of the big, blond, blue-eyed man standing over him, the man's cries faded and his flailing arms and legs lay still upon the ground.

Hunter raised the club for one more blow but stopped when the crackle of guns rose from the direction of the stagecoach. His heart shuddered. He hammered the second rapist's head once more, then kicked the still body, the dead eyes staring up at Hunter in silent castigation, into the ravine.

It landed with a thump near the other carcass.

Hunter whipped around, crouching and drawing the LeMat from its holster, facing in the direction from which guns blasted angrily and men shouted.

Another man screamed.

Yet another man bellowed, "Ah, ya lowdown dirty devils . . . !"

Hunter recognized the bellowing voice. It was followed by the twin blasts of Charley Anders's sawed-off shotgun and one more scream.

Charley's scream.

CHAPTER 3

Hunter turned to Miss Meyers.

She was sitting up, dirt and leaves in her mussed hair, which had fallen from the roll she'd had it pinned into atop her head. Her hat was gone. Her dress was torn. So were her petticoat and pantaloons.

Her hands seemed to be idly trying to close the flesh-revealing tears in her clothes as she stared up in shock at the jehu, her face pale, her eyes round and glassy. She had a bruise high on her right cheek. In a few hours, that eye would likely be black. The lace-edged bodice of her spruce green traveling dress had been ripped wide open, exposing the bodice beneath it, which was also torn, revealing a good portion of one bosom and part of another.

The shooting continued, men shouting, hooves thudding.

"Stay here!"

Hunter bounded off through the forest, sprinting back in the direction of the stage road. He climbed the rise along the mountain's shoulder, ran down the other side.

Beyond the shrubs and rocks, he saw men milling around the stage on horseback, dust rising.

"Where the hell's the payroll money?" yelled one of the horseback riders. He was kneeling atop the coach. To his left sat the steel-banded strongbox, its lid open, bullet-torn padlock hanging askew. Envelopes of all shapes and sizes were strewn around the box; they were tugged this way and that by the breeze.

The highwaymen had blown the strongbox and had discovered that the mine payroll was not inside.

"It's not in the box?" asked one of the men on horse-back.

"No, it is not!"

The man on horseback—tall, bearded, and wearing a black hat—cursed and looked around wildly. "Where's Buchanon?"

"Who's Buchanon?" asked one of the others.

"The jehu!" returned the man in the black hat.

"Buchanon's right here!" Hunter said as he stepped onto the trail from between two rocks and a twisted cedar.

He'd seen Charley Anders and Wilfred Farley lying in bloody heaps on the ground beside the coach, so he was in no mood for discussion. He tripped the latch to engage the LeMat's stout, twelve-gauge shotgun barrel and blew a fist-size hole in the cheek of the man in the black hat before the man could level the carbine that he was holding barrel up from his right thigh.

The man gave a loud yip as the buckshot punched him back off the tail of his horse.

There were four or five others milling in a ragged circle around the Concord.

Hunter flicked the lever back to engage the LeMat's

main, .44-caliber barrel and shot the man on the coach next, then shot a rat-faced man with long red hair off the hip of his skitter-hopping cream. The redhead managed to trigger one shot, which spanged loudly off a boulder to Hunter's left, before his head slammed against the iron-shod rear wheel of the coach with a resounding thud.

He bounced off the wheel to the ground where he lay unmoving, his cracked skull leaking brains.

The sudden commotion had spooked the six-horse hitch, and now the team, whinnying shrilly and pitching, lunged forward, dragging the locked front wheel until the wood brake broke with a bark and fell to the ground. The team tore off up the trail, pulling the coach along behind it, dust blooming in its wake.

The coach didn't get far before it fishtailed suddenly. One of the front wheels must have hit a boulder or a tree leaning over the trail, for the contraption's front end lurched upward sharply. The coach crashed loudly onto its side. The terrified horses neighed shrilly and kept running, tearing free of the rigging and running, all six still har-nessed together, on down the trail.

Hunter was only partly aware of the fate of the coach, for he watched now as another killer booted his big Amer-ican horse through the coach's still-billowing dust toward him, leveling a Sharps carbine. Hunter calmly aimed and fired, but the man's large-caliber round burned across the nub of Hunter's left cheek, making him pull his own shot slightly wide.

Hunter's bullet plunged into the Sharps-wielding man's right arm clad in red and black calico.

The man dropped the rifle, grabbed the wounded limb

with his gloved left hand, and shouted, "Pull out! Pull out!" He'd lost his hat.

His bullet-shaped head was pink and bald as a baby's behind while a big walrus mustache mantled his mouth. He loosed a string of shrill curses as, neck-reining his horse around sharply, he cast a fiery glare over his right shoulder at Hunter. "You ain't seen the last of us, Buchanon!"

The three other surviving highwaymen swung their horses around to follow the other man, whom Buchanon had recognized as Ike Talon, head of a notorious bunch of thieving killers who'd been haunting the Black Hills in eastern Wyoming and western Dakota Territory for the past year. Hunter didn't know where the gang was from—he'd heard Utah—but when they'd arrived in the Black Hills, the route between Deadwood and Cheyenne had become fraught with even more peril than before—and that was saying something.

Hunter fired two more shots at the other three killers, but they triggered a fusillade from horseback at him as they fled, and he had to drop down behind the rocks to keep from getting his head blown off. As they galloped off up the trail to the south, Hunter ran out onto the trail and fired his last round at the trio—a wasted shot, for they were now out of short gun range.

Hunter lowered the smoking LeMat and turned toward where Charley Anders and Wilfred Farley lay in the dirt beside the coach's fresh wheel ruts.

Rage coursed through the big, blond-headed, blue-eyed rancher-turned-jehu, like poison in his veins. He dropped to a knee beside his old friend, a man he'd known for half of his life. Hunter's father, Old Angus, and Charley had been drinking buddies up in Tigerville, which was the town closest to the Buchanon Ranch.

When they'd had the ranch, that was. Now it was gone, burned to a crisp, Hunter's two brothers dead—courtesy of rival rancher and Confederate-hating Yankee, Graham Ludlow and his savage business partner, Max Chaney, not to mention the crooked county sheriff, Frank Stillwell. Chaney and Stillwell had died bloody for their sins, but Graham Ludlow was still alive, though a heart stroke had turned him into a shell of his former self. Now Hunter and his aging father, an ex-Confederate soldier who'd lost an arm in the War of Northern Aggression, lived in relative squalor in a seedy rooming house in Tigerville.

"Ah, Charley."

Hunter patted the dead man's shoulder. Charley and Old Angus had known each other during the war. Hunter had fought in the war, too, but not with his father. His hunting prowess, including his stealth and knife-fighting skills, had earned him a position in a small, elite group of guerrilla warriors who'd worked mostly at night, killing Union officers and blowing up trains and munitions dumps behind enemy lines.

Charley Anders had been shot three times—twice in the chest, once in his upper left thigh. He was a bloody mess. He'd lost his hat in the ambush, and his thin, gray-brown hair slid around his liver-spotted scalp in the breeze. His washed-out blue eyes glinted in the sunlight dancing down through the pines from a faultless sky as blue as fresh snowmelt.

"Crazy damn time to die. Such a nice day . . ."

Hunter looked at the drummer, Farley. The man lay belly-up, arms and legs spread as if offering himself, body and soul, to the gods above. The coat of his cheap checked suit was spread to each side, like the wings of some shabby angel.

A bullet had torn a hole in the drummer's shoulder. Another bullet had carved a puckered blue hole just above his right eye. Both eyes stared skyward, bright with reflected sunlight, opaque in death.

A soft yip sounded.

Hunter gave a start, reaching for the bowie knife sheathed over his left hip as he turned his head to look over his shoulder. He silently berated himself for not having reloaded the LeMat.

He knew a moment's relief as Bobby Lee moved out of the brush with the dead cottontail hanging limp in his jaws. The coyote dropped the half-eaten rabbit with a plop in the dirt and looked around, sniffing the air and narrowing his eyes. He walked tentatively up to Hunter.

"We lost a good friend, Bobby Lee."

The coyote walked slowly, mewling softly, over to Charley Anders. Bobby sniffed the man's left ear, turned to Hunter as though in question. The coyote lifted his long, clean snout and gave a mournful wail.

"My God."

The woman's voice had come from behind Hunter. He swung around to see her standing at the edge of the trail, looking as though she'd been dragged and rolled. She'd managed to arrange her torn dress some, so the rips and tears weren't quite so revealing, but only a little. Dirt and needles still clung to her hair and in the lace along her low-cut bodice.

That bruise under her eye was growing darker, swelling. She studied the two dead men in shock, then slid her gaze to Hunter. He pulled the LeMat from its holster, broke it open, and turned the wheel slowly as he shook out the five spent .44-caliber cartridges.

They plunked into the dirt at his feet, clinking together.

When he'd reloaded the five main chambers, he plucked a twelve-gauge wad from the back of his cartridge belt, replaced the spent wad with the new one, and snapped the frame closed.

The singular LeMat was as fine a piece of shooting equipment as Hunter had ever used. It was hand-engraved with tiny oak leaves and a breach lever in the shape of a miniature saber. His own initials, HB, had been carved into each side of the long, sleek main barrel by the man who'd gifted him with the gun after Hunter had saved the man's life from a sharpshooter's bullet.

That man had been none other than the Confederate General Pierre Gustave Toutant-Beauregard, or "Little Creole" as he'd been known though there'd been nothing little about G. T. Beauregard's fighting spirit.

The LeMat had been the general's own, designed by himself and fashioned on commission by a French gunsmith in New Orleans. After Hunter had saved the general from a sharpshooter's bullet at Shiloh, taking the bullet himself, Beauregard had ordered the crafty gunmaker to change the monogram. He then gifted the handsome piece to the young Georgia Rebel who'd saved his life and whose own fighting spirit had already made Hunter Buchanon something of a legend, his name spoken nightly in admiring tones around Confederate cook fires.

G. T. Beauregard, a dusky skinned little man with dark eyes and a dark mustache, had handed the weapon over to the starry-eyed young warrior late one night in a hospital tent on one condition—that Hunter recover from his leg wound and continue killing the venal Yankees.

Hunter had vowed he would.

And he'd done just that.

Now he returned the handsome smoke wagon to its holster and turned to see Bobby Lee lifting his leg over the man who'd been wearing the black hat when Hunter had blown him off his horse. The coyote sent a fine yellow drizzle into the man's beleaguered-looking face and half-open eyes.

As he inspected the other three dead killers, Hunter saw that one wasn't dead but only wounded, albeit gravely. This man, the one Hunter had shot off the stage, lay off the trail's far side, grunting and groaning softly as he reached for an ivory-gripped Bisley revolver lying just beyond his outstretched fingers.

Hunter glanced at the woman, who also stared at the surviving killer, her mouth opening, eyes widening in re-newed fear.

"Turn away," Hunter told her as he slid the LeMat from its holster.

The woman looked at him, frowning as though not quite understanding.

"Turn away," Hunter repeated a little louder.

She looked at the big pistol in Hunter's right hand, and turned away, lowering her head slightly and closing her hands over her ears.

Hunter walked over to the wounded killer, who turned his head to gaze up at Hunter standing over him, the man's eyes turning wary. His ruddy, bluntly chiseled face was a mask of sweat and misery. Long, greasy, auburn hair hung in tangles down his back. An angry grimace curled his lips back, showing two silver front teeth.

"Why'd you attack the stage?" Hunter asked the man in a cold, even voice, staring down the LeMat's main barrel at the man's sweating face.

"Payroll, ya damn fool," the man wheezed out, gritting his teeth in dread and fury. He slid his gaze to Laura and added with a faint, lewd smile, "An' the woman."

"You weren't supposed to know about the payroll."

The man gave a taut smile.

"How did you know about the money?" Hunter asked him.

"Go to hell!" the man spat out, glaring.

The LeMat barked, flames and smoke lapping from the barrel.

Bobby Lee hurried over to anoint the dead man.

"Couldn't have done it better myself, Bobby Lee."

CHAPTER 4

Buchanon plucked out the spent shell and replaced it with fresh. He spun the cylinder and dropped the LeMat back into its holster.

He turned to the woman.

She still had her back to him. She still had her hands over her ears. She was shaking, head bobbing. Sobbing.

He looked around for the dead killers' horses. He didn't see a single one. They'd likely fled with the other men and mounts.

Now in the aftermath of the attack, Hunter realized the direness of his and the woman's situation. Ike Talon would likely be back. Not only had Hunter identified him and his men, but Talon wanted the payroll money. He and his men hadn't had time, thanks to Hunter, to give the coach a thorough going-over.

They'd return to do just that, and to kill the witnesses to the murders. Two of his men, apparently having gone rogue, had attacked the woman. The gang had likely been closing on the stage from the wooded ridges to either side, and the two men Hunter had killed and thrown into the ravine had gotten distracted when they saw Laura leave the trail alone.

Somehow, they'd lost track of Buchanon himself.

Hunter considered himself damned lucky they had, or both he and the girl would have gone the way of Charley and the drummer.

Hunter glanced along the trail to the south. Seeing no sign of Talon and the three others, he strode quickly down the trail to the north. The coach lay on its side only fifty feet away, in the middle of the trail.

Hunter leaped up onto the coach's right side, which was now the top, opened the door, and dropped inside. He hoisted himself up and out through the same door less than a minute later. He crawled up to the driver's boot and grabbed his canteen, which he'd tied by its lanyard from the wood seat's steel frame. He slung the canteen's woven lanyard over his head and left shoulder, and leaped back down to the trail.

He slung the saddlebags he'd found inside the coach over his left shoulder and walked over to the woman who had turned to watch him with a strange mix of fear and curiosity.

"Where did those come from?" she asked.

"Under the seat."

"You mean Mister Farley and I were sitting on the pay-roll money?"

"That's right."

It had been Buchanon's idea to hollow out the seat and carry inside what most owlhoots would look for in the strongbox. Why flaunt valuable cargo by carrying it up top in a strongbox that anyone could see from half a mile away, and that anyone could open with a single pistol shot?

He grabbed the canteen and unscrewed the cap. "Water?"

She shook her head.

Buchanon swirled the canteen. About half-full. Good enough for now. He took a sip, returned the cap, and slid the canteen out of the way behind him.

"Come on. We can't stay here." Hunter grabbed the woman's arm and pulled her along behind him as he headed along the trail to the north.

"What do you mean?" The woman pulled back on her arm. "Why don't I stay here while you go for help? How far are we from Tigerville?"

Hunter held fast to her arm despite her resistance. "Fifteen miles. I wouldn't make it on foot before dark. Besides, those killers will be back. Likely, soon."

"Why?"

"They know the money's on the coach. Don't ask me how they know. Nobody was supposed to know besides the mine superintendent, the bank in Cheyenne, and me and Charley. They must have inside help. Which means they'll be back for it, all right." Hunter turned to her sharply. "Why the hell are you resisting me, lady? Do you want to die out here?"

She pulled her arm free of Buchanon's hand, brought both hands to her face, and sobbed. "I'm injured. I'm tired. I'm scared . . . and . . . and I *just want to go home*!"

She dropped to her knees in the trail and leaned forward, lowering her head to the dirt. "I just want to go home!"

Hooves thudded in the south. The thuds grew louder, kicking up a wicked rataplan on the hard-packed trail.

Talon . . .

"Come on, dammit!" Buchanon reached down and pulled the woman brusquely to her feet. He gazed up trail again, seeing three hatted heads jostling into view near the crest of the first hill to the south. "They're back!"

Bobby Lee snarled and yipped, then ran into the brush.

Hunter pulled the woman off the trail's right side and into the forest. He pulled her up the slope. She no longer resisted, but she couldn't run as fast as he could, so he half-dragged her at times.

When they came to snags of blowdown, he wrapped his arm around her waist and carried her over obstructions before setting her down, grabbing her wrist again, and pulling her along behind him.

Halfway up the ridge, she dropped to her knees. "No!" She lowered her head, gasping for breath. "I can't! I can't! My feet . . . my boots . . . !"

Buchanon gazed back down the ridge. He could see bits of the trail through the trees. He couldn't see the riders. He didn't know if they'd seen him and the girl before Hunter had pulled her off the trail.

But he couldn't see them yet. A good sign. Still, they had to keep moving.

"Here." Buchanon dropped to a knee, picked up her left foot.

"What are you doing?"

"What's it look like?"

He quickly unbuttoned the shoe, removed it from her

foot, and tossed it over his shoulder. It thumped onto the ground.

"No!" she cried. "It's my only pair of . . ."

Hunter held up the other one. "You want to die for these boots? You can't run in them and, lady, you need to run!"

He tossed the other shoe back over his shoulder. It struck the soft forest duff and rolled several feet down the decline.

Hoof thuds sounded from below.

Hunter gazed down the slope. Four riders were just then swinging off the trail and into the trees, climbing, batting their heels against their horses' flanks. Hunter heard the squawk of tack and the raking sounds of the horses' straining lungs.

He cursed, pulled the woman to her feet, headed straight up the hill, and ran, grabbing at the ground with his booted feet, pulling the woman with his right hand.

He glanced behind and below.

There were quite a few trees between him and his pursuers, offering some cover. He couldn't tell if the riders had spotted him yet. They'd likely seen where his and the woman's tracks had left the trail, but if they'd laid eyeballs on him, they gave no indication.

Ahead, at the top of the ridge, lay a cap of mottled gray rock with strewn boulders offering cover.

He ran harder. The woman dropped to her knees with a groan. He dragged her into a niche in the wall of caprock. The niche, partly concealed by a wagon-size boulder, was like a closet that angled back slightly from the door, maybe six feet deep. Hunter shoved the woman in ahead of him.

She slumped against the wall, head down, breathing hard. She was as limp as a rag, long hair hiding her face.

Hunter slid the LeMat from its holster, clicked the hammer back, and held the revolver barrel up in front of his chest. He doffed his tan Stetson and leaned his head to one side, edging a look out over the slope.

The four riders rode abreast, roughly fifteen feet apart. They were coming hard, their horses lurching off their hind feet, the killers jouncing in their saddles, flapping their elbows.

Hunter saw that the second rider from the left was Ike Talon—a big, bald-headed, dark-eyed, dark-faced man riding low in his saddle, letting his wounded right arm hang straight down his side. Talon's walrus-mustached upper lip was stretched back from his picket-fence teeth in the agony of his wound.

Hooves thudded resoundingly, crunching dead leaves and pine needles.

As the four approached the caprock, they reined up and looked around, the sun angling through the pine crowns dappling them with gold. The brims of their hats half-shaded their hard, unshaven faces.

Hunter slid his head back into the niche, his heart beating in his ears. The killers were close enough that Hunter could smell the sour stink of their sweaty bodies mixing with the musk of their blowing horses.

The killers didn't say anything, but Buchanon could hear one of them wheezing loudly. That would be Talon sucking breaths in and out through his gritted teeth. Hunter could sense not only the pain in the man—his bullet had probably shattered the bone in his right arm—but the fury.

To his mind, he'd been outfoxed. In reality, Buchanon had gotten lucky. If two of the man's goatish renegades hadn't tried to rape the woman, all likely would have been lost. But since they had, thus luring Hunter away from the coach, Buchanon and the woman were still alive.

And Hunter had the saddlebags containing the mine payroll draped over his left shoulder.

So far so good.

So far . . .

Just keep riding, Buchanon silently urged the four men spread out before him now, looking around and listening intently for the slightest sound that would betray their quarry's position.

Just keep riding. Nothing to see here. They're gone. You've lost 'em. Go back to your snakepit. Tomorrow's another day . . .

Buchanon heard the squawk of saddle leather and a faint grunt as one of the men must have gestured to the others. Hooves thumped and bridles clanked against toothy jaws as the riders put the spurs to their mounts. He could tell from the thuds that the group was dispersing as it continued on up the slope, to each side of the caprock.

The sounds dwindled quickly.

Hunter canted his head to the left, sliding that eye around the niche's covering wall to stare out over the forested slope again. He saw only the arched tail of one horse to the far left as one of the killers continued on up the slope to the south of the caprock.

Buchanon exhaled a breath he hadn't realized he'd held.

He turned to the woman. She sagged low against the wall on his right.

"They're gone."

She didn't look at him.

He touched her arm. "We have to keep moving."

Keeping her chin down, she shook her head. "Leave me."

"No."

She lifted her chin, weakly shook her hair back from her face. "I'm too tired. I'm too exhausted. Leave me. I'll stay here. Come back for me . . . later."

That wouldn't work. He may not get back to her before morning. On her own, she'd be fair game for any predator in the area, and he knew there were more than a few—wildcats and grizzlies included.

And then there were the human kind, the most dangerous predators of all.

He couldn't leave her. He didn't much care for her. Too prissy and bossy. But he couldn't leave her.

"We're going together." Hunter tugged on her arm. "Come on—let's go."

She pulled her hand out of his and glared up at him, hardening her jaws. "I told you to leave me here! I don't care how"—she looked him up and down, critically, and with more than a little revulsion, as well—"large and brutish you are! You can't make me come with you when I've told you I want to stay here! You can't force me to do something against my will! Doing so would make you little better than them!"

She tossed her head to indicate their pursuers.

"All right." Buchanon nodded. "Have it your way. I'll try to make it back. I don't know when, but I have a feelin' you're gonna have a long night out here."

"I don't care. I'll be fine."

"All right." Buchanon stepped out of the niche. He

turned back as if in afterthought. "Oh, if that wildcat returns before I do, just bang two rocks together. That *might* frighten him off."

He turned away again. She grabbed his arm.

"What wildcat?" she asked skeptically, anger glinting in her pretty hazel eyes contrasting the tangled chestnut hair hanging down both sides of her face and across her shoulders.

"The one that holed up in here last night."

"How do you know a wildcat *holed up in here* last night?"

Hunter pointed at the finely ground gravel and dirt on the floor of the niche. "Wildcat scat."

It was rabbit scat, but he didn't think she'd know that.

She looked down, frowning. "That's not wildcat scat! You're a bald-faced liar!"

"All right."

Still holding the LeMat barrel up in his right hand, he looked around and then began striding along the base of the caprock and the strewn boulders, heading toward the northern end, intending to work his way around the stony crest of the ridge.

"Wait for me!"

Hunter turned to see the woman step out of the niche and, holding her skirts above her bare, dirty feet, followed him along the base of the caprock. She glared up at him from beneath her brows and wrinkled a nostril in disgust.

Hunter snorted and continued walking, looking around cautiously. She moaned and groaned behind him, and he, as tired of her as she was of him, tossed a glare at her from over his shoulder. "Keep it down!"

She gave him another cold-eyed glare. "You try walking barefoot over sharp rocks!"

"You'll soon be toe-down if you don't shut up."

Behind him, she made a soft, guttural cry of rage.

Hunter approached the north end of the caprock. He stopped and looked around the side of the rock humping up darkly from its pediment-like base of gravel and small boulders. Spying no movement in the forest to his left or ahead, he continued walking, setting his boots down quietly.

"Ouch!" the woman cried.

Hunter looked behind him again, glaring. She returned his glare, hardening her jaws again. "That one really hurt!"

Hunter cursed. He holstered the LeMat, swung around, crouched, and drew the woman up over his left shoulder.

She gave a deep grunt of surprise and exasperation.

"Be quiet!"

"Put me down!"

"I said be quiet or I'm gonna put you down and shoot you!"

It was no idle threat. He was ready to do it.

CHAPTER 5

Carrying the angrily chuffing and grunting woman like a sack of feed grain over his left shoulder, Hunter hurried forward along the side of the caprock, peering down the slope ahead and to his left.

The branches on the columnar pines didn't start until roughly twenty feet up from the ground, so he had a good view through the forest around him. He spied no sign of his pursuers.

He considered returning to the trail, where the walking would be easier for his barefoot charge, but quickly nixed the idea. Talon and the others would sooner or later swing back to the trail and run him and the woman down.

Dead Horse Canyon was only a half a mile or so to the east, straight ahead of him. The canyon ran more or less north and south, so following that canyon, giving him better cover than the trail offered, would eventually bring him near the southeastern outskirts of Tigerville.

The canyon was a badland maze of rock, timber, and chalky buttes carved long ago by Dead Horse Creek, which was usually only a slow-moving stream now in the mid-summer. Plenty of cover down there. And water. They'd need water.

"Put me down, damn you!" the woman berated him under her breath.

"Be quiet."

"Put me down this instant!" She slammed the heel of her fist against his lower back.

"Be quiet."

"Damn you!"

"As soon as we reach the bottom of the next slope, I'll set you down. But for now, we can't be lollygaggin'."

"I wasn't lollygaggin'!" she said tightly, mocking his Southern accent.

He stopped at the rear of the caprock and looked around again. The ridge dropped away before him, through more pines and scattered aspen. Green, sunlit leaves glinted in the warm, humid breeze. Spying no movement either to his left or down the slope ahead, or behind the caprock to his right, he started forward, negotiating the declivity carefully.

He'd taken only three strides when his right boot came down in a fresh pile of horse apples, which he didn't see until that boot slipped out from beneath him. The slope was steep—nearly forty-five degrees—and the trees widely spaced. He fell awkwardly and struck the ground hard on his right hip and shoulder, the girl tumbling off his other shoulder, and rolled.

So did the girl, groaning shrilly, skirts and hair flying wildly around her.

"Damn!" Hunter heard himself exclaim as the ground hammered him.

He bounced as he rolled, sharp twigs, branches, and

pine needles gouging his skin through his shirt, the ground ruthlessly shoving dirt and needles between his lips. The woman rolled against him—hard.

She cried out and continued rolling, Hunter's body slamming down on hers, his broad chest smashing against her lumpy one, making her cry out again, more loudly. Then she inadvertently kicked him across his left temple as they continued rolling, limbs entangled, down the steep decline.

At least, he thought the kick was inadvertent. As mad as she was, she might have kicked him on purpose. He couldn't really blame her. Damn foolish move, thinking he could carry even something as light as she down the steep ridge.

Finally they both piled up a few feet away from each other at the base of the ridge.

Hunter quickly took stock as he lay on his back, facing skyward. He didn't think anything was broken. He hurt like hell, but he'd broken bones before, even dislocated a couple back during the Fight for Southern Independence, but he didn't hurt that bad.

He turned to where the woman lay beside him, also on her back.

"You all right?"

She didn't say anything. Was she passed out?

Maybe dead?

He sat up to get a better look at her. She wasn't dead. She was crying. Quietly crying, her body quivering, her face scrunched up, eyes squeezed shut.

She lifted her head and cast another fierce look through her tears. "I would have been safer with that wildcat!"

Hunter spied movement to the east, straight out away

from him. A horse and rider were galloping toward him. One of the killers had a rifle raised, his right cheek pressed up against the stock.

Hunter flung himself onto the woman beside him.

She screamed as, rolling onto his right shoulder, he picked her up and hurled her over him, to his left, behind a tree. As he rolled toward her, a bullet thudded into the ground where she'd been lying a moment before, blowing up a gout of dirt and grass.

The thud of the bullet was followed by the whip-crack of the rifle of the fast approaching rider, the rataplan of the scissoring hooves now reaching Hunter's ears, as well.

Hunter threw himself behind the tree as yet another bullet ripped into the ground behind him, followed by the rifle's crashing report. The girl sat up, looking around wildly, sobbing fearfully.

"Stay down!" Hunter told her.

As she hunkered low, Hunter looked around the right side of the tree. The rider was within fifty yards and angling straight toward him, raising the rifle to his cheek again.

Hunter removed his hat, waved it out to the right of the tree, and dropped it. He'd no sooner dropped it than a bullet buzzed through the air to skin off the tree's right side, flinging bark and bits of wood in all directions.

Hunter unholstered his LeMat and aimed it around the tree's left side, lining up the sights on the rider plunging toward him.

He fired once, twice, three times.

The man had jerked back after the first shot. As the other two bullets hammered into him, he sagged even farther back in his saddle, pulling the reins back sharply.

His cream gelding whinnied fiercely as its head went up, snout aimed nearly skyward.

The horse dropped its rear and skidded forward on its belly. The rider plunged down the horse's left hip and the cream tumbled onto him.

The man screamed.

He screamed again as the cream gained its feet, trampling its wounded rider, kicking him. The man wailed. "Oh . . . oh . . . oh Christ!"

"Wait here!" Hunter told the woman and ran forward.

The cream shook itself as though to clear the cobwebs. Its saddle hung down its left side.

"Whoa boy, whoa boy," Hunter said, approaching the mount, holding both hands up, palms out, trying to calm the beast. The horse might be his and the woman's only chance to make it to Tigerville alive.

He continued forward too quickly.

The horse wanted nothing to do with him. As it turned sharply, Hunter dove for the reins. He got one ribbon in his right hand, but the horse, wheeling sharply a hundred and eighty degrees, tugged the leather free before Hunter could make a fist around it.

Loosing another angry neigh, it lunged off its rear hooves and galloped back the way in which it and its rider had come. It ran as though it were running a Fourth of July race with tin cans tied to its tail.

Hunter punched the ground and cursed.

The thuds of the fleeing cream's hooves dwindled. They were replaced by the growing rataplan of at least two more horses.

"Oh God!" the woman sobbed, staring toward the north.

Hunter looked beyond her. Sure enough, two more of

the stage-robbing gang members were heading toward him and the woman, coming hard and fast.

Hunter scrambled to his feet. He glanced at the cream's rider, who lay still now in the grass and sage, his body twisted and broken, his chest a bib of fresh blood.

Dead.

Good. One down, three to go . . .

Hunter rose and ran back to where the woman sat on her knees, head down, bawling. The two killers were two hundred yards away and closing, whipping their horses with their rein ends. They rode straight toward Hunter and the woman from the north, between the base of the ridge on Hunter's left and a long sweep of pine forest on his right.

Hunter looked around for the saddlebags. He'd dropped them in his tumble down the ridge.

He ran up the ridge, suppressing the aches and pains incurred in the plunge. Fortunately, he found the bags not far away, piled up against the base of a large cedar. He slung the bags over his right shoulder, ran the fifty feet back down the slope, knelt beside the bawling Miss Meyers, and palmed the LeMat.

That's all it took to cause both riders to rein their horses in suddenly. They'd been privy to Hunter's work with the LeMat earlier, and they weren't about to make themselves such easy targets again. The black horse of the rider on the right whinnied and reared. The man on the right, riding a steeldust, curveted his own horse, swung down from his saddle, and sheathed what appeared a Winchester carbine. He dropped his horse's reins and took a knee.

The other man dismounted, as well, throwing down his own reins, hefting the rifle he was holding, and stood near where his horse casually lowered its head to tug at the shin-high yellow wheat grass.

"Turn over the money and the woman, and we'll let you go, Buchanon!" The standing man was sixty yards away; Hunter could see the line of his teeth as he grinned.

The woman moaned.

"All right." It was Hunter's turn to grin. "Come an' get her!"

"Oh God! Oh God!" the woman cried into her hands.

"Don't worry! This ain't my first rodeo, sweetheart!"

"Oh God! Oh God!" the woman cried again.

Still grinning, Hunter extended the LeMat, and fired. The standing man flinched and slapped his hand over the left side of his neck. The kneeling man returned fire. The bullet plunked into the sod three feet in front of Hunter.

Buchanon slid the LeMat toward the kneeling man and fired. Just as he did, the standing man yelled to the other one, "Take cover, Emory, fer Christ-damn-sakes!" and bolted to his feet.

Hunter's bullet blew up dirt and grass just beyond him.

Both of the killers' horses had run off when Hunter fired the first shot, so the kneeling man, cursing loudly, ran back north and to Hunter's right, the flaps of his broadcloth coat winging out around him.

The other man joined him, also cursing, as they lumbered, spurs ringing like sleigh bells at Christmas, for the cover of the trees. Hunter aimed but didn't shoot. He didn't want to waste another bullet. Neither man was running fast, but they were just out of the LeMat's accurate shooting range.

Hunter wished he had his Henry repeater, which had belonged to his older, now-deceased brother, Shep, but he rarely packed the handsome sixteen-shooter on stage runs. When you had your hands full of leather ribbons leading out to a six-horse hitch, you couldn't handle much more than a hogleg. In the past, his LeMat and Charley's twelve-gauge shotgun had been more than sufficient for holding off some of the gnarliest owlhoots in the territory.

Charley . . .

In his mind's eye, Hunter saw Charley lying piled up on the trail beside the drummer, and his rage renewed itself, a fist of fire opening around his heart.

He pulled the LeMat down, glared off toward where the two killers were just then approaching the trees, and muttered, "Till we meet again, you sons of Satan . . ."

He holstered the LeMat, grabbed Miss Meyers's arm, and pulled her to her feet. "Come on!"

"Oh God, no—I can't!"

"Yes, you can!"

"No!"

"If you think those two will treat you any better than I have, I'll leave you. That what you want?" He was running hard, pulling the unwilling woman along behind him.

"No, but . . . oh, go to hell!"

The killers shouted angrily behind Hunter. He could no longer see them, because he and the woman were running through the trees now themselves. But he knew they were fetching their horses.

They'd resume the chase soon. They had no choice. They had to kill Buchanon, because he could identify them as killers, and they wanted the money and the woman. It was anyone's guess which they wanted more, but glancing behind him at Miss Meyers and the torn dress that could just barely contain her assets, he had a pretty good idea.

Money was one thing. The satisfaction of male lust was another.

There weren't many women who looked like Laura Meyers anywhere in the territory. She'd be a hell of a prize though she probably wouldn't live through the celebration following her acquisition.

"You're welcome, lady," Hunter said, chuckling drolly as he ran, leaping deadfalls, pulling, sometimes carrying, her along behind him.

Finally, Dead Horse Canyon opened ahead of him. The dark gash grew wider as he and the woman approached.

As the forest drew back behind him, he pushed through thirty feet of brush and wended his way around small boulders until he stood on the lip of the canyon. The woman dropped to her knees behind him, too exhausted now to even cry.

The canyon was roughly two hundred yards wide at this point, its shelving walls of salmon and pink sandstone and limestone dropping two hundred feet to the canyon floor. Dead Horse Creek, roughly twenty feet wide, was a glinting black snake curving between banks of high, green grass, green shrubs, and towering pines and Douglas firs. Water-carved caverns with gently arching portals, and of all sizes, lined the base of both cliffs.

Hunter knew the layout of the canyon, because he and his brothers had often hunted and fished along the meandering chasm, which was a font of game including deer, elk, and wild turkeys. Here, he and the woman had the advantage. It wouldn't be a hard descent, because the walls shelved relatively gently, offering good footing and plenty of handholds.

Men on horseback, however, wouldn't make it. At least, not here. They'd have to find an easier way down.

Hearing hoof thuds in the forest behind him, Hunter grabbed the woman's hand again. "Come on. We're almost there."

She shook her bowed head. "Where?"

"To the bottom of this canyon."

She looked up wearily, her pale features slack. When she saw the canyon dropping before her, her eyes widened and sharpened again in horror. "Oh God, no!"

CHAPTER 6

The thumping of the oncoming horses was growing louder.

Hunter pulled Laura to her feet. He sandwiched her face in his big hands and gazed into her pretty hazel eyes, forcing her to look back at him. "You're gonna follow me down. It's steep but it's easy. Lots of places for your hands and feet. Now, take a deep breath and follow me!"

She gazed back at him, and gradually, the terror left her gaze.

She drew a breath, released it, and nodded.

Hunter stepped over the lip of the canyon, setting his boots down on the small shelves of rock jutting out from the side of the ridge.

"Hurry, now," he said. "Don't look down. Just look at your hands and feet."

She stepped over the lip and started her descent, slow at first, but when she saw that there were plenty of hand- and footholds, she seemed to grow more confident and hurried her pace. Occasionally, she looked down at Hunter crawling down the wall directly below her, where he could catch her if she fell.

Seeing him near seemed to calm her, encourage her, and she continued crabbing down the wall just above him.

The sounds of approaching riders along with the shouts of their pursuers ebbed down into the canyon, echoing faintly. A few rocks rained down from above, bouncing off the wall several feet to Hunter's right.

He stopped and looked up just as one of the killers angled his head over the lip for a look into the canyon. He was above Hunter and the woman and a little to their right. The man pointed, shouting, "There they are!"

Hunter stepped to the right and said, "Keep coming, Miss Meyers!"

"Oh God," she gasped, looking up.

Hunter unsheathed the LeMat. "Don't look up! Keep going down!"

The other killer poked his head over the canyon's lip, the breeze bending the brown brim of his high-crowned Stetson. Both men raised their rifles to their shoulders and angled the barrels down at their prey.

Hunter had already raised the LeMat and was aiming down the barrel. He squeezed the trigger. The LeMat roared, and the man to his left on the canyon's rim stumbled back away from the wall without firing his weapon. The other man triggered his own rifle, but Hunter's shot made him fire wide—into the wall only a few feet below Buchanon.

Hunter fired at that man, too, driving him back away from the rim.

Laura cried out as her bare feet slipped off the narrow ledge she was on. She dropped straight down.

As she shot past Hunter on his left, Hunter reached out with his left hand and grabbed her right arm. The force of her fall made him lose his own precarious footing, made even more precarious by the fact that he was no longer holding on to anything with his hands, his left one holding her arm, his right one clutching the LeMat.

An acidic dread churned in his belly as he dropped straight down the wall, involuntarily releasing Miss Meyers's arm as well as the LeMat and raking all ten fingers along the rock wall sliding up past him in a gray-brown blur.

Madly, he tightened his jaws and clawed for purchase.

The woman gave a clipped scream. Vaguely, he heard a thump close on his left. A half an eye blink later, his boots slammed onto a strangely yielding surface and then he fell on his back, ears ringing, vision swimming.

He lifted his head. The girl lay beside him, writhing on the wiry green bushes they'd both fallen onto, cushioning the drop. God had reached out his hand in the form of evergreen shrubs growing up from an outward bulge in the ridge wall to catch them before they could fall the last fifty feet to their deaths.

Hunter still had the saddlebags, to boot. They were hanging over his left arm. He'd fallen on the canteen. He winced at the ache in his lower left back as he reached around to slide the canteen out to his side.

"There. Better . . ."

As the ringing slowly receded from Buchanon's ears, the whip-cracks of rifles assaulted them, as did the sharp spangs of bullets ricocheting off the rocks around him. He blinked his eyes to clear them, then gazed straight up the ridge.

Again, acidic dread bubbled in his belly.

One of the riflemen was aiming straight down the ridge wall at him, the rifle as still as stone in the man's gloved hands. Hunter could feel the burn of the rifle's sights on his forehead.

"Enjoy that last breath," he silently told himself.

But then the rifle jerked suddenly to Hunter's left, orange flames lapping from the barrel. The shooter screamed. Growls and snarls sounded from the ridge, and Hunter got a quick glimpse of some gray-brown, four-legged beast hanging from the man's arm by its jaws until man and clinging beast fell away from the ridge wall.

"Cussed vermin!" the man cried in terror. "I'm being attacked by a damned coyote! Quick, shoot him, A.J. *Shoot him!*"

A rifle cracked. Bobby Lee gave a sharp yelp.

Buchanon had wondered vaguely where the beast had gone. But then, Bobby Lee had never cottoned to gunfire. He'd likely been following his master and his master's female charge from a good distance, not wanting to take any of the lead meant for them. But just like he had done in the past, when he'd seen the chips were down for Hunter, he'd leaped in to help.

"God bless the beasts," Buchanon muttered, hoping Bobby Lee hadn't taken a bullet for his loyalty.

Looking around quickly, he saw his LeMat laying to his left, between himself and the woman.

He grabbed the big popper in his right hand, grabbed the woman's wrist in his left hand, said, "Come on!" and heaved them both to their feet.

Further good fortune showed itself in the form of a gentler slope below the evergreens, as well as a two-foot shelf of downward angling trail pocked here and there with deer pellets and rodent tracks.

Hunter stopped. Miss Meyers was a dead weight behind

him. He turned to see that she was on her knees, head hanging back, eyes closed.

Unconscious or nearly so.

He didn't know if she'd been brained by the fall or if she'd taken a bullet. He didn't have time to find out.

He had to get them both off the ridge.

He crouched, settled her over the saddlebags on his left shoulder, swung around, and hurried off down the gently sloping trail. The narrow trace angled downward to the left and leveled off on the canyon floor beneath a broad, bulging belly of striated rock giving good cover from the ridge crest above. The narrow, slow-moving stream of water, as black as indigo ink, murmured softly in its shallow bed to the right. Pines, shrubs, and green grass abutted it closely on the far side, several boughs hanging down over the water.

Hunter followed the clear, gravelly ground between the stream and the ridge wall, heading roughly northeast as he followed this section of the twisting canyon.

The woman was light. He doubted she weighed much over a hundred pounds. Still, as tired and sore as he was, she, in addition to the burden of the saddlebags, was becoming a heavy weight on his shoulder.

Still, he had to keep moving. He knew of a small cavern another quarter mile down the canyon in which they could hole up relatively safely for the night. One where he himself had stocked dry firewood the last time he'd overnighted there, when he'd hunted Dead Horse Canyon alone.

That had been two years ago, before the war with Ludlow and Chaney, before he'd lost his ranch as well as his two brothers—one older, one younger—and he and his father had been forced to move into Tigerville.

If the wood was still there, it would likely be in good burning condition. The cavern was protected by brush and boulders screening it from the canyon floor as well as from the tops of both ridge walls. As he remembered, it got cold in the canyon at night even in the summer. The woman was not dressed for a cold night; she'd need a fire.

His boots were growing as heavy as lead by the time he reached a natural bridge of rock hanging low down over the canyon. He was glad to see the bridge, for he remembered the cavern he was heading for lay just beyond it.

He hurried under the bridge, having to crouch so the stone underbelly didn't rake his hat off his head. The air beneath the bridge smelled of mold and dank stone. Coming out the other side he saw the oval-shaped opening of the cavern atop an outcropping of sand and gravel roughly twenty feet up from the canyon floor.

He climbed the outcropping, grunting and wheezing with the effort. He wasn't in the prime shape he'd been in during the war, he vaguely reflected. Back then he could run all night, barefoot, with a rucksack of high explosives strapped to his back, armed with only a Griswold & Gunnison .36-caliber cap-and-ball revolver tucked behind his belt, and a bowie-style knife he'd fashioned himself from a plow blade hanging from a leather sheath around his neck.

He gained the crest of the outcropping capped with small boulders and brush including a gnarled cedar, and dropped to his knees, his vision dimming with fatigue. The woman groaned, moved around on his shoulder.

"Hold on," he said.

He turned to peer into the cavern. When he'd over-nighted in the cave before, there had been no sign that anything more dangerous than foxes or coyotes had called the place home. There didn't appear to be any now either. In fact, there were no recent tracks or scat or rabbit bones at all.

There was, however, a stone fire ring and the short stack of firewood he'd gathered before he'd pulled out after his own last visit.

Things were looking up.

He rose and stepped into the cavern, crouching, for the ceiling wasn't as high as he was tall. He bent forward and eased Miss Meyers down onto the cave floor. She sat up, raised her knees, rested her arms on them, and pressed the heels of her hands to her temples.

"God . . . I hurt all over. What happened?" She lowered her hands and looked around.

"A cave."

Hunter sat down heavily and leaned back against the wall. He slid the saddlebags off his shoulder. He removed his hat, set the hat down on the saddlebags beside him, and swept his hand through his long, thick blond hair. "Where you hurt?"

She rested her head in her hands again. "Everywhere."

"Were you hit?"

She lowered her hands again, looked at her body as though seeing it for the first time. She ran her hands down her sides, down her legs over the torn and dirty dress, then shook her head, making her tangled, dirty hair jostle. "No. My head aches."

Hunter closed his eyes. Fatigue weighed heavy on him. "We took a fall."

"I know. I'm sorry. I was frightened."

He unscrewed the cap and held out the canteen to her. "Have some. It's warm but I'll refill it after dark."

She shook her head and sat back against the wall on the opposite side of the fire ring from him. She stretched her long legs out beneath her torn and rumpled dress and underclothes, and crossed her dirty, bloody feet at her ankles.

"Where are they?" she asked.

Hunter took a couple of sips of the brackish water, then capped and set the canteen near his hat and saddlebags. "Up on the rim, last I checked. If they want us bad enough, they'll be along soon. There are plenty of places on the western ridge where they can ride or lead their horses into the canyon."

"Do you think they'll come?"

He looked at her. Would he come for her, if he was such a man as his stalkers were?

Hard to say. Even beaten and dirty, she was still a fine figure.

The skin above the bridge of her nose creased as she gazed back at him, vaguely curious. As if reading his mind, her pale, dusty cheeks turned pink. She frowned and looked down at her exposed flesh. Her eyes settled on her lap. She closed her eyes and choked back a sob.

He tossed the canteen onto the dirt beside her. "You'll feel better if you have some water."

"I'm so tired and sore I don't want water."

"It'll make you feel better is what I'm saying."

She didn't respond to that.

Hunter glanced at her feet. "Do your feet hurt?"

Numbly she shook her head and drew her feet up, covering them with the folds of her torn dress. "Please leave me alone, Mister Buchanon. I just want to rest."

"All right."

He didn't realize it but he was dead asleep less than five seconds after he'd said those last words. He slid slowly down the cavern wall to settle onto his left shoulder. The next thing he was aware of was a cold snout roughly the texture of a gutta percha gun grip pressed against his left ear.

He woke with a start, hand automatically closing over the LeMat on his right hip. He rose and in the cavern's dusky light saw the long gray snout flanked by two yellow eyes regarding him from a few inches away.

Two V-shaped ears were pricked, and the animal before him made a soft whimpering sound in his throat.

"Bobby Lee!" Hunter exclaimed.

The woman must have conked out just as Hunter had, for she sat up now with a groan. When she opened her eyes, shook her hair back, and saw the coyote in Hunter's burly arms, she screamed.

CHAPTER 7

Laura Meyers stared across the cavern at the big, rugged, blond-headed, blue-eyed man in a buckskin tunic and buckskin pants and with a bear claw necklace curving across his broad chest, and wondered what kind of a man has a coyote for a pet.

A coyote he obviously loved, judging by how he hugged the wild animal so tightly to his chest, brusquely patting it, ruffling its neck, scratching its ribs, and exclaiming over it, as though it were a child. Judging by how the coyote laid its ears back and wagged its tail and licked the big man's lips, the coyote returned every bit of the big man's affection.

Laura had never seen such a thing in her life.

The whole display revolted her. It also intrigued her but only in the same fashion as a grisly traffic accident on a bustling Denver street. The big man himself interested her in a similar way. He looked very much like a Viking warrior straight out of some Norse fairy tale.

A large, crude man of the Western frontier. One whom she'd watched kill men with horrifying efficiency and violence, but also a man who obviously very much loved the wild beast in his arms and was not afraid of displaying such sentiment to a total stranger.

But, then again, why would he hide it? He was obviously as wild as the coyote he loved. Wild things were not afraid of anything. Least of all revealing themselves to a mere woman and a vexingly helpless one at that.

Of course, under the circumstances, she couldn't blame him. Despite her pique, he had saved her life, she reminded herself. She supposed she should feel grateful. All she really felt, however, was weariness and rage at the fates that had placed her in such a horrid and downright deadly situation.

She looked again at the man now lowering his head to closely inspect a bloody gash on the coyote's back. His bushy blond brows above his ice blue eyes furled with concern.

Yes, she had to admit he intrigued her. She also had to admit that he was rather handsome in a crude and uncivilized sort of way. Big and rawboned, with a face that could have been chiseled from red-hued granite, complete with anvil-like jaws, high, broad cheeks, broad forehead beneath the thick blond hair, and a deep cleft in his ship's prow chin.

A warrior's face.

He was nothing at all like Jonathan, who'd been smaller and more delicately featured. Jonathan had owned the features of a civilized man. A man of fine breeding and learning. A man who read books and studied the law—who was a member, in fact, of the Colorado Bar.

Jonathan had been a man who'd looked heart-thumpingly handsome in a wool and brocade suit, his black derby hat tipped at a jaunty angle as he leaned against the front of his law office on Larimer Street in Denver, shiny half-boots crossed, twirling his pearl-handled walking stick in his beringed right hand, a disarming smile showing his fine white teeth under his upswept handlebar mustache, waxed daily by the same barber.

Unfortunately, other women had found him handsome, as well, and beguiling with his aura of civilized power, his learned and witty conversation, his wealth—or the pretention of wealth, anyway.

She'd never known a man so different as this man was from Jonathan. She'd seen Buchanon's ilk on the streets of Denver, of course—rough-hewn men from the cattle ranches or from the mines in the mountains. Big, brash men with fists like hams, who carried themselves with almost arrogant confidence and erupted easily into ribald laughter.

Rowdy, violent men. Dangerous men.

Laura had never actually met such a man, talked to such a man, had anything at all to do with such a man except to look away from their insinuating glances and brashly ogling eyes when she traveled by hansom cab downtown to have dinner with Jonathan in the early evening on Market Street.

She realized now as she studied the man across from her that she was deeply afraid of him, as she was afraid of the foul-smelling beast he loved. He'd saved her life. For that she should be grateful. But all she felt was fear.

At least, she thought it was fear. Wasn't it fear that made the blood turn oddly warm in her belly while lifting chicken flesh across her slender shoulders?

Of course, it was fear. What else could it be? She was deeply afraid of this savage brigand and his feral pet.

Hunter Buchanon radiated power and physical strength. As he moved, administering to the wild beast in his arms, his muscles strained the seams of his tunic and his tight buckskin pants. She looked at the long, thick arms, the broad, calloused brown hands. Such a man could do anything he wanted to her and there was absolutely nothing she could do about it.

She gave a shiver as she averted her eyes from him.

She thought that deep down he was probably not all that different from the men who'd attacked the stagecoach and who'd dragged her off to satisfy their lust. Tonight, once the sun went down and darkness closed over the canyon, no doubt his own goatish cravings, coupled with his wildness fully revealed, would uncover itself behind the curtain of his rugged affability.

Laura crossed her arms on her barely concealed breasts, closed her eyes, and said a silent prayer for safety. She'd never felt more helpless and vulnerable in her life.

My God—what woman in such a situation would?

Soon, she hoped, she and this wild man and his wild beast would part ways and she would be safe and warm and comfortable in her new life—her new life without Jonathan—in Tigerville.

"I'll be hanged, Bobby Lee, if that son of a buck with the rifle didn't carve a nice notch in your hide." Hunter parted the coyote's fawn gray fur with his fingers to inspect the bloody gash across Bobby Lee's left hip.

The coyote turned his head back to sniff the cut, working his leathery nostrils. He looked up at his concerned master, blinked his red eyes slowly, then lifted his head and gave a soft, low wail.

"Oh, stop feelin' sorry for yourself!" Hunter laughed. "Hell, I've cut myself worse shaving. Just keep your consarned snout out of it and it should heal faster'n a pig can find a mud waller."

He glanced at the woman. She was frowning over her raised knees at him and Bobby Lee. "What's the matter, Miss Meyers? You look like you drank milk left out on the table too long."

"I'm just wondering how on earth you, uh . . . be-friended . . . this . . . animal."

"I found him wandering alone in a little valley near my family's ranch. I assumed some other rancher killed his mother, maybe his father, and likely the rest of the pups."

"And you took him in . . . ?"

"Yes."

"Why?"

"I don't know."

Hunter shrugged as he turned to gather wood from the stack behind him. He and the woman must have slept for well over an hour. Long shadows were stretching into the canyon. It would be dark soon. And cold soon, as well.

"I reckon for the same reason I took you in," Hunter said with a smile. "He was alone and in trouble."

"I was a passenger on your stagecoach," she pointed out tartly. "It was your duty to make sure I arrived at my destination safely. You not only failed to do that, but I left two portmanteau as well as a steamer trunk aboard that coach. Both contained all the items I have left to my name."

He glanced over his shoulder at her. Her words as well as the haughty tone she'd spoken them in riled him. She might have lost luggage, but he'd lost his good friend Charley Anders in that attack. He started to point that out but checked himself.

There was no point in arguing. To a woman like her, Charley had probably been only one or two steps up from the coyote she was regarding again distastefully, as Bobby Lee sat near the cave door, scratching behind his left ear with his left hind foot.

"I do apologize. I'll have a fire going in a minute. Then I'll go down and refill the canteen and we'll get your feet cleaned up. You don't want infection to set into those cuts and scrapes. I wish we had some whiskey, but since we don't, water will have to do."

"I can clean my own feet."

"All right. I'll help if you need it."

She scowled at him suspiciously. "I just bet you would."

Hunter found his own cheeks warming as he said, "I apologize, Miss Meyers. That was forward of me. I didn't mean anything inappropriate."

She sighed and shook her hair back. "I just want this to be over, Mister Buchanon. I want to be in Tigerville. How long do you think that's going to take us?"

Hunter had set a small, pyramidal pile of tinder in the center of the stone ring. He'd piled kindling and large chunks of wood nearby, ready to bring into action as the fire grew. "Hard to say. If we still have those hounds on our trail, longer than if we didn't."

As of a couple of hours ago, he absently reflected, he'd seen only two on his and the woman's trail. He wondered where the third one—Ike Talon himself—was. Talon had taken one of Hunter's bullets. Maybe he'd holed up to lick that nasty arm wound or to get it tended.

Probably too much to hope for that he might have bled to death.

Hunter produced a flat tin box from his shirt pocket, slid the lid open, and plucked a sulfur-tipped lucifer match from the box, and lit the tinder. He tended the flame carefully, tenderly, building it up slowly, then adding more tinder and then some of the smaller bits of kindling in the form of feathersticks and small chunks of dry pine bark.

When the flames looked strong enough, he added a small chunk of wood and then another. Certain the fire was going well enough now that he could leave it for a while, he picked up the canteen and stepped out of the cavern, looking around carefully.

He stood just outside the cave, watching and listening. Hearing or seeing nothing that troubled him, he moved through a gap in the rocks and brush fronting the cave and peered out over the canyon.

It was almost dark down there. The air was cool and damp. He could hear the murmuring stream, see the fading light angling into the canyon from his right reflected off the water. The trees and brush rustled in a faint breeze.

Deciding that there were enough shadows offering cover, he stepped back out of the rocks and crouched to peer into the cave. She sat watching him from over the knees she'd drawn taut against her chest, hugging them tightly, a concerned, worried expression on her pretty face. The fire's dancing flames shone gold in her hazel eyes.

Bobby Lee sat in the cave entrance, staring up at Hunter expectantly.

Hunter held up the canteen. "I'll be right back."

"You won't be gone long?" she asked, a faint tremor in her voice.

"Just a minute's all." Hunter looked at the coyote. "Stay here and keep watch, Bobby. Let me know if you hear or see anything, all right?"

He knew the coyote would.

He gave his beloved pet a warm pat on the head and then headed down the slope toward the water.

CHAPTER 8

When Hunter returned to the cave, Laura gave a silent sigh of relief.

He'd been gone longer than she had expected. Alone here, with just the coyote, she'd found herself feeling even more fearful than before he'd left. The coyote gave a mewl of greeting, wagging its tail and clawing at the big man's pantleg.

Hunter crouched to pat the beast's head.

"What took you so long?" Laura asked, hating the tremor she again heard in her voice.

She didn't want to feel as dependent on him as she did. She wasn't sure why, but she sensed there might be danger in it. She didn't know why that should be either. She just knew that she was feeling strangely, and she wasn't sure she could blame it all on fear, though she wanted to.

His voice was low, soft, almost intimate. He was such a big man that he seemed to fill most of the cave himself. "Decided to take a little tramp up stream and down, just making sure no one was on the scout out there. I think we're alone. Those two killers either decided to head to town for a warm meal and a soft bed, or they're holed up on the rim, maybe waiting for us to show ourselves in the morning."

"What will we do come morning?"

"I take another careful look around. If all's clear, we'll start up the canyon toward Tigerville."

"Will the canyon take us to town?"

"Close." Hunter had walked up to her, crouching under the cavern's low wall. He held out the canteen to her with one hand. He held out a strip of jerky in his other hand. "Have some fresh water and jerky. Gotta keep your strength up."

"What about you?"

"I had a big drink down at the stream."

"What about jerky?"

"That was the only one in my pocket. But go ahead. Hunger makes my senses keener."

"No."

She took the canteen and set it down beside her. She took the jerky, tore it in two, and gave him half. She smiled. "Fair is fair."

He returned her smile. "All right."

He stuffed part of the jerky into his mouth and then dropped to a knee, stirred the fire, and added another log. He sank down on his butt, removed his hat, ran a hand through his long hair, then leaned back against the wall.

The coyote yipped and came over and lay down beside its master, resting its long snout on Hunter's left thigh. It gave a satisfied groan, closed its eyes, and appeared almost instantly asleep.

Laura sank back against the wall, nibbling the jerky. She swallowed a bite and sipped the water. It tasted so good that the first sip made her realize how thirsty she was. Downright parched. She tipped the canteen back and drank hungrily, some of the water oozing out from between her lips and the spout and dribbling down her neck and onto her chest.

It made her shiver, but still she drank.

She lowered the canteen, sloshed the water in it, then arched her brows at Hunter, who sat watching her from the other side of the cave. "Sorry. I guess I didn't realize how dry I was."

Hunter shoved the rest of his jerky into his mouth and brushed his hands on his pants. Chewing, he said, "Take all you want. The stream's near."

She tossed him the canteen two-handed and with a grunt. "I've had enough for now. You take the rest. You worked hard." She hesitated, then found herself adding, "to save my life."

No one could have been more surprised by this sudden switch of sentiment. She found herself continuing with, "I'm sorry I wasn't more grateful before."

"It's all right. You were frightened and angry. I don't blame you. We'll get your bags, though. I'll send someone out for them once we reach Tigerville. Those killers would have no use for a woman's luggage."

More words came spilling out of her, further surprising her. "I want to apologize for my condescending attitude, Mister Buchanon. That's not who I am. At least, I'd rather not think that's who I am."

"Oh, hell," he said, hiking a shoulder, then taking a drink from the canteen. He was a bashful man. Big and rough but also bashful. At least, around a woman.

Around her.

She found that appealing for some reason.

"On the other hand, maybe it is who I am." She lifted her chin resolutely. It felt liberating, stating thoughts and feelings she'd been only halfway feeling and understanding for the past several weeks. "But I'm going to change. Just as the rest of my life is changing. I'm going to be a simpler, humbler human being."

"How is your life changing, Miss Meyers?"

"I am divorcing my husband and I'm moving to Tigerville. Mister Buchanon, you saved the life of the Tigerville Public School's new teacher."

"Pshaw! You don't say."

"Oh, yes."

"You're a teacher?"

"I attended a teaching academy for two years in Saint Louis. That was before I married Jonathan Gaynor and took up housekeeping for him."

Deep lines of befuddlement cut across the big man's broad forehead. "Jonathan Gaynor, Jonathan Gaynor. Where have I heard that name?"

"He's an attorney and a mining magnate in Denver. He has a town named after him in the Rockies."

"Oh, yeah," Hunter said, widening his eyes in realization. "Gaynorville. Sure, sure—I've heard of Gaynorville." He paused, studying her closely, incredulously. "You're married to *him*?"

"I'm divorcing him," she corrected him. "I'm using my maiden name, Meyers, because I don't want Jonathan or any of his cronies to know where I am."

The look of astonishment stayed on Buchanon's face. "Why would you divorce a man like that? He must be one of the richest men in Colorado Territory."

"I have learned over the past six weeks, Mister Buchanon, that there is more to life than money."

"You have?" He seemed genuinely surprised to hear that.

"I have. An honest relationship with the man you love is far more important than money. Love, loyalty . . . fidelity."

"Okay . . ."

"I learned six weeks ago that Jonathan has been in a long-standing affair with another woman. A woman in Gaynorville. He became involved in that relationship— with none other than a whorehouse madam, I might add— only two months after he and I were married!"

She choked back a sob and shook her head. The sudden feeling of sorrow was short-lived. She lifted her head and shook back her tangled hair, drawing a deep breath and marveled at how much better she felt, having confessed so much about the tawdry turn her life had taken.

To a stranger, no less!

Or . . . maybe that's why it had been so easy. She didn't know.

But suddenly more than fear or exhaustion, more than the draining and soul-withering worry about her future that had assaulted her ever since she'd made the decision to divorce Jonathan, she felt an incredible liberation.

Hunter stared at her with his mouth and eyes wide. His eyes had a deeply sympathetic cast. Slowly, he shook his head.

He seemed deeply confounded.

"Why, that there is pure evil," he said, still astonished.

"Yes! I told him that myself. Just before I shot him."

His eyes opened wider. There was something so sweet

and boyish and innocent in his reaction to these tawdry doings that she suddenly wanted to run over to him and hug him like a big warm teddy bear.

"You . . ."

"Shot him," she proudly announced.

"Lordy."

"You see, I learned about Jonathan's infidelity when I took over balancing his accounts, when his accountant Herman Lightkeeper grew ill from smoking those foul-smelling Mexican cigarettes he so favored. As I told you, I attended an academy for young women before I married Jonathan, so I know my numbers as well as my letters.

"Well, when I saw that Jonathan was having his secretary, Mister Pound, write a check each month to one Magdalena Hennessey in Gaynorville, I became quite curious. I inquired with Jonathan about the matter, and after considerable hemming and hawing, he said that Miss Hennessey was a business associate who managed a saloon for him in Gaynorville, and that he was paying her one hundred and fifty dollars a month to run this saloon.

"Well, his flushed and uncertain demeanor, as well as his obvious pique at my curiosity, made me even more curious. One hundred and fifty dollars a month seemed an awful lot to pay a saloon manager."

Laura took another bite of her jerky and chewed it angrily. "When Jonathan went off on one of his three- or four-day business trips to Gaynorville, to oversee his share in the mine and other sundry business interests up that-away, I followed him a day later. I asked about and learned that Magdalena Hennessey ran the saloon and parlor house known as Maggie's Place. Well, I marched over to Maggie's Place—what a windowless perdition with nearly naked girls and just-as-naked men lounging about the place in alcohol and opium stupors! That was the first time I smelled opium, but I knew what it was, all right. Like I said, I'm educated.

"My inquiries regarding Jonathan nearly made a couple of the girls strangle on their tongues while several of the men laughed uproariously in my face. One told me where I could find him, so I hitched up my skirts, climbed the stairs, and I found him, all right."

"Oh boy . . ."

"How many respectable businessmen, Mister Buchanon, do you think take baths in the middle of the afternoon with their business associates?"

"Uh . . ."

"I was so enraged, seeing him there . . . a man who doted on me like a child and called me 'pet' and 'my little pretty one' and 'his fair little sprite,' and who daily vowed his everlasting love and loyalty to me, that before I knew it, I'd taken the over-and-under derringer from my reticule—I don't even remember packing it—and shooting the bastard!"

Hunter slapped his thigh, grinning from ear to ear. "Hot damn—good for you! Did you kill him?"

"No, but I did make sure that, um, *sleeping* with that jug-bosomed slattern will be quite a painful task for the next several months!"

Hunter slapped his thigh again and laughed. "Serves him right!"

"And then I went home, summoned a lawyer, and started a divorce proceeding. I went to the bank to demand half of Jonathan's money, and do you know what I learned from the president of the Territorial Bank and Trust, Mister Buchanon?"

"No idea."

"That the man was not only a lying, cheating son of Satan, but that he was in financial ruin, as well. In that bank, he had forty-one dollars and thirty-eight cents. Jonathan was in so much debt, the president told me, that his creditors were beginning to howl like wolves on the blood trail. In other words, I, too, was penniless."

Grief touched her again. Humiliation. The shame of having been taken such utter advantage of. She lowered her chin, choked back a sob, then heaved herself to her feet. She stepped forward and crouched to scoop the canteen off the cave floor.

She sat down again, took a sip from the canteen, then curled her legs inward and pulled her dress up to expose her dirty, bloody bare feet.

"I learned that he spent all of his money on women, gambling, drinking, and making risky business investments . . . while drunk. He spent most of his time in Gaynorville—drunk."

She dribbled water over her bare left foot, sniffed, and brushed her fist across her nose. "I had no idea. I thought he was working for both of us."

She rubbed the water around on her foot and looked up at Hunter, tears dribbling down her cheeks. "How could one woman—one who so arrogantly touts herself as well-educated—be so stupid and blind?"

Hunter rose and, crouching under the low ceiling, walked over to her. He extended his hand to her. "You'll never get those feet clean that way. You're only making mud. Let's go down to the stream."

"Is it safe?"

"Pretty close to dark. I'm betting those killers are holed up. If they make a play on us, they'll likely wait till morning."

She looked at his extended hand and nodded. "All right."

She set the canteen aside and let Hunter pull her to her feet and lead her out of the cave. "Here we go," he said, and swept her up in his arms.

She gasped, resisting a little at first, tensing her body. But then, as he started off down the slope toward the canyon floor, she yielded her body to him, sank back in his arms, and wrapped her own arms around his neck.

When they reached the canyon, he felt her lean her head back against his shoulder. She turned her face toward his and gazed up at him, her eyes shimmering in the light of the moon climbing the sky above the canyon, in the east.

He could feel her soft, warm breaths puffing against his neck.

"He was a small man," she said softly as he carried her toward the satiny black skin of the snake-like creek curving in the darkness, pearl moonlight skimming its inky surface. "Not like you. He was a small man in ways I didn't suspect until I saw him . . . in that brothel . . . with her."

"That was some betrayal."

"Would you ever do that to a woman?"

"No, I wouldn't." He set her down on a rock at the edge of the stream. He knelt beside her. "Why Tigerville, of all places?"

"I saw an ad for a teacher in the school there."

"Sure, they just built one. Been looking for a teacher for a time."

"Well, they finally found one. I sent a telegram post-haste, announcing my credentials. The superintendent of the school council telegrammed me the next day, informing me that I had been accepted for the position and that school would begin one week after my arrival. So"—she dropped her hands to her thighs—"here I am, starting a new life . . . in this canyon after nearly being ravaged by goatish desperadoes . . . on the run from more desperadoes wanting to . . ."

"Again, I do apologize."

Hunter dipped his left hand in the water and scooped it up and over her left foot.

She drew a sharp breath.

"Cold?"

"A little," she said, her voice soft and intimate in the near-silent canyon. "It stings."

"Sorry."

"No, it feels good. Refreshing. Thank you, Mister Buchanon."

"Miss Meyers, I'm on knees before you, washing your feet. I think that means you can call me by my first name."

"All right." She chuckled at that, sniffed. "Hunter it is. Please, I'm Laura."

"Pleased to meet you, Miss Laura."

She chuckled again as she tucked her hair behind her ears and stared down at him gently scooping the water over her feet and rubbing it in, cleaning the small scrapes and scratches. The water had been cold at first. But now, in his large hands, it felt warm. His hands felt warm, as well. She could feel the rough callouses on them, but he caressed her feet very gently.

Suddenly, she grew warm despite the coolness of the

canyon. Her heartbeat quickened. She closed her eyes, luxuriating in the soft caressing of her feet by this big man's big, warm hands.

She felt the heat rise from her feet and into her legs, climbing still higher.

"Do you live in Tigerville, Hunter?" she asked.

"Indeed, I do."

"What brought you to Tigerville?"

"The war, I reckon. I fought for the Confederacy—the losin' side. Afterward, my pa brought the family—except for Ma, who died in Georgia before the war was over—out here to make a new start. All was well until a year ago. We had trouble with a rival rancher and a couple of his cronies . . . including the county sheriff."

Hunter drew a deep breath and let it out slowly as he massaged Laura's right foot, working the water up between her toes that shone in the dark water in the moonlight, rubbing the ball of her foot with the inside of his right index finger.

He was enjoying the feel of her bare foot in his hand while at the same time trying not to, wishing suddenly that he'd let her clean her own feet.

Wasn't proper, cleaning a strange lady's feet. Especially the feet of a beautiful young woman he was feeling himself becoming attracted to.

He looked up at her sitting on the rock above him.

She sat with her head thrown back, eyes closed. Her breasts rose and fell heavily as she breathed.

He stopped cleaning her feet but held them still in his hands, feeling the cool water slide over them in the slow-moving current.

She lowered her chin, looked down at him. Her hair

fell forward to frame her face. Her eyes shone in the moonlight. She pushed up off the rock, dropped her feet in the stream, and stood. He straightened to his full six-feet-four-inches and looked down at her.

She stared up at him, her eyes wide and round and moist. He could see the miniature moon in the left one. She raised her hands and placed them on the bulging slabs of his chest, and said quietly, "Hunter . . ."

He raised his own hands, wrapped them around hers, and lowered their hands together. "I have a gal," he said quietly, trying to resist this woman's strong pull on him. It wasn't easy.

"I see."

"Leastways, I did. It might be over now. Still . . . I set store by the gal. I love her."

"And you want her back."

"Once I can afford to build a good life for us, yes. I had a cache of gold. I prospected that gold for several long years, wanting to have a big enough stake that she and I could be married. She came from a wealthy family. I didn't want her to want on my account. Well . . . someone stole that gold from me. I don't know who. I wanted to postpone the wedding until I could build up a stake again. Annabelle didn't want to wait. I couldn't do it. I thought . . . still think . . . she deserves more. It drove a wedge between us."

Laura pulled her hands out of his. "I see. Of course, you would have a young lady. I'm sorry." She shook her head, chuckling with self-deprecation. "What a pathetic fool I am!"

"No, please, don't—"

Hunter stopped abruptly when Bobby Lee cut loose

with a loud volley of hammering yips that ripped around the canyon, echoing.

Hunter wheeled, palming the LeMat.

Two shadows moved fifteen feet away from him—two men, their hats limned by the moonlight—running through the brush. A branch snapped. A man cursed.

The LeMat leaped and roared in Hunter's hand.

CHAPTER 9

The next morning around nine, Annabelle Ludlow was sweeping the boardwalk fronting Big Dan Delaney's Saloon & Gambling Parlor in Tigerville, in preparation for opening, when she spotted a figure standing in one of Big Dan's big plate-glass windows, staring out at her.

She stopped sweeping and peered back at the person watching her. Only, there was no one else in the saloon at this early hour. That person in the window was herself. She just hadn't recognized her own reflection—at least not from that brief glimpse out of the corner of her eye.

But now, staring straight back at her own image in Big Dan's window, she still felt as though she were staring back at a stranger.

The stranger was around twenty. Pretty and long legged, with emerald eyes set in a heart-shaped face framed by thick tresses of dark red hair spilling down her shoulders and back and curling around to caress her sides. That much was Annabelle Ludlow.

The clothes she wore—if you could call them clothes, for they covered little of her—were what made her appear a stranger to herself. Possibly an impostor merely pretending to be Annabelle Ludlow but getting the attire all wrong.

A ranching gal as accustomed to horses as she was to bread-making and house-keeping, Annabelle had customarily worn a wool or calico blouse, denim jeans, and boy-size stockmen's boots with jangling spurs. That was when she was helping her father's and her brother's ranch hands on the range, which had been her favorite thing to do.

(Or *had* been, rather, back before she'd exiled herself from her home ranch as well as *been exiled by* her father, Graham, and brother, Cass Ludlow.)

If she were tending chores inside the Ludlow lodge at the Broken Heart Ranch headquarters, helping the Ludlows' longtime Chinese housekeeper, Chang, prepare meals, launder clothes, or give the lodge a thorough cleaning on some breezy spring day, she would wear a simple gingham day dress over the obligatory corset, camisole, pantaloons, wool stockings, and ankle boots.

She'd gather her red hair, which she'd always been rather vain about, and had always worn long, back out of the way in a long queue.

Never once had she ever had a hankering to dress as skimpily as a parlor girl.

She inspected the girl in the window—the tall, long-legged, willow frame with all the right man-pleasing curves stuffed into a satin-lined cotton corset adorned with floral motifs embellished with guipure lace, tiny pearls, and clear sequins. She wore a short, ruffled cream skirt so sheer that she could see her equally sheer-stockinged legs from her hips all the way down to the high-heeled, black-satin shoes on her feet.

She wore part of her hair up, in curlicues secured

atop her head with an amber rose pin; the rest hung in free-flowing curls down her back. Long, shiny emerald earrings, matching the color of her eyes, dangled from her ears.

Annabelle chewed her thumbnail and smiled. She was a little chagrined by her vanity but also pleased by what she saw.

She saw the horse and rider in the window, beside her own reflection, before she'd heard them ride up. Suddenly the steeldust's sunbathed head was beside her own in the glass. The horse's rider appeared above her own reflection—a bizarrely masked individual appearing out of the bright sunny morning as though from the murky darkness of a waking nightmare.

"Good morning there, little sister! How you doin' this fine day?"

Annabelle gasped and swung around to face the street and her brother, Cass, sitting atop the steeldust and smiling behind the flour sack mask he wore with round holes cut out for the eyes and mouth. Despite the mask, Annabelle could still see the knotted, hideously scarred flesh around his lips as well as around his eyes, which also appeared bloodshot, as though forever irritated by the barn fire that had nearly killed him.

Before the fire, Cass Ludlow had been a dashingly handsome young man. Most would say devilishly handsome, with dimpled cheeks, a cleft chin, high tapering cheekbones, and a thick thatch of unruly brown hair.

He'd been popular with the single young ladies throughout the Black Hills—mostly with the wrong kind of single young ladies. The fire that changed his appearance so drastically, having burned him so terribly, had started when Annabelle had thrown a lamp at him, trying to fend him off when he'd attacked her in a drunken rage in the barn at the Broken Heart headquarters.

Cass had ridden in late and passed out drunk in a pile of hay. It hadn't been the first time. He'd awakened that night to find his young sister trying to steal away on a horse against their father's orders, to ride off to her ex-Confederate lover. Graham Ludlow had forbidden her from seeing Hunter Buchanon not only because Buchanon had fought for the Confederacy during the war, but because Ludlow had arranged for Annabelle to marry the dandy son of one of Ludlow's business associates.

That fire for which Cass blamed his sister had left him a mangled and tortured husk who concealed his hideously scarred face with a burlap mask shaded by the broad brim of his tan Stetson adorned with a band of gaudy Indian beads.

"Cass!" Annabelle said, shocked to see her brother this early in the morning. Cass usually drank, gambled, and caroused—now mostly with parlor girls with strong stomachs—until well after midnight, not rolling out of whatever flea-bit mattress he found himself in until well after noon. "I didn't hear you ride up. You frightened me!"

Unconsciously, holding the broom in her right hand, she dragged her arm across the bulging camisole, suddenly feeling as naked as the day she was born.

"Say, now," Cass said, leaning forward against his saddle horn, grinning behind the mask, letting his red-rimmed eyes wander down his sister's comely countenance, from her bare shoulders down her long legs to the high-heeled shoes on her feet. "Don't you look fine. Yessir, very fine indeed!"

Annabelle flinched under her brother's unnatural scrutiny.

"That getup sure does highlight your finer points, little sister."

"Please, Cass," Annabelle said, feeling her face and ears warm with shame, looking away. "Don't."

"Don't what? Appreciate a fine female form? Ain't that what that getup is supposed to do? Make men appreciate you?"

"Not my brother!" She swung around to the door. "Now, if you'll excuse me, I have a saloon to open."

"Fine, fine," Cass said. She saw in the door's upper glass pane her brother swing down from the steeldust's back. "I came to town to wet my whistle. I ran out last night, playin' poker in the bunkhouse. Can you believe that none of them raggedy-heeled hands of ours could come up with more than a spoonful of busthead?"

Annabelle fumbled the door open, stumbling on her high heels, wanting to get away from her brother's mocking scrutiny as fast as she could. She knew what Cass was doing. He blamed her for the fire that night, and his way of exacting revenge was to stalk her and mock her new way of life, to castigate her for choices she'd made, including the choice to side with her young man, Hunter Buchanon, and the entire Buchanon family against her own.

She turned the sign in the door's window to OPEN, then walked down the wood-floored room to the long, mahogany bar at the rear, under a half-dozen mounted animal heads gazing blankly at nothing. As she approached the bar, she watched Cass walk into the saloon behind her, pausing halfway through the door to scratch a lucifer match to life on his thumbnail and then to hold the flame to the long, black, Mexican cheroot poking out from between his scarred lips.

He drew deeply on the cheroot, then, closing the door behind him, moved forward, blowing a long plume of smoke into the air before him.

He was five years Annabelle's senior, and her only sibling. The only one who'd made it through infancy and the war, that was. An older brother had been killed by the Confederates, thus their father's raw hatred for anyone who'd fought with the Rebel graybacks, as Graham Ludlow called the Confederates.

Cass always dressed, as he was this morning, a little like a Mexican *caballero*, in a red shirt with gaudy Spanish-style embroidering and ruffles down the front, and bell-bottom, deerskin leggings trimmed with jouncing whang strings. A concho-studded shell belt encircled his waist. A fancy, horn-gripped .44 was snugged into a hand-tooled leather holster tied fashionably low on his right leg. The bright beads on the band of his Stetson flashed and winked in the golden morning light angling through a near window.

His masked face with the red-rimmed eyes and scarred pink lips stood out in stark contrast to his brightly stylish attire. Of course, he was aware of that. That's why as he approached the bar now, behind which Annabelle stood, seeking refuge from her older brother's brash appraisal, Cass kept his eyes off the mirror behind her.

Annabelle had set a crate of whiskey bottles atop the bar. She busied herself now with arranging the bottles on a shelf beneath the mahogany.

To her right and behind her, a large cast-iron pot of Big Dan's signature chili bubbled on the black range set in an opening cut into the back bar and flanked with shelves and cupboards of pots, pans, and wood-handled silverware. Annabelle had come early to the saloon, as she did every morning, to prepare for the lunch crowd that would begin arriving by mid-day for the locally famous chili from Dan's ancient, food-stained recipe. One of Big Dan's secrets was to simmer the chili a good long time and to every hour add a dollop or two of rotgut whiskey.

There was no shortage of rotgut whiskey in Tigerville.

"Set me up, sweet sister," Cass said, slapping both open, gloved hands down atop the bar. "Long ride in from the Broken Heart. I feel like I've just crossed the Mojave at high summer."

Annabelle had crouched to place two more bottles atop the shelf. Now she straightened and gave her brother an angry, pointed look, shaking her head with genuine befuddlement. "Why, Cass? Why are you here?"

Cass manufactured a look of hurt and surprise. "What do you mean, sweet sis? I'm your older brother, ain't I? Ain't it a girl's older brother's duty to look after her?" He lowered his eyes to the cleavage of her corset. "Especially when that sister's indiscreet life choices have caused her to become quite the topic of local scandal? Whoo-ee! I sure see why too. A vision you are, Annabelle. Quite the under-dressed one, I might add."

Annabelle planted her hands on the edge of the bar, leaning forward, anger hardening her jaws. "Go home and leave me alone, Cass."

"Set me up."

"No."

"Set me up."

"You hate me. You're not here to protect my honor. You're only here to remind me of what happened to you."

Cass reached out quickly, wrapped his right hand around her left one, and squeezed. His red-rimmed eyes blazed behind the mask. "Of what you did to me!"

"I was only fighting you off. You tried to take a bullwhip to me, Cass. Your own sister. You threatened to whip off every stitch of my clothes! I saw the lamp hanging on the nail, and I grabbed it. I didn't intend for what happened. I only wanted you to leave me alone." She struggled against his hand. "Let me go, Cass—you're hurting me!"

"Sure, sure." Cass curled a nostril behind the mask, making the sacking shift, and released her hand. "I'll let you go . . . so's you can set me up. Come on, pour your brother the good stuff!"

Rubbing her wrist, she said, "Go away and leave me alone. You've no business here. I'm sorry about what happened to you, but it wasn't my fault!"

"I know."

That rocked Annabelle back on her high heels. She blinked. "What?"

"Set me up."

She glanced at him skeptically. He looked directly back at her, his eyes unwavering.

She could see the pain in them—constant and excruciating, and which lay beyond the physical torment of pus constantly erupting from the scars behind the mask. Remembering the horrors of that night, the flames shooting out of the lamp as she smashed it against her brother's head, Annabelle could once again hear his wails piercing the night, smashing it wide open and cleaving her heart.

She'd gladly go back in time and change what had

happened that night if she could. She'd told herself that she didn't feel guilty. That what had happened to Cass hadn't been her fault. But she'd been lying to herself. She hadn't slept through an entire night since it had happened.

Maybe that was another reason she'd banished herself from the ranch, and taken the job here, humiliating herself right out in the open here in Tigerville. Maybe dolling up like a whore and letting men ogle her as though she were nothing more than a prime cut of beef was her way of punishing herself for what had happened to Cass, a once handsome young man. One with a drinking problem and a definite aversion to work, but one who, with his father's backing, still had had a bright future ahead of him.

Now he was a grisly specter every one turned away from with shudders of revulsion and clucks of sympathy. Annabelle didn't know if they were true, but she'd heard rumors that the only girls who'd sleep with him were two half-breed Sioux girls who ran a few cribs in Poverty Gulch at the western edge of Tigerville. Even they made him pay extra.

The least his sister could do was buy him a drink.

CHAPTER 10

Annabelle grabbed a bottle off a shelf on the back bar, a labeled bottle from one of the higher shelves. She set a goblet on the bar in front of her brother. She dug the cork out of the bottle, and half-filled the glass.

That was a lot of whiskey for this time of the morning. At least, for most people. Not for Cass. She used to begrudge him such a destructive indulgence. Not anymore.

He looked down at the drink. His pain-riddled eyes brightened. He smiled up at Annabelle, his teeth and pink gums showing inside the mask, then picked up the glass and threw back half of the whiskey.

He kept his head raised. He held the bourbon in his mouth for a good ten seconds, eyes closed, savoring the liquor, and then swallowed. Annabelle saw the swell roll down his throat in time with the liquid.

He blew out a held breath, lowered his head, and ran a hand across his mouth. His eyes locked on hers, and already she saw the shine of drunkenness in them. Of the beginning of a slight tempering of his pain.

She left the bottle on the bar and studied her brother uncertainly. "You don't blame me?"

"I said I didn't, didn't I?"

"Sometimes it's hard to know what you really mean. You often speak in riddles, Cass."

"All right. Let me be as plain as possible, little sis." Cass raised the glass, glanced at her bare shoulders and upper chest, and said, "Aren't you chilly?"

She glanced at the stove from which heat radiated. Besides, it was mid-summer, and already the temperature was likely in the upper seventies. But Cass knew she wasn't cold. He just wanted another reason to look at her in an unbrotherly fashion and to make mention of her skimpy attire. To rib her again, however indirectly.

As was his way. As had been his way even before the fire.

There was something bent in Cass Ludlow. Even their father knew it. Cass hadn't done a full day's job on the range in years. And he drank as though to quell some deep wound inside him, one even more severe than the scars on his face. One that must have been there since the moment he'd been conceived.

Cass grabbed the bottle and poured more whiskey into his glass. Staring down at the amber liquor, he said, "Let me make it as plain as possible, so there's no mistake. No, I don't blame you for what happened in the barn that night." He looked up at her, and all traces of humor left his eyes. "I blame that big grayback who charmed you senseless."

"Oh Christ, Cass!" Annabelle stepped back, folding her arms over her breasts. "How many men have to die before you and our father finally bury the hatchet?"

"Why do you admire him so, Annabelle? Look at all you've lost on account of him."

She looked at him, frowning. "What do you mean?"

"You've lost your family because you sold us out to him. To them—the Buchanons. And then, after you fought so hard with them *against your family*, and tended old Angus's wounds, all he did was turn his big, broad back on you." Cass laughed caustically and stretched his arms out to indicate her skimpy attire again. "Look at you! You're alone. Working in Big Dan's Saloon as a whore!"

Annabelle slapped the bar with her open palm. "I'm not a whore. I just serve food and sling drinks!"

"Well, you dress like a whore." Cass chuckled again without mirth and took another sip of his whiskey.

"Hunter didn't turn his back on me. You know as well as I do that he lost everything, and he doesn't want us to marry until he can afford to give me the life he thinks I deserve."

"He thinks you deserve this life?"

"He didn't know it would come to this."

"How could he not see this comin'?" Cass laughed and ogled her again. "What did he think would happen? You aligned yourself with him and got yourself exiled by your father. There are not a lot of opportunities for single young ladies in Tigerville. The pretty ones sometimes have to—"

"He wants me to make up with Pa. I refuse. I've told him the money doesn't matter. That all I care about is . . ." Annabelle let the words trail off as she walked over to the stove and gave the chili a stir. She frowned pensively down at the thick chunks of beef and pinto beans swimming in the spicy tomato sauce, and said, plaintively, "If only that poke hadn't been stolen."

She set down the spoon and returned the lid to the pot, swinging abruptly around to Cass, who'd just taken another sip of his drink and was setting the glass back down on the bar. "I wonder who stole it."

Cass looked at her, vaguely curious. "Stole what?"

"Hunter gathered gold dust into a sizable stake—over thirty thousand dollars' worth—so we could elope and start a new life together. He worked hard, prospecting in his spare time away from the ranch. He cached that dust away in an old mine shaft where he didn't think anyone would ever find it. When he and I went into the shaft to retrieve the gold, it was gone."

Annabelle settled her weight on one hip, cocked one foot forward, and studied her devious brother with growing suspicion. "Someone stole it out of that shaft. Someone who'd likely followed him or maybe followed *me* from the Broken Heart to the old cabin near the shaft where Hunter and I used to meet in secret. That person might have seen Hunter and me go into the shaft together, when Hunter first showed me the gold and asked me to marry him."

She paused, choking back tears of sorrow for all that might have been, the happiness that she and Hunter might have known had that gold not been stolen, had her father not waged war on the Buchanons. But she couldn't think about that now.

What was done was done.

She shook off her sorrow and felt her heart beat faster, her suspicion and anger growing as she studied Cass with narrowed eyes and ridged brows. "Who would be that cunning? That malicious? Who would want to sabotage our love so badly? Who could that possibly be, Cass?"

Maybe the black-hearted brother who'd aligned himself

with his Confederate-hating father? she silently added to herself.

Cass stared at her blankly. Then he stepped back and spread his arms, smoke from his cheroot writing a big gray circle in the air beside him. "Guilty as charged, sis. All right. You got me. Yep, it was me. Just couldn't deny myself that thirty thousand dollars. No, sir. Came in mighty handy, though, as you can judge by all them trips to Frisco and Mexico I been takin'. All the new duds I bought. Or . . . hmm."

He set his index finger against his bottom lip and furled his brows in a parody of deep thought. "Maybe I spent it all on the lovely young ladies here in Tigerville. Those that would allow me into their boudoirs, that is. But since the only ones who deign to let the monster into their lair are the sweet, plump little Mexican-Sioux gals over on Poverty Gulch, that's probably rather unlikely, isn't it?"

He brushed his fingers through the air beside him, indicating the grisly specter grinning out at Annabelle from behind the mask.

Annabelle's cheeks warmed with chagrin. If Cass had found that gold, he'd have spent it in grand fashion. He'd probably have left Tigerville right after he'd found it, in fact. He'd probably be in San Francisco or Mexico, haunting the whorehouses and gambling parlors at all hours of the day and night. Surely there he'd have found a woman who, for the right price, would overlook the horrible disfigurement of his face.

But he'd remained at the ranch with his and Annabelle's overbearing father. As far as Annabelle could tell, he hadn't even bought any new clothes over the year since that gold had disappeared. And he was riding the same horse, wearing the same six-gun.

Annabelle looked down at her hands now, sucking her cheeks in shame. "I'm sorry, Cass."

"Don't be. You know me only too well's all." Cass splashed more whiskey into his glass and flashed his sidelong, coyote-like grin. "I'd have suspected me too."

"Tell me something."

Cass sipped the whiskey, then set the glass down on the bar. "Anything, sweet sister. You know that." His words were becoming a little slurred.

"Does Pa really think I'm working as a whore?"

Cass snorted. "What do you care what Pa thinks?"

Annabelle looked away again. Indeed, why should she care what her father thinks? Graham Ludlow may have been her father but he was a ghastly human being, a murderer whom she'd disowned every bit as much as he'd disowned her.

Graham Ludlow could go to hell.

Still, she found herself caring whether he thought she was working the rooms upstairs with the two half-breed girls, the Chinese girl, and the white girl, Ginny, who were still asleep in their cribs and would likely remain asleep until right before noon, when their working day usually started. They'd stumble sleepily and grumpily downstairs for a late breakfast before retiring to their rooms again until the light taps of their "gentlemen" callers started sounding on their doors.

Annabelle would care no more about what her father thought. Doing so had been an old habit.

She'd been aware of Cass's eyes on her, studying her, for the past full minute. Now his voice came, quietly enticing: "Why don't you come back with me today?"

Annabelle turned to him where he stood crouched over his drink, arms encircling his refilled glass and the bottle, his cheroot sending up a slender, billowing smoke ribbon. Sounds from the street grew louder as the sun climbed and intensified.

"You know that's impossible."

Cass shook his head. "Things have changed." He drew the cheroot to his mouth, took a puff, and blew the smoke out against the back bar. He smiled at her, narrowing one devious eye. "Guess who we got for a guest out at the ranch these days?"

"Please, let's not play games, Cass. I have a lot of work to do before—"

"Earnshaw."

She stared at him, glowering incredulously. "Kenneth?"

"One and the same."

"What's he doing here?"

"What do you think?"

Annabelle shook her head obstinately. "He's not here for me!"

"His poppa's railroad has arrived in Buffalo Gap. Thus, young Earnshaw's attentions have returned to the woman who spurned him but who he still loves and is bound and determined to marry!"

Cass slammed his hand down atop the bar and laughed.

Annabelle leaned toward Cass, feeling fire lancing from her eyes. "You can ride back to the Broken Heart and tell Kenneth Earnshaw as well as our father to go to—"

She stopped when an elderly, potbellied man in checked shirt, suspenders, and frayed bowler hat opened the saloon door and leaned inside. He was Beaver Clavin, local drunk and town crier.

Beaver's eyes bugged with excitement as he yelled

around the fat cigar stub in his mouth, "Didja all hear that Marshal Winslow done found yesterday's stage in a broken heap beside the trail south of town? Looks like it was struck by outlaws, and *everyone's dead!*"

Beaver swung around and trundled off to continue spreading the grisly news on down the street.

CHAPTER 11

"Welcome to your new home, Laura," Hunter told Tigerville's new schoolteacher riding behind him on the paint horse he'd acquired in Dead Horse Canyon.

The paint had belonged to one of the killers whom Hunter had killed the night before. The horse he was trailing, a ewe-necked dun, had belonged to the other killer. It was over the dun that both killers now rode belly-down, wrists tied to ankles beneath the dun's broad barrel.

Bobby Lee rode the dun, as well, sitting between the two dead men, resembling nothing so much as a coyote sultan riding off to war on a camel.

Hunter glanced over his shoulder to see Laura looking around at the first shacks and stock pens and clapboard and log business buildings pushing up along the trail around them, where the old army and stagecoach trail dovetailed with Tigerville's main street. It was midmorning, and the booming town was bustling, with men and women—mostly women of the painted variety—milling every which way. Already, raucous piano music was pattering away behind swinging saloon doors, and men were standing around on boardwalks with soapy beer mugs in their fists.

Hunter saw that Laura's cheeks had gone a little pale as she continued to turn her head from left to right and back again, taking it all in. She probably hadn't expected to find such a wild frontier town way up here in the Black Hills, far from the beaten path. Looking around himself, Hunter had to admit that Tigerville was a wild little place.

The town consisted of a dozen or so streets and avenues, and most of those streets and avenues were well peppered with saloons, whorehouses, and gambling parlors in addition to the obligatory mercantiles, grocery stores, butcher shops, gun and feed stores, harness shops, and even a few ladies' fine dress shops and millineries. But mostly the impression, while riding down the main thoroughfare, was of a hectic little Sodom and Gomorrah. Not nearly as sin-soaked as, say, Deadwood Gulch, fifty miles north, but well on its way.

As Hunter kept the paint and the dun moving, he saw ladies acting unladylike, yelling obscenities down at the men from second- and third-floor balconies. Most had little on. He saw a couple wearing nothing at all but fur boas and high-heeled shoes.

He came upon a pretty young blond in a poke bonnet and frilly yellow dress handing out little scraps of paper from a wicker basket hooked over her arm. Smiling as sweetly as the parson's daughter on Easter Sunday, she strode along the street's right side, shoving the cards at the men standing in clusters or hurrying from one side of the street to the other. As she approached Hunter and Laura, she smiled a crooked-toothed smile up at Hunter and, squinting against the bright morning sunlight, shoved a card into his hand and said, "Here you go, sir. Come an' see us sometime—without the lady. Or you can both come. However you like it!"

She winked then flounced away, not so much as giving the grisly cargo on Hunter's packhorse so much as a second glance but merely greeting Bobby Lee with, "Hello, pretty puppy."

That wasn't surprising—at least the part about her not acknowledging the dead men wasn't. Lots of folks mistook Bobby Lee for a dog simply because they weren't used to seeing domesticated coyotes in town. The citizens of Tigerville witnessed shootings on the streets or in the saloons nearly every day, and nearly every day they woke to a body or two in the muddy gutters or squirreled away behind outhouses or wood piles.

"What does it say?" Laura asked, peering over Hunter's shoulder at the scrap of paper in his gloved left hand.

Buchanon glanced at her. "Sure you want to know?"

"Yes," she said.

"All right. Don't say I didn't warn you."

He held the card up for the woman to read the two sentences in ornate black typescript: *"Join the party at the Harem Club. Men taken in and done for just one dollar!"*

"Oh dear."

"Yeah."

Hunter let the breeze take the note as he continued walking the paint down the festive main drag of Tigerville, which, as wild as it was now, had been wilder only a few years ago, in the years right after the war when he and his father and two brothers had come to this country from Georgia.

Back then, Tigerville and the hills around it had been a hotbed of bloody violence. This was right after General George Armstrong Custer had opened the Hills to gold-seekers in 1874, despite the Hills still belonging to the Sioux Indians, as per the Laramie Treaty of 1868.

Men and mules and horses and placer mining equipment poured up the Missouri River from Kansas and Missouri by riverboat and mule- and ox-train, and the great Black Hills Gold Rush exploded.

Naturally, crime also exploded, in the forms of claim-jumping and bloody murder as well as the stealing of gold being hauled by ore wagons, called Treasure Coaches, southwest to Cheyenne, Wyoming, and the nearest railroad. Tigerville was on the Cheyenne-Custer-Deadwood Stage Line, and the coaches negotiating that formidable country were preyed upon even more than they were now by road agents.

For those bloody reasons, the commissioners of Pennington County, chief among them Annabelle's father Graham Ludlow, brought in so-called lawman Frank Stillwell and the small gang of hardtails who rode with him, also calling themselves "lawmen." Bona fide crime dwindled while the death rate went up. It was said in these parts that you couldn't ride any of the roads spoking out of Tigerville and into the surrounding hills without coming upon Stillwell's low-hanging "tree fruit" in the form of hanged men.

Men hanged without benefit of trial.

Many of those men had once fought for the Confederacy. It seemed that most of the "tree fruit" Stillwell "grew" hailed from the South, which wasn't one bit fishy at all, given Stillwell's history of being second-in-command of one of the worst Union prisoner-of-war camps during the Civil War and having a widely known and much-talked-about hatred for the warriors of the old South.

Animosity between the Northern and Southern fighters had abated since Stillwell had been killed in last year's trouble that had pitted him along with the Ludlows and Max Chaney against the Buchanons. War memories and grudges were fading at long last, but last year's eruption of trouble had left both families—the Buchanons and the Ludlows—badly scarred. Battered to the point they would likely never recover, Hunter reflected with an inward flinch as a rusty knife of his own personal pain twisted in his heart.

"Hey, Buchanon—what you got there?"

The man's query, shouted from a boardwalk fronting the Black Hills–Cheyenne stage manager's office sandwiched between Howell's Tonic Emporium and Thomas C. Wannamaker's Justice of the Peace office, lassoed Hunter's consciousness and dragged him back into present-day Tigerville and the situation at hand.

Five men were standing around outside the stage office, between the office itself and the hitchrack at which six saddled horses were tied. The horses were sweat-matted; they'd been ridden hard. The five men were obviously the ones who'd done the hard riding, for their suitcoats and Stetsons were liberally floured in trail dust.

Hunter recognized all five as men from right here in Tigerville. A couple—Mel Fitzgerald and Warren Davenport—were both businessmen who served on the city council. Another— the big, burly "Iron Bill Todd" was a blacksmith, market hunter, and sawyer. The other two—Denny Hutton and Marcus Wheeler—were shopkeepers. Deputy U.S. Marshal Walt Winslow had apparently gathered these men into a posse to ride out in search of the stage.

Winslow had been sent from the territorial capital of

Yankton to hold down the proverbial fort here in Tigerville since Sheriff Frank Stillwell's demise last year along with all of Stillwell's outlaw "deputies" having been turned down in what was locally known as the Buchanon-Ludlow-Chaney War. Stillwell's successor, a town marshal appointed by the city fathers until they could elect another sheriff and seat deputies, had only been in office six weeks before he was shot in the back by a drunk doxie in a whorehouse unfittingly if imaginatively called The Library. After that, for understandable reasons, it had been hard to find a man or men who valued their lives so little as to don the badge of Tigerville Town Marshal.

Or county sheriff, for that matter.

"We thought you was dead!" said Mel Fitzgerald, a small man in a bowler hat and holding an old, double-barrel shotgun on his left shoulder. A stogie smoldered between his thin lips.

Hunter drew the paint up to the hitchrack's right end. "It was close."

Big Bill Todd, who was as big as Hunter but a good ten years older, stepped up to the edge of the boardwalk, looked gravely up at Hunter, and said, "We rode out last night, about an hour after you was expected here in town. We found the coach."

He paused, drew his mouth corners down beneath his shaggy gray mustache. "We saw poor ol' Charley layin' there in the trail. Brought him and the other fella to town. They're at the undertaker's."

"We tried to track you, but it got too dark," said the other city councilman, Warren Davenport, a tall, flat-eyed, raw-boned man in early middle age. "Then this mornin', the trail was too damn cold for any of us old farts to track you.

Winslow brought us back to town. He's in the manager's office now, palaverin' with Sullivan about what to do next. Reckon he won't have to do *nothin'* next now, though, 'cept bury poor Charley, that is."

His baleful bulldog eyes shifted to the dun over which the two dead men drooped.

"Buchanon!" exclaimed the station manager, Scotty Sullivan, who, apparently having heard Hunter palavering with the others, had pulled open his office door to stare in shock at the big blond jehu and his badly rumpled female charge. "What the hell happened?"

His round-framed spectacles glinted in the sunlight. He quickly doffed his bowler hat, glanced sheepishly at Laura, and said, "Uh . . . pardon my French, please, Miss."

Hunter had swung down from his horse and was tying the paint at the hitchrack. Bobby Lee leaped down off the dun's back and shot after a cat he'd spied poking its head out from a break between buildings on the street's opposite side. "What can I tell you, Scotty?" Hunter said in disgust. "We got hit. Charley's dead. Bushwhacked."

U.S. Deputy Marshal Walt Winslow stepped up beside Sullivan in the open doorway of the stage manager's office—a short, gray-haired man who resembled a sharp-featured, straight-backed, flinty-eyed Lutheran minister in his black suit, bullet-crowned black hat, crisp white shirt, and black foulard tie. Only, Winslow was more of a minister of justice as attested the age-tarnished moon-and-star badge pinned to the vest and peeking out from behind his left coat lapel.

Winslow had his pale, slender fingers dipped into the pockets of his vest, near the silver-washed chain of a hidden pocket watch. A thin, carefully trimmed mustache mantled his small mouth.

"There's one more. Ike Talon."

Winslow widened his eyes and nodded once, slowly, obviously stirred by the information. He'd been after Talon ever since Talon had come to this country to haunt the Black Hills trails, so he was well aware of Talon's reputation. With fresh interest, Winslow glanced at the two dead men slumped over the dun, then turned to Buchanon, his flinty eyes sharp.

"Is Talon still out there?" He jerked his head to the south.

Hunter reached up to help Laura down from the paint's back. When he'd set her gently on the ground, he took her hand and led her up onto the boardwalk.

As he did, the five men in Winslow's posse doffed their hats and cleared their throats deferentially to the pretty but bedraggled young woman, shuffling aside to make way for her and the jehu as they would for any two survivors of any fierce battle.

Especially when they'd survived such an infamous group as Talon's notorious bunch.

Hunter moved up to where Sullivan and Winslow stood atop the three steps leading up to the office door, gazed directly at the marshal, and said, "I got a feeling I know where Talon is. I'll see to him . . ." He slid his glance to Scotty Sullivan and hardened his jaws as he finished his thought. ". . . for Charley."

Winslow said, "That's not your job, son."

"I'm makin' it my job."

"No vigilante justice." Winslow smiled coldly, narrowed

his hard eyes a little, and shook his head once, slowly. "Not on my watch."

"Don't worry," Buchanon said. "He'll get his chance." He looked at Sullivan and then at Laura, flanking Hunter. "Scotty, this is Miss Laura Meyers. She was the other passenger on the stage."

"Miss Meyers," Scotty said, "it is indeed a pleasure."

"The pleasure is mine," Laura said, taking one step forward on her battered bare feet. The posse men were trying hard not to stare at the revealingly torn dress that was all but hanging off of her. "I am the new schoolteacher here in Tigerville, Mister . . ."

"This is Scotty Sullivan, Laura," Hunter said.

He knew right away he shouldn't have used her first name. They'd spent a night together on the run. Now he was using her first name.

Hmmm.

That "Hmmm" was on every face around Buchanon and Laura.

"Laura Meyers," he quickly corrected. "She's here to teach school."

Hunter could feel eyes on them both, studying them both critically, especially the woman's torn dress and obvious beauty despite the beating she'd taken.

"Mister Sullivan!" a female voice called above the din of the bustling street. "Mister Sullivan!"

A familiar voice to Hunter's ears.

Hunter's heartbeat quickened.

He and all of the men around him as well as Laura turned to where a scantily clad redhead with long dangling earrings the same green color as her eyes pushed through a small crowd of men standing outside of the Justice of the Peace's office, listening in on Hunter's conversation with Sullivan. Annabelle Ludlow stepped up onto the boardwalk, looking flushed and shaken, her eyes wide with worry.

She strode a little uncertainly in her high heels toward Sullivan and said, "Scotty, is it true?" she fairly screamed. "Tell me Hunter's not—"

Her eyes found Buchanon and she stopped dead in her tracks. Relief instantly washed over her, her eyes opening even wider, lower jaw falling. She slid her eyes to the pretty albeit disheveled woman standing close beside Hunter, and deep lines cut across her otherwise smooth forehead.

Buchanon held his left hand out to take Annabelle's hand in his, to assure her that he was unharmed. The blood appeared to run out of her face. She stumbled backward in her high heels. Her eyes rolled back in her head, her chin shot up like the prow of a boat cresting a stormy ocean wave. She swung half-around to face the street, then fell straight back into Hunter's outstretched arms with a high-pitched, raking exhalation.

"Annabelle!" he said, wrapping his arms around her slender, curvy frame, looking into her face, her eyelids fluttering. "Annabelle!"

"Passed out, poor girl," said one of the posse members behind Hunter.

"Couldn't take the shock of it, I reckon," muttered another. "All of it."

Another man chuckled dryly.

Hunter crouched, shifting his left arm around Annabelle's shoulders while snaking his right arm under the girl's knees, lifting her off the boardwalk and up against his chest. He glanced a little sheepishly at the men around him. More men had gathered from the street, for there was obviously something interesting happening out in front of the stage manager's office—interesting even beyond what usually transpired on the streets of this rollicking boom-town on any given day.

"That's Annabelle?" Laura asked, gazing at the girl in Hunter's arms, obviously a little surprised to see his once-betrothed so scantily clad.

Hunter understood. He hadn't gotten used to it either.

Flushing with embarrassment as well as with shame at what his lovely Annabelle had become over the past year, in the wake of the war between his family and hers, he looked from Sullivan to Laura and said, "I best tend to her. Just appears a might overcome with the vapors. I'll get her into a bed over at Big Dan's and then come back to get you settled in over at the school, Laur—er, I mean, Miss Meyers."

Laura gave him a sympathetic smile.

Another man chuckled.

CHAPTER 12

Annabelle in his arms, Hunter started across the street, looking both ways and hurrying ahead of a wagon moving toward him from one direction and pausing to let another wagon, moving toward him from the other direction, pass in front of him.

As he did, through dust lifting from churning wagon wheels and pounding horse hooves, he caught sight of a man standing out front of Big Dan Delaney's Saloon & Gambling Parlor. He couldn't see the man well, because Hunter was too busy trying to avoid being run over, and the dust obscured the man, as well, but he had the vague impression of something off about the man's features.

When he'd let a couple of horseback riders pass then hurried to the opposite side of the street, he headed north along the various boardwalks fronting the shops, saloons, and pleasure houses. He looked ahead toward Big Dan's place again.

The man he'd seen before, and who'd appeared to be staring toward Hunter and Annabelle, was no longer on the boardwalk fronting the saloon. Vaguely, Hunter noticed a rider on a big steeldust horse riding away from Dan's, and he even more vaguely noticed that the man was brightly attired in the Mexican style, as the man staring at him had been, but Hunter's main consideration was Annabelle, so he let the observer slip from his mind.

He crossed a street intersecting with Dakota Avenue, avoided a nasty collision with an ore dray rolling into town from one of the mines in the surrounding bluffs, and skirted a couple of dogs skirmishing over a dead rabbit. Quickening his pace as he approached the saloon in which Annabelle had taken a job as, of all things, a saloon girl, he saw Big Dan striding toward him from the north.

Big Dan was broader than he was tall, and he carried most of that weight in his gut. But he was fancily attired in a green-checked suit with a silk-banded black opera hat and a long, green cutaway coat, with spats on his shoes. He was proudly adorned with gold cuff links, and a diamond stickpin impaled the knot of his black cravat.

Big Dan Delaney had worked the mines with picks, shovels, and water pumps before building a stake for himself and buying the saloon, formerly the Red Rooster, from a mean drunk named Paul Elsbernd. Looking at him now, you'd never suspect Big Dan of the lowly rock-breaker and notorious, thuggish carouser he once had been.

Now he played the part—or at least dressed the part—of a respectable businessman and gentleman of some repute, always attiring himself to the nines, wielding a cherry walking stick with a carved wooden handle, and smoking a meerschaum pipe. He walked with his spade-bearded chin in the air, lowering it only to nod at the ladies before twisting his head to appraise their retreating behinds.

"Good Lord!" Big Dan exclaimed as he and Hunter both approached the saloon's front door from equal distances but from opposite sides. "What happened to my gal?"

Dan's referring to Annabelle as "his gal" graveled Hunter. He'd heard Dan blustering before to others: "Have you seen my new gal?" "Come on over to Big Dan's and check out my new gal, fellas. Graham Ludlow's daughter is now slingin' drinks for me in fine form!" He'd guffaw loudly enough to be mistaken for an approaching thunderstorm.

"She's not your gal, Dan," Hunter said, shouldering through the saloon's batwing doors and starting across the dim, cave-like room toward the stairs at the far end. The aromas of cooking chili saturated the air, as they did all times of the day and night. Big Dan might not have had the most comely girls working his upstairs cribs, but they were only fifty cents, and the chili, thirteen cents a bowl but only ten with a five-cent beer, was the main attraction.

Until he'd hired Graham Ludlow's comely, redheaded daughter to sling drinks for him, that was.

"Don't tell me she got hit on the street!" Dan thundered behind Hunter. "This will not stand—oh dear Lord! She's my biggest moneymaker and she never even takes a turn on her back. Have you summoned a doctor?"

Folks were forever getting hit by passing wagons on the streets of Tigerville. Most of those folks getting hit, however, were usually intoxicated. But there were always one or two who'd simply made a miscalculation of the traffic currents and got themselves hammered by a horse or an iron-shod wheel.

As he mounted the stairs, Hunter glanced at the big, garishly clad man standing in the middle of the room behind him, Big Dan's eyes and furred mouth wide in shock, likely anticipating a big drop in business if Annabelle was to be bedridden or worse, and not flouncing about the saloon to the delight of Big Dan's lusty, lowly regulars.

"She just fainted," Hunter said. "I'm gonna put her in a bed."

"Oh, thank heavens!" Dan exclaimed through a blowing exhalation. "She alone has nearly doubled my business over the past month!"

Hunter's cheeks warmed with rage as he continued up the stairs and into the musty second-floor hall. He saw a door standing partway open on his right. He kicked the door wide, stepped into the room, and stopped.

He glowered at a half-naked man lying on the bed before him, belly-down, arms spread out to either side of his head—a skinny gent, with a tangled mess of long, ginger-colored hair. The man was loudly sawing logs and muttering in his sleep.

"Christ," Hunter grumbled as he swung around and headed back out the door.

The man must have been a leftover customer from the night before. He'd probably passed out drunk and the girls hadn't been able to wake him so they could usher him out after the business transaction had been completed.

"Annabelle! Oh, my good heavens—what *happened*?"

Hunter turned to see a girl dressed in only a camisole, pantaloons, pink slippers, and with feathers in her sleep-mussed hair, staring at him from a half-open door ahead and on his left. She was a little brunette named Ginny, Hunter knew only because once Annabelle had started working at Big Dan's, Hunter had learned everything he could about the place.

"She'll be all right," Hunter told the girl. "Which one is her room?"

Ginny hurried out of her room, glancing with concern at Annabelle in Hunter's arms, dragging the heels of her overlarge slippers, and opened a door on the hall's left side. "This one's Annabelle's. Are you sure she'll be all right?"

"Yes. Thanks, Ginny."

"What happened?"

"I'll let her tell it."

"She didn't get hit out in the street, did she?"

"No."

"I had a friend—Millie—who got flattened by a lumber dray. Deader'n a door nail, poor girl!"

Hunter carried Annabelle into the room and gentled her onto the double brass bed. Remaining in the doorway, Ginny placed one slippered foot atop the other and twisted a finger into her long, straight hair. "You're Hunter Buchanon, ain't ya?"

She flashed a coquettish smile.

Hunter crouched over Annabelle, feeling her neck for a pulse. "That's right."

Hunter was no *medico*, but her pulse felt strong.

"How could you let her get away?" Ginny looked at Annabelle. "She's just about the prettiest girl in town. Too bad she ain't workin' the line. If she was, she'd make a whole lot more money than she is just—"

Hunter turned to the girl in the doorway, glaring. "Annabelle's not a whore!"

Ginny widened her eyes with a start, then cast Hunter a boldly skeptical look. "Sometimes, you know, Mister Buchanon, when a girl don't have a man to look after her, she often has to turn to the world's oldest profession just to survive."

"Would you leave us alone, Ginny?"

"Just sayin'," Ginny said, turning away haughtily and shuffling loudly off down the hall.

Hunter felt a hand close over his left one, which he'd wrapped around Annabelle's forearm. He looked down at Annabelle's hand atop his. She stared up at him through green eyes that complemented so beautifully her copper red hair.

"Are you all right?" Hunter asked.

Annabelle sat up, gazing into his eyes, her own eyes round as silver dollars, worry lines creasing their corners. "Are you?"

"I'm fine. No worse for the wear."

"Beaver Clavin said the stage was hit, that you were dead."

"He was only half-right."

Annabelle sagged back against the pillow with a sigh, her eyes remaining on his. "Oh, Hunter . . ."

"Yeah," he said, glancing down at her half-clad body. "I know." His tone was grave and not so subtly pitched with reproach. "Look at you."

"It's a job."

Hunter gave a caustic grunt. He opened his mouth to speak but stopped when Ginny's footsteps sounded in the hall again. He turned to the partly open door as the doxie poked her head into the room, extending a glass of water. "For Annabelle," she said timidly.

Annabelle lifted her head from the pillow. "Thank you, Ginny."

Hunter walked to the door and accepted the water from the doxie, who glanced around him to say, "You gonna be all right, Annabelle? Big Dan's awful worried."

"Tell Dan I'll be back down to tend the chili in a minute."

Ginny laughed as she turned and shuffled back down the hall.

Hunter returned to the bed, gave Annabellethe water, and sat down on the bed's edge. "Why'd you faint?"

Annabelle shrugged a shoulder, glanced toward the curtained window. "I was just so certain you were dead. Then, when I saw you standing there . . . I don't know, I never figured myself for the fainting type of girl, but . . ." She returned her gaze to his. "I don't know what I'd do if anything happened to you, Hunter."

He smiled and squeezed her hand. "Nothing's going to happen to me."

"It came close."

"Dumb luck. They caught us sitting like a rabbit in the grass."

"Why?"

"Ah, hell," Hunter said, wanting to avoid the subject. "I'd best get back over to the stage office. You sure you're gonna be all right?"

"Who is she?"

Hunter frowned. "Who's who?"

"You know very well who's who." Annabelle's tone had turned to tart anger. She glared up at him with a slow-boiling suspicion. "The pretty woman whose torn dress was hanging in ribbons off her buxom body."

"Oh, her." Hunter turned away, feeling his ears turn as hot as glowing coals. "She's the new schoolteacher here in Tigerville."

"What's her name?"

"Laura."

"Pretty name for a pretty woman. Married?"

"Not for long."

Annabelle glared up at him, her eyes hard as jade. "Hmm. Sounds right scandalous."

Hunter grinned. "Jealous?"

"No," Annabelle said pointedly, but her eyes gave the lie to her words. "You're a free man . . . just as I'm a free woman. That's the way you wanted it. That's the way you have it."

"Only because I couldn't give you the life you deserve."

"As if it's your place to decide what I deserve!" Her voice was getting louder, her tone sharper.

"I have nothing, Annabelle. A few dollars in my pocket, the clothes on my back. Pa can't work, so I'm supporting him too. Most everything I make goes to the boarding house." Sorrow and frustration building in him, Hunter placed his hand on Annabelle's face, caressed her cheek with his thumb. "I'm off driving the stage more than I'm here in town. That's no life for a girl like you."

Tears glazed Annabelle's eyes. She punched the bed with the end of one fist and brushed her other fist across her nose. "Dammit all, Hunter! What happened to us?"

"Your father happened to us!" he heard himself blurt out through clenched teeth.

She stared up at him in shock. "You blame me, don't you?"

"No!"

"Yes, you do. I see it in your eyes." More tears glazed her eyes as she studied him probingly.

"It's not true, Annabelle."

Was it? No. He could never blame Annabelle for her father's actions.

But maybe deep inside he did harbor some resentment toward her, for the mere fact that she was a Ludlow. And that the Ludlows had killed his two brothers, almost killed his father, burned their ranch, and ruined whatever future he and Annabelle might have had together.

No. It wasn't true. He loved Annabelle more than life itself. That was why he hadn't gotten a decent night's sleep over the past year and walked around feeling as though he had a knife in his guts.

He loved her and couldn't have her. Oh, they could go ahead and get married. They could go through the motions. But what then? They might have a few good loving weeks together . . . before the strain of living in dire poverty drove a wedge between them.

Theirs had been a storybook romance. A story of secret trysts in remote cabins, of quiet afternoon horseback rides in sun-washed beaver meadows. Of making love in the soft grass and ferns lining a chuckling mountain stream in the shade of breeze-brushed aspens, to the piping of nuthatches and bluebirds.

If they married now, the way things were—both of them penniless—they'd soon share one of those sad marriages Hunter bore witness to every day around the old prospector shacks on Poverty Gulch and elsewhere in scattered claims throughout the Black Hills. They would be two sullen, sour, haggard people toiling for dimes, hating their lives and soon hating each other. Rarely speaking or touching. Just putting up with each other as they toiled to stay alive as though their lives were not worth living.

He couldn't abide such a life. Not for him and Annabelle.

"I think it's true, Hunter," Annabelle said, placing her hand on his own cheek now, gazing into his eyes as though trying to peer into his soul. "You blame me."

"I don't." Hunter rose from the bed and gazed down at her. "But don't you think it's time you stopped punishing me for my decision not to marry you and ruin your life?"

She frowned again, puzzled. "What are you talking about?"

"This." Hunter gestured at her skimpy attire. "You took this job . . . dress like this . . . to punish me." He shook his head defiantly. "It's not going to work. I won't ruin everything just because you've chosen to humiliate yourself in public. Go home, Annabelle. Your father can give you the life you deserve. I hate the bastard, but he can give you a better life than I can!"

Annabelle scrunched her face up with rage. "You go to hell, Hunter Buchanon!"

"All right." Hunter drew a breath, hardened his jaws, nodded slowly. "That's the last I'll say on the subject. You live however you want to live. I wash my hands of you."

Annabelle sat up and dropped her feet to the floor, screaming, "You go to hell!"

Hunter strode to the door, stopped, and turned back to her. He glanced at her corset again, at her long legs clad in sheer, skin-colored stockings, and said, "Be careful, Annabelle. If you start enjoying this life . . . how men look at you and fawn over you . . . you might not find a way out of it."

He turned and walked out.

Behind him, Annabelle screamed, "*Go to hell with Miss Meyers and don't you ever come back, you bastard!*"

CHAPTER 13

Fuming, Hunter descended the stairs to Big Dan's main drinking hall.

Dan stood at the bar, a beer, a shot of whiskey, and his opera hat on the mahogany bar before him. Ginny sat at a table near the potbellied stove in the room's center, pale bare legs crossed, smoking a cigarette. She hunched as though chilled.

Both pimp and whore stared dubiously at Hunter walking angrily down the stairs, blond brows sharply ridged above his eyes. He glanced at the pair only once, embarrassed by the outburst they'd obviously overheard upstairs.

As he gained the bottom of the stairs, a four-legged creature scurried into the saloon beneath the batwing doors, toenails clickety-clacking on the wood floor.

"Bobby Lee!" Hunter said, scowling curiously down at the coyote. "What in tarnation . . . ?"

"It's all right," Big Dan said, taking a drag off a stogie. "We've gotten used to that brush wolf in here. Follows the li'l gal around like a loyal dog, shows his teeth at the men who get too handsy." He grinned. "That's all right. Keeps 'em in line. Besides, some o' the boys regard him as a curiosity. A brush wolf in a saloon following around the purtiest li'l gal in Tigerville!" Ignoring Ginny's glare, he winked at Buchanon. "He adds interest in my place. I like that."

Bobby Lee was sniffing the floor like a dog on a scent, nails clacking. He must have caught the scent he was after because he suddenly shot past Hunter without so much as a glance at his master, then bolted up the stairs.

Hunter turned around to scowl after the brush wolf. "Well, I'll be damned. I was wonderin' where he disappeared to. I thought he was out in the countryside, hunting rabbits. That disloyal little snipe!"

Oh well, he thought. *At least he's looking after Annabelle.* It appeared that someone needed to. He'd always thought she'd had more sense than she obviously did.

To hell with her!

He continued on outside and then negotiated his way back across the street. The small crowd fronting the stage manager's office had dispersed. Laura was no longer there either. Neither was the dun horse hauling the dead killers. The only ones still present were Marshal Winslow and the stage manager, Scotty Sullivan. They were conversing on the boardwalk fronting the office.

As Hunter mounted the boardwalk, he looked around and said, "Where's the teacher?"

Sullivan and Winslow turned to him.

Winslow smiled and said, "We figured you had enough woman trouble on your hands, Buchanon. I had Warren Davenport take her over to the school in that fancy chaise of his, and help get her settled in. I'm having the luggage from the stage hauled back to town in a wagon. She and her portmanteaus should be reunited soon."

Hunter ignored the faintly mocking glint in both men's eyes.

"Dahl should take a look at her." Dr. Norton Dahl was the *medico* here in Tigerville.

"I suggested it," Winslow said. "She wouldn't hear of it."

"Pretty woman." Sullivan's mouth corners came up as his devious glance darted to Winslow before he continued to Hunter. "She looked a might reluctant to leave with Davenport. Kept calf-eyein' Big Dan's place, like maybe she'd prefer you introduced her to her new place of employment. The big blond Viking berserker who saved her from certain death at the hands of Ike Talon."

"Maybe you curled her pretty toes for her last night," opined Winslow.

He winked at Sullivan, who snorted and cleared his throat.

Hunter muttered peevishly under his breath, his mood still foul in the wake of his dustup with Annabelle. He had more important things to do than stand around here, being mocked by a Deputy U.S. Marshal getting too old for his job and the stage manager who spent as much time in the whorehouses around Tigerville as he did managing his part of the stage line.

Hunter stepped off the boardwalk and headed south.

"Where you headed, Buchanon?" the marshal called behind him.

Hunter didn't respond to the man's question. He just kept walking, his torment over Charley's unprovoked killing bubbling to the surface of his general malaise.

A good friend dead. His girl—his *former* girl—slinging drinks in a cathouse.

What next?

He stopped when he came to the shingle marked DOCTOR NORTON DAHL, MD. He climbed a set of outdoor stairs to a rickety wood door. He tried the doorknob. Finding it locked, he knocked on the door. He could smell cigarette smoke oozing through the vertical cracks between the boards comprising the door. Loud, hacking coughing resounded from within the office as did the shambling of heavy feet.

Hunter knocked on the locked door again.

"I'm coming, for God's sake!" came Dahl's raspy voice. "I'm coming! I'm coming!" As the lock clattered and the door jerked inward, a large, round, bespectacled eye stole a look around the edge of the door. "By God, you better have money or your next stop is the bone orchard!"

That eye widened in recognition. A loosely rolled quirley dangled from one corner of the *medico*'s mustached mouth. "Oh, Buchanon." He coughed again, violently, then drew the door open a little wider. He exclaimed around the cigarette, "I'm damn tired of not getting paid. I gotta eat, too, same as everyone else!"

"Who didn't pay you?"

"The last fella I treated."

"Did he have a bullet in his arm? A big bald fella with a walrus mustache?"

Dahl nodded. "Took me almost an hour to dig out that slug. I had to call three men in from the street to hold him down or I'd likely have cut his arm off!"

"Is he still here?" Hunter looked into the doctor's office behind the *medico*.

"No. He should be. He lost a lot of blood. He stumbled out of here—without paying me one bloody cent!—

muttering something about how he'd get better treatment at the Payday Club. I told him to go on over to the Payday and die howling from the pony drip, and I would dance a happy little jig on his grave!"

In his late thirties, jaded, rumpled, and seedy, Dahl blew his own whiskey breath at Hunter. Cigarette smoke jetted from his nostrils.

"Thanks, Doc." Hunter whipped around and started down the stairs.

Behind him, the sawbones yelled, "Hey, the word goin' around is you're dead!"

"Not yet, Doc!"

Hunter negotiated his way across the busy main street again. A couple of street urchins, the orphan spawn of parlor girls, hounded him for pennies for rock candy. He dug what few coins he could spare from his pants and tossed them back over his shoulder. The orphans converged on them, snarling like wolves.

Hell, Hunter didn't have enough money for his own rock candy.

What he needed, though, was a drink. He'd get one soon to settle his nerves. First, though, he intended to kill Ike Talon. That right there would likely settle his nerves just fine. He would celebrate with a steak and all the trimmings, if he had that much coinage left in his pockets.

He found the Payday on the corner of Second Street and Third Avenue. It had been the first saloon and hotel in Tigerville, but now the town's growing heart had shifted to the east, abandoning and antiquating the place. Its second floor was a pleasure parlor and opium den run by a Chinaman everyone called Steve because they couldn't pronounce his real name. You patronized the Payday when you'd been kicked out of every other house in town or didn't have the jingle for better busthead and more attractive or talented women.

Hunter stepped over a black man passed out on the front step and pushed through the batwings. He took a quick look around at the shabby saloon boasting a half dozen tables at which a half dozen sullen men—mostly miners and ore haulers—nursed drinks and smoked. Two old-timers were playing checkers.

A tall gaunt man stood behind the bar with pomaded hair and a pinstriped shirt and bow tie. He stood like a statue, staring straight at Hunter without expression. The man's chest jerked as though something had suddenly come alive inside him, and he brought a white handkerchief to his mouth. The handkerchief was already spotted red but after he coughed into it so violently that he made Hunter's lungs feel like ground beef, and pulled it away from his mouth, it was redder.

He opened and closed his mustached mouth several times as he set the handkerchief down on the bar, and swallowed, eyes looking rheumy and sick.

A lunger.

Not seeing Talon in the dingy, smoky shadows around him, Hunter moved into the room and stopped six feet from the bar. The barman continued to look at him without interest. Hunter could hear the Chinaman, Steve, speaking a mix of Chinese and broken English beyond a curtained doorway flanking the barman, and another man speaking English, trying to understand what Steve was saying but apparently having a devil of a time.

"Big man, bald-headed gent with a walrus mustache," Hunter said to the barman.

The barman drew his mouth corners down. He slid his oily-eyed gaze to the stairs on his right. "Upstairs. End of the hall on the left."

Hunter swung around and headed for the stairs, taking the steps two at a time but moving quietly on the balls of his feet. He crossed the landing and then continued to the second floor.

He walked through the lingering fetor of the second-floor hall lit by only the single window at the end. He winced as the floorboards complained against his tread, moaning and groaning like old women on their deathbeds.

He stopped at the last door on his left, tilted his head toward the upper panel.

On the other side of the door, a young woman's voice said, "What are you doin', hon? You'd best stay in bed and—"

A man's deep voice said throatily, "Shut up, you damn fool!"

Hunter stepped back, drew the LeMat, clicked the hammer back, and smashed the underside of his right foot against the door, just beneath the knob. As the door exploded inward, wood slivers flying from the frame, Hunter saw Talon, clad in only red longhandles and a gun belt and pistol, raise a double-barrel shotgun and level it on the doorway.

Talon gave a savage grin, the white line of his teeth showing beneath his thick, black walrus mustache.

Hunter threw himself to the left a half a wink before rose-colored flames blossomed from one of the shotgun's two large maws. The buckshot caromed through the open door and blew a pumpkin-size hole in the wall on the hall's opposite side. The second blast came another half a wink on the heels of the first, carving another generous hole in the wall two feet above where Hunter had struck on his left shoulder and hip on the hall floor.

Inside Talon's room, the soiled dove screamed shrilly.

Hunter rose to his knee and thrust his LeMat through the open door in time to see big Ike Talon drop the shotgun and hurl himself out the window on the room's far side. Glass shattered as Talon dropped straight down beneath the window and out of sight.

A loud thump and a groan sounded from below.

Hunter rose and ran across the room. The whore, sitting up on the bed and covering herself with a sheet, pressing her hands to her ears, was still screaming as though she were being tortured by a dozen Apache braves with sharp knives.

Hunter poked the LeMat through the broken window.

Below, a secondary roof sloped down away from the main building. Talon had just gained his feet. His left arm was in a bloodstained sling. As he ran down the sloping roof toward the far edge, he twisted around and hurled a shot from the Colt in his right fist toward Hunter, who flinched as the bullet screeched past his left ear to break the dresser mirror behind him.

The whore screamed even louder. The screams felt like two open palms slammed again and again against Hunter's ears.

"Christalmight, lady—shut up!" he yelled as he poked the LeMat out the broken window again.

He fired two rounds but one round only chewed wood from the edge of the roof and the other flew through the air where Talon's big, longhandle-clad body had been a moment before, just before he'd hurled himself with a loud curse off the roof and into the alley flanking the Payday.

A wooden crash came from below.

Hunter leaped through the window.

He struck on the roof ten feet below, bending his knees and hurling himself forward, rolling twice, then rising to his feet and gazing out over the edge of the roof and into the alley. He raised the LeMat and tracked Talon as the man ran, limping, down the alley to Hunter's right. Buchanon fired just as the man darted around the front corner of a building on the alley's opposite side.

Hunter's slug struck brick and mortar with a resounding spang.

Buchanon cursed.

Talon slid his face out around the corner of the building covering him. He grinned at Hunter and made a lewd gesture, then pulled his head back out of sight.

CHAPTER 14

Hunter cursed again, fury burning in him.

He quickly replaced the LeMat's spent cartridges with fresh, spun the wheel, then leaped off the edge of the roof and onto the now-scattered pile of shipping crates that Talon had used to cushion his fall. The crates were no longer piled as high as they had been for Talon, but they broke Hunter's fall enough that, bending his knees to distribute the impact, then rolling onto his right shoulder, he managed not to break any bones.

He gained his feet and ran. He stopped near the front corner of the brick building around which Talon had disappeared and edged a look around the wall, half-expecting Talon to be waiting for him in ambush. Talon was just then dashing between two buildings roughly fifty yards east along the narrow street that was home to a livery stable, a farrier's shop, small orphanage, and three or four whores' cribs. Talon was heading east, back toward the main drag.

He was probably hoping to lose himself in Tigerville's hustling, bustling Dakota Avenue crowd.

Hunter pushed away from the brick building and ran north. He darted into the break into which Talon had vanished. He ran through the break, crossed another side street, then ran through another break, frightening a trash-scrounging cur that gave a sharp yip and ran away with its tail between its legs. When Hunter surfaced from the break, he found himself on Dakota Avenue, confronted by a swelter of dusty traffic and the din of men and women selling and bartering, dogs barking, horses whinnying, and by the sharp cracks of mule skinners' whips over the backs of ore drays' six-mule hitches.

Hunter looked around, catching a brief glimpse of red in a thinly roiling dust cloud ahead and on his right. He ran toward the splash of faded red ensconced in clay-colored dust. As he gained on the fleeing figure, Ike Talon glanced over his left shoulder at the man in pursuit. Talon stopped and wheeled, whipping up his revolver.

Hunter ducked as the gun belched, flames lapping from the barrel. The bullet thumped into an awning support post to Hunter's left, making a stout basket matron in a feathered hat scream in fear.

Hunter straightened, extended the LeMat, and steadied the big popper in his right hand, not wanting to send a bullet into a passing bystander. As Talon turned to run nearly straight north down the middle of the street, Hunter fired. Talon screamed, grabbed the back of his left leg, and fell.

Hunter ran forward.

He dove beneath a parked farm wagon on his left when Talon whipped his gun around again and fired two more angry rounds from his right shoulder and hip. The killer bellowed an enraged curse, then stiffly gained his feet and ran forward, dragging his left leg.

He stopped as two horses materialized out of the

swirling dust before him. They were the first two horses of a four-horse hitch pulling a big, high-sided mine supply wagon.

"Outta the way, you simple fool!" yelled the burly teamster sitting on the wagon's driver's seat a good six feet above the street.

The word "fool" hadn't entirely left his lips before the first two horses bulled into Talon. It was as though the man was swallowed by a maelstrom of charcoal dust inside of which horse heads bobbed. The killer disappeared completely from Hunter's view as the horses and wagon thundered toward Buchanon and then passed him on his right.

The driver screamed, *"WHO-AHHH! WHO-AHHHH, you mangy no-good cayuses!"*

As the wagon slowed, out from beneath it rolled the dusty bedraggled form of Ike Talon. Talon rolled onto his belly and lay writhing, mewling like a gut-shot dog. He was nearly straight out in the street beyond Hunter, who had gained his feet and regarded the battered killer with his heart chugging heavily, pumping poison blood through his veins.

Good. Talon was still alive.

Traffic had come to a standstill to the north and south. The dust still sifted over Talon. The driver of the wagon that had turned him into a battered human andiron came running from the front of the wagon, duster flopping at his sides and swaying around the high tops of his mule-eared boots.

"Oh lordy, lordy, lordy!" the mule skinner howled, stopping and staring down, aghast, at Ike Talon. "I didn't see ya there, pard!"

Hunter walked out into the street.

The driver looked at him from beneath the brim of his weather-stained sombrero. "I didn't see him. Honest, I didn't. What blame fool runs down Dakota Avenue half-dressed this time of the day?"

"A dead one."

Hunter kicked Talon onto his back. Talon groaned and snarled like a wounded wolf. He was all scraped and scratched. His torn longhandle top hung down over his right shoulder. His left arm was broken. Hunter saw the telltale bulge.

Hunter smiled down at the man. "How you feelin', Ike?"

Talon cursed and howled and kicked his legs. Blood stained the dirt around the left one. "Call the doc! Call the doc!"

"I don't think the doc is gonna let you crap on his step again, you old dog." Hunter pressed his left boot down on Talon's left arm, over the bulge.

Talon's eyes opened wide and all the blood drained out of his face. He made a high-pitched strangling sound in his throat.

"How's that feel, Ike? Doesn't look too good at all. But then, Charley Anders didn't look too good layin' out on that trail after you ambushed him, killin' him in cold blood, neither."

The mule skinner looked at Hunter slack-jawed, then backed away slowly. "Holy crap in the deacon's privy— you two got history . . ."

He continued to back away as though he'd just found himself confronted by an escaped lion from a traveling circus show.

Hunter had made little note of him. His attention was

on the man who'd led the gang that had attacked his stage and murdered his friend. Hunter raised the LeMat, angling it down at a forty-five-degree angle, and drew a bead on Talon's left arm, just above the bulge.

Talon stared up at him, eyes glazed with horror. "What're you . . . what're you . . . *ach-ohhhh!*" he screamed on the heels of the flat, resounding crack of the big LeMat and the bullet drilling into the bone of his left arm, halfway between his elbow and shoulder.

Talon lay writhing and bawling, rocking from side to side, clenching his hands together over his belly.

"That was for Charley," Hunter said.

He shot the man in his other arm, near the previous wound.

"That was for the drummer."

Talon kicked and screamed. He ground his spurs into the ground and tried to shove himself forward along the ground.

Hunter shot the man in his left knee. "That was for the young lady your men tried to savage."

Talon yelped and cried. "Stop! You're crazy! Someone . . ."

Hunter drew a bead on the man's other leg, and fired.

He stared down into Talon's puffed up mask of misery, and said, "That was for me."

Talon writhed, sobbing.

Hunter finished him with a bullet through his forehead. Talon lay back with a stupid, cross-eyed expression on his broad, meaty face.

Silence descended over the street.

Hunter looked around. He'd been so intent on making Ike Talon pay for his sins that he hadn't realized a large crowd had gathered in a complete circle around him, about twenty feet away. Men, women, children, and even a few dogs stared at him in wide-eyed fascination. Brightly dressed doxies perched like exotic birds on second- and third-floor balconies on both sides of the street, staring hang-jawed down at him and the dead Ike Talon, their wraps and dusters and hair feathers ruffling in the breeze.

The light wind kicked up dust and swirled it this way and that, making the on-lookers squint their eyes against it.

One face in particular caught Hunter's attention. Annabelle's.

He hadn't realized he was standing out front of Big Dan's Saloon. Annabelle stood on the boardwalk with Ginny and Big Dan and several of Big Dan's regulars clutching beers in their fists. Bobby Lee sat at Annabelle's feet, his copper eyes on Hunter.

Annabelle wore a dubious expression. One part enthrallment, two parts repulsion.

Slowly, she turned away and walked back into Big Dan's. Bobby Lee yipped softly and followed her.

The rest of the crowd remained in place, mired in grisly fascination.

"All right," someone finally said. "Holster the hogleg."

Walt Winslow stepped out from the crowd on the street's east side. He held a double-barrel shotgun in his hands, the large maws aimed at Hunter's belly.

"You're under arrest, Buchanon."

A collective murmur rose from the crowd.

"That was cold-blooded murder," Winslow said around the three-cent cheroot dangling from one corner of his mouth, his moon-and-star badge glinting in the late-morning sunlight.

Hunter saw another badge-wearing man flanking Winslow, one hand on the revolver jutting from the holster on the man's right hip, in front of the tucked-back flap of his clawhammer coat. That was Roy Birmingham, another federal assigned to the Black Hills and who often partnered up with Winslow.

Birmingham was Winslow's age, early sixties—a stout beer barrel of a man in a black suit, black slouch hat, and a red foulard tie. A shaggy gray mustache concealed his mouth beneath a flat-tipped, bright-red nose upon which little round spectacles perched, brightly reflecting the sun.

Birmingham didn't unholster his revolver. He just kept his hand over it and, chin lowered, smiled deviously over the tops of his spectacles at Hunter.

Hunter glared at Winslow holding the shotgun on him. "You're gonna arrest me for killing this killer?"

"That's right," Winslow said. "Holster the hogleg. It don't matter if he deserved it or not. Murder is murder. You murdered the man, Buchanon. I can't let that go." He slid his flinty yet somehow bemused gaze toward two little boys, one a head taller than the other, standing in the crowd to the south, in front of their mother clad in a long green dress trimmed with white lace. "What kind of a lesson would that be for the children?"

Hunter looked at the boys and their mother, who gazed at him with dark fascination.

He sighed and holstered the LeMat.

CHAPTER 15

"Here we go, Miss Meyers—home sweet home! What do you think?"

Warren Davenport, riding on the chaise buggy's front seat beside Laura, turned to the new schoolmarm and smiled broadly, showing large, square teeth the color of old ivory. He was a tall, rawboned man with a crudely chiseled face. Brown eyes burrowed deep in sockets above his wedge-shaped nose with a slight bulge at the end.

He looked more like a farmer than a businessman; that's why his three-piece black suit with paisley vest looked almost silly on him.

No, it did look silly. But Laura was in no mood for laughing.

However, she did find herself impressed by the schoolhouse set on a slight rise on the west edge of Tigerville. But then, after arriving in Tigerville only an hour ago, she'd had to lower her expectations concerning just about all aspects of the humble, crude, dirty, smoky, stinky, violent little cesspool of human wretchedness.

As the leather buggy climbed the hill behind the sleek black Morgan horse, following the gently curving trail between scattered evergreen shrubs and small pines, she could see more and more of the building. It was a simple frame structure with a hipped roof and a closed front porch rising from a half dozen steps. A bell tower jutted from the roof of the porch; a rope for ringing the bell hung down over the top step.

The unpainted pine boards comprising the school were so new that the smell of pine resin was thick and heady.

Despite the school superintendent's reassurances that a new school had recently been built, she'd come to expect a far humbler structure than the one she was seeing. The good residents of Tigerville had put some thought, time, and labor, not to mention taxpayer dollars, into a fine and respectable public school building.

That made Laura's heart lighten a bit. But only a bit. The licentious behavior she'd seen on the streets of Tigerville, and the wretched appearance of most of its citizens, was still a large, cold brick holding steadfast in the pit of her stomach.

Still, she painted a smile on her face and turned to Mister Davenport. The man was obviously proud of his town's accomplishment here, and he deserved to be.

"This looks quite wonderful, Mister Davenport. Quite wonderful, indeed."

He'd stopped the Morgan on the cinder-paved area fronting the school. Taking both ribbons in his black-gloved right hand, he closed his left hand around the buggy's brake handle. "Would you like a tour? I've been right eager to show it to you, Miss Meyers!"

"Uh . . ." Laura glanced down at her dress, over which she wore a blanket that Mr. Sullivan had accommodated her with from his office, and dirty bare feet still streaked with dry blood and which rested on the buggy floor, one hooked around the other.

"Oh, of course." Davenport threw his head back and laughed self-deprecatingly. "How callous of me. My God, you not only just pulled into town, but you were attacked by bandits on the way here! Good Lord!"

Still laughing heartily, Davenport reined the Morgan around the school's right side and down along the side to the rear. Turning to Laura again, he said, "I'm afraid the teacher's quarters are . . . well . . . you'll see . . ."

Laura didn't like the tone of that.

Davenport steered the horse around the pair of new privies flanking the school, complete with half-moons carved into the doors. He and Laura rode around what she assumed was a shed for storing firewood, and up to a gray log cabin with a shake-shingled roof.

Yes, now she saw. A shack.

Davenport reined the Morgan to a stop on a patch of hard-packed, bald ground fronting the shack and set the brake.

Laura stared at the shack, trying not to cry.

This was her new home?

The cabin couldn't have been cruder. It also couldn't have been much larger than her and Jonathan's bedroom back home in their large, mansard-roofed house on Grant Avenue in Denver.

Davenport, obviously sensing her discomfort, hemmed and hawed for a time before saying, "You see, Miss Meyers, we built the school here on old Homer Laskey's mining claim. He dug for gold in the ravine behind the cabin, and he ran a few hogs and chickens. A loner, Homer was. A bit, well . . ."

Davenport twirled his finger in the air by his left ear.

"Loco, some would say. He died five years ago now, and no one's lived here since. The cabin and Homer's claim went back to the town on account of how Homer left behind no living relatives. So, you see, since the lot already belonged to the city, and it had a cabin on it—a good and tight cabin, too, I might add—we thought we'd build the school on the old claim and then the new teacher . . . well, she could—"

"Live in the cabin," Laura finished for the man in a voice that sounded thin and forlorn even to her own ears. She gazed at the humble shack before her, feeling her upper lip tremble.

"Now, it don't look like much on the outside," Davenport said. The buggy tilted to his side as he clambered down, all knees and elbows. He walked around behind the buggy and came up on Laura's side, extending both roast-size hands toward her, smiling ingratiatingly. "Let me show you the inside, Miss Meyers. I think you'll like it. I really do."

Laura rose from the quilted leather buggy seat. Davenport wrapped his hands around her waist, pulled her off the buggy, and set her gently down on the hard-packed ground. As he did, his gaze lingered a little too long on her, his eyes roaming over her in a way that made her feel uncomfortable. Especially after the incident with the stage.

She lowered her gaze from his, hugged herself, and shivered inside the blanket though it must have been around eighty degrees out here, and humid.

Seeing her reaction, Davenport's ear tips reddened. He turned away, took her hand, and led her to the cabin's front door. She winced as grass stubble and small bits of gravel bit into her feet.

Davenport muttered nervously as he fished in his pocket for a key, then stuck it into the locking plate beneath the cast iron handle. He grunted for a time, stretching his lips back from his teeth, trying to turn the key. Finally, it made a low scraping sound as the locking bolt retreated into the door, and the door shuddered as it hung limp in its frame.

"Here we are," Davenport said, pushing the door open as he stepped into the cabin.

Laura stood in the open doorway, staring into her new home.

She'd been wrong. The shack was maybe a little larger than her and Jonathan's bedroom, but not by much. It was a single room with a kitchen area to the right, with a small stove, an eating table, and shelves housing rudimentary utensils, and a parlor area, if you could call it that, to the left. There was a rocking chair, a horsehair sofa that sagged badly in the middle, and a small wooden tea table carved from a log. To the rear of the parlor area, and abutting the left and rear walls, lay a small bed covered in threadbare wool blankets.

"See?" Davenport said. "Not so bad, eh?"

He smiled broadly, and again his eyes danced over her, making her skin crawl.

"No," she said, stepping into the cabin. The rough wood floor was partly covered by a couple of sun-faded, dusty, sour-smelling hemp rugs. "Not bad at all."

She was trying to sound jovial. The man made her nervous, self-conscious. She didn't like being alone with him. She wished she'd waited for Hunter, but he'd obviously and quite literally had his hands full with that saloon girl who'd passed out at the sight of him.

"You see there's an indoor spigot," Davenport said, pointing to a pump head and handle poking up out of the plank cupboard against the cabin's back wall, to the right, flanking the stove. "Ol' Homer was an odd one but he'd had the good sense to dig a well under the cabin."

"All the comforts of home," Laura said, stepping forward and poking a hand out of the blanket draping her shoulders to rake it across the three-by-four-foot eating table. The tip of her finger was gray-black with dust and grime.

Again, she shivered. She felt her knees quake. She wanted very much to drop to the floor, grimy as it was, and bawl her eyes out. But she could not. She could not afford to make a fool of herself. She needed the teaching job, and she had nowhere else to go.

That thought alone almost broke her.

She swallowed down a hard knot of homesickness, shook her head to clear the raw emotions swirling around in her brain, then tossed her hair back and turned her wooden smile to the big man hovering over her. "Home sweet home!"

"See—I knew you'd like it!"

"I do. Now, if you'll forgive me, Mister Davenport, I'd really like to clean myself up a bit."

"Oh, you're wanting to be alone, of course!" He threw his head back again and laughed, but the laugh sounded nearly as wooden as Laura's own smile had been.

Instead of retreating to the door, he lingered, a smile working at the muscles in his hard, unevenly featured face. He opened his mouth to speak, then, as if in afterthought, reached up to remove his hat from his head.

Holding the hat in his thick hands, he said, "Miss Meyers . . . uh . . . I have an idea. Won't you join me for dinner this evening?"

"What?" She couldn't believe what she was hearing.

"Well, I mean . . . I did send a boy from the grocery store over with the basics—sugar, flour, and coffee—that sort of thing—but surely you're not up to cooking so soon after arriving. After all you've been through! I could take you to dinner at the Imperial. It's a hotel. Best vittles in town! I can introduce you to a couple of the other school-board members who dine there regularly."

"That's a generous offer, Mister Davenport, but I think I'm just going to take a long, hot bath, put some salve on my feet, and go to bed early. Tomorrow I'll head down-town for groceries and stock the larder, so to speak." She tittered a nervous, phony laugh, just wishing the man would go. She hated how his eyes lingered on her and how his lingering gazes lifted a flush in the harsh curves and shaded hollows of his face.

She could smell him—the stench of unwashed male. She could hear the stentorian rasps of his breathing.

"I'd be happy to send the boy from the grocery store. If you'd like to make out a list, I could stop by later and pick it up."

"Oh, no. Thank you, Mister Davenport. I like to do my own shopping." That wasn't true. She'd rarely done her own grocery shopping. She and Jonathan had always had a servant for such tedium, but she wanted this man out of the cabin . . . and out of her life . . . as soon as possible. She didn't want him thinking she needed him for anything.

What a scoundrel! Laura was standing here feeling as though she'd just wrestled a grizzly bear in its own cave and wanting nothing more than to heat water and bathe her battered and weary body, to rub arnica into her poor, abused feet, and to go to bed and escape in dreams the harsh reality the fateful turn her life had taken.

Why did Hunter Buchanon just slip into her mind? Was that what—or whom—she was wanting to go to sleep and dream about? Was the contrast with her Viking warrior-savior what made Warren Davenport look so bedraggled and unappealing?

Get your mind off Hunter. You can't have him. He already has a girl. Besides, you don't need a man. Men will break your heart. You're here to prove your independence. You don't need your heart broken again. Besides, you're only attracted to Buchanon because any woman would be (though she hadn't thought she could ever be attracted to so big and rough a character) and because he got you out of a bad situation and you're just grateful to be alive.

Don't forget that Buchanon is the one who got you into that situation in the first place.

What an inept pair—him and the shotgun messenger, Charley Anders (God rest the poor man's soul)! You must blame Mister Buchanon for the poor, miserable state you're in, not fantasize about having him wrap those big, bulging arms around you and draw you against that enormous, thick chest of his.

Suddenly, she realized that Warren Davenport was standing before her, waving one of his big paws in front of her face, yelling, "Miss Meyers! Miss Meyers! Are you all right, Miss Meyers?"

She snapped out of her trance, her cheeks tingling with what she was sure was a crimson flush. "I'm sorry, Mister Davenport. I'm afraid . . . I . . . just feel a little dizzy is all. It must be the exhaustion."

"Whew! For a minute there, I thought you were gonna pull what Miss Ludlow pulled in front of the stage manager's office!"

"Yes, yes . . . so did I . . ."

Laura looked up at the man plaintively. "I hate to be rude, Mister Davenport. I do appreciate the ride over here and all, but I'm afraid . . ."

"Oh, of course, I'll take my leave. But don't you worry—I'll stop by to check on you later." He cleared his throat, looking a little sheepish. "Just to, um, you know—make sure your luggage arrived safely an' all."

"Oh, that won't be nec—"

"No problem at all, Miss Meyers. Well, then . . ." A little reluctantly, he planted his hat on his head, carefully adjusted the angle, then turned to the door. "I'll leave you to your bath." At the door, he turned back to her.

She was on the verge of screaming.

Was he ever going to leave???

"Welcome to Tigerville, Miss Meyers. I think you're gonna like it here. I know I for one am going to like having you here." Did he really wink at her? Yes, he did. "Just so's you know, Miss Meyers . . ."

"Yes, Mister Davenport?" Laura said, her knees weakening so that she was afraid she was going to pass out from the strain of needing to be rid of this wheedling boob. If he'd noted the weariness and desperation in her voice, he didn't let on.

"Um . . . just so's you know, Miss Meyers, I am a widower. Just so you know that . . . well . . . there won't be anything improper when we do have dinner together."

He cast her a broad smile. An unsettling smile. A smile with an off-putting edge to it. Almost as though there'd been a threat in it.

It was as though he'd just shown her a knife.

"Good day, now, teacher."

He dipped his chin, ducked through the door, and closed the door behind him.

He took his own good time climbing into his buggy and turning the Morgan back the way they'd come. When the thuds of the horse's hooves and the rattle of the wagon wheels had dwindled to silence, Laura finally drew a breath, slumped down in a chair, lay her head on the grimy table, and bawled.

CHAPTER 16

"Get in there, ya damn miscreant! Hangin's too good for ya—you know that, don't you?"

"Ow! Stop pokin' me with that damned shotgun, Winslow!"

"Get in there, then. Stop lollygaggin', you mangy polecat," barked Walt Winslow, ramming his shotgun into Hunter's back again as the big jehu stumbled over the threshold and into the Tigerville jail office.

"Ow!" Hunter wheeled and glared at the much smaller man wielding the double-barrel shotgun, flanked by his badge-wearing crony, the pot-gutted and bespectacled Roy Birmingham, who had a dung-eating smile on his suety, sun-burned face. "What the hell's gotten into you, Winslow? You're treating me like some hardened killer!"

"Well, maybe you ain't had time to get hardened, but you are a cold-blooded killer!"

"No, I'm not. Talon had it comin'. He killed Charley!"

"That don't matter," Birmingham said, stepping into the office behind the shotgun-wielding Winslow. "He was down and he was no longer armed and you still shot him anyway."

"Get in there!" Winslow bellowed, his hoarse voice going so high it had almost sounded like a girl's scream. He jerked the shotgun toward one of the four cells lined up against the squat stone building's rear wall. Only one cell was occupied—by an old wiry gent, probably a prospector, with a long bib-beard. The man was sound asleep on one of the cell's two cots and sawing logs like a practiced sawyer.

Of course, there were more men under lock and key. In a town like Tigerville, there were almost always a few men incarcerated for one thing or another. Usually a woman or two, to boot. But most were housed over at the county courthouse two blocks to the east, where they'd await a visit from the circuit judge while under the watch of two full-time jailers.

Reluctantly, ears burning with fury—no man had ever deserved to die bloody more than Ike Talon—Hunter stepped into the cell left of the one housing the prospector, who, judging by the stench reeking from his direction, had been arrested for drunk and disorderly conduct the night before. Probably more drunk than disorderly; any man who reeked as badly as he did had likely been far too drunk to have been all that disorderly.

Winslow slammed the door behind Hunter, who swung around to face the smaller, badge-wearing man, who said, "You got any more weapons on you?" He'd already confiscated Hunter's LeMat and bowie knife.

"No."

"You sure?"

"I said so, didn't I?"

"I should make you take your boots off," Winslow threatened.

"No, don't do that!" bellowed Birmingham, who'd taken a seat in Winslow's swivel chair flanking Winslow's cluttered rolltop desk. "No one's got smellier feet than a damn Rebel!" He pinched up his little pig eyes behind his little round spectacles and, cheeks growing even redder with mirth, said, "Most Southern boys only got two pairs of socks and they rarely change 'em!"

Birmingham slapped the desk and roared.

Winslow's stony face cracked a smile.

Hunter told the pot-gutted Deputy U.S. Marshal to do something physically impossible to himself.

Birmingham's smile faded though the flush remained.

It was Winslow's turn to laugh, though he, like Birmingham, had fought on the side of the Bluebellies during the War of Northern Aggression and Southern Independence. Most folks in the Hills had either fought for the Union or been Union sympathizers. That had always made it tough for the Southerners drawn here after the war, lured by the gold and, like the Buchanons, rich grazing land.

"I'm gonna dance at his hangin'," Birmingham told Winslow, though his now-angry gaze was on Hunter. "Gonna dance me a fine old jig, and I might even have a beer, though the doc done waved me off of the stuff on account of my ticker. Only for the rare special occasion, Doc said. Well, I'm gonna call that a rare special occasion."

"I'll buy," Winslow said, finally lowering the shotgun.

"You were friends with Charley, too, Winslow," Hunter said. "Hell, everybody was friends with Charley."

"That doesn't mean you can break the law. Not in front of me and the whole damn town!"

Hunter gave a guttural cry of frustration, then went over and sat down on his cot. He leaned forward, elbows on his knees. He scrubbed his hat off his head and ran his hands through his hair in frustration. "If you could've seen what they did to him. Bushwhacked him! Him an' the drummer. Two of 'em dragged the girl off into the woods."

"I'm sure they did," Winslow said, sagging into a straight-backed chair by his desk. "That's Talon for you." He leaned his shotgun against the desk and dragged a slender cheroot from a box on the desktop. "You got a light, Roy?"

"I do." Birmingham dug a lucifer from the breast pocket of his suitcoat, scratched it to life on the top of Winslow's desk, and held it to the end of the marshal's cigar.

Hunter continued raking his fingers across his scalp, frustrated by the unfairness of it all. He thought of his father, Old Angus. He thought of Annabelle. He supposed Winslow and Birmingham were right. He had killed Talon after the man was down. Not only killed him, but tortured him, to boot.

Right in front of half the town.

He inwardly cursed himself for a fool. Now he was going to hang, and Old Angus was going to be alone. Who'd look after him?

Who would look after Annabelle?

He cursed again and then threw himself back on the cot and crossed his boots at the ankles. He folded his arms behind his head and stared at the lone stone ceiling that bore the scratched initials of the many prisoners this old cell had housed over the years since Tigerville was nothing more than a logging camp and cavalry outpost, back before the boom.

He'd best settle in, he told himself. It might be a while before the judge, Devlin Baker, a Yankee, made his way up to Tigerville. When he did, Hunter would likely be hanging from the town's makeshift gallows the next day at high noon. Baker was notorious for showing little or no leniency for men who'd once fought for the Confederacy. It was widely known that Hunter as well as his father, Old Angus, had fought for the Stars & Bars.

That Hunter, in fact, had been a Southern war hero.

Soon, the Yankees of Tigerville would get their long-sought deserts.

He jerked his head up. He'd been so deep in thought, grieving his bleak end, that he hadn't realized that both Deputy U.S. Marshals, Winslow and Birmingham, had moved up to stand just outside his cell, staring in at him, their brows raised skeptically.

Hunter scowled. "What the hell do you two want? If you think I'm gonna piss myself, you're gonna have to wait till after the trapdoor drops."

"We've been thinkin', Roy and me," Winslow said.

"Yeah? That's a first."

"All sass, ain't ya?" Birmingham said, flaring a pudgy nostril. "All fire and fury. Typical Buchanon."

"Typical Buchanon."

"Like I said," Winslow said, louder this time. "We've been thinkin' it over."

Hunter's curious frown further ridged his brows. "Thinkin' what over?"

"The hangin'."

Birmingham said, "We're ready to make you a deal. You don't deserve it, but we find ourselves in kind of a tight spot, Walt an' me."

Hunter dropped his feet to the floor, rose from the cot, and walked over to the cell door. He gazed skeptically through the iron bands. "I'm listening."

"You see," Winslow said, "Roy and I have been assigned to check out whiskey runners over on the Sioux Reservation. That means we have to leave Tigerville, and since I have yet to find a man willing to occupy this office, I have no one to leave in charge . . ." He dug a tin badge out of his vest pocket and held it up between his fingers. The words TOWN MARSHAL had been stamped into the tin face. "Till now."

Hunter frowned at the badge, then shifted his incredulous stare to Winslow. "You mean . . . you want me to be the *new town marshal*?"

"Just till Walt here gets back to Tigerville," Birmingham said.

"Unless you want to wear that star full-time," Winslow said. "Looks like I'm gonna have to look out of town for a man, and that's a heap of paper-pushing nonsense I don't have time for—what with my federal assignments and all. That trouble you were involved in last year . . . all them deputies of Stillwell's getting killed . . . then the unfortunate circumstances of the last town marshal's, um, unexpected expiration . . ."

"You mean Lon Lonnigan's gettin' shot in the back over at the Library by a drunk whore?"

Birmingham snorted and then brushed his hand across his mustache.

"Indeed," Winslow said. "The whole damn mess has made it a might difficult to find a lawman. At least, a good one. One who won't go and get himself shot the moment he steps out onto the boardwalk."

Winslow flattened out his hand in which the badge now rested belly-up. He slid his hand through the bars of the cell door. "Go ahead, kid. Pin that to your shirt. Just till I get back. Who knows—you might even warm to the job. Better pay than your stage drivin' job, and without the dust and holdups."

"How much?"

"Huh?"

"How much you offerin'?" Hunter asked.

"Oh, say . . ." Fingering his clipped mustache, Winslow glanced at Birmingham. "How 'bout thirty a month? A little steep, but I think the city fathers would agree to that amount."

Birmingham shrugged, nodded.

"The stage line pays me thirty-five a month," Hunter said.

"They do?" both Deputy U.S. Marshals said at the same time.

Hunter grinned cagily. "You know they do."

"All right," Winslow said. "How 'bout forty a month?"

"Fifty or call the hangman. Hangin' would be quicker. Lonnigan lingered for three days after the doc cut that bullet out of his liver. His yells could be heard all over town."

"All right, all right," Winslow said. "Fifty it is. When I talk to the city council, I'll call it hazard pay. They shouldn't balk . . . given the circumstances." He shook his hand, making the badge on his palm dance. "Here you go, kid. Deal's a deal."

Hunter frowned down at the badge. Why was he feeling as though he'd just been cheated by a crooked faro dealer and a rigged dealer's box?

Slowly, he plucked the badge out of Winslow's hand,

held up the badge, and looked at it as though it were a poisoned cookie. Birmingham tossed Winslow a big ring of keys. Winslow poked the key in the lock and opened the door.

"Congratulations on the new job, kid." The lawman smiled and held out the ring of keys. "Here—that's yours."

"Good luck!" Birmingham said as both he and Winslow grabbed rifles and bedrolls waiting by the door.

Hunter remained standing inside the cell, the badge in his hand. He looked from the badge to the two gray-headed lawmen grabbing their gear and fumbling the door open, both men chuckling like two school boys who'd just turned a frog loose in the girls' privy.

"Hey—you two weren't planning on hangin' me at all, were you?" Hunter called.

"For killin' Ike Talon?" Winslow asked, widening his eyes in shock. "Hell, no! Old Ike's been needin' killin' since he graduated from rubber pants!"

Birmingham was wheezing in red-faced laughter as he hustled through the door and out to where two saddled horses were waiting for him and Winslow at the hitchrack.

"See you when we get back, kid," Winslow said, grinning, eyes glittering devilishly. He turned toward the hitchrack, then turned back to Hunter, saying, "Oh, and . . . just a word of advice. Stay out of the Library unless absolutely necessary. I found out for myself that that place is a nest of rattlesnakes best steered well clear of. Poor ol' Lonnigan didn't have a chance!"

Both oldsters were roaring now as they strapped their bedrolls to their saddles, shoved their rifles into their saddle scabbards, and swung up into the leather.

They were still roaring as they turned their horses out into the afternoon traffic and headed south at spanking trots.

Hunter walked slowly out of the cell and over to the open office door. His ears burned from the fleecing he'd just taken. He felt as though he'd been gunny-sacked, rolled, kicked, had his pockets cleaned, and his boots stolen. He looked at the badge in his hand, scowling, then shuttled his gaze to where the two old federals had galloped off along Dakota Avenue, their laughter still echoing.

Hunter sighed. "I gotta feelin' they were prepared to offer me better pay, too, dammit."

CHAPTER 17

Once back at his family's Broken Heart Ranch, Cass Ludlow handed his horse over to the half-breed stable boy and followed the well-worn path up the rise to the impressive, stately main house situated on the crest of a low bluff.

The arrangement afforded the Broken Heart's proud founder, Graham Ludlow, a prime view from virtually every window in the house of his well-appointed headquarters with its immaculately maintained bunkhouse, barns, stables, and corrals that formed a half circle around the house to the west. The view also comprised a good portion of Ludlow's lush and massive range stretching to all horizons, the green valleys between pine- and cedar-stippled ridges liberally peppered with his prime, white-faced cattle.

That "beef on the hoof," as Ludlow called it, was the envy of nearly every other rancher in southwestern Dakota and eastern Wyoming Territories.

Cass left the cinder-paved path sheathed by transplanted shrubs of various varieties as well as by aromatic pines and cedars, and started up the lodge's broad wooden steps rising to the wraparound veranda. As he did, he heard men's voices above, and paused on the third step up from the bottom. He'd been rolling a cigarette as he walked, and now, rolling the paper closed around the tobacco, he lifted his gaze to the veranda ten feet above.

His father sat out there, in the push chair he'd had to start using on account of his weak ticker. The summer day was warm, over eighty degrees, but still the old man's legs were covered with a red plaid blanket. He wore his traditional hickory shirt and bolo tie under his traditional black cowhide vest, from a pocket of which hung a gold watch chain. Ludlow had once been a big man, his broad face chiseled out of granite and split with a formidable, liver-spotted nose. He hadn't been tall, but broad, with thick shoulders and arms, giving the overall impression of intimidating strength.

Cass, himself, had been intimidated, not to mention the victim, of that intimidating strength for most of his childhood, the beatings having ended after Cass had turned eighteen and Ludlow had given up hope of ever "bringing him around" to do a full day's work or to turn him into the bootstrapper, business-minded stockman Ludlow had so wanted him to be instead of the whoremongering sluggard he was.

That big strong man, however, was gone.

Ludlow, with his failing heart and refusal to give up strong drink and cigars, was a droopy-eyed, haggard-faced, slump-shouldered husk of his former self. He must have lost a good half of his previous weight over the past year, since the end of the violence that had begun after Ludlow had learned that his daughter, Annabelle, had been secretly planning to wed the former grayback, Hunter Buchanon, who hailed from a family of ex-Confederates, which meant, to Ludlow's way of thinking, that they had blood on their hands.

The blood of Ludlow's son who'd died in the war.

Anger burned in Cass when he saw the young popinjay sitting in a wicker chair beside Cass's father, and to whom Graham Ludlow was conversing in such quiet, conspiratorial, almost intimate tones. Kenneth Earnshaw, in his late twenties, was a short, slender young man with a boyish face still a little plump with baby fat he would never outgrow, and an almost feminine mop of carefully combed, strawberry blond hair, with sideburns of the same color, and a thick, bushy strawberry mustache. He'd grown a goatee to try to disguise the fact that his chin was as weak as his character.

Uncharacteristically, he was dressed in range gear though Cass had seen the young nancy-boy on a horse only once, and Earnshaw had looked as though he were sitting on the back of a giant porcupine. He took a couple of turns around the corral, with the stable boy leading the horse, then scrambled off the uncomfortable perch so quickly he'd got a boot caught in his stirrup and had struck the ground on his head.

He'd screeched like a girl with a pigtail caught in a wagon wheel's spokes.

Now he sat there beside Cass's father, decked out in cowboy garb. At least, what a nancy-boy from the East wanting to look like a thirty-a-month-and-found cow puncher would wear though no cowboy Cass had ever known wore doeskin trousers stuffed into polished black patent boots adorned with red piping, and a silk shirt with ruffles down the front. The trousers themselves had some kind of fancy stitching up around the legs and probably down the legs. He couldn't see the legs because they were obscured by the hand-tooled, elk hide leggings he wore over them.

The man's hat was as white as a wedding gown, and Sir Kenneth, as Cass called him behind his back, wore it with one side pinned up against the crown.

Now, Cass himself enjoyed wearing attire, often in the Spanish style, that made him stand out in a crowd and that attracted the ladies. (At least, it had before the fire. Now it was the scars from the fire that made him stand out in a crowd.) But not even he would be caught in a getup as outlandish as Sir Kenneth's.

He didn't like the way Kenneth and Graham Ludlow were talking either. As though Kenneth was the man's son. His favorite one, at that. Of course, everyone knew who Ludlow's favorite son was—or had been. But Mighty John Ludlow, as Cass thought of his older brother with an inward sneer, was lying in itty-bitty, blown-up pieces on a forgotten battlefield in Tennessee, leaving behind Cass to unsuccessfully fill his shoes.

Only, there was no filling the shoes of a dead man. Especially a proud man's firstborn son.

The two up there were talking in tones as hushed and intimate as those of lovers. Cass knew what they were talking about. He'd overheard them on several occasions. Cass's father was still banking on Kenneth marrying Annabelle, and Ludlow was schooling Kenneth on the fineries of ranch and stock management, and how to hire and fire and keep a good, working bunch of men on your payroll. How to earn and keep their respect.

That last one was going to be a steep climb for young Kenneth in those hand-tooled elk hide leggings of his.

"What the hell's goin' on up there?" Cass said abruptly, loudly, pounding the steps with his boots as he climbed to the top of the veranda. "You two forming your own secret government or something?"

"Cass! For God's sake, boy, you startled the hell out of me! You know starts aren't good for my ticker!"

"Neither are those, Pa," Cass said, nodding to indicate the fat stogie in Ludlow's right hand and the glass of whiskey on a small table to the left of his chair.

"Oh, go to hell!" Ludlow curled a red-rimmed nostril and took a couple of puffs off the stogie.

Kenneth turned to Cass and fought a snide grin from his lips like a persnickety widow woman trying to swat a couple of mongrel strays off her porch with a broom. Cass backed up to the porch rail, hiked a hip on it, and folded his arms across his chest, casting the dandy a bald stare.

Ludlow looked at him, impatient, scowling. "Well . . . ?"

"Well, what?"

"What did you find out? Is Annabelle really working at Big Dan's place in Tigerville?"

"She is, Pops, I'm sorry to say. Rather embarrassing to see her in there, like that. She looks good, though, in that little corset that don't cover half of her, uh, *attributes*, and those fishnet stockings." He turned his head to cast a mocking glance at Kenneth, whose cheeks instantly mottled red.

Kenneth looked quickly away from Cass. He didn't have the stomach for regarding the younger Ludlow's masked countenance for more than a second or two at a time. Earnshaw turned to Ludlow and pounded the arms of his wicker chair with his fists. "Why is she degrading herself this way?"

"Because she's mixed up and confounded—that's why! That grayback got into her head and twisted her thinking. He turned her against her own family, and even now, after he's turned his back on her, she remains in town, taking a job like some commoner, or worse. She's cutting off her nose to spite her face. She's humiliating me as well as herself!" Ludlow looked at Cass. "Tell me she's not working upstairs."

"I don't know, Pop," Cass lied, shaking his head doubtfully. "I really don't know."

Earnshaw twisted in his chair toward Ludlow, his pale neck swollen with anger beneath his red silk bandanna. "We have to get her out of there, Graham. We have to get her out of there *now*!"

Cass gave a quiet, caustic snort. *Graham, now, is it? When Pop starts calling him son, I'm gonna take young Earnshaw out to teach him to hunt and he's gonna get a bullet right between his skinny little shoulders. "I mistook him for a deer, Pa. Honest, I did. Tragic mistake . . ."*

"What the hell are you laughing at?"

Cass suddenly realized his father was glaring at him, hard-jawed, Ludlow's watery eyes somewhat resembling the tough twin gimlets that had resided in those deep sockets not all that long ago.

"Oh, hell!" Cass pushed away from the porch rail. "The errand boy did the job you ordered him to do. I rode to town and I told you what I saw. I'm gonna go upstairs and rub some salve into these burns, a gift from the little princess you two seem to still hold such store by."

"Cass, wait!"

But Cass had already pulled the heavy oak door open and gone inside. He crossed the sunken parlor to the broad, carpeted stairs and climbed to the second story. Anger surged hotly inside him.

Errand boy. That's what he had been relegated to. His father was grooming Earnshaw to take over the ranch once he'd wedded Annabelle. Cass really had no place here anymore. All he'd really hung around for was to make sure that the Pretty Little Princess didn't marry the big gray-back, Buchanon. Not after what she'd done to him in the barn that horrible night.

Why should she be happy when he never could be? Hell, the only whores who'd spend time with him were the half-breeds and Mexicans in the squalid cribs along Poverty Gulch. His life had been turned to ashes the night the barn fire had consumed his face. His father couldn't even look at him anymore. Ludlow could look at him maybe a second or two longer than that preening Earnshaw could, but after a few seconds even Ludlow had to flinch a little and avert his gaze.

What the hell was Cass hanging around here for?

He had a stake. A good one. He had enough money for a fresh start.

Where he'd make that start, he had no idea. Anywhere but here.

Cass walked into his room. He looked both ways along the hall, making sure he was alone, always fearful the family's longtime Chinese servant, Chang, might uncover Cass's secret. He knew he was just being paranoid, but that stake meant everything to him.

Satisfied that Chang was likely in the kitchen preparing the evening meal—Ludlow always wanted a large spread though the old invalid couldn't eat more than a few bites anymore—Cass closed the door and twisted the key in the lock. Enough sunlight pushed through his western window despite the green velvet curtain drawn over it, that he felt no need for a lamp.

He opened his dresser's bottom drawer, opened an old, falling apart cigar box housing trinkets from his childhood from scavenging expeditions he'd taken on horseback here and there about the Ludlow range. There were arrowheads, the fletched end of a Sioux arrow, a dried muskrat head, a "good luck" jingle bob, potsherds from an ancient Indian encampment, some Spanish coins, a miniature clipper ship he'd built from matchsticks, and a small photograph of his mother, jagged on one edge because he'd cut it away from a wedding photo that had included his father. There was also a thin sheaf of penciled letters from a Swedish hony-ocker's daughter he'd once loved—or thought he'd loved—the summer he was fifteen.

Beneath the letters that were tethered together with a powder blue hair ribbon little Beret had given him to re-member her by, lay a key. He plucked the key from the box and walked over to the closet door on the other side of his wood-framed bed covered with a star quilt his mother and Chang had sewn one winter.

He opened the door, knelt down, and pulled an ancient army footlocker out from beneath a pile of old clothes and boots. It didn't come easily. He grunted as he gave it sev-eral tugs until it sat on the closet floor just inside the door. His heart in his throat, he poked the key into the padlock securing the lid, turned it. The shank sprang free, and Cass opened the lid.

He released a held breath as he gazed down at the

four swollen burlap pouches each roughly the size of a ten-pound bag of sugar. He was always afraid it wouldn't be here the next time he opened the lid. He checked the locker regularly, just to make sure the contents were still inside. Of course, it would be. Chang was no thief; Graham Ludlow had never snooped in Cass's room. He'd never had enough interest in his son to care one whit what Cass had stowed in his room.

Still, a heavy, nettling paranoia weighed heavy in the younger Ludlow.

He untied the string from around the neck of one of the bags, slipped his hand inside, dug his fingers into the sugary dust, and removed his clenched fist from the bag. Carefully holding his hand over the bag, he opened it.

He smiled, eyes and mouth widening inside the cutout holes of the mask. He let the rich dust slide slowly out of his hand and back into the bag. It made a soft, sibilant sound, the soft snick of a snake moving through dry grass. As the gold tumbled back into the bag, it glittered in the few stray strands of sunshine angling into the closet from over Cass's shoulder.

His heart quickened. He heard himself breathing.

He'd estimated that there was nearly forty thousand dollars in gold here in these four bags, which he'd plundered from the mine shaft in which Hunter Buchanon had hid them after prospecting the gold himself, building a cache he'd intended to use for a marriage stake for himself and Annabelle.

Cass laughed devilishly through his teeth.

He'd followed the pair out from town, to the remote little prospector's cabin they'd met to make love in. He'd followed them out from the cabin when Hunter had showed the gold to his lovely betrothed.

After the lovebirds had left the shaft hand in hand, certain of their future together, Cass had stolen into the shaft and plundered their stash.

Again, he laughed.

All his now. He deserved it after what Annabelle had done to his face.

What she deserved was to marry the pasty little nancy-boy, Kenneth Earnshaw, and rot away here with Sir Kenneth and Graham Ludlow, right here at the appropriately named Broken Heart Ranch.

As for Cass, what he deserved was to head to Mexico, hole up in a shack along the Sea of Cortez, learn to play the mandolin, and pay the dusky-eyed, copper-skinned *señoritas*—whose constitutions were stronger than those of the *norteamericano* whores—to haul his ashes from time to time.

Not the ones in his fireplace either.

A knock sounded on Cass's door. "Cass!"

He leaped with a start.

CHAPTER 18

Cass opened his door to see Chang, their middle-aged Chinese housekeeper, standing before him in the Chinaman's crisp white smock and red silk cap. A gray-brown mustache, that appeared a little grayer every day, dropped down both sides of his mouth.

He studied Cass with his muddy eyes, deep lines cut across the doughy skin of his broad forehead. Chang seemed suspicious. Did the Chinaman have some mystical Eastern way of knowing that Cass was up to no good, or did he just know Ludlow's son well enough to know that it was always a good bet that Cass was up to no good?

"Your father wants see you downstairs!" Chang said with customary vehemence.

As if to corroborate the Chinaman's story, Graham Ludlow's voice thundered from below: "Cass! Cass, come down here! I want to talk to you! We have an important matter to discuss!"

Chang glanced once more at Cass, nodded once as if to say, "See?" then turned and shuffled off down the hall to Cass's right, heading for the narrow stairs that dropped down to the kitchen at the house's rear.

Cass cursed, drew a calming breath. He felt as though he'd almost been caught with the stolen gold, though he knew that wasn't true. Hiding that gold in the house was fraying his nerves.

Stolen gold. His sister's dower, so to speak.

Did Cass feel guilty for having stolen it?

Hell, no!

Cass adjusted his hat and his mask, then stepped into the hall, drew the door closed, locked it, pocketed the key, and headed down the stairs.

His father sat in his push chair in the parlor, near the overstuffed leather elkhorn chair by the fireplace. The chair was scuffed and scratched from years of use. The seat cushion was permanently bowed inward by the old man's behind. An unlit cigar lay on the chair's right arm, near a pair of Ludlow's wire-rimmed reading spectacles.

On the low table fronting the chair were several stacks of leather-bound books on cattle and horse breeds as well as on rangeland management. There they remained though Cass doubted his father had looked at any of them in over a year.

"What can I do for you, Pa?"

"Why do you have to be so damned emotional?" Ludlow said, beetling his wiry gray brows and slapping a claw-like hand down on an arm of his pushchair. "What was that display out there about?" He canted his head to indicate the veranda beyond the long, recessed windows.

The drapes were pulled back to let in the afternoon sunlight. Cass saw Earnshaw still sitting out there in the wicker chair, gazing off over the Broken Heart holdings as though they were already his.

"I get tired of seein' you and that rube bein' all cozy.

Like he was already your son-in-law when Annabelle doesn't want anything to do with the man."

"Annabelle doesn't know her own mind. She's high-strung, just like her mother was. She entertains crazy fantasies, and they separate her from reality. Kenneth comes from a good, high-bred family. A wealthy one. As you know, his father is a friend of mine. Annabelle's marriage to Kenneth will benefit both families. It will mean the continuation of this ranch after I am gone. That should please you. Kenneth may not be as good on a horse as some, but with his business and investment sense, he can run this ranch. You know as well as I do that you can't. You won't! You've proven that time and time again!"

"It's just not in my blood, Pa."

"You're a Ludlow!"

"I'm more like Mother was. You know—pretty to look at but otherwise useless?" Cass clapped his hands and laughed loudly, ironically, plucking at the mask. He stopped abruptly because he could feel it turning into a sob.

No man sobbed in front of Graham Ludlow.

"Good God." Ludlow looked away, taking an exasperated drag off his stogie. He stared through the window but he didn't appear to be seeing anything. He was probably thinking about his first-born son lying dead on that Southern battlefield, thinking of all that could have been if only John had come home.

John had been the rancher. He'd ridden as though he'd been born on a horse. He was breaking wild broncs by the time he was fifteen years old, and sleeping out in the barn with the hands because he wanted to learn the ways of the range from the old salts who'd worked for his father for years.

At least, that was how Ludlow told it. John was so long ago now that Cass barely remembered his older brother. He'd been only thirteen when the news had arrived that John was dead.

"Is that all, Pa? I'm a might tired. I could use a nap."

"No, it's not all. Come over here and sit down." Ludlow indicated the short sofa on the other side of the low table on which his books sat untouched. "We have to talk about Annabelle."

Cass sighed. He moved into the room and slacked into the sofa with another weary sigh. "When are you gonna let her go, Pa? I saw her. I talked to her. There's no budge in that girl."

Ludlow chuckled. Despite his disdain for what Annabelle had become, pride glinted in his eyes. "She's like me that way. Some ways like her ma, some ways like me. Like me, she's a fierce fighter. Always been that way. If you told that child it was night and time for bed, she'd say it was morning and time to rise, just out of sheer defiance."

"Ain't she a caution!" Cass laughed again with irony.

"Left to her own devices," Ludlow continued, ignoring his son's bizarre behavior out of long habit, "she'd come around. But we can't wait that long. If she keeps on at Big Dan's, something bad will happen. She'll end up with child. We have to save her from herself. We have to intervene."

"Intervene?"

"Kidnap her."

"*What?*" Again, Cass laughed, this time in disbelief.

"She's a herd quitter." Ludlow tossed an imaginary lariat. "Lasso and dally her in!"

Cass squinted at his father. "Could you make that a little plainer?"

Ludlow scowled at his son. "What's plainer than a lariat and a loop?"

"You know I was never a natural roper."

"Just because you didn't want to be." Ludlow leaned forward in his chair, rested the elbow of the hand holding the cigar on the chair's right arm. He cast his son a direct look, eyes wide, brows raised. "I haven't given up on you, boy. Not by a long shot. If you can take a few men into town and long-loop that spirited filly of mine, and drag her back here to the Broken Heart, I'll give you a bigger cut of my inheritance after I'm gone."

"How much am I getting now?" Cass had figured he'd just keep his usual, paltry allowance of thirty-a-month-and-found despite his rarely doing a lick of ranch work. That's why he'd been so happy to get his hands on Buchanon's gold.

"My will calls for a trust that would pay you fifty dollars a month."

"Ah, so I get a raise when the old boy kicks off. How you feelin', Pa? Think you'll be around much longer?"

Ludlow pointed the wet end of his stogie at Cass. "If you keep that up, I'll outlive you, and that's a natural fact though there won't be nothin' natural about your passing!"

"There's that big fatherly heart."

"If you can get Annabelle back to the ranch, and help me see that she marries Earnshaw, I'll write you back in for a third. Just leave the day-to-day operations to Earnshaw and Cassidy." Cole Cassidy was Ludlow's trusted ranch foreman, a fairly new man in the role but not in the ranching business. "You stay out of it. You'll just muck things up like you've always done and make it harder for them to do their jobs."

Ludlow puffed the stogie.

Rage a runaway six-horse hitch inside him, making even his eyes burn, Cass pushed himself up and off the sofa. He stepped over the table, knocking over a stack of his father's books, and crouched over the old man in the push chair gazing up at him dubiously.

Cass placed his hands on the arms of the push chair and shoved his hideous, masked face up close to his father's, so close that he knew Ludlow could smell the still-open sores that cracked and bled and oozed yellow puss. The old man drew his own head back and to one side, his face deeply lined with revulsion.

"You go to hell, old man," Cass said slowly, darkly. "You can take that third ownership of the Broken Heart and shove it where the sun don't shine. I don't want your money or your charity. I'm sick of it. I'm sick to death of you and this ranch. I'm pullin' out on you, my beloved father. I'm gonna leave you to rot here in that chair, pining for your dead favorite son pushing up daisies in Tennessee.

"I'm gonna leave you here with that fairy out there and your daughter who hates your guts. For what you did to Buchanon's family, she'll hate your guts till the day they kick you out with a cold shovel. Me? I hate you for other reasons. And for those reasons, I'll get her back for you. Because I hate you and I hate her for what she did to me. The Little Princess deserves nothing more than to marry that prissy parrot out there who makes water sittin' down, and live here with you till you die. My only regret is that you're likely to go all too soon to be the just punishment she deserves for doing *this* to me!"

With that, Cass reached up, swiped his hat off his head, and pulled the mask from his face.

"Oh!" Ludlow cried, tipping his head far back in his chair, his eyes huge and bright with revulsion. He stared at the horror of his offspring's hideously scarred and oozing features, and wailed, "Oh God! Oh God! Oh God! *Chang—my pills!*"

Cass straightened as he grinned down at his father. That was the first time Ludlow had laid eyes upon the evidence of his daughter's wickedness. He'd never entered Cass's room all those weeks and months he'd lain shivering and howling with pain.

Only the doctor from town and Chang had seen what Annabelle had done to her brother. Only them. No one else had seen the monster residing inside the flour sack mask.

Until now.

"*My God—what's wrong?*" Young Earnshaw's plaintive wail had come from the doorway behind Cass.

Cass turned to where Kenneth stood just inside the open front door.

Earnshaw's eyes moved to Cass, who stood grinning his death's head grin at the young dandy. All the blood fell from the little man's face.

"Oh," Earnshaw choked out, gasping as he stumbled back against the wall. "Oh . . . oh God!"

He covered his mouth with his forearm, then turned and stumbled back onto the veranda. Cass heard the rumble of the dandy's boots on the wood steps as Kenneth hurried off the porch and into the yard. Outside, Kenneth retched.

The soft thumps of slippered feet rose from the direction of the kitchen.

"What happen? What happen?"

Chang entered the room from an arched doorway.

"Chang," Ludlow bellowed. "My pills! Hurry!"

Chang stopped when he saw Cass standing bareheaded and unmasked before the old, wailing man. Chang clucked and shook his head as he came forward, holding a small brown bottle in his hand.

"You very bad, Mister Cass! Cover up! Cover up! Look what you do to your father!"

"Yeah, look what I do to him," Cass said, glancing down at the sobbing old man again.

He pulled the mask down over his face and crouched to retrieve his hat from the floor. He set the hat on his head and walked across the parlor to the house's open front door.

"Fortunately, that's nothin' compared to what she'll do to him." Cass stopped at the door and turned to regard Ludlow again.

Chang had splashed whiskey into a glass and was now feeding the old man a pill and the whiskey to wash it down with.

"I'll see you again soon, old man," Cass said, smiling through the mask at his flushed and haggard father. "I'll see you again soon with the Little Princess in tow!"

Laughing, he left.

CHAPTER 19

Laura Meyers lolled in the sudsy water.

Well, not lolled, exactly. The corrugated tin washtub was too small for any kind of lolling. She sat scrunched down in the tub with her knees drawn up to her bosoms. So, no, she wasn't lolling. At least, not most of her was. But she was enjoying the hot bath, anyway.

It was the third one she'd taken since she'd arrived at her humble little abode here in Tigerville. She'd been here three days, and she'd taken a bath at the end of each day despite how much work she'd discovered went into preparing one. First, she had to build a fire in the stove with what little split wood there was in the woodshed. There was a sizable stack of logs, but little of it had been split. She wasn't yet willing to attempt that formidable task. She wasn't sure she could even lift a splitting maul.

(Just learning to build fires alone had nearly sent her screaming into the hills!)

Then she had to pump and heat the water in a cast-iron pot. She had only one pot, so it took a good long time to get enough water heated and to fill the tub while adding more wood to the fire from her precious supply.

The first time she'd had to go through all that, on the first evening after the bizarre Warren Davenport had finally left her, she'd had a good cry. She'd had several good cries since, over various aspects of her life here in this small cabin, but she so far hadn't cried over this particular bath.

She supposed she was too exhausted to cry. Or maybe she was getting used to the odious work it took to have a bath. Or maybe, with the perspective she'd acquired after all the work it had taken her to clean out this wretched little hovel and make it habitable for a civilized woman accustomed to the finer things in life, the work that went into heating water for a bath wasn't really all that much work at all.

She was enjoying her bath here near the end of another long day of toil. The water felt good against her skin. Before, in her previous life, she'd never realized how good a bath really felt. Probably because she herself had never had to do the work of preparing one, and because she'd never before worked so hard . . . or perspired so much . . . as to so badly need one.

She smiled at that. Then she noted her smile and the rather pleased, satisfied feeling that the smile had spawned. Every minute of the short time she'd spent here felt as though she were on the verge of resigning her new job, of giving up the cabin, and of returning to Denver.

The only thing that stopped her was the fact that if she returned to Denver she'd likely be jailed for having shot her husband. As anyone could imagine, that was a large deterrent. There had been a few times when she'd thought that going to jail might be a welcome exchange for the tedium and toil of life in the perdition that was Tigerville in general and in this cabin in particular, but, having weighed all options, she'd decided to stick it out here rather than go to prison.

She had nowhere else to go. In her situation, any other place might be just as bad as Tigerville. Besides, while she still hated it here, she didn't hate it quite as much as she had when she'd first arrived. So that was something. Maybe . . . just maybe . . . she would keep finding more satisfaction in doing things for herself and not having to rely so heavily on others.

Especially on a man who'd betrayed her so badly.

As far as Jonathan was concerned, she didn't think he'd send the authorities after her. Not after what she'd caught him doing and with whom he'd been doing it. That would only arouse the scandal-mongers around Denver, and his reputation would be ruined. His business might suffer. However, if Laura returned to Denver, he might have her arrested just because he couldn't stand to see the woman who'd injured him so severely . . . and possibly permanently . . . walking around scot-free.

He might even sic a henchman on her. She knew he had henchmen. She didn't know what they did, exactly. She hadn't wanted to know. But she knew from overheard bits of his conversations that he did, indeed, employ such beasts. Now she could only imagine what they did . . . what they might do to *her* . . . and those imaginings made her wince.

She jerked her head from her knees with a quiet gasp.

She'd heard something outside.

Cocking her head slightly, she listened, frowning at the window just ahead of her, in the front wall. She'd pulled the flour sack curtains closed before she'd stepped into her bath, but they were so thin and tattered that she could still see through them. But all she could see was tree boughs nodding and bobbing in the wind.

She could hear only a burned log fall in the stove, the soft crackling of the soap suds, and the intermittent whisperings of the breeze outside the cabin. Occasionally there was the soft thud of a pine cone tumbling from one of the surrounding trees.

And birdsong, of course.

Nothing else.

She rested her chin down on her knees again. Her imagination had only been sparked by her wild imaginings of Jonathan's henchmen. That was all. Nothing else.

The thought had no sooner passed through her mind than something moved in the window to her left. She jerked her head in that direction.

Again, nothing.

She gasped again, louder, when someone snickered outside the cabin.

"Who's there?" Laura yelled, heart pounding as she drew her knees up tighter against her chest. "Who's there? I heard you! Go away. You're trespassing on private property!"

Silence.

Outside, someone whispered. The whisper was answered by another person—another *man*—and then there was a quiet rustling noise as though of someone moving.

Two men were skulking around outside the cabin.

"Go away! Whoever you are, go away or I will summon the authorities!"

As she swept her gaze from window to window, she spied the flicker of a shadow between two of the logs in the front wall, left of the door. Narrowing her eyes, she peered between the two logs. The chinking had crumbled and disappeared from between many of the logs and now she could clearly see an eye staring in at her through one of those gaps.

Laura hugged her knees even tighter against her breasts and screamed, "Oh my God, you're depraved scoundrels! Go away! I'm warning you! Go away—do you hear?"

More snickers.

A man said raspily, "Get away, Andy! Let me have a look!"

The eye disappeared.

Shadows moved through sunlit gaps in the chinking.

Another eye reappeared in the gap through which the first eye had stared.

"Go away, you beasts!" Laura cried, trying to make herself as small as possible. "Go away! Go away! Oh, please—go away!"

"She's a looker, I'll give her that," said one of the depraved peeping toms.

A little louder, one of the men said, "Hey, teacher, we'll give you a nickel if you lower your knees!"

They both wheezed with ribald laughter.

"Go away, you devils!" Laura screamed. "You're sick and depraved!"

Both peeping toms continued to wheeze with goatish laughter . . . until a large shadow appeared in the window straight above where the men were hunkered down, taking turns peeping through the gap.

The shadow dropped down beneath the window.

As the shadow rose again, the two toms cried out, "Hey, let us go! Let us go, ya big—"

Two shadows moved violently.

There was a cracking sound, as of two heads being smacked together.

The peeping toms cried out in agony.

"Now, get out of here!" a man shouted. "If I catch either of you two over here again, I'll gut-shoot you both! Understand?"

"Oh, my head, my head!" one of the toms screeched.

"Mine too!" the other one sobbed. "I think . . . I think you done scrambled my brains!"

"You don't have any brains to worry about, Andy. Neither of you Cullen idiots does. Now, get out of here!"

There was a sharp thump. In her mind's eye, Laura pictured Hunter Buchanon's boot slamming into the backside of one of the toms. She slapped a hand over her mouth in shock but felt a smile tug at her lips.

More thuds and thumps followed as the two toms, sobbing, went stumbling away through the brush.

Laura snorted into her hand. Her heart lightened as her fear evaporated.

He was back. She'd been wondering about him in the back of her mind, wondering if she'd ever see him again. He couldn't have reappeared at a more opportune time.

Two solid knocks sounded on the cabin's front door, making the rickety door shudder in its frame.

"Come in!" Laura cried out in delight, sitting straight up in the tub.

As the door opened, she realized that she'd just invited a man into the cabin in which she sat naked in a bathtub.

"Oh, no—wait!" she screeched, holding one hand out toward the door while covering her bosoms with her other arm. "I'm in a bath but I'll be presentable in a minute!"

She saw his big shadow in the door, saw his blue-eyed

gaze find her in the tub. His eyes widened and then he stepped abruptly back and drew the door closed with a scrape and a click.

"Sorry!" he said through the door.

"No apologies warranted! Please, don't go anywhere! Stay right there!"

She scrambled up out of the tub and toweled herself off. She shook her wet hair out, wishing she had time to dry and brush it so she'd look more presentable. She suddenly felt self-conscious and wanted very much to look as good as possible to her gentleman caller, Hunter Buchanon—if she could call him that—but that would take too long.

She scrambled breathlessly into pantalettes, a chamise, petticoat, and pantaloons over which she drew the pretty but conservative and relatively comfortable day dress she'd purchased the day before in town, having realized after going through her single trunk and two portmanteaus that she hadn't brought—nor did she own—a single garment that would be comfortable for physical exertion.

And this place certainly needed some physical exertion.

She buttoned the dress to her throat, tossed her wet hair back behind her shoulders, and opened the door.

He stood a way off, boots spread, thumbs hooked behind his cartridge belt. A pair of brown leather gloves were hooked behind the belt, as well. He was looking around the yard, at the furniture she'd dragged outside to give a thorough scrubbing. She'd also hung both braided rugs on a rope line she'd strung between two trees, and given them a good beating with a stick.

The bedding that had come with the place was out

there, as well. She'd scrubbed the sheets and quilts on a washboard in the tub and hung them to dry from another line.

"You've been busy," he said, blond brows arched beneath his hat brim. "I'm a little surprised you're still here."

He genuinely was. He'd thought she'd be gone by now. He was glad he'd been wrong.

"Yes, well," she said, "it hasn't been easy."

Buchanon looked at the rundown cabin. "No, I bet it hasn't. They should have fixed the place up for you."

Laura glanced beyond him toward the new school building roughly fifty yards to the south, its rear wall facing the teacher's cabin. "I'm grateful to have a new school building. Perhaps they spent all their money on the school."

"Hell," Hunter growled. "The men on the school council, especially Davenport, have more money than they know what to do with. They just have a hard time spending it. 'Tighter'n the bark on a tree,' as my old man would say."

He chuckled under his breath, averting his blue eyes a little sheepishly, then hooked a thumb over his shoulder. "Sorry about those two. The Cullen twins. A couple of raggedy-heeled prospectors. They live in a cabin in a gulch to the north. They won't bother you again, though."

He gave her a direct look with those warm yet commanding eyes of his. "I promise."

She believed him.

"Please, don't look at me too closely," she said, looking away from him as she ran her hands back through her wet hair. "I look like a drowned rat."

"Not any drowned rat I've ever seen."

Her freshly scrubbed cheeks flushed beautifully, he thought. He couldn't help feasting his eyes on her. A rare beauty. Seeing her took a little of the sting out of the situation with Annabelle. The sting of what she'd become. It was time to forget her now, he realized.

It was time he moved on.

"Say," Laura said, flouncing out from the cabin to stand before him and brush her thumb across the badge on his chest. "What's this?"

"What's it look like? A nickel's worth of tin. A step up from a few marshals back who had to cut their own badges out of a fruit can."

"How'd you come about it?" She gave him a cockeyed, jeering grin. "Did you steal it? Maybe you pinned it on to impress me."

"It impresses you, does it?"

"Oh, I think any woman is impressed by a handsome man in a badge. Especially one who'd proven himself so capable in saving her life."

Before he knew what he was doing, he'd drawn her to him and kissed her. She gasped and stiffened at first, but once she was in his arms, her body turned to warm mud, yielding to him. She returned his kiss with a passionate one of her own.

"My," she said, her chest rising and falling heavily as they finally pulled apart. "I have to say . . . that took me a little by surprise."

"Sorry. Me too."

"Don't apologize."

He smiled down at her, loving how her cheeks were flushed again. The flush had stretched all the way into her ears, and her eyes were positively radiant.

"What about," she said slowly, studying him closely, "the young lady who fainted in your arms the other day.

The lovely young lady, I might add, who had been wearing even less than I was at the time."

"That's over," Hunter said resolutely.

"Oh? That happened awfully fast."

"Not really. It happened months ago. I just wasn't willing to accept it. But I am now." Hunter could still hear the angry words she'd hurled at him the last time they'd been together in Big Dan's Saloon: "*Go to hell with Miss Meyers and don't you ever come back, you bastard!*"

Now he ran his hands down Laura's arms. "I'm sorry I didn't come sooner. When I got roped into the town marshal's job, the two rapscallions who roped me into it gave me the impression that all I'd be doing was locking up drunks and fetching widows' cats out of trees. Well, I've been a lot busier than that. And I've been studying a law book, as well, so I have some idea what and what not to do. Those two federals didn't tell me anything about that either."

Laura laughed and then reached up to flick his hat brim with her thumb. "I think you could use a cup of coffee."

Buchanon smiled. "I think I could."

"Have a seat at my dining table," she said, pointing at the crude wood table and two chairs sitting in the yard near one of the clotheslines.

She wheeled and headed back into the cabin, announcing, "I'll be right out with the pot, Marshal Buchanon!"

CHAPTER 20

"I heard what happened with Ike Talon," Laura said as she set the black coffeepot and two stone mugs—both with many fine cracks in them—on the table.

Hunter had taken a seat in one of the two chairs, sitting sideways to the table, right elbow on the table, one ankle resting atop the other knee. He'd doffed his hat and hooked it over an edge of the table.

"You did? Who told you?"

Laura poured coffee into his cup. "I walked to town the other day for groceries and other supplies." She glanced down at her sensible dress. "While I was in the ladies' dress shop, I heard a couple of the women talking about how that *lowly former Rebel soldier* shot a man dead in the street and then tortured him."

She glanced at him with a wince then filled her own mug.

"Lowly former Rebel soldier," Hunter said, arching a mock accusatory brow at her. "Now, why would you assume that was me?"

"Only because the name Talon was mentioned," Laura said with a coy smile. She sat down in her chair and lifted her coffee to her lips, continuing to smile at him through the steam rising from the mug. "You could have had him arrested, you know."

"I could have. But then, I wouldn't be wearin' this shiny new star."

"Oh, so it was sort of an audition?"

"A what?"

"Never mind."

Buchanon furled a brow at her in mock indignation. "Listen, if you're gonna try to intimidate this lowly ex-Rebel with big words, I'm not gonna come around here anymore."

"I apologize!" She reached across the table and placed her hand on his wrist. "Only simple words from now on."

Hunter smiled. "That's better."

Keeping her hand on his wrist, she frowned across the table at him. "You have such a warm smile and kind eyes. How did such a decent man learn to kill with such brutality?"

"I like to call it efficiency."

"All right. Efficiency, then."

"The war."

"I had a feeling you were going to say that."

"It's my least favorite trait. I hate what I did during the war. I killed innocent men who were only doing their duty, just like I was. But I discovered I was uncommonly good at it. An inherited trait, no doubt. A barbaric one. I have to tell you that I got so's I even enjoyed it . . . until I killed one particular young man. A young Union picket. He couldn't have been much over . . . well, my own age. Sixteen or so. He looked younger somehow. I stuck a bowie knife in him."

Laura sucked a sharp breath through her teeth.

"I want to tell you this about me but it's not going to make you feel any better about who I am . . . or what I've done."

Laura dragged her hand back over to her side of the table but kept her gaze on his. "Go on."

Buchanon sipped his coffee.

"It was late—one or two in the morning—and I'd been sent to blow up several supply wagons along the Tennessee River, using the Union's own Ketchum grenades. Those wagons were heavily guarded, and the young man I killed had been one of those guards.

"There was a clear half-moon, and that creamy light was reflected in the young soldier's eyes as I stole up on him and closed my hand over his mouth to muffle any scream, and jerked him over backward from behind. I pulled the bloody knife out of his belly and found myself staring into a pair of young, anguished, terrified eyes gazing back at me in bald horror.

"As I remember—and I remember every detail and likely will till they nail the lid down on my coffin—the kid was tall and willowy, a face speckled with red pimples. Just a kid. I dragged him back into the woods along the river. He was bleeding out, dying fast. I laid him out on the ground and slid my hand away from his mouth.

"'Oh God,' the kid wheezed out at me. 'I'm dyin'—ain't I?'"

Hunter blinked a sheen of emotion from his eyes, swallowed a growing knot in his throat.

"I just stared down at him. For a while, I couldn't move. I'd killed so many men almost without thinking about it. That's what you had to do as a soldier. You had to numb yourself against killing. You killed for the greater good.

You killed for the freedom of the Confederacy, to stamp out the uppity Yankee aggressors. But as much as I wanted to ignore the innocent eyes staring up at me on that moon-lit night along the Tennessee, my mind flinched in horror and revulsion at the fear in that boy's eyes.

"He whispered so softly that I could barely hear him. He said, 'Ma an' Pa . . . never gonna see 'em again. My lovely May!'" Hunter sniffed, brushed tears from his eyes with his left forearm. "'We was gonna be married as soon as I went home!' he told me.

"Grief and sorrow exploded inside me. I dropped the bloody knife, grabbed the kid by his collar, and drew his head up to my own." Hunter made the motions with his own hands. "'I'm sorry!' I told him. 'I'm sorry!'

"The kid just stared back at me, two half-moons float-ing in his eyes like on the surface of a night-dark lake. He opened his mouth. He wanted to say something but he couldn't get the words out. Then his eyes rolled back and he was dead."

Hunter blinked more tears from his eyes, saw the dark marks they made on the freshly scrubbed table. "That kid haunts me every day and night. I can't get him out of my head. After the war, I hung up my guns. I thought I'd hung them up for good . . . till the trouble last summer. Till my brothers were killed. I had to strap them on again, and that's the problem with killing. Once it starts it just never seems to end. Especially when you're cursed with being good at it."

He turned to Laura who sat staring back at him from across the table, her own eyes bright with tears.

"As for Ike Talon, I shouldn't have killed him that way. But once I got going . . . and I remembered what he did to Charley . . . and what his men did to you . . . something just broke loose in me and I couldn't control it anymore."

Hunter shook his head in disgust with himself. He lifted his mug and sipped his coffee. He sat back in the chair and turned to Laura once more. "There you have it. Those are this tiger's stripes."

She slid her hand back across the table. She closed it over his wrist again and squeezed. "Can I ask you for a favor?"

"Anything."

"Would you help me get everything back inside the cabin? And then come inside with me?" She paused, gazing directly into his eyes, her chest rising and falling sharply as she breathed. "Do you have time?"

Hunter placed his hand over hers. "I'll make time."

The cabin door opened an hour later, and Hunter stepped out, yawning, stretching, and scrubbing his hands through his hair, making it stick up in spikes.

He glanced back into the cabin. Laura lay curled on her side beneath the single sheet, her hair down and hanging in love-mussed tangles about her flushed cheeks and her bare shoulders.

She smiled, and her eyes caught the light angling into the cabin through the door.

Hunter drew the door closed. He wore only his buckskin pants and boots. The Black Hills' heat and humidity could be as brutal as the winters were long and cold.

He thumbed his suspenders up his bare shoulders, then walked straight out away from the cabin. He walked past the tree to which he'd tied his handsome cream stallion,

Ghost. Earlier, before he'd helped Laura get her cabin back in order, he'd unsaddled the horse and set a bucket of water down for him.

Now Ghost watched Hunter, curiously twitching his ears. He lowered his head and pawed the ground with his left front hoof, playful.

Hunter snorted then headed into the woodshed behind the school. A minute later, he came out pushing a wheelbarrow loaded with logs. He dumped the logs in front of the cabin, then returned to the woodshed three more times, each for another load of logs. On his last trip, he hauled the splitting maul as well as the logs over to the cabin, then set to work splitting the logs into stove-size chunks of firewood.

It was late in the day, the shadows growing long and wide, but it was still hot. Sweat soon cloaked his broad chest in a golden sheen. He set each log on a larger log he used as a base, raised the maul high above his head, and cleanly cleaved the wood with the maul's steel blade.

He'd always enjoyed the pure raw exercise of woodsplitting, and he had the chest and arms and washboard belly to prove it. Soon, he had a sizable pile of split wood stacked neatly in front of the cabin. He set another log on the chopping block, raised the maul, and swung it down with a grunt. The blade disappeared for a moment in the pine chunk, and the chunk exploded into four equal pieces, leaving the maul stuck in the chopping block.

As he gathered the pieces and stacked them, the cabin door opened with a groan of dry hinges, the bottom of the door scraping the floor.

He turned to see Laura step out of the cabin with a blanket wrapped around her otherwise naked body. She was barefoot, and her nearly dry hair was lovely as it hung in fetching tangles. The late sunlight shone gold in the chestnut tresses.

"Don't mind me," she said, tossing her hair back away from her smooth, still-flushed cheeks, smiling admiringly at the muscles rippling and bulging in his arms and flexing beneath the blond hair of his broad chest. "I'm just going to watch you work."

She leaned back against the door frame.

Hunter chuckled, set another log on the block, split it, then left the pieces where they lay. He left the maul on the chopping block and walked over to the pretty girl standing outside the cabin. He stood over her, hooking his thumbs behind the waistband of his trousers, sweating, and glanced at the door.

"Those hinges need grease, and the bottom of the door needs planing. I think your chimney's fouled. That's why the range leaks smoke. Probably a squirrel nest or a bird's nest in there. That needs cleaned out too. I'll be by in the next few days to take care of that for you. And that leak in the roof."

He glanced up at a gap between the moss-covered shakes. "There's probably more than one. I'll make sure those logs get chinked for you too."

"You don't have to do that. You have a job to do."

"Every man gets a break."

"You know what I think?"

"What's that?"

She moved up close to him, twisted a finger in the sweat-damp hair curling on his chest, and gave him a crooked, coquettish smile. "I think you might be striving for reasons to come calling again."

Hunter wrapped his arms around her, placed a finger beneath her chin, and tipped her head back, her swollen lips only inches from his own. "No striving here. I'll be back. You can count on—"

He stopped when the rataplan of a galloping horse sounded, accompanied shortly by a man's voice yelling, "Marshal Buchanon! Marshal Buchanon!"

Hunter lowered his arms, then shoved Laura toward the cabin door. "You'd best go inside!"

Giving him a worried look, she swung around, her hair and the tail of the blanket swishing, and hurried inside. As she closed the door, frowning through the narrowing crack, Hunter stepped away from the cabin just as a horse and rider appeared, galloping around the woodshed and heading straight for the cabin.

"Marshal Buchanon! Marshal Buchanon!"

As the rider approached, the door behind Hunter moaned and scraped, and he turned as Laura tossed his shirt out through the three-foot gap. "Here!"

Laura glanced beyond Hunter as the rider approached. Her eyes widened and she drew the door closed quickly.

Pulling the buckskin tunic over his head, Hunter turned to the rider, recognizing Otis Crosby, a beefy, moon-faced odd-job man in his early thirties clad in dungarees, work boots, and a blue work shirt. Otis was riding a horse Hunter recognized as belonging to a local faro dealer, Luther Sorenson. Hunter frowned up at Otis, whose gaze had drifted to the door before shuttling back toward Buchanon, the skin above Otis's nose furled incredulously.

"What on God's green earth is the matter, Otis?" Hunter said, shoving the shirttails down into his trousers.

Otis's vaguely questioning gaze drifted from Hunter to

the door again, then back to Hunter, and the odd-jobber's sunburned cheeks turned redder.

"Come on, Otis—out with it!" Hunter said, feeling his ears burn with chagrin. Otis had obviously seen him standing out here with his shirt off as well as Laura's quickly retreating figure clad in only an old striped trade blanket.

Otis was a reliable roofer and woodcutter—one who could also be relied upon to spread gossip as fast and as broadly as the ladies from the Tigerville Lutheran Church Sobriety League. And that was saying something. What Otis had seen here was sure to spread like a wildfire in a drought on a windy summer afternoon.

"Big trouble, Marshal Buchanon!" he said. "Six Injuns done rode into town, waltzed right into the Goliad Saloon— never mind the signs that says no Injuns, half-breeds, Mescins, Chinamen, darkies, or Easterners allowed—and shot Phil Scudder outright! Then they robbed the place, sayin' they was gettin' even for their people who Scudder poisoned.

"They shot the faro dealer when Mister Sorenson bore down on 'em with that big greener of his! Then the other men in the place started shootin' at the Injuns and the Injuns returned fire . . . and when I slipped out of there to fetch you, they was all pinned down behind tables an' such, still inside the Goliad, swappin' lead like hell wouldn't have it!"

Hunter had told Otis where he'd be in the event trouble erupted so the odd-job man would know where to fetch him. Buchanon just hadn't counted on trouble erupting this early in the evening, nor on being caught in a compromising position with Laura though he'd felt himself becoming attracted to her over the past few days.

Hunter didn't have time to worry about his and, more importantly, Laura's reputation. He swung around, pushed through the cabin door, scooped his hat off the table, and grabbed his gun belt and LeMat and bowie knife off a wall peg. As he strapped the belt around his waist and headed back to the door, he glanced at Laura standing near the front window, holding the blanket taut around her shoulders.

Judging by the concern in her eyes, she'd overheard everything.

"Be careful," she said.

He grabbed her, kissed her hastily, then hurried out the door.

CHAPTER 21

Otis was still waiting outside the shack on the faro dealer's horse as Hunter hurried out the door and strode across the yard at an angle toward his own mount.

A minute later, mounted on Ghost's back, Hunter raced around the side of the school and then onto the newly graded trail that rose and fell over two low rises peppered with settlers' sad shacks, stock pens, and hay barns. As he crested one of these rises and started down the other side, he checked Ghost down slightly. Warren Davenport rode toward him in his red-wheeled, two-seater chaise buggy.

Davenport's big, raw-boned frame was clad in what appeared a new black suit with a fawn wool vest, bowler hat, and red pocket square. A gold watch chain flashed in the sun. As Buchanon trotted Ghost toward where the man was slowing his own horse, scowling up at him curiously, Hunter regarded the man with what must have been a similar expression. When Hunter, still approaching, saw a spray of brightly colored flowers—a mix of roses and pansies likely recently purchased from a local flower shop—lying on the seat beside the man, his own curiosity swelled inside him.

As the men's gazes held, Davenport's brows ridged and his own eyes glinted with suspicion. More than just suspicion—bald disdain and indignation.

Now hearing muffled gunfire crackling from the town center, Hunter batted his heels to the stallion's flanks, and Ghost shot on up the trail. As he crested the next rise, he glanced back over his left shoulder. Davenport had now stopped his chaise and was talking to Otis Crosby, who'd stopped the faro dealer's horse beside the buggy. As the two men talked, both men turned their heads to glance along the trail toward Hunter.

Buchanon turned his head forward and galloped on down the rise, not so vaguely musing on Davenport's destination with that new suit and those fresh flowers, though it took little musing to cipher out that there was really only one place the businessman could be going.

To the home of the pretty new schoolteacher, of course.

As Hunter weaved his way around shacks and stock pens, he absently hoped Laura had a derringer lying around the cabin. Living on her own, she'd need it, and not only to fend off the Cullen boys . . .

As he cut through a break between the bank and the assay office, and swung Ghost to the south, he turned his attention to the trouble at hand. The gunfire was growing louder, angrier, and he could hear men shouting and yelling and a woman screaming. A man seemed to be screaming, as well, as though in horrible agony.

There was little street traffic. Most of the men and women normally heading for the saloons this time of the day were gathered in small clusters on the boardwalks, looking tense and wary and conversing in low tones, obviously unsettled by the sounds of the foofaraw coming from the direction of the Goliad, which sat on a side street one block east of the main avenue.

Hunter swung Ghost hard left at the side street.

Men were clustered on both sides of the street, crouching carefully and staring down the side street toward the Goliad, a large, plain, white frame building with a peaked roof and a balcony running along the outside of the second floor. Several men either lay or were crawling, obviously wounded, on the street fronting the saloon/hotel/whorehouse. A horse was down, as well, near one of the two hitchracks fronting the building, flopping and trying futilely to stand.

One man lay half in and half out of a window on the side of the building facing Hunter. He wasn't moving.

Meanwhile, the thunder of gunfire swelled until two men came running out of the saloon's front door and onto the front gallery, where several more men lay unmoving or, in one case, sitting up with his back to the Goliad's front wall, wailing, "I'm hit! I'm hit! Those savages shot me!"

He wasn't the only one squawking. More men yelled and wailed inside the hotel. A girl loosed shrill screams over and over again, every other second, as though she were in a screaming contest.

Three more men followed the first two out of the building. All five had long black hair and were wearing buckskin pants, shirts, and moccasins. All five wore six-shooters around their hips and were wielding Winchester carbines. Ochre, white, and blue war paint streaked their broad, dark-eyed, cinnamon-colored faces. A couple wore their hair in braids woven with dyed buckskin.

As Hunter checked Ghost down to a skidding halt,

curveting the mount, pointing his right shoulder at the hotel, the five Sioux ran toward a hitchrack on the other side of the street and maybe forty yards beyond the hotel. A tall white man walked out of the Goliad's front door. Stopping at the edge of the gallery, he raised a long-barrel New Army Colt straight out in his right hand, and shouted, "Stop, you red devils!"

The Colt bucked and roared, red flames lancing from the barrel.

All five redskins stopped in the street before their horses, wheeled, crouched, raised their rifles, and sent a volley of lead back toward the Goliad.

"Oh, damn you!" the tall man yelped as the bullets punched him straight back into the hotel, firing the Colt straight up in the air.

Hunter shucked his brother's Henry out of the saddle scabbard, leaped out of the leather, and swatted Ghost with the rifle's butt, yelling, "Get out of the way, Ghost!"

As the horse wheeled and, whinnying shrilly, galloped back in the direction from which it and its rider had come, Hunter dropped to a knee. But then he saw that all five savages were drawing beads on him.

He leaped back to his feet just as one of the maws bearing down on him sprouted smoke and flames. The bullet sang past his left ear as he turned and ran to his right, gritting his teeth at the furious belching of the Indians' rifles. He launched himself off his heels and into the air, diving over a stock trough and landing on the ground beyond it on his back with a sharp grunt.

He damn near knocked the wind out of himself, he noted as the redskins' bullets thumped into the stock trough and tore chunks out of its upper edges, slinging the slivers onto Hunter's face and chest.

No. He *did* knock the wind out of himself!

He rolled over onto his belly and lay gasping for breath. When he was finally able to suck some air into his lungs, he realized that beneath the tolling of cracked bells in his ears caused by the wicked slamming of the bullets into the trough just inches from his head, he'd heard the hard, fast thuds of fleeing horses.

He raised his head, now hatless, as well as the rifle.

The five Indians were galloping east, away from the hotel, their long black hair bouncing on their shoulders.

Hunter jacked a round into the Henry's chamber and aimed. He held his fire and lowered the barrel. They were too far away, fleeing fast.

He rose to a knee then, taking another painful breath, pushed off the knee to his feet. He crouched to scoop his hat off the ground and set it on his head.

He looked around at the carnage in the street and on the boardwalk on his side of the street. He walked over and put the wounded horse out of its misery. The other horses tied to the hitchrack must have fled after this one had taken a bullet through one of the Goliad's several broken out windows during the height of the melee inside the saloon.

Hunter turned to a dozen or so men clumped behind him, gazing beyond him toward the scene of the chaos, and yelled, "Somebody fetch the sawbones!"

Buchanon strode along the boardwalk, then stepped up onto the Goliad's front gallery. The man who'd been sitting there announcing that he was hit was still sitting there but he was no longer saying anything. Wearing a nicely groomed beard framing his pale face, he sat back against the wall, beneath a shattered window, his crossed eyes staring up over Hunter's right shoulder. Hunter recognized him as the local haberdasher, Vincent Kozlowski.

The man had taken at least two rounds to the chest, another just above his groin.

No wonder he'd been yelling.

Hunter stepped through the bullet-riddled batwing doors. The place looked as though a tornado had ripped through it. Men were only now rising from behind overturned tables and chairs, looking ready to duck again at the first sign of more lead. Four scuttled out from behind the player piano on the right side of the room, beneath an oil painting of a nude, ivory-skinned red-haired woman with a jade necklace reclining on a green fainting couch.

She and the couch had weathered the lead swap little better than the rest of the room had. She'd taken a bullet to the forehead and another to a knee, but neither wound had faded her come-hither smile.

There were more men sprawled on the floor and over tables and chairs, bleeding out in the sawdust, than there were stepping warily out of the smoky shadows. A dead Indian lay against the wall to Buchanon's left, beneath a red blood smear on the wall above him. The dead Indian's Winchester lay across his right shoulder.

One of the six was dead. Five remained.

At least the girl had stopped screaming. Hunter didn't see any girls down here, dead or otherwise, so the doves must have fled to the second story.

Good choice.

Hunter picked out one man, a beefy gent with curly red hair and wearing a shaggy beard on his freckled, ruddy face—a bouncer here at the Goliad, and said, "Llewelyn, what the hell had them Injuns' necks in a hump?"

He'd heard it once from Otis Crosby, but he wanted to hear it again from a man who'd been in the thick of it.

Llewelyn had taken a bullet to his shoulder. He was breathing hard through gritted teeth as he walked unsteadily toward Buchanon. He spat to one side, furious, and said, "They accused Scudder of sellin' illegal whiskey on the reservation and then they shot him and then two of them mangy devils leaped behind the bar to clean out the cash box. Sorenson had his double-barrel like he always does, and he tried to cut down on 'em, but them Injuns was ready for him."

The big bouncer hooked his thumb over his shoulder, indicating a man in a snappy green suit with an orange brocade vest still seated in his chair though he and the chair had been overturned onto the floor. The faro dealer's blood-splattered shotgun lay nearby. There was a pump-kin-size hole in the ceiling above him, where he'd discharged both barrels of the greener.

"There he lays," the bouncer said. "Dead before he hit the gallblamed floor!"

Hunter said, "Was Scudder sellin' illegal whiskey?"

"Hell, I don't know. I just bounce here during the day and over at the Queen of Hearts at night. I was just about to get off here when them six savages rode into town like it's ten years ago and Red Cloud is still raisin' hob!"

He cursed and, gritting his teeth again, looked down at his bloody shoulder.

Hunter swung around and left the saloon. He hadn't seen that much carnage in any one place since the Big

Trouble of the previous year. He hadn't expected to see something like this in Tigerville. He'd have expected it a few years ago, when the town had been about as wide open as any mining hub on the frontier.

And, as Llewelyn had said, back when the Sioux were still on the prod.

Hunter didn't mind admitting to himself that he was shaken. Not only by the carnage and by the fact that it had been instigated by Indians, but by his own responsibility in the matter.

He found himself the unlikely, not to mention reluctant, town marshal of Tigerville, with the problem falling soundly . . . and *resoundingly* . . . in his lap.

He had to try to run down those murdering Sioux before they disappeared into the ravines and canyons of the Pine Ridge Reserve, some of the remotest, ruggedest country in the territory.

It was his job.

As he walked out into the street, poked a finger between his lips, and whistled for his horse, he silently opined that those two old federal lawdogs, Winslow and Birmingham, were going to have the last laugh, after all.

True, when those Indians left town, they'd officially left Buchanon's jurisdiction and strayed into Winslow's and Birmingham's. Still, any town marshal worth his salt would go after them since there was no one else to do it. If only to follow them and find out where they ended up so he could pass the information on to the federals.

He considered forming a posse but nixed the idea outright. That would take too long. Those redskins would be splitting the wind. It was too close to sundown. He had to pick up their trail before dark and follow them and wait for an opportunity to take them down. Their horses were likely not shod, as Indians didn't shoe their horses. Nothing turned colder faster than the trail of an unshod horse.

Ghost came galloping back down the cross-street, shaking his head, cream mane waving. The stallion didn't like the carnage it saw around it, nor the smell of it, but he'd come back because he was well-trained and loyal and just one hell of a good, all around horse. He and Hunter had fought last year's war together; they'd been baptized together in blood.

Hunter caught the ribbons, swung into the saddle, slid the Henry into the scabbard, then booted Ghost back toward Dakota Avenue. He'd seen the Indians head east, but he knew they'd swing south at the edge of town. Pine Ridge lay to the south and east.

Hunter knew a shortcut to the trail that led to the main trail to Pine Ridge.

If the Indians followed a trail, that was. They might head cross-country.

He turned left onto Dakota Avenue and galloped down the street still lined with shocked, wary faces of men and some women exclaiming and wagging their heads at the killings at the Goliad. One of those shocked faces stood out in the crowd. It was an uncommonly pretty one framed by thick tresses of deep red hair.

It belonged to Annabelle Ludlow, who stood outside Big Dan's Saloon in her gallingly scanty getup. Her bosom buddy, Bobby Lee, sat on the boardwalk beside her, staring at Hunter, ears pricked.

Buchanon cursed.

CHAPTER 22

Hunter was going to ride on past Annabelle but when she stepped into the street, he checked Ghost down but kept his head forward, not looking at her directly.

Bile still churned in his loins not only for the angry words she'd spewed at him, but for the shameful way she was acting, standing out here on the street wearing no more than Hunter could pack into his mouth and still eat a full meal around.

She walked up to him in her high-heeled shoes to stand just off his right stirrup. "What happened?"

"Some Indians shot up the Goliad. I'm going after them."

He clucked to Ghost, putting him ahead, but drew back on the reins when Annabelle reached up to place her hand on his thigh. "Hunter, wait!"

"What is it?" he snarled at her, looking at her finally.

She gazed up at him, worry carving ladder rungs across her forehead. "You're going alone? After *Indians*?"

"No choice. If I wait, I'll lose 'em." Hunter glanced at Bobby Lee standing to the right of Annabelle's fishnet stocking–clad right leg and shiny green canvas shoe adorned with a cream satin ribbon. Many a time Bobby Lee had helped him and his father and brothers track cattle-rustling bronco braves. Bobby had a good sniffer when it came to Injuns.

"I could use help tracking, Bobby . . . if you think you can leave this . . . uh"—he raked his eyes across Annabelle's nearly nude body, and wrinkled his nose distastefully—"*parlor girl* unchaperoned for a few hours."

"I'm not a parlor girl, you big, simple-minded ass!" Annabelle squawked, cheeks turning crimson with fury.

But Hunter had already booted Ghost on down the street to the south. He glanced over his shoulder to see Annabelle squaring her shoulders at him, glowering at him hatefully, fists on her hips. Bobby Lee stood looking from Hunter to Annabelle then back again. Annabelle looked down at him then swung her arm forward, indicating Buchanon.

The coyote gave an eager yip and came running, catching up to Hunter and running along beside him, gracefully avoiding horseback riders, buggies, and drays weaving through the street around them.

Hunter, still miffed at the coyote for his questionable alliance with the girl who'd broken his heart, kept his head forward, muttering angrily under his breath. Yes, it was she who'd broken *his* heart, he told himself. Not the other way around. *Everything I did, all the choices I made, were for her benefit. She was only dressing like some one-dollar doxie, attracting the attention of every male in town, to spite him.*

Cunning, vindictive little wench!

Well, he'd moved on.

Time now to turn his full attention to those war-painted redskins.

At the south edge of town, he swung east on a shaggy two-track, a former freighting trail that slithered up over the prairie from Ogallala, Nebraska. Hunter, with Bobby Lee dogging him from behind, followed the trail at a hard gallop. He rounded the base of a haystack butte, then continued hard, crouched forward over the saddle horn, looking around for those crazy, red-skinned killers.

He continued his hell-for-leather pace for a good mile, then reined in Ghost and sat atop a low, grassy, cedar-stippled rise, looking around cautiously, frowning, peering into the long shadows stretching eastward from rocks, trees, sage brush, and steeply sloping, pine-clad ridges.

He'd thought he'd have seen the killers by now.

They'd had to have come down that valley ahead of him, that angled down from the northwest to curve around between steep, piney ridges before making another turn to jog off to the south and west, straight out beyond Hunter's position. That was the only way out of Tigerville from the east.

Bobby Lee gave a low moan. Hunter turned to the coyote seated on a rocky outcropping to Hunter's left. The coyote shifted his front feet edgily, looking at Hunter sharply, then turned his head to the south, tilted his long, arrow-shaped snout nearly straight up in the air, and gave a low wailing cry.

The coyote leaped down off the outcropping, landing on the trail directly ahead of Ghost, then shot off the trail's right side and into the shallow valley to the south.

"Where the hell you goin'?" Hunter said, keeping his voice down. Those redskins might be anywhere.

They wouldn't be headed south. Not yet. At least, not directly. Dead Horse Canyon lay that way, beyond a steep jog of rocky bluffs.

Bobby might only be tracking a rabbit but Hunter had known the coyote long enough to know that Bobby wouldn't lead him after a rabbit. He reined Ghost off the trail and booted the horse into a lope. Bobby Lee was a small shadow against the blond grass and sage now over a hundred yards ahead. He was heading to the left of the steep, pine-clad ridge jutting steeply straight to the south.

"I don't know where you're goin', Bobby Lee," Hunter said to himself, looking around. "I just hope you're not leadin' me off on a wild goose chase . . ."

Ahead, Bobby ran around the steep ridge's left side and disappeared from Hunter's view.

"No way, Bobby," Hunter told himself, scowling over Ghost's pricked ears. "Not a chance—there's a stone wall back in there—a bastion of solid rock. It angles down from the top of that piney ridge. Them Injuns wouldn't have headed that way because there's no *trail* through there!"

Having hunted this country for years, Hunter knew most of the trails around Dead Horse Canyon.

Still, he followed the coyote though he was beginning to be more and more convinced that Bobby Lee was on the trail of a cottontail or jackrabbit. If so, by following the crazy coyote, Hunter was losing precious time. He needed to find the Indians' trail before dark, and sundown was only a half hour away.

He and Ghost loped around the side of the pine-clad ridge. Now that stone wall loomed high ahead of him, set back a little from the forested one. Its steep face was strewn with boulders that had likely fallen from its crest over the eons, and lightly stippled with pines, cedars, and junipers growing from cracks in the rock wall.

Bobby Lee was a shadow sliding across the ground dead ahead of Hunter, angling gradually from Hunter's right to his left. He appeared to have his nose to the ground.

Hunter scanned the ground around him. Spying something, he checked Ghost down, stepped out of the leather, and dropped to a knee.

Fresh horse apples lay in a ragged line before him, dropped by a fast-moving horse. Hunter didn't have to touch one of the apples to know they were fresh; he could smell the green of the recently dropped dung.

Around the dropping, squinting and straining his eyes, he could see the faint impressions of unshod hooves. He also saw wagon tracks. The ground here was hard and carpeted in short, tough, strawberry blond grass that didn't accept impressions easily, but there was definitely recent sign left by passing riders on unshod ponies as well as wagon tracks. Several sets of wagon tracks, in fact.

The wagon tracks were older. A wagon had passed through here multiple times the past several months.

His heart quickening hopefully, Buchanon swung back up onto Ghost's back and booted the mount ahead. He could no longer see Bobby Lee. He looked from left to right then back again.

Nothing.

It was as though the brush wolf had been swept up into

the sky; he appeared to be nowhere around. If he was out here, Hunter would see him, for there was little cover out here to hide him—none, in fact.

Had he climbed the ridge?

Slowing Ghost to a fast walk, Hunter gazed up the steep inclination, looking for any sign of Bobby Lee's small, gray, fast-moving form.

Movement nearly straight ahead of him pulled his gaze down from the ridge to its base. A small, four-legged beast, the west-angling sun glinting gold in Bobby Lee's faun coat and yellow eyes, moved out from the base of the ridge and then leaped onto a wagon-size boulder that had tumbled down the ridge a long time ago. Bobby sat atop the boulder, lifted his long, pointed snout, and gave a chortling yowl.

Hunter booted Ghost into another gallop, covering the ground between himself and Bobby Lee quickly. When he was twenty feet from the boulder, Bobby leaped fleetly, gracefully down from the top of the rock, striking the ground on all fours with a thud. He ran back to the base of the ridge . . . and disappeared before Hunter's very eyes!

It was as though the ridge had absorbed him.

Hunter shook his head and rubbed his eyes. He looked at the ridge base again.

No Bobby.

What the hell . . . ?

He kept Ghost moving. As he did, the base of the ridge acquired an odd shape. The gray wall seemed to shift and separate. There appeared to be a gap in it, one that he could see better when he canted his head to the right.

Hunter swung Ghost to the right and continued forward, letting the stallion take a few more long strides.

Sure enough, he saw a gap that had been partially hidden from view by the boulder Bobby had been sitting on. The problem was the ridge wall was the same gray as the boulder, giving the illusion that the base of the wall was all one stony gray slab. But tucked away at an angle behind the boulder was a notch angling back into the rock wall, like a half-open door opening to the inside.

The notch was filled with dark shadows, and those shadows grew as Hunter steered Ghost around the boulder and into the notch.

Bobby Lee appeared before him, sitting just inside the notch and at the opening of what appeared to be a cave with a portal roughly the size of a large barn's open stock doors.

Bobby Lee gazed smugly up at Hunter, tongue hanging down over his lower jaw with its small, curved white teeth.

"Bobby Lee, I'll be damned if you ain't smarter'n I've given you credit for!"

Bobby Lee growled as though annoyed, then wheeled and disappeared into the cave.

Hunter followed. The cave ceiling was high enough that he didn't have to dismount or even duck. The walls of the cave moving up around him were roughly twenty feet apart. The floor of the cave was hard rock, but there were small stretches of gravel and loamy gray dirt bearing the impressions of unshod hoof and wagon tracks.

"They came this way," Hunter muttered to himself, hearing the astonishment in his voice, the mutters echoing off the close rock walls around him. "I'll be damned if Bobby Lee ain't right!"

Seeing gray light ahead, and Bobby Lee's small shadow jostling against it, he booted Ghost into a faster walk. Obviously, this wasn't a cave but a hidden passage through the stony bulwark. It had likely been carved by a long-ago river.

As he neared the light, he glanced at the walls on either side of him. The walls were painted with zigzags, sunbursts, and wavy lines in bright reds and yellows. There were also scenes depicting stick figures in elaborate costumes floating above hunting scenes—stick figures with long hair impaling a deer or an elk, sometimes a bear standing upright. These scenes were interspersed with representations of buffalo and bird tracks.

The Black Hills caves, and there was a veritable labyrinth of caves in the Hills, were filled with such paintings. A man who'd called himself an archaeologist had spent a few weeks on the Buchanon ranch several summers back while he'd been exploring the Hills. He'd informed Hunter, who'd seen many such paintings on his hunting and curiosity-driven expeditions around the Hills, that some of those cave paintings, or "petroglyphs" as the learned man had called them, were over eight thousand years old.

Seeing those scenes depicting activities so long ago always gave Hunter a ghostly chill, and they did now, as well.

He followed Bobby Lee into the wash of dimming gray light. He'd thought that they were coming to the far side of the ridge and would be out in the open when they gained the light. Now he saw that wasn't true. Halting

Ghost and staring straight up toward the sky, he saw that the light was coming down through a thirty-foot, straight up-and-down gap in the rock.

Ahead lay more stone-walled passage.

Bobby had continued, so Hunter could no longer see him but he could hear the soft ticking of the coyote's nails on the stone floor, and the rapid pants. Something told Hunter that Bobby Lee was as curious about this passage as he himself was.

Also, the coyote was being led by the fresh scent of the Sioux warriors, who'd passed through here less than a half hour ago.

"Hold on, Bobby," Hunter called, gigging Ghost on ahead, hearing his voice echoing off the close stone walls. "Wait for me, *amigo*. Being this deep in a mountain makes my insides quiver, an' that's a natural fact!"

Now the floor of the passage began dropping.

Ghost was careful to keep his footing, slowing his pace and taking cautious, mincing, herky-jerky steps. Suddenly, it was almost as dark as the inside of a well. Fortunately, for only a short time. Soon, more faint light shone ahead. And then, as the passage floor continued dropping, Hunter could again see Bobby's small figure silhouetted against it.

The light grew until it formed a ragged-edged oval.

The oval grew closer . . . closer . . . and Hunter blew a sigh of relief as the passage walls slipped back behind him and he and Ghost rode out into fresh air filled with birdsong. Above was the vast sky, green with late light and bayoneted with lemon-colored streaks from the setting sun.

The horse gave a nervous snort and a whicker, shook

his head. He hadn't liked that dark passage any more than Hunter had.

Buchanon looked around and whistled. The passage had led him into Dead Horse Canyon. The north wall of the canyon shot straight up above him. The southern ridge loomed ahead, on the far side of the slender stream of Dead Horse Creek, whose far bank was peppered with shrubs and small pines.

Bobby Lee stood in the middle of the stream, lowering his head to the water, drinking thirstily. Hunter gigged Ghost up to the stream and let him drink. He swung down from his saddle, lay belly-down, and cupped water to his mouth. He returned to the horse for his canteen, poured out the brackish stuff from earlier in the day, and refilled it.

As he did, he looked around warily, keeping one hand close to the LeMat on his hip. He also watched Bobby Lee, relieved that the coyote didn't look edgy, which meant there was no imminent danger. When Bobby Lee had slaked his thirst at the stream, the coyote sat down on the far bank, putting his back to Hunter and staring straight across the canyon toward the southern ridge.

Hunter could hear the coyote sniffing and growling very softly, eerily.

The Indians must have continued straight across the canyon.

Brows ridged with befuddlement, Hunter returned his canteen to his saddle horn. Chicken flesh rose across his shoulders.

Were the Indians planning to hole up in the canyon till morning?

If so . . . and if he continued across the gorge . . . he might ride into an ambush. On the other hand, Bobby Lee would likely warn him if they started to get close.

Urgency prodding Buchanon forward, he stepped back into his saddle, booted Ghost across the stream, and followed Bobby Lee to the south, nearly straight across the canyon. He followed the coyote into yet another, partly disguised gap in the ridge wall.

This gap did not let into another tunnel, however. It traced a slender side canyon running perpendicular to the main one. It rose gradually, hardly winding Ghost at all, until Hunter found himself on the canyon's southern rim, under a vastly arching, velvet-black sky aglitter with stars so bright that they resembled a million tiny Christmas tree candles.

It was dark enough that he decided to find a sheltered place to set up camp for the night. He'd continue after the Indians in the morning. He didn't want to risk Ghost stepping into a gopher hole, and there were plenty of gophers out here.

He dry-camped, ate jerky from his saddlebags, washed it down with fresh water, and slept well, Bobby Lee curled up in a tight ball against his left hip. He saddled and set out just after dawn.

Dogging Bobby Lee, who kept his nose to the ground, he rode all that day . . . and all the next day too.

On the afternoon of the third day, still following the killers' trail as well as a set of well-worn wagon tracks, he checked Ghost down suddenly. Bobby Lee had stopped and now stood in the middle of the trail, ahead of Hunter, lifting his nose and sniffing.

"What is it, Bob—"

Hunter stopped when his eyes picked out the thick, black smoke rising above the next rise to the southeast. The crackle of gunfire reached his ears, faint with distance.

So did what could only be the war cries of rampaging Sioux warriors.

CHAPTER 23

Three days before, a few minutes after Hunter had galloped away from her cabin, Laura returned to the cabin's front window.

A horse had whinnied, and for a moment she thought . . . hoped . . . that Hunter must be returning. But, no. With a cold, wet feeling inside her, she saw Warren Davenport's Morgan horse trot around from behind the wood shed flanking the new school building and pull the sleek black chaise carriage toward the cabin. Davenport's tall, hammer-headed figure, clad in what appeared a new three-piece suit, sat in the front seat, his gloved hands manipulating the reins.

Laura gave a rare curse and stepped quickly away from the window, letting the ragged, flour sack curtains settle back into place. Her heart quickened. She splayed her fingers over her chest, a wash of emotions racing through her.

The primary one was dread.

Warren Davenport was the last person she wanted to see. Her body had been tingling with the feminine fulfill-ment she'd felt after her hour with Hunter Buchanon. That glorious, storybook feeling that had taken all of the edges off her anxiousness about having come to this rough-and-tumble place vanished the very instant she'd seen that horse and buggy and the crude face with wedge-shaped nose and cold, deep-set eyes of the man driving it.

She looked around, wanting desperately to flee. But the cabin had no back door.

Should she hide?

Should she lock the door and pretend she wasn't here?

She backed away from the door, her hand on her chest, feeling the throbbing of that tortured organ just beneath her breastbone. She drew a breath and held it, seeing the shadow of the buggy as well as of the man driving it slide and jostle beyond the window left of the door.

The hoof thuds and the rattling of the chaise's wheels fell silent.

The horse blew, shook its head. Laura heard the bit rattle in its teeth.

Davenport cleared his throat and called, "Miss Laura?"

Staring at the door, holding her breath, Laura shivered. There was a harsh, toneless quality about his voice. It perfectly matched the agate-hardness of his eyes set deep in their raw-boned sockets.

"Miss Laura—I brought you something, my dear!"

Laura flinched, felt her shoulders quiver. *My dear?*

She stood staring at the door, heart racing. She'd pretend she wasn't here. Yes, she was taking a walk, getting the lay of the land. She wasn't here. She was elsewhere.

Anywhere but here!

She gasped when three loud knocks sounded on the door. They were as loud as pistol shots.

"Laura!"

Why did he think he could call her by her first name?

Anger joined the mix of emotions roiling inside her.

Three more knocks. Again, she gasped.

He called her name, louder. His voice was angry now. His boots thudded outside the door, and Laura gasped again, louder, when a shadow moved in the window. She leaped back when she saw his face, half-shaded by the brim of his crisp derby hat, glowering in at her, exasperation in his round, bulging eyes. He held both hands up to the window, to each side of his face. He held a spray of brightly colored flowers in his right fist; he was using the flowers to help block the light.

"Laura! It's Warren! Haven't you heard me knocking, dear?"

Embarrassment scalded the blood rising in her cheeks and ears. He was staring right at her as she stood six feet back from the door. There was no longer any denying him.

She fashioned a smile and, smoothing her day dress down across her thighs, she stepped to the door and opened it with another flinch of dread. "Oh, Mister Davenport! Why, I . . . I . . ."

He moved toward her from the window, frowning angrily. "Didn't you hear me knock?"

"No, I'm sorry—I'd fallen asleep. I was taking a nap."

"Sound sleeper."

"Yes, well . . ."

"Here. These are for you."

He thrust the flowers at her, smiling broadly. Odd, how his eyes remained as cold and dark as ice on a deep winter pond. She accepted them, frowning at them. "I don't know what to say."

"Oh, I have one more thing! Wait here!"

Davenport wheeled and strode back out to the chaise.

From the carriage's back seat he lifted a box wrapped in tissue paper and trimmed with a dark-blue ribbon. Smiling, he walked back to the door and shoved the package through it.

Laura gazed at it dully. "What on earth?"

"Open it."

"It can't be for me."

Davenport frowned suddenly, his heavy brows forming a long, brooding mountain over his eyes. "Why not?"

"Because I . . . because I . . ." Go ahead and say it, she told herself. *Because I can't accept gifts from a man whose advances are unwanted.* Say it!

She couldn't. He'd been nice to her. He was a widower and probably lonely. She didn't want to hurt his feelings.

"Please, Laura," he said, his voice suddenly gentle as he smiled down at her, having to tip his head downward to do so. The top of her head only came up to his chin.

She looked at the neatly wrapped package and then at the flowers.

"Um . . . all right . . ."

She set the flowers and the package on the table. She untied the ribbon, gently removed the paper, and opened the box. More tissue paper resided therein. She opened the paper, uncovering a neatly folded pile of dark blue velvet trimmed with gold satin.

She turned to Davenport quickly. "Oh, I can't. I'm sorry . . . I just can't—"

Still smiling sweetly, he blinked slowly and lowered his chin. "Go ahead," he urged in a voice just above a whisper. "Pull it out of there and hold it up to yourself. I think once you see it, you'll be smitten. At least, that's what Mrs. Hughes down at the dress shop said. She helped me pick it out. She'd seen you and remembered your chestnut hair, and she thought the dark blue would complement your hair as well as your eyes so beautifully."

Laura stared down at the dress. Indeed, it was beautiful. But she felt as though she were staring down at a box full of writhing rattlesnakes. She looked up at Davenport, frowning, about to reject the gift outright, but the sweet smile on his face tugged at her heartstrings.

He was lonely and sweet and kind—if a little awkward— and he probably missed his wife terribly. His grief and loneliness had probably caused this brazen advance on Laura despite that she'd given him no encouragement whatsoever.

At least, she didn't think she had.

Had she?

Perhaps she should have been more careful. Some men— especially older, lonely men—often misread a woman's words and gestures, or gave them too much import. That's probably what had happened here. A simple misunderstanding.

The least she could do was open the dress, and then, once she'd shown her appreciation for it, she could gently explain why she couldn't accept it, thereby letting him down as gently as she could. She'd take this bit of awkwardness as a lesson that she had to be more careful in the future.

She'd been married for five years. She hadn't been in such a situation as this one in a long time, and she'd just stumbled, that's all.

"Oh, it's lovely," she said as she held the gown out in front of her. It was, indeed, of sapphire velvet with a white taffeta collar and gold satin running along the low-cut bodice and around the cuffs.

It had likely been shockingly expensive. He must have paid thirty dollars for it, maybe even more in so remote a place as Tigerville.

She lowered the dress and smiled sweetly up at the man. "It really is lovely, Mister Davenport. But I can't possibly—"

Her interrupted her with: "I met that grayback marshal on the way out here. He didn't happen to stop here, did he?" He was still smiling sweetly, only, as before, the smile did not show in his eyes, which were alarmingly flat and cold once more.

Laura's mouth was still open, shaping the next word she'd wanted to say though the breath for those words had gotten held up on her vocal cords. She stared up at him, feeling her cheeks once again turn warm.

"Was he out here? The grayback?" Suddenly, Davenport was scowling, his jaws tight, his eyes glinting with anger. He grabbed Laura's wrist, squeezed it. "If he was out here pestering you—that bottom-feeding Rebel scum!—you let me know, Laura, and I will make damn good and sure he never does it again. That U.S. Marshal appointed him town marshal, but Winslow has no business poking his nose in the affairs of this town. I sit on the town council—am business partners with the mayor, in fact— and we'll take an emergency vote and have him run out of tow—"

"*No!*" Laura pulled her wrist free of Davenport's grip and stepped back. "He wasn't pestering me, Mister Davenport!" She stared up at him, incredulous, and rubbed her wrist. He'd squeezed it so hard that she could still see the marks of his fingers in her skin.

Davenport studied her for a long time. He looked around the cabin, his eyes finally resting on the bed. Laura glanced over her shoulder at it. The covers were thrown back and rumpled, which was how she'd left them when she'd risen and discovered Hunter outside splitting wood.

Davenport returned his gaze to her. She shrank beneath the severity of the man's look. She wanted him to leave even worse than before, but she found herself feeling afraid of him. He was much bigger and stronger than she was.

She felt a building anger in him. She also felt that that anger could erupt in violence. He seemed like a human volcano, throwing up small mushroom clouds of invisible smoke as the lava roiled and rose inside him.

"He's nothing."

Davenport had said the words so quietly, making a raking sound, that Laura wasn't quite sure she'd heard him correctly.

"Wh-What?"

"He's nothing. I realize you're new here, Laura. You don't know how we folks live here in Tigerville. The social layout. Who's good people, who's not. The Buchanons are lowly folk. The lowest of the low. They are gutter-wallowing Rebel trash. That one and his father live in a seedy little rooming house next door to a bordello. He drives the stage. Or he did until that smug old federal lawman pinned a badge to his shirt. Why, he shot a man in cold blood on Dakota Avenue—in the heart of Tigerville!—and Winslow rewarded him for it by making him town marshal. By God, I'm gonna get a lawyer and prove it's illegal!"

He removed his hat and slapped it against his leg.

Davenport's crudely structured face turned brick red, and his neck swelled as he barked so loudly that Laura took another couple of stumbling steps backward— *"Trash! You see? Trash!"* He paused, and then his voice came oddly gentle again, and he smiled like an idiot, eyes as opaque as a bear's eyes. "I've taken you under my wing. I intend to look out for you. I will not allow you to see him ever again."

"What?" she fairly exploded, unable to believe her own ears. She gave a caustic laugh and glared up at this crazy monster in hang-jawed exasperation. "You have no right to—"

He cut her off with: "Put it on." He canted his head toward the dress on the table.

She looked at the gown, then switched her gaze back to Davenport. "No."

"I'm taking you out to supper. To the Dakota Territorial Hotel. Finest vittles in town. Every table covered in white linen! We're gonna celebrate the beginning of a long relationship that will, I have a sneaking suspicion, lead to a wedding."

He smiled stupidly down at her, taking a step forward, holding his hat down in front of him, working the brim with his oversized thumbs. "I have money, you see. Don't worry—I don't care about your past. Why you've come here. You're accustomed to money, are you not? To the finer things? I can tell the cut of woman you are. I can afford all those things. After dinner, I'll show you my house. It's damn near the biggest one in town—uh, pardon my French. I don't normally curse in front of a lady." He chuckled. "And that's what you are. Aren't you?"

As if in afterthought, he held his hat up in one hand

and held up the other hand, palm out. "Oh, don't worry. I don't intend for anything inappropriate, Miss Laura. Not until we're married." He winked, blushing. "But then it won't be inappropriate, will it?"

He gave a hissing, self-satisfied laugh through his teeth.

She glared up at him, at once terrified and enraged. The words exploded out of her in a chortling wail: "*You go to hell!*"

He sprang forward, swinging his right hand back behind his shoulder. It arced toward her in a blur until it smashed against her face, picking her up off her feet and hurling her back and sideways.

She struck the floor hard and rolled up against the side of the range.

She rolled onto her back, ears ringing. She gazed up in numb shock. Her cheek was iron-hot where he'd struck her.

His ugly face with its supercilious smile slid back into view. He gazed down at her and said with a single, slow bob of his head, "Now, you put the dress on. I've made reservations for six. We don't wanna be late."

He gestured toward the window with his hat. "I'll be waiting right outside."

He winked, set the hat on his head, and went out.

CHAPTER 24

Hunter galloped to within a few yards of the crest of the rise, watching black smoke roil thickly from the other side of the hill into the clear blue sky, hearing the angry crackle of gunfire and the tooth-gnashing whoops and yowls of Sioux war cries.

He reined Ghost to a stop, shucked his Henry from its sheath, leaped out of the saddle, and dropped the reins. He reached into a saddlebag pouch for his spyglass, then, looping the lanyard of the glass's leather sack around his neck, ran crouching to the top of the rise.

Bobby Lee ran panting along behind him, keeping his head down and mewling. The gray-brown fur around the coyote's neck stuck straight up in the air.

Hunter dropped to his belly, removed his hat, and set it down beside him. He lifted a cautious gaze over the rise and stretched his lips back from his teeth in a grimace.

An old trading post sat in the bowl-shaped hollow below. A big barn and a corral and stable sat to the left, the long, L-shaped, two-story log main building lay to the right, divided by the trading trail that ran up from Ogallala and wended its way northward through the Hills all the way to Deadwood. The place was a legendary trading post established twenty years ago by the now-deceased Blinky Bill Weatherspoon. It was apparently still in operation— or had been until today.

Hunter had never visited the post, for it was too far south from where he normally ventured, on the edge of the Pine Ridge Reservation, but he'd heard the stories about Blinky Bill's old trading stop from the old market and buffalo hunters and cavalrymen who'd frequented Blinky Bill's back when the Sioux were still on the rampage and Blinky Bill's had been repeatedly threatened by Sioux warriors.

It appeared the Sioux were again on the war path. At least five of them were—the same five that Hunter had been following, no doubt. Blinky Bill's barn was almost entirely consumed by bright orange flames. Shouting and screaming rose from the main lodge, which boasted a high false façade bearing the words BLINKY BILL'S TRADING POST in ornate though now faded letters set against faded canary yellow. Faded as the paint was, it could still be clearly seen by Hunter from his distance of two hundred yards without even using the spyglass.

Several saddled horses were fleeing the yard, dragging their bridle reins. Four men, apparently bushwhacked, had fallen in the yard between the burning barn and the main lodge. Two Indians in buckskins and war paint, mounted on war-painted ponies, were hazing a half dozen horses away from the barn and into the meadow behind it. Another Indian was just then walking through the yard, inspecting the fallen men around him.

Hunter uncased the spyglass and raised it, quickly adjusting the focus.

The Indian in the yard paused near one of the fallen men around him. The man on the ground before him had long yellow hair and was also dressed in buckskins. He lifted his head and arms pleadingly, and wailed. The Indian aimed his carbine out and down from his right shoulder, and shot the wailing man in the head.

The crack of the warrior's shot was still snaking around the hollow, echoing, when a woman's scream rose from inside the trading post. A stout, brown-haired, female figure burst out of the trading post's swinging doors and onto the broad, peeled log gallery fronting it. As she started running down the steps toward the main yard, a white apron flapping around her thick hips, an Indian in a yellow calico shirt and black braids and war paint stepped out of the trading post behind her.

He cocked his Winchester and fired into the woman's back as the Indian in the yard fired into her chest. She stopped, jerked forward and then back, loosed a yodeling wail, then twisted around and fell back against a hand rail angling along the steps. The doomed woman slid slowly down to sit on the bottom step, head down, as if she were only dozing.

"That tears it!"

Hunter returned the spyglass to its case and scuttled a few feet back down the rise before gaining his feet, donning his hat, and dropping the spyglass back into a saddlebag pouch. He turned to Bobby Lee regarding him curiously, head cocked to one side, one ear up, one ear down.

"Stay here with Ghost, Bobby. You've done your work. Time for me to do mine."

The coyote sat down and raised his other ear, mewling very quietly and shifting his delicate front feet.

Hunter cocked a round into the Henry's action, off-cocked the hammer, then climbed to the crest of the rise. He dropped to both knees, doffed his hat, and peered into the hollow.

The two Indians on horseback were out of sight behind the flames and black smoke of the burning barn. The other killers must have gone into the cabin, from which more male and female screams sounded, as did the whooping and hollering of the savage killers and the sound of shattering glass.

A shallow ravine ran along the base of the rise Hunter was on, forming a semicircle around the trading post. Between the ravine and the trading post yard was a thin scattering of cedars and junipers, offering a modicum of cover. If Hunter could make that ravine and then those cedars, he might have a chance of bringing the killers down before they spotted him.

Heart quickening, he drew a deep breath, rose to his feet, and, holding the Henry at port arms across his chest, ran crouching down the rise, leaping willows and wending his way around stunt pines and small cottonwoods and aspens. He kept one eye on the cabin and one eye on the area around the barn, ready to go to ground if one of the Indians should reappear in the yard.

Horrific cries and screams continued issuing from the trading post cabin. The savages were killing the folks in there in grand Sioux fashion—slow and painful.

Hunter gained the ravine and dropped to his hands and knees. He took a moment to catch his breath, then removed his hat again and edged a look up over the lip of the draw, stretching a gander toward the lodge.

He could smell kerosene riding the waves of the smoke wreathing around the yard. The savages had likely used the coal oil to set the barn on fire. They were probably using it in the cabin now, as well, for he could see smoke issuing through a partly open window in the second story.

As he gazed at that window, another shrill scream rose from the lodge. A half second later, the window through which the smoke was curling burst outward, the glass shattering. A slender figure, clad in what appeared a gauzy pink wrap, came hurling out the window and angling groundward, the wrap rising straight up as did the girl's long, curly blond hair as she fell.

The girl, probably a whore working the second story cribs, gave another ear-rattling cry just before she hit the ground with a loud, cracking thud and a grunt. She lay in a broken heap right where she'd fallen, the gauzy wrap and her long hair blowing around her in the breeze.

"*Jesus!*" Hunter said. She'd escaped the only way she could the torture she'd witnessed around her.

Buchanon set his hat on his head and started to gain his feet but stopped when a footfall sounded behind him, just before a hand closed down over his left shoulder.

Hunter wheeled with a startled grunt. His eyes snapped wide when he saw the pain-racked countenance of Deputy U.S. Marshal Walt Winslow on his knees behind him.

"Winslow!" he said under his breath. "What the hell're you doing here?"

Winslow sagged back on his butt on the ravine bottom. His hat was gone and his short, steel gray hair was mussed. His blue eyes were bright, scrunched up at the corners with pain. He held his gloved left hand across his bloody belly, only a few inches above the brass buckle of his cartridge belt. The holster perched high on his right hip was empty.

"A small pack of Injuns howlin' like devils jumped me an' Birmingham. We were arresting three men from the post when they came at us all at once, from three directions. Roy got hit first. He's still in the yard with the men we were arresting for sellin' poisoned whiskey at Pine Ridge."

Winslow glanced down at the dark red blood oozing out from between his fingers, and cursed. He shook his head. Tears of pain came to his eyes. "I took this bullet, emptied my pistol, and tried climbing into the saddle. Got my foot caught in the stirrup, and my horse dragged me into this ravine here. The Injuns gave me up for dead, I reckon. Anyways, they haven't come lookin' for me. I lost my gun. My rifle's on my horse . . . wherever he is."

"This is starting to make sense."

"What is?"

"Those Injuns on the warpath. They shot up the Goliad in Tigerville, shot Phil Scudder first and then a good dozen of the patrons. They struck the trading post here on their way back to the rez."

Winslow grunted, winced, nodded his head. "We intercepted a wagon headed for Pine Ridge last night. It was loaded to the gills with whiskey. Likely poisoned whiskey. Several people have died on the rez from what the Indian agent down there thinks was strychnine-laced whiskey that came from the trading post.

"The driver of the wagon told me an' Roy that the whiskey originated at the Goliad in Tigerville. Scudder freighted the rotgut out from Tigerville via some old, secret trail gold miners used back when gold hunting was illegal in the Black Hills. The whiskey was always hauled on a moonless night, to avoid suspicion. Scudder hauled it out here to Blinky Bill's in secret. The trading post's past indiscretions involving selling whiskey to the Indians got it banned to sell any whiskey at all, to anyone. That didn't keep the devil now managing the place—a scurvy reprobate named Calvin Holte and his wife and two sons— from selling firewater to the Indians at Pine Ridge."

Winslow grunted again, shook his head, blinked tears of agony from his eyes. "Christ, this hurts! Why can't I just die, dammit? I'm so damn thirsty!"

"Hold on, Winslow. I'll fetch my canteen when I've taken those Injuns down."

"Don't try it! There's five of 'em, and they're madder'n stick-teased snakes. Scudder an' Holte and Holte's sons were poisoning the whiskey—dumping strychnine into it."

"Why in hell were they poisoning their own customers?"

"Meanness. Pure meanness. None of them had any love for the Sioux. Hated the whole tribe, in fact. Leftover animosity from Red Cloud's raids."

"Can't say as I blame them braves for bein' piss-burned, but they've carved too broad a swath, killed too many innocent people. I'm takin' 'em down."

"What?" Winslow gave a caustic laugh. "You're a real lawman now?"

Hunter brushed his thumb across the badge on his chest. "You're the one who ramrodded me into wearing this tin star, aren't you?"

Winslow grinned despite his pain. "I'll be damned if you're not one to ride the river with, Buchanon. I'm sorry I won't get to ride it with you."

Hunter patted the old lawman's shoulder. "You hold on, Walt. I'll be back with water."

"Go with God, kid," Winslow said. "And give the devil the hindmost!"

Hunter glanced up over the crest of the ravine bank.

All was clear. The Indians were still inside the main lodge, stomping around and grunting and yelling. More smoke was oozing out more windows, and a fresh dose of coal oil rode thick and cloying on the breeze. Since they were setting fire to the main lodge, the raiders were likely getting ready to pull their picket pins.

Hunter leaped up out of the ravine and made a beeline toward the lodge.

Just as he did, the two Indians he'd seen earlier came riding around the barn's far side and into the yard. They were leading three other war-painted horses with colorful blanket saddles by the mounts' rope bridles. They saw Hunter at the same time he saw them.

Hunter stopped walking. He was halfway between the burning lodge and the ravine.

The two braves stopped their horses roughly sixty feet away from him. The smoke from the burning barn wafted through the air of the yard, obscuring them occasionally, obscuring him from them. Hunter stared at them.

They stared at him, their eyes inky dark in their copper-colored, war-painted faces.

A guidon of black smoke swept between him and them, blotting them out entirely. When the guidon passed, they were both in mid-stride, galloping toward him and yowling like the devil's hounds.

CHAPTER 25

Hunter dropped to a knee and raised the Henry to his shoulder as the two warriors galloped toward him, both firing their Winchesters with their rope reins in their teeth.

Their mistake had been remaining mounted against an unmounted opponent. They weren't mounted for long. Hunter blew the left one off his horse, cocked the Henry, slid the barrel to the right, and blew the other one off his horse.

Both now-riderless mounts broke their routes off wide as they approached Buchanon, each horse coming within arm's length of trampling him into the earth before veering off to his right and left and buck-kicking into the distance. The two warriors were still rolling like discarded oversized children's dolls when one of the Indians from inside the burning lodge stepped out onto the front veranda. He was holding two burlap sacks, bulging with what was no doubt plunder from inside the trading post, by rope ties down his back.

He stopped in his tracks and widened his eyes at his two cohorts just now rolling to still, bloody heaps in the yard before him. He swung his shocked brown eyes toward Hunter, dropped both sacks to the veranda floor, and reached for the Colt holstered on his right, buckskin-clad thigh.

Hunter planted a bead on the warrior's chest and fired.

The bullet punched through the Sioux's chest, throwing him straight back over the balcony rail and into the yard. His six-shooter clattered onto the floor where his moccasin-clad feet had just been. Another brave came running out through the smoky open doorway, yowling and raising a carbine to his shoulder, sliding the barrel around, looking for a target.

His target found him first. Hunter's bullet carved a neat round hole through the warrior's forehead, throwing him back through the lodge's open door through which gray smoke slithered like ghosts.

Remaining on one knee, Buchanon ejected his last spent cartridge casing and pumped a fresh round into the chamber. He aimed at the open door, waiting.

There was one more plunderer inside the lodge. He'd have to come out soon. The flames and the smoke would drive him out.

Unless he escaped through a window or a back door.

Hunter's heart quickened anxiously. He caressed the spur of the Henry's cocked hammer with his thumb, tapped the trigger with his gloved right index finger.

Come on . . .

He glanced at the front windows, spying no movement aside from the jostling of orange flames chewing away at the inside of the lodge.

"Dammit!"

He leaped to his feet, strode quickly to the lodge, climbed the veranda's steps, and moved slowly, keeping the Henry aimed straight out from his shoulder, through the open front door. The room's shadows were obscured with clouds of roiling gray smoke. The smoke peppered his eyes; he tried to blink the sting away.

He moved inside what appeared a saloon area with a bar at the rear. A staircase angled up over the bar's right side. To the left, through an open doorway, lay the store area.

Hunter took two more strides into the main room, sliding the rifle this way and that, looking for the fifth and final warrior. A savage grunt sounded behind him and then a man leaped onto his back, snaking his calico-clad left arm over Hunter's shoulder, trying to pull Buchanon's left arm back.

Light from a window glinted off the blade of a knife in the Indian's right hand, which was rushing around from behind Hunter's right shoulder, heading for his throat.

A shrill howl rose from the door followed by the quick patter of four padded feet and the manic clicking of toe nails. A deep growl followed. The person on Hunter's back yelped as Bobby Lee sunk his teeth into him. That delayed the would-be stabber's fatal thrust.

Stumbling forward against the weight on his back, Hunter dropped the Henry and raised his right hand straight up before him, grabbing the hand holding the bowie knife within inches of his carotid artery. Behind him, Bobby Lee growled fiercely; Hunter thought the coyote must be chomping into one of his assailant's legs, making the man on his back grunt and groan fiercely.

Hunter wrapped his right hand around the right hand of the Indian and around the knife's wooden handle. Still hearing Bobby Lee growl fiercely as he shook whichever of the assailant's legs he was chomping into, Hunter fell forward onto a table littered with bottles, glasses, and playing cards. As he hit the table, he turned onto his right shoulder, slamming the Indian onto his back on the table. Buchanon ground his big body against the lighter body of the Indian's.

As he did, he thrust the hand of the Indian holding the knife in front of his neck straight out away from him, squeezing the hand until a shrill cry rose from beneath him. The hand opened and the bowie fell to the floor. The warrior was kicking at Bobby Lee, who had his teeth sunk into the renegade's left calf, shaking the leg as though trying to tear the limb from the brave's body.

Gaining his feet, Hunter palmed his LeMat and yelled, "Let him go, Bobby!"

No sooner had Bobby released the buckskin-clad leg than the warrior sprang off the table, quick as a striking rattlesnake, and dashed in a copper blur toward Hunter, long black hair flying, teeth showing between stretched-back lips. Hunter swung the LeMat up above his left shoulder then slashed it forward and down, smashing the barrel against the brave's forehead.

That stopped the warrior in his tracks.

No. *Her* tracks. The warrior before Buchanon looked in nearly every way like the other four—slender but well-muscled, built for savage fighting. But unlike the others, the copper-skinned, war-painted face owned the gentler curves of a female.

Just now, that female's brown eyes rolled back into her head and she sagged backward toward the table. Astonished at his discovery, Hunter thrust his left hand forward, grabbed the girl's collar, and eased her back against the table and then down to the floor.

He looked at her lying there, slumped on her left side, her oval face obscured by the thick strands of her coarse, straight, blue-black hair.

"I'll be damned," he said, eyes stinging as the smoke from an upstairs fire filled the room. Flames were licking through the ceiling and slithering down the stairway at the rear of the drinking hall.

Bobby Lee was mewling and looking around fearfully at the flames and smoke, clacking his little nails on the floor.

Hunter holstered the LeMat and, crouching, drew the warrior princess over his left shoulder and headed for the door. "Come on, Bobby Lee. I don't know about you, but it's gettin' too hot in here for me!"

He carried the Indian girl out into the yard and lay her down near the body of Deputy U.S. Marshal Roy Birmingham. The poor old gent had been shot at least six times. His revolver was still in its holster. Moving quickly, for the lodge was burning more hotly and would likely soon be engulfed in flames, he felt around on Birmingham's corpse for a set of handcuffs.

All he found was a set of small handcuff keys.

He turned to the other three men—one old, the other two much younger—lying around Birmingham. All three had their hands cuffed behind their backs. They sported even more bullet wounds than Birmingham did. Hunter removed the cuffs from the wrists of the older, buckskin-clad gent with long grizzled yellow-gray hair and who lay near the bottom of the porch steps.

Bobby Lee, he saw, was properly anointing the bodies

of the dead renegades in typical Bobby Lee fashion, one hindleg hiked high.

Hunter chuckled under his breath then took the cuffs over to the Sioux girl. She moaned, squeezing her eyes closed as though in pain. Hunter had smacked her pretty hard. She'd had a lot of fight in her; in fact, if Bobby Lee hadn't shown up when he had, Hunter would likely be lying inside the burning lodge about now, his own blood boiling in the flames where it would have oozed out around his neck.

He quickly snapped the cuffs closed around the girl's wrists, then, wincing against the heat of the crackling flames now thoroughly gorging themselves on the lodge's shake-shingled roof and on the big false façade, he dragged Birmingham a good hundred feet away from the burning building.

He left the Indians where they lay. They could burn up in their own fire.

As for the girl, he'd take her back to Tigerville. He didn't like playing favorites just because her shirt was lumpier than the men's, but he couldn't kill her in cold blood. He'd leave her fate for a judge to decide.

Besides, he'd been reading up on the law and had a little better understanding of a citizen's rights. Not that he regretted torturing and killing Ike Talon. Ike Talon was another matter altogether.

When he had Birmingham safely away from the flames, he went back over and picked up the princess, slinging her over his shoulder, then tramped back in the direction of the ravine in which he'd left Walt Winslow. Bobby Lee trotted dutifully along beside him, panting from the heat of the growing fire that was roaring like a fire-breathing dragon behind them.

Hunter stopped at the lip of the ravine. "Hey, Winslow, I got 'em all but—"

He stopped. Winslow lay where Buchanon had left the man. Only now he wasn't moving. He lay flat on his back, both hands on his bloody belly, staring straight up at the puffy white clouds floating high across the blue arch of the prairie sky.

Hunter sighed. He lay the girl on the ground.

"Let me know if she wakes up," Hunter told Bobby Lee.

The coyote sat beside the girl, curling his thick, bushy gray tail around his right hindleg. He looked down at the girl, showing his teeth.

Hunter walked down into the ravine. He dropped to a knee beside Winslow and placed a finger against the man's neck and gave a ragged sigh. "Dead, all right. Poor devil."

Bobby Lee growled and snarled.

Hunter turned to see the coyote crouching forward, chest down, butt in the air. He was snapping and snarling at the Indian girl who tossed her head from side to side, blinking her eyes and pushing up off the ground.

Hunter rose. "Hold on."

She rolled onto her belly and lifted her chin, glaring at him. She snarled at him in much the same way Bobby Lee was snarling at her. Hunter didn't know how she did it so easily, for her wrists were cuffed behind her back, but she managed to spring to her feet. Bobby was instantly on her, chomping into her ankle. She gave a raking scream of raw fury, and kicked Bobby away from her.

Bobby yelped and rolled.

She tossed her hair from her wild eyes and screamed at him in Lakota, *"White devil! Murdering coward!"*

She turned and started running away. She ran fast for someone with her wrists tied behind her. Hunter ran up out of the ravine and sprang off his heels, diving forward and swiping his right hand across a once moccasin-clad foot, tripping her. She hit the ground with another enraged scream.

She sounded like a wolverine with a leg in a trap.

She rolled onto her back and somehow managed to leap to her feet again.

Hunter was just regaining his own feet when she sprang forward, ramming her head and shoulders against him. He hadn't yet got his feet settled, so her sudden attack caused him to pitch over backward, striking the ground on his back.

Hissing like an enraged mountain lion, she slammed her head against his—over and over again—heedless of the goose egg swelling on her own forehead—until he managed to roll her off of him. His head aching, vision swimming, he didn't see her come at him until she was on him again, hissing and spitting and sinking her teeth into his shoulders and chest.

Bobby Lee danced circles around them, barking and growling and showing his teeth.

Hunter felt like he was under attack by a crazed catamount, wincing as her teeth tore into his flesh, ripping his shirt.

Realizing he wasn't going to be able to fend this feral she-beast off until he got serious, he pulled her head up off his chest by her hair, then, rolling up off his right hip and shoulder, slammed her onto the ground. She was still snarling and hissing and snapping her teeth, still trying to bite him.

"Girl, I'm sorry about this, but . . ." He ripped the LeMat from its holster and smashed the barrel against her head again.

She screamed and slumped back, the fight suddenly gone from her.

Buchanon sat back on his boot heels and looked down at his torn shirt, blood-stained where her teeth had ripped his flesh. He turned to Bobby Lee standing nearby and staring at him dubiously.

"Damn," Hunter said. He sleeved the girl's saliva from his cheek. "Now, ain't she a caution?"

CHAPTER 26

Laura stepped onto the boardwalk fronting the Tigerville jail and town marshal's office, knocked once on the jailhouse door, then tripped the latch and shoved the door halfway open.

Inside, the beefy odd-job man, Otis Crosby, lifted his chin from his chest and dropped his work boot–clad feet from the edge of the cluttered desk to the floor and turned his moon-shaped face toward Laura with a surprised expression.

The look of surprise turned to chagrin. He smiled sheepishly as he said, "Caught me sleepin' on the job, Miss Meyers."

Laura had formally met Otis several days ago, when she'd come looking for Hunter. The town's mayor had assigned Otis the task of keeping an eye on the jailhouse while Hunter was off trying to run down the Indians who'd murdered so many people in the Goliad Saloon nearly a week ago now. The town was without a lawman while Hunter was gone. Laura had never seen Otis do anything here at the jailhouse but sleep in the chair with his boots on the desk.

She'd stopped here several times, desperate to talk to Hunter about the lunatic Warren Davenport, who kept bestowing gifts on her and paying her unwanted visits at her little shack flanking the school. She was so alarmed by the man's bizarre behavior—actually having forced her under threat of physical harm to have supper with him—that she couldn't sleep or eat and wanted very desperately for the fool to leave her alone.

She was deathly afraid of the man; the cut on her cheek proved she had good reason to be. She was horrified when she looked at her image in the mirror. Her black eye, incurred during Talon's attack on the stage, had all but disappeared. But now she would be facing her students in a few days, on the first day of school, with a scab on her cheek.

"Any sign of Hunt . . . I mean, Marshal Buchanon?" she asked Crosby hopefully.

Otis had gained his feet and was holding his hat in his hands.

He shook his head. "N-no, ma'am. Ain't seen hide nor hair, I'm sorry to say."

"I wonder what could be keeping him," she said, half to herself as she turned away from the man, crestfallen.

"The mayor said he's gonna form a posse and hire a good tracker if Hunter ain't back by tomorrow. No one's seen the two federal fellas—Winslow and Birmingham—neither."

"By tomorrow it might be too late." Laura drew the door closed and turned to the street. *But, then, it might already be too late.*

Her heart felt swollen and heavy with worry. Over the

past several days, she'd kept imagining Hunter lying dead somewhere out in the Hills or on the prairie. Or wounded and on foot, dying slowly. The thought haunted her. She was deeply worried about him; deeply worried for herself, as well.

If he was gone, killed by those renegade Sioux, she would have no one here in town to protect her from the unwanted advances of Warren Davenport.

She turned and began to walk up the street to the north but stopped suddenly when whom did she see but none other than Warren Davenport himself!

She gasped and rocked back on her heels. She felt as though he'd slapped her in the face again.

Davenport stood facing her from the end of the next block. He stood outside his business office, staring right at her. He wore his usual ominous-looking black, three-piece suit and derby hat, a gold watch chain dangling from a pocket of his black wool vest. He stood with his black shoes spread wide, his fists on his hips holding the flaps of his coat back, puffing the cigar that angled from one corner of his mouth.

He was too far away for Laura to see his expression clearly, but she knew he was scowling at her severely. With remonstration. He knew she'd come to the jailhouse searching for Hunter.

He looked the specter of death itself bearing down on her with flat, soulless, darkly judging eyes.

Laura turned away quickly with a chortling sound of terror rising from her throat. She gave her back to the man, as though no longer seeing him would mean he would no longer be there. Automatically, she began moving south, away from him, wanting to put as much distance between her and him as possible.

She crossed a side street after nearly being run down by a horse, then, blinking from the dust wafting around her, mounted the boardwalk on the street's other side. She was staring at the walk's scarred, tobacco-stained boards, her thoughts bleak and hopeless. Something made her look up. She blinked against the dust and harsh sunlight, frowning curiously.

The stage from Cheyenne must have just rolled into town. It was parked in front of the stage manager's office half a block away. Dust was still sifting around it, the lathered horses blowing and shaking their heads. Passengers were climbing out of the carriage door facing the boardwalk.

One of these passengers attracted the brunt of Laura's attention. He was a finely dressed gentleman in a butterscotch bowler hat and coat, black foulard tie, and black trousers of the finest wool. He'd just stepped down from the stage and was using a cane to negotiate the boardwalk between the parked coach and the manager's office.

The cane had a silver horse-head handle.

Instantly, Laura stopped and, turning toward the shop on her left, trying to hide her face, stumbled forward, knees weakening. Her heart hammering painfully, she dared another glance toward the stage.

The finely dressed man with the cane was her husband, Jonathan Gaynor. She couldn't see his face because he hadn't looked her way—thank God!—but she saw his neatly trimmed dark brown hair beneath the hat and the neat little muttonchops framing his regular-featured face that she'd once thought was handsome.

Now she didn't think she'd ever seen an uglier man. Aside from Warren Davenport, that was. She was being stalked by two devils—one large and blunt-faced, the other dressed to the nines and dapper, complete with a silver horse-head cane!

Oh God—what was Jonathan doing here in Tigerville? Did he have business interests here?

Of course, he didn't have business interests in Tigerville. He was here for one reason and one reason only—to find the wife who'd shot him in his private parts!

Laura dared one more glance toward the stage. Jonathan appeared to be with another man—taller, slightly broader through the shoulders, with a thick mustache. He wore a dark blue pinstriped suit with a red ribbon tie and black, low-crowned hat. A badge glinted on the lapel of the man's coat. Laura had seen such badges before in Denver.

It was a Pinkerton's badge.

A Pinkerton detective had tracked her down and accompanied Jonathan here to see that Laura received her just deserts!

Dizzy with terror, Laura swung around and, holding up a hand to shield her face from the direction of the stage manager's office, she stepped off the boardwalk and strode headlong into the street. She only became aware of men yelling at her and of traffic stopping or swerving sharply to avoid her after she'd gained the boardwalk on the other side of Dakota Avenue.

She hurried into the shadows beneath a boardwalk awning and stepped up to the front of a shop. Leaning forward, she placed one gloved hand on the shop's front wall and drew deep, even breaths, trying to calm her racing heart. She placed her other hand over her mouth, aghast at what was happening to her.

Not only did she have the crazed Warren Davenport after her, but Jonathan was now pursuing her, as well. And the one man who could protect her from both pursuers was probably lying dead out in the prairie!

Someone walked up to her. She could hear the tapping of shoes, see a shadow merge with her own on the boardwalk. "Take a breath," said a woman's voice to her right.

Laura opened her eyes. A sheer, peach stocking–clad foot resided in a high-heeled pink satin shoe on the boardwalk beside her.

She turned her head slowly, slowly lifted her gaze to follow the slender, nicely turned, stocking-clad leg up past the stocking, which ended mid-thigh, to a sexy satin peach camisole and pink satin pantalettes. She continued on up the nicely endowed camisole to the pretty, green-eyed, heart-shaped face complimented beautifully by thick, tumbling and curling tresses of thick red hair.

The young woman Hunter had intended to marry regarded Laura skeptically. Almost with—what? Concern?

"I beg your pardon?" Laura said.

"Take a deep breath. Slowly." Miss Ludlow placed her hand on her tummy and drew a slow, deep breath, as though to demonstrate.

Laura drew a breath deep into her lungs.

"Let it out, take another. Deep and slow."

Laura nodded and drew another deep, slow breath. Almost instantly, her heart had begun to slow its frantic pace. Now it slowed even further.

"Keep going," Miss Ludlow said, ignoring the whistles

and goatish looks of the men passing on the boardwalk. "A few more."

Laura drew another deep breath, then another.

"Thank you," she said with a sigh. "That helps." Remembering Jonathan, she cast a quick glance back in the direction of the stagecoach parked in front of the station manager's office. Fortunately, he was no longer anywhere Laura could see him. He and the Pinkerton agent must have gone into the manager's office.

Again, Laura's heart quivered, hiccupping.

"You look like you could use a drink."

Laura turned to the pretty redhead, startled. "What? Oh, no . . . I'm the new teacher here in town."

"I know who you are."

Laura studied the girl, but her expression, one eye cocked, that brow slightly furled, was vague. Laura nodded. "Yes, I know who you are too." She looked the girl up and down in open admiration. "You're very pretty."

"Hunter has good taste in women." Miss Ludlow returned Laura's admiring smile, and Laura instantly felt her guard go down.

She also felt the heat of embarrassment rise in her cheeks.

"Come on," said the pretty redhead, canting her head toward the front door of the saloon called Big Dan's, which was where Laura knew that she worked. "I'll buy you a drink."

"Thank you, but like I said . . ."

"We have a back door." Miss Ludlow smiled and then extended her right hand. "Annabelle."

Again, Laura returned the girl's smile. She squeezed her hand. "Laura."

"Follow me, Laura."

Annabelle turned, stepped into an alley, and walked along the side of the building toward the rear. Holding the skirt of her copper-patterned cream day dress above her ankles, reticule dangling from her left wrist, Laura followed the redhead around to the back of Big Dan's and through a rear door.

She felt dangerously self-conscious. If she were to be seen entering a saloon and whorehouse, she'd likely have unemployment added to her list of woes.

On the other hand, Jonathan would likely know soon where to find her. He and the Pinkerton man would ask around, flash a few photographs of the treacherous woman he was looking for, and they'd find her in no time. Soon, she'd either be dead or in jail.

Oh, Hunter—where are you?

She followed Annabelle up a creaky back stairway to the second floor.

"Don't worry," Annabelle said, keeping her voice low as they walked along the dingy, sour-smelling hall. She'd taken her shoes off and was walking barefoot, cradling the shoes in her arm. "The only ones up here are you and me and the whores. They'll be asleep till noon and it's only ten."

"Aren't I taking you away from your work?"

"I started the chili downstairs for Dan. He'll be in soon to take over. He likes to take the credit for his chili. We don't get much business until noon."

Annabelle stopped at a door, twisted the knob, shoved the door open, and walked into the room beyond it, glancing over her shoulder at Laura. "Please."

Laura stepped timidly into the room. Before her was a brass-framed bed littered with female clothes and under-clothes, a dressing table, a chest of drawers, a washstand, and a pitcher and bowl.

One very small, dusty window let in a little light through badly faded velvet curtains flanking two motley-looking, mismatched brocade arm chairs sitting to either side of a round eating table. The ornate paper on the walls, above the wainscoting, was also faded and peeling.

Annabelle walked to the chest of drawers. "Take a seat over there by the window. I have a bottle around here somewhere. I'm not much of a drinker—I've seen what it's done to my brother Cass—but I like a little nip before bed to help me sleep."

Laura sat in one of the chairs, leaning back to take the breeze blowing through the partly open window. She was warm—perspiring, in fact—and her heart was still beating fast. She felt as though her skin had been peeled back to expose every nerve in her body. She kept seeing Warren Davenport glaring at her, and Jonathan leaning on his cane.

As Annabelle brought a bottle and two small water glasses, Laura leaned forward with her elbows on the table and massaged her temples with her fingers. Annabelle poured some liquor into one of the glasses and slid it toward Laura.

"Here you go—drink that. If anyone could use a drink, it's you." She splashed whiskey into the second glass, then set the bottle on the table and sank into the chair across from Laura.

Laura reached for her glass with a trembling hand, and threw back the entire shot. She swallowed, lifting her chin and savoring the warm, calming feeling the whiskey touched her with. She choked a little on the whiskey's harshness, like pepper at the back of her throat, but still relished its soothing properties.

"Oh, yes . . . yes, that's good."

"Whoa!" Annabelle laughed and threw back her own entire shot.

She smacked her lips, set her glass down, refilled Laura's glass and then her own.

"What the hell? I think I deserve a day off."

Laura lifted her glass to her lips, drank half, then set the glass back down on the table. She lowered her hands to her lap, straightened her back, tightened her shoulders, and closed her eyes, luxuriating in the nerve-calming properties of the liquor.

"What happened?" Laura opened her eyes to see Annabelle gazing at her from the other side of the table. "You look like a dozen ghosts danced across your grave," the pretty redhead added.

"If only it were that delightful." Laura threw back the rest of the shot and swallowed. She raised her hand to her lips as she coughed, then rested her hand on the table before her, squeezing it worryingly with the other one. "Can I trust you?" A wave of emotion swept through her, tugging on her heart and bringing tears to her eyes. "I have no one to talk to. Hunter's gone and . . . I . . . I . . ."

Annabelle's green eyes widened sympathetically as she stretched her arms across the table and closed both of her hands around Laura's. "If you can't trust another lost woman, who can you trust?"

Laura laughed at that but it was partly a sob. She'd never felt so afraid . . . so lost, but it felt good being here in this small, shabby room with this young woman she found herself feeling a kinship with despite their loving . . . or having loved on Annabelle's part . . . the same man.

Laura sniffed, cleared her throat, and returned Annabelle's frank, sympathetic gaze with a direct one of her own. "I shot my husband, an important man, in Denver."

Annabelle's eyes widened, glinting in obvious surprise. Her full lips parted slowly, brows rising. "Oh . . ."

CHAPTER 27

"Did you kill him?" Annabelle asked.

"Unfortunately, no."

Annabelle clamped her hand over her mouth and laughed with guilty delight.

"I caught him in a bathtub with another woman. I'd learned that he and this other woman—a parlor house madam—had been carrying on behind my back since only a few months after we were married. That he was taking weekly trips to Gaynorville to see her, in fact."

"Gaynorville? The mining town near Denver?"

"That's the one." Laura smiled with chill irony. "My husband named the town after himself. He's Jonathan Gaynor."

"Wow!"

"I'm using my maiden name though I should have come up with something more imaginative. I just didn't know that he would actually follow me here. All the way here from Denver."

"He's here . . . in Tigerville?"

"I just saw him step down from the stage . . . with a decided limp as well as a Pinkerton detective."

"Gosh, Laura—no wonder you looked as pale as a freshly laundered sheet out there!"

"That's not my only problem."

Annabelle held up her hand, palm out. "Hold on." She plucked the cork out of the bottle's lip. "If I need another one, you most certainly do." She poured another half inch of whiskey into each glass and set the bottle down.

Laura held up her glass. "To keeping secrets and female alliances?" she asked with a hopeful arch of her brows.

Annabelle touched her glass to the teacher's, smiling brightly. "Hear! Hear!"

The two each took down half of the whiskey in their glasses at the same time and then set the glasses back down on the table.

Annabelle wiped her hand across her mouth and leaned forward, eyes wide and expectant. "All right. I'm all ears."

"Do you know Warren Davenport?"

"Enough to not like the way he looks at me," Annabelle said darkly.

Laura brushed her finger across her cheek, to indicate the scab. "See this?"

"Yes," Annabelle said, again darkly.

"He gave me that after I rebuffed his advances. He's stalking me, threatening me."

Annabelle slapped the table. "That son of a—"

"I don't know who I'm more afraid of—him or Jonathan."

"I've always known there was something off about that morbid old man. For years before she died, hardly anyone but their close neighbors ever saw his long-suffering wife, Beatrice. She was much younger than him—a mail-order bride from the Midwest. Pretty, to boot. After she moved here to marry Davenport, and he saw the way other men looked at her, with their tongues hanging out, the way men do—you know how it is . . ."

"Yes."

"Davenport made her stay home. For years and years no one saw her except her neighbors fetching wood from the wood shed behind their house or pinning wash on her clothesline. Word was he forbade her to leave the house. She died two years ago. Her death was and still is a mystery. Davenport only said she'd died in her sleep after a long illness and that she was too proud to seek medical help."

"Do you think he killed her?" Laura asked.

"I wouldn't put it past him."

"I wouldn't either." Laura crossed her arms, hugging herself, trying to quell the chill in her bones despite the warm breeze ebbing through the window behind her. "Not after seeing his eyes when he gets angry."

Again, fear washed through Laura. She lowered her head and sobbed. "I'm so frightened. I don't know what I'm going to do. If Davenport doesn't kill me, Jonathan most surely will!"

Annabelle reached across the table and squeezed Laura's hand reassuringly. "We need to hide you away somewhere. Until Hunter gets back from chasing those renegades."

"Do you think he'll return?"

"Of course, he'll return," Annabelle said, smiling reassuringly. "He's Hunter, isn't he? Besides, he's got Bobby Lee by his side. There's nothing those two Rebels can't get through together." A deep sadness shone in the redhead's eyes as she added, "Side by side."

It was her turn to tear up. She shook her head as though to dislodge the emotion.

"You love him—don't you?" Laura said.

Annabelle had turned her head to gaze out the window. She shook her head. "Not anymore, but I did once." She looked at Laura, quirking her mouth corners in understanding. "You love him, don't you?"

Laura nodded. "I'm sorry, Annabelle! I didn't mean for it to happen. Honestly, I didn't!"

"Don't worry. I know how it is with him." Annabelle shook her head, drawing her mouth corners down regretfully. "But it's over between us. There's no man more stubborn. I hope it works out for you, because I can tell you're a good woman. After all you've been through, you deserve a good man. As stubborn as he is, Hunter is all that . . . and more."

She quickly brushed a tear from her cheek with her thumb.

Laura stretched her own hand across the table this time, and squeezed Annabelle's left one. She smiled into the pretty redhead's jade eyes with knowing sympathy.

"Now, then," Annabelle said, sniffing and blinking the emotion from her eyes. "We need to hide you away somewhere." She turned abruptly to the open window behind her and Laura, frowning curiously.

Hoof thuds sounded through the open window. So did men's voices. The men were speaking quietly, as though afraid of being overheard.

"What is it?" Laura asked.

Her frown deepening, Annabelle held up her hand and rose slightly from her chair, peering over the sill and down into the alley behind the saloon.

"See here," one of the men was saying, "we gotta be real patient. We gotta go in this back door and sneak upstairs and hole up in her room. We wait for her to leave the saloon and return to her room, because there's no way the men down there, including Big Dan, are gonna let us take her. Not without a fight, and we'll likely be outgunned."

Another man said something too quietly for Laura to hear.

She said, "Annabelle, who are those men talking—"

Again, Annabelle held up her hand for silence. She continued gazing through the window into the alley below.

The man who'd been speaking before said, "Don't worry. I got it on good word she goes upstairs regularly to check on the whores, make sure their clients are bein' nothin' but gentlemen. She dotes on them girls like an ol' mother hen."

Laura rose and angled her own gaze down through the window. Three men stood around four horses. One of the men, who wore a Spanish-cut red shirt and low-crowned black hat, was rummaging around inside a saddlebag pouch. As he pulled a length of rope out of the pouch, Laura turned to her new friend and whispered, "Annabelle, are those men talking about *you*?"

The pretty redhead turned her face, mottled red and white with her own brand of fear, and said, "The one in the black hat is my brother Cass. He's here for me. My depraved old father must have sent him to kidnap me and take me against my will back to the Broken Heart and marry the sniveling son of one of his business partners!"

Laura gasped, slowly closing her hand across her mouth. Annabelle had serious trouble of her own to deal with. No wonder she'd so readily commiserated with Laura's own dire scrape.

As Laura stared down into the alley, the three men were talking too quietly to overhear while passing a bottle around. Getting themselves fortified with liquid courage. Their hat brims concealed their faces.

Annabelle grabbed Laura's hand. "We have to get out of here! If they find me up here, they'll take me. If they find you up here . . ." She shook her head ominously. "No telling. They're drunk. My brother is not a gentleman."

"Is there another back way out of here?" Laura asked as Annabelle led her to the door.

Annabelle paused to step into her shoes. "Only through the saloon. Don't worry. It's not yet noon. Probably not all that busy yet."

"Annabelle, I can't be seen down there!"

Annabelle swung toward Laura, her own eyes anxious. "You can't stay up here. Too dangerous. There are no locks on the doors. I'm going to go down and tell Dan what Cass is up to. Dan and our bouncer, Eugene, will put a stop to it straightaway—believe me!"

"Annabelle—I'm in enough trouble! If I'm seen in a saloon—"

"Here!" Annabelle had grabbed a hooded cape off a wall hook. "This is mine but one of the doves often borrows it. She's always cold in the mornings and wears it when she goes downstairs to sit by the potbellied stove."

Annabelle dropped the cape down over Laura's head. "Ginny has lighter hair, but you're similarly shaped, so if you keep the hood up and your head down, you should make it out the front door without being recognized. Just drag your feet and try to look pouty and hungover."

Laura raised the hood and drew it as far forward as it would go to conceal her features. "How's this?"

"Lead-pipe cinch!" Annabelle said, and cracked the door.

She peered both ways along the hall. Deeming it clear, she stepped into the hall and led Laura along behind her. They hurried together toward the stairs. Annabelle paused and tilted her head toward a door at the end of the hall, on the hall's right side. That was the door that led to the rear stairs and back door.

The creaking of furtive bootsteps sounded on the rear stairs. A couple of the men coming up those stairs snickered and chuckled. One sounded as though he had his hand over his mouth, trying not to laugh.

"Come on!" Annabelle said, squeezing Laura's hand.

As they started down the main stairs to the saloon, the door to the rear stairs opened behind them. Footsteps sounded on the floor of the hall now above and behind the women. Men grunted and murmured.

One said, "Wait—stop, Annabelle!"

Annabelle swung a look over her left shoulder. Her masked brother stood at the top of the stairs, his drink-bright eyes wide and angry behind the slit cuts in the flour sack.

"Annabelle, you wait, dammit!"

Laura's heart raced as she heard heavy foot thuds on the stairs behind her.

"Dan!" Annabelle called. "Dan—help!"

The big, red-faced, portly man in the gaudy suit and with an apron around his rotund waist turned from the range behind the bar. He'd been sampling chili from a wooden spoon. Now, still holding the spoon up to his mouth, he scowled up the stairs, and his red face turned redder.

"What the hell's goin' on?"

Annabelle, with Laura in tow, had just gained the bottom of the stairs and was heading toward the bar. Annabelle glanced at Laura walking on her right, released Laura's hand, and jerked her chin toward the saloon's front door.

Laura nodded and put her head down, sort of shrinking like a turtle back inside the shell of the cape's hood. There were maybe ten men in the room, most sitting at tables, hunched over mugs of beer and bowls of chili.

As she headed for the door, Laura was relieved to see that all eyes were on the striking, scantily clad redhead who, angling toward the bar, yelled bitterly, "My drunk brother and a few friends snuck up the back stairs to kidnap me and take me back to the Broken Heart! Dan, would you please remind him I have no intention ever returning to the Broken Heart again—so help me God!"

"Be my pleasure, darlin'!"

Laura cut a look toward the bar on her left. Big Dan dropped the spoon and reached for a double-barrel shotgun leaning against the backbar. He glanced at a beefy, younger man with red-blond muttonchops and goatee eating chili at the end of the bar, and yelled, "Eugene—stop feeding your face and grab the bung starter! We got some heads to break!"

"Hold on, Dan! Hold on!" Cass Ludlow yelled from the stairs.

Fascinated by what was happening, Laura had stopped and turned toward the rear of the room. Cass Ludlow, wearing a flour sack mask beneath his black hat, had stopped halfway down the stairs, flanked by the two others. Ludlow held one gloved hand up, palm out.

"Hold on! Hold on! I just wanna talk to dear sis, is all!" His words were slurred from drink. He held on to the banister to his right to steady himself.

As both Big Dan and the man called Eugene hurried toward the stairs, Big Dan wielding the shotgun and Eugene slapping what appeared a small leather-wrapped club against the palm of his left hand, Laura turned forward and continued toward the door.

She'd taken only two strides before she tripped over something.

She stopped and looked down as a cane tumbled from the chair it had been leaning against to the floor. Laura stared down in horror as the cane rolled toward her, the silver horse head at its top glinting in the sunlight from a near window.

Her terror grew a hundred-fold when the man sitting in the chair turned to her, and she found herself staring hang-jawed into the face of her husband, Jonathan Gaynor.

CHAPTER 28

Jonathan Gaynor was so preoccupied with the pretty redhead standing with her back to the bar, pointing and yelling at the three men clad in trail garb on the stairs while Big Dan and the bouncer hurried toward them—shouting threats and warnings—that Jonathan hardly even glanced at his wife who'd shot him in his unmentionables.

He merely glanced down at the cane she'd kicked onto the floor, scowled up at her fleetingly and with deep annoyance ridging his slender, dark brown brows, then nudged the Pinkerton sitting beside him with his elbow. While the Pinkerton reached down to retrieve the cane, Jonathan's gaze returned to Annabelle, saying to the detective, "I'll be damned if that pretty little redhead isn't about to burst right out of that corset!"

The Pinkerton laughed as he leaned the cane against Jonathan's chair.

Her knees nearly buckling in relief at her husband's distraction, even though he was distracted by another woman—no surprise there!—Laura drew the hood tighter about her face and strode quickly toward the batwing doors. Once outside, she turned to peer over the doors and into the saloon.

Annabelle's brother and his two accomplices were stomping angrily up the stairs, still arguing with Big Dan and the bouncer called Eugene. In a few seconds, all three ranch men who'd come to kidnap Annabelle had retreated through the door at the top of the staircase leading to the rear alley.

Laura stepped to one side, pressing her back against the saloon's front wall, and heaved a long sigh of deep relief. She and Annabelle were both safe. At least, for the time being.

That time was short-lived.

She closed her eyes to gather herself. When she opened them, she sucked a sharp breath in renewed terror.

Warren Davenport stood before her, towering over her, glowering furiously down at her darkly with his stony eyes, pointing a big, thick, crooked index finger at her. "I saw you come out of there! Why, you slattern! Whore!" He bellowed the insults as loudly as he could, trying to shame her in public. He'd realized he couldn't have her, so now he'd bury her. "Look here, everybody—Tigerville's new schoolteacher just came out of Big Dan's whorehouse! Is this the kind of teacher we—"

He stopped as Laura turned to run away from him.

"Oh, no, you don't! You won't run away from me, you whore!"

Davenport grabbed Laura's shoulder and spun her around. A half second later the back of his right hand crashed into her left cheek in roughly the same place he'd struck her the other night. Laura screamed as she spun and fell to the boards.

"*Slattern! Witch! Whore!*" Davenport bellowed at the tops of his lungs, moving toward her threateningly once more.

"No!" Laura screamed.

Davenport jerked back, frowning as he turned around. Laura had just seen a large brown hand grab the man's left shoulder. Now as Davenport stumbled back toward the saloon's front wall, Hunter Buchanon moved toward him, swinging his right fist back behind his right shoulder before throwing it forward with an enraged grunt.

Hunter's fist smashed against Davenport's mouth with a solid smacking sound. The man's lips instantly turned red as he screamed and, throwing his arms out for a balance he never achieved, flew straight back through the saloon's large plate-glass window. The words BIG DAN'S SALOON forming an arc across the window in large, gold-leaf lettering disappeared as the window shattered inward with the din of a dozen little girls screaming at the tops of their lungs.

Davenport disappeared inside the saloon amidst the raining glass.

Rage was a wildfire inside Buchanon as he stepped through the shattered window.

Davenport lay in the glass several feet inside the saloon, peppered with more glass, gazing in wide-eyed shock at the big man moving toward him. Davenport scuttled back on his butt. He'd lost his hat; broken glass glistened across the bald top of his head.

"You Southern devil!" Davenport raged, spitting blood from his smashed lips.

He scrambled to his feet. As Hunter moved on the man quickly, Davenport brought a roundhouse punch up from his knees. The man's fist glanced off of Hunter's left temple.

Buchanon didn't even flinch. He stepped into the man, who was nearly as tall as he was, and hammered the man's mouth again with his own right fist. Davenport's head jerked back with a startled grunt. When his head jerked back forward, Buchanon slammed his fist against his nose.

Blood from the broken nose now mixed with the blood from the ruined lips, dribbling in several streams down Davenport's chin. He brushed his fist across his nose, eyes watering. He shook his head, bellowed with rage, stepped forward, and swung another punch at Hunter, who easily ducked it.

Moving in on Davenport again, Buchanon punched the man in the gut once, twice, three times. The man screamed and jackknifed. Stepping forward, Hunter smashed his right knee into the point of the man's chin, lifting him up off his knees and sending him stumbling backward with another wailing cry. He piled up on a table from which three men in business suits had one second ago scrambled, clutching their chili bowls and beer mugs.

Buchanon's wolf was off its leash. Hunter couldn't get what Davenport had done to Laura out of his head. He crouched, pulled the man to his feet, and went to work on his face once more, driving him back onto the table again. Hunter was about to pull Davenport off the table yet again to continue the savage beating, when Big Dan shouted, "Eugene—grab that crazy grayback!"

A second later, a man leaped onto Hunter from behind, pulling his arms behind his back and hauling him away from Davenport, shouting, "Hold on, Buchanon. You're gonna kill him!"

"He needs killin'!" the former Rebel heard himself bellow.

He'd torn one arm loose from Big Dan's bouncer and had started to move toward Davenport once more when two other men leaped onto his back, yelling and driving him to the floor. One of the men sat on his head while another sat on his chest. Yet another sat on his knees, pinning him flat to the floor.

They were big men. Buchanon wasn't getting up until they let him.

"All right," Hunter said. "Let me up, dammit. I'm done!"

The fire inside him was dampened down enough that he thought he could get his wolf back on its leash. He felt grateful for the three men, including Eugene, who'd intervened. He'd wanted to kill Davenport. The man deserved killing. But he was done with that. At least, he wanted to be.

He didn't want to pull another stunt like the one he'd pulled on Ike Talon. The berserker inside him had to die. He didn't want to be that man anymore. The war was over.

"Thanks, fellas," Hunter said, as, breathing hard, big Eugene Donleavy helped him to his feet.

One of the other two men handed Hunter his hat.

Hunter regarded the bloody-faced, wheezing Davenport and then glanced a little sheepishly around the room before turning toward the door. Laura was peering in at him through the broken window.

As Hunter moved toward her, she lifted her chin slightly to look past him. Her eyes widened; she slapped both hands across her mouth.

Behind Hunter, several men shouted. Annabelle's voice yelled, "Hunter, look out!"

Buchanon swung around, ripping his LeMat from its holster. Davenport had gained his feet and was extending an over-and-under derringer at Hunter in his right hand.

On the heels of Annabelle's warning, Davenport turned his head, as did Hunter, to see Annabelle standing eight feet away from Davenport, aiming Big Dan's double-barrel shotgun straight out from her right shoulder at Laura's assailant.

As Davenport began to swing the derringer toward the redhead, Annabelle triggered both barrels.

Orange flames ripped from the steel maws. Annabelle screamed as the big barn-blaster's savage kick flung her and the shotgun straight back over a table behind her. At the same time, both fist-size clumps of buckshot blew Davenport back through the long, rectangular window on Hunter's left, in the side wall opposite the bar.

The shotgun's blast echoed around the room like the deafening blast of a Napoleon cannon.

Hunter stared, stunned, at the billowing smoke from the shotgun. He looked at the shattered window on his left and then at where Annabelle had been standing a moment ago, before the shotgun's kick had thrown her over the table. Several men stood around where she lay on the floor between the table and the bar, looking down at her, shaking their heads and muttering.

Hunter lowered the LeMat and pushed his way through the crowd.

"Now, that was a spectacle!" chuckled a dapper little man holding a cane with a silver horse head.

Buchanon gave the man only a passing glance and only because the man he was standing with, near the table over which Annabelle had been thrown, wore the copper shield of a Pinkerton detective.

"Annabelle! Annabelle!" said Big Dan Delaney, owner of the saloon. He was pushing through the crowd, as well, catching Hunter's glance and saying, "She grabbed my shotgun off the bar. I didn't know she even knew how to shoot it!"

Hunter pushed a couple more men aside and stepped up to where Annabelle lay on the floor, groaning and shaking her head slowly from side to side. He dropped to a knee beside her, placed his hand on her arm.

"Honey, you all right?"

She turned her head to stare up at him. Her face was pale. "I . . . I think so . . ."

She raised her hand to him. Hunter took it, eased her slowly up off the floor, wrapped his arms around her, and, holding her up against his chest, rose to his feet.

Big Dan stepped aside and waved his arms to clear a path for Hunter and Annabelle. "Make way, now, fellas! Please, make way!"

Hunter crossed the room and climbed the stairs. He looked down at the pretty redhead in his arms. She stared up at him, her own arms wrapped around his neck.

"This is getting to be a habit," she said with a faint wry flicker of one mouth corner.

"You got a habit of doin' some pretty crazy things, and that down there was one of 'em."

He turned to her door. It stood partway open. He kicked it wide and carried Annabelle into the room and lay her down on the bed that was a mess of rumpled sheets and quilts and strewn dresses and frilly underwear. The room smelled like Annabelle. It was a poignant smell. It went straight to his heart. He didn't think he'd ever get that smell out of his head if he lived to be a million years old though he'd just now realized that fact.

He was going to miss that smell.

He was going to miss a lot of things about her. For years now he'd thought he and she would grow old together, that they'd die side by side. But now he realized that wasn't true. They'd die apart.

Hunter eased her onto the bed, adjusted the pillow beneath her head.

"How do you feel? Anything broken? Should I call the doc?"

Annabelle shook her head, making her thick red hair shift on the pillow. "My shoulder's just sore." She worked her arm a little, wincing. "I'm going to have a helluva bruise tomorrow."

"You're starting to talk like the men downstairs."

"Yeah, well, they like the way I talk," she said crisply, narrowing one fiery jade eye at him.

"Well, I don't."

"I don't care what you like or don't like."

"Oh hell—enough of this! Why in the hell was Warren Davenport going at Laura like that?"

"She said he's been pestering her something awful. Giving her things. Forcing her to dine with him. At least he *was*. He won't be doing that again." A horrified expression flashed across her face. "Do you think I killed him?"

"Well, you triggered both barrels of that twelve-gauge

into him. Blasted him through a window." Buchanon chuckled caustically. "Yeah, I think you killed him!"

Annabelle ground her elbows into the bed and raised her head and shoulders, the fires of anger returning to her eyes. "Well, if I hadn't killed him, he would have killed you. But now, since you don't seem any too grateful, I'm starting to think I should have just let him go ahead and shoot you in the back!"

"Have you talked to Laura?"

"What?"

"Have you talked to her?"

Annabelle gazed up at him, frowning bewilderedly. "Yes." The frown twisted her brows more severely. "Why?"

"I was just . . . I was just . . ."

"Don't worry. We didn't get together to compare notes on you. In fact, we didn't exchange one word about you at all!" Annabelle lied.

"What brought you two together?" He wasn't sure why, but he felt vaguely suspicious.

"She's in a heap of trouble." Annabelle placed her hand on his forearm and squeezed it urgently. "You best get down there and find her before that nasty husband of hers does . . ."

"Her husband?" Buchanon scowled down at her. "What're you talkin' about, Annabelle?"

"Just go to Laura, Hunter." Annabelle sat up higher, stared into his eyes from only a few inches away. "She needs you! You're not needed here. You're no longer needed here. Go to the woman who loves you and needs you. Go!"

She swung her arm toward the door.

As she stared at him, face flushed with fury, her upper

lip quivered. A sheen of emotion shimmered in her eyes. She tucked her upper lip under her lower front teeth to stop the quiver. "Just go to her," she said again, and let her head sink slowly back onto the pillow.

She turned her face to one side, away from him.

Hunter backed away from her, feeling as rotten as he had the last time they'd parted, with her screaming down the hall at him. When would that hard, wooden knot in his belly ever loosen?

He turned to the door just as he heard the clacking of nails in the hall, and the familiar manic pants of—who else?

Bobby Lee.

Buchanon poked his head into the hall. Sure enough, the coyote was running toward him a tad uncertainly, his padded feet slipping on the bare wooden floor. Hunter hadn't seen his coyote friend for over an hour. As he'd been approaching town with the Indian woman in tow, Bobby Lee had run off with his nose to the ground—likely on the scent of a jackrabbit or a deer.

Now, having sensed trouble, here he was.

"Bobby, I was just . . ."

Hunter let his voice trail off as Bobby Lee slipped past him into Annabelle's room.

Bobby stopped by the bed and placed his front paws on the edge of it, sniffing and mewling softly as he studied Annabelle who had her back to him. The girl's shoulders jerked as she cried silently.

Bobby glanced at Hunter, who stood in the doorway feeling as hollowed out as an old log. The coyote raised his upper lip to show his teeth at him in silent reproof, then leaped up onto the bed and lay in a tightly curled ball at the base of it.

Hunter nodded. "Look after her, Bobby."

He stepped out of the room and drew the door closed behind him.

CHAPTER 29

Buchanon hurried back down the stairs and into Big Dan's main drinking hall.

Very few of Big Dan's customers were sitting at the tables. They all appeared to be standing at the window Annabelle had shot Warren Davenport out of, on the room's right side now as Hunter headed for the swing doors at the front.

"Any sign of life in him?" Hunter called to the group crowded around the window, loudly conversing.

One of the men turned to Hunter, removed a fat stogie from his mouth, and said, "Deader'n last year's Christmas goose!"

"Somebody better fetch an undertaker." There were a good half dozen undertakers in Tigerville. In a mountain boom town like this one, where it seemed the more ore that was pulled out of the surrounding hills, the more men ended up dead in back alleys and dusty streets . . . or blown out of saloon windows . . . undertaking was almost as prosperous as mining.

"Already sent for one!" another man called.

"When he's finished there, send him over to the jail. I have two more for him."

Big Dan was standing near the front window that Hunter had punched Davenport through from the outside. The big saloon owner was scowling down at the broken glass. He turned to Buchanon, glowering and shaking his big, red-faced head. "This is going to cost me a pretty penny! Do you know how much it costs to have plate-glass windows shipped up here from Cheyenne?"

Hunter continued striding past the man. He was in no mood to listen to caterwauling about broken windows. Pushing through the swing doors, he said, "Best keep servin' up the chili, Dan."

He paused on the boardwalk and looked around for Laura. She was nowhere in sight. He recalled Annabelle's words: "She's in a whole heap of trouble!"

What kind of trouble?

Had her husband come looking for her?

Hunter wanted to go to her, but he'd only just ridden up to the jail office when he'd heard and seen Davenport berating Laura out front of Big Dan's. He'd left his horse as well as the horse his prisoner was tied to, and run over to intervene on Laura's behalf. He was glad to see his prisoner still sitting on the back of the Indian pony he'd tied her to, head down, hands cuffed behind her back.

The two horses over which he'd hauled the dead federals, Winslow and Birmingham, back to town were also still standing before the hitchrack fronting his office.

He had to get his prisoner in a jail cell and Winslow and Birmingham ready for the undertaker. It was a hell of a job, this law business. He wasn't sure he was cut out for it. At the moment, he just wanted to go back to driving the stagecoach. No—really what he wanted to do at this moment was hunt Laura down and find out if she was all right.

But that would be a while.

He negotiated his way across the street. Several men had gathered around the horses carrying his prisoner and the two dead marshals. A couple of little boys, maybe eight and ten years old, were snooping around the horses carrying Winslow and Birmingham, squatting down to get a look at the heads of the blanket-wrapped bodies.

Hunter chased the boys away and turned to the young Indian woman sitting the Indian pony sporting war paint. Ignoring the men standing on the boardwalk, muttering amongst themselves and eyeing the young woman speculatively, Hunter fished his barlow knife out of his pants pocket and opened the blade. Stepping up to the girl's left foot hanging down the horse's left side, he looked up at her and said, "I'm gonna cut the rope off your foot. If you kick me, you're gonna get the point of this knife in your leg."

He showed her the knife.

Over their past three days traveling together, she'd tried to kick him more than once. Several times, she'd turned wildcat on him, once almost snatching his cast-iron pan off a cook fire and bashing his head in with it. He'd grabbed her just in time, wrestled her to the ground, and got the cuffs back on her while she spat and snarled and cursed him in Sioux. That had been a particularly close one.

One of many.

He had to admit that a couple of times he'd considered putting a bullet into her rather than continue to risk his own life getting her back to Tigerville. For some reason, he hadn't done it. Who would have known? They'd been all alone out there.

But he would have known. Of all the crazy damn things he'd found himself doing in his wild life, he now found himself trying to impress himself as a man of the law. As a good one. That damned badge on his shirt weighed heavy on him, and however half-consciously, he wanted to honor it. He wanted to live up to it.

At least until he could find a more willing man than he was to wear the damn thing—a nickel's worth of cheap tin!

For now, though, he had work to do.

The Indian girl didn't even look at him, much less respond to his warning. She hadn't said anything to him in all the days they'd ridden together, and had sat around campfires at night. Mostly, she'd stared at him, upper lip curled, eyes hard as black granite, as though wanting to tear his heart out with her fingernails and dine on it in front of him. That had been a little unsettling.

Now he cut the rope from around her left ankle and stepped back.

She didn't try to kick him.

Well, that was something, anyway.

He walked around to the other side of the horse and cut the rope from around her other ankle. Again, he stepped back quickly, and arched one brow in surprise.

Again, she hadn't tried to kick him.

Maybe this really was progress . . .

"All right," he said, taking another step back away from her horse and placing his hand on the grips of his LeMat. "Come on down. Nice and slow."

She turned her head to him and looked at him coldly through the black strands of her hair. Suddenly, she smiled.

But her eyes were still cold, bright with primal hatred. She was toying with him, making him wonder what she would try next.

"I'll gut-shoot you," he warned.

Slowly, she raised her moccasin-clad left foot, swung it over her horse's mane, and dropped straight down to the ground in front of him. She was a head shorter than he was, and she weighed half what he did. Her hands were cuffed behind her back. Still, he knew from experience that she could move rattlesnake quick and do some serious damage.

Apprehension quickened his heart. He'd be glad to have her in a jail cell.

He canted his head toward the jailhouse door.

She turned slowly, reluctant to take her smiling gaze from his. She stepped up onto the boardwalk, and the men standing on the boardwalk, watching her and Hunter curiously, made way for her as they would for some dangerous wild animal that had escaped a circus.

Hunter stepped onto the boardwalk behind her.

He took one more step before she swung back toward him in a blur of quick motion. With a cat-like scream, she thrust her right foot up between his legs, the sharp toe connecting decisively with his crotch. She screamed again and smashed her forehead against his mouth.

Hunter dropped to his knees, sunbursts of pain flaring in his eyes, the worst kind of male agony radiating in all directions from his loins. He felt the oily wetness of blood on his lips.

Despite the grinding pain, he kept his eyes on her feet. A good thing he did. She was about to ram her knee into his face when he heaved himself forward, flinging his hands out before him, and ripped both feet out from under her.

She fell with another even more piercing scream and struck the boardwalk on her back, the back of her head smacking the boards and bouncing with a resounding double-thud. Hunter leaped up off his feet, trying desperately to suppress the fireballs of pain rolling through him, one after another, and crouched over her.

Quickly, before she could renew her attack, he jerked her head up off the boardwalk by her hair, grabbed her left arm, and heaved her up over his shoulder.

Imagine carrying an enraged mountain lion on your shoulder. That's what she was like—snarling and screaming and kicking her legs and shaking her head, trying to bash his head with her own, a couple of times succeeding.

As Hunter started forward in a desperate rush, the office door opened inward. The moon-faced Otis Crosby stood in the doorway looking bleary-eyed from a nap.

He blinked in hang-jawed surprise.

"Why, Marshal—"

"Fetch the cell keys, Otis! Got a live one!"

Otis moved his wide-eyed, hulking form to the left as Hunter bulled through the door with the panther-like girl on his shoulder, snapping her jaws and grunting and hissing. She managed to close her sharp teeth over his left ear.

More javelins of pain lanced through him.

"Ow, dammit! Ow, dammit! Let go, you crazy squaw!"

Hunter turned sharply, knocking her head against the office's stone wall until her jaws opened, releasing his ear. Buchanon headed for one of the four open cell doors, carried the crazy Indian inside, and dropped her without ceremony on the cell's single cot.

She bounced once, then lay wincing—eyelids fluttering—slowly raising her deerskin-clad knees to her chest. The blow against the wall had knocked her semi-unconscious. Blood shone darkly in her blue-black hair.

Good.

Hunter staggered out of the cell, crouching, clamping one hand over his ear, the other over his privates, and shouting, "Hurry—close the damn door and lock it tight!"

Otis lumbered past him to the cell, fiddling with the key ring. "I'm tryin', Marshal—I'm tryin'!"

"Hurry up!"

"These damn old keys are rusty!"

"Lock the damn door, Otis!"

Otis grunted as he turned the key in the door. "There—got her locked in good, Marshal!"

"Christ!" Hunter sank into the chair at the cluttered desk, leaning forward over his bruised oysters.

"Boy, she sure took a nasty turn on you!" Otis observed. "Hard to believe such a little thing—"

"She's not all that little and I've encountered mountain lions a whole lot friendlier."

"Who is she? What'd she do?"

"She was one of the six warriors who shot up the Goliad."

"No! *Her?*"

Hunter had pulled a handkerchief out of his pants pocket and was holding it over his split lip. His head ached, his ears rang, his vision was still blurry, and he felt as though he'd been spitted on a Sioux war lance.

He pulled the desk's bottom drawer open and peered inside, vaguely noting that a mouse had built a nest out of some shredded wanted circulars. "Where's my bottle?"

Otis flinched. "What bottle?"

"The bottle I kept in this . . ." Hunter looked up at the husky odd-jobber standing before him, guiltily worrying the key ring in his big, dirt-stained hands. Hunter gave a caustic chuff. He knew exactly where the bottle had gone. Otis was not known as a regular drinker, but his occasional benders were legendary.

"I got a job for you."

"Sure, sure," Otis said, brightening. He ambled over to the wall fronting the desk and hung the keys on a railroad spike embedded in the stone. "I had me a nap so I'm fresh."

"Glad one of us is fresh," Hunter grumbled.

He opened another drawer and pulled out a lined tablet and a pencil. "Both Winslow and Birmingham are dead. I need to wire word to the U.S. Marshal's office in Yankton. They need to let me know what to do with the bodies. They also need to alert the circuit court judge and send him quick to try that wildcat in yonder."

He quickly scribbled the missive on the paper, then ripped the sheet from the pad and held it out to Otis.

"Take that over to Western Union. Make sure Mike Quinn taps it out today. Not tomorrow. Today. Tell him to bill the city council. I don't have more than a few cents to my name an' me an' Pa's rent is already late over at Mrs. Brumvold's boarding house."

"You got it, Marsh—"

Otis stopped when the office door opened suddenly. Two men stepped in, one behind the other. Hunter recognized both from Big Dan's.

The first man was the dapper little gent in a tailored butterscotch suitcoat, side whiskers, and a handlebar mustache, the facial hair looking especially dark given the creamy color of his unblemished face. He was leaning on the silver horse head of his cane carved from what appeared a fine grade of wood—possibly cherry.

The man behind him, several inches taller, was the long-faced, mustached Pinkerton with the copper shield on his left coat lapel. The detective was more subtly attired in brown checked wool over a white shirt with a celluloid collar and a brown foulard tie. A bulge in his coat denoted a hogleg of considerable caliber residing in a shoulder holster.

His eyes were coldly serious. He didn't look like a man who smiled all that much even on his best days.

"Hello, Mister Buchanon," greeted the dapper gent with the cane, limping into the room. Each time he put weight on the silver horse head, his mouth tightened in a flinch. "I understand you're the law enforcement here in Tigerville."

Hunter and Otis shared a skeptical glance.

Looking back at the dandy, Hunter said, "That's right." His voice was still a little tight. The rolling waves of agony down south of his cartridge belt were not yet finished with him.

"I was told as much by Big Dan."

"What can I help you with?" Hunter didn't want to help him with anything. He wanted to find a bottle, swill his pain away, and take a nap. At the moment, in his current condition, he wouldn't be much help to anyone.

The dandy held out his pale, beringed hand and gave an oily smile. "My name is Jonathan Gaynor."

CHAPTER 30

Buchanon had had a sneaking suspicion that Gaynor was who the popinjay was, so he wasn't completely taken off guard. He thought he probably did a pretty good imitation of a disinterested party as he said, "If the name's supposed to impress me, it doesn't."

"It impresses quite a few people, Marshal." This from the Pinkerton, who stood behind and a little to one side of Gaynor, studying Hunter with severely ridged brows, hands clutching his coat lapels. He had a humorless, schoolmasterly look, chin dipped toward his chest.

Hunter instinctively didn't like him. But then he didn't like Gaynor, either, though his dislike for Gaynor was for obvious reasons that had been made clear to him by the man's wife.

Buchanon shrugged and turned to the dandy, who was leaning on his cane, his pale face red with anger. "I'm not one of them. Now, if you wanna preen, do it outside. If you have business, state it and get the hell out of my office. I have a prisoner and two dead deputy U.S. marshals to tend to, not to mention a split lip and sore balls!"

He dabbed at his mouth again with the handkerchief.

Gaynor and the Pinkerton shared a look. The Pinkerton shrugged and shook his head in disgust. Gaynor turned back to Hunter, his jaws hard, his thin lips compressed in a taut line beneath his ostentatious mustache. He reached into a pocket of his butterscotch coat and set a small photograph on the desk before Hunter.

Buchanon looked at the picture. He felt his belly tighten as he stared down at the elegantly beautiful woman he'd made love with only a few days ago.

Laura was decked out in a ruffled shirtwaist secured at the neck with a cameo pin, a velvet waistcoat, and a flowered picture hat. Her thick hair was coifed in a roll atop her head, the hat secured to the roll. The wide eyes—appearing brown in the black-and-white photo—were warm, intelligent, and lustrous. The photo was an egg-shaped, upper body shot with a floral background. Probably taken in Gaynor's own stylishly furnished living room.

Again, Hunter manufactured a disinterested expression as he looked at the preening pigeon before him. "Suppose I know her—then?"

The Pinkerton took one step forward and gazed at Hunter with his typically officious, pompous air. "You'd have to tell us where we can find her. This woman is wanted for attempted murder."

Buchanon kept his eyes on Gaynor. "Maybe he had it coming."

Gaynor bunched his lips and rammed his cane down on the floor. "I did *not* have it coming!"

"Carrying on with another woman for most of your marriage while professing false loyalty is about as lowdown-dirty a thing as a man can do to a woman." Hunter flared a nostril at him. "I'd say you had it coming, all right."

Unexpectedly, Jonathan Gaynor's thin lips twitched in a smile. He nodded knowingly. "Ahh . . . yes . . . you've met her, all right. Even gotten to know her, I daresay."

"Well enough to know that if I see you anywhere near her, I'll gut-shoot you and leave you to the stray dogs in a back alley." Buchanon flashed his threatening glare on the Pinkerton. "That goes for you, too, Mister Pink."

Gaynor and the Pinkerton shared another look, both men shaping grim smiles and shaking their heads, as though reflecting on a shared secret.

Turning back to the Tigerville town marshal, Gaynor said, "Look, Marshal, I see you've come to know my wife rather well. That's not unexpected. You've probably even been *seduced* by her—in more ways than one, I might add. It would be true to Jane's character to form an alliance with a man of power here where she has apparently fled in an attempt to escape the repercussions of her reprehensible behavior."

Jane? Hunter wanted to blurt out but caught himself.

Buchanon said, "She didn't find you in a bathtub with a whorehouse madam in Gaynorville?"

"No!" Gaynor laughed, stumbling back and stabbing his cane at the floor to help him regain his balance. He glanced at the suddenly smiling Pinkerton—he did smile, after all—then returned his mirthful gaze to Buchanon and said, "Dear Lord—is that the story she told you?"

He looked at the Pinkerton again, chuckling. The Pinkerton didn't laugh but he did keep smiling. He looked at the floor and shook his head as though he'd heard everything now.

"Let's hear your side of it," Hunter said.

"Do you mind if I sit down?" Gaynor asked sharply. "I took a bullet in a precarious area. Certainly, you—a man suffering an injury in a similar region—would understand."

"Help yourself." Hunter glanced at a spool-back chair abutting the wall behind the dandy.

Gaynor snapped his fingers at the chair, and the Pinkerton hustled into action, pulling the chair out away from the wall and positioning it carefully behind his boss. The dandy slacked into the chair with a long, ragged sigh and another painful flinch.

Resting his cane across his thighs, he leaned forward, pinned Hunter with a frank, direct look, and said, "Jane is a woman of profoundly duplicitous character. She married me . . . as I have recently discovered . . . just as she married three other men before me. Imagine it. She's twenty-seven years old, and already she's been married four times. To wealthy men. Wealthy men she fleeced and fled!"

Hunter's cheeks warmed with anger. "You're a damn liar."

"Am I?" Gaynor reached behind again and snapped his fingers.

Again, the Pinkerton rushed into action, pulling a thin sheaf of folded papers out of his coat pocket and handing them up to his boss. Gaynor unfolded the sheets and shoved them at Hunter. "Take a look for yourself."

Buchanon looked at the top page:

$5000 REWARD!

Mr. GEORGE JASON UNDERHILL of Leadville
in the Colorado Territory was found *murdered*
in his home on October 14th, 1878.
Mr. Underhill had recently *married* an attractive
Young Lady known as "Marie,"
one of several believed aliases.

(*see photo below*)

It is believed that "Marie" murdered Underhill
before *pillaging* his home of all *valuables*
and fleeing by way of stagecoach or train.
A REWARD of $5000 will be paid by the
Undersigned for the Arrest and Conviction
of "Marie Underhill" for the wanton Murder and
Robbery of George Jason Underhill.

Signed for the Pinkerton Detective Agency
by CHAZ R. MOODY
Superintendent Pinkerton Western District Office
Denver, Colorado Territory

Hunter merely glanced at the other dodgers.

The photograph on each was of Laura or Jane or whoever in hell she was posing in varying costumes in various
photographers' artificial scenes. One photo owned a railroad flavor—probably taken in a photographer's studio
outfitted with a faux parlor car complete with a brass railroad lantern mounted beside a small, curtained window.

All of the alleged crimes were similar in nature—the
fleecing and murdering of moneyed, older men.

Hunter's numb fingers released the pages. They fluttered to the floor.

He stared down at them in shock, his mind a whirl.

"Don't feel too bad, Marshal," Jonathan Gaynor said gently. "You're by no means the first man she's duped. She's a professional."

Buchanon looked up at the two men. "You don't go near her until I've checked into it. Understand?"

The two men glanced at each other skeptically.

Hunter rose from his chair, uncoiling like a big cat to his full six-feet-four. He stared down at both men. He was more than a head taller than Gaynor and half a head taller than the Pinkerton. He probably outweighed the Pinkerton by fifty pounds, all of it muscle. The Pinkerton had skinny legs and a slight paunch.

Both men looked up at him, wary expressions creeping over their faces.

The threat was obvious.

Gaynor nodded slowly. "All right. We'll check back with you, Marshal." He frowned with admonishment. "Be forewarned—Jane can be very convincing."

Gaynor turned and, employing his cane, headed out the door. The Pinkerton glanced once more at Buchanon. He nodded twice—arching his brows—then followed his employer out of the jailhouse and into the busy street.

Hunter just then realized that Otis was still in his office, standing about seven feet back from where Gaynor had sat in the spool-back chair. The conversation had likely proven far too interesting for Otis to tear himself away. No doxie in town spread more gossip than Otis Crosby.

"I thought I told you to take that note to the Western Union office," Hunter barked at the man.

Otis jerked with a start, his beefy face instantly reddening. "I was just . . . I just . . . was headin' that way right now, Mar—!"

"Hold on!"

Otis wheeled from the open doorway. "Huh?"

Hunter pointed at him commandingly and with no little threat in his flashing blue eyes. "I know you're good at spreading gossip, but keep your mouth shut about what those two and I said in here. Instead, you can spread this— if anyone says one word to that dapper little flamingo and his Pinkerton sidekick, they'll be paying the piper."

He mashed his thumb against Otis's chest. "And the piper is me!"

"Oh . . . oh . . . all right, Marshal!" Otis smiled delightedly. "I'll spread the word—sure enough. You can count on me!"

He turned again and lumbered out the door.

"I know I can," Buchanon muttered to himself.

He kicked the door closed, raked his hand down his face, avoiding contact with his lip, then turned to see the Sioux woman staring at him through her cell door. Her black eyes were as flat as the surface of a deep well. She curled her upper lip and said, "Woman trouble?"

Hunter glowered at her. "I didn't know you could speak English."

She shook her tangled hair back behind her shoulders, pulled her shoulders back proudly, and said, "I went to a boarding school in Cheyenne. I killed one of the schoolmasters who snuck into my room one night. He got a broken lamp across his throat for his trouble. Then I went back to my people and vowed to fight the white man forever."

"Yeah, well, now you're gonna hang for *your* trouble."

Hunter looked around for his hat. Through the window by the door he saw the Stetson lying on the boardwalk where he'd lost it in the dustup with his prisoner.

He stepped out, plucked the hat off the floor, then strode back into the office. He grabbed a padlock off his desk. He started for the door again but stopped when the girl said, "That Scudder—he was sellin' my people poison whiskey. Him and Calvin Holte. The last batch killed seven men and made six more so sick they're still sick. They scream, and their women scream!"

"I know." Hunter looked at her pointedly. "But what you did, riding into town and killing innocent men at the Goliad—that was wrong too. Scudder and Holte and those two sons of Holte—those are the ones who should hang. But now you're gonna hang."

"You white men—you're all alike."

Hunter's ears burned with anger. "Those two Deputy U.S. Marshals you killed out there had been sent to arrest Holte and his sons. You killed them when they were doing just that. They would have come back to town and arrested Scudder. But now they're dead—two good men despite what you might think about all white men. The five warriors you rode to town with are dead. And you're going to hang."

She stared back at him through the steel bars, her eyes as cold and dark as before.

Something in those eyes touched him, though. Deep

down, he understood why she'd done what she'd done. He might have done the same thing in her place.

Who was he kidding?

He'd have done *exactly* what she'd done.

And he'd hang for it.

He sighed heavily, went to a water bucket, and filled a tin cup. He walked over to her, shoved the cup through the bars at her.

"You must be thirsty."

She smacked the cup out of his hands. Water splashed across the floor.

"All right." He nodded. "Have it your way."

He turned to the door. "I'm gonna be gone awhile."

He went out, secured the padlock on the door, and mounted his horse.

Wretched damn day and it was only going to get worse.

CHAPTER 31

Hunter pulled Ghost up to one of the two hitchracks fronting the boarding house on the corner of Third Avenue and Second Street, not far from the abandoned English Tom Mine, and studied the two old men sitting out on the building's front veranda, to the right of the door.

Both spidery and gray-bearded, with faces like raisins, they sat in wooden rockers, trade blankets covering their skinny legs.

One of those old coots was Hunter's father, Angus Buchanon, who'd just taken a sip from a flat brown bottle. Angus furtively passed the bottle to the old coot sitting beside him. That was Joe Ryan, who'd been a mine superintendent a few years ago, before a bad ticker and arthritis had put him out of commission and he'd moved into Mrs. Brumvold's boarding house, which was where old men . . . and raggedy-heeled younger men, it seemed . . . came to molder and eventually die.

Ryan took a quick sip of the locally distilled firewater, passed the bottle back to Angus, who corked the bottle and slipped it furtively into a large pocket of the old Confederate greatcoat he wore as an open affront to the

Yankees who outnumbered former Confederate freedom fighters in the area by around ten to one. The two old men muttered to each other, chuckling devilishly, like two schoolboys eager to learn the effect of the frog they'd left in the girls' privy.

Neither had seen the younger Buchanon ride up to the boarding house. Their chairs were angled so that they could look across the empty lot sitting catty-corner to the boarding house and over to where half a dozen whores' cribs sat on the banks of a creek and out front of which the whores, young enough to be the old coots' granddaughters, paraded around their laundry lines half-dressed. None of the girls was out there today, but they'd be out there again soon, and the old men would be parked out here, sharing a bottle of busthead, snorting, elbowing each other, and generally enjoying the show.

The two graybeards hadn't heard Hunter approach because both were nearly as deaf as fence posts.

Still seated on Ghost's back, Hunter cleared his throat and said loudly enough to penetrate the two oldsters' logy hearing: "If Mrs. Brumvold catches you two old scudders out here passin' that devil juice back an' forth, she's gonna have Big Syd throw you both out in the street." Big Syd was the three-hundred-pound Chinaman in Mrs. Brumvold's employ.

Both men whipped their heads around with starts.

Old Angus's blue eyes flared with customary rancor as he said, "Where the hell you been?"

"Chasin' owlhoots."

"What for?"

Hunter brushed his thumb across the badge pinned to his shirt. He swung down from Ghost's back, tossed the reins over the rack, and mounted the porch steps. He crossed to the door but stopped when old Angus said, "Get over here."

"What do you want, old man?"

"I want you to get over here—that's what I want." Angus beckoned with his one arm. He'd lost the left one in the War of Northern Aggression. For Joe Ryan's benefit, he added, "And don't backtalk your father or I'll take you over my knee and quirt your naked behind so raw you won't be able to sit down for a week."

Joe Ryan snorted and continued to stare out, piningly, toward the whores' cribs.

Hunter gave a chuff, brushing his thumb across his nose, and ambled over to where the old men sat in their rockers. Hunter leaned down and planted an affectionate kiss on his father's leathery cheek. He squeezed Angus's skinny shoulder through the greatcoat, hating how insubstantial it felt. Both men looked him up and down, eyes lingering on the badge on his shirt as well as on his cut lip and bruised forehead.

"You look like you was rode hard an' put up wet!" observed Joe Ryan, who had a face like a cadaver. He no longer smoked but he'd smoked cigars so long that the one corner of his mouth wore a permanent brown indentation. His watery blue eyes were milky from cataracts.

"What the hell are you wearin' that star for?" Angus wanted to know.

"I got hornswoggled by two old federals. Don't ask me how. It's so long ago now, I don't even remember. I gotta get inside and get cleaned up. I got a nasty chore to run."

Hunter turned and started for the boarding house's front door.

"I thought you was drivin' the stage," Angus said, craning his neck to scowl at his son.

"Long story, Pa. I'll fill you in later."

He pushed through the front door over which a wooden sign ordered: LEAVE THY SINS OUTSIDE WITH THE SOIL FROM YOUR SHOES! He loved his father dearly, but he didn't have time to palaver with the two old coots. Hell, they wouldn't remember half of what he told them, anyway. He had to find Laura . . . or whatever in hell her name was . . . and get the lowdown on Jonathan Gaynor's story about her.

His new job weighed heavy on him. The Indian girl weighed heavy on him. So did the death of his good friend Charley Anders as well as the deaths of Winslow and Birmingham. His mouth and south of his cartridge belt still ached. He kept hearing Annabelle's sad, haunting cries as she lay on her bed at Big Dan's.

But Laura was foremost on his mind at the moment.

He tramped down the boarding house's wood-floored hall, making his way back past the parlor on one side and the communal dining room on the other and past the stairway that rose to the second and third floors. Angus's muffled voice called angrily from the porch, "Gallblastit, Hunter, get back here! I ain't done talkin' to you yet, boy!"

He sounded like an angry old crow.

Hunter walked past Mrs. Brumvold's tick-tocking grandfather clock and opened a door on the hall's left side. He could hear the little widow lady, Mrs. Reed, chastising her long-dead husband behind the door directly across the hall from Hunter and Angus's room. He could also smell the odors of several earlier meals, as well as the one Mrs. Brumvold and Big Syd were currently whipping up in the kitchen off the dining room. It was nearly noon. The new smells were of pork roast, gravy, boiled beets, and fresh biscuits.

Buchanon's belly growled as he tossed his hat on one of the room's two beds and then removed his gun and cartridge belt. He tugged his shirttails out of his pants and walked over to the washstand. He peered into the small round mirror on the wall above the stand, giving his lip a quick inspection. He retrieved a whiskey bottle from a shelf, popped the cork, stuck out his torn lower lip, and poured some of the whiskey over the cut.

"Oh Jesus!" He leaned forward, one hand on the wall beside the mirror, stretching his lips back from the burn.

"Serves ya right!" Angus said, limping into the room behind Hunter.

Hunter had heard the old man shuffling down the hall, using the cane he'd whittled out of an oak branch while sitting on the veranda ogling the soiled doves with Joe Ryan. Buchanon watched his father hobble into the room, looking little more than a stick over which the ancient greatcoat hung, and Hunter's heart ached with anguish.

"Old Angus," as everyone had called him for the past thirty years, had recovered from the bullet he'd taken last year, during the war with Ludlow, Chaney, and Stillwell, but the long recuperation had taken the shimmer out of his eyes, the vitality out of his countenance, whittling him down to sagging hide and sinew. His long, craggy face, the color of old leather, was carpeted in a long, silky white beard through which warts and liver spots shone. Hunter could hear the old man's wheezing—each breath a chore.

Hunter returned his attention to his lip, splashed more whiskey on it.

Again, he leaned forward, head down, and sucked a breath through gritted teeth.

"Serves you right—turnin' your back on your father. What's gotten into you, boy? Treatin' Old Angus like a second-rate citizen. I swear, I'm beginning to wonder if there wasn't a Yankee in the woodshed."

Hunter shelved the whiskey bottle, turned to the old man standing a few feet inside the door, glaring across the tiny room at his big, strapping son. "Sorry, Pa. I've had a bad coupla days, and this one isn't getting any better soon."

Angus shuffled over to a chair, slacked stiffly into it, and heaved a sigh of his own, leaning forward on his cane. "When you was gone so long I started hopin' maybe you'd come to your senses and stole off with that purty little red-head of yours to get hitched in Cheyenne."

Hunter shrugged out of his shirt, tossed it toward a wall peg but missed. "That's off, Pa. Not gonna happen."

"You know she ain't like them other Ludlows. Hell, Annabelle is different from her pa and that demented brother of hers. I swear there must've been a Rebel in the Ludlow wood shed." Old Angus's spindly shoulders rose and fell like pistons inside the coat as he laughed deep in his throat.

Hunter poured water from the pitcher into the porcelain bowl atop the washstand and bent forward. "You know that's not why I'm not marrying her, Angus."

"Why, then?"

"You know why—I'm flat broke. Hell, I don't have enough money right now to pay Mrs. Brumvold this month's rent, and she'll likely be around soon lookin' for it. I'm gonna have to get down on my hands and knees and beg her to give us another week."

Hunter splashed water on his face. Wincing against the sting of his cut lip, he lathered his face with the soap then dunked his face in the bowl, rinsing off. When he lifted his face from the water, his father said, "Don't worry about Mrs. Brumvold. I'll sweet-talk her. Maybe even have to curl the old gal's toes for her."

In the mirror, Hunter saw Angus's eyes twinkle dimly with bawdy humor.

Hunter gave a caustic snort, chuckled, and splashed water on his chest and under his arms.

"What else is eating you, boy?" his father asked. "What else is goin' on?"

Buchanon rubbed the soap into his skin. Getting rid of a week's worth of sweat and trail dust felt good. He'd soak in a tub soon, when time allowed, but for now the whore's bath would suffice. "Nothin' for you to worry about, Pa."

"Well, I am worried. Why'd you go and pin that badge to your shirt, anyway? Drivin' stagecoach is dangerous enough in this country."

"They didn't have anybody else."

"That's 'cause nobody else is fool enough to take that job in this town!"

"Thanks, Pa," Hunter said with a caustic grunt.

"You know what I mean."

"Yeah, I do."

Hunter grabbed a towel and dried his face, chest, and under his arms. He looked at his old father sadly, and sighed. "I'm sorry, Pa. I'll tell you all about it when I have time."

Angus drew his mouth corners down and nodded. "I know you will, son. I'm sorry to be an extra burden. I wish the Good Lord would just go ahead and take me, and then you wouldn't have me to worry about anymore."

"That's the last thing I want, you old scudder." Hunter dropped to a knee before his father. "You're all I have, Pa. You an' Bobby Lee. I want you to live long enough to see that ranch rebuilt. To live and work on our own land again."

Angus shook his head. "That's not gonna happen, son. Look at us—both sittin' here with our pockets turned inside out."

Hunter reached up and wrapped an arm around the old man's shoulders, cupping the back of his neck with his right hand. "I know, Pa. I just keep hopin', is all. I'm sorry we've come to this. You an' me, livin' in a seedy little boarding house in this cesspool of a town."

"We're getting by, boy. We had us a nice run out at the 4-Box-B. Now we're in town but we're gettin' by."

"If I could only get that gold back."

"That gold's gone, son. Besides, that was for you and Annabelle."

"If I ever got it back—and I know it ain't likely—I'm gonna use it to rebuild the ranch. Get you back on that nice front veranda where you had such a pretty view of those Black Hills you love. You're a good man. You been the best pa a boy could hope for. You deserve to die at home."

Angus smiled at his son, blue eyes filling with tears. He blew out his cheeks, shook his head, and looked down. "It's Shep an' Tye I miss. I sure wish I had those strappin' sons of mine back." He blew a ragged breath, his lips quivering with sorrow.

"I know, Pa." Hunter rose and pressed his lips to the old man's age-freckled, liver-spotted forehead.

Straightening, he went over to his chest of drawers, found a passingly clean blue chambray shirt, and pulled it on. Old Angus sat in his chair, head bowed, tears dribbling down his leathery cheeks to his hands wrapped over the head of his cane.

Hunter buttoned his shirt and strapped his gun and cartridge belt and bowie knife around his waist. "I'll be back for supper, Pa. Maybe even have time for a game of cribbage afterwards."

Angus blew his nose into an old red handkerchief with white polka dots. "I'd like that, son."

Hunter's heart twisted again at his father's grief.

He turned and walked out of the room.

CHAPTER 32

Hunter swung Ghost onto the freshly graded trail that climbed the rise to Homer Laskey's old mining claim and pig farm and on which now stood the town's new schoolhouse. It was a fine-looking building. One that he and the other residents of Tigerville should be proud of. Finally, school would be in session.

Or maybe not just yet . . .

Hunter felt a rat of dread gnawing in his belly as he walked Ghost up the rise. He was about to leave the trail and ride around to the building's rear, to Laskey's old cabin, when another glance at the school showed him the front door was open. Sweeping sounds came from the door. He saw the moving straw head of a broom inside a small cloud of dust blowing out the door and onto the front step.

A second later, Laura stepped out of the enclosed porch and onto the step, making quick, almost desperate sweeping sounds, her hair falling from the bun atop her head. She gave a soft grunt with every sweep of the broom. She appeared to be fighting off a pack of wolves—wolves of frustration. Of desperation.

Of fear of being exposed, maybe . . .

Hunter swung Ghost up to the bottom of the steps. As she swept the dust down the steps, Laura glanced at him, glanced away, then turned her gaze back to him, and stopped sweeping. She stared at him, frozen in place, dust wafting around her.

The bun of her hair hung down over her right ear. Her face was pale. It steadily grew paler, her eyes darker.

She fell back against one of the rails angling down the steps, keeping her eyes on his, studying him, trying to read him. Then, as though his thoughts were all too obvious, she gave an ironic little laugh, turned her head to one side, dropped her chin, and squeezed her eyes closed. She remained like that for nearly a minute.

Hunter didn't say anything. No words came to him. He felt like he'd drank sour goat's milk. Anger came on the heels of that sick feeling. Anger and indignation. He realized then that while he hadn't known her long, he'd fallen in love with her. Maybe she'd been a buoy the fates had thrown him on the heels of Annabelle.

But, still, he'd fallen in love with her. She'd been a rare glimmer of hope in what had become a hopeless life.

She drew a deep breath, turned away from him, climbed the steps, leaned the broom against the porch, and disappeared into the school.

Hunter continued just riding away. There was no point in remaining here. Her look had told him everything. Every rotten thing he didn't want to hear. But he couldn't ride away. Not yet.

He swung heavily down from Ghost's back.

He dropped the reins, climbed the steps, and doffed his hat as he stepped into the school. The air was heavy with the tang of green pine. A dozen new student desks formed four straight lines, two lines to each side of him as he walked slowly down the aisle between them, toward the dais atop which sat the teacher's desk—also new and shiny with varnish.

Laura sat at the desk, head down, staring at her entwined hands before her. Stacks of open boxes stood around the desk. Books and chalk slates sat on the teacher's desk as well as on shelves behind her. A black chalkboard on castors stood to the right of the desk, facing the room. On the chalkboard was written in flowing, feminine script—*Welcome To Tigerville School!* Below that: *Your Teacher Is Miss Meyers*.

Hunter had lost track of time, but he thought that school had been scheduled to start the next day. He'd seen posters advertising that fact around town, encouraging parents to enroll their children.

"Is it?" he asked, stopping roughly halfway down the room from the front. He held his hat in his hands before him and cast her a cold, severe look.

She looked up at him, one brow arched curiously. She nodded slowly with bleak understanding. "You talked to Jonathan."

"I did."

"And he told you—what? That I'm some money-grubbing charlatan?"

"Something like that."

"And you believe him?"

"I don't know. I came here to get the truth."

"I don't think you did," Laura said. "I think you've already made up your mind."

Hunter took a step forward. "Tell me it's not true, Laura . . . or whatever your name is."

She smiled coldly. Some color returned to her cheeks, and her eyes flashed gold with indignation. "Go to hell, Hunter."

His heart kicked with anger. He'd had enough.

He wheeled, set his hat on his head, and strode to the door. "*You go to hell!*" she screamed behind him, the last word choking off in a sob.

He left the school, dropped down the front steps, picked up his reins, and swung up onto Ghost's back. He galloped down the rise, heading back toward the heart of town. As he crested the next rise, a horse and buggy clomped and clattered toward him. The man driving the buggy was the Pinkerton. The man sitting beside the Pinkerton, of course, was Jonathan Gaynor.

Hunter cursed, then rammed his heels into Ghost's flanks. He galloped down the hill and drew rein beside the buggy as the Pinkerton, smoking a long, slender cheroot, stopped the sorrel in the buggy's traces.

Hunter said, "How did you know where to find her?"

"Amazing what kind of information you can buy from the right drunk for the cost of a drink." Gaynor smiled. "What's the point of prolonging things, Marshal? She's coming back to Denver one way or another."

"Don't worry, Buchanon," the Pinkerton said. "She'll get a fair hearing." He touched a black-gloved thumb to his badge. "I wear this shield proudly and take my job seriously. Mister Gaynor has assured me he will pay for her to have competent representation at his own expense."

"I just want to put the matter behind me," Gaynor told Hunter. "And I want to make sure that what happened to me never happens to anyone else. That said, I am going to recommend the judge give her probation, not a prison sentence. The West is not an easy place for a woman. I'm sure she did what she did because she was driven to it by circumstances beyond her control."

"That's mighty charitable of you," Buchanon said snidely. "Given what she did to you. Where she shot you."

"Yes, well." Gaynor's cheeks colored, and he glanced away. Returning his gaze to Hunter, he shrugged with embarrassment and said, "Despite it all . . . well . . . I find myself still in love with her. Imagine that."

Somehow, Hunter found himself understanding the sentiment.

"The next stage to Cheyenne doesn't leave until Saturday," he told the pair.

Gaynor nodded. "I know. I thought we'd take her over to the Imperial, put her up in her own room where we can keep an eye on her until the stage leaves."

"Sounds rather generous under the circumstances," said the Pinkerton, blowing cigar smoke into the wind. "Don't you think, Marshal?"

Hunter thought it was, indeed. The Imperial was the best hotel in town—with thirty suites, a fine restaurant, and a saloon second to none in the Black Hills. Not even Deadwood claimed better. He didn't respond to the man's question, though.

He just grunted, turned Ghost away from the buggy, and put him into another rocking lope. Like Gaynor, he wanted to put the matter of Laura Meyers behind him as fast as possible.

* * *

Slow, heavy thuds sounded on the school's front steps.

Laura lifted her head from her desk, frowning curiously. Her curiosity diminished as the staccato thuds continued. They incorporated a shuffling sound as well as the taps of what could only be a cane.

She felt a cold stone drop in her stomach as Jonathan Gaynor stepped into the school, clad in his dandyish butterscotch suitcoat with matching bowler hat. His black-gloved right hand shoved the cane ahead of him. Stepping forward, he leaned into the cane, gritting his teeth with every awkward, obviously painful step.

The Pinkerton she'd seen earlier in Big Dan's Saloon walked slowly along behind Jonathan. The man's cold eyes bore into Laura's, as did those of Jonathan himself, as the two men walked down the center aisle between the desks that no students would sit at any time soon.

Not until the town found another teacher.

Thump-shuffle-thud. Thump-shuffle-thud.

Jonathan's pale face was a mask of pent-up rage. His eyes reminded her of those of the now-deceased Warren Davenport. Only, Jonathan's were smaller, even colder and more shrewdly cunning.

He stopped ten feet from Laura's desk.

The Pinkerton stopped several feet behind him. He waited there, a guard dog relegated to a corner until he was needed.

Jonathan stood staring contemptuously at Laura for nearly a full minute before his face twisted bitterly and he said through a contemptuous smile, "How far did you really think you'd get?"

"To be honest," Laura said, "not this far." She was

amazed by the calmness she heard in her own voice. All hope was gone. Her fear had mutated into a grim resignation.

He was a powerful man. She was merely a woman. Mostly, women were a commodity in the West. They owned the rights of beef and poultry.

"Do I have to come with you now?"

"Yes."

"Are you going to turn me over to the police?"

"No."

Laura drew a deep breath, stared down at her hands. "Are you going to kill me?"

"No." Jonathan glanced back at the man behind him. "My associate Mister Blanchard and I have devised a far more fitting and colorful punishment."

"What is it?" Still, she felt no fear. Only weariness. Only a desire to have it all done and over with.

Gaynor turned back to Laura but said to his associate, "You tell her, Mister Blanchard."

Blanchard smiled. "We're sending you up to Leadville. Outside of Leadville, you'll never be seen or heard from again. At least, not by anyone . . . any *man* . . . who doesn't patronize you and the rest of the whores at the Purple Palace."

"Hurdy-gurdy house," Jonathan said with grim amusement.

That sent a chill through her veins.

But only a momentary one. She could have guessed that enslaving her to a whorehouse in the wilds of the Colorado Rockies, and in an even darker perdition than

Tigerville, would be the punishment Jonathan would devise. He did have imagination—she would give him that.

She looked at Jonathan's associate. "You're not really a Pinkerton, are you?"

"No," Jonathan answered for the man. "He's one of my, uh—"

"Henchmen," Laura finished for him.

Jonathan smiled. "You see, my dear, there will be no divorce. We've concocted a complete, sordid history for you. One as a practiced charlatan. You see what happened is I caught you trying to fleece me and you shot me and ran out on me. Just as you've done to several wealthy men in your disreputable past. We tried the story out on Marshal Buchanon. I have to say it worked pretty well."

"Pretty well, but not well enough." Hunter walked slowly into the schoolhouse from the enclosed front porch, his rifle resting on his shoulder.

Blanchard whipped around, shoving his right hand inside his coat.

"Bad idea," Hunter said, stopping a few feet inside the open door, leaving the rifle on his shoulder.

He stopped, boots spread, easing his weight back on his left hip.

Jonathan whipped around, as well. He moved faster than his injury would allow. He screamed a curse and fell with a hard thud and a groan, his cane clattering onto the floor.

Hunter said, "Anybody can have wanted dodgers printed. Anybody with a few dollars and a friend in a print shop. I grew suspicious when I heard your tale of sweet understanding. You didn't come all this way to give her a fair hearing. I figured I might should drift this way and clear up any doubts lingering in my fool brain."

He looked at Laura. "I doubted you. I'm sorry."

She didn't say anything but only stared back at him while Jonathan grunted and groaned on the floor in front of her desk.

Hunter stepped forward, lowering the Henry from his shoulder and clicking the hammer back. He aimed the barrel at Blanchard. "You two are under arrest."

"Please, don't," Laura objected. "Let them go. I want to put this all behind me. I came here to make a fresh start, and I can't do that under a cloud of scandal. Especially after Warren Davenport . . ."

Hunter frowned at the young woman. "They tried to kidnap you . . . sell you into slavery. I can't let that—"

"Please," Laura said, pointedly. "You doubted me. I'll forgive you under one condition. Let them go." She cast her fiery gaze to each of her two would-be assailants in turn. "I don't want to see either of their ugly faces ever again!"

Hunter thought it over. He wanted to turn the key on Gaynor and his henchman in the worst way. But Laura would be on trial, then too. After what had happened with Davenport on Dakota Avenue, she'd never live it down. She wouldn't have a chance here in Tigerville.

Fury burning in him, he curled his upper lip at Blanchard and indicated the man's diminutive boss moaning on the floor behind him. "Scrape that dung off the floor and get the hell out of here. If I ever see either one of you again, I'll kill you."

Blanchard hurried over to Gaynor. With effort, and with Jonathan cursing and grunting, Blanchard helped the man to his feet and gave him his cane. Blanchard wrapped an arm around his boss's shoulders and helped him down the aisle to the door.

As they walked past him, Hunter turned to keep his rifle as well as his threatening glare leveled on them both.

Blanchard didn't look at him. Gaynor looked up at him, flaring an angry nostril, eyes hard with self-righteous indignation.

They left the schoolhouse, descended the front steps, piled into their buggy, and spun away.

His eyes still on the open front door, watching the buggy dwindle into the distance, Hunter said, "You'd best pack a bag and come with me. I have a feeling you won't be safe until those two leave town on the next stage."

When no response came from behind him, he turned to look toward the front of the room. Laura was gone. The schoolhouse's back door stood open.

The vacant dais said it all. She might have forgiven him, but it was over.

Again, he'd been a fool.

CHAPTER 33

Cass Ludlow galloped into the Broken Heart head-quarters and checked his steeldust gelding down to a skidding halt, dust wafting in a heavy cloud around him.

The masked Ludlow swung down from the saddle, got his left boot caught in the stirrup, and fell hard on his head and shoulders. The bottle he'd been holding plunked to the ground beside him.

"Ow—damn!" Cass wailed, flopping his arms, at once trying to free his boot from the stirrup and wanting to pick up the bottle before all the liquor ran out of it.

The half-breed hostler came running out of the stable, yelling, "Mister Cass! Mister Cass!"

"Yes, yes—it's Mister Cass, Deuce. Get the bottle!"

"Mister Cass!" the boy cried, grabbing the gelding's reins. It had just dug its rear hooves into the dirt and was about to gallop off, frightened by its rider's raucous high jinks.

"Yes, it's Mister Cass, Deuce." Cass didn't know if that was the boy's real name, but it's what everyone called him. He was the bastard child of a former hand who'd run off with a blond dancer he'd met at an opera house in Spearfish. "Let's get beyond that to the bottle, now, shall we?"

Ignoring the bottle, and holding the gelding's reins in his left hand, Deuce crouched over the stirrup and used his left arm to wrench up Cass's left ankle then yank the toe free of the stirrup.

"Ow!" Cass yelped as his foot dropped to the ground. "Christalmighty, you little devil—I think you broke my ankle!"

"Mister Cass!" the boy cried, in shock to see his employer's son flopping around on the ground like a landed fish.

The boy had dropped the gelding's reins, and the steel-dust had lunged off to sidle up to the wall of the stable, anxiously stomping and blowing.

Cass rolled onto his side, grabbed the bottle, and held it up to gauge the level. A good bit had darkened the dirt around where it had fallen, but there was still a couple of swallows left in the bottom. He drew the bottle to his mouth, raised it high.

The unseemly display was too much for the frantic stable boy. He'd witnessed such antics before but he'd never become used to it. He turned away, grabbed the gelding's reins, and led the mount, as confused and frightened as he himself was, through the stable's open double doors.

Cass drained the bottle, tossed it aside, and sat up. He chuckled, drunkenly amused by his inelegant dismount and by the half-breed stable boy's anxious reaction. Cass extended his left leg and turned his foot this way and that, wincing.

The ankle hurt but it probably wasn't broken. Just twisted a little.

On the other hand, maybe he'd broken it but was too drunk to feel the pain . . .

Hmmm.

Cass rose to a knee. He pushed off the knee to his feet, gingerly testing the injured limb.

No, it wasn't broken. He'd know even through all the busthead he and his cronies had drunk on their way to town . . . in town . . . and then after they'd fled town like jackasses with tin cans tied to their tails. They'd fled laughing and then split up, Phil and Dave heading back to the wood-cutting camp in which Cass had found them and drafted them into his scheme to kidnap his sister.

Yes, his father had wanted him to use some of his own Broken Heart men in the scheme, but Cass, preferring as usual to mix business with pleasure, had enlisted the help of two of "his *amigos*," as he called his fun-loving, skirt-chasing, card-playing, part-time outlaw cronies.

Now, of course, he realized his mistake. The realization sobered him a little. Maybe they should have waited to get drunk *after* the deed had been accomplished rather than before and during.

Cass turned to stare up at the Ludlow lodge looming on the eastern rise like a foreboding storm cloud. The sight of the rambling house, his father's domain, sobered him further. The windows were cold eyes glaring down on him, teeming with judgment. He wouldn't have been surprised to see the big house shake from side to side, like a man—like Graham Ludlow himself—wagging his head in grieved disdain for his pathetic son.

Cass looked at the bottle lying in the finely churned dust and horse manure of the yard. What he wouldn't give for just one more drink!

He kicked the bottle. It rose, dropped, bounced, and slid along the ground, parting the scattered straw.

He made the decision right then and there. He knew it was the right one, because he suddenly felt as though an anvil had been lifted from his shoulders.

He laughed to himself. He should have made the decision a long time ago.

How much happier he'd have been! He could see his future before him—long stretches of rocky red desert, tile-roofed adobe huts, the clear blue waters of the Sea of Cortez glinting in the background. And the *señoritas*.

Oh, the *señoritas*!

He walked a little unsteadily to the open stable doors. The boy stood back in the shadows, rubbing the claybank down with a thin cotton towel.

"Deuce, saddle that big roan of mine. Have him ready to ride in ten minutes."

He didn't wait for a response. Giddy from his decision, he walked up the path that climbed the hill, past the circular, cinder-paved area where several wrought-iron hitch-racks stood near the base of the porch steps.

He climbed the steps, chuckling through his teeth. He crossed the porch, opened the front door, and stepped inside.

The old man and Kenneth Earnshaw were seated close together, Earnshaw on one of the parlor's leather sofas, Graham Ludlow on his left in the pushchair. They were both leaning forward, staring at a large plat open on the coffee table before them.

Each held a drink in one hand, a cigar in the other.

They'd been talking together like a couple of conspirators plotting a gold heist when Cass had entered, but now they looked up at him, eyes widening expectantly. They looked around behind him and then returned their gazes to the masked countenance of Cass himself, frowning.

"Where is she?" Earnshaw asked.

Cass threw up his hands. "Decided not to go through with it." He chuckled tauntingly. "She seemed to be having so much fun, parading around in that little getup of hers, I didn't have the heart. You know, when I saw her today, she wasn't wearing more than what I could tuck into one back pocket. Ha!"

He delighted in the crimson flush his words caused to rise in his father's and wannabe brother-in-law's cheeks.

"You useless bastard!" Earnshaw said, standing so quickly he spilled some of his drink.

"If you want her so damn bad, why don't you go fetch her yourself instead of sitting around here pretending you're the next Graham Ludlow?" Cass looked at his father and pointed at Earnshaw. "If you want that little nancy-boy to marry your daughter so damn bad, send him to fetch her. Make him earn her, for God's sake. Make him earn *something*. I for one, however, don't think he can stay on her any longer than he can stay on the best broke horse in the Broken Heart remuda."

Cass laughed again caustically, and turned to the stairs.

He stopped, having seen a rosy-cheeked, shrewd smile light up his father's face. He turned his gaze back to Ludlow, frowning curiously. "What in the hell are you—"

"You failed," the old man croaked out. He puffed the stogie in his left hand, the smoke nearly obliterating him from Cass's view for a few seconds. He blew the thick, white smoke out his mouth and nostrils, grinning. "You failed again just as you've always failed in the past. Look at you. You're so drunk you're about to fall down."

Ludlow set his goblet down and clapped his hands, grinning bizarrely and cackling like a warlock. "Bravo, dear boy! Bravo! One more failure in a string of failures! At least you're predictable—I'll give you that!"

"Go to hell—both of you!" Cass started up the stairs. His left boot slipped off the bottom step. He stumbled forward, causing his father to roar even louder.

"True to your nature!" Ludlow roared as Cass stumbled up the stairs, leaning heavily on the rail. "You're nothing but a drunk and sluggard! My God—how did such a mongrel grow from the seed of my loins?"

Cass gained the second floor and hurried into his room.

He fished the key from the drawer, picked up a pair of saddlebags from the floor near his bed, and opened the closet. He worked quickly, anger burning in him like venom in his veins. The anger was souring the effect of the alcohol coursing through those same veins, corrupting the drunk, turning it into something sick and foul.

He had to work quickly before he lost his courage.

That's really the thing that had been lacking in his character all of these years, the one thing that had been holding him back from leaving his arbitrary, sadistic, and tyrannical father. Lack of confidence. Lack of spine.

He'd had both things mocked and beaten out of him, so he'd become the one thing Graham Ludlow had been most afraid he'd turn out to be:

Nothing.

Well, here he was: nothing. But this nothing man, who didn't even have his good looks anymore, was hightailing it out of here. He was going to take that gold and start afresh.

God, he needed a drink!

Once he had all four gold sacks safely ensconced in both saddlebag pouches, he scoured his room for a bottle. He found three—all dry. He found a small brown bottle of chokecherry wine he'd pilfered from Chang's own private supply. It contained only a teaspoonful. Still, it was something.

He threw it back, the sweet cherry taste mixing with his bile and only making him feel fouler. He shouldered the bulging saddlebags, grunting under the weight, and left his room. He wouldn't pack anything else. Just the clothes on his back and the gold. He wanted to leave everything behind.

Everything!

He walked down the hall and stopped at the top of the stairs. His father and Earnshaw were speaking more loudly, a little contentiously.

"What are you saying?" Earnshaw said in a tone of incredulity.

"I'm saying my son does have a point. You're going to marry her. Perhaps you should be the one to fetch her."

Earnshaw hemmed and hawed.

Ludlow said, "Maybe she's been wanting you to stand up to her, to take charge. Don't *ask* her to marry you. Annabelle doesn't respond to weakness. Annabelle is the kind of woman who responds only to strength. A raised fist! That's one reason she chose Buchanon—aside from merely wanting to defy me, of course, which I know was the *main* reason she chose him. She wants a man who can prove himself to her by taming her. By not taking no for an answer. You have to be as strong as she is. Stronger!"

Cass threw his head back, laughing, and started down the stairs, his boots under the fifty pounds of gold making loud hammering sounds. "Sounds like a winning plan, Pops. Sure, sure. Nothing about sending that pigeon after Annabelle can go wrong at all!"

Cass laughed again as he clomped down the last step to stand at the bottom of the stairs.

He turned to see Kenneth Earnshaw sitting back on the sofa, shoulders slumped, chin down, looking like a tow-headed, baby-faced midget dressed like Buffalo Bill Cody ready for a performance in his Wild West show. Wild Bill with a bad case of stage fright, that was. Kenneth's shoulders bowed forward, and he was looking forlornly down at the drink in his hands.

He didn't seem nearly as enthused about Ludlow's plan as Ludlow himself did.

Ludlow scowled at Cass. "Where in the hell are you going? What's in those bags?"

"This here?" Cass shifted the bags on his shoulders. "This here is my ticket out of this dump. This devil's lair you call the Broken Heart. I'll be seein' you, Pops . . . never again!" he added with a laugh.

He crouched to fumble the front door open.

"Where in the hell do you think you're going?" Ludlow said, hardening his bulldog jaws.

"Mexico!"

"That's crazy—get back here!"

"*Adios, Padre!*" Cass said, descending the porch steps.

Deuce had already brought up the saddled roan and was walking back down the hill toward the stable, obviously wanting nothing to do with the disturbance in the house.

"Thanks, Deuce!" Cass called.

The boy gave no response, just kept walking, head down.

"Cass, get back here!"

Cass glanced behind him. His father sat on the porch, Earnshaw behind him, holding the chair's push handles.

"Cass!" Ludlow wailed, pounding the arms of his chair with both fists. "You get back here, dammit. You can't survive on your own. You need to stay here and be provided for!"

To be kicked around like a mangy cur, you mean, you old buzzard.

"Go to hell," Cass quietly snarled as he draped his saddlebags over the roan's back.

"Cass, dammit—you can't leave. I forbid it! Dammit, Cass, get down off that horse!" Ludlow's voice was shrill. "If you leave this yard, you will get no more money from me. Not a dime. I will disown you. Your handouts end as soon as you pass through that gate!"

Cass cast a lewd gesture over his shoulder and put the roan into a rocking gallop.

CHAPTER 34

Three days later, Laura Meyers walked forthrightly along Dakota Avenue, her chin in the air, smiling through the gauzy veil hanging down from the brim of her small, green felt hat. She smiled so brightly that she felt that at any moment she might break into song. Or that she might sprout wings and fly. The joyous feeling had just come over her though she'd felt it building for several days.

The fact was she'd never felt so good in her life. Who'd have expected she could feel so at home in a town as . . . well, *colorful* . . . as Tigerville?

She didn't just feel at home. For the first time in her life, she felt light and free and independent and proud. She also felt successful. Along with that feeling came a feeling of great confidence.

She'd never been a successful, confident woman. She'd realized lately that she'd felt comfortable and secure in her old lifestyle, with Jonathan back in their grand home in Denver. But that comfort and security had been an illusion. A lie. She'd never known who Jonathan really was. Nor had she known who she was.

She'd never felt anything akin to the joy and independence she felt now. The terror she'd felt on her way here, fleeing Jonathan's wrath, had now after she'd successfully completed her first three days of school-teaching in the new schoolhouse been set on its head. Now she couldn't imagine ever going back to her old life, much less of ever leaving Tigerville.

She glanced around at the cowboys and drifters, the bearded mule skinners and the Chinamen and black men and the dusky-skinned men with obvious Indian blood milling around her, snorting and spitting and yelling and cursing and laughing and, in one case out front of a beer parlor on the opposite side of the street, smacking each other's faces with their bare fists while other men around them yelled encouragement.

Laura's smile did not waver.

Colorful, jovial, raucous, rowdy Tigerville!

She crossed a side street then stepped up onto the boardwalk fronting Big Dan's Saloon. She stopped in front of the door, hesitating, suddenly self-conscious. But then she looked down at the linen-covered wicker basket whose handle was hooked over her arm, and proceeded inside. As the batwings swung back into place behind her, she looked around.

All faces turned toward her, turned away, then quickly returned and held on her, eyes widening.

What in God's green earth was Tigerville's new school-teacher doing in Big Dan's place? was the question passing over the minds of the dozen or so customers regarding her incredulously. Annabelle, standing behind the bar and running a cloth over its glistening varnished surface, glanced at her in the same fashion as the others, jerking a second, startled look at the woman standing in front of the batwings.

Annabelle froze, mouth and eyes opening. Leaving the cloth on the mahogany, she hurried out from behind the bar and over to Laura, smiling a little scandalously at the pretty teacher dressed in a conservative silk dress and velvet waistcoat. Wrapping her hand around Laura's free one, Annabelle whispered urgently, "Laura, what on earth are you doing in here?"

"I came to see my new friend," Laura said, not lowering her voice one iota. She extended the basket toward Annabelle. "And to bestow a couple of humble but well-deserved gifts on her."

"*Here?*" Annabelle cried under her breath. She rose onto the tips of her high-heeled shoes to gaze out over the doors behind Laura before turning a self-conscious look into the room over her own left shoulder.

"Yes, here. Where else would I find you?" Laura smiled affectionately. "Look, Annabelle—you saved my life. Besides, we're friends. If it's scandalous for the new schoolteacher to be friends with a saloon girl—well, then, so be it." She shook the basket. "These are for you."

Annabelle chuckled throatily, looked around once more, then led Laura over to a table against the wall on Laura's left, on the other side of the potbellied stove, which would give them a little concealment from the front windows. "Have a seat here," Annabelle said, pulling a chair out from the table. "Would you like a cup of tea? I just boiled water for some. I was about to take a badly needed break. It may be too late to renovate your reputation, but at least none of the ladies from the sobriety and morality leagues will see us mingling if they deign to peer through the batwings."

She snorted a laugh.

Laura sat down and set the basket on the table, smiling up at Annabelle. "I would love some tea."

"Be right back!"

Annabelle walked back around the bar in her customary skimpy outfit and high-heeled shoes and returned a minute later, holding a smoking china teapot in one hand, two china cups in the other hand. "I'm taking a fifteen-minute tea break, Eddie," she told the tall, gray-haired, gray-mustached man drying a beer schooner behind the bar.

Eddie flared a nostril at her, then used his towel to swat a fly on the bar.

"Big Dan's taking a nap upstairs," Annabelle told Laura.

She set the teapot and two cups on the table. "Here we are." She filled Laura's cup first and then filled her own, set down the teapot, and took a seat in the chair across from Laura, frowning curiously at the linen-covered basket. "Now, then—what's this about gifts for me, humble or otherwise?"

"Oh, believe me—they're humble. Especially in light of what you did for me."

Annabelle leaned across the table and keeping her voice furtively low, her eyes sharp and angry, said, "You mean shooting that scalawag and perverted moron, Warren Davenport? Someone should have shot him long ago. He probably intended to imprison you the way he did his poor, dearly departed wife . . . may God rest her tortured soul." She lifted her cup and blew on the steaming tea. "Besides, it was Hunter he was about to shoot. I should've let him shoot that big cork-headed Rebel first and *then* shot Davenport!"

"You don't mean that."

"Oh, yes, I do."

Laura smiled knowingly and sipped her tea. "Still, by killing him, you saved me every bit as much as you saved Hunter."

"As for saving you from Davenport—for that I am grateful. You don't owe me a damn thing." Annabelle snickered and lifted her hand to her mouth. "Listen to me. I believe Hunter's right—I've learned to cuss and I'm enjoying it."

Laura laughed and lifted the linen cloth from the basket. "This is a pie I made from the currants growing behind my cabin. My mother used to make currant pie. I hadn't had one in nearly twenty years, until I made two last night. I'm not much of a cook but I fumbled my way through it. I made one for you and one for me. This is an embroidered doily made by one of my little girls."

"One of your . . . ?"

"Students."

"Oh, how nice!" Annabelle said. "They must have taken a shine to you if they're already making you doilies!"

Annabelle picked up the yellow cotton doily in the shape of a daisy, and fingered it admiringly.

"Little Audra Bernum gave me two. One for me and one to give to my best friend."

Annabelle looked at her. A sheen of emotion shone in her eyes. "Do you know you're the first female friend I've ever had?"

"I am?"

"I was raised out at the Broken Heart around all men.

Not a single other female. I went to school out near the ranch, but there were more boys than girls. None of the girls were my age—either younger or older—and I didn't get to spend time with any of them outside of school. Our ranches were just too far apart."

Laura smiled sweetly. "I'm so glad we're friends, Annabelle."

"Me too." Annabelle returned Laura's smile, sipped her tea, swallowed, and said, "So, tell me—how is school going? How many days have you been in session now?"

"I just finished the third day. It's going rather well, I'm happy to say. I have only seven students. Most are from the local orphanage, but the banker's wife, Mrs. Carmichael, spoke to me after school. She's interested in enrolling her son and daughter when they return from visiting her husband's family in the East."

"That's wonderful."

"It is wonderful. The children currently enrolled are generally sweet, seem to like me, I like them, and, best of all, they all seem eager to learn. We are hard at work each day on penmanship, grammar, reading, and mathematics. We finished up today with a discussion on the wonders of gravity. I did a demonstration by taking my shoes off and leaping off my desk." Laura winced. "And nearly broke my ankle, I think . . ."

She reached down to rub the appendage of topic.

"Oh, dear!"

"I'll be all right. At least they had a good laugh."

"And . . . no sign of . . . ?"

"My soon-to-be former husband?" Laura turned her mouth corners down. "No, thank God. Hunter made sure he and his henchman were on the last stage out of

Tigerville. He assured me he watched them board and leave town."

"You're lucky to have Hunter watching over you. He's good at that."

"Annabelle, I want you to know that's all he's doing."

Annabelle frowned. "What do you mean?"

"He's just watching over me. I mean, he watched over me in the case of Jonathan, but I haven't seen him in a couple of days now. We're not . . . we're not together."

"I don't understand," Annabelle said, tapping both index fingers against the rim of her half-empty teacup. "I thought you two—"

"It's over."

"Why? Because he believed Jonathan's story? Laura, I know that was silly of him, but we all make mistakes."

"That's not it. At least, it's not all of it." Laura sipped her tea, set her cup down, and cast her new friend a frank, knowing look. "You're still in love with him."

"No, no—"

Laura reached across the table and placed her right hand down on Annabelle's left one, quieting her.

"What's more—he's still in love with you, Annabelle. He's always going to be in love with you. I know it the way only another woman can know such a thing."

Annabelle looked at her, vaguely incredulous.

"Beyond that," Laura continued, "I know that you are still very much in love with Hunter. You always will be."

Annabelle laughed and shook her head. "Nothing could be further from the truth. I assure you, Laura, I care nothing for the man. He turned his back on me when I needed him most."

"He turned his back on you because he loves you. He

wanted you to go back to your father because he knew your father could provide for you. He couldn't. Maybe that was another mistake on his part. But his gold was gone. The disappointment of that bit him deep. Imagine all the work that went into building that marriage stake for the two of you only to find it gone just when you were about to get married."

Laura squeezed her hand again. "Please, Annabelle . . . give him another chance. Stop punishing him. All men are fools in many ways. Women are fools in fewer ways, but we can be fools just the same. Don't let pride make you turn your back on a man who loves you as much as Hunter does—especially when, deep down in your heart, you return every ounce of his love—in spades."

Annabelle stared at her, looking a little dumbfounded. Her cheeks were drawn and pale.

Laura slid her chair back, rose, and hooked the handle of the basket over her arm. "Thanks for the tea."

She rose, walked around the table, crouched, and gave Annabelle's cheek an affectionate kiss, her shoulders a sisterly squeeze.

She turned and left Big Dan's Saloon. She retraced her steps to the south. When she was halfway down the next block, she thumbed a tear from her cheek.

CHAPTER 35

Only a few minutes after Laura had left Big Dan's, Kenneth Earnshaw drove his blue-wheeled surrey with a leather canopy and a brass oil lamp into Tigerville.

As soon as he gained the heart of town, rolling from north to south along Dakota Avenue, heads swung toward him and held on the little, pale, blond-haired man in the three-piece suit of bleached buckskin complete with red necktie, white silk shirt, and a fringed buckskin coat, the flaps of which blew out behind the little man in the wind.

On his head was his bullet-crowned cream hat, trimmed with a red ostrich feather, one side pinned to the crown.

Around him, men hooted and painted ladies cackled from parlor house balconies. Ignoring the slovenly minions, his spade-bearded chin in the air, Kenneth pulled to a stop in front of the Tigerville marshal's office, engaged the surrey's brake, and stepped down from the seat. He tied the blooded, blue-black mare of both Morgan and Arabian blood—a gift from young Kenneth's father on Kenneth's last birthday, which was celebrated in the Parisian Hotel on Madison Avenue in New York City—and mounted the jail office's small front boardwalk.

He tapped on the door and opened it. A large, beefy gent in work shirt and dungarees was sitting kicked back in the swivel chair behind the desk to Kenneth's left, his mule-eared boots crossed on the desk's edge. The man's arms were crossed on his chest, and his head sagged over them.

Sound asleep.

He woke as Kenneth opened the door, grunting with a start and dropping his thick-soled boots to the floor.

A sheepish expression and a bright red blush rose in his broad, ruddy cheeks. As Kenneth stepped into the room in all his gallant glory, that expression of chagrin was quickly replaced by a forehead-crumpling frown of fascination and curiosity. To Otis Crosby's eyes, the little man walking into the office resembled nothing so much as one of the fancy-plumed roosters Mrs. Van Camp had running around her place, just behind his own tumble-down shack. Those roosters crowed all day and night till he wanted to shoot the lot of them; that's why he never seemed to get enough sleep.

Sure enough, this little man here looked just like one of them red-combed, double-laced cocks that strutted around the Van Camp place, pecking at the hens.

To Kenneth, Otis Crosby was indistinguishable from all the other unwashed minions in this backwater perdition.

"Can I . . . uh . . . help you . . . ?" Otis asked.

Kenneth glanced around, frowning, tentative. The only other person he saw in the room was a bedraggled-looking female, obviously of aboriginal heritage, sitting on a cot in one of the office's four cells. She sat with her back against the wall, one ankle resting atop a raised knee—a most unladylike arrangement of the female form.

Savages.

"Yes, yes . . . I was wondering if Marshal Buchanon was around?"

"No, he ain't," Otis said, rising from the chair. "He had to leave town when some cork-headed fool robbed the Parthenon Parlor House's madam at gunpoint, then lit out like a coyote after a jackrabbit. No tellin' when he'll be back. The marshal, I mean. Is there anything—"

But before he could finish the question, the little man in the feathered hat had backed out the door and was just then letting the latch click into place behind him. Earnshaw turned to the street, unable to keep a grin from flicking at the corners of his mouth.

He'd assumed Buchanon would be gone, but he'd wanted to check just to make sure that, according to plan, one of Ludlow's more dependable men with a fast horse had robbed the Parthenon and then safely "skinned out of town," as the colorful saying went, with Buchanon in tow.

Not that Earnshaw was afraid of the big ex-Confederate brigand. He just wanted to make sure today's scheme went down without a hitch.

He climbed back into the carriage, waited for an opening in the traffic, then swung the horse full around, angling toward Big Dan's Saloon on the opposite side of the street. He drove back north for only a hundred feet and then stopped the surrey behind a parked lumber dray. Again, he set the brake, clambered down to the street, and opened his coat to make sure his .44-caliber British bulldog was secure in his shoulder holster.

Seeing that the snub-nosed, double-action wheel gun with ivory grips was right where it was supposed to be, he stepped up onto the boardwalk and entered Big Dan Delaney's Saloon & Gambling Parlor. It being mid-afternoon, there were only maybe a dozen men in the place, most standing at the bar, a few sitting at tables between Earnshaw and the bar. A couple were playing roulette on the bar's far side, in the saloon's apparent gambling area.

Right away, he saw Annabelle.

As Earnshaw closed the door behind him, she finished setting a pair of beer schooners onto the table of two men clad in business suits. One of the businessmen said something to Annabelle, who laughed affably, batted her eyelashes coquettishly, and swung around, saying, "Why, thank you, kind sir. It's not every day a gal gets a compliment like that!"

As she headed back to the bar in her high-heeled shoes, half her back left uncovered by the black corset she wore, both businessmen swung their heads around to ogle her retreating, half-naked figure. One elbowed the other and said to Annabelle, "If you'd finally accept my marriage proposal, you'd get a compliment like that every day of the week and twice on Sunday!"

Fury setting Kenneth's eyes on fire, he strutted forward and said loudly above the low din of desultory conversation, "She's spoken for."

All heads in the saloon swung toward him. Including Annabelle's.

She'd just set her empty serving tray on the bar and now, locking her eyes on his, said in open astonishment, "Kenneth!"

Earnshaw strode toward her, his chin in the air, the

feather in his hat dancing. "Annabelle, I've had enough of this foolishness. You are to accompany me back to the Broken Heart at once." He stopped before her, setting one polished, hand-tooled boot down resolutely beside the other one with a click, and said, "You will be my wife, and I will not take no for an answer!"

A hush fell over the room.

Annabelle stared at Kenneth in glassy-eyed astonishment.

Suddenly, every man in the place, including the skinny bartender flanking Annabelle, erupted with a near-deafening roar of laughter.

Annabelle laughed then, too, briefly bringing a hand to her mouth, jerking her shoulders. She looked Earnshaw up and down, and, as though seeing him now the way the men saw him, laughed again, uncontrollably. Regaining some of her composure, she said, "Did my father put you up to this?"

"This was my decision," young Earnshaw lied. "I am bound and determined to take you out of this hell hole and return you to the ranch where you rightly belong and where you and I will be married and raise a family. Dammit, Annabelle, that's my final decision. I will not be swayed. Now, come along—we are going home!"

Again, the room interrupted in laughter.

Kenneth's cheeks burned with embarrassment. He glanced around skeptically. Why were they laughing at him? He'd done what Annabelle's father had instructed him to do—to speak his mind and brook no argument. He'd spoken his demands as forcefully as any man could.

And still they laughed . . .

Even Annabelle smiled again, mockingly.

"The carriage is waiting outside, Annabelle," Kenneth said firmly, narrowing his eyes. "You must come with me now. I will brook no defiance!"

"Go to hell, you damn toad!" This from the man sitting to Earnshaw's right—the same man who'd made Annabelle blush with his fawning only a moment ago.

Rage caused Kenneth's heart to hammer his breastbone. Before he knew what he was doing, he'd reached into his jacket and pulled the Bulldog from his shoulder holster. He extended the snub-nosed revolver out to his right and planted the barrel against his tormentor's forehead. He clicked the hammer back and stared at Annabelle, who, seeing the gun, gave a strangled cry and leaped back against the bar, placing her hand on her throat.

"Kenneth, what are you doing?"

"Either come with me now or I am going to blow this man's brains out!"

"Kenneth!"

The man—a middle-aged gent with a trimmed black beard, pomaded black hair, and pudgy red nose—stared in shock and terror up along the cocked revolver and the arm extending it, at Kenneth's deadly resolute eyes.

Another man leaped to his feet nearby, yelling, "No, you're not!" The man reached for a revolver on his hip but managed only to close his hand around the weapon's grips before Kenneth shot him.

Pow!

The whole room jumped. Annabelle stared in shock as the man cursed sharply and fell back over his chair, the bullet in his upper left thigh oozing thick, red blood. He hit the floor and yelled with shrill exasperation, "The Eastern daisy shot me!"

Kenneth stared down at him. He was half in disbelief himself. He hadn't planned on shooting the man. It was as if another man had squeezed the Bulldog's trigger. He'd shot a man once before—in fact, he'd shot Sheriff Frank Stillwell back at the end of last year's trouble. But shooting Stillwell had been an accident. This was something he'd done on purpose although he hadn't planned to do it ahead of time.

He'd just done it. He'd shot him!

Looking around through his own wafting powder smoke, he was glad he'd done it. Because all the faces regarding him now did so with no more of their previous mocking but with no little amount of apprehension and possibly even respect.

He aimed the Bulldog once more at the bearded man before him, who sat holding both his hands straight up in the air, palms forward.

Earnshaw stared with menace bordering on lunacy at his bride-to-be. "Are you coming, Annabelle—or must this man, too, suffer for your defiance?"

Annabelle thrust her hands out in supplication. "Put the gun down, Kenneth!"

Kenneth thrust his left hand toward her. "Come!"

"All right. Just let me—"

"No—now. Come!"

He snapped his fingers and pressed the Bulldog harder against the bearded man's forehead. The bearded man winced, closed his eyes, and turned his head to one side in trepidation.

"All right," Annabelle said, reaching for Kenneth's extended hand. "I'll come. Just put the gun down, Kenneth!"

Kenneth wrapped his left hand around her right wrist

and jerked her toward him. At the same time, he pulled
the Bulldog from the bearded man's head. He backed himself and Annabelle toward the batwing doors, waving the
gun around and yelling, "Everybody stay right where you
are. If you try to follow me, someone's likely to get hurt!"

He glanced with menace at Annabelle.

He was so enraged by her behavior, by the way she
and the others had treated him, that he felt an almost un-
deniable urge to put a bullet in her lovely head. The only
reason he didn't was because she was Graham Ludlow's
daughter . . . and his bride-to-be, of course. The day he'd
finally broke her to his rein would be a satisfying one,
indeed.

He gave a caustic laugh at the thought as he backed
through the batwings. What a defiant bitch she was. Rest
assured, he'd tame her. He was the man to do it even if he
had to employ a bullwhip!

Quickly, he holstered the Bulldog and then grabbed
Annabelle and threw her into the carriage. He ripped the
reins from the tie rail and climbed aboard and released
the brake handle. He glanced to his right in time to see
Annabelle try to leap over the carriage's right front wheel.

Kenneth grabbed her with his right hand and jerked her
back toward him. "No, you don't!"

"Ow—you're hurting my arm!"

"Be quiet!"

Keeping a vice-like grip on her left wrist with his right
hand, he took the reins in his left hand, shook them over
the back of the mixed Morgan-Arab, and they were off,
heading north toward the Broken Heart at a full gallop.

CHAPTER 36

Buchanon drew sharply back on Ghost's reins.

The horse locked its rear hooves up, skidding forward, curveting to the right. Hunter looked down at the zebra dun gelding lying dead in the trail, and winced.

The poor beast must have stepped in a gopher hole. Its left front leg was badly broken, the bone showing through a jagged tear in the hide. A bloody hole in the horse's head, just behind its left ear, showed where its rider had put it out of its agony.

Hunter had just lifted his head to look around at the blond hills stippled with widely scattered pines around him, when a mewling wail rose off his right flank.

He threw himself off the left side of his horse a half a blink before a rifle belched. Twisting around in mid-air, Buchanon struck the two-track ranch trail on his left shoulder and hip.

He palmed the LeMat and, quickly finding the man in the pine behind him and off the trail's left side as Hunter gazed back toward the south, flung two quick shots into the branches.

The man who'd been perched in a fork in the tree,

roughly fifteen feet up from the ground, yelped, sagged back, and dropped his rifle. He tumbled down out of the branches, smacking several, breaking one with a crunching sound, then hit the ground with a grunt.

His pale Stetson with a funneled brim sailed lightly to the ground between its owner and the coyote standing ten feet away from the man, head down, tail arched, growling softly.

The man lay still on his belly, cheek pressed to the ground. A pair of saddlebags lay near the base of the tree, near where the man's Winchester now lay.

Hunter gained his feet, wincing against a new set of ailments, silently opining that he was getting too long in the tooth to be hurling himself out of the saddle with such regularity. He retrieved his hat, set it on his head, then, limping slightly on his left leg, walked over to his would-be back-shooter.

Bobby Lee was still growling, showing his teeth.

Buchanon kicked the man onto his back. Blood shone on his chest where bullets had torn through his shirt.

"It's all right, Bobby Lee," Hunter said. "You can get the hump out of your neck. This one's dead."

Bobby Lee gave a little yip, then went over and anointed the man's left, spurred boot.

Hunter stared down at the man—a bull-chested, thick-armed, short-legged gent with an angular face and a thick brown mustache in which jerky crumbs resided. Buchanon recognized him as Wrench Kinkaid, one of Graham Ludlow's rowdier hands who'd made a reputation for himself by often stomping a little too high with his tail up on Saturday nights in Tigerville and ending up getting hauled off to the hoosegow until he sobered up and Ludlow's foreman rode to town to pay his fine.

Hunter frowned, a growing suspicion pricking the hair under his shirt collar.

What was Wrench Kinkaid doing in town on a weekday afternoon? And why was he robbing a seedy sporting parlor like the Parthenon? It didn't make sense.

Ludlow might have fired the man, but that didn't explain why the man would rob the Parthenon. Kinkaid knew Tigerville well enough to know there were riper plums to be picked.

Unless the robbery had been a smokescreen to divert Buchanon from something even more nefarious . . .

His pulse quickened. He had to get back to town pronto.

He grabbed Kinkaid's saddlebags but did not bother opening them. The seventy dollars and change Kinkaid had taken off Mary Jane Quinn, the Parthenon madam, would be inside. Hunter hurried over to where Ghost stood off the side of the trail, contentedly grazing.

He tossed the saddlebags over the mount's back, stepped into the leather, said, "Come on, Bobby. We gotta make haste back to town. This whole thing smells like rotten eggs!"

He booted Ghost into a run.

Tigerville spread out ahead of him twenty minutes later.

Hunter was glad that Kinkaid hadn't gotten far before his horse had plundered that gopher hole. He was sorry for the horse. He liked horses more than he liked men—

especially men like Wrench Kinkaid—but especially given his suspicions concerning Kinkaid's motives, he was glad he'd found the man before he could get any farther than a twenty-minute ride away.

He'd been gone from town a little over an hour. Not long. But something had happened while he'd been away. He'd sensed it the minute he turned left at the fork in the trail and headed straight south into town, where the trail became Dakota Avenue.

The town seemed quieter than it usually was this time of the day. There were plenty of men in the street, but most were clustered straight ahead of Buchanon now as he slowed Ghost to a trot. Bobby Lee trotted along beside him, tongue hanging after the long run. As Hunter gained the heart of the business district, he canted his head to the right, peering closely at the tightly grouped men who appeared to be in silent discussion.

As Buchanon approached the crowd, his pulse quickened even more, for now he saw that the men were gathered in front of Big Dan's Saloon. Big Dan himself stood at the center of the crowd, yelling orders to what appeared somewhat reluctant listeners.

"Now, see here," one man yelled back at big Dan Delaney, "that's Graham Ludlow's daughter. Who are we to interfere in Ludlow's private affairs? I say let her and the fancy-Dan settle the matter their ownselves!"

Most of the other men in the crowd nodded and yelled in agreement.

Bobby Lee gave a low growl as he stared at the group.

Hunter started to boot Ghost up to the clustered men but stopped when a man to his right laughed and said, "Looks like you went an' lost her for sure now."

Hunter turned to see Cass Ludlow sitting on the board-walk, legs extended straight out before him, leaning back against the front wall of a little hovel of a watering hole called Quiet Sam's Beer Emporium though the so-called emporium sold rotgut whiskey, to boot.

The masked Ludlow son grinned behind his flour sack mask. Around the edges of the cutouts, Hunter could see the scarred and twisted skin caused by the fire.

Young Ludlow held a bottle between his legs. He lifted the bottle to his lips, took a deep pull, causing the bubble to jerk back and forth between the bottom and the neck.

"What happened?" Hunter asked.

"She's gone."

"Where?"

"Why you so interested? I thought you gave her up."

"Tell me, dammit," Hunter said through gritted teeth, feeling his face burn with rage, "or so help me I'll come down there an'—"

"What?" Cass said, grinning through the mask. "Beat me till I'm ugly?" He chuckled drunkenly.

Hunter sat his horse, fuming.

Again, Bobby Lee gave a low, dark growl. He clipped it off with a quiet wail.

"Looks like the better man won," Cass said. "Least-ways, maybe little Earnshaw cared more for her than you do. The little rube came for her. Plans to marry her. Left town not ten minutes ago. Dragged her out of Big Dan's at gun point. Shot poor Mort Lawton in the leg, sure enough. He meant business, Earnshaw did. He wasn't takin' no for an answer. It was quite the scuffle!"

Buchanon only distantly heard that last sentence, for

by then he'd already spun Ghost around and galloped back in the direction from which he'd come, Bobby Lee hot on his trail.

"Where the hell you goin'?" Cass yelled behind him. "I thought you done gave her up?"

That's what Hunter had thought. He realized his mistake. It hadn't taken that popinjay kidnapping her to do it. He'd known it all along. He'd just been too damn proud to admit it. Poor as he was, he was poorer without Annabelle, and she was poorer without him.

Crouching low in the saddle, he spurred Ghost into a lunging gallop. He shot out of town and up the trail, heading straight north at the three-tined fork. Fifteen minutes later, he crested a rise and drew Ghost to a halt, blinking as his own dust caught up to him.

His eyes widened as he stared straight north. A black carriage with a leather canopy and blue-painted wheels was just then climbing another rise a hundred yards beyond, following the trail's gradual right curve. The fine horse pulling the carriage had slowed for the rise, sunlit dust rising around both horse and surrey.

That had to be them. No one but Earnshaw would drive a citified rig out here.

"Let's go, Ghost!" Buchanon urged, crouching low and ramming his heels into his loyal mount's loins again.

Bobby Lee panted along frantically behind him.

The stallion caromed down off the rise, gained the bottom, and dug its front hooves into the trail, climbing hard. The carriage just now crested the rise and disappeared from sight.

It came into view again as Ghost reached the top of the

hill. It was only fifty yards away now, following the trail near the edge of a narrow gorge that slid toward it from the east, on Hunter's right side. Dust laced off the carriage's spinning, iron-shod wheels and churned in the air behind it.

"Stop, Earnshaw!" Hunter shouted, urging even more speed from Ghost, the wind pasting the brim of his hat against his forehead. "Stop the damn buggy—I'm right behind you!"

He heard Annabelle scream beneath the wind and the drumming of Ghost's hooves. Earnshaw shouted. The man poked his head out from under the canopy. He snaked his right hand out, as well, angling it back. Sunlight flashed off a silver-chased gun barrel.

The gun cracked. Smoke puffed. The bullet plumed dust several feet in front of Ghost's scissoring hooves.

Earnshaw pulled his head back into the carriage. He and Annabelle were both yelling, arguing. There was the sharp crack as though of a hand against flesh. Horse and carriage jerked sharply off the trail, to the right side, and swerved up to within only a few feet of the gorge.

"Rein in, Earnshaw! Dammit, rein in!"

Earnshaw poked his head out of the carriage again. The gun followed. The wind blew his outlandish hat off his head, tossed it high and back toward Buchanon. Kenneth aimed the pistol toward Hunter.

Again, it popped.

The horse pulling the carriage whinnied shrilly and swerved sharply to the right.

"No!" Hunter cried.

The horse was angling toward the gorge, the surrey bouncing crazily along behind it over sagebrush and rocks.

Hunter reined Ghost off the trail and into the surrey's billowing dust. "Earnshaw—rein in, you fool!"

Buchanon's heart shot straight up into his throat when Earnshaw's horse ran over the lip of the gorge and dropped like a stone. It drew the surrey down behind it, the carriage rolling onto its right side an eye blink before it disappeared from Hunter's view.

Annabelle screamed, her horrified voice lancing the wind.

A second later, the horse's brief, agonized whinny rose like the screams of a dozen witches. It was drowned by the heart-rending crunching and clattering of the surrey smashing to smithereens on the floor of the canyon.

"Oh God, no!" Hunter wailed. "Oh God, no—*Annabelle!*"

CHAPTER 37

Hunter checked Ghost to a dusty halt, hurled himself from the saddle, and ran to the edge of the gorge. He dropped to his knees, rested his hands on his thighs, and leaned forward to cast his terrified gaze toward the canyon floor.

Bobby Lee came running up beside him. The coyote, too, cast his gaze into the gorge, yipping and yowling.

Hunter couldn't believe it when he did not see Annabelle's body lying in a broken heap near where Kenneth Earnshaw lay near the crumpled heap of the dead horse and the carriage lying smashed flat, all four wheels broken, spokes flung every which way, on the canyon floor.

Hunter blinked several times in astonishment. No, Annabelle did not lay dead on the canyon floor.

She hung maybe thirty feet straight below him, both hands wrapped around what appeared to be the branch of an ancient, petrified tree jutting six feet out from the canyon's stone wall. She stared wide-eyed up at Hunter, cheeks ashen. The knuckles of her hands wrapped around the end of the petrified branch were as white as snow.

"Hold on!" Hunter shouted.

"Finally you give me some good if overly obvious advice!" Annabelle's thick red hair blew around her head and pale shoulders in the wind. "But this tree isn't gonna hold for long!"

"What?"

"It's not gonna hold, I said!" Desperation had crept into her voice.

Hunter looked at where the tree met the ridge wall. Small rocks and gravel were slithering out around the branch and rolling off down the wall into the canyon. The branch was bending downward, shuddering ever so faintly.

It was slowly crumbling, breaking at the point it protruded from the wall.

Annabelle's scantily clad body shuddered in time with the bending of the disintegrating tree. She'd lost both shoes; she moved both bare feet as though she were treading water.

"All right—I'm comin' down!" Hunter brushed his hat off his head, quickly unbuckled his cartridge belt, and flung it away.

"If so, you'd better hurry!"

"That's always been the main problem with you, Annabelle," he said, his voice quavering with desperation as he kicked out of his boots and whipped off his socks.

"What has?" she said, staring up at him, her round, jade eyes dark with fear.

"You're a harpy."

As Hunter lowered his bare feet into the canyon, turning to face the canyon wall, Bobby Lee mewled and whined and gave Hunter's cheek a couple of licks with his rough tongue as though in encouragement.

"Be right back, Bobby," Hunter said. "Entertain the

guests while I'm away—will you? Don't let the fiddler stop playin'!"

The coyote only canted his head this way and that at him, befuddled, eyes worried. He switched his weight from one foot to the other, whining.

"Some men need a harpy," Annabelle said throatily.

Hunter moved down the nearly sheer wall, grabbing chucks of rock with both his feet and hands, not liking how unstable all his foot- and handholds seemed. Some crumbled clean away and he had to grab another one, not finding that one much more supportive than the former one.

Not good.

He might get down. But would he and Annabelle be able to climb back up again?

He moved quickly, wincing against the scuffs and scrapes to his feet and hands. He glanced up to watch Bobby Lee watching him closely, flicking each ear forward and back at a time, cocking his head this way and that.

Continuing to spider down the wall, rocks and gravel tumbling down from his hands and feet, he glanced down at Annabelle. She gazed up at him, eyes widening when the branch bobbed violently and a crunching sound rose from its base.

More rocks and gravel tumbled away from where the branch met the ridge wall, bouncing against the wall as they tumbled to the canyon floor.

"Oh God," Annabelle said. "Oh God . . . oh God . . ."

"Hold on, honey!"

"Tell it to this damn branch!"

"There's that language again."

She said something far worse.

"Now, you're really making me blush," Hunter quipped,

lowering his right foot, releasing his left hand, lowering his left foot, then his right hand.

Again, the branch bobbed violently.

"Oh God!" Annabelle screamed.

The branch was breaking where it joined the wall, the end that Annabelle was holding on to pitching downward. Hunter set his bare feet on a slender rock ledge, bent his knees, and thrust his hand out toward the end of the branch.

"Grab my hand!"

Annabelle threw her hand toward his just as the branch gave with a sickening crunch. Hunter wrapped his hand around hers and drew her toward him, stretching his lips back from his teeth and grunting fiercely as her weight threatened to pull them both off the wall and into the canyon.

She slammed against the ridge wall and hung there, several feet below him, dangling, kicking her bare legs and thrusting her other hand against the wall, desperately seeking purchase.

"Oh God, oh God!" she panted, staring in bald terror straight up at Hunter.

Digging his bare feet into the rock ledge and clinging to the knob of rock with his left hand, he pulled her up toward him. His right bicep bulged through his shirt-sleeve.

He growled through gritted teeth, "I do believe you've been dining on too much of Big Dan's chili, honey!"

"Some men like a lady with a little curve!" Annabelle cried as he pulled her far enough up toward him that she could place her feet on the ledge. She threw herself against the ridge wall, hugging it like a long-lost friend, right cheek pressed to the uneven surface.

Hunter squeezed her left hand in his right one.

"You all right?"

"No." She was breathing hard and fast.

"Take deep breaths."

"What's that supposed to do?"

"Calm you down."

"I'm not gonna calm down until we're off this wall. There's one thing you don't know about me, Hunter."

"Oh boy—here we go . . ."

"I'm deathly afraid of heights!"

"Honey, in this situation, no one likes heights." Hunter was staring straight up, trying to figure out how he and Annabelle were going to climb the crumbling wall. Bobby Lee was staring down at them, yipping and mewling frantically and pawing at the lip of the ridge as though trying to dig down to them.

All he was doing was tossing sand and gravel down the wall, peppering Hunter's face.

"Thanks for the help, Bobby Lee, but we'll figure somethin' out from our end!"

The coyote stopped pawing and studied him curiously, his eyes bright with worry.

The narrow stone ledge that Hunter and Annabelle were standing on shifted precariously.

Annabelle said, "Oh no!"

Hunter cursed and looked down at the shelf. Just like the petrified tree branch, it was breaking free of the ridge wall.

"We gotta start climbing, honey!"

Hunter reached up and grabbed a knob of rock protruding from the ridge wall above him. It broke free of the wall, bounced off his shoulder, and sailed down into the canyon.

Annabelle reached up, as well—to the same effect.

Again, the ledge shuddered, shifted, the edge facing the canyon angling downward.

Annabelle looked at Hunter, tears in her eyes, sobbing. "Hunter!"

He was thinking the same thing she was: they were doomed.

Buchanon reached out and wrapped his right hand around her neck, drawing her close and pressing his lips to her forehead. "I love you, Annabelle. I always have. I'm sorry I was such a stubborn idiot!"

"I love you, too, Hunter Buchanon—despite your stubborn idiot streak!"

She sobbed. Hunter wrapped his arm around her shoulders, drew her taut against him. The ledge beneath their feet dropped a few more inches, sand and gravel slithering out around it, falling to the canyon floor.

They had maybe ten, fifteen seconds left . . .

"Here, lovebirds!" came a voice from above.

A yielding object smacked Hunter's head and shoulder. He looked up. A broad noose hung down before him and Annabelle. He lifted his gaze beyond the rope toward the crest of the ridge, and blinked in surprise.

Cass Ludlow peered down at him and Annabelle. He lay belly-down two feet to the right of where Bobby Lee sat looking down, as well.

"Cass!" Annabelle exclaimed in surprise.

Ludlow grinned behind his flour sack mask and jerked the rope. "Grab the loop! I got the other end dallied around my saddle horn!"

Hunter had already grabbed the noose. He pulled it

over Annabelle's head first, then his own. He drew the rope up beneath their arms then wrapped his arms around Annabelle. He held her so tightly that she grunted, the air being forced from her lungs. No sooner had he drawn Annabelle to him than the stone ledge gave way beneath their feet.

Annabelle screamed.

Hunter clenched his teeth and looked down at the stone ledge dropping in pieces toward the canyon floor.

"Hold on, honey!" he shouted as he and Annabelle dropped three or four feet before stopping suddenly, the tightening rope cutting into their armpits. They slammed as one against the ridge wall. They hung together, dangling over the canyon, shuddering against the wall.

Suddenly, the rope grew tauter, squeaking with the strain of being pulled from above. Slowly, Hunter and Annabelle began rising, facing each other, their bodies mashed together in a near suffocating embrace. Hunter had turned his back to the wall so that he absorbed the scraping of the flaking stony surface, the rocks and sharp ledges tearing at his shirt.

He and Annabelle gazed deeply, hopefully into each other's eyes.

He had never loved this woman more than he did now, when only seconds ago he'd almost lost her.

Slowly, they inched up the wall, his body dislodging stones and gravel and bits of petrified wood. It all clattered together on the canyon floor, where the horse and carriage and smashed body of Kenneth Earnshaw lay within a fifty-foot radius.

Finally, the lip of the ridge drew to within three feet . . . two feet . . . then they were pulled up over it, Annabelle

on top of Hunter now. Buchanon winced at the scraping
of the canyon's edge against his back. They were drawn
up onto the ground, dragged as one package, still entwined in their lovers' embrace, the rope drawn taut
around them.

The rope grew slack, bowing before them. They
stopped moving.

Bobby Lee had been following them from the lip of the
ridge, yipping and yowling and licking their faces.

Now Hunter lifted the slack rope up over him and
Annabelle, tossed it aside, and closed his mouth over hers.
Lying atop him, her body flat against his, she lifted her
hands to his face and returned his affectionate kiss with
an even hungrier one of her own.

Bobby Lee yipped and ran around the reunited lovers
in joyous circles.

At long last, Buchanon became aware of a fancy-
topped pair of boots standing two feet away from him and
Annabelle, to his left, Annabelle's right. He and Annabelle
looked up at Cass gazing down at them, an ironic expression in his drink-bright eyes.

"Cass!" Annabelle said, rolling off of Hunter and staring up in amazement at her brother.

The question must have been plain in both her and
Hunter's eyes.

Cass shrugged and raised his hands. "You're wonderin'
what possessed me—I know."

"Yes," Annabelle agreed, sitting up, still staring incredulously up at her brother. "*What possessed you to save
our lives?*"

Cass plopped down on his butt before them, shoved

his legs half out, and draped his arms over his knees. "I got no idea."

He tossed a rock as though in frustration. "Well . . . maybe . . . it's just that what I saw in the Reb's eyes back in town was genuine worry. Real love. I guess I had myself hornswoggled. I thought all you two really saw in each other was a way to be bones in ol' Graham's craw. An' mine, as well."

He shook his head and stared at the pair in genuine amazement. "I'll be damned if you two aren't about as gone for each other as two people ever been gone for each other on good ol' mother earth. I just couldn't watch you plunge into that canyon. Not without trying to do something about it." He paused, said softly, "You two have what I'll never have. I was jealous of that. It made me mean and angry. I do apologize."

His eyes were gravely sincere.

Annabelle sobbed and threw herself into her brother's arms, hugging him tight. "Thank you, Cass."

"Same here," Hunter said, reaching out to squeeze the man's arm. "Thank you."

As Annabelle pulled away from him, Cass grimaced and said, "Yeah, well, I'm no saint." He sat with his arms on his knees and looked off for a time. Finally, he turned back to Hunter and Annabelle sitting before him, and said, "I'm the one who stole your gold."

Hunter and Annabelle shared another surprised glance.

"Yeah, I took it, all right." Cass nodded, spat to one side. "I had a devilish notion to head on down Mexico-way and spend your wedding stake." He grinned sardonically. Suddenly, he frowned, perplexed. "I had a whole year to start the trip, but I never got around to goin'. I don't know why. Just the other day I left the ranch. Had a final falling out with Pa and decided it was time to head to Mexico."

He shrugged again, looked off. "Still didn't make it. Just holed up in Tigerville, whoring and drinking. Hell, I'll never go to Mexico. Too tied here. To *him*."

He shook his head.

With a grunt, he gained his feet, dusted off his pants, and turned to his roan horse standing head-to-head with Ghost. He swung up into the leather, then turned to gaze down at the lovers once more.

"It's back near where you cached it. The gold. It's in the root cellar of the old prospector's shack. Don't be too surprised when you see that every grain of dust is still there." Cass gave a wry chuff and shook his head. "Never even bought a drink with it. Not a single one. Don't ask me why."

"I know why," Annabelle said.

Cass raised a curious brow inside his mask.

"Because you have more self-respect than you give yourself credit for. You always have, Cass."

"Oh, I don't know if I'd go that far." Cass laughed and reined his sorrel around, pointing it back in the direction of Tigerville. "Now, if you'll forgive me, I'll just leave you two alone. I got me a date with a fresh bottle of tarantula juice and a dusky-eyed little gal along Poverty Gulch."

Cass winked, nudged spurs to his horse's flanks, and rode away.

Annabelle turned to Hunter.

Neither one said a word for a long time. It was too much to comprehend. They had the gold. They had their marriage stake.

They could get married and rebuild the ranch. They could raise a family out at the 4-Box-B.

Old Angus might even be able to enjoy the view of his beloved Black Hills from his front porch again before he dies.

Annabelle shook her head slowly, her eyes grave, wonder-struck. "I don't know what to say," she whispered.

"Two words will do." Hunter smiled, thumbed a streak of dust from her cheek.

"I do, you big stubborn fool." Annabelle wrapped her arms around him and sobbed. "I do!"

"Always have to defy me, don't you?"

"I do!"

Keep reading for a special excerpt...

PREACHER'S CARNAGE
WILLIAM W. JOHNSTONE
and J. A. JOHNSTONE

In the bloody aftermath of a wagon ambush, a suspect flees, a woman disappears, and a mountain man searches for truth, justice, and revenge. They call him Preacher . . .

Preacher is no hired killer. When a wagon train is brutally ambushed on the Sante Fe Trail, though, he can't say no to the St. Louis businessman willing to pay him for justice. It's not the stolen gold that's convinced Preacher to take the job And it's not the missing body of one of the wagon train's crew, a prime suspect who may have plotted the ambush and taken off with the gold. No, it's the suspect's lovely fiancé, Alita Montez. She believes her boyfriend is innocent—and has run off to find him. Preacher can't abide the idea of a young woman alone on the Sante Fe Trail. If the Comanche don't get her, the coyotes will. And Preacher can't have that.

But to save the girl and get the gold, the legendary mountain man will have to forge a path that's as twisted as a nest of rattlers, face off with trigger-happy kidnappers, backstabbers, and bounty hunters— and match wits with Styles Mallory, the biggest, baddest frontiersman of them all . . .

Look for **PREACHER'S CARNAGE.**
On sale now.

CHAPTER 1

Preacher's arm drew back and then flashed forward. The heavy hunting knife in the mountain man's hand turned over once in mid-air as it flew straight and true through the shadows along the hard-packed dirt street, past the man in the beaver hat.

With Preacher's powerful muscles behind it, the foot of cold steel buried itself in the chest of a man about to fire a pistol into Beaver Hat's back.

The would-be killer grunted and reeled a step to the side. His gun arm sagged. In his death throes, he might have jerked the trigger anyway, but that was a chance Preacher had had to take. He couldn't prevent the callous murder any other way.

The man in the beaver hat might have seen the knife fly past him, or maybe he'd just heard it cutting through the air close to his head. But he heard the grunt of pain behind him and whirled around with surprising speed and grace for a man of his bulk. The cane he carried lifted and came down sharply on the wrist of his assailant's gun hand. The unfired pistol thudded to the street.

Beaver Hat drew the cane back to strike again, but it wasn't necessary. After pawing for a second at the knife in his chest, the assailant's knees buckled. As he fell, Beaver Hat stepped back to give him room to pitch forward on his face.

Beaver Hat turned to face Preacher as the mountain man approached. He lifted his cane and said, "I warn you, sir, if that man is your partner and you intend to continue in the same vein, I shall deal with you harshly."

Preacher said, "Just who you reckon flung that pig-sticker into the varmint's chest, mister?"

"You?"

"Damn right."

Preacher stepped past the man in the beaver hat, hooked a booted toe under the corpse's shoulder, and rolled the dead man onto his back. He reached down, grasped the knife's handle, and pulled the weapon free.

After wiping blood from the blade on the dead man's rough, homespun shirt, Preacher straightened and slid the knife back into the sheath at his belt. He had a pair of flintlock pistols tucked behind that belt as well, but in the poor light, he had trusted his knife more than a gun when he spotted the man about to bushwhack Beaver Hat.

"Should we summon the authorities?" Beaver Hat asked as he looked down disdainfully at the corpse.

"Only if you want to stand around for an hour answerin' some constable's foolish questions. Did you know this fella?"

Beaver Hat leaned forward slightly to study the dead

man's face in the faint light that came from a window in a nearby building.

"I don't believe I've ever seen him before."

"Then he didn't have any personal reason for wantin' to hurt you?"

"I can't imagine what it would be."

Preacher nodded, satisfied by that answer.

"The only explanation that makes any sense is that he planned to kill you, then rob you. A fancy-dressed gent like you, most folks in this part of town would figure you've got money in your pockets."

"So you're saying it's *my* fault this miscreant tried to attack me?" Beaver Hat asked rather testily.

"Take it however you want to," Preacher said. "It don't matter to me."

Beaver Hat stood there frowning for a moment, then said, "Well . . . at any rate . . . I owe you my thanks. I heard someone behind me, but I doubt if I would have been able to turn around and disarm that dolt before he shot me."

"Not hardly," Preacher agreed. "Usually, thieves like him would rather knife their victims or strangle 'em. But I reckon he figured a shot wouldn't draw enough attention around here to worry about. He'd have time to go through your pockets before anybody came to check on things. And shootin' a fella *is* a quicker, simpler way to kill him than those other ways."

"You sound as if you speak from experience."

"Mister," Preacher said, "if there's a way to kill a varmint who needs killin', chances are I've done it."

The man stared at him for a couple of seconds, then

said, "Well, that's an audacious claim, anyway. I still owe you a debt of gratitude, and although a drink hardly has the same value as my life, at least to me, I'd very much like to buy one for you, sir."

"In that case," Preacher said, "I ain't gonna argue, and I know a good place."

Red Mike's Tavern was only a few blocks from the waterfront where the Mississippi River flowed majestically past the settlement of St. Louis.

Actually, calling it a settlement understated the situation. By this time, more than seventy-five years after its founding as a trading post by French fur traders Pierre Laclède and Auguste Chouteau, St. Louis had grown into a full-fledged town. So much so that Preacher, accustomed to the more-lonely reaches of the Rocky Mountains, always felt a mite uneasy among so many people and so many buildings. Not to mention, the air stunk of dead fish, smoke, and unwashed flesh.

However, he had spent some time in New Orleans recently, and that city at the mouth of the Mississippi was ten times worse in every way Preacher could think of.

Red Mike's catered to both rivermen and fur trappers, necessitating an uneasy truce between the two factions. The tavern was as close to a home away from home as Preacher had.

"Judging by all the greetings that were shouted as we came in, it appears that everyone here knows your name," Beaver Hat commented as he and Preacher sat down at a table. Each man had a big mug of beer.

"Maybe so," Preacher allowed, "but that don't mean they're all my friends. I could point out half a dozen fellas in here who wouldn't mind a bit seein' my carcass skinned and the hide hung up to dry."

Beaver Hat shuddered and said, "That's a rather grisly image. I suppose that in your travels you've actually witnessed such things, though."

Preacher shrugged and took a drink from his mug.

Beaver Hat drank, too, and continued, "It occurs to me that we haven't been introduced. My name is Daniel Eckstrom."

"Folks call me Preacher."

Eckstrom was a heavyset man with jowls, side whiskers, and bushy eyebrows. Those eyebrows climbed up his forehead as his eyes widened in surprise.

"Preacher?" he repeated.

"That's right. Do we know each other?"

"No, but I've heard of you. In fact, I ventured into this part of town tonight specifically in search of you."

Preacher frowned and said, "You were lookin' for me?"

"That's right. I inquired among my acquaintances in the fur trading industry as to the identity of a dependable, knowledgeable man of the frontier, and your name came up repeatedly. Well, your *nom de guerre*, as it were. I assume your mother did not name you Preacher."

As a matter of fact, Preacher's mother had named him Arthur, and he had gone by Art during his childhood and adolescence, which had been cut short when he left his family's farm and headed west to see the elephant. After a few detours, including one to New Orleans where he'd fought the bloody British with Andy Jackson's army, he had wound up in the mountains where he had learned the fur trapping business and earned the special enmity of the Blackfoot Indians. An encounter with the Blackfeet that almost cost him his life had resulted in the nickname Preacher, and it had stuck with him ever since, to the point that sometimes he felt like he barely remembered his real name.

He looked darkly across the table at Daniel Eckstrom, who went on, "I was also told that my best chances of locating you would be in this section of town. Several people whose opinions I sought knew that you had been in St. Louis in recent days but weren't sure if you were still here."

"I was fixin' to light a shuck for the mountains pretty soon. Too many people in these parts. I don't cotton much to bein' crowded."

"Then it's fortunate in more ways than one that I encountered you tonight. Not only did you save my life from that robber, but now I can tell you why I wanted to talk to you."

"Yeah, I was a mite curious about that," Preacher said dryly.

"I have a proposition for you," Eckstrom said. "I'd like to hire you."

Preacher nodded slowly as he pondered whether to hear Eckstrom out or grab the man by the collar of his expensive coat, drag him to the door, and boot his rump into the street. This wasn't the first time somebody had sat down with him in Red Mike's and tried to hire him for some chore. Every time he agreed—usually against his better judgment—he'd wound up in a heap of trouble. Every instinct in Preacher's body told him that this time probably wouldn't be any different.

But his curiosity got the better of him, and he said, "What kind of job are we talkin' about?"

"One that involves a considerable amount of gold coin," Eckstrom replied smoothly. "And the distinct possibility that you might encounter one or more of those . . . how did you phrase it? . . . varmints who need killin'."

CHAPTER 2

More intrigued than he wanted to be, Preacher took another healthy swallow of his beer and told Eckstrom, "Go on."

"I'm a businessman, as you probably surmised."

"In that outfit, I didn't take you for a keelboater."

"I have an interest in several enterprises here in St. Louis," Eckstrom continued as if he hadn't heard Preacher's comment, "but a partner and I also own a retail establishment . . . a general store, if you will . . . in Santa Fe, a town in the Mexican province of Nuevo Mexico."

Preacher nodded and said, "I know Santa Fe. Been there quite a few times."

"I'm aware of that fact. That was another question I asked of my acquaintances. I wanted a man who knew the ground, so to speak."

Eckstrom was the bush-beating sort, Preacher realized, and you couldn't hurry those fellas. He sat back and waited for Eckstrom to go on.

"My partner is a man named Armando Montez," Eckstrom went on. "A native of Santa Fe and a man of impeccable character. I supply the goods, sending wagon trains full of merchandise several times a year to Santa Fe, where Señor Montez sells them and we divide the profits equally. Twice a year, he sends me my share, in the form of gold coins, sending them back with the empty wagons since those wagon trains are always well guarded against the brigands who lurk along the Santa Fe Trail."

"Plenty of outlaws along the Santa Fe Trail, all right," Preacher said, "along with Kiowa and Comanch'. It's rugged country."

The mountain man recalled a journey he had made along the Santa Fe Trail a few years earlier, accompanying a wagon train full of immigrants. They had run into plenty of trouble along the way, including a huge grizzly bear that had seemed hellbent on killing Preacher.

"In order to make the whole process safer," Eckstrom said, "no one knows exactly which trip will contain one of those money shipments except myself, Señor Montez, and his assistant, a young man named Toby Harper."

Preacher had told himself to be patient, but his restraint was starting to wear thin. He drained the rest of his beer, signaled to Red Mike behind the bar for another, and then said, "From the way you were talkin' a few minutes ago, I'm guessin' something happened to one of those shipments."

Eckstrom sighed heavily and nodded.

"Indeed it did. The last time Armando sent my share to me, the wagon train was ambushed and the gold was stolen. All the men traveling with the wagons were slain . . . with the exception of Toby Harper. He seems to have, ah, disappeared."

Preacher cocked an eyebrow and said, "Sounds to me

like this fella Harper set up the whole deal and was behind the ambush."

"Armando refuses to believe that. Harper was his assistant for several years, and Armando insists that he is absolutely trustworthy."

"You don't believe that, though," Preacher said.

"I've met the young man only twice. He seemed genuine enough, but no, in the face of the evidence, I have no reason to believe he's honest. However, Armando has another reason for feeling the way he does: Toby Harper was supposed to become his son-in-law. The young man is engaged to marry Armando's daughter Alita."

One of the serving girls brought Preacher's beer over and set the mug on the table in front of the mountain man. She bent forward as she did so, giving him an enticing view and a suggestive smile. Preacher was too rugged to ever be considered handsome, but the ladies seemed to like him anyway.

Normally he might have been happy to spend what he'd expected to be his last night in St. Louis with this gal, but he'd gotten interested in Daniel Eckstrom's story and wanted to hear more. So he returned the serving girl's smile but without any sort of commitment in the expression.

The girl recognized that and flounced away in mingled annoyance and disappointment. Preacher said to Eckstrom, "I can see why your partner don't want to believe the worst of Harper. It's possible there's some other reason his body wasn't with the others. If Injuns jumped that wagon train, they could've carried him off, plannin' to take him back to their camp and torture him to death."

"Would the savages do such a thing?"

Preacher shrugged and said, "Kiowa and Comanch' ain't as bad about that as some of the other tribes, like the Blackfeet up north or the Apache farther west, but it's been known to happen."

"Isn't it just as likely he arranged the whole thing and is responsible not only for the loss of the gold but the deaths of all those other men, as well?"

"Based on what you've told me . . . yeah, I reckon it is. But what you *haven't* told me, Mr. Eckstrom, is what you want me to do about it."

"Naturally, quite a bit of time has passed since this occurred. Communication between here and Santa Fe is not swift, needless to say. But before the trail gets any . . . colder, isn't that how you'd say it? . . . Before the trail gets any colder, I need a good man to take it up, find Toby Harper, and discover the truth of his involvement, and recover that gold. And if Harper *is* to blame and the gold *can't* be recovered . . . then my representative can deliver some justice for those men who were murdered by killing Toby Harper."

For a long moment, Preacher didn't respond. He just sat there looking across the table at Eckstrom, his fresh mug of beer forgotten for now.

Finally he said, "That's putting it mighty plain."

"I'm a plain-spoken man," Eckstrom said.

For the most part, that wasn't true, Preacher thought. Eckstrom was a man who loved the sound of his own voice. But clearly he knew when to be blunt, too.

The mountain man shook his head and said, "I'm not a hired killer, mister. If you'd said what you just did to any

of the folks you asked about me, they'd have told you that.
You'll have to find yourself somebody else."

"From what I've heard, there *isn't* anyone else with
your skills. Besides, I'm more interested in recovering
those gold coins than in settling the score with Harper."

Preacher took a long swallow from the mug and
thumped it back down on the table.

"Nope. My gut says this is something I don't want to
get mixed up in, and I'm old enough to have learned to
listen to it."

Eckstrom leaned forward and said, "There's actually
more at stake than I've mentioned so far."

"I don't reckon there's anything you could say that
would change—"

"What about a young woman's life being in danger?"

Preacher's eyebrows lowered. He said, "You must be
talkin' about that gal who's your partner's daughter."

"Alita Montez," Eckstrom confirmed.

"I can see why she'd be mighty upset that the fella she
figured on gettin' hitched with has disappeared and is
mostly likely dead. And if he ain't dead, that means he's
probably turned outlaw. But I don't see how that puts her
life in danger."

"The last letter I received from Armando," Eckstrom
said, "he told me that Alita was determined to prove
Harper's innocence. He fears that she plans to launch a
search of her own for him. A couple of the men who work
for him are fiercely devoted to her, and she would have
no trouble convincing them to accompany her." The businessman spread his hands. "Given the lag in communications, it's entirely possible that she's already set out from

Santa Fe by now, even though her father assured me that he intends to keep a close eye on her. In my experience, it's quite difficult to keep a determined woman from doing what she wants to do."

Preacher grunted and said, "You're right about that. But you don't know for sure she's gone to look for Harper."

"Indeed, I don't. But the possibility certainly exists. She could be out there now, somewhere along the Santa Fe Trail—"

"All right, all right," Preacher interrupted him. "You done made your point."

"Sufficiently to persuade you to accept the proposition?"

"Well, you ain't exactly *made* a proposition yet, because you ain't said anything about what's in this for me."

Eckstrom placed both hands flat on the table and said, "Half of whatever money you recover."

"What if it's all gone?"

"Then you'll have the satisfaction of knowing that you did the right thing. And, as I said, perhaps will have dealt with the man responsible for committing such a foul act. So, you see, I'm not offering to pay you for killing Toby Harper. Not exactly."

Preacher made a little growling sound deep in his throat and said, "You talk around and around a thing, mister, until I ain't sure just what it is you're sayin'. But if there's a chance there's a gal out there gettin' herself into trouble—"

"A very good chance, I'd say."

"Then I can't hardly turn my back on the deal. Just out

of curiosity, though . . . how much money are you talkin' about?"

"Armando sent me approximately two thousand dollars with the wagon train. So your share of the recovered funds could be as much as a thousand."

Preacher kept his face impassive, but he was impressed. One thousand dollars was a lot of money. More than he'd ever made in a season of trapping furs. After hearing about the girl, he'd already been leaning toward accepting the job from Eckstrom, but the chance of such a windfall clinched the deal.

Not that he would live his life any differently if he had that much money, he told himself. As long as he had enough for supplies to get him to the mountains, that was really all he needed. He could live off the land as well as the Indians.

Might be nice to spend some time in Santa Fe with plenty of *dinero*, though, he mused. There was a cantina there he liked almost as much as Red Mike's, as well as a few señoritas who had professed undying devotion to him. And then, when the money started to run low, he could get himself an outfit and head north through the Sangre de Cristos toward the big ranges of the Rockies. That was where he'd wanted to wind up all along.

Eckstrom was watching him with an eager expression on his beefy face. Preacher said, "All right. The way I see it, I'm goin' after three things: the money, the girl—if she's there—and the truth."

"If you find all three," Eckstrom said, "you'll have definitely earned your reward!"

"You are such *a jerk, Lieutenant Catalanotto!" Veronica snapped.*

"Why can't you take me seriously for one damned minute? Or are you *trying* to foul this up, so you won't have to place yourself in danger?"

Joe's smile disappeared instantly, and Veronica knew with deadly certainty that she'd gone too far. He took a step toward her, and she took a step back. He was very tall, very broad—and *very* angry.

Then he reached out and, with one finger underneath her chin, lifted her head so that she was forced to look up into his eyes.

The connection was there between them again—instant and hot. The look in his eyes was mesmerizing. It erased everything—all the angry words, all the misunderstandings—and left only this almost primitive attraction, this simplest of equations. Man plus woman.

"You're wrong, Veronica," he murmured. "I take you *very* seriously...."

Dear Reader,

We've got some great reading for you this month, but I'll bet you already knew that. Suzanne Carey is back with *Whose Baby?* The title already tells you that a custody battle is at the heart of this story, but it's Suzanne's name that guarantees all the emotional intensity you want to find between the covers.

Maggie Shayne's *The Littlest Cowboy* launches a new miniseries this month, THE TEXAS BRAND. These rough, tough, ranchin' Texans will win your heart, just as Sheriff Garrett Brand wins the hearts of lovely Chelsea Brennan and her tiny nephew. If you like mysterious and somewhat spooky goings-on, you'll love Marcia Evanick's *His Chosen Bride*, a marriage-of-convenience story with a paranormal twist. Clara Wimberly's hero in *You Must Remember This* is a mysterious stranger—mysterious even to himself, because his memory is gone and he has no idea who he is or what has brought him to Sarah James's door. One thing's for certain, though: it's love that keeps him there. In *Undercover Husband*, Leann Harris creates a heroine who thinks she's a widow, then finds out she might not be when a handsome—and somehow familiar—stranger walks through her door. Finally, I know you'll love *Prince Joe*, the hero of Suzanne Brockmann's new book, part of her TALL, DARK AND DANGEROUS miniseries. This is a royal impostor story, with a rough-around-the-edges hero who suddenly has to wear the crown.

Don't miss a single one of these exciting books, and come back next month for more of the best romance around—only in Silhouette Intimate Moments.

Yours,

Leslie Wainger

Leslie Wainger
Senior Editor and Editorial Coordinator

PRINCE JOE

SUZANNE
BROCKMANN

Published by Silhouette Books
America's Publisher of Contemporary Romance

SILHOUETTE BOOKS

ISBN 0-373-07720-3

PRINCE JOE

Copyright © 1996 by Suzanne Brockmann

This edition published by arrangement with Harlequin Books S.A.

Printed in U.S.A.

Books by Suzanne Brockmann

Silhouette Intimate Moments

Hero Under Cover #575
Not Without Risk #647
A Man To Die For #681
*Prince Joe #720

*Tall, Dark and Dangerous

SUZANNE BROCKMANN

wrote her first romance novel in 1992, and fell in love with the genre. She writes full-time, along with singing and arranging music for her professional a cappella singing group called Vocomotive, organizing a monthly benefit coffeehouse at her church and managing the acting careers of her two young children, Melanie and Jason. She and her family are living happily ever after in a small town outside of Boston.

For Eric Ruben, my swim buddy.

Prologue

Baghdad, January 1991

Friendly fire.

It was called friendly because it came from U.S. bombers and missile launchers, but it sure as hell didn't feel friendly to Navy SEAL Lieutenant Joe Catalanotto, as it fell from the sky like deadly rain. Friendly or not, an American bomb was still a bomb, and it would indiscriminately destroy anything in its path. Anything, or anyone, between the U.S. Air Force bombers and their military targets was in serious danger.

And SEAL Team Ten's seven-man Alpha Squad was definitely between the bombers and their targets. They were deep behind enemy lines, damn near sitting on top of a factory known to manufacture ammunition.

Joe Catalanotto, commander of the Alpha Squad, glanced up from the explosives he and Blue and Cowboy were rigging against the Ustanzian Embassy wall. The city was lit up all around them, fires and explosions hellishly illuminating the night sky. It seemed unnatural, unreal.

Except it was real. Damn, it was *way* real. It was dangerous with a capital *D*. Even if Alpha Squad wasn't hit by
friendly fire, Joe and his men ran the risk of bumping into
a platoon of enemy soldiers. Hell, if they were captured,
commando teams like the SEALs were often treated like
spies and executed—after being tortured for information.

But this was their job. This was what Navy SEALs were
trained to do. And all of Joe's men in Alpha Squad per-
formed their tasks with clockwork precision and cool confidence. This wasn't the first time they'd had to perform a
rescue mission in a hot war zone. And it sure as hell wasn't
going to be the last.

Joe started to whistle as he handled the plastic explosives, and Cowboy—otherwise known as Ensign Harlan
Jones from Fort Worth, Texas—looked up in disbelief.

"Cat works better when he's whistling," Blue explained
to Cowboy over his headset microphone. "Drove me nuts
all through training—until I got used to it. You *do* get used
to it."

"Terrific," Cowboy muttered, handing Joe part of the
fuse.

His hands were shaking.

Joe glanced up at the younger man. Cowboy was new to
the squad. He was scared, but he was fighting that fear, his
jaw tight and his teeth clenched. His hands might be shaking, but the kid was doing his job—he was sticking it out.

Cowboy glared back at Joe, daring him to comment.

So of course, Joe did. "Air raids make you clausty, huh,
Jones?" he said. He had to shout to be heard. Sirens were
wailing and bells were ringing and antiaircraft fire was
hammering all over Baghdad. And of course there was also
the brain-deafening roar of the American bombs that were
vaporizing entire city blocks all around them. Yeah, they
were in the middle of a damned war.

Cowboy opened his mouth to speak, but Joe didn't let
him. "I know how you're feeling," Joe shouted as he put
the finishing touches on the explosives that would drill one
mother of a hole into the embassy foundation. "Give me a
chopper jump into cold water, give me a parachute drop
from thirty thousand feet, give me a fourteen-mile swim,

hell, give me hand-to-hand with a religious zealot. But this... I gotta tell you, kid, inserting into Baghdad with these hundred-pounders falling through the sky is making me a little clausty myself."

Cowboy snorted. "Clausty?" he said. "You? Shoot, Mr. Cat, if there's anything on earth *you're* afraid of, they haven't invented it yet."

"Working with nukes," Joe said. "That sure as hell gives me the creeps."

"Me, too," Blue chimed in.

The kid wasn't impressed. "You guys know a SEAL who *isn't* freaked out by disarming nuclear weapons, and I'll show you someone too stupid to wear the trident pin."

"All done," Joe said, allowing himself a tight smile of satisfaction. They'd blow this hole open, go in, grab the civilians and be halfway to the extraction point before ten minutes had passed. And it wouldn't be a moment too soon. What he'd told Ensign Jones was true. Jesus, Mary and Joseph, but he hated air raids.

Blue McCoy stood and hand-signaled a message to the rest of the team, in case they'd missed hearing Joe's announcement in the din.

The ground shook as a fifty-pound bomb landed in the neighborhood, and Blue met Joe's eyes and grinned as Cowboy swore a blue streak.

Joe laughed and lit the fuse.

"Thirty seconds," he told Blue, who held up the right number of fingers for the rest of the SEALs to see. The squad scrambled to the other side of the street for cover.

When a bomb is about to go off, Joe thought, there's always a moment, sometimes just a tiny one, when everything seems to slow down and wait. He looked at the familiar faces of his men, and he could see the adrenaline that pumped through them in their eyes, in the set of their mouths and jaws. They were good men, and as always, he was going to do his damnedest to see that they got out of this city alive. Forget alive—he was going to get them out of this hellhole untouched.

Joe didn't need to look at the second hand on his watch. He knew it was coming, despite the fact that time had seemed to slow down and stretch wa-a-a-ay out....

Boom.

It was a big explosion, but Joe barely heard it over the sounds of the other, more powerful explosions happening all over the city.

Before the dust even settled, Blue was on point, leading the way across the war-torn street, alert for snipers and staying low. He went headfirst into the neat little crater they had blown into the side of the Ustanzian Embassy.

Harvard was on radio, and he let air support know they were going in. Joe was willing to bet big money that the air force was too busy to pay Alpha Squad any real attention. But Harvard was doing his job, same as the rest of the SEALs. They were a team. Seven men—seven of the armed forces' best and brightest—trained to work and fight together, to the death if need be.

Joe followed Blue and Bobby into the embassy basement. Cowboy came in after, leaving Harvard and the rest of the team guarding their backsides.

It was darker than hell inside. Joe slipped his night-vision glasses on just in time. He narrowly missed running smack into Bobby's back and damn near breaking his nose on the shotgun the big man wore holstered along his spine.

"Hold up," Bob signaled.

He had his NVs on, too. So did Blue and Cowboy.

They were alone down there, except for the spiders and snakes and whatever else was slithering along the hard dirt floor.

"Damned layout's wrong. There's supposed to be a flight of stairs," Joe heard Blue mutter, and he stepped forward to take a look. Damn, they had a problem here.

Joe pulled the map of the embassy from the front pocket of his vest, even though he'd long since memorized the basement's floor plan. The map in his hands was of an entirely different building than the one they were standing in. It was probably the Ustanzian Embassy in some other city, in some country on the other side of the damned globe. Damn! Someone had really screwed up here.

Blue was watching him, and Joe knew his executive officer was thinking what *he* was thinking. The desk-riding genius responsible for securing the floor plan of this embassy was going to have a very bad day in about a week. Maybe less. Because the commander and XO of SEAL Team Ten's Alpha Squad were going to pay him a little visit.

But right now, they had a problem on their hands.

There were three hallways, leading into darkness. Not a stairway in sight.

"Wesley and Frisco," Blue ordered in his thick Southern drawl. "Get your butts in here, boys. We need split teams. Wes with Bobby. Frisco, stay with Cowboy. I'm with you, Cat."

Swim buddies. Blue had read Joe's mind and done the smartest thing. With the exception of Frisco, who was baby-sitting the new kid, Cowboy, he'd teamed each man up with the guy he knew best—his swim buddy. In fact, Blue and Joe went back all the way to Hell Week. Guys who do Hell Week together—that excruciating weeklong torturous SEAL endurance test—stay tight. No question about it.

Off they went, night-vision glasses still on, looking like some kind of weird aliens from outer space. Wesley and Bobby went left. Frisco and Cowboy took the right corridor. And Joe, with Blue close behind him, went straight ahead.

They were silent now, and Joe could hear each man's quiet breathing over his headset's earphones. He moved slowly, carefully, checking automatically for booby traps or any hint of movement ahead.

"Supply room," Joe heard Cowboy breathe into his headset's microphone.

"Ditto," Bobby whispered. "We got canned goods and a wine cellar. No movement, no life."

Joe caught sight of the motion the same instant Blue did. Simultaneously, they flicked the safeties of their MP5s down to full fire and dropped into a crouch.

They'd found the stairs going up.

And there, underneath the stairs, scared witless and shaking like a leaf in a hurricane, was the crown prince of

Ustanzia, Tedric Cortere, using three of his aides as sand-
bags.

"Don't shoot," Cortere said in four or five different languages, his hands held high above his head.

Joe straightened, but he kept his gun raised until he saw
all four pairs of hands were empty. Then he pulled his NVs
from his face, squinting as his eyes adjusted to the dim red
glow of a penlight Blue had pulled from his pocket.

"Good evening, Your Royal Highness," he said. "I am
Navy SEAL Lieutenant Joe Catalanotto, and I'm here to get
you out."

"Contact," Harvard said into the radio, having heard
Joe's royal greeting to the prince via his headset. "We have
made contact. Repeat, we have picked up luggage and are
heading for home plate."

That was when Joe heard Blue laugh.

"Cat," the XO drawled. "Have you looked at this guy?
I mean, Joe, have you really looked?"

A bomb hit about a quarter mile to the east, and Prince
Tedric tried to burrow more deeply in among his equally
frightened aides.

If the prince had been standing, he would have been about
Joe's height, maybe a little shorter.

He was wearing a torn white satin jacket, reminiscent of
an Elvis impersonator. The garment was amazingly tacky.
It was adorned with gold epaulets, and there was an entire
row of medals and ribbons on the chest—for bravery under
enemy fire, no doubt. His pants were black, and grimy with
soot and dirt.

But it wasn't the prince's taste in clothing that made Joe's
mouth drop open. It was the man's face.

Looking at the Crown Prince of Ustanzia was like looking into a mirror. His dark hair was longer than Joe's, but
beyond that, the resemblance was uncanny. Dark eyes, big
nose, long face, square jaw, heavy cheekbones.

The guy looked exactly like Joe.

Chapter 1

A few years later
Washington, D.C.

All of the major network news cameras were rolling as Tedric Cortere, crown prince of Ustanzia, entered the airport.

A wall of ambassadors, embassy aides and politicians moved forward to greet him, but the prince paused for just a moment, taking the time to smile and wave a greeting to the cameras.

He was following her instructions to the letter. Veronica St. John, professional image and media consultant, allowed herself a sigh of relief. But only a small one, because she knew Tedric Cortere very well, and he was a perfectionist. There was no guarantee that Prince Tedric, the brother of Veronica's prep-school roommate and very best friend in the world, was going to be satisfied with what he saw tonight on the evening news.

Still, he would have every right to be pleased. It was day one of his United States goodwill tour, and he was looking his best, oozing charm and royal manners, with just enough blue-blooded arrogance thrown in to captivate the royalty-crazed American public. He was remembering to gaze directly into the news cameras. He was keeping his eye movements steady and his chin down. And, heaven be praised, for a man prone to anxiety attacks, he was looking calm and collected for once.

He was giving the news teams exactly what they wanted—a close-up picture of a gracious, charismatic, fairy-tale-handsome European prince.

Bachelor. She'd forgotten to add "bachelor" to the list. And if Veronica knew Americans—and she did; it was her business to know Americans—millions of American women would watch the evening news tonight and dream of becoming a princess.

There was nothing like fairy-tale fever among the public to boost relations between two governments. Fairy-tale fever—and the recently discovered oil that lay beneath the parched, gray Ustanzian soil.

But Tedric wasn't the only one playing to the news cameras this morning.

As Veronica watched, United States Senator Sam McKinley flashed his gleaming white teeth in a smile so falsely genuine and so obviously aimed at the reporters, it made her want to laugh.

But she didn't laugh. If she'd learned one thing during her childhood and adolescence as the daughter of an international businessman who moved to a different and often exotic country every year or so, she'd learned that diplomats and high government officials—particularly royalty—take themselves very, *very* seriously.

So, instead of laughing, she bit the insides of her cheeks as she stopped several respectful paces behind the prince, at the head of the crowd of assistants and aides and advisers who were part of his royal entourage.

"Your Highness, on behalf of the United States Government," McKinley drawled in his thick Texas accent, shaking the prince's hand, and dripping with goodwill, "I'd like to welcome you to our country's capital."

"I greet you with the timeless honor and tradition of the Ustanzian flag," Prince Tedric said formally in his faintly British, faintly French accent, "which is woven, as well, into my heart."

It was his standard greeting; nothing special, but it went over quite well with the crowd.

McKinley started in on a longer greeting, and Veronica let her attention wander.

She could see herself in the airport's reflective glass windows, looking cool in her cream-colored suit, her flame-red hair pulled neatly back into a French braid. Tall and slender and serene, her image wavered slightly as a jet plane took off, thundering down the runway.

It was an illusion. Actually, she was giddy with nervous excitement, a condition brought about by the stress of knowing that if Tedric didn't follow her instructions and ended up looking bad on camera, she'd be the one to blame. Sweat trickled down between her shoulder blades, another side effect of the stress she was under. No, she felt neither cool nor serene, regardless of how she looked.

She had been hired because her friend, Princess Wila, knew that Veronica was struggling to get her fledgling consulting business off the ground. Sure, she'd done smaller, less detailed jobs before, but this was the first one in which the stakes were so very high. If Veronica succeeded with Tedric Cortere, word would get out, and she'd have more business than she could handle. *If* she succeeded with Cortere...

But Veronica had also been hired for another reason. She'd been hired because Wila, concerned about Ustanzia's economy, recognized the importance of this tour. Despite the fact that teaching Wila's brother, the high-strung Prince of Ustanzia, how to appear calm and relaxed while under the watchful eyes of the TV news cameras was Veronica's first major assignment as an image and media consultant, Wila trusted her longtime friend implicitly to get the job done.

"I'm counting on you, Véronique," Wila had said to Veronica over the telephone just last night. She had added with her customary frankness, "This American connection is too important. Don't let Tedric screw this up."

So far Tedric was doing a good job. He looked good. He sounded good. But it was too early for Veronica to let herself feel truly satisfied. It was her job to make sure that the prince *continued* to look and sound good.

Tedric didn't particularly like his younger sister's best friend, and the feeling was mutual. He was an impatient, short-tempered man, and rather used to getting his own way. *Very* used to getting his own way.

Veronica could only hope he would see today's news reports and recognize the day's success. If he didn't, she'd hear about it, that was for sure.

Veronica knew quite well that over the course of the prince's tour of the United States she was going to earn every single penny of her consultant's fee. Because although Tedric Cortere was princely in looks and appearance, he was also arrogant and spoiled. And demanding. And often irrational. And occasionally, not very nice.

Oh, he knew his social etiquette. He was in his element when it came to pomp and ceremony, parties and other social posturing. He knew all there was to know about clothing and fashion. He could tell Japanese silk from American with a single touch. He was a wine connoisseur and a gourmet. He could ride horses and fence, play polo and waterski. He hired countless aides and advisers to dance attendance upon him, and provide him with both his most trivial desires and the important information he needed to get by as a representative of his country.

As Veronica watched, Tedric shook the hands of the U.S. officials. He smiled charmingly and she could practically hear the sound of the news cameras zooming in for a close-up.

The prince glanced directly into the camera lenses and let his smile broaden. Spoiled or not, with his trim, athletic body and handsome face, the man was good-looking.

Good-looking? No, Veronica thought. To call him good-looking wasn't accurate. Quite honestly, the prince was gorgeous. He was a piece of art. He had long, thick, dark hair that curled down past his shoulders. His face was long and lean with exotic cheekbones that hinted of his mother's Mediterranean heritage. His eyes were the deepest brown, surrounded by sinfully long lashes. His jaw was square, his nose strong and masculine.

But Veronica had known Tedric since she was fifteen and he was nineteen. Naturally, she'd developed a full-fledged crush on him quite early on, but it hadn't taken her long to realize that the prince was nothing like his cheerful, breezy, lighthearted yet business-minded sister. Tedric was, in fact, quite decidedly dull—and enormously preoccupied with his appearance. He had spent endless amounts of time in front of a mirror, sending Wila and Veronica into spasms of giggles as he combed his hair, flexed his muscles and examined his perfect, white teeth.

Still, Veronica's crush on Prince Tedric hadn't truly crashed and burned until she'd had a conversation with him—and seen that beneath his facade of princely charm and social skills, behind his handsome face and trim body, deep within his dark brown eyes, there was nothing there.

Nothing *she* was interested in, anyway.

Although she had to admit that to this day, her romantic vision of a perfect man was someone tall, dark and handsome. Someone with wide, exotic cheekbones and liquid brown eyes. Someone who looked an awful lot like Crown Prince Tedric, but with a working brain in his head and a heart that loved more than his own reflection in the mirror.

She wasn't looking for a prince. In fact, she wasn't looking, period. She had no time for romance—at least, not until her business started to turn a profit.

As the military band began to play a rousing rendition of the Ustanzian national anthem, Veronica glanced again at their blurry images in the window. A flash of light from the upper-level balcony caught her eye. *That was odd.* She'd been told that airport personnel would be restricting access to the second floor as a security measure.

She turned her head to look up at the balcony and realized with a surge of disbelief that the flash she'd seen was a reflection of light bouncing off the long barrel of a rifle—a rifle aimed directly at Tedric.

"Get down!" Veronica shouted, but her voice was drowned out by the trumpets. The prince couldn't hear her. No one could hear her.

She ran toward Prince Tedric and all of the U.S. dignitaries, well aware that she was running toward, not away from, the danger. A thought flashed crazily through her head—*This was not a man worth dying for.* But she couldn't stand by and let her best friend's brother be killed. Not while she had the power to prevent it.

As a shot rang out, Veronica hit Tedric bone-jarringly hard at waist level and knocked him to the ground. It was a rugby tackle that would have made her brother Jules quite proud.

She bruised her shoulder, tore her nylons and scraped both of her knees when she fell.

But she saved the crown prince of Ustanzia's life.

When Veronica walked into the hotel conference room, it was clear the meeting had been going on for quite some time.

Senator McKinley was sitting at one end of the big oval conference table with his jacket off, his tie loosened, and his shirtsleeves rolled up. Henri Freder, the U.S. ambassador to Ustanzia, sat on one side of him. Another diplomat and several other men whom Veronica didn't recognize sat on the other. Men in dark suits stood at the doors and by the windows, watchful and alert. They were FInCOM agents, Veronica realized, high-tech bodyguards from the Federal Intelligence Commission, sent to protect the prince. But why were they involved? Was Prince Tedric's life still in danger?

Tedric was at the head of the table, surrounded by a dozen aides and advisers. He had a cold drink in front of him, and was lazily drawing designs in the condensation on the glass.

As Veronica entered the room, Tedric stood, and the entire tableful of men followed suit.

"Someone get a seat for Ms. St. John," the prince ordered sharply in his odd accent. "Immediately."

One of the lesser aides quickly stepped away from his own chair and offered it to Veronica.

"Thank you," she said, smiling at the young man.

"Sit down," the prince commanded her, stony-faced, as he returned to his seat. "I have an idea, but it cannot be done without your cooperation."

Veronica gazed steadily at the prince. After she'd tackled him earlier today, he'd been dragged away to safety. She hadn't seen or heard from him since. At the time, he hadn't bothered to thank her for saving his life—and apparently he had no intention of doing so now. She was working for him, therefore she was a servant. He would have expected her to save him. In his mind, there was no need for gratitude.

But she wasn't a servant. In fact, she'd been the maid of honor last year when his sister married Veronica's brother, Jules. Veronica and the prince were practically family, yet Tedric still insisted she address him as "Your Highness," or "Your Majesty."

She sat down, pulling her chair in closer to the table, and the rest of the men sat, too.

"I have a double," the prince announced. "An American. It is my idea for him to take my place throughout the remaining course of the tour, thus ensuring my safety."

Veronica sat forward. "Excuse me, Your Highness," she said. "Please forgive my confusion. Is your safety still an issue?" She looked down the table at Senator McKinley. "Wasn't the gunman captured?"

McKinley ran his tongue over his front teeth before he answered. "I'm afraid not," he finally replied. "And the Federal Intelligence Commission has reason to believe the terrorists will make another attempt on the prince's life during the course of the next few weeks."

"Terrorists?" Veronica repeated, looking from McKinley to the ambassador and finally at Prince Tedric.

"FInCOM has ID'd the shooter," McKinley answered. "He's a well-known triggerman for a South American terrorist organization."

Veronica shook her head. "Why would South American terrorists want to kill the Ustanzian crown prince?"

The ambassador took off his glasses and tiredly rubbed his eyes. "Quite possibly in retaliation for Ustanzia's new alliance with the U.S.," he said.

"FInCOM tells us these particular shooters don't give up easily," McKinley said. "Even with souped-up security, FInCOM expects they'll try again. What we're looking to do is find a solution to this problem."

Veronica laughed. It slipped out—she couldn't help herself. The solution was so obvious. "Cancel the tour."

"Can't do that," McKinley drawled.

Veronica looked down the other side of the table at Prince Tedric. He, for once, was silent. But he didn't look happy.

"There's too much riding on the publicity from this event," Senator McKinley explained. "You know as well as I do that Ustanzia needs U.S. funding to get their oil wells up and running." The heavyset man leaned back in his chair, tapping the eraser end of a pencil on the mahogany table. "But the prospect of competitively priced oil isn't enough to secure the size funds they need," he continued, dropping the pencil and running his hand through his thinning gray hair. "And quite frankly, current polls show the public's concern for a little-nothing country like Ustanzia—beg pardon, Prince—to be zilch. Hardly anyone knows who the Ustanzians are, and the folks who *do* know about 'em don't want to give 'em any of their tax dollars, that's for sure as shootin'. Not while there's so much here at home to spend the money on."

Veronica nodded her head. She was well aware of everything he was saying. It was one of Princess Wila's major worries.

"Besides," the senator added, "we can use this opportunity to nab this group of terrorists. And sister, if they're who we think they are, we want 'em. Bad."

"But if you know for a fact that there'll be another assassination attempt...?" Veronica looked down the table at Tedric. "Your Majesty, how can you risk placing yourself in such danger?"

Tedric crossed his legs. "I have no intention of placing myself in any danger whatsoever," he said. "In fact, I will remain here, in Washington, in a safe house, until all danger has passed. The tour, however, will continue as planned, with this lookalike fellow taking my place."

Suddenly the prince's earlier words made sense. He'd said he had a double, someone who looked just like him. He'd said this person was an American.

"This man," McKinley asked. "What was his name, sir?"

The prince shrugged—a slow, eloquent gesture. "How should I remember? Joe. Joe Something. He was a soldier. An American soldier."

"'Joe Something,'" McKinley repeated, exchanging a quick, exasperated look with the diplomat on his left. "A soldier named Joe. Should only be about fifteen thousand men in the U.S. armed forces named Joe."

The ambassador on McKinley's right leaned forward. "Your Highness," he said patiently, "when did you meet this man?"

"He was one of the soldiers who assisted in my escape from the embassy in Baghdad," Tedric replied.

"A Navy SEAL," the ambassador murmured to McKinley. "We should have no problem locating him. If I remember correctly, only one seven-man team participated in that rescue mission."

"SEAL?" Veronica asked, sitting up and leaning forward. "What's a SEAL?"

"Part of the Special Forces Division," Senator McKinley told her. "They're *the* most elite special-operations force in the world. They can operate anywhere—on the sea, in the air and on the land, hence the name, SEALs. If this man who looks so much like the prince really is a SEAL, standing in as the prince's double will be a cakewalk for him."

"He was, however, quite unbearably lower-class," the prince said prudishly, sweeping some imaginary crumbs from the surface of the table. He looked at Veronica. "That is where you would come in. You will teach this Joe to look and act like a prince. We can delay the tour by—" he frowned down the table at McKinley "—a week, is that what you'd said?"

"Two or three days at the very most, sir." The senator grimaced. "We can announce that you've come down with the flu, try to keep up public interest with reports of your health. But the fact is, after a few days, you'll no longer be news and the story will be dropped. You know what they say: Out of sight, out of mind. We can't let that happen."

Two or three days. Two or three days to turn a rough American sailor—a Navy SEAL, whatever that really meant—into royalty. Who were they kidding?

Senator McKinley picked up the phone to begin tracking down the mysterious Joe.

Prince Tedric was watching Veronica expectantly. "Can you do it?" he asked. "Can you make this Joe into a prince?"

"In two or three *days?*"

Tedric nodded.

"I'd have to work around the clock," Veronica said, thinking aloud. If she agreed to this crazy plan, she would have to be right beside this sailor, this SEAL, every single step of the way. She'd have to coach him continuously, and be ready to catch and correct his every mistake. "And even then, there'd be no guarantee...."

Tedric shrugged, turning back to Ambassador Freder. "She can't do it," he said flatly. "We *will* have to cancel. Arrange a flight back to—"

"I didn't say I couldn't do it," Veronica interrupted, quickly adding, "Your Majesty."

The prince turned back to her, one elegant eyebrow raised.

Veronica could hear an echo of Wila's voice. "I'm counting on you, Véronique. This American connection is too important." If this tour were canceled, all of Wila's hopes for the future would evaporate. And Wila's weren't the only hopes that would be dashed. Veronica couldn't let herself forget that little girl waiting at Saint Mary's....

"Well?" Tedric said impatiently.

"All right," Veronica said. "I'll give it a try."

Senator McKinley hung up the phone with a triumphant crash. "I think we've found our man," he announced with a wide smile. "His name's Navy Lieutenant Joseph P.—" he glanced down at a scrap of paper he'd taken some notes on "—Catalanotto. They're faxing me an ID photo right now."

Veronica felt an odd flash of both hot and cold. Good God, what had she just done? What had she just agreed to? What if she couldn't pull it off? What if it couldn't be done?

The fax alarm began to beep. Both the prince and Senator McKinley stood and crossed the spacious suite to where the fax machine was plugged in beneath a set of elegant bay windows.

Veronica stayed in her seat at the table. If this job couldn't be done, she would be letting her best friend down.

"My God," McKinley breathed as the picture was slowly printed out. "It doesn't seem possible."

He tore the fax from the roll of paper and handed it to the prince.

Silently, Tedric stared at the picture. Silently, he walked back across the room and handed the sheet of paper to Veronica.

Except for the fact that the man in the picture was wearing a relaxed pair of military fatigues, with top buttons of the shirt undone and sleeves rolled up to his elbows, except for the fact that the man in the picture had dark, shaggy hair cut just a little below his ears, and the strap of a submachine gun slung over one shoulder, except for the fact that the camera had caught him mid-grin, with good humor and sharp intelligence sparkling in his dark eyes, the man in this picture could very well have been the crown prince of Ustanzia. Or at the very least, he could have been the crown prince's brother.

The crown prince's *better-looking* brother.

He had the same nose, same cheekbones, same well-defined jawline and chin. But his front tooth was chipped. Of course, that was no problem. They could cap a tooth in a matter of hours, couldn't they?

He was bigger than Prince Tedric, this American naval lieutenant. Bigger and taller. Stronger. Rougher edged. Much, *much* more rough-edged, in every way imaginable. Good God, if this picture was any indication, Veronica was going to have to start with the basics with this man. She was going to have to teach him how to sit and stand and walk....

Veronica looked up to find Prince Tedric watching her.

"Something tells me," he said in his elegant accent, "your work is cut out for you."

Across the room, McKinley picked up the phone and dialed. "Yeah," he said into the receiver. "This is Sam McKinley. *Senator* Sam McKinley. I need a Navy SEAL by the name of Lieutenant Joseph—" he consulted his notes "—Catalanotto. Damn, what a mouthful. I need that lieutenant here in Washington, and I need him here yesterday."

Chapter 2

Joe lay on the deck of the rented boat, hands behind his head, watching the clouds. Puffs of blinding white in a crystal blue California sky, they were in a state of constant motion, always changing, never remaining the same.

He liked that.

It reminded him of his life, fluid and full of surprises. He never knew when a cream puff might turn unexpectedly into a ferocious dragon.

But Joe liked it that way. He liked never knowing what was behind the door—the lady or the tiger. And certainly, since he'd been a SEAL, he'd had his share of both.

But today there were neither ladies nor tigers to face. Today he was on leave—shore leave, it was called in the navy. Funny he should spend the one day of shore leave he had this month far from the shore, out on a fishing boat.

Not that he'd spent very much time lately at sea. In fact, in the past few months, he'd been on a naval vessel exactly ninety-six hours. And that had been for training. Some of those training hours he'd spent as an instructor. But some of the time he'd been a student. That was all part of being a Navy SEAL. No matter your rank or experience, you always had to keep learning, keep training, keep on top of the new technology and methodology.

Joe had achieved expert status in nine different fields, but those fields were always changing. Just like those clouds that were floating above him. Just the way he liked it.

Across the deck of the boat, dressed in weekend grunge clothes similar to his own torn fatigues and ragged T-shirt, Harvard and Blue were arguing good-naturedly over who had gotten the most depressing letter from the weekly mail call.

Joe himself hadn't gotten any mail—nothing besides bills, that is. Talk about depressing.

Joe closed his eyes, letting the conversation float over him. He'd known Blue for eight years, Harvard for about six. Their voices—Blue's thick, south-of-the-Mason-Dixon-Line drawl and Harvard's nasal, upper-class-Boston accent—were as familiar to him as breathing.

It still sometimes tickled him that out of their entire seven-man SEAL team, the man that Blue was closest to, after Joe himself, was Daryl Becker, nicknamed Harvard.

Carter "Blue" McCoy and Daryl "Harvard" Becker. The "redneck" rebel and the Ivy League-educated Yankee black man. Both SEALs, both better than the best of the rest. And both aware that there was no such thing as prejudices and prejudgments in the Navy SEALs.

Out across the bay, the blue-green water sparkled and danced in the bright sunshine. Joe took a deep breath, filling his lungs with the sharp salty air.

"Oh, Lord," Blue said, turning to the second page of his letter.

Joe turned toward his friend. "What?"

"Gerry's getting married," Blue said, running his fingers through his sun-bleached blond hair. "To Jenny Lee Beaumont."

Jenny Lee had been Blue's high school girlfriend. She was the only woman Blue had ever talked about—the only one special enough to mention.

Joe exchanged a long look with Harvard.

"Jenny Lee Beaumont, huh?" Joe said.

"That's right." Blue nodded, his face carefully expressionless. "Gerry's gonna marry her. Next July. He wants me to be his best man."

Joe swore softly.

"You win," Harvard conceded. "Your mail was much more depressing than mine."

Joe shook his head, grateful for his own lack of entanglement with a woman. Sure, he'd had girlfriends down through the years, but he'd never met anyone he couldn't walk away from.

Not that he didn't like women, because he did. He certainly did. And the women he usually dated were smart and funny and as quick to shy away from permanent attachments as he was. He would see his current lady friend on occasional weekend leaves, and sometimes in the evenings when he was in town and free.

But never, ever had he kissed a woman good-night—or goodmorning, as was usually the case—then gone back to the base and sat around daydreaming about her the way Bob and Wesley had drooled over those college girls they'd met down in San Diego. Or the way Harvard had sighed over that Hawaiian marine biologist they'd met on Guam. What was her name? Rachel. Harvard *still* got that kicked-puppy look in his brown eyes whenever her name came up.

The truth was, Joe had been lucky—he'd never fallen in love. And he was hoping his luck would hold. It would be just fine with him if he went through life without *that* particular experience, thank you very much.

Joe pushed the top off the cooler with one bare toe. He reached into the icy water to pull out a beer, then froze.

He straightened, ears straining, eyes scanning the horizon to the east.

Then he heard it again.

The sound of a distant chopper. He shaded his eyes, looking out toward the California coastline, to where the sound was coming from.

Silently, Harvard and Blue got to their feet, moving to stand next to him. Silently, Harvard handed Joe the binoculars that had been stowed in one of the equipment lockers.

One swift turn of the dial brought the powerful lenses into focus.

The chopper was only a small black dot, but it was growing larger with each passing second. It was undeniably heading directly toward them.

"You guys wearing your pagers?" Joe asked, breaking the silence. He'd taken his own beeper off after it—and he—had gotten doused by a pailful of bait and briny seawater.

Harvard nodded. "Yes, sir." He glanced down at the beeper he wore attached to his belt. "But I'm clear."

"Mine didn't go off, either, Cat," Blue said.

In the binoculars, the black dot took on a distinct outline. It was an army bird, a Black Hawk, UH-60A. Its cruising speed was about one hundred and seventy miles per hour. It was closing in on them, and fast.

"Either of you in any trouble I should know about?" Joe asked.

"No, sir," Harvard said.

"Negative." Blue glanced at Joe. "How 'bout you, Lieutenant?"

Joe shook his head, still watching the helicopter through the binoculars.

"This is weird," Harvard said. "What kind of hurry are they in, they can't page us and have us motor back to the harbor?"

"One damn big hurry," Joe said. God, that Black Hawk could really move. He pulled the binoculars away from his face as the chopper continued to grow larger.

"It's not World War Three," Blue commented, his troubles with Jenny Lee temporarily forgotten. He had to raise his voice to be heard above the approaching helicopter. "If it was World War Three, they wouldn't waste a Hawk on three lousy SEALs."

The chopper circled and then hovered directly above them. The sound of the blades was deafening, and the force of the wind made the little boat pitch and toss. All three men grabbed the railing to keep their footing.

Then a scaling rope was thrown out the open door of the helicopter's cabin. It, too, swayed in the wind from the chopper blades, smacking Joe directly in the chest.

"Lieutenant Joseph P. Catalanotto," a distorted voice announced over a loudspeaker. "Your shore leave is over."

Veronica St. John went into her hotel suite, then leaned wearily back against the closed door.

It was only nine o'clock—early by diplomatic standards. In fact, if things had gone according to schedule today, she would still have been at a reception for Prince Tedric over at the Ustanzian Embassy. But things had gone very much *not* according to schedule, starting with the assassination attempt at the airport.

She'd gotten a call from the president of the United States, officially thanking her, on behalf of the American people, for saving Prince Tedric's life. She hadn't expected that. Too bad. If she'd been expecting the man in the White House to call, she might have been prepared to ask for his assistance in locating the personnel records of this mysterious navy lieutenant who looked so much like the crown prince of Ustanzia.

Nobody, repeat *nobody* she had spoken to had been able to help her find the files she wanted. The Department of Defense sent her to the Navy. The Navy representatives told her that all SEAL records were in the Special Forces Division. The clerk from Special Forces was as clandestine and unhelpful as James Bond's personal assistant might have been. The woman wouldn't even verify that Joseph Catalanotto existed, let alone if the man's personnel files were in the U.S. Special Forces Office.

Frustrated, Veronica had gone back to Senator McKinley, hoping that he could use his clout to get a fax of Catalanotto's files. But even the powerful senator was told that, for security reasons, personnel records for Navy SEALs were never, repeat *never*, sent via facsimile. It had been a major feat just getting them to fax a picture of the lieutenant. If McKinley wanted to see Joseph P. Catalanotto's personnel file, he would need to make a formal request, in writing. After the request was received, it would take a mandatory three days for the files to be censored for his—and Ms. St. John's—level of clearance.

Three *days*.

Veronica wasn't looking to find Lieutenant Catalanotto's deepest, darkest military secrets. All she wanted to know was where the man came from—in which part of the country he'd grown up. She wanted to know his family background, his level of education, his IQ scores and the results of personality and psychological tests done by the armed forces.

She wanted to know, quite frankly, how big an obstacle this Navy SEAL himself was going to be in getting the job done.

So far, she only knew his name, that he looked like a rougher, wilder version of Tedric Cortere, that his shoulders were very broad, that he carried an M60 machine gun as if it were a large loaf of bread, and that he had a nice smile.

She didn't have a clue as to whether she'd be able to fool the American public into thinking he was a European prince. Until she met this man, she couldn't even guess how much work transforming him was going to take. It would be better to try not to think about it.

But if she didn't think about this job looming over her, she would end up thinking about the girl at Saint Mary's Hospital, a little girl named Cindy who had sent the prince a letter nearly four months ago—a letter Veronica had fished out of Tedric's royal wastebasket. In the letter, Cindy—barely even ten years old—had told Prince Tedric that she'd heard he was planning a trip to the United States. She had asked him, if he was going to be in the Washington, D.C., area, to please come and visit her since she was not able to come to see him.

Veronica had ended up going above the prince—directly to King Derrick—and had gotten the visit to Saint Mary's on the official tour calendar.

But now what?

The entire tour would have to be rescheduled and replanned, and Saint Mary's and little Cindy were likely to fall, ignored, between the cracks.

Veronica smiled tightly. Not if *she* had anything to say about it.

With a sigh, she kicked off her shoes.

Lord, but she ached.

Tackling royalty could really wear a person out, she thought, allowing herself a rueful smile. After the assassination attempt, she had run on sheer adrenaline for about six hours straight. After that had worn off, she'd kept herself fueled with coffee—hot, black and strong.

Right now what she needed was a shower and a two-hour nap.

She pulled her nightgown and robe out of the suitcase that she hadn't yet found time to unpack, and tossed them onto the bed as she all but staggered into the bathroom. She closed the door and turned on the shower as she peeled off her suit and the cream-colored blouse she wore underneath. She put a hole in her hose as she took them off, and threw them directly into the wastebasket. It had been a bona fide two-pairs-of-panty-hose day. Her first pair, the ones she'd been wearing at the airport, had been totally destroyed.

Veronica washed herself quickly, knowing that every minute she spent in the shower was a minute less that she'd be able to sleep. And with Lieutenant Joseph P. Catalanotto due to arrive anytime after midnight, she was going to need every second of that nap.

Still, it didn't keep her from singing as she tried to rinse the aches and soreness from her back and shoulders. Singing in the shower was a childhood habit. Then, as now, the moments she spent alone in the shower were among the few bits of time she had to really kick back and let loose. She tested the acoustics of this particular bathroom with a rousing rendition of Mary Chapin Carpenter's latest hit.

She shut off the water, still singing, and toweled herself dry.

Her robe was hanging on the back of the bathroom door, and she reached for it.

And stopped singing, mid-note.

She'd left her robe in the bedroom, on the bed. She hadn't hung it on the door.

"No...you're right. You're *not* alone in here," said a husky male voice from the other side of the bathroom door.

Chapter 3

Veronica's heart nearly stopped beating, and she lunged for the door and turned the lock.

"I figured you didn't know I was in your room," the voice continued as Veronica quickly slipped into her white terry-cloth bathrobe. "I also figured you probably wouldn't appreciate coming out of the bathroom with just a towel on—or less. Not with an audience, anyway. So I put your robe on the back of the door."

Veronica tightened the belt and clutched the lapels of the robe more closely together. She took in a deep breath, then let it slowly out. It steadied her and kept her voice from shaking. "Who are you?" she asked.

"Who are *you*?" the voice countered. It was rich, husky, and laced with more than a trace of blue-collar New York. "I was brought here and told to wait, so I waited. I've been hustled from one coast to the other like some Federal Express overnight package, only nobody has any explanations as to why or even *who* I'm waiting to see. I didn't even know my insertion point was the District of Columbia until the jet landed at Andrews. And as long as I'm complaining I might as well tell you that I'm tired, I'm hungry and my shorts have not managed to dry in the past ten hours, a situation that makes me very, very cranky. I would damn near sell my soul to get into that shower that you just stepped out of. Other than that, I'm sure I'm very pleased to meet you."

"Lieutenant Catalanotto?" Veronica asked.

"Bingo," the voice said. "Babe, you just answered your own question."

But had she? "What's your first name?" she asked warily.

"Joe. Joseph."

"Middle name?"

"Paulo," he said.

Veronica swung open the bathroom door.

The first thing she noticed about the man was his size. He was big—taller than Prince Tedric by about two inches and outweighing him in sheer muscle by a good, solid fifty pounds. His dark hair was cut much shorter than Tedric's, and he had at least a two-day growth of beard darkening his face.

He didn't look as exactly like the prince as she'd thought when she saw his photograph, Veronica realized, studying the man's face. On closer inspection, his nose was slightly different—it had been broken, probably more than once. And, if it was possible, this navy lieutenant's cheekbones were even more exotic-looking than Tedric's. His chin was slightly more square, more stubborn than the prince's. And his eyes ... As he returned her inquisitive stare, his lids dropped halfway over his remarkable liquid brown eyes, as if he was trying to hide his innermost secrets from her.

But those differences—even the size differences between the two men—were very subtle. They wouldn't be noticed by someone who didn't know Prince Tedric very well. Those differences certainly wouldn't be noticed by the array of ambassadors and diplomats Tedric was scheduled to meet.

"According to the name tag on your suitcase, you've gotta be Veronica St. John, right?" he said, pronouncing her name the American way, as if it were two words, *Saint* and John.

"Sinjin," she said distractedly. "You don't say Saint John, you say 'Sinjin.'"

He was looking at her, examining her in much the same way that she'd looked at him. The intensity of his gaze made her feel naked. Which of course, underneath her robe, she was.

But he didn't win any prizes himself for the clothing he was wearing. From the looks of it, his T-shirt had had its sleeves forcibly removed without the aid of scissors, his army fatigues had been cut off into ragged shorts, and on his feet he wore a pair of dirty canvas deck shoes with no socks. He looked as if he hadn't showered in several days, and, Lord help her, he smelled that way, too.

"Dear God," Veronica said aloud, taking in all of the little details she'd missed at first. He wasn't wearing a belt. Instead, a length of fairly thick rope was run through the belt loops in his pants, and tied in some kind of knot at the front. He had a tattoo—a navy anchor—on his left biceps. His fingers were blackened with stains of grease, his fingernails were short and rough—a far cry from Prince Tedric's carefully manicured hands. Lord, if she had to start by teaching this man the basics of personal hygiene, there was no way she'd have him impersonating a prince within her three-day deadline.

"What?" he said with a scowl. Defensiveness tinged his voice and darkened his eyes. "I'm not what you expected?"

She couldn't deny it. She'd expected the lieutenant to arrive wearing a dress uniform, stiff and starched and perfectly military—and smelling a little more human and a little less like a real-life marine mammal-type seal. Wordlessly, she shook her head no.

Joe gazed silently at the girl. She watched him, too, her eyes so wide and blue against the porcelain paleness of her skin. It was hard for him to tell the color of her hair—it was wet. It clung, damp and dark, to the sides of her head and neck.

Red, he guessed. It was probably some shade of red, maybe even strawberry blond, probably curly. Yet, if there really was a God and He was truly righteous, she would have nondescript straight hair, maybe the color of mud. It didn't seem fair that this girl should have wealth, a powerful job, refined manners, a pair of beautiful blue eyes *and* curly red hair.

Without makeup, her face looked alarmingly young. Her features were delicate, almost fragile. She wasn't particularly pretty, at least not in the conventional sense. But her cheekbones were high, showcasing enormous crystal blue eyes. And her lips were exquisitely shaped, her nose small and elegant.

No, she wasn't pretty. But she was incredibly attractive in a way he couldn't even begin to explain.

The robe she wore was too big for her. It drew attention to her slight frame, accentuating her slender wrists and ankles.

She looked like a kid playing dress up in her mommy's clothes.

Funny, from the cut and style of the business suits that had been neatly packed in her suitcase, Joe had expected this Veronica St. John—or "Sinjin," as she'd pronounced it with her slightly British, extremely monied upper-class accent—to be, well . . . less young. He'd expected someone in their mid-forties at least, maybe even older. But this girl couldn't be a day over twenty-five. Hell, standing here like this, just out of the shower, still dripping wet, she barely looked sixteen.

"You aren't what I expected, either," Joe said, sitting down on the edge of the bed. "So I guess that makes us even."

He knew he was making her nervous, sitting there like that. He knew she was nervous about him getting the bedspread dirty, nervous about him leaving behind the lingering odor of dead fish—bait from the smelly bucket Blue had knocked over earlier that morning. Hell, he was nervous about it himself.

And damn, but that made him angry. This girl was somehow responsible for dragging him away from his shore leave. She was somehow responsible for the way he'd been rushed across the country without a shower or a change of clothes. Hell, it was probably her fault that he was in this five-star hotel wearing his barnacle-scraping clothes, feeling way out of his league.

He didn't like feeling this way. He didn't like the barely concealed distaste he could see in this rich girl's eyes. He didn't like being reminded that he didn't fit into this opulent world of hers—a world filled with money, power and class.

Not that he *wanted* to fit in. Hell, he wouldn't last more than a few months in a place like this. He preferred his own world—the world of the Navy SEALs, where a man wasn't judged by the size of his wallet, or the price of his education, or the cut of his clothes. In *his* world, a man was judged by his actions, by his perseverance, by his loyalty and stamina. In his world, a man who'd made it into the SEALs was treated with honor and respect—regardless of the way he looked. Or smelled.

He leaned back on the big, fancy, five-star bed, propping himself up on his elbows. "Maybe you could give me some kind of clue as to what I'm doing here, honey," he said, watching her wince at his term of endearment. "I'm pretty damn curious."

The rich girl's eyes widened, and she actually forgot to look disdainful for a few minutes. "Are you trying to tell me that no one's told you *any*thing?"

Joe sat up. "That's *exactly* what I'm telling you."

She shook her head. Her hair was starting to dry, and it was definitely curly. "But that's impossible."

"Impossible it ain't, sweetheart," he said. A double wince this time. One for the bad grammar, the other for the "sweetheart." "I'm here in D.C. without the rest of my team, and I don't know why."

Veronica turned abruptly and went into the hotel suite's living room. Joe followed more slowly, leaning against the frame of the door and watching as she sifted through her briefcase.

"You were supposed to be met by—" she pulled a yellow legal pad from her notebook and flipped to a page in the back "—an Admiral Forrest?" She looked up at him almost hopefully.

The navy lieutenant just shrugged, still watching her. Lord, but he was handsome. Despite the layers of dirt and his dark, scowling expression, he was, like Prince Tedric, almost impossibly good-looking. And this man was nearly dripping with an unconscious virility that Tedric didn't even *begin* to possess. He was extremely attractive underneath all that grime—if she were the type who went for that untamed, rough-hewn kind of man.

Which, of course, Veronica wasn't. Dangerous, bad-boy types had never made her heart beat faster. And if her heart seemed to be pounding now, why, that was surely from the scare he'd given her earlier.

No, she was not the type to be attracted by steel-hard biceps and broad shoulders, a rough-looking five o'clock shadow, a tropical tan, a molten-lava smile, and incredible brown bedroom eyes. No. Definitely, positively not.

And if she gave him a second glance, it was only to verify the fact that Lieutenant Joseph P. Catalanotto was *not* going to be mistaken for visiting European royalty.

Not today, anyway.

And not tomorrow. But, for Wila's sake, for her own career, and for little Cindy at Saint Mary's, Veronica was going to see to it that two days from now, Joe would be a prince.

But first things first. And first things definitely included putting her clothes back on, particularly since Lieutenant Catalanotto wasn't attempting to hide the very, *very* male appreciation in his eyes as he looked at her.

"Why don't you help yourself to something to drink," Veronica said, and Joe's gaze flickered across the suite, toward the elaborate bar that was set up on the other side of the room. "Give me a minute to get dressed," she added. "Then I'll try to explain why you're here."

He nodded.

She walked past him, aware that he was still watching right up to the moment she closed the bedroom door behind her.

The man's accent was atrocious. It screamed New York City—blue-collar New York City. But okay. With a little ingenuity, with the right scheduling and planning, Joe wouldn't have to utter a single word.

His posture, though, was an entirely different story. Tedric stood ramrod straight. Lieutenant Catalanotto, on the other hand, slouched continuously. And he walked with a kind of relaxed swagger that was utterly un-princely. How on *earth* was she going to teach him to stand and sit up straight, let alone *walk* in that peculiar, stiff, princely gait that Tedric had perfected?

Veronica pulled fresh underwear and another pair of panty hose—number three for the day—from her suitcase. Her dark blue suit was near the top of the case, so she pulled it on, then slipped her tired feet into a matching pair of pumps. A little bit of makeup, a quick brush through her almost-dry hair...

Gloves would cover his hands, she thought, her mind going a mile a minute. Even if that engine grease didn't wash off, it could be hidden by a pair of gloves. Tedric himself often wore a pair of white gloves. No one would think that was odd.

Joe's hair was an entirely different matter. He wore his hair short, while Tedric's flowed down past his shoulders.

They could get a wig for Joe. Or hair extensions. Yes, hair extensions would be even better, and easier to keep on. Provided Joe would sit still long enough to have them attached...

This was going to work. This was *going* to work.

Taking a deep breath and smoothing down her suit jacket, Veronica opened the door and went back into the living room.

And stopped short.

The living room of her hotel suite was positively crowded.

Senator McKinley, three different Ustanzian ambassadors, an older man wearing a military dress uniform covered with medals, a half-dozen FInCOM security agents, Prince Tedric *and* his entire entourage all stood frozen and staring at Joe Catalanotto, who had risen to his feet in front of the sofa. The tension in the room could have been cut by a knife.

The man in uniform was the only one who spoke. "Nice to see that you dressed for the occasion, Joe," he said with a chuckle.

Joe crossed his arms. "The guys who shanghaied me forgot to bring my wardrobe trunk," he said dryly. Then he smiled. It was a genuine, sincere smile that warmed his face and touched his eyes. "Good to see you, Admiral."

Joe looked around the room, his gaze landing on Prince Tedric's face. Tedric was staring at him as if he were a rat that had made its way into the hotel room from the street below.

Joe's smile faded, and was replaced by another scowl. "Well," he said. "I'll be damned. If it isn't my evil twin."

Veronica laughed. She couldn't help it. It just came bubbling out. She bit down on the inside of her cheek, and all but clamped her hand across her mouth. But no one seemed to notice—no one but Joe, who glanced over at her in surprise.

"Don't you know who you're talking to, young man? This is the crown prince of Ustanzia," Senator McKinley said sternly to Joe.

"Damn straight I know who I'm talking to, Pop," Joe said tightly. "I'm the kind of guy who never forgets a face—particularly when I see it every morning in the mirror. My team of SEALs pulled this bastard's sorry butt out of Baghdad." He turned back to Tedric. "Keeping free and clear of war zones these days, Ted, you lousy bastard?"

Everyone in the room, with the exception of Joe and the still-grinning admiral, drew in a shocked breath. Veronica was amazed that her ears didn't pop from the sudden drop in air pressure.

The crown prince's face turned an interesting shade of royal purple. "How dare you?" he gasped.

Joe seemed to grow at least three feet taller and two feet broader. He took a step or two toward Tedric, and everyone in the room—with the exception of the admiral—drew back.

"How dare *you* put yourself into a situation where my men had to risk their lives to pull you back out?" Joe all but snarled. "One of my men spent *months* in intensive care because of you, dirtwad. I'll tell you right now, you're damned lucky—*damned* lucky—he didn't die."

The deadly look in Joe's eyes was enough to make even the bravest man quiver with fear. They were *all* lucky that Joe's friend hadn't died, Veronica thought with a shiver, or else they'd be witnessing a murder. And unlike the morning's assassination attempt, she had no doubt that Joe would succeed.

"*Mon Dieu,*" Tedric said, hiding the fact that his hands were shaking by slipping into his native French and turning haughtily to his aides. "This . . . this . . . *creature* is far more insolent than I remembered. Obviously we cannot risk sending him into public, masquerading as *me*. He would embarrass my heritage, my entire *country*. Send him back to whatever rock he crawled out from under. There is no other option. Cancel the tour."

On the other side of the room, one of the senator's assistants quickly translated Tedric's French into English, whispering into McKinley's ear.

With a humph, the prince stalked toward the door, taking with him Senator McKinley's hopes for lower-priced oil and Wila's dreams of economic security for her country.

But McKinley moved quickly, and cut Prince Tedric off before he reached the door.

"Your Highness," McKinley said soothingly. "If you're serious about obtaining the funding for the oil wells—"

"He's a monster," Tedric proclaimed loudly in French. McKinley's assistant translated quietly for the senator. "Even Ms. St. John cannot turn such a monster into a prince."

Across the room, Joe watched as Veronica hurried over to the prince and Senator McKinley and began talking in a lowered voice. Turn a monster into a prince, huh? he thought.

"You always did know how to liven up a party, son."

Joe turned to see Admiral Michael "Mac" Forrest smiling at him. He gave the older man a crisp salute.

The admiral's familiar leathery face crinkled into a smile. "Cut the bulldinky, Catalanotto," he said. "Since when did you start saluting? For criminy's sake, son, shake my hand instead."

The admiral's salt-and-pepper hair had gone another shade whiter, but other than that, the older man looked healthy and fit. Joe knew that Mac Forrest, a former SEAL himself, still spent a solid hour each day in PT—physical training—despite the fact that he needed a cane to walk. Ever since Joe first met him, the Admiral's left leg had been shorter than his right, courtesy of the enemy during the Vietnam War.

Mac's handclasp was strong and solid. With his other hand, he clapped Joe on the shoulder.

"It's been nearly a year and you haven't changed the least bit," Admiral Forrest announced after giving Joe a once-over. The older man wrinkled his nose. "Including your clothes. Jumping Jesse, what hole *did* we drag you out of?"

"I was on leave," Joe said with a shrug. "I was helping Blue pull in a major tuna and the bait bucket spilled on me. The boys in the Black Hawk didn't give me a chance to stop at my apartment to take a shower and pick up a change of clothes."

"Yeah." The admiral's blue eyes twinkled. "We were in kind of a hurry to get you out here, in case you didn't notice."

"I noticed," Joe said, crossing his arms. "I take it I'm here to do some kind of favor for him." With his chin, Joe gestured across the room toward Prince Tedric, who was still deep in discussion with Senator McKinley and Veronica.

"Something tells me you're not happy about the idea of doing Tedric Cortere any favors," Mac commented.

"Damn straight," Joe said, adding, "sir. That bastard nearly got Frisco killed. We were extracting from Baghdad with a squad of Iraqi soldiers on our tail. Frisco took a direct hit. The kid nearly bled to death. What's maybe even worse, at least in his eyes, is that his knee was damn near destroyed. Kid's in a wheelchair now, and fighting hard to get out.''

Mac Forrest stood quietly, just letting Joe tell the story.

"We'd reached the Baghdad extraction point when Prince Charming over there refused to board the chopper. We finally had to throw him inside. It only gave us about a thirty-second delay, but it was enough to put us into the Iraqi soldiers' firing range, and that's when Frisco was hit. Turns out His Royal Pain-in-the-Butt refused to get into the bird because it wasn't luxurious enough. He nearly got us all killed because the interior of an attack helicopter wasn't painted in the colors of the Ustanzian flag.''

Joe looked steadily at the admiral. "So go ahead and reprimand me, Mac,'' he added. "But be warned—there's nothing you can say that'll make me do any favors for *that* creep.''

"I'm not so sure about that, son,'' Mac said thoughtfully, running his hand across the lower part of his face.

Joe frowned. "What's going on?''

"Have you seen the news lately?'' Mac asked.

Joe looked at him for several long moments. "You're kidding, right?''

"Just asking.''

"Mac, I've been in a chopper, a transport jet and a jeep tonight. None of them had in-flight entertainment in the form of the evening news,'' Joe said. "Hell, I haven't even seen a newspaper in the past eighteen hours.''

"This morning there was an assassination attempt on Tedric.''

Aha. Now it suddenly all made sense. Joe nodded. "Gee, sir,'' he said. "And I already smell like bait. How appropriate.''

Mac chuckled. "You always *were* a smart mouth, Catalanotto.''

"So what's the deal?'' Joe asked. "Where am I inserting? Ustanzia? Or, oh joy, are we going back to Baghdad?''

Inserting. It was a special-forces term for entering—either stealthily or by force—an area of operation.

The admiral perched on the arm of the sofa. "You've already inserted, son,'' he said. "Here in D.C. is where we want you—for right now. That is, if I can convince you to volunteer for this mission." Briefly, he outlined the plan to have Joe stand in for the crown prince for the remainder of the American tour—at least until the terrorists made another assassination attempt and were apprehended.

"Let me get this straight," Joe said, sitting down on the couch. "I play dress-up in Cortere's clothes—which is the equivalent of painting a giant target on my back, right? And I'm doing this so that the United States will have more *oil?* You've got to do better than that, Mac. And don't start talking about protecting Prince Ted, because I don't give a flying fig whether or not that bastard stays alive long enough to have his royal coffee and doughnut tomorrow morning."

Mac looked across the room, and Joe followed the older man's gaze. Veronica was nodding at Prince Tedric, her face serious. Red. Her hair was dry, and it was definitely red. Of course. It *had* to be red.

"I don't suppose working with Veronica St. John would be an incentive?" Mac said. "I had the opportunity to meet her several weeks ago. She's a real peach of a girl. Rock-solid sense of humor, though you wouldn't necessarily know it to look at her. Pretty, too."

Joe shook his head. "Not my type," he said flatly.

"Mrs. Forrest wasn't my type when I first met her," Mac stated.

Joe stood. "Sorry, Mac. If that's the best you can do, I'm outta here."

"Please," Mac said quietly, putting one hand on Joe's arm. "I'm asking for a personal favor here, Lieutenant. Do this one for me." The admiral looked down at the floor, and when he looked back at Joe, his blue eyes were steely. "Remember that car bomb that took out a busload of American sailors in London three years ago?"

Silently, Joe nodded. Oh, yeah. He remembered. Mac Forrest's nineteen-year-old son had been one of the kids killed in that deadly blast, set off by a terrorist organization called the Cloud of Death.

"My sources over at Intelligence have hinted that the assassins who are gunning for Prince Tedric are the same terrorists who set off that bomb," the admiral said. His voice trembled slightly. "It's Diosdado and his damned Cloud of Death again. I want them, Lieutenant. With your help, I can get them. Without your help..." He shook his head in despair.

Joe nodded. "Sir, you've got your volunteer."

Chapter 4

It was nearly two-thirty in the morning before Veronica left the planning meeting.

All of the power players had been there—Senator McKinley, whose million-dollar smile had long since faded; Henri Freder, the Ustanzian Ambassador; Admiral Forrest, the salty-looking military man Veronica had met several weeks ago at an embassy function in Paris; stern-faced Kevin Laughton, the Federal Intelligence Commission agent in charge of security; and Prince Tedric's four chief aides.

It had been decided that Prince Tedric should be spirited away from the hotel to a safe house where he'd be guarded by FInCOM agents and Ustanzian secret service men. The American sailor, Joe Catalanotto, would simply move into Tedric's suite of rooms on the tenth floor, thus arousing no suspicion among the hotel staff and guests—or even among the prince's own lesser servants and assistants, who would not be told of the switch.

After convincing the prince to give Veronica St. John a chance to work with the sailor, McKinley had gotten the ball rolling. Prince Tedric was gone, much to everyone's relief.

Veronica and the prince's main staff were working to re-schedule the beginning of the tour. The idea was to organize a schedule that would require Joe to have the least amount of contact with diplomats who might recognize that he was not the real prince. And the FInCOM agents put in *their* two cents worth, trying to set up times and places for Joe to appear in public that would provide the assassins with an obvious, clear target without putting Joe in more danger than necessary.

"Where's Catalanotto?" Admiral Forrest kept asking. "He should be here. He should be part of this op's planning team."

"With all due respect, Admiral," Kevin Laughton, the FInCOM chief, finally said, "it's better to leave the strategizing to the experts." Laughton was a tall man, impeccably dressed, with every strand of his light brown hair perfectly in place. His blue eyes were cool, and he kept his emotions carefully hidden behind a poker face.

"In that case, Mr. Laughton," Forrest said tartly, "Catalanotto should definitely be here. And if you paid close attention, sir, you might even learn a thing or two from him."

"From a navy *lieutenant*?"

"Joe Cat is a Navy SEAL, mister," Forrest said.

There was that word again. SEAL.

But Laughton didn't look impressed. He looked put-upon. "I should've known this was going too smoothly," he said tiredly. He turned to Forrest. "I'm sure you're familiar with the expression, Admiral: Too many cooks spoil the broth?"

The admiral fixed the younger man with a decidedly fishlike stare. "This man is going to be your bait," he said. "Can you honestly tell me that if your roles were reversed, you wouldn't want in on the planning stages?"

"Yes," Laughton replied. "I can."

"Bulldinky." Forrest stood. He snapped his fingers and one of his aides appeared. "Get Joe Cat down here," he ordered.

The man fired off a crisp salute. "Yes, sir." He turned sharply and disappeared.

Laughton was fuming. "You can't pull rank on me. I'm FInCOM—"

"Trust me, son," Forrest interrupted, sitting down again and rocking back in his chair. "See these do-hickeys on my uniform? They're not just pretty buttons. They mean when I say 'stop,' you stop. And if you need that order clarified, I'd be more than happy to call Bill and have him explain it to you.''

Veronica bit the insides of her cheeks to keep from smiling. By Bill, the admiral was referring to the President. Of the United States. The look on Kevin Laughton's face was not a happy one.

The admiral's young aide returned and stood patiently at attention just behind Forrest's chair. Forrest tipped his head to look up at him, giving him permission to speak with a nod.

"Lieutenant Catalanotto is unable to attend this meeting, sir," the aide said. "He's getting a tooth capped, and... something done with his hair, sir. I think."

"Thank you, son," Forrest said. He stood, pushing his chair back from the conference table. "In that case, I suggest we adjourn and resume in the morning, when Lieutenant Catalanotto can attend."

"But—"

The admiral fixed Laughton with a single look. "Don't make me make that phone call, mister," he said. "I may have phrased it kind of casually, but my suggestion to adjourn *was* an order." He straightened and picked up his cane. "I'm going to give you a little hint, Laughton, a hint that most folks usually learn the first day of basic training. When an officer gives an order, the correct response is, 'Yes, sir. Right away, sir.'"

He glanced around the table, giving Veronica a quick wink before he headed toward the door.

She gathered up her papers and briefcase and followed, catching up with him in the corridor.

"Excuse me, Admiral," she said. "I haven't had time to do any research—I haven't had time to *think*—and I was hoping you could clue me in. What exactly is a *SEAL?*"

Forrest's leathery face crinkled into a smile. "Joe's a SEAL," he said.

Veronica shook her head. "Sir, that's not what I meant."

His smile became a grin. "I know," he said. "You want me to tell you that a Navy SEAL is the toughest, smartest, deadliest warrior in all of the U.S. military. Okay. There you have it. A SEAL is the best of the best, and he's trained to specialize in unconventional warfare." His smile faded, giving his face a stern, craggy cast. "Let me give you an example. Lieutenant Catalanotto took six men and went one hundred miles behind the lines during the first night of Operation Desert Storm in order to rescue Tedric Cortere—who was too stupid to leave Baghdad when he was warned of the coming U.S. attack. Joe Cat and his Alpha Squad—they're part of SEAL Team Ten— went in undetected, among all the bombs that were falling from U.S. planes, and pulled Cortere and three aides out without a single fatality."

Admiral Forrest smiled again as he watched an expression of disbelief flit across Veronica's face.

"How on earth . . . ?" she asked.

"With a raftload of courage," he answered. "And a whole hell of a lot of training and skill. Joe Cat's an expert in explosives, you know, both on land and underwater. And he knows all there is to know about locks and security systems. He's a top-notch mechanic. He understands engines in a way that's almost spiritual. He's also an expert marksman, a sharp-shooter with damn near any ordnance he can get his hands on. And that's just the tip of the iceberg, missy. If you want me to continue, then we'd better find a place to sit and get comfortable, because it's going to take a while."

Veronica tried hard to connect everything she'd just heard with the grimy, unkempt, seemingly uneducated man who had appeared in her hotel room. "I see," she finally said.

"No, you don't," Forrest countered, a smile softening his words. "But you will. Best thing to do is go find Joe. And when he talks to you, really listen. You'll know soon enough what being a SEAL means."

Joe sat in the hairdresser's portable chair, looking at himself in the hotel-room mirror.

He looked . . . different.

A dentist had come in and capped the tooth he'd chipped three years ago while on a training mission and had never had fixed.

Joe had stopped noticing it after a while. He'd had the rough edges filed down the day of the accident, but he'd never had the time or inclination to get the damn thing capped.

The capped tooth wasn't the only thing different about him now. Joe's short dark hair was about six inches longer—and no longer short—thanks to the hair extensions the tired-looking stylist had almost finished attaching.

It was odd, seeing himself with long hair like this.

Joe had grown his hair out before, when he'd had advance warning of covert operations. But he liked wearing his hair short. It wasn't military-regulation short, just a comfortable length that was easy to deal with.

Long hair got in the way. It worked its way into his mouth, hung in his face, and got in his eyes at inopportune moments.

And it made him look like that cowardly idiot, Tedric Cortere.

Which was precisely the point, right now.

God help them, Joe vowed, if they expected him to wear those satin suits with the ruffles and metallic trim, and those garish rings on his fingers. No, God help *him*. This was a job, and if the powers that be wanted him to dress like an idiot, he was going to have to dress like an idiot. Like it or not.

Joe stared into the mirror at the opulence of the hotel room. This place gave him the creeps. He was nervous he might break something or spill something or touch something he wasn't supposed to touch. And his nervousness really annoyed him. Why *should* he be nervous? Why *should* he feel intimidated? It was only a lousy hotel room, for Pete's sake. The only difference between this room and the cheap motel rooms he stayed in when he traveled was that here the TV wasn't chained down. Here there was a phone in the bathroom. And the towels were thick and plentiful. And the carpets were plush and clean. And the wallpaper wasn't stained, and the curtains actually closed all the way, and the furniture wasn't broken and mismatched. Oh yeah, and the price tag for a one-night stay—that was different, too.

Sheesh, this place was as different from the places he usually stayed as night was to day, Joe reminded himself.

But the truth was, he wished he *was* staying at a cheap motel. At least then he could lie on the bed and put his feet up without being afraid he'd ruin the bedspread. At least he wouldn't feel so goddammed out of his league.

But he was stuck here until another assassination attempt was made or until the prince's U.S. tour ended in five weeks.

Five weeks.

Five weeks of feeling out of place. Of being afraid to touch anything.

"Don't touch!" he could still hear his mother say, when as a kid, he went along on her trips to Scarsdale, where she cleaned houses that were ten times the size of their tiny Jersey City apartment. "Don't touch, or you'll hear from your father when we get home."

Except Joe didn't have a father. He had a whole slew of stepfathers and "uncles," but no father. Still, whoever was temporarily playing the part of dear old dad at home would have leaped at any excuse to kick Joe's insolent butt into tomorrow.

Jeez, what was wrong with him? He hadn't thought about *those* "happy" memories in years.

The hotel-room door opened with an almost-inaudible click and Joe tensed. He looked up, turning his head and making the hairdresser sigh melodramatically.

But Joe had been too well-trained to let someone come into the room without giving them the once-over. Not while he was looking more and more like a man who'd been an assassin's target just this morning.

It was only the media consultant. Veronica St. John.

She posed no threat.

Joe turned his head, looking back into the mirror, waiting for the rush of relief, for the relaxation of the tension in his shoulders.

But it never came. Instead of relaxing, he felt as if all of his senses had gone on alert. As if he'd suddenly woken up. It was as if he were about to go into a combat situation. The colors in the wallpaper seemed sharper, clearer. The sounds of the hairdresser behind him seemed louder. And his sense of smell heightened to the point where he caught a whiff of Veronica St. John's subtle perfume from all the way across the room.

"Good God," she said in her crisp, faintly British-accented voice. "You look . . . amazing."

"Well, thank you, sweetheart. You're not so bad yourself."

She'd moved to where he could see her behind him in the mirror, and he glanced up, briefly meeting her gaze.

Blue eyes. Oh, baby, those eyes were blue. Electric blue. Electric-*shock* blue.

Joe looked up at her again and realized that the current of awareness and attraction that had shot through him had gone through her, as well. She looked as surprised as he felt. Surprised, no doubt, that a guy from his side of the tracks could catch her eye.

Except he didn't look like himself anymore. He looked like Prince Tedric.

It figured.

"I see you had the opportunity to take a shower," she said, no longer meeting his eyes. "Did your clothes get taken down to the laundry?"

"I think so," he said. "They were gone when I got out of the bathroom. I found this hotel robe.... I'd appreciate it if you could ask Admiral Forrest to send over a uniform in the morning. And maybe some socks and shorts . . . ?"

Veronica felt her cheeks start to heat. Lord, what was wrong with her? Since when did the mention of men's underwear make her face turn as red as a schoolgirl's?

Or maybe it wasn't the mention of unmentionables that was making her blush. Maybe it was the thought that this very large, very charismatic, very handsome, and very, *very* dangerous man was sitting here, with absolutely nothing on underneath his white terry-cloth robe.

From the glint in his dark brown eyes, it was clear that he was able to read her mind.

She used every ounce of her British schooling to keep her voice sounding cool and detached. "There's no need, Your Majesty," she said. "We go from here to your suite. A tailor will be arriving soon. He'll provide you with all of the clothing you'll need for the course of the next few weeks."

"Whoa," Joe said. "Whoa, whoa! Back up a sec, will ya?"

"A tailor," Veronica repeated. "We'll be meeting with him shortly. I realize it's late, but if we don't get started with—"

"No, no," Joe said. "Before that. Did you just call me 'Your *Majesty*'?"

"I'm done here," the hairdresser said. In a monotone, he quickly ran down a quick list of things Joe could and could not do with the extensions in his hair. "Swim—yes. Shower—yes. Run a comb through your hair—no. You have to be careful to comb only above and below the attachment." He turned to Veronica. "You have my card if you need me again."

"Find Mr. Laughton on your way out," Veronica said as Joe stood and helped the man fold up his portable chair. "He'll see that you get paid."

She watched, waiting until the hairdresser had closed the hotel-room door tightly behind him. Then she turned back to Joe.

"Your Majesty," she said again. "And Your Highness. *And* Your Excellency. You'll have to get used to it. This is the way you're going to be addressed."

"Even by *you?*" Joe stood very still, his arms folded across his chest. It was as if he were afraid to touch anything. But that was ridiculous. From the little information Veronica had gleaned from Admiral Forrest, Joe Catalanotto, or Joe Cat as the admiral had called him, wasn't afraid of *any*thing.

She crossed the room and sat down in one of the easy chairs by the windows. "Yes, even by me." Veronica gestured for him to sit across from her. "If we intend to pull off this cha rade—"

"You're right," Joe said, sitting down. "You're absolutely right. We need to go the full distance or the shooters will smell that something's not right." He smiled wryly. "It's just, after years of 'Hey, you!' or 'Yo, paesan!' 'Your Majesty' is a little disconcerting."

Veronica's eyebrows moved upward a fraction of an inch. It figured she'd be surprised. She probably thought he didn't know any four-syllable words.

Damn, what *was* it about her? She wasn't pretty, but...at the same time, she *was*. Her hair was gorgeous—the kind of soft curls he loved to run his fingers through. Joe found his eyes drawn to her face, to her delicate, almost-pointed nose, and her beautifully shaped lips. And those eyes...

His gaze slid lower, to the dark blue blazer that covered her shoulders, tapering down to her slender waist. She wore a matching navy skirt that ended a few inches above her knees, yet still managed to scream of propriety. Her politely crossed legs were something else entirely. Not even the sturdy pumps she wore on her feet could hide the fact that her legs were long and graceful and sexy as hell—the kind of legs a man dreams about. *This* man, anyway.

Joe knew that she was well aware he was studying her. But she had turned away, pretending to look for something in her briefcase, purposely ignoring the attraction he knew was mutual.

And then the phone rang—a sudden shrill noise that broke the quiet.

"Excuse me for a moment, please," Veronica said, gracefully standing and crossing the room to answer it.

"Hello?" she said, glancing back at Joe. As she watched, he leaned his head back and closed his eyes.

Thank goodness. He couldn't undress her any further with eyes that were closed. And with his eyes closed, she didn't have to be afraid that the warmth that spread throughout her entire body at his unmasked interest would somehow show. Heaven help her if this man got the idea that he could make her heart beat harder with a single look. She had enough to worry about without having to fight off some sailor's amorous advances.

"The tailor has arrived," one of Tedric's aides told her. "May I ask how much longer you'll be?"

"We'll be up shortly," Veronica said. "Please arrange to have coffee available. And something to eat. Doughnuts. Chocolate ones." Lt. Joe Catalanotto looked the chocolate-doughnut type. They could all certainly use some extra sugar to keep them awake.

She hung up the phone and crossed back to Joe. His head was still back, and his eyes were closed. He'd slumped down in the chair as if he had no bones in his entire body.

He was totally, absolutely and quite soundly asleep.

Veronica sat down across from him and leaned forward, studying his face. He'd shaved and somehow managed to get all of the grease and dirt off in the shower. Even his hands were free of grime. His hair was clean and now, with the extensions, quite long. To the average eye, he might have looked quite a bit like Prince Tedric, but Veronica knew better.

Tedric had never been—and never would be—this handsome.

There was an edge to Joe Catalanotto's good looks. A sharpness, a definition, an *honesty* that Tedric didn't have. There was something vibrant about Joe. He was so very alive, so vital, as if he took each moment and lived it to its very fullest. Veronica had never met anyone quite like him before.

Imagine taking a squad of seven men deep behind enemy lines, she thought, with bombs falling, no less. Imagine having the courage and the confidence to risk not just one's own life, but six other lives, as well. And then imagine actually *enjoying* the danger.

Veronica thought of the men she knew, the men she was used to working with. They tended to be so very...careful. Not that they weren't risk takers—oftentimes they were. But the risks they took were financial or psychological, never physical. Not a single one would ever put himself into any real physical danger. A paper cut was the worst they could expect, and *that* usually required a great deal of hand-holding.

Most men looked softer, less imposing when asleep, but not Joe. His body may have been relaxed, but his jaw was tightly clenched, his lips pulled back in what was almost a snarl. Underneath his lids, his eyes jerked back and forth in REM sleep.

He slept ferociously, almost as if these five minutes of rest were all he'd get for the next few days.

It was strange. It was very strange. And it was stranger still when Veronica sighed.

It wasn't a particularly weighty sigh, just a little one, really. Not even very loud.

Still, Joe's eyes flew open and he sat up straight. He was instantly alert, without a hint of fatigue on his lean face.

He took a sip directly from a can of soda that was sitting on the glass-topped end table and looked at Veronica steadily, as if he hadn't been fast asleep mere seconds earlier. "Time for the tailor?" he said.

She was fascinated. "How do you do that?" she asked, leaning forward slightly, searching his eyes for any sign of grogginess. "Wake up so quickly, I mean."

Joe blinked and then smiled, clearly surprised at her interest. His smile was genuine, reaching his eyes and making the laugh lines around them deepen. Lord, he was even more attractive when he smiled that way. Veronica found herself smiling back, hypnotized by the warmth of his eyes.

"Training." He leaned back in his chair and watched her. "SEALs take classes to study sleep patterns. We learn to catch catnaps whenever we can."

"Really?" Joe could see the amusement in her eyes, the barely restrained laughter curving the corners of her mouth. Her natural expression was a smile, he realized. But she'd taught herself to put on that serious, businesslike facade she wore most of the time. "Classes to learn how to sleep and wake up?" she asked, letting a laugh slip out.

Was she laughing *at* him or *with* him? He honestly couldn't tell, and he felt his own smile fade. Damn, what was it about this particular girl that he found so intimidating? With any other woman, he'd assume the joke was shared, and he'd feel glad that he was making her smile. But *this* one . . .

There was attraction in her eyes, all right. Genuine animal attraction. He saw it there every time she glanced in his direction. But there was also wariness. Maybe even fear. She didn't want to be attracted to him.

She probably didn't think he was good enough for her.

Damn it, he was a Navy SEAL. There was nobody better. If she wanted to ignore the fire that was ready to ignite between them, then so be it. Her loss.

He would find plenty of women to distract him during this way-too-simple operation, and—

With a hiss of silk, she crossed her long legs. Joe had to look away.

Her loss. It was her loss. Except every cell in his body was screaming that the loss was *his*.

Okay. So he'd seduce her. He'd ply her with wine—no, make that expensive champagne—and he'd wait until the heat he saw in her eyes started to burn out of control. It would be that easy. And then... Oh, baby. It didn't take much to imagine his hands in her soft red hair, then sweeping up underneath the delicate silk of her blouse, finding the soft, sweet fullness of her breasts. He could picture one of those sexy legs wrapped around one of his legs, as she pressed herself tightly against him, her fingers reaching for the buckle of his belt as he plundered her beautiful mouth with his tongue and . . .

Sure, it might be that easy.

But then again, it might not.

He had no reason on earth to believe that a woman like this one would want anything to do with him. From the way she dressed and acted, Joe was willing to bet big bucks that she wouldn't want any kind of permanent thing with a guy like him.

Veronica St. John—"Sinjin," she pronounced it with that richer-than-God accent—could probably trace her bloodline back to Henry the Eighth. And Joe, he didn't even know who the hell his father was. And wouldn't *that* just make dicey dinner conversation. *"Catalanotto... Italian name, isn't it? Where exactly is your father from, Lieutenant?"*

"Well, gee, I don't know, Ronnie." He wondered if anyone had ever called her Ronnie, probably not. *"Mom says he was some sailor in port for a day or two. Catalanotto is her name. And where* she *came from is anyone's guess. So is it really any wonder Mom drank as much as she did?"*

Yeah, that would go over *real* well.

But he wasn't talking about marriage here. He wasn't talking about much more than quenching that sharp thirst he felt whenever he looked into Veronica St. John's eyes. He was talking about one night, maybe two or three or four, depending on how long this operation lasted. He was talking short-term fling, hot affair—not a lot of conversation required.

It was true, he didn't have a lot of experience with debutantes, but hell, her money and power were only on the surface. Peel the outer trappings away, and Veronica St. John was a woman. And Joe knew women. He knew what they liked, how to catch their eye, how to make them smile.

Usually women came to him. It had been a long while since he'd actively pursued one.

This could be fun.

"We trained to learn how to drop instantly into rapid-eye-movement sleep," Joe said, evenly meeting the crystal blueness of Veronica's eyes. "It comes in handy in a combat situation, or a covert op where there may be only brief stretches of time safe enough to catch some rest. It's kept more than one SEAL alive on more than one occasion."

"What else do SEALs learn how to do?" Veronica asked.

Oh, baby, what you don't know ...

"You name it, honey," Joe said, "we can do it."

"My name," she declared in her cool English accent, sitting back in her chair and gazing at him steadily, "is Veronica St. John. Not honey. Not babe. Veronica. St. John. Please refrain from using terms of endearment. I don't care for them."

She was trying to look as chilly as her words sounded, but Joe saw heat when he looked into her eyes. She was trying to hide it, but it was back there. He knew, with a sudden odd certainty, that when they made love, it was going to be a near religious experience. Not *if* they made love, *When*. It *was* going to happen.

"It's a habit that's gonna be hard to break," he said.

Veronica stood, briefcase in hand. "I'm sure you have a number of habits that will be a challenge to break," she said. "So I suggest we not keep the tailor waiting a minute longer. We have plenty of work to do before we can get some sleep."

But Joe didn't move. "So what am I supposed to call you?" he asked. "Ronnie?"

Veronica looked up to find a glint of mischief in his dark eyes. He knew perfectly well that calling her "Ronnie" would not suit. He was smiling, and she was struck by the even whiteness of his teeth. He may have chipped one at one time, but the others were straight and well taken care of.

"I think Ms. St. John will do quite well, thank you," she said. "That *is* how the prince addresses me."

"I see," Joe murmured, clearly amused.

"Shall we?" she prompted.

"Oh, yes, please," Joe said overenthusiastically, then tried to look disappointed. "Oh ... you mean shall we *leave?* I thought you meant ..." But he was only pretending that he misunderstood. He couldn't keep a smile from slipping out.

Veronica shook her head in exasperation. "Two days, Lieutenant," she said. "We have two days to create a miracle, and you're wasting time with sophomoric humor."

Joe stood, stretching his arms above his head. His feet and legs were bare underneath his robe. So was the rest of him, but Veronica was determined not to think about that.

"I thought you were going to call me 'Your Majesty.'"

"Two days, *Your Majesty,*" Veronica repeated.

"Two days is a breeze, Ronnie," he said. "And I've decided if I'm the prince I can call you whatever I want, and I want to call you Ronnie."

"No, you most certainly will not!"

"Why the hell not? I'm the prince," Joe said. "It's your choice—Ronnie or Honey. I don't care."

"My Lord, you're almost as incorrigible as Tedric," Veronica sputtered.

"'My Lord,'" Joe mused. "Yeah, you can call me that. Although I prefer 'Your All-Powerful Mightiness.' Hey, while I'm making royal decrees, why don't you go ahead and give the serfs a day off."

He was laughing at her. He was teasing her, and enjoying watching her squirm.

"You know, this is going to be a vacation for me, Ron," he added. "Two days of prep is a cakewalk."

Veronica laughed in disbelief. How *dare* he...? "Two days," she said. "You're going to have to completely relearn how to walk and talk and stand and sit and *eat.* Not to mention memorizing all the names and faces of the aides and ambassadors and government officials that the prince is acquainted with. And don't forget all the rules and protocols you'll have to learn, all of the Ustanzian customs and traditions..."

Joe spread his hands and shrugged. "How hard could it be? Give me a videotape of Tedric and half an hour, and you'll think I'm the same guy," he said. "I've gone on far tougher missions with way less prep time. Two days—forty-eight hours—is a luxury, sweetheart."

How could he think that? Veronica was so stressed out by the rapidly approaching deadline she could barely breathe.

"*Less* than forty-eight hours," she told him sharply. "You have to sleep some of that time."

"Sleep?" Joe smiled. "I just did."

Chapter 5

"And never, *ever* open the door yourself," Veronica said. "Always wait for someone—a servant—to do it for you."

Joe gazed at her across the top of his mug as he sat on the other side of the conference table in Tedric's royal suite. "Never?" he said. He took a sip of coffee, still watching her, his dark eyes mysterious, unreadable. "Old Ted never opens the door for anyone?"

"If he were with a king or a queen, he might open the door," Veronica said, glancing down at her notes. And away from those eyes. "But I doubt you'll be running into any such personages on *this* tour."

"What does Ted do when he's all alone?" Joe started to put his mug down on the richly polished oak tabletop, but stopped as if he were afraid to mar the wood. He pulled one of Veronica's file folders closer and set his mug down on top of the stiff manila. "Just stand there until a servant comes along to open the door? That could be a real drag if he's in a rush to use the head." He rested his chin in the palm of his hand, elbow on the table, as he continued to gaze at her.

"Your Highness, an Ustanzian prince never rests his elbows on the top of a table," Veronica said with forced patience.

Joe smiled and didn't move. He just watched her with half-closed bedroom eyes that exuded sexuality. They'd been working together all night, and not once had he let her forget that she was a woman and he was a man. "I'm not a Ustanzian prince," he said. "Yet."

Veronica folded her hands neatly on top of her notes. "And it's not called a 'head,'" she said. "Not john, not toilet, not bathroom. It's a water closet. W.C. We went through this already, remember, Your Majesty?"

"How about I call it the Little Prince's Room?" Joe asked.

Veronica laughed despite her growing sense of doom. Or maybe because of it. What was she going to do about Joe Catalanotto's thick New Jersey accent? And what was she going to do about the fact that this man didn't, for even one single second, take *any*thing they were doing seriously?

And to further frustrate her, she was ready to drop from exhaustion, while he looked ready to run laps.

"My mother's name is Maria. She was an Italian countess before she met my father. My father is King Derrick the Fourth, *his* father was Derrick the Third," Joe recited. "I was born in the capital city on January 7, 1961.... You know, this would be a whole lot easier on both of us if you would just hand me your file on this guy, and give me a videotape so I can see firsthand the way he walks and stands and..."

"Excuse me, Lieutenant." A FInCOM agent by the name of West stood politely to one side.

Joe looked up, an instant Naval Officer. He sat straighter and even looked as if he was paying attention. Now, why couldn't Veronica get him to take *her* that seriously?

"At Admiral Forrest's request, Mr. Laughton requires your consultation, sir, in planning the scheduling of the tour, and the strategy for your protection," West continued. "That is, if you wish to have any input."

Joe stood. "Damn straight I do," he said. "Your security stinks. Fortunately those terrorists took the night off, or I'd already be dead."

West stiffened. "The security we've provided has been top level—"

"What I'm saying is your so-called top-level security isn't good enough, pal," Joe countered. He looked back at Veronica. "What do you say you go take a nap, Ronnie, and we meet back at . . ." He glanced at his watch. "How's eleven-hundred hours? Just over two hours."

But Veronica stood, shaking her head. She wanted desperately to sleep, but unless she attended this meeting, the visit to Saint Mary's would be removed from the tour schedule. She spoke directly to the FInCOM agent. "I'd like to have some input in this meeting, too, Mr. West," she said coolly. "I'm sure Mr. Laughton—or Admiral Forrest—won't mind if I sit in."

Joe shrugged. "Suit yourself."

"Princes don't shrug, Your Highness," Veronica reminded him as they followed West out into the corridor and toward the conference room.

Joe rolled his eyes.

"And princes don't roll their eyes," she said.

"Sheesh," he muttered.

"They don't swear, either, Your Majesty," Veronica told him. "Not even those thinly veiled words you Americans use in place of the truly nasty ones."

"So you're *not* an American," Joe said, walking backward so he could look at her. "Mac Forrest must've been mistaken. He told me, despite your fancy accent, that you were."

Joe had talked about her with Admiral Forrest. Veronica felt a warm flash of pleasure that she instantly tried to squelch. So what if Joe had talked with the admiral about her. *She'd* talked to the admiral about Joe, simply to get some perspective on whom she'd be dealing with, who she'd be working closely with for the next few weeks.

"Oh, I'm American," Veronica said. "I even say a full variety of those aforementioned nasty words upon occasion."

Joe laughed. He had a nice laugh, rich and full. It made her want to smile. "That I won't believe until I hear it."

"Well, you won't hear it, Your Majesty. It wouldn't be polite or proper."

Her shoe caught in the thick carpeting, and she stumbled slightly. Joe caught and held her arm, stopping to make sure she had her balance.

Veronica looked really beat. She looked ready to fall on her face—which she just about did. Joe could feel the warmth of her arm, even through the sleeve of her jacket and blouse. He didn't want to let her go, so he didn't. They stood there in the hotel corridor, and FInCOM Agent West waited impatiently nearby.

Joe was playing with fire. He knew that he was playing with fire. But, hell. He was a demolitions expert. He was used to handling materials that could blow sky-high at any time.

Veronica looked down at his hand still on her arm, then lifted enormous blue eyes to his.

"I'm quite all right, Your Royal Highness," she said in that Julie Andrews accent.

"You're tired as hell," he countered bluntly. "Go get some sleep."

"Believe it or not, I do have some information of importance to add to this scheduling meeting," she said hotly, the crystal of her eyes turning suddenly to blue flame. "I'd truly appreciate it if you'd unhand me so we could continue on our way, Your Majesty."

"Wait," Joe said. "Don't tell me. A prince never offers a helping hand, is that it? A prince lets a lady fall on her face, right?"

"A prince doesn't take advantage of a lady's misfortune," Veronica said tightly. "You helped me—thank you. Now let me go. Please. Your Excellency."

Joe laughed. This time it was a low, dangerous sound. His hand tightened on her arm and he drew her even closer to him, so that their noses almost touched, so that Veronica could feel his body heat through the thin cotton shirt and dark slacks the tailor had left him with after the early-morning fitting.

"Babe, if you think this is taking advantage, you've never been taken advantage of." He lowered his voice and dropped his head down so he was speaking directly into her ear. "If you want, I'll demonstrate the differences. With pleasure."

She could feel the warmth of his breath on her neck as he waited for her to react. He was expecting her to run, screaming, away from him. He was expecting her to be outraged, upset, angry, offended.

But all she could think about was how utterly delicious he smelled.

What would he say, what would he do if she moved her head a fraction of an inch to the right and pressed her cheek against the roughness of his chin. What would he do if she lifted her head to whisper into *his* ear, "Oh, yes"?

It wouldn't be the response he was expecting, that was certain.

But the truth was, this wasn't about sex, it was about power. Veronica had played hardball with the big boys long enough to know that.

It wasn't that he wasn't interested—he'd made that more than clear in the way he'd looked at her all night long. But Veronica was willing to bet that right now Joe was bluffing. And while she wasn't going to call his bluff, she was going to let him know that merely because he was bigger and stronger than she, didn't mean he'd automatically win.

So she lifted her head and, keeping her voice cool, almost chilly, said, "One would think that a Navy SEAL might be aware of the dangers of standing too long in a public corridor, considering someone out there wants Tedric—whom, by the way, you look quite a bit like these days—dead."

Joe laughed.

Not exactly the response *she* was expecting after her verbal attack. Another man might have been annoyed that his bluff hadn't worked. Another man might have pouted or glowered. Joe laughed.

"I don't know, Ron," he said, letting her go. His dark eyes were genuinely amused, but there was something else there, too. Could it possibly be respect? "You sound so...proper, but I don't think you really are, are you? I think it's all an act. I think you go home from work, and you take off the Margaret Thatcher costume, and let down your hair and put on some little black sequined number with stiletto heels, and you go out and mambo in some Latin nightclub until dawn."

Veronica crossed her arms. "You forgot my gigolo," she said crisply. "I go pick up my current gigolo and then *we* mambo till dawn."

"Let me know when there's an opening, honey," Joe said. "I'd love to apply for the job."

All humor had gone from his eyes. He was dead serious. Veronica turned away, afraid he'd see just from looking at her how appealing she found the thought of dancing with him until dawn, their bodies clasped together, moving to the pulsing beat of Latin drums.

"We'd best not keep Mr. Laughton waiting," she said. "Your Majesty."

"Damn," Joe said. "Margaret Thatcher's back."

"Sorry to disappoint you," Veronica murmured as they went into the secret-service agents' suite. "But she never left."

"Saint Mary's, right here in Washington," Veronica said from her seat next to Joe at the big conference table. "Someone keeps taking Saint Mary's off the schedule."

"It's unnecessary," Kevin Laughton said in his flat, almost-bored-sounding Midwestern accent.

"I disagree." Veronica spoke softly but firmly.

"Look, Ronnie," Senator McKinley said, and Veronica briefly shut her eyes. Lord, but Joe Catalanotto had all of them calling her Ronnie now. "Maybe you don't understand this, dear, but Saint Mary's doesn't do us any good. The building is too small, too well protected, and too difficult for the assassins to penetrate. Besides, it's not a public event. The assassins are going to want news coverage. They're going to want to make sure millions of people are watching when they kill the prince. Besides, there's no clear targeting area going into and out of the structure. It's a waste of our time."

"This visit's been scheduled for months," Veronica said quietly. "It's been scheduled since the Ustanzian secretary of press announced Prince Tedric's American tour. I think we can take one hour from one day to fulfill a promise the prince made."

Henri Freder, the Ustanzian ambassador to the United States, shifted in his seat. "Surely Prince Tedric can visit this Saint Mary's at the end of the tour, after the Alaskan cruise, on his way back home."

"That will be too late," Veronica said.

"Cruise?" Joe repeated. "If the assassins haven't been apprehended before the cruise to Alaska is scheduled, there's no way in hell we're getting on that loveboat." He looked around the table. "A cruise ship's too isolated. It's a natural target for tangos."

He smiled at their blank expressions. "Tangos," Joe repeated. "T's. Terrorists. The bad guys with guns."

Ah. There was understanding all around.

"Unless, of course, we're ready and waiting for 'em," Joe continued. "And maybe that's not such a bad idea. Replace the ship's personnel and passenger list with platoons of SEALs and—"

"No way," Laughton said. "FInCOM is handling this. It isn't some military operation. SEALs have no place in it."

"Terrorists are involved," Joe countered. "SEAL Team Ten has had extensive counterterrorist training. My men are prepared for—"

"War," Laughton finished for him. "Your men are prepared and trained for *war*. This is not a war, Lieutenant."

Joe pointed to the cellular phone on the table in front of Laughton. "Then you'd better call the terrorists. Call the Cloud of Death, call up Diosdado. Call him up and tell him that this is not a war. Because *he* sure as hell thinks it's one."

"Please," Veronica interjected. "Before we continue, may we all agree to keep Saint Mary's on the schedule?"

McKinley frowned down at the papers in front of him. "I see from the previous list that there weren't going to be any media present at the event at Saint Mary's."

"Not all of the events scheduled were for the benefit of the news cameras, Senator," Veronica said evenly. She glanced around the table. "Gentlemen. This rescheduling means hours and hours of extra work for all of us. I'm trying my best to cooperate, as I'm sure you are, too. But I happen to know that this appearance at Saint Mary's was of utmost importance to Prince Tedric." She widened her eyes innocently. "If necessary, I'll ring up the prince and ask for *his* input and—"

"No need to do that," Senator McKinley said hastily.

Getting self-centered Prince Tedric in on this scheduling nightmare was the last thing *any*one wanted, Veronica included. His so-called "input" would slow this process down to a crawl. But she was prepared to do whatever she had to do to keep the visit to Saint Mary's on the schedule.

McKinley looked around the table. "I think we can keep Saint Mary's on the list." There was a murmur of agreement.

Joe watched Veronica. Her red curls were up in some kind of feminine arrangement on the top of her head. With her delicate features and innocent blue eyes, she looked every inch the demure, cool English lady; and again, Joe was struck by the feeling that her outward appearance was only an act. She wasn't demure *or* cool, and if his gut feelings were right, she could probably outmanipulate the entire tableful of them. Hell, she just had. But she'd done it so subtly that no one was even aware they'd been manipulated.

"About the Alaskan cruise," Senator McKinley said.

"That's not until later in the tour." Joe leaned back in his chair. "Let's keep it off the public schedule for now. We don't want the T's—terrorists—choosing that opportunity above everything else. We want 'em to strike early on. But still, we can start making arrangements with the SEAL teams, start getting 'em prepped for a potential operation aboard ship."

"No SEALs," Kevin Laughton said tersely.

Joe gave the FInCOM agent a disbelieving look. "You *want* high casualties? Is that your goal here?"

"Of course not—"

"We're all on the same team, pal," Joe said. "We all work for the U.S. Government. Just because I'm Navy and you're Fink—"

"No SEALs." Laughton turned to an aide. "Release this schedule to the news media ASAP, keeping the cruise information off the list." He stood. "My men will start scouting each of these sites."

Joe stood up, too. "You should start right here in this hotel," he said. "If you're serious about making the royal suite secure, you're understaffed. And the sliding door to the balcony in the bedroom doesn't lock. What kind of security is that?"

Laughton stared at him. "You're on the *tenth* floor."

"Terrorists sometimes know how to climb," Joe said.

"I can assure you you're quite safe," Laughton said.

"And I can assure you that I'm not. If security stays as is, if Diosdado and his gang decide to come into this hotel to rid the world of Prince Tedric, then I'm as good as dead."

"I can understand your concern," Laughton said. "But—"

"Then you won't have any objection to bringing the rest of my Alpha Squad out here," Joe interrupted. "You're obviously undermanned, and I'd feel a whole hell of a lot better if—"

"No," Laughton said. "Absolutely not. A squad of Navy SEALs? Utter chaos. My men won't stand for it. I won't have it."

"I'm going to be standing around, wearing a damned shooting target on my chest," Joe retorted. "I want my own guys nearby, watching my back, plugging the holes in FInCOM's security net. I can tell you right now, they won't get in your boys' way."

"No," Laughton said again. "*I'm* in charge of security, and I say *no*. This meeting is adjourned."

Joe watched the FInCOM chief leave the room, then glanced up to find Veronica's eyes on him.

"I guess we're going to have to do this the hard way," he said.

The man known only as Diosdado looked up from his desk as Salustiano Vargas was shown into the room.

"Ah, old friend," Vargas greeted him with relief. "Why did your men not say it was you they were bringing me to see?"

Diosdado was silent, just looking at the other man as he thoughtfully stroked his beard.

Vargas threw himself down into a chair across from the desk and casually stretched his legs out in front of him. "It has been too long, no?" he said. "What have you been up to, man?"

"Not as much as you have, apparently." Diosdado smiled, but it was a mere shadow of his normally wide, toothy grin.

Vargas's own smile was twisted. "Eh, you heard about that, huh?" His smile turned to a scowl. "I would have drilled the bastard through the heart if that damned woman hadn't pushed him out of the way."

Diosdado stood. "You are lucky—very, *very* lucky—that your bullet missed Tedric Cortere," he said harshly.

Vargas stared at him in surprise. "But—"

"If you had kept in touch, you would have been aware of what I have spent *months* planning." Diosdado didn't raise his voice when he was angry. He lowered it. Right now, it was very, *very* quiet.

Vargas opened his mouth to speak, to protest, but he wisely shut it tightly instead.

"The Cloud of Death intended to take Cortere hostage," Diosdado said. "Intends," he corrected himself. "We still intend to take him." He began to pace—a halting, shuffling process as he dragged his bad leg behind him. "Of course, now that you have intervened, the prince's security has been strengthened. FInCOM is involved, and my contacts tell me that the U.S. Navy is even playing some part in Cortere's protection."

Vargas stared at him.

"So what," Diosdado continued, turning to face Salustiano Vargas, "do you suggest we do to bring this high level of security and protection back to where it was before you fouled things up?"

Vargas swallowed, knowing what the other man was going to tell him, and knowing that he wasn't going to like what he heard.

"They are all waiting for another assassination attempt," Diosdado said. "Until they *get* another assassination attempt, security will be too tight. Do you know what you are going to do, my old friend Salustiano?"

Vargas knew. He knew, and he didn't like it. "Diosdado," he said. "Please. We're friends. I saved your *life*—"

"You will go back," Diosdado said very, very softly, "and you will make another attempt on the prince's life. You will fail, and you will be apprehended. Dead or alive—your choice."

Vargas sat in silence as Diosdado limped, shuffling, from the room.

"Tell me what it is about Navy SEALs that makes Kevin Laughton so upset, Your Majesty," Veronica said as she and Joe were delivered safely back to Prince Tedric's hotel suite. "Why doesn't he want your Alpha Squad around?"

"He knows his guys would give him problems if my guys were brought in to do their job," Joe said. "It's a slap in the face. It implies I don't think FInCOM can get the job done."

"But obviously, you don't think they can."

Joe shook his head and sat down heavily in one of the plush easy chairs in the royal living room. "I think they're probably top-notch at mid-level protection," he said. "But my life's on the line here, and the bad guys aren't street punks or crazy people with guns. They're professionals. Diosdado runs a top-notch military organization. He's a formidable opponent. He could get through this kind of security without blinking. But he couldn't get through the Alpha Squad. I *know* my SEALs are the best of the best. SEAL Team Ten is elite, and the Alpha Squad is made up of the best men in Team Ten. I want them here, even if I have to step on some toes or offend some FInCOM agents. The end result is I stay alive. Are you following me?"

Veronica nodded, sitting down on the sofa and resting her briefcase on a long wooden coffee table.

The sofa felt so comfortable, so soft. It would be so easy to let her head fall back and her eyes close. . . .

"Maybe we should take a break," Joe said. "You can barely keep your eyes open."

"No, there's so much more you need to learn," Veronica said. She made herself sit up straight. If *he* could stay awake, she could, too. "The history of Ustanzia. The names of Ustanzian officials." She pulled a file from her briefcase and opened it. "I have fifty-seven pictures of people you will come into contact with, Your Highness. I need you to memorize these faces and names, and—Lord, if there were only another way to do this."

"Earphone," Joe said, flipping through the file.

"Excuse me?"

He looked up at her. "I wear a concealed earphone," he said. "And you have a mic. We set up a video camera so that you can see and hear everything I'm doing while you're some safe distance away—maybe even out in a surveillance truck. When someone comes up to shake my hand, you feed me his name and title and any other pertinent info I might need." He flipped through the photos and handed them back to Veronica. "Pick out the top ten and I'll look 'em over. The others I don't need to know."

Veronica fixed him with a look, suddenly feeling extremely awake. What did he mean, the others he didn't need to know?

"All fifty-seven of these people are diplomats Tedric knows quite well. You could run into any one of these people at any time during the course of this tour," she said. "The original file had over three hundred faces and names."

Joe shook his head. "I don't have time to memorize faces and names," he said. "With the high-tech equipment we have access to—"

"*You* don't have time?" Veronica repeated, eyebrows lifted. "We're *all* running out of time, Lieutenant. It's *my* task to prepare you. Let me decide what there is and isn't time for."

Joe leaned forward. "Look, Ronnie, no offense, but I'm used to preparing for an operation at my own speed," he said. "I appreciate everything you're trying to do, but in all honesty, the way that Ted walks and talks is the least of my concerns. I've got this security thing to straighten out and—"

"That's Kevin Laughton's job," she interrupted. "Not yours."

"But it's my ass that's on the line," he said flatly. "FInCOM's going to change their security plans, or this operation is not going to happen."

Veronica tapped her fingernails on the legal pad she was holding. "And if you don't look and act enough like Prince Tedric," she said tartly, "this operation is not going to happen, either."

"Get me a tape," Joe countered. "Get me a videotape and an audiotape of the guy, and I promise you, I *swear* to you, I will look and act and sound exactly like Ted."

Veronica's teeth were clenched tightly together in annoyance. "Details," she said tightly. "How will you learn the details? Assuming, of course, that you are able to miraculously transform yourself into European royalty simply by viewing a videotape?"

"Write 'em down," Joe said without hesitation. "I retain written information better, anyway." The telephone rang and he paused briefly, listening while West answered it. "Lieutenant, it's for you," the FInCOM agent said.

Joe reached for the extension. "Yo. Catalanotto here."

Yo. The man answered the phone with "Yo" and Veronica was supposed to believe he'd be able to pass himself off as the prince, with little or no instruction from her?

"Mac," Joe said into the telephone. It was Admiral Forrest on the other end. "Great. Thanks for calling me back. What's the word on getting Alpha Squad out here?"

How did a lieutenant get away with calling an admiral by his first name, anyway? Veronica had heard that Forrest had been a SEAL himself at one time in his long navy career. And from what little she knew about SEALs so far, she suspected they were unconventional in more than just their warfare tactics.

Joe's jaw was tight and the muscles in the side of his face were working as he listened to Forrest speak. He swore sharply, not bothering to try to disguise his bad language. As Veronica watched, he rubbed his forehead—the first sign he'd given all day that he was weary.

"FInCOM has raised hell before," he said. "That hasn't stopped us in the past." There was a pause and he added hotly, "Their security *is* lax, sir. Damn, you know that as well as I do." Another pause. "I was hoping I wouldn't have to do that."

Joe glanced up and into Veronica's watching eyes. She looked away, suddenly self-conscious about the fact that she was openly eavesdropping. As she shuffled through the file of photographs, she was aware of his gaze still on her.

"Before you go, sir," he said into the telephone. "I need another favor. I need audio- and videotapes of Tedric sent to my room ASAP."

Veronica looked up at that, and directly into Joe's eyes.

"Thanks, Admiral," he said and hung up the phone. "He'll have 'em sent right over," he said to Veronica as he stood.

He looked as if he were about to leave, to go somewhere. But she didn't even get a chance to question him.

"FInCOM's having a briefing about the tour locations here in D.C.," Joe said. "I need to be there."

"But—"

"Why don't you take a nap?" Joe said. He looked at his watch, and Veronica automatically glanced at hers. It was nearly five o'clock in the evening. "We'll meet back here at twenty-one hundred hours."

Veronica quickly counted on her fingers. Nine o'clock. "No," she said, standing. "That's too long. I can give you an hour break, but—"

"This briefing's important," Joe said. "It'll be over at twenty-hundred, but I'll need an extra hour."

Veronica shook her head in exasperation. "Kevin Laughton doesn't even *want* you there," she said. "You'll spend the entire time arguing—"

"Damn straight, I'm going to argue," Joe said. "If FInCOM insists on assuming the tangos are going to mosey on up to the front door and ring the bell before they strike, then I've got to be there, arguing to keep the back door protected."

Joe was already heading toward the door. West and Freeman scrambled to their feet, following him.

"Put those details you were talking about in writing," Joe suggested. "I'll see you in a few hours."

Veronica all but stamped her foot. "You're supposed to be working with me," she said. "You can't just . . . leave. . . ."

But he was gone.

Veronica threw her pad and pen onto the table in frustration. Time was running out.

Chapter 6

Veronica woke up from her nap at seven-thirty, still exhausted but too worried to sleep. *How* was Joe going to learn to act like Prince Tedric if he wouldn't give her any time to properly teach him?

She'd made lists and more lists of details and information Joe had no way of knowing—things like, the prince was right-handed. That was normally not a problem, except she'd noticed that Joe was a lefty. She'd written down trivial information such as the fact that Tedric always twirled the signet ring he wore on his right hand when he was thinking.

Veronica got up from the table and started to pace, alternately worried, frustrated and angry with Joe. Who in blazes actually *cared* what Tedric did with his jewelry? Who, truly, would notice? And why was she making lists of details when basic things such as Tedric's walk and ramrod-straight posture were being ignored?

Restless, Veronica pawed through the clothes in her suitcase, searching for a pair of bike shorts and her exercise bra. It was time to try to release some of this nervous energy. She dug down farther and found her favorite tape. Smiling grimly, she crossed to the expensive stereo system built into the wall and put the tape into the tape deck. She pushed Play and music came on. She cranked the volume.

The tape contained an assorted collection of her favorite songs—loud, fast songs with pulsating beats. It was good music, familiar music, *loud* music.

Her sneakers were on the floor of the closet near the bathroom. As Veronica sat on the floor to slip them onto her feet and tie them tightly, she let the music wash over her. Already she felt better.

She scrambled up and into the center of the living room, pushing the furniture back and away, clearing the floor, giving herself some space to move.

With the furniture out of the way, Veronica started slowly, stretching out her tired muscles. When she was properly warmed up, she closed her eyes and let the music embrace her.

And then she began to dance.

Halfway through the tape, it came to her—the answer to her frustration and impotent anger. She had been hired to teach Joe to act like the prince. With his cooperation, the task was formidable. Without his cooperation, it was impossible. If he failed to cooperate, she would have to threaten to withdraw.

Yes, that was exactly what she had to do. At nine o'clock, when she went down the hall to the royal suite, she would march right up to Joe and look him in the eye and—

A man wearing all black was standing just inside her balcony doorway, leaning against the wall, watching her dance.

Veronica leaped backward, her body reacting to the unannounced presence of a large intruder before her brain registered the fact that it was Joe Catalanotto.

Heart pounding, chest heaving, she tried to catch her breath as she stared at him. How in God's name had *Joe* gotten into her room?

Joe stared, too, caught in the ocean-blueness of Veronica's eyes as the music pounded around them. She looked frightened, like a wild animal, uncertain whether to freeze or flee.

Turning suddenly, she reached for the stereo and switched the music off. The silence was abrupt and jarring.

Her red curls swung and bounced around her shoulders as she turned rapidly back to look at him again. "What are you doing here?" she asked.

"Proving a point," he replied. His voice sounded strained and hoarse to his own ears. There was no mystery as to why that was. Seeing her like this had made his blood pressure rise, as well as other things.

"I don't understand," she said, her eyes narrowing as she studied his face, searching for an answer. "How did you get in? My door was locked."

Joe gestured to the sliding door that led to the balcony. "No, it wasn't. In fact, it was open. Warm night. If you breathe deeply, you can almost smell the cherry blossoms."

Veronica was staring at him, struggling to reconcile his words with the truth as she knew it. This room was on the tenth floor. Ten stories up, off the ground. Visitors didn't simply stroll in through the balcony door.

Joe couldn't keep his gaze from sliding down her body. Man, she was one hot package. In those skintight purple-and-turquoise patterned shorts and that tight, black, racer-backed top that exposed a firm, creamy midriff, with all those beautiful red curls loose around her pale shoulders, she looked positively steamy. She was slender, but not skinny as he'd thought. Her waist was small, her stomach flat, flaring out to softly curving hips and a firm, round rear end. Her legs were incredible, but he'd already known that. Still, in those tight shorts, her shapely legs seemed to go on and on and on forever, leading his eyes to her derriere. Her breasts were full, every curve, every detail intimately outlined by the stretchy fabric of her top.

And, God, the way she'd been dancing when he'd first climbed onto the balcony had exuded a raw sensuality, a barely contained passion. He'd been right about her. She *had* been hiding something underneath those boxy, conservative suits and that cool, distant attitude. Who would have guessed she would spend her personal time dancing like some vision on MTV?

She was still breathing hard from dancing. Or maybe—and more likely—she was breathing hard from the sudden shock he'd given her. He'd actually been standing inside the balcony door for about ten minutes before she looked up. He'd been in no hurry to interrupt. He could have stayed there, quite happily, and watched her dance all night.

Well, maybe not *all* night . . .

Veronica took a step back, away from him, as if she could see his every thought in his eyes. Her own eyes were very wide and incredibly, brilliantly blue. "You came in...from the *balcony?*"

Joe nodded and held something out to her. It was a flower, Veronica realized. He was holding a rather tired and bruised purple-and-gold pansy, its petals curled up for the night. She'd seen flowers just like it growing in flower beds outside the hotel.

"First I climbed down to the ground and got this," Joe said, his husky voice soft and seductive, warmly intimate. "It's proof I was actually there."

He was still holding the flower out to her, but Veronica couldn't move, her mind barely registering the words he spoke. A black band was across his forehead, holding his long hair in place. He was wearing black pants and a long-sleeved black turtleneck, with some kind of equipment vest over it, even though the spring night *was* quite warm. Oddly enough, his feet were bare. He wasn't smiling, and his face looked harsh and unforgiving. And dangerous. Very, *very* dangerous.

Veronica gazed at him, her heart in her throat. As he stepped closer and pressed the flower into her hand, she was pulled into the depths of his eyes. The fire she saw there became molten. His mouth was hard and hungry as his gaze raked her body.

And then his meaning cut through.

He'd climbed *down* to the *ground*...? *And* back up again? Ten *stories?*

"You climbed up the outside of the hotel and no one stopped you?" Veronica looked down at the flower, hoping he wouldn't notice the trembling in her voice.

He crossed to the sliding door and pulled the curtain shut. Was that for safety's sake, or for privacy? Veronica wondered as she turned away. She was afraid he might see his unconcealed desire echoed in her own eyes.

Desire? What was wrong with her? It was true, Joe Catalanotto was outrageously good-looking. But despite his obvious physical attributes, he was rude, tactless and disrespectful, rough in his manners and appearance. In fact, he was about as far from a being a prince as any man she'd ever known. They'd barely even exchanged a civil conversation. All they did was fight. So why on earth could she think of nothing but the touch of his hands on her skin, his lips on hers, his body. . . ?

"No one saw me climbing down *or* up," Joe said, his voice surrounding her like soft, rich velvet. "There are no guards posted on this side of the building. The FInCOM agents don't see the balcony for what it is—a back door. An accessible and obvious back door."

"It's so far from the ground," she countered in disbelief.

"It was an easy climb. Under an hour."

Under an hour. *This* is what he'd been doing with his time, Veronica realized suddenly. He should have been working with *her,* learning how to act like Tedric, and instead he was climbing up and down the outside of the hotel like some misguided superhero. Anger flooded through her.

Joe took a step forward, closing the small gap between them. The urge to touch her hair, to skim the softness of her cheek with his knuckle, was overpowering.

This was *not* the scenario he'd imagined when he'd climbed up the side of the hotel and onto her balcony. He'd expected to find Veronica hard at work, scribbling furiously away on the legal pad she always carried, or typing frantically into her laptop computer. He'd expected her to be wearing something that hid her curves and disguised her femininity. He'd expected her hair to be pinned up off her neck. He'd expected her to look up at him, gasping in startled surprise, as he walked into the room.

And, yeah, he'd expected her to be impressed when he told her he'd scaled the side of the hotel in order to prove that FInCOM's security stank.

Instead, finally over her initial shock at seeing him there, Veronica folded her arms across her delicious-looking breasts and glared at him. "I can't *believe* this," she said. "I'm supposed to be teaching you how to fool the bloody world into thinking you're Prince Tedric and you're off playing commando games and climbing ten stories up the outside of this hotel?"

"I'm not a commando, I'm a SEAL," Joe said, feeling his own temper rise. "There's a difference. And I'm not playing games. FInCOM's security stinks."

"The President of the United States hasn't had any qualms about FInCOM's ability to protect *him,*" Veronica said tersely.

"The President of the United States is followed around by fifteen Finks, ready to jump into the line of fire and take a bullet for him if necessary," Joe countered. He broke away, pulling off the headband and running his fingers through his sweat-dampened hair. "Look, Ronnie, I didn't come here to fight with you."

"Is that supposed to be an apology?"

It wasn't, and she knew it as well as he did. "No."

Veronica laughed in disbelief at his blunt candor. "No," she repeated. "Of course not. Silly me. Whatever could I have been thinking?"

"I can't apologize," Joe said tightly. "Because I haven't done anything wrong."

"You've wasted time," Veronica told him. "*My* time. Maybe you don't understand, but we now have less than twenty-four hours to make this charade work."

"I'm well aware of the time we have left," Joe said. "I've looked at those videotapes Mac Forrest sent over. This is *not* going to be hard. In fact, it's going to be a piece of cake. I can pose as the prince, no problem. You've gotta relax and trust me." He turned and picked up the telephone from one of the end tables Veronica had pushed aside to clear the living-room floor of furniture. "I need you to make a phone call for me, okay?"

Veronica took the receiver from his hand and hung the phone back up. "No," she said, icily. "I need *you* to stop being so bloody patronizing, to stop patting my hand and telling me to relax. I need *you* to take me seriously for one damned minute."

Joe laughed. He couldn't help himself. She was standing there, looking like some kind of hot, steamed-up-windows dream, yet sounding, even in anger, as if she was trying to freeze him to death.

"Ah, you find this funny, do you?" Her eyes were blue ice. "I assure you, Lieutenant, you can't do this without me, and I am very close to walking out the bloody door."

She was madder than hell, and Joe knew the one thing he *shouldn't* do was keep laughing. But damned if he couldn't stop. "Ronnie," he said, pretending he was coughing instead of laughing. Still, he couldn't hide his smile. "Ronnie, Ronnie, I *do* take you seriously, honey. Honest."

Her hands were on her hips now, her mouth slightly open in disbelief. "You are *such* a...a jerk!" she said. "Tell me, is your real intention to...to...foul this up so royally that you won't have to place yourself in danger by posing as the prince?"

Joe's smile was wiped instantly off his face, and Veronica knew with deadly certainty that she'd gone too far.

He took a step toward her, and she took a step back, away from him. He was very tall, very broad and *very* angry.

"I *volunteered* for this job, babe," he told her, biting off each word. "I'm not here for my health, or for a paycheck, or for fame and fortune or for whatever the hell *you're* here for. And I'm sure as hell *not* here to be some kind of lousy martyr. If I end up taking a bullet for Prince Tedric, it's going to be despite the fact that I've done everything humanly possible to prevent it. Not because some pencil-pushing agency like FInCOM let the ball drop on standard security procedures years ago."

Veronica was silent. What could she possibly say? He was right. If security wasn't tight enough, he could very well be killed. She couldn't fault him for wanting to be sure of his own safety. And she didn't want to feel this odd jolt of fear and worry she felt, thinking about all of the opportunities the terrorists would have to train their gunsights on Joe's head. He was brave to have volunteered for this mission—particularly since she knew he had no love for Tedric Cortere. She shouldn't have implied otherwise.

"I'm sorry," Veronica murmured. She looked down at the carpet, unable to meet his eyes.

"And as for taking you seriously..." Joe reached out and with one finger underneath her chin, he lifted her head so that she was forced to look up into his eyes. "You're wrong. I take you *very* seriously."

The connection was there between them—instant and hot. The look in Joe's eyes was mesmerizing. It erased everything, *every*thing between them—all the angry words and mistrust, all the frustration and misunderstandings—and left only this basic, almost primitive attraction, this simplest of equations. Man plus woman.

It would be so easy to simply give in. Veronica felt her body sway toward him as if pulled by the tides, ancient and unquestioning. All she had to do was let go, and there would be only desire, consuming and overpowering. It would surround them, possess them. It would take them on a flight to paradise.

But that flight was a round trip. When it ended, when they lay spent and exhausted, they'd be right here—right back where they'd started.

And then reality would return. Veronica would be embarrassed at having been intimate with a man she barely knew. Joe would no doubt be smug.

And they would have wasted yet another hour or two of their precious preparation time.

Joe was obviously thinking along the exact same lines. He ran his thumb lightly across her lips. "What do you think, Ronnie?" he asked, his voice husky. "Do you think we could stop after just one kiss?"

Veronica pulled away, her heart pounding even harder. If he kissed her, she would be lost. "Don't be foolish," she said, working hard to keep her voice from shaking.

"When I make love to you," he said, his voice low and dangerous and *very* certain, "I'm going to take my sweet time."

She turned to face him with a bravado she didn't quite feel. *"When?"* she said. "Of all the macho, he-man audacity! Not *if,* but *when* I make love to you.... Don't hold your breath, Lieutenant, because it's not going to happen."

He smiled a very small, very infuriating smile and let his eyes wander down her body. "Yes, it is."

"Ever hear the expression 'cold day in hell'?" Veronica asked sweetly. She crossed the room toward her suitcase, found a sweatshirt and pulled it over her head. She was still perspiring and was still much too warm, but she would have done damn near anything to cover herself from the heat of his gaze.

He picked up the telephone again. "Look, Ronnie, I need you to call my room and ask to speak to me."

"But you're not there."

"That's the point," he said. "The boys from FInCOM think I'm napping, nestled all snug in my bed. It's time to shake them up."

Careful to keep her distance, careful not to let their fingers touch, Veronica took the phone from Joe and dialed the number for the royal suite. West picked up the phone.

"This is Ms. St. John," she said. "I need to speak to Lieutenant Catalanotto."

"I'm sorry, ma'am," West replied. "He's asleep."

"This is urgent, Mr. West," she said, glancing up at Joe, who nodded encouragingly. "Please wake him."

"Hang on."

There was silence on the other end, and then shouting, as if from a distance. Veronica met Joe's eyes again. "I think they're shaken up," she said.

"Hang up," he said, and she dropped the receiver into the cradle.

He picked up the phone then, and dialed. "Do you have a pair of sweats or some jeans to pull on over those shorts?" he asked Veronica.

"Yes," she said. "Why?"

"Because in about thirty seconds, fifty FInCOM agents are going to be pounding on your door— Hello? Yeah. Kevin Laughton, please." Joe covered the mouthpiece with his hand and looked at Veronica who was standing, staring at him. "Better hurry." He uncovered the phone. "Yeah, I'm still here."

Veronica scrambled for her suitcase, yanking out the one pair of blue jeans she'd packed for this trip.

"He is?" she heard Joe say into the telephone. "Well, maybe you should interrupt him."

She kicked off her sneakers and pulled the jeans on, hopping into them one leg at a time.

"Why don't you tell him Joe Catalanotto's on the line. Catalanotto." He sighed in exasperation. "Just say Joe Cat, okay? He'll know who I am."

Veronica pulled the jeans up and over her hips, aware that Joe was watching her dress. She buttoned the waistband and drew up the zipper, not daring to look in his direction. *When I make love to you . . .* Not if, *when.* As if their intimate joining were already a given—indisputable and destined to take place.

"Yo, Laughton," Joe said into the telephone. "How's it going, pal?" He laughed. "Yeah, I thought I'd give you a little firsthand demonstration, and identify FInCOM's security weak spots. How do you like it so far?'' He pulled the receiver away from his ear. ''That good, huh? Yeah, I went for a little walk down in the gardens.'' He met Veronica's eyes and grinned, clearly amused. ''Yeah, I was struck by the beauty of the flowers, so I brought one with me up to Ms. St. John's room to share with her, and—''

He looked at the receiver, suddenly gone dead in his hands, and then at Veronica.

''I guess they're on their way,'' he said.

Chapter 7

"I need more coffee," Veronica said. How could Joe be so *awake?* She hadn't seen him yawn even once as they'd worked through the night. "I think my laryngitis idea might work—after all, we've been giving the news media reports that Prince Tedric is ill. You wouldn't have to speak and—"

"You know, I'm not a half-bad mimic," Joe insisted. "If I work on it more, I can do a decent imitation of Prince Tedric."

Veronica closed her eyes. "No offense, Joe, but I seriously doubt you can imitate Tedric's accent just from listening to a tape," she said. "We have better things to do with your time."

Joe stood and Veronica opened her eyes, gazing up at him.

"I'm getting you that coffee," he said. "You're slipping. You just called me 'Joe.'"

"Forgive me, Your Royal Highness," she murmured.

But he didn't smile. He just looked down at her, the expression in his eyes unreadable. "I like Joe better," he finally said.

"This isn't going to work, is it?" she asked quietly. She met his eyes steadily, ready to accept defeat.

Except he wasn't defeated. Not by any means. He'd been watching videotapes and listening to audiotapes of Prince

Tedric in all of his spare moments. It was true that he hadn't had all that many spare moments, but he was well on his way to understanding the way Tedric moved and spoke.

"I can do this," Joe said. "Hell, I look just like the guy. Every time I catch my reflection and see my hair this way, I see Ted looking back at me and it scares me to death. If it can fool *me*, it can fool everyone else. The tailor's delivering the clothes he's altered sometime tomorrow. It'll be easier for me to pretend I'm Tedric if I'm dressed for the part."

Veronica gave him a wan smile. Still, it *was* a smile. She was so tired, she could barely keep her eyes open. She'd changed out of her jeans and back into her professional clothes hours ago. Her hair was up off her shoulders once again. "We've got to work on Tedric's walk. He's got this rather peculiar, rolling gait that—"

"He walks like he's got a fireplace poker in his pants," Joe interrupted her.

Veronica's musical laughter echoed throughout the quiet room. One of the FInCOM agents glanced up from his position guarding the balcony entrance.

"Yes," she said to Joe. "You're right. He does. Although I doubt anyone's described it quite that way before."

"I can walk that way," Joe said. He stood, and as Veronica watched, he marched stiffly across the room. "See?" He turned back to look at her.

She had her face in her hands and her shoulders were shaking, and Joe was positive for one heart-stopping moment that she was crying. He started toward her, and knelt in front of her and— She was laughing. She was laughing so hard, tears were rolling down her face.

"Hey," Joe said, faintly insulted. "It wasn't *that* bad."

She tried to answer, but could get no words out. Instead, she just waved her hand futilely at him and kept on laughing.

Her laughter was infectious, and before long, Joe started to chuckle and then laugh, too.

"Do it again," she gasped, and he stood and walked, like Prince Tedric, across the room and back.

Veronica laughed even harder, doubling over on the couch.

The FInCOM agent was watching them both as if they were crazy or hysterical—which probably wasn't that far from the truth.

Veronica wiped at her face, trying to catch her breath. "Oh, Lord," she said. "Oh, God, I haven't laughed this hard in years." Her eyelashes were wet with her tears of laughter, and her eyes sparkled as, still giggling, she looked up at Joe. "I don't suppose I can talk you into doing that again?"

"No way," Joe said, grinning back at her. "I draw the line at being humiliated more than twice in a row."

"I wasn't laughing at you," she said, but her giggles intensified. "Yes, I was," she corrected herself. "I *was* laughing at you. I'm so sorry. You must think I'm frightfully rude." She covered her mouth with her hand, but still couldn't stop laughing—at least not entirely.

"I think I only looked funny because I'm not dressed like the prince," Joe argued. "I think if I were wearing some sequined suit and walking that way, you wouldn't be able to tell the two of us apart."

"And *I* think," Veronica said. "*I* think . . . I think it's hopeless. I think it's time to give up." Her eyes suddenly welled with real tears, and all traces of her laughter vanished. "Oh, *damn*. . ." She turned away, but she could neither stop nor hide her sudden flow of tears.

She heard Joe's voice, murmuring a command to the FInCOM agents, and then she felt him sit next to her on the sofa.

"Hey," he said softly. "Hey, come on, Veronica. It's not that bad."

She felt his arms go around her and she stiffened only slightly before giving in. She let him pull her back against his chest, let him tuck her head in to his shoulder. He was so warm, so solid. And he smelled so wonderfully good . . .

He just held her, rocking slightly, and let her cry. He didn't try to stop her. He just held her.

Veronica was getting his shirt wet, but she couldn't seem to stop, and he didn't seem to mind. She could feel his hand in her hair, gently stroking, calming, soothing.

When he spoke, his voice was quiet. She could hear it rumble slightly in his chest.

"You know, this guy we're after?" Joe said. "The terrorist? His name's Diosdado. One name. Kind of like Cher or Madonna, but not so much fun. Still, I bet he's as much of a celebrity in Peru, where he's from. He's the leader of an organization with a name that roughly translates as 'The Cloud of Death.' He and a friend of his—a man named Salustiano Vargas—have claimed responsibility for more than twelve hundred deaths. Diosdado's signature was on the bomb that blew up that passenger flight from London to New York three years ago. Two hundred and fifty-four people died. Remember that one?"

Veronica nodded. She most certainly did. The plane had gone down halfway across the Atlantic. There were no survivors. Her tears slowed as she listened to him talk.

"Diosdado and his pal Vargas took out an entire busload of U.S. sailors that same year," Joe said. "Thirty-two kids—the oldest was twenty-one years old." He was quiet for a moment. "Mac Forrest's son was on that bus."

Veronica closed her eyes. "Oh, God . . ."

"Johnny Forrest. He was a good kid. Smart, too. He looked like Mac. Same smile, same easygoing attitude, same tenacity. I met him when he was eight. He was the little brother I never had." Joe's voice was husky with emotion. He cleared his throat. "He was nineteen when Diosdado blew him to pieces."

Joe fell silent, just stroking Veronica's hair. He cleared his throat again, but when he spoke, his voice was still tight. "Those two bombings put Diosdado and The Cloud of Death onto the Most Wanted list. Intel dug deep and came up with a number of interesting facts. Diosdado had a last name, and it was Perez. He was born in 1951, the youngest son in a wealthy family. His name means, literally, 'God's gift.'" Joe laughed a short burst of disgusted air. "He wasn't God's gift to Mac Forrest, or any of the other families of those dead sailors. Intel also found out that the sonuvabitch had a faction of his group right here in D.C. But when the CIA went to investigate, something went wrong. It turned into a firefight, and when it was over, three agents and ten members of The Cloud of Death were dead. Seven more terrorists were taken prisoner, but Diosdado and Salustiano Vargas were gone. The two men we'd wanted the most got away. They went deep underground. Rumor was Diosdado had been shot and badly hurt. He was quiet for years—no sign of him at all—until a few days ago, when apparently Vargas took a shot at Prince Tedric."

Joe was quiet again for another moment. "So there it is," he said. "The reason we can't just quit. The reason this operation *is* going to work. We're going to stop those bastards for good, one way or another."

Veronica wiped her face with the back of her hand. She couldn't remember the last time she'd cried like this. It must have been the stress getting to her. The stress and the fatigue. Still, to burst into tears like that and . . .

She sat up, pulling away from Joe and glancing around the room, alarmed, her cheeks flushing with embarrassment. She'd lost it. She'd absolutely lost it—and right in front of Joe and all those FInCOM agents. But the FInCOM agents were gone.

"They're outside the door," Joe said, correctly reading her thoughts. "I figured you'd appreciate the privacy."

"Thank you," Veronica murmured.

She was blushing, and the tip of her nose was pink from crying. She looked exhausted and fragile. Joe wanted to wrap her back in his arms and hold her close. He wanted to hold her as she closed her eyes and fell asleep. He wanted to keep her warm and safe from harm, and to convince her that everything was going to be all right.

She glanced at him, embarrassment lighting her crystal blue eyes. "I'm sorry," she said. "I didn't mean to—"

"You're tired." He gave her an easy excuse and a gentle smile.

They were alone. They were alone in the room. As Joe held her gaze, he knew she was aware of that, too.

Her hair was starting to come free from its restraints, and strands curled around her face.

He couldn't stop himself from reaching out and lightly brushing the last of her tears from her cheek. Her skin was so soft and warm. She didn't flinch, didn't pull away, didn't even move. She just gazed at him, her eyes blue and wide and so damned innocent.

Joe couldn't remember ever wanting to kiss a woman more in his entire life. Slowly, so slowly, he leaned forward, searching her eyes for any protest, alert for any sign that he was taking this moment of truce too far.

Her eyes flickered and he saw her desire. She wanted him to kiss her, too. But he also saw doubt and a flash of fear. She was afraid.

Afraid of what? Of him? Of herself? Or maybe she was afraid that the overwhelming attraction they both felt would ignite in a violent, nearly unstoppable explosion of need.

Joe almost pulled back.

But then her lips parted slightly, and he couldn't resist. He wanted a taste—just a taste—of her sweetness.

So he kissed her. Slowly, gently pressing his lips to hers.

A rush of desire hit him low in the gut and it took every ounce of control to keep from giving in to his need and pulling her hard into his arms, kissing her savagely, and running his hands along the curves of her body. Instead, he made himself slow down.

Gently, so gently, he ran his tongue across her lips, slowly gaining passage to the softness of her mouth. He closed his eyes, forcing himself to move still more slowly, even slower now. She tasted of strawberries and coffee—an enticing combination of flavors. He caressed her tongue with his own and when she responded, when she opened her mouth to him, granting him access and deepening their kiss, he felt dizzy with pleasure.

This was, absolutely, the sweetest kiss he'd ever shared.

Slowly, still slowly, he explored the warmth of her mouth, the softness of her lips. He touched only her mouth with his, and the side of her face with the tips of his fingers. She wasn't locked in his arms, their bodies weren't pressed tightly together. Still, with this gentle, purest of kisses, she had the power to make his blood surge through his veins, to make his heart pound in a wild, frantic rhythm.

He wanted her desperately. His body was straining to become joined with hers. And yet . . .

This kiss was enough. It was exhilarating, and it made him feel incredibly happy. Happy in a way he'd never been even while making love to the other women he'd had relationships with—women he'd been attracted to and slept with, but hadn't particularly cared for.

He felt a tightness in his chest, a weight of emotion he'd never felt before as, beneath his fingers, Veronica trembled.

He pulled back then, and she looked away, unable to meet his eyes.

"Well," she said. "My word."

"Yeah," Joe agreed. He hadn't intended to whisper, but he couldn't seem to speak any louder.

"That was . . . unexpected."

He couldn't entirely agree. He'd been expecting to kiss her ever since their eyes first met and the raw attraction sparked between them. What was unexpected was this odd sense of caring, this emotional noose that had somehow curled itself around his chest. It was faintly uncomfortable, and it hadn't disappeared even when he'd ended their kiss.

She glanced at him. "Maybe we should get back to work."

Joe shook his head. "No," he said. "I need a break, and you do, too." He stood, holding out his hand to her. "Come on, I'll walk you to your room. You can take a nap. I'll meet you back here in a few hours."

Veronica didn't take his hand. She simply gazed up at him.

"Come on," he said again. "Cut yourself some slack."

But she shook her head. "There's no time."

He gently touched her hair. "Yes, there is. There's definitely time for an hour of shut-eye," he said. "Trust me, Ronnie, you're gonna need it to concentrate."

Joe could see indecision on her face. "How about forty minutes?" he added. "Forty winks. You can crash right here on the couch. I'll order some coffee and wake you up at—" he glanced at his watch "—oh-six-twenty."

Slowly she nodded. "All right."

He bent down and briefly brushed her lips with his. "Sleep tight," he said.

She stopped him, touching the side of his face. "You're so sweet," she said, surprise in her voice.

He had to laugh. He'd been called a lot of things in his life, and "sweet" wasn't one of them. "Oh, no, I'm not."

Veronica's lips curved into a smile. "I didn't mean that to be an insult." Her smile faded and she looked away, suddenly awkward. "Joe, I have to be honest with you," she said quietly. "I think that kiss . . . was a mistake. I'm so tired, and I wasn't thinking clearly and, well, I hope you don't think that I… Well, right now it's not… We're not… It's a *mistake*. Don't you think?''

Joe straightened. The noose around his chest was so damn tight he could hardly breathe. A mistake. Veronica thought kissing him had been a mistake. He shook his head slowly, hiding his disappointment behind a tight smile. "No, and I'm sorry *you* think that," he replied. "I thought maybe we had something there."

"Something?" Veronica echoed, glancing up at him.

This time it was Joe who looked away. He sat down next to her on the couch, suddenly tired. How could he explain what he meant, when he didn't even know himself? Damn, he'd already said too much. What if she thought by "something" he meant he was falling in love with her?

He pushed his hair back with one hand and glanced at Veronica.

Yeah, she wanted him to fall in love with her about as much as she wanted a hole in the head. In the space of a heartbeat, he could picture her dismay, picture her imagining the restraining order she'd have to get to keep him away from her. He was rough and uncultured, blue-collar through and through. *She* hung out with royalty. It would be embarrassing and inconvenient for her to have some crazy, rough-edged, lovesick sailor following her around.

Gazing into her eyes, he could see her trepidation.

So he gave her a cocky smile and prayed that she couldn't somehow sense the tightness in his chest. "I thought we had something great between us," he said, leaning forward and putting his hand on her thigh.

Veronica moved back on the couch, away from him. His hand fell aside.

"Ah, yes," she said. "Sex. Exactly what I thought you m ant."

Joe stood. "Too bad."

She glanced at him but didn't meet his gaze for more than a fraction of a second. "Yes, it is."

He turned away, heading for the bedroom and his bed. Maybe some sleep would make this pressure in his chest lighten up or—please, God—even make it go away.

"Please, don't forget to wake me," Veronica called.

"Right," he said shortly and closed the door behind him.

The knock on the door came quickly, no less than five minutes after Joe had called for coffee from room service. Man, he
thought, people really hopped to it when they thought a guy
had blue blood.

West and the other FInCOM agent, Freeman, both drew
their guns, motioning for Joe to move away from the door. It
was an odd sensation. He was the one who usually did the protecting.

The door opened, and it was the room-service waiter. West
and Freeman handed Joe two steaming mugs of fragrant coffee. Joe carried them to the coffee table and set them down.

Veronica was still asleep. She'd slid down on the couch so
that her head was resting on the seat cushion. She clutched a
legal pad to her chest.

She looked incredibly beautiful. Her skin was so smooth and
soft looking, it was all he could do not to reach out with one
knuckle to touch her cheek.

Veronica St. John.

Who would have guessed he would have a thing for a prim-
and-proper society girl named Veronica St. John? "Sinjin," for
Pete's sake.

But she wasn't interested in him. That incredible, perfect kiss
they'd shared had been "a mistake."

Like *hell* it had.

Joe had had to force himself to fall asleep. Only his extensive training had kept him from lying on the bed, staring at the
ceiling and expending his energy by playing their kiss over and
over and over again in his mind. He'd spent enough time doing that while he was in the shower, after he woke up. Each time
he played that kiss over in his head, he tried to figure out what
he'd done wrong, and each time, he came up blank. Finally
he'd had to admit it—he'd done nothing wrong. That kiss had
been perfect, not a mistake.

Now all he had to do was convince Veronica of that fact.

Yeah, right. She was stubborn as hell. He'd have a better
chance of convincing the Mississippi River to flow north.

The hell of it was, Joe found himself actually *liking* the girl, trying to make her smile. He wanted to get another look behind her so-very-proper British facade. Except he wasn't sure exactly where the facade ended and the real girl began. So far, he'd seen two very conflicting images— Veronica in her prim-and-proper work clothes, and Veronica dressed down to dance. He was willing to bet that the real woman was hidden somewhere in the middle. He was also willing to bet that she would never willingly reveal her true self. Especially not to *him*.

Joe had more than just a suspicion that Veronica considered him substandard. He was the son of a servant, while she was a daughter of the ruling class. If she had a relationship with him, it would be a lark, a kick. She'd be slumming.

Slumming.

God, it was an ugly word. But, so what? So she'd be slumming. Big deal. What was he going to do if she approached him? Was he going to turn her down? Yeah, right. Like hell he'd turn her down.

He could just picture the scenario.

Veronica knocks on his door in the middle of the night and he says, "Sorry, babe, I'm not into being used by curious debutantes who want a peek at the way the lower half lives and loves."

Yeah, right.

If she knocked on his door, he'd fling it open wide. Let her go slumming. Just let him be the one she was slumming with.

Veronica stirred slightly, shifting to get more comfortable on the couch, and the legal pad she'd been holding fell out of her arms. Joe moved quickly and caught it before it hit the floor.

Her hair was starting to come undone, and soft red wisps curled around her face. Her lips were slightly parted. They were so soft and delicate and delicious. He knew that firsthand.

It didn't take much to imagine her lifting those exquisite lips to his for another perfect kiss—for a deep, demanding, soulful kiss that would rapidly escalate into more. *Way* more.

And then what?

Then they'd be lovers until she got tired of him, or he got tired of her. It would be no different from any of the other relationships he'd had.

But so far, everything about this *was* different. Veronica St. John wasn't some woman he'd met in a bar. She hadn't approached him, handed him the keys to her car or her motel room and asked if he was busy for the next twenty-four hours. She hadn't even approached him at all.

She wasn't his type. She was too high-strung, too uptight.

But something he'd seen in her eyes promised a paradise the likes of which he'd never known. Hell, it was a paradise he was probably better off never knowing.

Because what if he never got tired of her?

There it was. Right out in the open. The big, ugly question he'd been trying to avoid. What if this noose that had tightened around his chest never went away?

But that would never happen, right?

He couldn't let Veronica's wealth and high-class manners throw him off. She was just a woman. All those differences he'd imagined were just that—imagined.

So how come he was standing there like an idiot, staring at the girl? Why was he too damned chicken to touch her, to wake her up, to see her sleepy blue eyes gazing up at him?

The answer was clear—because even if the impossible happened, and Joe actually did something as idiotically stupid as fall in love with Veronica St. John, she would never, not in a million years, fall in love with him. Sure, she might find him amusing for a few weeks or even months, but eventually she'd come to her senses and trade him in for a more expensive model.

And somehow the thought of that stung. Even now. Even though there was absolutely nothing between them. Nothing, that is, but one perfect kiss and its promise of paradise.

"Yo, Ronnie," Joe said, hoping she'd wake up without him touching her. But she didn't stir.

He bent down and spoke directly into her ear. "Coffee's here. Time to wake up."

Nothing.

He touched her shoulder, shaking her very slightly.

Nothing.

He shook her harder, and she stirred, but her eyes stayed tightly shut.

"Go away," she mumbled.

Joe pulled her up into a sitting position. Her head lolled against the back of the couch. "Come on, babe," he said. "If I don't wake you up, you're going to be madder than hell at me." He gently touched the side of her face. "Come on, Ronnie. Look at me. Open your eyes."

She opened them. They were astonishingly blue and very sleepy. "Be a dear, Jules, and ring the office. Tell them I'll be a few hours late. I'm bushed. Out too late last night." She smiled and blew a kiss into the air near his face. "Thanks, luv." Then she tucked her perfect knees primly up underneath her skirt, put her head back down on the seat cushions and tightly closed her eyes.

Jules?

Who the hell was Jules?

"Come on, Veronica," Joe said almost desperately. He had no right to want to hog-tie this Jules, whoever the hell he was. No right at all. "You wanted me to wake you up. Besides, you can't sleep on the couch. You'll wake up with one hell of a backache."

She didn't open her eyes again, didn't sigh, didn't move.

She was fast asleep, and not likely to wake up until she was good and ready.

Gritting his teeth, Joe picked Veronica up and carried her into the bedroom. He set her gently down on the bed, trying to ignore the way she fit so perfectly in his arms. For half a second, he actually considered climbing in under the covers next to her. But he didn't have time. He had work to do. Besides, when he got in bed with Veronica St. John, it was going to be at her invitation.

Joe took off her remaining shoe and put it on the floor, then covered her with the blankets.

She didn't move, didn't wake up again. He didn't give in to the desire to smooth her hair back from her face. He just stared down at her for another brief moment, knowing that the smart thing to do would be to stay far, far away from this woman. He knew that she was trouble, the likes of which he'd never known.

He turned away, needing a stiff drink. He settled for black coffee and set to work.

Chapter 8

Veronica sat bolt upright in the bed.

Dear Lord in heaven, she wasn't supposed to be asleep, she was supposed to be working and—

What time was it?

Her watch read twelve twenty-four. Oh, no, she'd lost the entire morning. But she must have been exhausted. She couldn't even remember coming back here to her own room and—

Oh, Lord! She realized she wasn't in her own room. She was in the prince's bedroom, in the prince's bed. No, not the prince's. *Joe's. Joe's* bed.

With a dizzying flash, Veronica remembered Joe pulling her into his arms and kissing her so slowly, so sensuously that every bone in her body seemed to melt. He had rid them of their clothes like a seasoned professional and . . .

But . . . she was still dressed. Right down to her hose, which were twisted and uncomfortable. She'd only *dreamed* about Joe Catalanotto and his seductive eyes and surprisingly gentle hands.

The kiss had been real, though; and achingly, shockingly tender. It figured. Joe would know exactly how to kiss her to make her the most vulnerable, to affect her in the strongest possible way.

She'd expected him to kiss her almost roughly—an echo of the sexual hunger she'd seen in his eyes. She could have handled that. She would have known what to say and do.

Instead, Joe had given her a kiss that was more gentle than passionate, although the passion had been there, indeed. But Veronica was still surprised by the restraint he'd shown, by the sweetness of his mouth against hers, by the slow, lingering sensuality of his lips. She could very well have kissed him that way until the end of time.

Time. Lord! She'd wasted so much *time*.

Veronica swung her legs out of bed.

She'd *told* Joe to wake her up. Obviously, he hadn't. Instead of waking her, he'd carried her here, into his bedroom.

She found one of her shoes on the floor, and searched to no avail for the other. Perfect. One shoe off and one shoe on, having slept away most of the day, her dignity in shreds, she'd have to go out into the living room where the FInCOM agents were parked. She'd have to endure their knowing smirks.

She was a wimp. She'd fallen asleep—and stayed asleep for *hours*—while on the job.

And Joe . . . Joe hadn't kept his promise to wake her up.

She'd been starting to . . . like him. She'd been attracted from the start, but this was different. She actually, genuinely *liked* him, despite the fact that he came from an entirely different world, despite the fact that they seemed to argue almost constantly. She even liked him despite the fact that he clearly wanted to make their relationship sexual. Despite all that, she'd thought he had been starting to like her, too.

Her disappointment flashed quickly into anger. How *dare* he just let her sleep the day away? The *bastard* . . .

Veronica fumed as she tucked her blouse back into the top of her skirt and straightened her jacket, thankful her suit was permanent-press and wrinkle-proof.

Her hair wasn't quite so easy to fix, but she was determined not to emerge from the bedroom with it down and flowing around her shoulders. It was bad enough that she'd been sleeping in Joe's bed. She didn't want it to look as if he'd been in there with her.

Finally, she took a deep breath and, single shoe in her hand and head held high, she went into the living room.

If the FInCOM agents smirked condescendingly, Veronica refused to notice. All she knew was, Joe was not in the room. Good thing, or she might have lost even more of her dignity by throwing her shoe directly at his head.

"Good afternoon, gentlemen," she said briskly to West and Freeman as she gathered up her briefcase. Ah, good. There was her missing shoe, on the floor in front of the sofa. She slipped them both onto her feet. "Might I ask where the lieutenant has gone?"

"He's up in the exercise room," one of them answered.

"Thanks so very much," Veronica said and breezed out the door.

Joe had already run seven miles on the treadmill when Veronica walked into the hotel's luxuriously equipped exercise room. She looked a whole lot better. She'd showered and changed her clothes. But glory hallelujah, instead of putting on another of those Margaret Thatcher suits, she was wearing a plain blue dress. It was nothing fancy, obviously designed to deemphasize her femininity, yet somehow, on Veronica, it hugged her slender figure and made her look like a million bucks. Her shoes were still on the clunky side, but oh, baby, those legs . . .

Joe wiped a trickle of sweat that ran down the side of his face. When had it gotten so hot in here?

But her greeting to him was anything but warm.

"I'd like to have a word with you," Veronica said icily, without even a hello to start. "At your convenience, of course."

"Did you have a good nap?" Joe asked.

"Will you be much longer?" she asked, staring somewhere off to his left.

That good, huh? Something had ticked her off, and Joe was willing to bet that that something was him. He'd let her sleep. Correction—he'd been unable to wake her up. It wasn't his fault, but now he was going to pay.

"Can you give me five more minutes?" he countered. "I like to do ten miles without stopping."

Joe wasn't even out of breath. Veronica could see from the computerized numbers lit up on the treadmill's controls, that he'd already run eight miles. But he didn't sound winded.

He was sweating, though. His shorts were soaking wet. He wasn't wearing a shirt, and his smooth, tanned skin was slick as his muscles worked. And, dear Lord, he had so *many* muscles. Beautifully sculpted, perfect muscles. He was gorgeous.

He was watching her in the floor-to-ceiling mirrors that covered the walls of the exercise room. Veronica leaned against the wall near the door and tried not to look at Joe, but everywhere she turned, she saw his reflection. She found herself staring in fascination at the rippling muscles in his back and thighs and arms, and then she started thinking about their kiss. Their fabulous, heart-stoppingly romantic kiss. Despite his nonchalant attitude, that kiss had been laced with tenderness and laden with emotion. It was unlike any kiss she'd experienced *ever* before.

Veronica had been well aware that Joe had been holding back when he kissed her that way. She'd felt his restraint and the power of his control. She had seen the heat of desire in his eyes and known he wanted more than just a simple, gentle kiss.

Veronica couldn't forget how he'd searched her eyes as he'd leaned toward her and . . .

Excellent. Here she was, standing there reliving Joe's kiss while staring at his perfect buttocks. Veronica glanced up to find his amused dark eyes watching her watch his rear end. No doubt he could read her mind. Of course the fact that she'd been nearly drooling made it all the easier for him to know what she'd been thinking.

She might as well give in, Veronica admitted to herself. She might as well sleep with the man and get it over with. After all, he was so bloody positive that it was going to happen. And after their kiss, despite her best intentions, all Veronica could think about was "When was he going to kiss her again?" Except he hadn't woken her up, which meant that he probably didn't even *like* her, and now *she* was mad as hell at him. Yes, kissing him *had* been a royal mistake. Although at the time, when she'd said those words, she'd meant another kind of mistake entirely. She'd meant their timing had been wrong.

She'd meant it had been a mistake to add a romantic distraction to all of the other distractions already driving her half mad.

Then, of course, he'd said what *he'd* said, and . . .

The fact that Joe saw their growing relationship as one based purely on sex only added to Veronica's confusion. She knew that a man like Joe Catalanotto, a man accustomed to intrigue and high adventure, would never have any kind of long-term interest in a woman who worked her hardest to be steady and responsible and, well, quite frankly, *boring*. And even if that wasn't the case, even if by some miracle Joe fell madly and permanently in love with her, how on earth would she handle his leaving on dangerous, top-secret missions? How could she simply wave goodbye, knowing she might never again see him alive?

No, thank you very much.

So maybe this pure sex thing didn't add to her confusion. Maybe it simplified things. Maybe it took it all down to the simplest, most basic level.

Lord knew, she *was* wildly attracted to him. And so what if she was watching him?

Veronica met Joe's gaze almost defiantly, her chin held high. One couldn't have a body like that and expect people *not* to look. And watching Joe run was like watching a dancer. He was graceful and surefooted, his motion fluid and effortless. She wondered if he could dance. She wondered—not for the first time—what it would feel like to be held in his arms, dancing with him.

As Veronica watched, Joe focused on his running, increasing his speed, his arms and legs churning, pumping. The treadmill was starting to whine, and just when Veronica was sure Joe was going to start to slow, when she was positive he couldn't keep up the pace a moment longer, he went even faster.

His teeth were clenched, his face a picture of concentration and stamina. He looked like something savage, something wild. An untamed man-creature from the distant past. A ferocious, barbaric warrior come to shake up the civility of Veronica's carefully polite twentieth-century world.

"Hoo-yah!" someone called out, and Joe's face broke into a wide smile as he looked up at three men, standing near the weight machine in the corner of the room. As quickly as his smile appeared, the barbarian was gone.

Odd, Veronica hadn't noticed the other men before this. She'd been aware of the FInCOM agents lurking near her, but not these three men dressed in workout clothes. They seemed to know Joe. SEALs, Veronica guessed. They had to be the men Joe had asked Admiral Forrest to send.

Joe slowed at last, returning the treadmill to a walking speed as he caught his breath. He stepped off and grabbed a towel, using it to mop his face as he came toward Veronica.

"What's up?"

Joe was steaming. There was literally visible heat rising from his smooth, powerful shoulders. He stopped about six feet away from her, clearly not wanting to offend her by standing too close.

His friends came and surrounded him, and Veronica was momentarily silenced by three additional pairs of eyes appraising her with frank male appreciation. Joe's eyes alone were difficult enough to handle.

Joe glanced at the other men. "Get lost," he said. "This is a private conversation."

"Not anymore," said one of them with a Western twang. He was almost as tall as Joe, but probably weighed forty pounds less. He held out his hand to Veronica. "I'm Cowboy, ma'am."

She shook Cowboy's hand, and he held on to hers far longer than necessary, until Joe gave him a dark look.

"All right, quick introductions," Joe said. "Lieutenant McCoy, my XO—executive officer—and Ensigns Becker and Jones. Also known as Blue, Harvard and Cowboy. Miss Veronica St. John. For you illiterates, it's spelled Saint and John, two words, but pronounced *Sinjin*. She's Prince Tedric's media consultant, and she's on the scheduling team for this op."

Lt. Blue McCoy looked to be about Joe's age—somewhere in his early thirties. He was shorter and smaller than the other men, with the build of a long-distance runner and the blue eyes, wavy, thick blond hair and handsome face of a Hollywood star.

Harvard—Ensign Becker—was a large black man with steady, intelligent brown eyes and a smoothly shaven head. Cowboy's hair was even longer than Blue McCoy's, and he wore it pulled back into a ponytail at the nape of his neck. His eyes were green and sparkling, and his smile boyishly winsome. He looked like Kevin Costner's younger brother, and he knew it. He kept winking at her.

"Pleased to meet you," Veronica said, shaking hands with both Blue and Harvard. She was afraid if she offered Cowboy her hand again, she might never get it back.

"The pleasure's all ours, ma'am," Cowboy said. "I love what you've done with the captain's hair."

"Captain?" Veronica looked at Joe. "I thought you were a Lieutenant."

"It's a term of endearment, ma'am," Blue said. He,too, had a thick accent, but his was from the Deep South. "Cat's in command, so sometimes he gets called Captain."

"It's better than some of the other things they call me," Joe said.

Cat.

Admiral Forrest had also called Joe by that nickname. Cat. It fit. As Joe ran on the treadmill, he looked like a giant cat, so graceful and fluid. The nickname, while really just a shortened form of Catalanotto, wasn't too far off.

"Okay, great," Joe said. "We've made nice. Now you boys get lost. Finish your PT, and let the grown-ups talk."

Lt. McCoy took the other two men by the arms and pulled them toward weight-lifting equipment. Harvard began to bench-press heavy-looking weights while Cowboy spotted him, one eye still on Joe and Veronica.

"Now let's try this one more time," Joe said with a smile. "What's up? You look like you want to court-martial me."

"Only if the punishment for mutiny is still execution," Veronica said, smiling tightly.

Joe looped his towel around his neck. "Mutiny," he said. "That's a serious charge—especially considering I did my damnedest to wake you up."

Veronica crossed her arms. "Oh, and I suppose your 'damnedest' included putting me in a nice soft bed, where I'd be sure to sleep away most of the day?" she said. She glanced around, at both the FInCOM agents and the other SEALs, and lowered her voice. "I might *also* point out that it was hardly proper for *me* to sleep in *your* bed. It surely looked bad, and it implied . . . certain things."

"Whoa, Ronnie." Joe shook his head. "That wasn't my intention. I thought you'd be more comfortable, that's all. I wasn't trying to—"

"I'm an unmarried woman, Lieutenant," Veronica interrupted. "Regardless of what you intended, it is not in my best interests to take a nap in any man's bed."

Joe laughed. "I think maybe you're overreacting just a *teeny* little bit. This isn't the 1890s. I don't see how your reputation could be tarnished simply from napping in my bed. If I were in there with you, it'd be an entirely different matter. But if you want to know the truth, I'd be willing to bet no one even noticed where you were sleeping this morning, or even that you were asleep. And if they did, that's their problem."

"No, it's *my* problem," Veronica said sharply, her temper flaring. "Tell me, Lieutenant, are there many women in the SEALs?"

"No," Joe said. "There're none. We don't allow women in the units."

"Aha," Veronica retorted. "In other words, you're not familiar with sexual discrimination, because your organization is based on sexual discrimination. That's just perfect."

"Look, if you want to preach feminism, fine," Joe said, his patience disintegrating, "but do me a favor—hand me a pamphlet to read on the subject and be done with it. Right now, I'm going to take a shower."

By now they had the full, unconcealed attention of the three other SEALs and the FInCOM agents, but Veronica was long past caring. She was angry—angry that he had let her sleep, angry that he was so macho, angry that he had kissed her—and particularly angry that she had liked his kiss so damn much.

She blocked Joe's way, stabbing at his broad chest with one finger. "Don't you *dare* run away from me, Lieutenant," she said, her voice rising with each word. "You're operating in *my* world now, and I will not have you jeopardizing my career through your own *stupid* ignorance."

He flinched as if she'd slapped him in the face and turned away, but not before she saw the flash of hurt in his eyes. Hurt that was rapidly replaced by anger.

"Jesus, Mary and Joseph," Joe said through clenched teeth. "I was only trying to be nice. I thought sleeping on the couch would screw up your back, but forget it. From now on, I won't bother, okay? From now on, we'll go by the book.''

He pushed past her and went into the locker room. The FInCOM agents and the three other SEALs followed, leaving Veronica alone in the exercise room. Her reflection gazed back at her from all angles.

Perfect. She'd handled that just perfectly.

Veronica had come down here to find out why he'd let her sleep so long, and wound up in a fierce argument about sexual discrimination and her pristine reputation. That wasn't the real issue at all. It had just been something to shout about, because Lord knew she couldn't walk up to him and shout that his kiss had turned her entire world upside down and now she was totally, utterly and quite thoroughly off-balance.

Instead, she had called him names. *Stupid. Ignorant.* Words that had clearly cut deep, despite the fact that he was anything but stupid and far from ignorant.

What Veronica had done was take out all her anger and frustration on the man.

But if anyone was to blame here, it was herself. After all, she was the one foolish enough to have fallen asleep in the first place.

"Hey, Cat!" Cowboy called loudly as he showered in the locker room. "Tell me more about fair Veronica 'Sinjin.'"

"There's nothing to tell," Joe answered evenly. He glanced up to find Blue watching him.

Damn. Blue could read his mind. Joe's connection to Blue was so tight, there were few thoughts that appeared in Joe's head that Blue wasn't instantly aware of. But what would Blue make of the thoughts Joe was having right now? What would he make of the sick, nauseous feeling Joe had in the pit of his stomach?

Stupid. Ignorant.

Well, that about summed it all up, didn't it? Joe certainly knew now exactly what Veronica St. John thought of him, didn't he? He certainly knew why she'd thought that kiss was a mistake.

Cowboy shut off the water. Dripping, he came out of the stall and into the room. "You sure there's nothing you can tell us about Veronica, Cat? Oh, come on, buddy, I can think of a thing or two," he said, taking a towel from a pile of clean ones and giving himself a perfunctory swipe. "Like, are you and she doing the nightly naked two-step?"

"No," Joe replied flatly, pulling on his pants.

"You planning on it?" Cowboy asked. He slipped into one of the plush hotel robes that were hanging on the wall.

"Back off, Jones," Blue said warningly.

"No." Joe answered Cowboy tersely as he yanked his T-shirt over his head and thrust his arms into the sleeves of his shirt.

"Cool," Cowboy said. "Then you don't mind if I give her a try—"

Joe spun and grabbed the younger man by the lapels of his robe, slamming him up against a row of metal lockers with a crash. "Stay the hell away from her," he snapped. He let go of Cowboy, and turned to include Blue and Harvard in his glare. "All of you. Is that clear?"

He didn't wait for an answer. He turned and stalked out of the room, slamming the door behind him.

The noise echoed as Cowboy stared at Harvard and Blue.

"Shoot," he finally said. "Anybody have any idea what the hell's going on?"

Chapter 9

Room service arrived at the royal suite before Joe did.

"Set it out on the table, please," Veronica instructed the waiter.

She'd ordered a full-course meal, from appetizers to dessert, complete with three different wines.

This afternoon's lesson was food—or more precisely, *eating* food. There was a hundred-dollar-a-plate charity luncheon in Boston, Massachusetts, that had been left on the prince's tour schedule. Both the location and the visibility of the event were right for a possible assassination attempt, but it was more than a hi-and-bye appearance. It would involve more than Joe's ability to stand and wave as if he were Prince Tedric.

The hotel-suite door opened, and Joe came inside, followed by three FInCOM agents. His shirt was unbuttoned, revealing his T-shirt underneath, and he met Veronica's eyes only briefly before turning to the laden dining table. It was quite clear that he was still upset with her.

"What's this?" he asked.

"This is practice for the Boston charity luncheon," Veronica replied. "I hope you're hungry."

Joe stared at the table. It was loaded with dishes covered with plate-warmers. It was set for two, with a full array of cutlery and three different wineglasses at each setting. What, didn't Miss High-and-Mighty think he knew how to eat with a fork? Didn't she know he dined with admirals and four-star generals at the Officers' Club?

Stupid. Ignorant.

Joe nodded slowly, wishing he was still pissed off, wishing he was still nursing the slow burn he'd felt upstairs in the exercise room. But he wasn't. He was too tired to be angry now. He was too tired to feel anything but disappointment and hurt. Damn, it made him feel so vulnerable.

The room-service waiter was standing next to the table, looking down his snotty nose at Joe's unbuttoned shirt. Gee, maybe the waiter and Veronica had had a good laugh about Joe before he'd arrived.

"This is unnecessary," he said, turning back to look at Veronica. Man, she looked pretty in that blue dress. Her hair was tied back with some kind of ribbon, and— Forget about her, he told himself harshly. She was just some rich girl who'd made it more than clear that they lived in two different worlds, and there was no crossing the border. He was stupid and ignorant, and kissing him had been a mistake. "Believe it or not, I already know which fork is for the salad and which fork is for the dessert. It might come as a shock to you, but I also know how to use a napkin and drink from a glass."

Veronica actually looked surprised, her blue eyes growing even wider. "Oh," she said. "No. No, I knew that. That's not what this is." She let a nervous laugh escape. "You actually thought *I* thought I'd need to teach you how to eat?"

Joe was not amused. "Yeah."

My God, he was serious. He was standing there, his powerful arms folded across his broad chest, staring at her with those mystifying dark eyes. Veronica remembered that flash of hurt in Joe's eyes when they'd argued in the exercise room. What had she said? She'd called him stupid and ignorant. Oh, Lord. She *still* couldn't believe those words had come out of her mouth.

"I'm so sorry," she said.

His eyes narrowed slightly, as if he couldn't believe what he was hearing.

"I owe you an apology," Veronica explained. "I was very angry this afternoon, and I said some things I didn't mean. The truth is, I was frustrated and angry with myself. *I* was the one who fell asleep. It was all my fault, and I tried to take it out on you. I shouldn't have. I *am* sorry."

Joe looked at the waiter and then at the FInCOM agents who were sitting on the sofa, listening to every word. He crossed to the door and opened it invitingly. "You guys mind stepping outside for a sec?"

The FInCOM agents looked at each other and shrugged. Rising to their feet, they crossed to the door and filed out into the corridor. Joe turned to the waiter. "You, too, pal." He gestured toward the open door. "Take a hike."

He waited until the waiter was outside, then closed the door tightly and crossed back to Veronica. "You know, these guys *will* give you privacy if you ask for it," he said.

She nodded. "I know," she said. She lifted her chin slightly, steadily meeting his gaze. "It's just...I was rude to you in public, I felt I should apologize to you in public, too."

Joe nodded, too. "Okay," he said. "Yeah. That sounds fair." He looked at her, and there was something very close to admiration in his eyes. "That sounds really fair."

Veronica felt her own eyes flood with tears. Oh, damn, she was going to cry. If she started to cry, she was going to feel once more just how gentle Joe's hard-as-steel arms could be. And Lord, she didn't want to be reminded of that. "I *am* sorry," she said, blinking back the tears.

Oh, *damn,* Veronica was going to cry, Joe thought as he took a step toward her, then stopped himself. No, she was trying hard to hide it. It was better if he played along, if he pretended he didn't notice. But, man, the sight of those blue eyes swimming in tears made his chest ache, reminding him of this morning, when he'd held her in his arms. Reminding him of that unbelievable kiss...

Veronica forced a smile and held out her hand to him. "Still friends?" she asked.

Friends, huh? Joe had never had a friend before that he wanted to pull into his arms and kiss the living daylights out of.

As he gazed into her eyes, the attraction between them seemed to crackle and snap, like some living thing.

Veronica was okay. She was a decent person—the fact that she'd apologized proved that. But she came from miles on the other side of the railroad tracks. If their relationship became intimate, she'd still be slumming. And *he'd* be . . .

He'd be dreaming about her every night for the rest of his life.

Joe let go of Veronica's hand as if he'd been stung. Jesus, Mary and Joseph, where had *that* thought come from . . . ?

"Are you all right?" The concern in her eyes was genuine.

Joe stuffed his hands in his pockets. "Yeah. Sorry. I guess I'm . . . After we do this dining thing, I'm going to take another short nap."

"A three-minute nap this time?" Veronica asked. "Or maybe you'll splurge, and sleep for five whole minutes . . . ?"

Joe smiled, and she gave him an answering smile. Their gazes met and held. And held and held and held.

With another woman, Joe would have closed the gap between them. With another woman, Joe would have taken two short steps and brought them face to face. He would have brushed those stray flame-colored curls from the side of her beautiful face, then lifted her chin and lowered his mouth to meet hers.

He had tasted her lips before. He knew how amazing kissing Veronica could be.

But she wasn't another woman. She was Veronica St. John. And she'd already made it clear that sex wasn't on their agenda. Hell, if a kiss was a mistake, then making love would be an error of unbelievable magnitude. And the truth was, Joe didn't want to face that kind of rejection.

So Joe didn't move. He just gazed at her.

"Well," she said, slightly breathlessly, "perhaps we should get to work."

But she didn't cross toward the dining table, she just gazed up at him, as if she, too, were caught in some kind of force field and unable to move.

Veronica was beautiful. And rich. And smart. But more than just book smart. She was people smart, too. Joe had seen her manipulate a tableful of high-ranking officials. She couldn't have done that on an Ivy League diploma alone.

He didn't know the first thing about her, Joe realized. He didn't know where she came from, or how she'd gotten here, to Washington, D.C. He didn't know how she'd come to work for the crown prince of Ustanzia. He didn't know why she'd remained, even after the assassination attempt, when most civilians would have headed for the hills and safety.

"What's your angle?" Joe asked.

Veronica blinked. "Excuse me?"

He reworded the question. "Why are you here? I mean, I'm here to help catch Diosdado, but what are *you* getting out of this?"

She looked out the window at the afternoon view of the capital city. When she glanced back at Joe, her smile was rueful. "Beats me," she said. "I'm not getting paid nearly half enough, although it could be argued that working for royalty is a solid career boost. Of course, it all depends on whether we can successfully pass you off as Prince Tedric."

She sank down onto the couch and looked up at him, elbow on her knee, chin in her hand. "We have less than six hours before the committee makes a decision." She shook her head and laughed humorlessly. "Instead of becoming more like Tedric, you seem more different from him than when we started. I look at you, Joe, and you don't even *look* like the prince anymore."

Joe smiled as he sat next to her on the couch. "Lucky for us, most people won't look beneath the surface. They'll expect to see Ted, so... they'll see Ted."

"I *need* this thing to work," Veronica said, smoothing her skirt over her knees. "If this doesn't work..."

"Why?" Joe asked. "Mortgage payment coming due on the castle?"

Veronica turned and looked at him. "Very funny."

"Sorry."

"You don't really want to hear this."

Joe was watching her, studying her face. His dark eyes were fathomless, and as mysterious as the deepest ocean. "Yes, I do."

"Tedric's sister has been my best friend since boarding school," Veronica said. "Even though Tedric is unconcerned with Ustanzia's financial state, Wila has been working hard to make her country more solvent. It matters to her—so it matters to me." She smiled. "When oil was discovered, Wila actually did cartwheels right across the Capital lawn. I thought poor Jules was going to have a heart attack. But then she found out how much it would cost to drill. She's counting on getting U.S. aid."

Jules.

Be a dear, Jules, and ring the office. Veronica had murmured those words in her sleep, and since then, Joe had been wondering, not without a sliver of jealousy, exactly who this Jules was.

"Who's Jules?" Joe asked.

"Jules," Veronica repeated. "My brother. He conveniently married my best friend. It's quite cozy, really, and very sweet. They're expecting a baby any moment."

Her brother. Jules was her brother. Why did that make Joe feel so damned good? He and Veronica were going to be friends, nothing more, so why should *he* care whether Jules was her brother or her lover or her pet monkey?

But he *did* care, damn it.

Joe leaned forward. "So that's why Wila didn't come on this tour instead of Brain-dead Ted? Because she's pregnant?"

Veronica tried not to smile, but failed. "Don't call Prince Tedric that," she said.

He smiled at her, struck by the way her eyes were the exact shade of blue as her dress. "You know, you look pretty in blue."

Her smile vanished and she stood. "We should really get started," she said, crossing to the dining table. "The food's getting cold."

Joe didn't move. "So where did you and Jules grow up? London?"

Veronica turned to look back at him. "No," she replied. "At first we traveled with our parents, and when we were old enough, we went away to school. The closest thing we had to a permanent home was Huntsgate Manor, where our Great-Aunt Rosamond lived."

"Huntsgate Manor," Joe mused. "It sounds like something out of a fairy tale."

Veronica's eyes grew dreamy and out of focus as she gazed out the window. "It was so wonderful. This big, old, moldy, ancient house with gardens and grounds that went on forever and ever and ever." She looked up at Joe with a spark of humor in her eyes. "Not really," she added. "I think the property is only about four or five acres, but when we were little, it seemed to go to the edge of the world and back."

Night and day, Joe thought. Their two upbringings were as different as night and day. He wondered what she would do, how she would react if she knew about the rock he'd crawled out from under.

Veronica laughed, embarrassed. "I don't know why I just told you all that," she said. "It's hardly interesting."

But it *was* interesting. It was fascinating. As fascinating as those gigantic houses he'd gone into with his mother, the houses that she'd cleaned when he was a kid. Veronica's words were another porthole to that same world of "Look but don't touch." It was fascinating. And depressing as hell. Veronica had been raised like a little princess. No doubt she'd only be content to spend her life "happily ever after," with a prince.

And he sure as hell didn't fit *that* bill.

Except, what was he doing, thinking about things like happily ever after?

"How about you, Joe?" she asked, interrupting his thoughts. "Where did you grow up?"

"Near New York City. We really should get to work," he said, half hoping she'd let the subject of his childhood drop— and half hoping that she wouldn't.

She wouldn't. "New York City," she said. "I've never lived there, I've only visited. I remember the first time I was there as a child. It all seemed to be lights and music and Broadway plays and marvelous food and . . . *people,* people everywhere."

"I didn't see any plays on Broadway," Joe said dryly. "Although when I was ten, I snuck out of the house at night and hung around the theater district, trying to spot celebrities. I'd get their autograph and then sell it, make a quick buck."

"Your parents probably *loved* that," Veronica said. "A ten-year-old, all alone in New York City . . . ?"

"My mother was usually too drunk to notice I was gone," Joe said. "And even if she had, she wouldn't have given a damn."

Veronica looked away from him, down at the floor. "Oh," she said.

"Yeah," Joe said. "Oh."

She fiddled with her hair for a moment, and then she surprised him. She looked up and directly into his eyes and smiled—a smile not without sorrow for the boy he'd once been. "I guess that's where you learned to be so self-reliant. And self-confident."

"Self-reliant, maybe. But I grew up with everyone always telling me I wasn't good enough," Joe said. "No, that's not true. Not everyone. Not Frank O'Riley." He shook his head and laughed. "He was this mean old guy who lived in this grungy basement apartment in one of the tenements over by the river. He had a wooden leg and a glass eye and his arms were covered with tattoos and all the kids were scared sh— Scared to death of him. Except me, because I was the toughest, coolest kid in the neighborhood—at least among the under-twelve set.

"O'Riley had this garden—really just a patch of land. It couldn't have been more than twelve by four feet. He always had something growing—flowers, vegetables—it was always something. So I went in there, over his rusty fence, just to prove I wasn't scared of the old man.

"I'd been planning to trample his flowers, but once I got into the garden, I couldn't do it," Joe said. "They were just too damn pretty. All those colors. Shades I'd never even imagined. Instead, I sat down and just looked at them.

"Old Frank came out and told me he'd loaded his gun and was ready to shoot me in my sorry butt, but since I was obviously another nature lover, he'd brought me a glass of lemonade instead."

Why was he telling her this? Blue was the only person he'd ever mentioned Frank O'Riley to, and never in such detail. Joe's friendship with Old Man O'Riley was the single good memory he carried from his childhood. Chief Frank O'Riley, U.S.N., retired, and his barely habitable basement apartment had been Joe's refuge, his escape when life at home became unbearable.

And suddenly he knew why he was telling Veronica about Frank, his one childhood friend, his single positive role model. He wanted this woman to know where he came from, who he really was. And he wanted to see her reaction; see whether she would recognize the importance old Frank had played in his life, or whether she would shrug it off, uncaring, uninterested.

"Frank was a sailor," Joe told Veronica. "Tough as nails, and with one hell of a foul mouth. He could swear like no one I've ever known. He fought in the Pacific in World War Two, as a frogman, one of the early members of the UDTs, the underwater demolition teams that later became the SEALs. He was rough and crude, but he never turned me away from his door. I helped him pull weeds in his garden in return for the stories he told."

Veronica was listening intently, so he went on.

"When everyone else I knew told me I was going to end up in jail or worse, Frank O'Riley told me I was destined to become a Navy SEAL—because both they and I were the best of the best."

"He was right," Veronica murmured. "He must be very, *very* proud of you."

"He's dead," Joe said. He watched her eyes fill with compassion, and the noose around his chest grew tighter. He was in big trouble here. "He died when I was fifteen."

"Oh, no," she whispered.

"Frank had one hell of a powerful spirit," Joe continued, resisting the urge to pull her into his arms and comfort her because *his* friend had died more than fifteen years ago. "Wherever I went and whatever I did for the three years after he died, he was there, whispering into my ear, keeping me in line, reminding me about those Navy SEALs that he'd admired so much. On the day I turned eighteen, I walked into that navy recruitment office and I could almost feel his sigh of relief."

He smiled at her and Veronica smiled back, gazing into his eyes. Again, time seemed to stand totally still. Again, it was the perfect opportunity to kiss her, and again, Joe didn't allow himself to move.

"I'm glad you've forgiven me, Joe," she said quietly.

"Hey, what happened to 'Your Highness'?" Joe asked, trying desperately to return to a more lighthearted, teasing tone.

She was getting serious on him. Serious meant being honest, and in all honesty, Joe did *not* want to be friends with this woman. He wanted to be lovers. He was *dying* to be her lover. He wanted to touch her in ways she'd never been touched before. He wanted to hear her cry out his name and—

Veronica looked surprised. "I've forgotten to call you that, haven't I?"

"You've been calling me Joe lately," he said. "Which is fine—I like it better. I was just curious."

"You're nothing like the real prince," she said honestly.

"I'm not sure if that's a compliment or an insult."

She smiled. "Believe me, it's a compliment."

"Yeah, that's what I thought" Joe said. "But I wasn't sure exactly where *you* stood."

"Prince Tedric . . . isn't very nice," Veronica said diplomatically.

"He's a coward and a flaming idiot," Joe stated flatly.

"I guess you don't like him very much, either."

"Understatement of the year, Ronnie. If I end up taking a bullet for him, I'm gonna be really upset." He smiled grimly. "That is, if you can be upset and dead at the same time."

Veronica stared at Joe. If he ended up taking a bullet . . .

For the first time, the reality of what Joe was doing hit her squarely in the stomach. He was risking his life to catch a terrorist. While Tedric spent the next few weeks in the comfort of a safe house, Joe would be out in public. Joe would be the target of the terrorists' guns.

What if something went wrong? What if the terrorists succeeded, and killed Joe? After all, they'd already managed to kill hundreds and hundreds of people.

Joe suddenly looked so tired. Were his thoughts following the same path? Was he afraid he'd be killed, too? But then he glanced up at Veronica and tried to smile.

"Mind if we skip lunch?" he asked. "Or just postpone it for a half hour?"

Veronica nodded. "We can postpone it," she said.

Joe stood, heading toward the bedroom. "Great, I've gotta crash. I'll see you in about thirty minutes, okay?"

"Do you want me to wake you?" she asked.

Joe shook his head, no. "Thanks, but . . ."

Oh, baby, he could just imagine her coming into his darkened bedroom to wake him up. He could just imagine coming out of a deep REM sleep to see that face, those eyes looking down at him. He could imagine reaching for her, pulling her down on top of him, covering her mouth with his. . . .

"No, thanks," he said again, reaching up with one hand to loosen the tight muscles in his neck and shoulders. "I'll set the alarm."

Veronica watched as he closed the bedroom door behind him.

They were running out of time. Despite his reassurances, Veronica didn't believe that Joe could pull it off.

But those weren't the only doubts she was having.

Posing as Prince Tedric could very easily get Joe killed.

Were they doing the right thing? Was catching these terrorists worth risking a man's life? Was it fair to ask Joe to take those risks when Tedric so very clearly wouldn't?

But out of all those doubts, Veronica knew one thing for certain. She did not want Lieutenant Joe Catalanotto to die.

Chapter 10

Veronica was ready nearly thirty minutes before the meeting was set to start.

She checked herself in the mirror for the seven thousandth time. Her jacket and skirt were a dark olive green. Her silk blouse was the same color, but a subtle shade lighter. The color was a perfect contrast for her flaming-red hair, but the suit was boxy and the jacket cut to hide her curves.

Joe would call it a Margaret Thatcher suit. And he was right. It made her look no-nonsense and reliable, dependable and businesslike.

So, all right, it wasn't the height of fashion. But she was sending out a clear message to the world. *Veronica St. John could get the job done.*

Except, in a few minutes, Veronica was going to have to walk out the hotel-room door and head down the corridor to the private conference room attached to Senator McKinley's suite. She was going to go into the meeting and sit down at the table without the slightest clue whether or not she had actually gotten this particular job done.

She honestly didn't know whether or not she'd been able to pull off the task of turning Joe Catalanotto into a dead ringer for Prince Tedric.

Dead ringer. What a horrible expression. And if the security team of FInCOM agents didn't protect Joe, that's exactly what he'd be. Dead. Joe, with his dancing eyes and wide, infectious smile... All it would take was one bullet and he would be a thing of the past, a memory.

Veronica turned from the mirror and began to pace.

She'd worked with Joe all afternoon, going over and over rules and protocols and Ustanzian history. She had shown him the strange way Prince Tedric held a spoon and the odd habit the prince had of leaving behind at least one bite of every food on his plate when eating.

She had tried to show Joe again how to walk, how to stand, how to hold his head at a royal angle. Just when she thought that maybe, just *maybe* he might be getting it, he'd slouch or shrug or lean against the wall. Or make a joke and flash her one of those five-thousand-watt smiles that were so different from any facial expression Prince Tedric had ever worn.

"Don't worry, Ronnie. This is not a problem," he'd said in his atrocious New Jersey accent. "I'll get it. When the time comes, I'll do it right."

But Veronica wasn't sure what she should be worrying about. Was she worried Joe wouldn't be able to pass for Prince Tedric, or was she worried that he *would?*

If Joe looked and acted like the prince, then he'd be at risk. And damn it, why should Joe have to risk his life? Why not let the prince risk his *own* life? After all, Prince Tedric was the one the terrorists wanted to kill.

Veronica had actually brought up her concerns to Joe before they'd parted to get ready for this meeting. He'd laughed when she'd said she thought it might be for the best if he couldn't pass for Tedric—it was too dangerous.

"I've been in dangerous situations before," Joe had told her. "And this one doesn't even come close." He'd told her about the plans and preparations he was arranging with both Kevin Laughton's FInCOM agents and the SEALs from his Alpha Squad. He'd told her he'd wear a bulletproof vest at all times. He'd told her that wherever he went, there would be shielded areas where he could easily drop to cover. He'd reminded her that this operation had minuscule risks compared to most other ops he'd been on.

All Veronica knew was, the better she came to know Joe, the more she worried about his safety. Frankly, this situation scared her to death. And if this *wasn't* dangerous, she didn't want to know what dangerous meant.

But danger was part of Joe's life. Danger was what he did best. No wonder he wasn't married. What kind of woman would put up with a husband who risked his life as a matter of course?

Not Veronica, that was for sure.

Although it wasn't as if Joe Catalanotto had dropped to his knees and begged her to marry him, was it? And he wasn't likely to, either. Despite the incredible kiss they'd shared, a man like Joe, a man used to living on the edge, wasn't very likely to be interested in anything long-term or permanent. *Permanent* probably wasn't even in his vocabulary.

Veronica shook her head, amazed at the course her thoughts had taken. *Permanent* wasn't in *her* vocabulary, either. At least not right now. And certainly not when attached to the words *relationship* and *Joe Catalanotto*. At least fifty percent of the time, the man *infuriated* her. Of course, the rest of the time he made her laugh, or he touched her with his gentle sweetness, or he burned her with that look in his eyes that promised a sexual experience the likes of which she'd never known before.

Either Veronica was fighting with Joe, or fighting the urge to throw herself into his arms.

There'd been one or two...or three or so times—certainly no more than six or eight, at any rate—this afternoon, when Veronica had found herself smiling foolishly into Joe's deep brown eyes, marveling at the length of his eyelashes, and finding her gaze drawn to his straight, white teeth and his rather elegantly shaped lips.

In all honesty, once or twice, Veronica had actually thought about kissing Joe again. Well, maybe more than once or twice.

So, all right, she admitted to herself. He *was* rather unbearably handsome. And funny. Yes, he was undeniably funny. He always knew exactly what to say to make her damn near choke with laughter on her tea. He was blunt and to the point. Often tactless at times—most of the time. But he was always honest. It was refreshing. And despite his rough language and unrefined speech, Joe was clearly intelligent. He hadn't had the best of educations, that much was true, but he seemed well-read and certainly able to think on his own, which was more than Veronica could say for Prince Tedric.

So, okay. Maybe now that she and Joe had had a chance to really talk, maybe now he didn't infuriate her fifty percent of the time. Maybe he only infuriated her, say, twenty percent of the time. But spending twenty percent of her time angry or annoyed or worrying about him was still too much—even for the kind of casual, sexual relationship Joe wanted.

Obviously, Veronica had to continue to keep her distance. Squaring her shoulders, she resolved to do precisely that. She'd stay far, far away from Joe Catalanotto. No more kisses. No more lingering looks. No more long talks about her personal life. From now on, her relationship with Joe would be strictly business.

Still a few minutes early, Veronica took her purse and briefcase and locked her hotel room door behind her. Down at the end of the corridor, she could see FInCOM agents standing outside the royal suite where Joe was getting dressed. More agents were farther down the hall, outside the conference room.

The conference-room door was ajar, so Veronica went in.

This was it. Tonight they would decide whether or not they could successfully pass a Navy SEAL off on the American public as Prince Tedric of Ustanzia.

If the answer was yes, Veronica's friend Wila would be one step closer to getting her American funding, and Joe would be one step closer to catching Diosdado, the terrorist.

She sat down at the empty oval conference table and crossed her legs.

If the answer was no, Joe would return to wherever it was Navy SEALs went between missions, and Veronica would sleep easier at night, knowing that assassins weren't trying to end his life.

Except, if Joe wasn't on *this* mission, he'd probably be on some other, what he considered *truly* dangerous mission. So really, whatever happened, Veronica was going to end up worrying, wasn't she?

Veronica frowned. She was certainly expending a bit of energy thinking about a man she had decided most definitely to stay away from.

Besides, after this meeting, she probably wasn't ever going to see Joe Catalanotto again. And the pang of remorse she felt was *surely* only because she'd failed at her assignment. It wouldn't be long before Veronica had trouble remembering Joe's name. And he certainly wouldn't give *her* a second thought.

Senator McKinley came into the room, followed by his aides and the Ustanzian ambassador and *his* aides. Both men nodded a greeting, but Veronica's attention was pulled away by a young woman taking orders for coffee or tea.

"Earl Grey," Veronica murmured, smiling her thanks.

When she looked up, Kevin Laughton and some of his FInCOM security team had come into the room, along with Admiral Forrest.

The older man caught Veronica's eye and winked a hello. He came around the oval table and pulled out the seat next to hers. "Where's Joe?" he asked.

Veronica shook her head, glancing around the room again. Even in a crowd like this, Joe would have stood out. He was bigger than most men, taller and broader. Unless he was crawling across the rug on his hands and knees, he hadn't yet arrived.

"Still getting changed, I guess," she said to Mac Forrest.

"How's the transformation going?" Forrest asked. "You got him eating lady fingers with his pinky sticking out yet?"

Veronica snorted and gave him a disbelieving look.

"It's going *that* well, huh? Hmm." The admiral didn't seem disappointed. In fact, he gave her a downright cheerful smile. "He'll get it. Did he tell you, he's a pretty darn good mimic? He's got a real ear for language, Joe Cat does."

An ear for language? With his thick accent? Oh, come on.... Veronica didn't want to offend the admiral by rolling her eyes—at least not outwardly.

"Joe's a good man," Forrest told her. "A little too intense sometimes, but that's what makes him a good commander. You win his loyalty, and he'll be loyal to the end. He demands loyalty in return—and gets it. His men would follow him to hell and back." He chuckled. "And they have, on more than one occasion."

Veronica turned toward him. "Joe doesn't think this operation is dangerous," she said. "If that's true, what exactly *is* dangerous?"

"To a SEAL?" Forrest mused. "Let's see. . . . Breaking into a hostile high-security military installation to track down a pilfered nuclear warhead might be considered dangerous."

"*Might* be?"

"Depends on the location of the military installation, and how well-trained that hostile military organization actually is," he said. "Another dangerous op might be to make a HAHO jump from a plane—"

"A what?"

"HAHO," Forrest repeated. "A high-altitude high-opening parachute jump. It's when you get the green light to jump from the plane at about thirty thousand feet—way up high where the bad guys can't hear the sound of your airplane approaching. You yank the cord, the chute opens and you and your squad parasail silently to the landing zone. And maybe, when you get there, you rescue fifteen hostages—all children—from a bunch of tangos who wouldn't bat an eye over spilling the blood of innocent kids. And maybe before you can pull the kids out of there, the op goes from covert to full firefight. So you rock and roll with your HK, knowing that your body is the only thing shielding a nine-year-old from the enemy's bullets."

Veronica frowned. "Would you mind repeating that last bit in English? Before you can pull the kids out of there...what?"

Forrest grinned, a twinkle in his blue eyes. "The terrorists become aware of your presence and open fire. You've got an instant battlefield—a full firefight. You return fire with your HK—your submachine gun—scared to death because there's a tiny little girl standing directly behind you."

Veronica nodded. "I thought that was what you said." She studied Admiral Forrest's weathered face. "Are these actual operations you're describing or merely hypothetical scenarios?"

"That's classified information," the old man said. "Of course, you're a smart girl. You can probably figure out they wouldn't be classified if they were hypothetical, right?"

Veronica was silent, digesting all he had said.

"Heads up, missy," Forrest whispered. "Looks like this meeting's about to start."

"Let's get this show on the road," Senator McKinley said, his voice cutting above the other conversations from his seat at the head of the table. "Where the hell is Catalanotto?"

McKinley was looking directly at Veronica, as were most of the other people at the table. They honestly expected her to provide them with an answer.

"He said he'd be here," she said calmly. "He'll be here." She glanced at her watch. "He's only a few minutes late."

Just then, West, one of the FInCOM agents, stepped through the door. "Crown Prince Tedric of Ustanzia," he announced.

Aha. *That* was why Joe was late. He was coming to this meeting dressed in the prince's clothes. The tailor had dropped off several large garment bags late this afternoon. No doubt Joe had wanted to wear one of the resplendent suits to make him look more like Tedric.

Any minute now he'd saunter into the room, wearing a garish sequined jacket and a sheepish grin.

But West stepped back and a figure appeared in the doorway.

He was dressed in gleaming white pants and a short white jacket that clung to his broad shoulders and ended at his waist. There were no sequins in sight, but plenty of medals covered his chest, along with a row of golden buttons decorated with the royal Ustanzian shield. The shield also glittered from the bejeweled ring he wore on his right hand. His gleaming black hair was combed directly back from his face.

It was Joe. It had to be Joe, didn't it?

Veronica searched his eyes, looking for the now quite-familiar differences between Joe's and Prince Tedric's faces. But with his shoulders back, his head held at that haughty angle, and no sign of a smile curving his lips, Veronica wasn't sure exactly *who* was standing in the doorway.

And then he spoke. "I greet you with the timeless honor and tradition of the Ustanzian flag," he said in the prince's unmistakable faintly British, faintly French accent, "which is woven, as well, into my heart."

Chapter 11

Nobody moved.

Everyone stared at Prince Tedric. It *was* Prince Tedric, not Joe. That voice, that accent... Except, what was the real prince doing here, away from the safety of his secure room on the other side of town? It didn't make sense. And his shoulders seemed so broad....

As Veronica watched, the prince took several steps into the room with his peculiar, stiff royal gait. He walked like he had a fireplace poker in his pants, as Joe had so inelegantly described. Veronica fought the urge to giggle. This had to be the prince, indeed. About half-a-dozen dark-suited FInCOM agents followed him inside, and one of them closed the door tightly behind them.

One royal eyebrow lifted a fraction of an inch at the people still sitting at the conference table, and the Ustanzian ambassador scrambled to his feet.

"Your Highness!" he said. "I didn't realize you'd be attending...."

McKinley stood, too. The rest of the table followed suit.

Still, as Veronica rose to her feet, she stared. This man wasn't Joe. Or was it? Tedric had never seemed so tall, so imposing.

But this couldn't be Joe. That voice had been Tedric's. And that walk. *And* that haughty look.

The prince's gaze swept around the table. His eyes passed over Veronica without the slightest hint of familiarity, without the tiniest bit of recognition or warmth. He looked through her, not at her. No, it wasn't Joe. Joe would have winked or smiled. And yet . . .

He held out a hand decorated with a huge gold and jeweled ring for the Ustanzian ambassador to bow over.

Senator McKinley cleared his throat. "Your Majesty," he said. "It was dangerous for you to come here. I should have been informed." He glanced at his chief aide and hissed, "Why wasn't I informed?"

The prince affixed the senator with a very displeased stare. "I am not used to asking permission to leave my room," he said.

He was the prince. Veronica tried to tell herself that she was now convinced of that fact, yet doubt lingered.

"But, Your Majesty," Kevin Laughton chimed in. "It's just not safe." He looked over at the FInCOM agents who had arrived with the prince. "I *must* be told of any movement." He looked more closely at the men and a funny look crossed his face. Veronica tried to follow his gaze, to see what he saw, but he quickly looked back at the prince, his face once again expressionless.

"If there was something you needed," Henri Freder, the Ustanzian ambassador, interjected, "all you had to do was ask, Your Majesty. We will provide you with all your requests, I can assure you."

"Sit, please, sit. Sit, sit," the prince said impatiently.

Everyone sat. Except the prince. He stood pointedly next to Senator McKinley's seat at the head of the table.

Rather belatedly, McKinley realized his mistake. He hastily stood and offered the prince his chair, moving around to one of the empty seats on the side of the oval table.

On the other side of the room, one of the FInCOM agents coughed. When Veronica glanced at him, he gave her a quick wink. It was Cowboy—one of the SEALs from Joe's Alpha Squad. At least, she thought it was. She did a double take, but when she looked again, he was gone.

She turned and stared at the man who was settling himself in the now vacant chair at the head of the table. "I'll need something to write on and a pen," he announced to no one in particular. "And a glass of water."

Had she imagined Cowboy standing there? Was this really Joe, or was it Prince Tedric? Veronica honestly did not know.

Around her, all of the aides and assistants were scrambling. One of them provided the prince with a smooth white pad of paper, another with a plastic ballpoint pen that the prince simply looked at in disdain. Yes, he had to be the real prince. No one could possibly imitate that disgusted look, could they? Another assistant produced a gold-plated fountain pen, which the prince took with a nod, and yet another presented him with a tall, ice-filled glass of water.

"Thank you," he said, and Veronica sat up.

Thank you? Those words weren't in Tedric's vocabulary. At least, Veronica had never heard him say them before.

Senator McKinley was giving the prince a detailed report on all that had been done over the past several days, and on the changes to the scheduled tour.

Veronica stared down the table at the man now sitting at its head. Prince Tedric never said thank-you. This man was Joe. It *had* to be Joe. But... he didn't look or act or sound *any-*thing like the Joe she was starting to know so well.

The prince took a sip of his water, removed the cap from his pen.

This would prove it. Joe was left-handed; the prince only used his right.

The prince took the pen in his right hand and jotted a quick note on his pad of paper.

Oh, my God, it wasn't Joe. It was the prince. Unless...

As the senator continued to talk, the prince tore the piece of paper from the pad and folded it neatly in half. He glanced over his shoulder and one of the aides was instantly behind him. He handed the aide the piece of paper and whispered a few words into the young man's ear before turning back to Senator McKinley.

Veronica watched as the aide came around the table, directly toward her. The young man handed her the folded piece of paper.

"From Prince Tedric," the aide whispered almost sound-lessly in her ear.

She glanced down the table toward the prince, but he wasn't paying her the slightest attention. He was absently twisting his ring as he listened to McKinley.

Why would Prince Tedric write *her* a note?

Hardly daring to breathe, she unfolded the paper.

"Hey, Ronnie," she read, printed in big, childish block let-ters. "How'm I doing? Love, Prince Joe."

Veronica laughed. Aloud. McKinley stopped talking mid-sentence. The entire table turned and looked at her. Including Joe, who gave her a withering look, identical to those she'd re-ceived from Prince Tedric in the past. "It's Joe," she said.

Nobody understood. They all just stared at her as if she'd gone mad—except Kevin Laughton, who was nodding, a small smile on his face, and Admiral Forrest, who was rocking back in his seat and chuckling.

Veronica gestured down toward the head of the table, to-ward Joe. "This is not Prince Tedric," she explained. "It's Lieutenant Catalanotto. Gentlemen, he's fooled us all."

Everyone started talking all at once.

The prince's haughty expression turned into a slow, friendly smile as he gazed down the table at Veronica. His cold eyes turned warm. Oh, yes, this was definitely Joe.

"You're amazing," she mouthed to him. She knew he wouldn't be able to hear her over the din, but she had no doubt he could read her lips. She wouldn't be surprised to find there was nothing Joe Catalanotto couldn't do, and do well.

He shrugged. "I'm a SEAL," he mouthed back, as if that explained everything.

"I knew it was the lieutenant," Veronica heard Kevin Laughton say. "But only because I knew three of the men who came in with him weren't on my staff."

"I knew it was him, too," Senator McKinley's loud voice boomed. "I was waiting to see when y'all would catch on."

Still, Veronica gazed into Joe's dark eyes. "Why didn't you tell me?" she silently asked.

"I did," he answered.

And he was right. He *had* told her. "Don't worry, I'll get it," he'd said. "I'm a pretty good mimic."

Pretty good?

Veronica laughed. He was *amazing*.

Joe smiled back at her as everyone around them continued to talk at once. But they might have been alone in this room, for all the attention she paid anyone else.

That was admiration he could see in Veronica's blue eyes. Admiration and respect. She wasn't trying to hide it. She was sending him a message with her eyes as clear as the one she'd sent with her lips.

Joe could also see traces of the attraction she was never really able to conceal. It was always back there, lurking, waiting patiently for the moment when her defenses were down, waiting for her to temporarily forget that he wasn't a regular of the country-club set.

And, God, he was waiting, too.

Except she wasn't going to forget. It was only at times like this, when they were safely across the room from each other, that Veronica gazed into his eyes. It was only when she was safely out of reach that she let him drown in the swirling ocean-blueness of her eyes.

It didn't take much to imagine what being Veronica St. John's lover would be like, to see her with her red curls tumbled down her back, dressed only in the skimpiest of satin and lace, desire turning her sea-colored eyes to blue flames. As Joe gazed into her eyes, he felt himself going under for the third and final time.

He wanted her so desperately, he was nearly dizzy with desire. Somehow, some way, he was going to change her mind, break through that flimsy wall she'd thrown up between them.

Admiral Forrest raised his voice to be heard over the noise. "I think this meeting can be adjourned," he said. "We can announce to the press that Prince Tedric's tour will resume as of oh-eight-hundred hours tomorrow. Are we in agreement?"

Veronica reluctantly pulled her eyes away from the molten lava of Joe's gaze. Her heart was pounding. Good Lord, the way that man looked at her! If they had been alone, he would have kissed her again. Or if he hadn't, maybe *she* would have kissed *him!*

Lord save her from herself.

She shuffled the papers in front of her, attempting to regain her equilibrium as the room slowly cleared.

Senator McKinley shook her hand briefly, commending her on a job well-done before he rushed off to another appointment.

Veronica could feel Joe's eyes still on her as he stood and talked to Admiral Forrest. The FInCOM men tried to escort them out of the room, but Joe hung back, clearly waiting for her.

Taking a deep breath, she gathered her briefcase and went to join them.

Joe was looking down at the ring on his hand. "Did you know this ring is worth more than a new car?" he mused. "And did you know old Ted has about twenty of 'em?"

Mac Forrest grinned at Veronica, slapping Joe on the back one more time as they walked down the hotel corridor. "You couldn't tell it was Joe, could you?" Forrest asked her.

Veronica glanced up at Joe. She wasn't prepared for the jolt of warmth and energy that surrounded her as she met his dark eyes. He was smiling at her, and she found herself smiling foolishly back, until she realized the Admiral had asked her a question. She tore her eyes away.

"No, sir, I couldn't," she answered hoping that she didn't sound as breathless as she felt. "Except . . ."

"What?" Joe asked.

She looked up at him, bracing herself before meeting his hypnotizing eyes again. "You said 'Thank you,'" she replied. "Tedric wouldn't dream of thanking a servant."

"Well, maybe ol' Ted's been reading up on the American version of Miss Manners," Joe said. "Because for the next five weeks, he's going to be saying 'thank you' to all the lowly servants. And maybe even 'please,' every now and then."

"That's fine with me. I think everyone should say thank-you. I think it's rude not to," Veronica said.

"The equipment you ordered is coming in late tonight," Admiral Forrest said to Joe. "It'll be ready for tomorrow."

"We leave the hotel at oh-eight-hundred?" Joe asked.

Veronica dug into her briefcase and checked the schedule. "That's right," she said. "There're a number of public appearances—just visual things—a chance for the news reporters to get footage of you climbing in and out of limousines and waving. Tomorrow night there's an optional embassy function, if you feel up to it. There *will* be people there who know Tedric quite well, though. You'll have to be ready to recognize them."

"Can *you* recognize them?" Joe asked.

"Well, yes," Veronica said. "Of course. But—"

"Then I'm ready," he said with a grin.

"We've ordered a surveillance van," Admiral Forrest said to her. "You'll have the seat of honor at the main mike. Joe will wear an earphone and a microphone so the communication can go both ways. He'll hear you and you'll hear him. *And* we'll have miniature video cameras set up, so you'll be able to see both Joe *and* from Joe's point of view."

They stopped outside the royal suite, waiting while West went inside to make a quick security sweep. "All clear," he said, coming back out. The entire group moved into the room.

Admiral Forrest clasped Joe's hand again. "Good job, son." He nodded at Veronica. "You, too, missy." He glanced at his watch. "I've got to make some status reports." As Mac turned to leave, he shook his finger at Joe. "No more unauthorized field trips down the outside of the building," he admonished. "No more games." He turned to the other SEALs, Blue, Cowboy and Harvard, who were standing by the door with the FInCOM agents. "You're on the same side as security now," he said to them. "You make sure Lieutenant Catalanotto stays secure. Have I made myself clear?"

"I gave them liberty tonight, Admiral," Joe interjected. "I figured—"

"You figured wrong," Forrest said. "As of thirty minutes ago, this operation has started."

Cowboy clearly wasn't happy about that.

The admiral opened the door to the hallway. "As a matter of fact, I need to see this security team in the corridor, pronto."

"But, sir—" Cowboy started.

"That was an order, Ensign," Forrest barked.

Still, the three SEALs didn't move until Joe gave them an almost-imperceptible nod.

The door closed behind them and the room was suddenly silent.

"What was *that* about?" Veronica asked Joe, suddenly aware of how close they were standing, of how delicious he smelled, of how he managed to make even that ridiculous white jacket look good.

He gave her one of his familiar sheepish smiles as he sat on the arm of the sofa. "I think Mac's realized that Diosdado could get lucky and take me out," he said. "He doesn't want to lose the commanding officer of the Alpha Squad."

"He doesn't want to lose a friend," Veronica corrected him.

"He's not going to," Joe said. "I have no intention of dying." It was a fact. His quiet statement combined with the certainty in his eyes and on his face convinced Veronica that it was, indeed, a fact. He looked hard and invincible, and quite possibly immortal.

But he wasn't immortal. He was human. He was flesh and blood, and starting tomorrow morning, he was going to be a target. When he stepped out the hotel door dressed as Prince Tedric, there could be an assassin's gun trained on him.

By tomorrow at this time, Joe could very well have been shot. He could be seriously injured. Or worse. He could be dead.

Permanently dead.

Joe might be able to disregard the danger, but Veronica couldn't. He was going to be out in public with a security team that wasn't up to par. Sure, the odds were better now that the three SEALs from the Alpha Squad had joined FInCOM's team, but there were no guarantees.

Veronica was going to be safely tucked away in some surveillance vehicle where, if the terrorists *did* get through the security force, she'd have a front-row seat to watch Joe die.

He was sitting there watching her, and she was struck by his casual bravery, his unassuming heroism. He was doing this for Admiral Forrest, for the admiral's dead son, and for all of the other U.S. sailors who'd been killed at Diosdado's hands. And for all the people, sailors and civilians, who would be hurt or killed by the terrorists if they were not stopped here and now.

Yes, there was a chance that he might die. But in Joe's eyes, it was obviously a risk worth taking if it meant they'd catch these killers. But what a tremendous risk, an incredible sacrifice. He'd be risking his life, his precious, irreplaceable life. It was the most he could possibly give. And to Joe, it was also the least he could do.

"Has anyone bothered to thank you for what you're doing?" Veronica asked, her throat feeling unnaturally tight as she gazed into Joe's eyes.

He shrugged, a loose casual move, echoed in his easygoing smile. "If it all works out, I'll probably get the Ustanzian Medal of Honor." He glanced down at the rows of Prince Tedric's medals on his chest and made a face. "Considering Ted's got four, I'm not sure I want one," he added. "Even if I can talk 'em out of giving me one, there'll be some kind of ceremony, and I'll have to smile for the cameras and shake Ted's sweaty hand."

"And if it doesn't work out . . . ?" Her voice trembled.

He shrugged and his smile became a grin. "Then I won't have to shake Ted's hand, right?"

"Joe."

He stood up. "Ronnie," he said, mimicking her intensity. "Lighten up, all right?"

But she couldn't. How could she lighten up when tomorrow he might very well be dead? Veronica glanced around the room, aware once again that they were alone. They were alone, and she might never have another chance to hold him in her arms.

Despite her resolve to stay away from Joe, Veronica stepped toward him, closing the gap between them, slipping her arms around his waist and holding him tightly, resting her head against his shoulder.

He was shocked. She'd seen the surprise in his eyes. She still felt it in the stiffness and tension in his entire body. Never in a million years had he expected her to put her arms around him.

As she started to pull back, she lifted her head and she could see a vulnerability deep in his eyes, a flash of almost childlike wonder. But it was gone so quickly, she was left wondering if she hadn't imagined it.

He almost didn't react. *Almost* didn't. But before she pulled away, he encircled her with his arms, holding her gently but quite firmly in place. He sighed very softly as he allowed his body to relax against hers.

Joe couldn't make himself release her. Veronica was in his arms, and he was damned if he was going to let her go. She fit next to him so perfectly, they might have been made for each other. She was soft in all the right places, and firm in all the others. Holding her like this was heaven.

Veronica stared up at him, her ocean blue eyes wide.

There were few things he wanted right this moment as much as he wanted to kiss her. He wanted to plunder her soft, sweet mouth with his tongue. To kiss her deeply, savagely, until she clung to him, dizzy from desire. He wanted to sweep her into his arms and carry her into the bedroom, where he'd undress her with his teeth and kiss every inch of her smooth, supple body before driving himself into her sweet, welcoming warmth.

He felt nearly delirious just thinking about it—the sheer bliss. And it would start with one small kiss . . .

He slowly lowered his head to kiss her.

Veronica gazed up into his eyes, transfixed, lips slightly parted.

He was a fraction of a second from paradise, and . . . she turned her head.

Joe's mouth landed on her cheek as she quickly pulled free of his arms.

Frustration made every muscle in his body tighten. *Damn* it. What had just happened here? Hell, *she'd* made the first move. She was the one who'd put her arms around him. And then . . .

"Veronica," he said, reaching for her.

But she stepped away from him, out of reach, as the door opened and the FInCOM agents and SEALs came back inside.

"I gotta run, Cat," Admiral Forrest called out, waving briefly through the open door. "We'll talk tomorrow. Be good."

"Well," Veronica said, her voice intentionally light as she collected her briefcase. "I'll see you in the morning, Lieutenant."

That was it? She was going to not kiss him and then just walk away?

She wouldn't meet his eyes as she made a beeline for the door, and short of running after her and tackling her, there was little that Joe could do to stop her.

"Thanks again," Veronica added, and she was out the door.

"Walk her to her room," Joe ordered West, suddenly afraid for her, walking alone in the hotel corridor, even the short distance to her own room.

The man nodded and followed Veronica, closing the door behind him.

"Thanks again?" Cowboy echoed her departing words. He wiggled his eyebrows suggestively at Joe. "Something happen in here we should know about?"

Joe shot him one long look. "Stop," he said.

Cowboy started to say something else, but wisely kept his mouth shut.

Thanks again.

Veronica's words echoed in Joe's head. *Thanks again.*

She had been thanking him. Of course. When she had put her arms around him, she wasn't giving in to the attraction that simmered between them. No way. She was *thanking* him. She was being the generous aristocrat thanking the lowly servant. Damn, he was *such* a fool.

Joe had to sit down.

"Everything all right, Cat?" Blue asked softly in his gentle Southern accent.

Joe stood again and headed for the bedroom. "Fine," he answered shortly, keeping his head turned away so his friend wouldn't see the hurt he knew was showing in his eyes.

Chapter 12

When the embassy party started at nine—twenty-one-hundred hours according to Joe—Veronica was feeling an old pro at handling the equipment in the surveillance van.

She wore a lightweight wireless headset with an attached microphone positioned directly under her lips. Joe could hear every word she spoke through a miniature receiver hidden in his right ear. And Veronica could hear him quite clearly, too. His wireless mike was disguised as a pin he wore in the lapel of his jacket.

She could see Joe, too, on a TV screen built into the side panel of the van. Another screen showed a different angle—Joe's point of view. Both views were courtesy of miniaturized video cameras discreetly held by several FInCOM agents. So far, Veronica hadn't had much use for the TV screen that showed the world from Joe's eyes. It would come in handy tonight, though.

The three SEALs from Alpha Squad were also wearing microphones and earphones patched into the same frequency that Veronica and Joe were using. It was easy to tell Blue's, Cowboy's and Harvard's voices apart, and of course, she would recognize Joe's voice anywhere.

More often than not, the SEALs used some kind of abbreviated lingo, using phrases like "LZ" and "recon" and "sneak and peek." They talked about the "T's" or "tangos," which Veronica knew to mean terrorists. But for every word she recognized, they used four others whose meanings were mysterious. It was like listening to another language.

Throughout the day, Veronica had reminded Joe when to bow and when to wave, when to ignore the news cameras, and when to look directly into their lenses and smile. She'd warned him when his smile became a bit too broad—too Joe-like—and he'd adjusted instantly in order to seem more like the real prince.

The high-tech equipment made the process infinitely easier than any other job she'd ever done.

What she was never going to get used to, however, was the slightly sick feeling in the pit of her stomach as she watched Joe on the video cameras and wondered when the assassins were going to strike.

"Okay," came the word from Kevin Laughton, who was also in the surveillance van. "The limo is approaching the embassy."

"Got it," West said over the van's speakers. "I see them coming up the drive." FInCOM was using a different frequency for their radio communication. Joe's earphone had been modified to maintain a direct link with them, too. If someone—SEAL or Fink—so much as breathed a warning, he wanted to hear it.

"Check, check," Veronica heard Joe say into his mike. "Am I on?"

"We're reading you," Laughton said. "Do you copy?"

"Gotcha," Joe said. "Ronnie, you with me?"

"I'm here," Veronica said, purposely keeping her voice low and calm. Her heart was beating a mile a minute at the thought of Joe walking into the Ustanzian Embassy and actually relying on her for the information he needed to pull off his masquerade as Prince Tedric. And if *she* was on edge, he must be incredibly nervous. He not only had to think about successfully portraying Tedric, but he also had to worry about not getting killed.

"Cameras are on," a FInCOM agent's voice reported. "Surveillance van, do you have picture?"

"Roger that, FInCOM," Veronica said, and Joe laughed, just as she'd known he would.

"What, are you getting into this?" he asked her.

"Absolutely," she said smoothly. "I don't know the last time I've so looked forward to an embassy party. I get to sit out here in comfort instead of tippy-toeing around all those dignitaries and celebrities, eating overcooked hors d'oeuvres and smiling until my face hurts."

Joe leaned across the limousine, closer to the camera. "Overcooked hors d'oeuvres?" he said, making a face. *"That's* what I have to look forward to here?"

"Ready to open the limo doors," West's voice announced. "Everyone in position?"

"Joe, be careful," Veronica murmured quickly.

He touched his ear briefly, giving her the signal that he heard her. She saw something flicker in his eyes before he looked away from the video camera.

What was he thinking? Was he thinking of last night, of the way he'd almost kissed her? He *would* have kissed her again, and she probably would have kissed him, too, if she hadn't heard the hotel-room door start to open.

Probably? Definitely—despite her better judgment. She should be grateful they had been interrupted when they were. She *knew* she was grateful that she'd heard the sound of the doorknob turning. How awful would it have been to have three FInCOM agents, three SEALs and one navy admiral open the door to find her locked in Joe's embrace.

Joe had been oddly distant this morning—no doubt a direct result of her rapid flight from his hotel room last night. Veronica felt guilty about running away. But if she'd stayed, and if he'd pursued her, she would have ended up in his arms again. And, quite probably, she would have ended up in his bed.

She had thought maybe a little time and a little distance would take the edge off the attraction she felt for this man. But when she had walked out of her room this morning, Joe had been dressed in one of Tedric's least flashy dark suits and was already waiting with the FInCOM agents in the corridor. She'd looked at him, their eyes had met, and that attraction had sparked again.

No, time and distance had done nothing. She'd wanted to kiss Joe as much this morning as she had wanted to kiss him last night. Maybe even more so.

The security team had led him down the hallway to the elevators and she'd followed a step or two behind. Once downstairs, they'd gone immediately to work.

Admiral Forrest had explained the array of equipment in the van, and Joe had stared unsmiling into the cameras as the screens and relays were checked and double-checked. She'd talked to him over her headset, and although his replies had started out terse and to the point, over the course of the long day, he'd warmed up to his usual self, with his usual sardonic humor.

"Doors are opening," West announced now, and the pictures on the TV screens jumped as the agents holding the cameras scrambled out of the limo.

The paparazzi's flashbulbs went off crazily as Joe stepped out of the long white car, and Veronica held her breath. If someone was going to shoot him, it would happen now, as he was walking from the car to the embassy. Inside the building, security was very tight. He would still be in some danger, but not half as much as out here in the open.

The FInCOM agents surrounded him and hustled him inside, one of them roughly pushing Joe's head down, out of target range.

"Well, *that* was fun," Veronica heard Joe say as the embassy doors closed behind them. "Warn me next time you decide to put me in a half nelson, would you, guys?"

"We're inside," West's voice said.

On Veronica's video screen, the Ustanzian ambassador approached Joe, followed by an entourage of guests and celebrities. Joe instantly snapped into character, shoulders back, expression haughty.

"Henri Freder, Ustanzian ambassador to the United States," Veronica told Joe. "He knows who you are. He was at the meeting last night, and he's available to help you."

"Your Highness." Freder gave Joe a sweeping bow. "It is with great pleasure that I welcome you to the Ustanzian Embassy."

Joe nodded in return, just a very slight inclination of his head. Veronica smiled. Joe had Tedric's royal attitude down cold.

"The man to Freder's left is Marshall Owen," Veronica said to Joe, calling up additional background on Owen on the computer. "Owen's a businessman from . . . Atlanta, Georgia, who owns quite a bit of real estate in Europe, Ustanzia included. He's a friend of your father's. You've only met him three or four times—once in Paris. You played racketball. You won, but he probably threw the game. Shake his hand and address him as 'Mr. Owen'—Daddy owes him quite a bit of money."

On-screen, Joe shook Marshall Owen's hand. "Mr. Owen," he said in Tedric's unmistakable accent. "A pleasure to see you again, sir. Will you be in town long? Perhaps you can come to the hotel for a visit? There are racketball courts next to the weight room, I believe."

"Excellent," Veronica murmured.

With this equipment and Joe's ability to mimic, it was going to be—what was that expression of Joe's?—a piece of cake.

Joe sat on the couch in the royal suite, drinking beer from the bottle and trying to depressurize.

There was a soft knock on the hotel-room door, and West moved to answer it, opening it only slightly. The FInCOM agent opened it wider and Veronica slipped inside.

She smiled when she saw Joe. "You were great today."

He felt his face relaxing as he smiled back at her. "You weren't so shabby yourself." He started to stand, but she waved him back into his seat. "Want a beer? Or something to eat? We could order up . . . ?"

Jesus, Mary and Joseph, could he sound any more eager for her company?

She shook her head, still smiling at him. "No, thank you," she said. "I really just wanted to stop in and tell you what a good job you did."

Joe had tried to keep his distance all day long. He'd tried to act cool and disinterested. Tried. Jesus, Mary and Joseph, after last night, after he realized Veronica had only put her arms around him as a gesture of thanks, he should have had no problem staying away from her. He should have known better. Even after she'd apologized for her angry outburst, for calling him stupid and ignorant, he should have known that just because she'd apologized for saying those things, it didn't mean that she didn't think they were true.

Veronica had told him that she wanted to be friends—yeah, probably the way she would befriend a stray dog.

But all day long, he'd found himself playing to the hidden video cameras, knowing she was watching him, enjoying the sound of her voice speaking so intimately into his ear.

It didn't matter that they were dozens, sometimes even hundreds of yards apart. Veronica was his main link to the surveillance van. Hers was the voice Joe heard most often over his miniaturized earphone. He had to depend on her and trust her implicitly when she gave him information and instructions. Whether she knew it or not, their relationship *had* become an intimate one.

And Joe suspected that she knew it.

He was staring at her again, he realized. Her eyes were so blue and wide as she gazed back at him.

He looked away first. Who was he kidding? What was he trying to do? Weren't two rejections enough? What did he want, three for three?

"It's getting late," he said gruffly, wanting her either in his arms or gone.

"Well," she said, clearly flustered. "I'm sorry. I'm..." She shook her head and fished for a moment in her briefcase. "Here is tomorrow's schedule," she added, handing him a sheet of paper. "Good night, then." She moved gracefully toward the door.

"Saint Mary's," Joe said aloud, his eyes catching the name halfway down the schedule.

Veronica stopped and turned back toward him. "Yes, that's right," she said. "I meant to ask you to wear something... special."

"What? My giant chicken suit?"

She laughed. "Not exactly what I had in mind."

"Then maybe you should be more specific."

"Blue jacket, red sash, black pants," Veronica instructed. "I think of it as Tedric's Prince Charming outfit. Didn't you get fitted for something like that?"

"I did and I'll wear it tomorrow." Joe bowed. "Your wish is my command."

Chapter 13

Veronica rode to Saint Mary's in the limousine with Joe.

He was wearing the Prince Charming-like suit she'd asked him to wear, and he looked almost ridiculously handsome.

"This is going to be a difficult one," she said, doing some last-minute work on her laptop computer.

"Are you kidding?" Joe said. "No media, no fanfare—how hard could it be?"

"I'm going in with you this time," Veronica said, as if she hadn't heard him.

"Oh, no, you're not," he countered. "I don't want you within ten feet of me."

She looked up from her computer screen. "There's no danger," she said. "Saint Mary's wasn't on the schedule we released to the press."

"There's always danger," Joe insisted. "There's always a possibility that we're being followed."

Veronica looked out the rear window. Three other limos, plus the surveillance van, were trailing behind them. "Goodness gracious," she said in mock surprise. "You're right! We're being followed by three *very* suspicious-looking limousines and—"

"Knock off the comedy routine, St. John," Joe muttered. "You're not going in there, and that's final."

"You don't want me to get hurt." Veronica closed her computer and slid it back into its carrying case. "That's so sweet."

"That's me," Joe said. "Prince Sweetie-Pie."

"But I *need* to go in."

"Ronnie—"

"Saint Mary's is a hospice, Joe," Veronica said quietly. "For children with cancer."

Joe was silent.

"There's a little girl named Cindy Kaye who is staying at Saint Mary's," she continued, her voice low and even. "She wrote a letter to Tedric, asking him to stop and visit her during his tour of the United States. She'd like to meet a real prince before—well—before she dies." She cleared her throat. "Cindy has an inoperable brain tumor. She's been writing to Tedric for months—not that he bothers to read the letters. But I've read them. Every single one. She's incredibly bright and charming. And she's going to die in a matter of weeks."

Joe made a low, pain-filled sound. He rubbed his forehead with one hand, shielding his eyes from her view.

"I spoke to her mother on the phone this morning," Veronica said. "Apparently Cindy's taken a turn for the worse. She's been practicing her curtsy for months, but as of last night, she's..." She cleared her throat again. "The tumor's affecting more and more of her motor functions, and she's now unable to get out of bed."

Joe swore, long and loud, as the limo pulled up outside the hospice.

It was a clean, white building, with lots of windows, and beautiful flowers growing in the neatly tended gardens outside. There was a statue of the Madonna, also gleaming white, in among the flowers. It was lovely to look at, so peaceful and serene. But inside . . . Inside were children, all dying of cancer.

"What am I supposed to say to a kid who's dying?" Joe asked, his voice hoarse.

"I don't know," Veronica admitted. "I'll come with you—"

"No way." Joe shook his head.

"Joe—"

"I said, *no*. I'm *not* risking your life, goddammit!"

Veronica put her hand on his arm and waited until he looked up at her. "Some things are worth the risk."

Cindy Kaye was tiny, so skinny and frail. She looked more like a malnourished six-year-old than the ten-year-old Veronica knew her to be. Her long brown hair was clean and she wore a pink ribbon in it. She was lying on top of her bedspread, wearing a frilly pink dress with lots of flounces and lace. Her legs, covered in white tights, looked like two slender sticks. She wore white ballet slippers on her narrow feet.

The little girl's brown eyes filled with tears, tears that spilled down her cheeks, as Joe came into the room and gave her his most royal of bows.

"Milady," he said in Tedric's unmistakable accent. He approached Cindy and the vast array of tubes and IVs and medical equipment that surrounded her without the slightest hesitation. He sat on the edge of Cindy's bed and lifted her skeletal hand to his lips. "It is a great honor to meet you at last. Your letters have brought great joy and sunshine to my life."

"I wanted to curtsy for you," Cindy said. Her voice was trembling, her speech slurred.

"When my sister, the Princess Wila, was twelve," Joe said, leaning forward as if he were sharing a secret with her, "she injured her back and neck in a skiing accident, and was confined to her bed, much the way you are now. Our great-aunt, the Duchess of Milan, taught her the proper social etiquette for such a situation. The duchess taught her the 'eyelid curtsy.'"

Cindy waited silently for him to continue.

"Close your eyes," Joe commanded the little girl, "count to three, then open them."

Cindy did just that.

"Excellent," Joe said. "You must have royal blood in your veins to be able to do the eyelid curtsy so elegantly your very first time."

Cindy shook her head, the corners of her mouth finally curving upward.

"No royal blood? I don't believe it," Joe said, smiling back at her. "Your dress is very beautiful, Cindy."

"I picked it out just for you," she said.

Joe had to lean close to understand. He looked up to meet the eyes of the woman seated beside the bed—Cindy's mother. She gave him such a sweet, sorrowful, thankful smile, he had to look away. Her daughter, her precious, beautiful daughter, was dying. Joe had always believed he was a strong man, but he wasn't sure he would have the strength to sit by the bedside of his own dying child, day after day, hiding all his frustration and helplessness and deep, burning anger, offering only comforting smiles and peaceful, quiet, reassuring love.

He felt some of that frustration and rage form a tornado inside him, making his stomach churn. Somehow, he kept smiling. "I'm honored," he said to Cindy.

"Do you speak Ustanzian?" Cindy asked.

Joe shook his head. "In Ustanzia we speak French," he said.

"Je parle un peu français," Cindy said, her words almost unrecognizable.

Oh, God, thought Veronica. Now what?

"Très bien," Joe said smoothly. "Very good."

Veronica relaxed. Joe knew a bit of French, too. Thank goodness. That might have been a real disaster. Imagine the child's disappointment to find that her prince was an imposter...

"I would love to see your country," Cindy said, in her stilted schoolgirl French.

Oh, dear. Veronica stood. "Cindy, I'm sure Prince Tedric would love for you to see his country, too, but he should really practice his English, now that he's visiting America."

Joe looked up at her. "It's all right," he murmured, then turned back to Cindy. "I know a way you can see my country," Joe replied in perfect French. His accent was impeccable—he spoke like a native Parisian. "Close your eyes, and I will tell you all about my beautiful Ustanzia, and you will see it as if you are there."

Veronica's mouth was hanging open. Joe spoke *French? Joe* spoke *French?* She pulled her mouth shut and listened in silence as he described Ustanzia's mountains and valleys and plains in almost poetic language—both in French and English, as he translated the too-difficult words for the little girl.

"It sounds wonderful," Cindy said with a sigh.

"It is," Joe replied. He smiled again. "Do you know some people in my country also speak Russian?" He then repeated his question in flawless Russian.

Veronica had to sit down. Russian? What *other* languages did he speak? Or maybe she should wonder what languages *didn't* he speak . . .

"Do you speak Russian?" Joe asked the little girl.

She shook her head.

"Say '*da*,'" Joe said.

"*Da*," she said.

"That's Russian for 'yes,'" he told her, and smiled—a big, wide, warm Joe smile, not one of Tedric's pinched smiles. "Now you speak Russian."

"*Da*," she said again, with a brilliant smile in return.

A FInCOM agent appeared in the doorway. When Joe looked up, the man touched his watch.

"I have to go now," Joe said. "I'm sorry I can't stay longer."

"That's okay," Cindy said, but once again her eyes filled with tears.

Joe felt his heart clench. He'd been there, visiting Cindy, for only thirty minutes. When they'd set up the schedule for the tour, McKinley had wanted to allot only five minutes for Saint Mary's, but Veronica had been adamant that they take a full half hour. But now, even a half hour didn't seem long enough.

"I'm so glad I got to meet you," Joe said, leaning forward to kiss her on the forehead as he stood.

"Your Majesty . . . ?"

"Yes, milady?"

"I heard on the news that there are lots of kids hungry in Ustanzia right now," Cindy said, laboring over the words.

Joe nodded seriously. "Yes," he said. "That news report was right. My family is trying to fix that."

"I don't like it when kids are hungry," she said.

"I don't either," Joe said, his voice husky. The tornado inside him was growing again. How could this child think of others' troubles and pain, when her own pain was so great?

"Why don't you share your food with them?" Cindy said.

"It's not always that easy," Joe said. But she already knew that. Surely she, of all people, knew that.

"It should be," she said.

He nodded. "You're right. It should be."

She closed her eyes briefly—an eyelid curtsy.

Joe bowed. What could he say now? Stay well? That would be little more than a cruel joke. I'll see you soon? An untruth. Both he and the child knew they would never meet again. His rage and frustration swelled up into his throat, making it difficult to speak. "Goodbye, Cindy," he managed to say, then moved toward the door.

"I love you, Prince," Cindy said.

Joe stopped, and turned back to her, fighting hard to smile. "Thank you," he said. "I'll treasure this day, Cindy—always—and carry you forever in my heart."

The little girl smiled, made happy by such a small thing, such a small pleasure.

Somehow Joe kept the smile on his face until he was outside the room. Somehow he managed to walk down the hall without putting his fist through a wall. Somehow he managed to keep walking—until the burning rage in his stomach and throat and behind his eyes grew too intense, and his feet wouldn't carry him another step forward.

He turned toward the wall—the same wall he hadn't put his fist through—and leaned his arms against it, burying his face in the crook of his elbow, hoping, *praying* that the pain that was burning him would soon let up.

But why should it? The pain Cindy was in wasn't going to let up. She was going to die, probably in a matter of days. The injustice of it all was like a knee to his groin. Bile filled his mouth and he wanted to shake his fist at the sky and curse the God Who could let this happen.

"Joe."

Ronnie was there, then. Leading him down the hall, she pulled him into the semiprivacy of a tiny chapel. Warm and soft, she put her arms around him and held him tightly.

"Oh, God," he said, fighting the hot rush of tears to his eyes. "Oh, *God!*"

"I know," she said. "I know. But you were so good. You made her smile. You made her *happy.*"

Joe pulled back to look at Veronica. Light filtered in through the stained-glass windows, glowing red and blue and gold on the tile floor. "I'm not even a real prince," he said harshly. "It was all just a lie."

Veronica shook her head. "Tedric would've disappointed her horribly," she said. "You've given her something good to dream about."

Joe laughed, but it came out sounding more like a sob. He stared up at the crucifix on the wall behind the altar. "Yeah, but for how long?"

"For as long as she needs good dreams," Veronica said quietly.

Joe felt his eyes fill with tears again. He tried to blink them back, but one or two escaped, rolling down his face. He was crying. God, he hadn't cried since he was fifteen years old. Embarrassed, he wiped at his face with the back of one hand. "This is why you insisted that Saint Mary's stay on the schedule," he said gruffly. "*You're* really the one responsible for making that little girl happy."

"I think it was teamwork," Veronica said, smiling at him through her own tears.

He'd never seen her look more beautiful. Nearly everything she'd done up to this point, he realized, she'd done for the sake of one little dying girl. Sure, she wanted to help catch the terrorists. And she wanted to help her friend, the princess of Ustanzia. But what *really* had driven her to make sure Joe could pass as Prince Tedric, was the little sick kid back in that bed.

He knew that as sure as he knew his heart was beating.

The noose around Joe's chest drew so tight, for one heart-stopping moment he was sure he'd never be able to breathe again. But then something snapped—not the noose, but something in his head—and a little voice said, "You're in love with this woman, you flaming idiot," and he knew it was true.

She was wonderful. And he was *crazy* in love with her.

Her smile faded and there was only warmth in her eyes, warmth and that ever-present flame of desire. She moved back into his arms, and lifted her mouth to his and . . .

God, he was kissing her. He was actually kissing her.

He took her lips hungrily, pulling her lithe body closer to him. He wanted to inhale her, devour her, become one with her. He kissed her again and again, his tongue sweeping fiercely past any pretense of civility, as he savagely claimed her mouth.

He could feel her arms around his neck, feel her pressing herself even tighter against him as she kissed him with equal abandon.

It was so right. It was so utterly, perfectly right. This woman, his arms around her, their two hearts beating—pounding—in unison. Two souls intertwined. Two minds so different, yet alike.

Joe knew with sudden frightening clarity what he'd been fighting and denying to himself for days now.

He wanted.

Ronnie St. John.

Permanently.

As in "till death do us part."

He wanted to make love to her, to possess her, to own her heart as completely as she owned his. He wanted to see her eyes widen in pleasure, hear her cry his name as he filled her, totally, absolutely, in a perfect act of total and binding love.

For the first time in his life, Joe understood the concept of happily ever after. It was a promise he'd never allowed himself before, an impossible rank he'd never thought to achieve.

But it was right there, staring him in the face whenever Veronica walked into the room. It was in the way she stood, the way she tilted her head very slightly as she listened to him talk, the way she tried so ineffectually to tuck her wild curls back up into her bun, the way her blue eyes danced as she laughed. And it was in the way she was kissing him, as if she, too, wanted to wrap her gorgeous mile-long legs around his waist and feel him inside her forever and ever and ever and *ever*.

But then, as suddenly as the kiss had started, it stopped.

Veronica pulled away, as if she suddenly realized that they were standing in the middle of the hospice chapel, surrounded by stained glass and soothing dark wood and candles, with a FInCOM agent watching them from the doorway. A nun knelt quietly before the altar. They'd been standing there, kissing, in front of a *nun,* for crying out loud....

Veronica's cheeks flushed pink as Joe looked into her eyes, trying to see what she was thinking. Was this just another "mistake"? Or was this simply a more emotional thank-you? Or was it more than that? Please, God, he wanted it to be more. He wanted it to mean she was feeling all of the things that he felt. But they weren't alone, and he couldn't ask. He couldn't even speak. All he could do was hope.

She looked away from him, the expression in her eyes unreadable as she murmured an apology.

An apology. Mistakes and accidents required apologies.

Joe's heart sank as the FInCOM agents quickly led them both back to the waiting limos. And when Kevin Laughton hustled Veronica into a different limousine and she didn't even glance in Joe's direction before getting inside, his heart shattered.

He had his answer. That kiss had been another mistake.

Joe was quiet on the charter flight to Boston. Even his friends from the Alpha Squad knew enough to stay away from him.

Veronica slipped into the seat next to his, and he glanced up, his eyes wary.

"Are you all right?" she asked quietly.

He smiled tightly. "Why wouldn't I be all right?"

Veronica wasn't sure how to answer that question. Because you just spent time with a dying child. Because you talked to her and you didn't try to pretend that she had a future, that she wasn't dying. Because it hurts like hell to know that there's nothing you or anyone else can do for that little girl, except make her smile a few more times. . . .

And because you kissed me as if your world were crumbling beneath your very feet, and when I pulled away, you looked at me as if I were ripping the heart from your chest. . . .

Joe shook his head. "You know, that's the problem when big, mean guys like me show we actually have a soul," he complained. "Everyone gets all worried, like, he lost it once, now he's gonna burst into tears every time someone says 'Boo.' Well, forget about it. I'm fine."

Veronica nodded, not daring to comment, certainly not daring to mention the kiss. Not yet. They sat for a moment in silence, and then she turned back to look at him. "I had no idea you spoke French," she said, tackling a much safer subject, hoping he'd be the one to bring up the topic of the kiss they'd shared. "*And* Russian?"

Joe shrugged. "I'm a language specialist," he said, shortly. "It's no big deal."

"How many languages do you speak?"

"Eight," he said.

"Eight," Veronica repeated. The way he said it, it was nothing. She spoke English and French and a very small bit of Spanish, and *that* hadn't been nothing. In fact, it had been a great deal of work.

"Someone in the team has to be able to communicate with the locals," he said, as if that explained everything. His SEAL Team needed him to speak eight different languages, so he'd learned eight different languages.

"What else do you specialize in?" she asked.

Joe shrugged. "The usual SEAL tricks."

"Balancing beach balls on your nose and barking like a dog?"

He finally smiled. "Not quite," he said.

"I assume some kind of swimming is involved," Veronica said. "Or else you wouldn't be called SEALs."

"Yeah, swimming," he said. "And scuba diving. Skydiving. Parasailing." He started ticking the list off on his fingers. "Explosives, underwater and on land. Weapons and other high-tech war toys. Martial arts and some less conventional hand-to-hand techniques. Computers. Locks. Alarm systems. And so on."

"Admiral Forrest said you were a sharpshooter," Veronica said. "An expert marksman."

"Everyone in SEAL Team Ten is," he replied, shrugging it off.

"Besides languages, what else do *you* specialize in?" Veronica asked.

He gazed at her for several long seconds. "I know a little more than the other guys when it comes to the high-tech war toys," he finally said. "I'm also a classified expert in jungle, desert and arctic survival. You know about the languages and my... ability to mimic. Comes in handy at times. I can fly any type of aircraft, from a chopper to a Stealth." He smiled, but it lacked the wattage of his usual grins. "Hell, I could probably handle the space shuttle if I had to. And I'm an expert mechanic. I could fix it if it breaks. There's some other stuff that you don't want to know, and some that I can't tell you."

Veronica nodded slowly. Admiral Forrest had told her much of this before, but she hadn't believed it. She probably still wouldn't believe it if she hadn't heard Joe speaking perfect French. He could do all those incredible things, superhuman things, and yet it was his humanity—his compassion and kindness for a dying child—that had moved her the most. Moved her profoundly.

She looked down at her hands, folded nervously in her lap. "Joe, about this morning," she started to say.

"It's okay, Ronnie. You can forget about it," he interrupted, knowing that she was talking about their kiss. His eyes were guarded as he glanced at her again. He looked away, out the window of the jet. "It was . . . something we both needed right then. But, it . . . didn't mean anything, and I know you're not going to let it happen again. No more mistakes, right? So we don't need to talk about it. In fact, I'd rather *not* talk about it."

"But . . ."

"Please," he said, turning to look at her again.

It didn't mean anything. His words suddenly penetrated, and Veronica stared at him, her mouth slightly open. She closed her mouth, and looked back down at her hands.

She sat there in silence, afraid to move, afraid to breathe, afraid to *think*, because she was afraid of what she'd feel.

It didn't mean anything.

That kiss had been more than a kiss. It had been an exchange of emotions, a joining of souls. It had been filled with feelings she didn't want to feel, powerful feelings for a man who scared her more than she wanted to admit. A man who specialized in making war. A man who risked his life as a matter of course. A man she'd tried to keep her distance from. Tried and failed.

She'd kissed him. In *public*. And he thought it didn't *mean* anything?

The seat-belt light flashed on, and the pilot's voice came over the loudspeaker.

"We're approaching Boston. Please return to your seats."

Joe stared out the window as if he'd never seen Boston before, as if the aerial view was infinitely more interesting than anything he could see inside the jet.

Veronica forced her voice to sound even and controlled. "We'll be arriving in Boston in a few minutes," she said. Joe lifted his head in acknowledgment, but still didn't look in her direction. "From the airport, it's only about a fifteen-minute drive downtown to the hotel where the charity luncheon is being held. Your speech will be on a TelePrompTer. It'll be brief and all you'll have to do is read it.

"This evening, there's a private party on Beacon Hill," she said, wishing she felt as cool and detached as she sounded. Wishing she didn't feel like crying. *It didn't mean anything.* "The host and hostess are friends of Wila's. And mine. So I won't be in the surveillance van tonight."

He turned and frowned at her, his dark eyes piercing. "What? Why not?"

"Ambassador Freder will be in the van," Veronica said, purposely not meeting the intensity of Joe's gaze. "I'll be attending my friends' party. There'll be virtually no risk for you. Consider this another one of Tedric's obligations that couldn't be gotten out of."

She could feel him watching her, giving her a long, measuring look. "There's never no risk," he said. "I'd feel much better if you were in the van."

"We won't stay long," she said, glancing up at him.

"Just long enough to get shot, maybe, huh?" Joe said. He forced a smile. "Relax, Ronnie, I was kidding."

"I don't think getting shot is ever funny," Veronica said tightly.

"Sorry," he said. God, she was strung as tight as he was. Probably the tension from worrying about his reaction to this morning's kiss. No doubt the relief hadn't set in yet.

Sitting next to her like this was torture. Joe jerked his thumb toward the window. "It's been a while since I've been in New England," he said. "Mind if I . . . ?"

Veronica shook her head. "No, that's . . . Go right ahead and . . ."

He'd already turned to look out the window.

She'd been dismissed.

Rather than stare at the back of Joe's head, agonizing over his impersonal words, Veronica ignored the seat-belt sign and stood, moving toward the front of the plane where there were several empty seats.

It didn't mean anything.

Maybe not to Joe, but that kiss *had* meant something to Veronica.

It meant *she'd* been a real fool.

Chapter 14

Salustiano Vargas, the former right hand of the man known by most of the world only as Diosdado, stared at the telephone in his cheap motel room as it rang. It was hotter than hell in there and the air conditioner chugged away to no avail.

He had told no one, *no one,* where he would be staying. Still, he knew damn well who was on the other end of the line. There was nowhere he could run where Diosdado couldn't find him.

He picked it up after the seventeenth ring, unable to stand it any longer. "Yes?"

Diosdado said only one word. "When?"

"Soon," Vargas replied, closing his eyes. "You have my word."

"Good." The line was cut without a goodbye.

Vargas sat in the heat for several moments, not moving.

It truly *was* hotter than hell in this cheap room.

When he stood, it took him only a few minutes to pack up his things. He carried his suitcase to his rented car and headed across town—toward a fancy, expensive resort. He couldn't afford to stay there, but he would put it on his credit card. He wanted luxury. He wanted clean sheets, a firm bed. He wanted room service and a view of a sparkling swimming pool with young girls lounging around it. He wanted the cool, sweet, fresh air of a fancy hotel room.

He didn't want hell. He'd be there soon enough.

As the applause died down, Joe smiled in the direction of the TV news cameras. "Good afternoon," he said. "It is an honor and a pleasure to be here today."

Veronica couldn't concentrate on his words. All her attention was on Blue and Cowboy and Harvard's voices as they kept a constant lookout for danger.

This was the perfect setting for an assassination attempt. There were TV cameras here from every network, including cable news, *and* the event was political—a hundred-dollars-a-plate fund-raiser for a well-known senator's reelection campaign.

But if the terrorists were going to try to shoot the prince—Joe—they hadn't set up in any of the obvious vantage points. If they were here, they were in with the crowd, sitting in the rows of banquet tables.

FInCOM agents were everywhere. Veronica could see them on her video screens, their eyes sweeping the crowd, watchful for any sign of danger or trouble.

Please, Lord, protect Joe and keep him safe—

There was a sudden commotion at one of the tables in the back, and Veronica's heart lodged in her throat.

She could hear the SEALs shouting and see the FInCOM agents running, all converging on one table, and one man.

"I have my rights!" the man was shouting as he was wrestled to the floor. "I've done nothing wrong! I'm a Vietnam veteran and I want to know—"

Noise erupted as people tried to get away from the commotion, and the FInCOM agents tried to get the man out of the room. And Joe... Joe was still standing at the podium, watching. Why didn't he get down, out of harm's way?

"Joe," Veronica said into her microphone. "Take cover!"

But he didn't move.

"Joe!" she said again. "Damn it, get down!"

He wasn't listening. He was watching as the man was dragged toward the door.

"Wait," he said sharply, his commanding voice echoing over the PA system, cutting through hubbub, through the sound of eight hundred voices all talking at once. "I said, *wait!*"

Blue froze. They all froze—the FInCOM agents and their prisoner, looking up toward Joe. A hush fell over the crowd.

"Is he armed?" Joe asked, more quietly now.

Blue shook his head. "No, sir."

"I only wanted to ask a question, Your Highness," the man called out, his voice ringing clearly across the room.

Veronica sat on the edge of her seat, watching. She could see the TV cameras catching every bit of the drama.

"He only wanted to ask a question," Joe repeated mildly. He turned to Kevin Laughton, who now stood on the stage next to him. "Has it become illegal in this country to ask a question?"

"No, sir," Laughton said. "But—"

Joe turned pointedly away from Laughton. "He would like to ask a question," he said to the watching crowd, "and I would like to *hear* his question, if the rest of you don't mind...?"

Someone started to clap, and after a brief smattering of applause, Joe bowed his head to the man.

"The question I wanted to ask you, Prince Tedric," the man said in his clear voice, "and the question I want to ask *all* of you," he added, addressing the entire crowd, "is how can you sit here in good conscience, spending so much money for one meal, when right next door a homeless shelter and soup kitchen for Vietnam veterans is about to be shut down from lack of funding?"

It was so quiet in the room, a pin could have been heard falling on the floor.

Joe didn't answer at first. He let the question sit, filling the air, surrounding all the luncheon guests.

"What is your name?" Joe asked the man.

"Tony Pope, sir," the man said. "Sergeant Tony Pope, U.S. Marines, retired."

"You served in Vietnam, Sergeant?" Joe asked.

Pope nodded. "Yes, sir."

Joe looked at Blue and the FInCOM agents who were still holding Pope's arms. "I think you can release him," he said. "I think we've determined he's not out for blood."

"Thank you, sir." Pope straightened his jacket and tie.

He was a good-looking man, Veronica realized, with a neatly trimmed goatee and mustache. His suit was well-tailored, if rather worn and fraying in spots. He held himself proudly, standing tall, with his shoulders back and head high.

"Do you run this homeless shelter, Sergeant Pope?" Joe asked.

"Yes, sir," Pope replied. "The Boylston Street Shelter. For ten years, sir." His mouth tightened. "We've had some tough times, but never like this. The few grants we had left ran out, and it'll be six months before we stand a chance of getting any additional funding. And now the city says we need to make repairs to the facility by the end of the month—Friday—or our site's condemned. We barely have enough cash to feed our residents, let alone make the kind of repairs they're demanding. To be bluntly honest, sir, the Vietnam vets that live at Boylston Street Shelter are getting screwed—again."

"How many men use your facility?" Joe asked quietly.

"Daily we average around two hundred and fifty," the man replied. "These are men who have nowhere else to go—no food, no place but the street to sleep."

Joe was silent.

"Our yearly overhead cost is twenty thousand dollars," Tony Pope said. He looked around the room. "That's what two hundred of you are paying right now, for one *single* meal."

"Is the Boylston Street Shelter serving lunch today?" Joe asked.

"Today and every day," Pope said. "Until they nail our doors shut."

"Do you mind if I come take a look?" Joe asked.

If Pope was surprised, he hid it well. "I'd be honored."

"No way," Veronica heard Kevin Laughton say vehemently. "Absolutely no way."

"Joe, what are you doing?" she asked. "You can't leave the building, it's not safe."

But Joe had already jumped down, off the stage, and was striding between the tables, toward Sgt. Tony Pope, U.S.M.C., retired.

As Veronica watched, Pope led Joe—surrounded by FInCOM agents and his three SEALs—out of the room. The TV news cameras and reporters scrambled after them.

The shelter was, quite literally, right next door to the hotel. Once inside, Pope gave Joe—and the camera crews—a tour of his modest facility, from the cafeteria to the kitchen. He pointed out the holes in the roof and the other parts of the building that needed repairs. He introduced Joe to many of the longtime residents and workers.

Joe addressed them by rank, even the grungiest, rag-clad winos, and spoke to them all with the utmost respect and courtesy.

And as Joe was leaving, he slipped the jeweled ring from his finger and handed it to Tony Pope. "Fix your roof," he said.

Tears sprang to the older man's eyes. "Your Majesty," he said. "You've already given us so much." He gestured to the TV cameras. "The publicity alone is priceless."

"You need some quick cash, and I have one ring too many," Joe said. "The solution is so obvious. So simple." He smiled into the TV news cameras. "Just like my friend Cindy says."

"Oh, Joe, that ring's not yours to give away," Veronica breathed, knowing that she would pay for the ring herself, if she had to.

The final scene in the evening news report showed all of the men in the Boylston Street Shelter sharply saluting Prince Tedric as he left the building.

"Sergeant Tony Pope asks that contributions be sent directly to the Boylston Street Shelter," the news anchor said, "at 994—"

The phone rang, and Veronica pushed the Mute button as she answered it.

"Did you see it?" It was Henri Freder, the Ustanzian ambassador. "Did you see the news? It's not just a local story, it's being run nationally, *and* by the cable network."

"I saw it," Veronica said.

"Gold," Freder said. "Pure, solid gold."

"I know that ring was valuable, sir," Veronica started to say. "But—"

"Not the ring," Freder enthused. "Prince Tedric's image! Absolutely golden! He is America's newest hero. Everyone *loves* him. We couldn't have done it better if we'd tried. I've got to go, my other phone is ringing—"

Veronica stared at the disconnected telephone and slowly hung up the receiver. Everyone loved Prince Tedric—who was really a sailor named Joe, and not a real prince at all.

Or was he?

He was more of a prince than Tedric had ever been.

Now, because of Joe, everyone loved Prince Tedric. Except Veronica. She was falling in love with a prince named Joe.

Veronica had two hours to rest before the party. She lay down on the bed and stared at the ceiling, trying not to let the words Joe had spoken on the plane echo in her mind.

The kiss they'd shared. *It didn't mean anything.*

She was in love with a man who had told her, on more than one occasion, that the best she could hope for with him was a casual sexual relationship. He'd told her that the kisses they'd shared meant nothing to him.

He *did* desire her, though.

Veronica knew that from looking into his eyes. She knew it, too, from the way he'd kissed her in the chapel at Saint Mary's. If they'd been alone, it wouldn't have taken much for that one, single kiss to escalate into lovemaking.

But he didn't love her.

So now what? Was she going to just sit around loving Joe from a distance until the terrorists were caught, until he went back to SEAL Team Ten's temporary base in California? Or was she going to do something foolish, like make love to the man, stupidly hoping that the physical act would magically make him fall in love with her, too?

It would never happen. He would have all he'd ever wanted from her—sex. And she would have a broken heart.

A single tear slid down the side of her face and lodged rather uncomfortably in her ear. Perfect. She was now one-hundred-percent pitiable and pathetic.

The telephone rang, and Veronica rolled over and looked at it. She contemplated letting the front desk take a message, but after three rings, she finally picked it up. She wasn't going to get any sleep anyway.

"Veronica St. John," she said on a sigh.

"Hey."

It was Joe.

Veronica sat up, hastily wiping the moisture from her face, as if he would somehow be able to tell she'd been crying. She hadn't expected the caller to be Joe. Not in a million years. Not after their dreadful conversation on the plane.

"Are you awake?" he asked.

"I am now," she said.

"Oh, damn," he said, concern tingeing his voice. "Did I really wake you?"

"No, no," she said. "I was just . . . No."

"Well, I won't take too much of your time," Joe said. His husky voice sounded slightly stiff and unnatural. "I just wanted to tell you that if you get any flak about me giving away that ring of Tedric's—"

"It's all right," Veronica interrupted. "The ambassador called and—"

"I just wanted to let you know that I'll pay for it," Joe said. "I don't know what I was thinking—giving away something that didn't belong to me. But—"

"It's all taken care of," Veronica said.

"It is?"

"Your popularity rating is apparently through the roof," she told him. "I think the Ustanzian ambassador is considering having you knighted or perhaps made into a saint."

Joe laughed. "I can see it now. Joe, the patron saint of celebrity impersonators."

"Don't you mean, the patron saint of dying children and struggling causes?" Veronica said softly. "You know, Joe, you never fail to surprise me."

"That makes two of us," he muttered.

"What?"

"Nothing. I should go—".

"You really are softhearted, aren't you?" Veronica asked.

"Honey, I'm not soft anywhere." She could almost see him bristle.

"I didn't mean that as an insult," she said.

"Look, I just have a problem with the way this country treats war veterans, all right?" he said. "I'm tired of seeing good men, soldiers and sailors who risked their lives fighting for this country, being forced to live in the lousy gutter."

Veronica pushed her hair from her face, suddenly understanding. This was personal. This had something to do with that old sailor Joe had known when he was a child. What was his name...? "Frank O'Riley," she said, hardly realizing she'd spoken aloud.

Joe was silent for several long seconds. "Yeah," he finally said. "Old Man O'Riley went on a binge and lost his job. Got himself evicted. It damn near killed him to think of losing his garden, and he sobered up, but it was too late. No one helped him. He was a war hero, and he was out on the street in the goddammed middle of the goddammed winter."

"And because of that, he died," Veronica guessed correctly.

"He caught pneumonia." Joe's voice was curiously flat, and she knew by his lack of inflection and emotion that Frank O'Riley's death *still* hurt him deeply.

"I'm sorry," Veronica murmured.

Joe was quiet again for a moment. Then he sighed. "What I don't get, is how the hell our armed forces can send our guys to fight a war without really preparing them. And if we *are* going to send out these . . . *kids,* then we shouldn't be so damned surprised when they come home and fall apart. And then—and this is *real* genius—we try to sweep the pieces under the rug so no one will see. Nice move, huh?"

"Those are pretty tough words for someone who specializes in making war," Veronica said.

"I'm not suggesting we demilitarize," Joe said. "I think that would be a mistake. No, I just think the government should take responsibility for the veterans."

"But if there were no wars, there'd be no veterans. If we spent money on diplomatic relations rather than guns and—"

"Right," Joe said. "But there are enough bad guys in the world that wouldn't hesitate to step forward and kick some butt if our country couldn't defend itself. I mean, sure we could hand out flowers and love beads, but we'd get back a round of machine-gun fire in our gut. There are some mean bastards out there, Ronnie, and they don't want to play nice. We need to be as tough and as mean as they are.''

"And that's where *you* come in," Veronica said. "Mr. Tough and Mean. Ready to fight whatever war pops up."

"I'm a fighter," Joe stated quietly. "I've been prepared for war my entire life." He laughed softly, his voice suddenly so intimate and low in her ear. "It's the other surprises in life that knock me over."

"You are so utterly un-knock-overable." Veronica wished the same were true of herself.

"You're wrong," Joe countered. "The past few days, I can barely remember what solid ground feels like."

Veronica was quiet. She could hear Joe breathing on the other end of the phone line, three doors down the hotel corridor. "Cindy?" she asked softly. He didn't say a word. "I'm sorry," she added. "I should have prepared you more for—"

"Not Cindy," he said. "I mean, going to see her *was* tough, but . . . I was talking about you."

Veronica felt all the air leave her lungs. "Me?" She couldn't speak in more than a whisper.

"God, would you look at the time? I gotta go."

"Joe, what—"

"No, Ronnie, I don't know why I said that. I'm just asking for trouble and—" He broke off, swearing softly.

"But—"

"Do yourself a favor tonight, babe," Joe said brusquely. "Stay the hell away from me, okay?"

The phone line was disconnected with a click.

Veronica sat on the bed for a long time, holding the receiver against her chest. Was it possible . . . ? Could it be . . . ? Did Joe think *she* was the one who didn't want any kind of relationship?

What was it that he'd said on the plane . . . ? About the kiss they'd shared . . . *It didn't mean anything, and I know you're not going to let it happen again.*

You're *not going to let it happen again.*

Not *we*. *You*. Meaning Veronica. Meaning...what? That she was the one who was preventing their relationship from growing?

The telephone began to emit a series of piercing tones, and Veronica quickly dropped the receiver into the cradle.

If Joe really thought she didn't want a relationship with him, then she was going to have to set him straight.

Veronica stood and crossed to the closet, her nap forgotten. She looked quickly through her clothes, glancing only briefly at the rather staid dress she'd intended to wear to the party tonight. That dress wouldn't do. It wouldn't do at all....

Chapter 15

Joe stood in the marble-tiled front hallway of Armand and Talandra Perrault's enormous Beacon Hill town house, chatting easily in French with the couple who were the host and hostess of tonight's party.

Armand Perrault was a charming and gracious silver-haired Frenchman who'd retired a millionaire from his import-export business. His wife, Talandra, was a tall, beautiful young black woman with a rich, infectious laugh.

Talandra had known Veronica from college. Apparently they'd been roommates and good friends. They'd even gone on vacations together—that was how Talandra had met Wila Cortere, Joe's supposed sister.

God, at times like this, Joe felt like such a liar.

"Where *is* Véronique, Your Highness?" Talandra asked him.

He fought the temptation to shrug. "She wasn't ready to leave the hotel when I was," he said instead in Tedric's royal accent. "I'm sure she'll be here soon."

Ambassador Freder was in the surveillance van, sitting in Veronica's seat, ready to provide names and facts and any other information Joe might need.

Damn, how he wished it was Veronica whispering in his ear. Even though this party was not public and therefore technically a low risk, Joe was on edge. He *liked* knowing that Veronica was safely tucked away in the van, out of danger. Tonight, he was going to spend all of his time wondering where she was, and praying that she was safe.

Damn, he hated not knowing where she was. Where *was* that other limousine?

"May I get you another glass of champagne?" Talandra asked.

Joe shook his head. "No, thank you."

He could feel Talandra's dark brown eyes studying him. "You're not as Wila and Véronique described you," she said.

"No?" Joe's gaze strayed back to the front door as several FInCOM agents pulled it open.

Please, God, let it be her . . .

The woman who came in the door was a redhead, but there was no way on God's earth it could be Veronica, wearing a dress that exposed so much skin and—

Hot *damn!*

It *was* her. It *was* Veronica.

Over his earphone, Joe could hear Cowboy. "Whoo-ee, boss, babe alert at eleven o'clock!"

Sweet God! Veronica looked . . . out of this world. The dress she was wearing was black and long, made of a soft silky fabric that clung to her every curve. Two triangles of black barely covered her breasts, and were held up by two thin strips of fabric that crossed her shoulders and met between her shoulder blades, at the cutaway back of the dress. There was a slit up the side of the skirt, all the way up to the top of her thigh, that revealed flashes of her incredible legs. Her shoes were black, with high, narrow heels that were a polar opposite to the clunky-heeled pumps she normally wore.

She was wearing her hair up, piled almost haphazardly on top of her head, with stray curls exploding around her face.

"Tell me, Your Majesty, does Véronique know how you feel?" Talandra whispered into his ear.

Startled, he glanced at her. "Excuse me?"

She just smiled knowingly and crossed the room toward Veronica.

"Yeah, Your Majesty," Harvard said over Joe's earphone as Joe watched Veronica greet her old friend with a warm hug and kiss. "You might want to keep that royal tongue *inside* your royal mouth, do you copy that?"

Joe couldn't see Cowboy or Harvard, but he knew that wherever they were, they could see him. But what exactly did they see? And what had Talandra seen in his face that made her make that very personal comment?

Was he *that* transparent? Or was this just the way being in love was? Was it impossible to hide? And if so, could Veronica see it just as easily? If so, he was in big trouble here.

Veronica turned her head, about to glance in his direction, and he abruptly turned away. He'd have to stay far, far away from her. He'd already revealed way too much this afternoon, when he'd talked to her on the phone. And damn it, he was trying hard *not* to be in love with her. How tough could it be? After all, he'd spent nearly his entire life not in love with Veronica. It shouldn't be too difficult to get back to that state.

What was love, anyway, but a mutated form of lust? And he'd easily walked away from women he'd lusted after before. Why, then, did his legs feel as if they were caught in molasses when he tried to walk away from Veronica?

Because love *wasn't* lust, and love *wasn't* something a man could turn off and on like a faucet. *And* he was crazy in love with this woman, no matter that he tried to convince himself otherwise.

And God, if she found out, her gentle pity would kill him.

"Hell, boss," Cowboy said. "She's heading straight toward you, and you're running *away?*"

"You've got it backward, Cat," Harvard chimed in. "A woman like that walks in your direction, you stand very, *very* still."

Blue's south-of-the-Mason-Dixon-Line accent made his voice sound gentle over Joe's earphone, but his words were anything but. "You boys gonna enjoy explaining to Admiral Forrest how you got Joe Cat killed while you were watchin' women instead of watchin' for T's?"

Cowboy and Harvard were noticeably silent as Joe moved around the corner into an enormous room with a hardwood floor.

It was the ballroom—not that he'd ever been in a ballroom in a private house before. But it was pretty damn unmistakable. A jazz trio was playing in one corner, the furniture was placed around the edges of the room and people were out in the middle of the floor, dancing. This had to be the ballroom. It sure as hell wasn't the bathroom or the kitchen.

Joe headed for a small bar set up in the far corner, across from the band. The bartender greeted him with a bow.

"Your Highness," the young man said. "What can I get for you?"

Whiskey, straight up. "Better make it a ginger ale," Joe said instead. "Easy on the ice."

"I'll have the same," said a familiar voice behind him. It was Veronica.

Joe didn't want to turn around. Looking at her from a distance had been hard enough. Up close, that dress just might have the power to do him in.

He closed his eyes briefly, imagining himself falling to his knees in front of her, begging her to...what? To marry him? Yeah, right. Dream on, Catalanotto.

He forced a smile and made himself turn. "Ms. St. John," he said, greeting her formally.

She smiled up at him. Light gleamed off her reddish gold hair, and her eyes seemed to sparkle and dance. She was unbelievably beautiful. Joe couldn't imagine that at one time he'd thought her less than gorgeous.

She lifted her hand, and he took it automatically, bringing it halfway to his lips before he realized what he was doing. God Almighty, all those hands he'd pretended to kiss over the past few days...But this time, he wasn't going to have to pretend. He brought Veronica's hand to his mouth and brushed his lips lightly across her delicate knuckles.

He heard her soft intake of breath, and when he glanced up, he could see that her smile had faded. Her blue eyes were enormous, but she didn't pull her hand away.

Joe stood there, like an idiot, staring into eyes the color of the Caribbean Sea. Her gaze flickered down to his lips and then farther, to the pin he wore in his lapel—the pin that concealed the microphone that would broadcast everything they said to the surveillance truck, the FInCOM agents and the SEALs.

Joe heard only silence over his earphone, and he knew they were all listening. All of them. Listening intently.

"How are you, Your Majesty?" Veronica asked, her voice cool and controlled.

Joe found his own voice. "I'm well, thanks," he said. Damn, he sounded hoarse, and not an awful lot like Prince Tedric. He cleared his throat, then moistened his dry lips, and realized that Veronica's eyes followed the movement of his tongue. God, was it possible that she wanted to kiss him . . . ?

Her eyes met his, and something flamed—something hot, something molten, something that seared him to his very soul, something that made his already dry mouth turn into something resembling the floor of Death Valley.

Veronica gently disengaged her hand from his and reached to take one of the glasses of ginger ale from the bar. "Have you met my friend Talandra?" she asked him.

"Yeah," Joe said, catching himself and correcting himself by saying, "Yes. Yes, I have." He concentrated on doing the Ustanzian accent. But as he watched, she took a delicate sip of her soda and all he could think about were her lips. And the soft curves of her creamy skin, and of her breasts, exposed by the fabulous design of that dress. "She seems . . . nice."

Their eyes met, and again, he was hit by a wave of heat so powerful it nearly knocked him over.

Veronica nodded politely. "Yes, she is."

What kind of game was this?

She turned to watch the dancers, and her arm brushed against his. She smiled an apology and moved slightly away. But when it happened again, Joe knew damn well it was no accident. At least he hoped it was no accident. His pulse began to race with the implications.

"I love to dance," she said, glancing at him.

Oh yeah, he knew that. He'd seen her dance. It hadn't been like this—all stiff and polite and formal. When she'd danced, she'd moved with a sensuality and abandon that would've shocked the hell out of half of the people in this room.

Veronica tucked her hand into the crook of his elbow, and Joe's heart began to pound.

She was coming on to him.

Not in any way that the video cameras and microphones could pick up, but she *was* coming on to him. It all made sense. The dress, the shoes, the fire she was letting him see in her eyes . . .

He couldn't figure out why the sudden change of heart.

Joe opened his mouth to speak, but quickly shut it. What could he ask her? What could he say? Certainly nothing that he wanted broadcast over the entire security network.

Instead, he put his hand over hers, covering her cool fingers with his. He gently stroked her smooth skin with his thumb.

Veronica turned to look up at him, and Joe could see her desire in her eyes. No doubt about it—she was letting him see it. She wanted him, and she wanted him to know it.

She smiled then—a beautiful, tremulous smile that brought his heart up into his throat. He wanted to kiss her so badly, he had to clench his teeth to keep from leaning toward her and caressing her lips with his own.

"Your Majesty," she said very softly, as if she couldn't find the air to do more than whisper, "may I have this dance?"

He could have her in his arms, right here, right now. Damn, wouldn't that be heaven?

But then, from across the room, came an earsplitting crash.

Joe reacted, pulling Veronica into his arms and shielding her with his body. What the hell was he thinking? What was he doing, standing here next to her like this, as if he weren't the target of assassins? She was close enough so that bullets meant for him could end her life in the beat of a heart.

"It's all right, Cat." He heard Blue's voice over his earphone. "It's cool. Someone dropped a glass. We do not have a situation. Repeat, there is *no* situation."

Joe pulled Veronica in even closer for a second, closing his eyes and pressing her tightly against him before he released her. Adrenaline was flooding his system and his entire body seemed to vibrate. Jesus, Mary and Joseph, he'd never been so scared. . . .

Veronica touched his arm. "I guess we're all on edge," she said with a small smile. "Are you all right?"

Joe looked wound tighter than a drum. There was a wildness in his eyes she'd never seen before and his hand actually trembled as he pushed his hair back, off his face.

"No," he said curtly, not bothering to disguise his voice with Tedric's odd accent. "No, I'm not all right. Ronnie, I need you to stay the hell away from me."

Veronica felt her smile fade. "I thought we were going to...dance."

Joe let out a short burst of exasperated air. "No way," he said. "Absolutely not. No dancing."

She looked down at the floor. "I see."

As Joe watched, Veronica turned and started to walk away, unable to disguise the flash of hurt in her eyes. My God. She thought he was rejecting her. He tried to catch her arm, to stop her, but she was moving faster now.

"No, you *don't* see," he called after her in a low voice.

But she didn't stop walking. Joe started to follow.

Damn! Short of breaking into a sprint, there was no way he could catch her. And although shouting "Yo, Ronnie!" was something Joe Catalanotto might not have hesitated to do even at a posh society party, Prince Tedric was not prone to raising his voice in public.

When Joe rounded the corner into the front hall, Veronica was nowhere in sight. Damn! Double damn! How could he follow her if he didn't know where she went?

He headed toward the living room and the spacious kitchen beyond, hearing the unmistakable sound of Talandra's laughter from that direction.

But Talandra stood near a large stone fireplace, sipping champagne and talking with a group of elegantly dressed women—none of whom were Veronica. "Oh, here's the prince now," Talandra said, smiling at Joe.

There was nothing he could do but go and greet the group of ladies as Talandra made introductions.

"Code Red," came Cowboy's voice, loud and clear over Joe's earphone. "We have an open window on the third floor! Repeat, open window, third floor. Possible break-in. Joe, get the *hell* out of here. Double time! This is not a drill. Repeat. This is *not* a drill!"

Everything switched into slow motion.

Joe had to get out of here. He had to get away from these ladies—God help them all if a terrorist burst into the room firing a submachine gun.

"Get down!" he shouted at the women. "Get to cover!"

Talandra was the first to react. Of course, she'd probably been warned about an assassination attempt. She led the entire group of ladies down a hallway to the back of the house.

God, all it would take was one man and one gun and— Jesus, Mary and Joseph! Ronnie was somewhere in this house.

"Blue, where's Ronnie?" Joe said into his mike, heading for the kitchen door as he pulled out the gun he kept hidden under his jacket. FInCOM had ordered he remain unarmed. He'd smiled and said nothing. He was damn glad now that he'd ignored that order. If someone was going to start shooting at him, damn it, he was going to shoot back. "Blue, I need you to find Ronnie!"

"I don't see her, Cat," his XO reported, his gentle drawl replaced by a staccato stream of nearly accentless words. "But I'm looking. Get your own butt under cover!"

"Not till I know she's safe," Joe retorted as he burst through the kitchen door. A man in a chef's hat looked up at him in shock, his eyes glued to the gun. "Get down," Joe ordered him. "Or get out. We've got trouble."

The chief scurried for the back door.

A new voice came over the earphone. It was Kevin Laughton, the FInCOM chief. "Veronica St. John's already in a limo, heading back to the hotel. Proceed to the emergency escape vehicle, Lieutenant," he ordered.

"Double-check that info, Alpha Squad," Joe said as he pushed open the pantry door, hard, and went inside, gun first. The small storage room was empty.

"Information verified," Harvard's calm voice reported. "Ronnie has left the building. Suggest you do the same, Cat."

Joe was filled with relief. Ronnie was safe. The relief mingled with adrenaline and made him almost light-headed.

"Kitchen's empty and clear," he announced over his mike.

"Move it out, Cat," Cowboy said. "We got this situation under control."

"Are you kidding?" Joe said into his microphone, pushing the door to the living room open an inch. "And leave all the fun to you guys?"

Joe could see about ten FInCOM agents heading toward him. He swore under his breath and stepped back as they came through the door. They surrounded him instantly. West and Freeman were on either side of him, shielding him with their own bodies as they moved him toward the back door.

There was a car idling outside the kitchen, waiting for exactly this type of emergency. The car door was thrown open, and West climbed into the back seat first, pulling Joe behind him. Freeman followed, and before the door was even closed, the driver took off, peeling out down the narrow alleyway and onto the dark city streets.

West and Freeman were breathing hard as they both holstered their weapons. They watched without much surprise as Joe rested his own gun on his lap.

"You're not supposed to be carrying," West commented.

"Kevin Laughton would throw a hissy fit if he knew," Freeman said. "'Course, he doesn't have to know."

"Imagine Kevin's shock," Joe said, "if he knew that I've got another gun in my boot and a knife hidden in my belt."

"And probably another weapon hidden somewhere else that you're not telling us about," West said blandly.

"Probably," Joe agreed.

The car was moving faster now, catching green lights at all of the intersections as it headed downtown. Joe took out his earphone—they were out of range. He leaned forward and asked the driver, "Any word on the radio? What's happening back there? Any action?" He hated running away from his squad like this.

The driver shook his head. "The word is it's mostly all clear," he said. "It's an alleged false alarm. One of the party guests claims she opened the window in the third-floor bathroom because she was feeling faint."

Joe sat back in his seat. False alarm. He took a deep breath, trying to clear the nervous energy from his system. His guys were safe. Ronnie was safe. *He* was safe. He holstered his gun and looked from Freeman to West. "You know, I had no idea you guys were willing to lay it on the line for me."

West looked out one window, Freeman looked out the other. "Just doing our job, sir," West said, sounding bored.

Joe knew better. It was odd, sitting here between two relative strangers—strangers who would have died for him today if they'd had to. It was odd, knowing that they cared.

With a sudden flash, Joe remembered a pair of crystal blue eyes looking at him with enough heat to ignite a rocket engine.

West and Freeman weren't the only ones who cared.

Veronica St. John cared, too.

Chapter 16

Veronica stood at the window, looking out over downtown Boston. With all the city lights reflected in the Charles River, it was lovely. She could see the Esplanade and the Hatch Shell, where the Boston Pops played free concerts in the summer. She could see Back Bay and the Boston Common. And somewhere, down there, hidden by the trees of the common was Beacon Hill, where Talandra lived, and where there was a party going on right this very moment—without her.

She took another sip of her rum and cola, feeling the sweet warmth of the rum spreading through her.

Well, *she'd* certainly made a fool of herself tonight. Again. Veronica could see her wavery reflection in the window. She looked like someone else in this dress. Someone seductive and sexy. Someone who could snap her fingers and have dozens of men come running. Someone who wouldn't give a damn if some sailor didn't want her near him.

She laughed aloud at her foolishness, but her laughter sounded harsh in the empty hotel suite. She'd gone to this party with every intention of seducing Joe Catalanotto. She'd planned it so perfectly. She'd wear this incredible dress. He would be stunned. They'd dance. She'd dance really close. He would be even more stunned. He would follow her back to the hotel. She'd ask him into her room under the pretense of briefing him for tomorrow. But he'd know better. He'd ask the FInCOM agents to wait outside, and once the hotel-room door closed, he would pull her into his arms and . . .

It was perfect—except that she'd forgotten one small detail. Her plan would work only if Joe wanted her, too.

She had thought she'd seen desire in his eyes when he looked at her tonight, but obviously, she'd been mistaken.

Veronica took another sip of her drink and turned from the window, unable to bear the silence another minute.

There was a radio attached to the television, and she turned it on. It was set to a soft-rock station—not her favorite kind of music, but she didn't care. Just as long as there was *some*thing to fill the deadly silence.

She knew she ought to change out of her dress. It was only helping to remind her what a total imbecile she'd been. She looked at herself again in the mirror that hung on the hotel-room wall. The dress was practically indecent. The silky fabric clung to her breasts, broadcasting the fact that she was wearing no bra, and the cut of the dress showed off all kinds of cleavage and skin and curves. Good grief, she might as well have gone topless. *Whatever had possessed her to buy this dress, anyway?* It was like wearing a nightgown in public.

Veronica stared at herself in the mirror. She knew why she had bought the dress. It was to be an unspoken message to Joe. *Here I am. I'm all yours. Come and sweep me off my feet.*

To which he'd responded quite clearly. *Stay the hell away from me.*

She sighed, fighting the tears ready to spring into her eyes. She should change into something more sensible—her flannel nightie, perhaps—instead of standing here, feeling sorry for herself. She wasn't here, in Boston, to be either sexy or romantic. She was here to do her job. She wasn't looking for sex or romance or even friendship, with Joe Catalanotto. She was simply looking to get a job done well. Period, the end.

"You are such a bloody liar," Veronica said aloud to her reflection, her voice thick with disgust.

"You're not talking to me, I hope."

Veronica spun around, nearly spilling her rum and cola down the front of her dress.

Joe.

He was standing no more than three feet away from her, leaning against the wall next to the mirror. He stepped forward and took the drink from her hand.

Veronica's heart was pounding. "What are you doing here?" she gasped. "How did you get in?"

There was no balcony this time. And she was *positive* that the room's single door had been securely locked. But of course, he *had* told her he was an expert at picking locks.

Joe just smiled.

He was still wearing his party clothes. He wore a navy blue military-style jacket that buttoned up both sides of his chest and ended at his trim waist. His pants were made of a khaki-colored fabric that looked soft to the touch. They fit him like a second skin, clinging to his muscular thighs and perfect derriere. They were tucked into a pair of shiny black, knee-high boots. He wore a red sash around his waist, and the splash of color completed the princely picture.

He looked devastatingly, heart-breakingly handsome. Veronica's stomach flip-flopped. Lord, the way he was smiling at her . . . But whatever he was doing here, it wasn't personal, she told herself. Joe had made it clear at the party that he wanted her to stay away from him.

As she watched, he set her drink down on the end table next to the sofa and crossed to the windows. He pulled the curtains shut. "I've been wearing my bull's-eye long enough for one day," he said.

Veronica glanced at her watch. It was only nine-thirty. "The Perraults' party was supposed to last until midnight or one o'clock," she said, unable to keep her surprise from sounding in her voice. "You were supposed to stay until at *least* eleven."

Joe shrugged. "We had a little incident."

Veronica took an involuntary step forward, fear propelling her toward him. An *incident?* "Are you all right?"

"It was a false alarm," he said with another of his easy smiles.

He was standing in front of her, relaxed and smiling, absolutely at ease—or so he wanted her to believe. But she knew better. Beneath his feigned calm, he was tense and tight and ready to burst at the seams. He was upset—or he'd been upset.

"Tell me what happened," she said quietly.

He shook his head, no. "I came to get my dance."

She didn't understand. His words didn't seem to make sense. "Your...what?" She looked around the room. This was the first time he'd been in her room at the Boston hotel—how could he have left something behind?

"You asked me to dance," Joe said.

All at once, Veronica understood. He'd come here, to her room, to *dance* with her. She felt her face flush with embarrassment. "You don't have to do this," she said tightly. "I suppose I got a little silly, and—"

"When I told you to stay away from me—"

"It's okay that you didn't want—"

"I didn't want to dance with you, because you're not wearing a bulletproof vest under that dress," Joe said.

Veronica glanced down at her barely covered chest and felt her blush grow even stronger. "Well," she said, trying to sound brisk and businesslike. "Obviously not."

Joe laughed, and she looked up, startled, into the warmth of his eyes.

"God, Ron," he said, holding her gaze. "I didn't even get a chance to tell you how...perfect you look tonight." The warmth turned to pure fire. "You're *gorgeous*," he whispered, moving closer to her, one step at a time.

Veronica closed her eyes. She didn't have the strength to back away. "Don't, Joe," she said quietly.

"You think I didn't *want* to dance with you at that party?" Joe asked. He didn't give her a chance to answer. He touched her, gently cupping her shoulders, and her eyes opened. He slid his hands down to her elbows in the sweetest of caresses. "Lady, tonight I would have sold my soul for one kiss, let alone a chance to hold you in my arms." Gently, he pulled her even closer, clasping her hand in a dance hold. "Like this."

Slowly, he began to dance with her, moving in time to the soft ballad playing over the radio.

Veronica was trapped. She was caught both by his powerful arms and by the heat in his eyes. Her heart was pounding. She'd wanted him to touch her, to hold her, to dance with her, but not this way. Not because he pitied her...

"But I would've sold *my* soul. Not yours." Joe's voice was a husky whisper in her ear as he pulled her even closer. "Never yours, baby. I wasn't about to risk your life for a dance."

Veronica felt her pounding heart miss a beat. What was he saying? She pulled back to look into his eyes, searching for answers.

"You were in danger just standing next to me," Joe explained. "I should've told you to get lost the minute you walked into that room."

Was he saying that he hadn't wanted to dance with her because he feared for her safety? Dear Lord, if so, then she'd misunderstood his sharp words of warning for a brush-off, for a rejection. When in reality...

"I don't know what I was thinking," Joe said, then shook his head.

In reality, maybe he'd wanted her as badly as she'd wanted him. Veronica felt a burst of hope and happiness so intense, she almost laughed out loud.

"Hell, I *wasn't* thinking," Joe added. "I was... I don't know what I was."

"Stunned?" Veronica supplied. She could smile again, and she smiled almost shyly up at him.

Joe's slow smile turned into a grin. "Yeah. You bet. 'Stunned' about says it all. When you walked into the party, I was totally blown away. And I was thinking with a part of my anatomy that has nothing to do with my brain."

Veronica had to laugh at that. "Oh, really?"

"Yeah," Joe said. His smile grew softer, his eyes gentler. "My heart."

And then he kissed her.

She saw it coming. She saw him lean toward her, felt him lift her chin to meet his mouth. She knew he was going to kiss her. She expected it—she wanted it. But still, the softness of his lips took her by surprise, and the sweetness of his mouth on hers took her breath away.

It was dizzying. The earth seemed to lose all its gravity as he pulled her even closer to him, as he slowly, sensuously, languidly explored her lips with his, as she opened her mouth to him, deepening the kiss.

And still they danced, the thin wool covering his thighs brushing the silk of her dress. The softness of her stomach pressed intimately against the hardness of his unmistakable desire. Her breasts were tight against his powerful chest.

It was heaven. Giving in to her passion, giving up trying to fight it was such an enormous relief. Maybe this was a mistake, but Veronica wasn't going to think about it anymore. At least not right now, not tonight. She was simply going to kiss Joe Catalanotto, and dance with him, and savor every last moment. Every delicious, wonderful, magnificent second.

"Yo, Ronnie?" Joe whispered, breaking the kiss.

"Yo, Joe?" she said, still breathless.

He laughed. And kissed her again.

This time it was hotter, harder, stronger. It was still as sweet, but it was laced with a volcanic heat. Veronica knew without a doubt that tonight she was in for the time of her life.

Joe pulled back, breathing hard. "Whoa," he said, freeing one hand to push his hair back, out of his face. He closed his eyes briefly, took in a deep breath then forced it quickly out. "Ronnie, if you want me to leave, I should go now, because if—"

"I don't want you to leave."

He looked into her eyes. *Really* looked. As if he were searching for the answers to the mysteries of the universe.

Veronica could see his sharp intelligence, his raw, almost brutal strength, and his gentle tenderness all mixed together in his beautiful deep brown eyes.

"Are you sure?" he asked, his voice a ragged whisper.

Veronica smiled. And kissed him. Lord knew, she'd found the answers to all of her questions in *his* eyes.

"Unh," he said, as she swept her tongue fiercely into his mouth. And then his hands were in her hair, on her throat, on her breasts. He was touching her everywhere, as if he wanted to feel all of her at once and didn't know where to start. But then his hands slid down her back to her derriere, pressing her hips tightly against him, holding her in place as he slanted his head and kissed her even harder.

She opened her legs, taking advantage of the slit up the side of her dress, and she rubbed the inside of her thigh against his. His hand caught her leg, and he pressed her still closer to him.

Joe's mouth slid down to her neck as his hand cupped her breast. The roughness of his callused fingers rasped against the silk as he stroked the hard bud of her nipple.

"Oh, man," Joe breathed between kisses, as he slipped his hand under the fabric of her top, and touched her, really touched her, with nothing between his fingers and her flesh. "For how many days have I been *dying* to touch you like this?"

Veronica's fingers fumbled with the buttons of his jacket. "Probably the same number of days *I've* been dying for you to touch me like that."

He lifted his head, looking into her eyes. "Really?" His gaze was so intense, so serious. "Maybe it was love at first sight, huh?"

Veronica felt her own smile fade as her pulse kicked into overtime. "Love?" she whispered, hardly daring to hope that this incredible man could possibly love her, too.

Joe looked away, down at his hand still cupping her breast. "Love…lust… Whatever." He shrugged and kissed her again.

Veronica tried to hide her disappointment. *Whatever.* Well, all right. "Whatever" was better than not being desired. "Whatever" was what she'd been expecting—what he'd told her to expect from him right from the start.

But she didn't want to think about that now. She didn't want to think about anything but the way he was making her feel as he kissed and caressed her.

Joe pulled back then, and looked into her eyes. Slowly he slid the dress's narrow strap off her right shoulder. As it fell away, the silk covering her breast fell away, too.

And still he gazed into her eyes.

Veronica felt the coolness of the air as it touched her skin. And then she felt Joe, as he lightly ran one finger across the tip of her breast. She felt her body tighten, felt her nipples grow more taut, even more fully aroused.

He held her gaze longer than she would have believed possible before his eyes dropped down to caress the bareness of her breast.

"God," he breathed, moistening his lips with the tip of his tongue. "You're so beautiful."

They were frozen in place as if time had somehow stopped. But time hadn't stopped. Her heart was still beating, and with every beat, every surge of blood through her veins, Veronica wanted him even more.

But still he didn't touch her; at least, no more than another of those light-as-a-feather brushes with one finger. And she wanted him to touch her. She wanted him, so very badly, to touch her.

"If you don't touch me, I'm going to *scream,*" she said from between clenched teeth.

Joe's smile turned hot. "Is that a threat or a promise?" he asked.

"Both," she said, lost in the heat of his eyes. She was begging now. "Touch me."

"Where?" he asked, his voice hoarse. "How?"

"My breast, your mouth," she said. "Now. *Please.*"

He didn't hesitate. He brought his mouth to her breast and swept his tongue across her sensitive nipple. Veronica cried out, and he drew her into his mouth, pulling hard.

She reached for him, pushing his jacket off his shoulders. The buttons on his shirt were so tiny, so difficult to unfasten. But she wanted his shirt off. She wanted to run her hands against all those incredible muscles in his chest and shoulders and arms. She wanted to feel the satiny smoothness of his skin beneath her fingers.

She could hear her voice moaning her pleasure as Joe suckled and kissed her again and again.

But then he lifted his head and, stopping only to kiss her deeply on the mouth, he gazed into her eyes again. "What else do you want?" he demanded. "Tell me what you want."

"I want this bloody shirt off you," she said, still worrying the buttons.

He reached up with both hands and pulled. Buttons flew everywhere, but the shirt was open. He yanked it off his arms.

Veronica touched his smooth, tanned muscles with the palms of her hands, closing her eyes at the sensation, running her fingers through the curly dark hair on his chest. Oh, yes. He was so beautiful, so solid.

"Tell me what you want," Joe said again. "Come on, Ronnie, tell me where you want me to touch you."

She opened her eyes. "I want you to touch every single inch of me with every single inch of you. I want you and me on that bed in the other room. I want to feel you between my legs, Joe—"

Joe picked her up. He simply swept her effortlessly into his arms and carried her into the bedroom.

Veronica had her hands on the button of his pants before he yanked back the bedcover and laid her on the clean white sheets.

As she unfastened his sash, he found the zipper in the back of her dress. As he peeled her dress down toward her hips, she unzipped his pants and pushed them over his incredible rear end.

Her dress landed with a hiss of silk on the carpet and Joe pulled back, nearly burning her with his eyes as he took her in, lying propped up on her elbows on the bed, wearing only her black lace panties and a pair of thigh-high stockings. Lord, when he looked at her like that, with that fire in his eyes, she felt like the sexiest woman in the world.

She sat up, taking the last of the pins from her hair.

Slowly, he pushed off his shoes and stepped out of his trousers, still watching her.

Veronica was watching him, too. She rolled first one and then the other stocking from her legs as she let herself look at Joe. He was wearing only a pair of white briefs. She'd seen him in running shorts before, shorts that were nearly as brief, that exposed almost as much of his magnificent body. But this time she really let herself look.

His shoulders were broad and solid as rock. His arms were powerful and so very big. She couldn't have even begun to span his biceps with both of her hands, although she wanted rather desperately to try. His chest was wide and covered with thick dark hair. His muscles were clearly defined, and they rippled sensually when he so much as breathed. His stomach was a washboard of ridges and valleys, his hips narrow, his legs as strong as steel.

Yes, when she'd seen him run, although she'd tried not to look, she'd managed to memorize his body in amazing, precise detail, down to the scars on his shoulder and left leg, and the anchor tattoo on his arm.

But tonight there *were* some differences. She let her eyes linger on the enormous bulge straining the front of his briefs.

Veronica looked up to find Joe watching her, a small smile playing across his lips.

"Part of me wants to stand here and just look at you all night," he said.

She glanced down at his arousal, then smiled into his eyes. "Another part of you won't be very happy if you do that."

"Damn straight," he said with a laugh.

"Do I really have to beg you to come over here?" Veronica asked.

"No."

And then he was next to her on the bed and she was in his arms, and Lord, he was kissing her, touching her, running his hands across her body, filling her mouth with his tongue, tangling her legs with his.

It was ecstasy. Veronica had never felt anything remotely like it before. It was the sweetest, purest, most powerful passion she had ever known.

This was love, she thought. This incredible whirlwind of emotions and heightened sensations was love. It carried her higher, to an intellectual and emotional plane she'd never before imagined, and at the same time, it stripped her bare of every ounce of civility she had, leaving her ruled by ferocious passion, enslaved by the burning needs of her body.

She touched him, reaching down between their bodies to press the palm of her hand against his hardness, and when he cried out, she heard herself answer—the primitive call and response between a savage animal and his equally savage mate.

His hands were everywhere and his mouth was everywhere else. His fingers dipped down inside the lace of her panties, and he moaned as he felt her wet heat.

"Yes," Veronica said. It was the only word she seemed able to form with her lips. "Yes."

She tugged at his briefs, pulling him free from their confines, moaning her pleasure at the sensation of him in her hands. He was silky smooth and so hard, and oh...

He sat up, pulling away from her to slide her panties down and off. She sat up, too, following him, kneeling next to him on the bed, reaching for him, unwilling to let him go.

Joe groaned. "Ronnie, baby, I got to get a condom on."

He turned to reach for his pants, now crumpled on the floor, but Veronica was faster. She opened the drawer of the bedside table and took out a small foil package—one of the condoms she'd bought just hours ago when she'd bought the dress. She'd put them in the drawer in hopes of using them precisely this way with precisely this man.

"Whoa," Joe said as she pressed it into his hand. He was surprised that she was prepared. "I guess it's stupid *not* to be ready for anything these days, huh?"

He was just holding the little package, looking at her.

Good Lord, did he actually think she kept these things on hand all the time? Was he imagining a steady stream of male visitors to her room? Veronica took it from him and tore it open. "I bought it for you. For you and me," she said, somehow finding her voice in her need to explain. "I was hoping we'd make love tonight."

She saw the understanding in his eyes. She'd bought it because she'd wanted to make love—to *him*.

Veronica touched him, covering him with her fingers, gazing from that most intimate part of him, to the small ring of latex in her hand. "I'm not sure exactly how this is supposed to work," she said. "It doesn't really look as if it's going to fit, does it?"

She gazed into the heat of his eyes as he took the condom from her. "It'll fit," he said.

"Are you sure?" she asked, her smile turning devilish. "Maybe I should have bought the extra-large Navy SEAL size."

Joe laughed as he quickly and rather expertly sheathed himself. "Flattery will get you *every*thing."

Veronica encircled his neck with her arms, brushing the hard tips of her breasts against his solid chest and her soft stomach against his arousal. "I don't want everything," she breathed into his ear. "I think I already told you precisely what I want."

He kissed her—a long, sweet, slow, deep kiss that made her bones melt and her muscles feel like jelly. Still kissing her, he pulled her onto his lap, so that she was straddling his thighs. Then, taking her hips in his hands, he slowly, so slowly, lifted her up, above him.

Veronica pulled back from Joe's kiss, her eyes open. He began to lower her down, on top of him, and as the very tip of him parted her most intimately, he opened his own eyes, meeting her gaze.

Slowly, impossibly slowly, a fraction of an inch at a time, he lowered her onto him, staring all the while into her eyes.

The muscles in his powerful arms were taut, but the sweat on his upper lip wasn't from physical exertion. He lifted her slowly back up, off him, and then brought her down again, so that he was barely inside her, setting a deliberate and leisurely teasing rhythm.

Veronica moaned. She wanted more. She wanted *all* of him. She tried to shift her weight, to bring herself down more fully on top of him, but his strong arms held her firmly in place. Her moan changed to a cry of pleasure as his mouth latched on to her breast, but still he didn't release her hips.

"Please," she cried, the words ripped from her throat. "Joe, please! I want more!"

He covered her mouth with his, kissing her fiercely as he arched his body up and pushed her hips down and filled her completely, absolutely, incredibly.

The sound she heard herself make was almost inhuman as he plunged into her, filling her again and again and again. The rhythm was frantic, feverish, and Veronica threw back her head, delirious from the sweet sensations exploding inside her as she found her release. Arrows of pleasure shot through her— straight to her heart.

Joe's fingers stabbed through her hair as he called out her name and she clung to his neck and shoulders. She rode his explosive release, letting his passion carry her higher, even higher, loving the way he held her as if he were never going to let her go.

And then it was over. Joe sank back on the bed, pulling her down along with him.

Veronica could feel his heart beating, hear him breathing, feel his arms still tightly around her. She waited, hoping he would be the first to speak.

But he didn't speak. The silence stretched on and on and on, and through it, Veronica died a thousand times. He was regretting their lovemaking. He was trying to figure out a way to get out of her room with the least amount of embarrassment. He was worrying about the rest of the tour, wondering if she was going to chase after him like a lovesick fool and . . .

He sighed. And stretched. And nuzzled the side of her face. Veronica turned toward him and he met her lips in a slow, lingering kiss.

"When can we do this again?" he asked, his voice husky in the quiet. He brushed her hair back so he could see her face.

His eyes were half-closed, but she could see traces of the everpresent flame still burning.

He *didn't* regret what they'd just done. How could he, if he already wanted to know when they'd make love again? She smiled, suddenly feeling ridiculously, foolishly happy. His answering smile was sleepy, and very, *very* content.

"You gonna answer my question?" he asked. His eyes opened slightly wider for a second. "Or is that smile my answer?"

Veronica slowly trailed her fingers down his arm, watching as they followed the contours of his muscles. "Are you in any hurry to leave?" she asked.

His arms tightened around her. "Nope."

"Good."

"Yeah."

Veronica glanced up at him and saw he was watching her. He smiled again, laughing softly as she met his eyes.

"What?" she asked.

"You really want to know?"

She nodded, making a face at him. "Of course. You look at me and laugh. I should say I'd want to know what you were thinking."

"Well, I was thinking, who would've guessed that proper Ms. Veronica St. John is a real screamer in bed."

Veronica laughed, feeling her cheeks heat. "But I'm not," she protested. "I mean, I *don't* . . . I mean, I never have before. . . . Made all that . . . noise, I mean."

"I loved it," Joe said. "And I love it even more, knowing that I'm the only one who makes you do it." His words were teasing, but his eyes were serious. "It's an incredible turn-on, baby." His voice got lower, softer, more intense. "*You're* an incredible turn-on."

"You're embarrassing me," she admitted, pressing her warm cheeks against his shoulder.

"Perfect," he replied, with his wonderful, husky laugh. "I also love it when you blush."

Veronica closed her eyes. He loved what she did, he loved when she blushed. What she would have given to hear him say that he loved *her*.

"You know what would absolutely kill me?" Joe asked, his voice still low and very, very sexy.

Oh, dear Lord, she could feel him growing inside her. She felt her body respond, felt her pulse start to quicken.

"If you danced for me," Joe said, answering his own question.

Veronica closed her eyes, imagining the nuclear heat that would be generated in the room if she danced for Joe—and only for Joe. She could imagine discarding various articles of clothing until she moved in time to music clad only in the tiniest black panties and the fire from his eyes. . . .

Veronica blushed again. Could she really dance for him that way? Without laughing or feeling foolish?

Joe hugged her tighter. "No pressure," he said quietly. "I only want you to dance for me if you want to. It's just a fantasy, that's all. I thought I'd share it with you. No big deal. Two out of three's not bad."

Veronica lifted her head. "Two out of three . . . ?"

"Fantasies that have come true," Joe said. He smiled. "The first one was making love to you. The second one was making love to you twice in the same night."

"But . . ."

Joe kissed her sweetly. Then he made his second fantasy come true.

Chapter 17

Chicago, Dallas and Houston were a blur. During the day and sometimes in the evening, Veronica sat in the surveillance van, feeding information to Joe via his earphone, praying that the man she loved wasn't about to be killed in front of her very eyes.

Joe would look into the hidden, miniaturized video cameras and smile—a sweet, hot, secret smile meant only for her.

At night, Joe came to her room. How he got out from under the watchful eyes of the FInCOM agents, Veronica never knew. How he got into her room was also a mystery. She never heard him. She would just look up, and he'd be there, smiling at her, heat in his eyes.

In Dallas, he came carrying barbecued chicken, corn on the cob, and a six-pack of beer. He was wearing jeans and T-shirt and an old baseball cap backward on his head. He wouldn't tell her where he got the food and beer, but she had the feeling he'd climbed down the outside of the building to the street below and walked a few blocks over to a restaurant.

They had a picnic on her living-room floor, and made love before they'd finished eating, right there on the rug in front of the sofa.

He always stayed until dawn, holding her close. They sometimes talked all night, sometimes slept, always woke up to make love again. But as the sun began to rise, he would vanish.

Then in Albuquerque, there was another "incident," as Joe called them. Veronica sat in the van, her heart in her throat after one of the FInCOM agents thought he saw a man with a concealed weapon in the crowd outside the TV station where "Tedric" had been interviewed.

The SEALs and the FInCOM agents had leapt into action, ready to protect Joe. They'd hustled him into the limousine and to safety, but Veronica was shaken.

She sat in her hotel room, fighting tears, praying Joe would arrive soon, praying his quicksilver smile would make her forget about the danger he was in, day in and day out, as he stood in for the real prince. But she had to remember that he was no stranger to dangerous situations. His entire life was filled with danger and risk. Even if he survived these particular assassins, it would only be a matter of time before he'd be facing some new danger, some other perhaps-even-more-deadly risk.

How could she let herself love a man who could die—violently—at any given moment?

"Yo, Ronnie."

Veronica turned around.

Joe. There he was, still dressed in his shiny white jacket and dark blue pants, his hair slicked back from his face. He looked tired, but he smiled at her, and she burst into tears.

He came across the room so quickly, she didn't see him move. Pulling her into his arms, he held her tightly.

"Hey," he said. "Hey."

Embarrassed, she tried to pull away, but he wouldn't let her go.

"I'm sorry," she said. "Joe, I'm sorry. I just..."

Joe lifted her chin and kissed her gently on the mouth.

"I'm all right," he told her, knowing, the way he always did, exactly what she was thinking. "I'm fine. Everything's okay."

"For right now," she said, looking up into the mysterious midnight depths of his eyes, wiping the tears from her face with the heel of her hand.

"Yeah," he said, catching a tear that hung on her eyelashes with one finger. "For right now."

"And tomorrow?" she asked. "What about tomorrow?" She knew she shouldn't say the words, but they were right on the tip of her tongue and she couldn't hold them back.

He gently ran his hand through her hair again and again as he gazed down into her eyes. "You really that worried about me?" he asked, as if he couldn't quite believe her concern.

"I was scared today," Veronica admitted. She felt her eyes well with tears again and she tried to blink them back.

"Don't be scared," Joe told her. "Blue and the other guys aren't going to let anything happen to me."

Nice words and a nice thought, but Blue and Cowboy and Harvard weren't superhuman. They were human, and there was no guarantee one of them wouldn't make a very human mistake.

Tomorrow at this time, Joe could very well be dead.

Tomorrow, or next week or next year...

Reaching up, Veronica pulled his head down and kissed him. She kissed him hard, almost savagely, and he responded instantly, pulling her against his body, lowering his hands to press her hips closer to him.

She found the buckle of his belt and started to unfasten it, and he lifted her up and carried her into the bedroom.

Veronica pulled him tightly to her and closed her eyes, trying to shut out her fears. With the touch of his hands, with his mouth and his body against hers, tomorrow didn't exist. There was only here and only now. Only ecstasy.

But when morning dawned, and Joe crept out of bed trying not to wake her, Veronica still hadn't slept. She watched him dress, then closed her eyes as he kissed her gently on the lips.

And then he was gone.

It was not beyond the realm of possibility that he could be gone forever.

Phoenix, Arizona.

The April sunshine was blazing hot, reflecting off the streets, heating the air and making it difficult to breathe.

Inside the protection of the limousine parked on the street in front of the brand-new Arizona Theatre and Center for the Arts building, Joe was cool and comfortable.

But he was glad for the sunglasses he wore. Even with them on, even with the tinted glass of the limo, Joe squinted in the brightness as he sat up to get a better look at the morning's location.

A broad set of shallow steps led to a central courtyard. It was flat and wide and surrounded by a series of marble benches placed strategically in the shade of flowering trees. The lobby of the theater was directly behind the courtyard, and the Center for the Arts offices surrounded it on the other two sides.

There was a stage in the courtyard, set up in the shade of the theater. That was where Joe—as Tedric—would go for the theater's dedication ceremony.

People were already milling around, trying to stay cool in the shade, fanning themselves with copies of the arts center's events schedule.

Joe could hear Veronica over his earphone as she sat in the surveillance van.

"Please test your microphones, Alpha Squad," she said.

Blue, Cowboy and Harvard all checked in.

"Lieutenant Catalanotto?" she said, her voice brisk and businesslike.

"Yo, Ronnie, and how are you this fine morning?" Joe said, even though he'd spent the night with her, even though he'd left her room mere hours earlier and knew *exactly* how well she was.

"A simple check would be sufficient," she murmured. "Cameras?"

Joe grinned into the miniaturized video camera that the FInCOM agent sitting across from him was carrying. God forbid someone should find out about the incredible steamy nights they spent together—the high-class media consultant and the sailor from a lousy part of New Jersey. Veronica always played it so cool in public, often addressing him as "Lieutenant Catalanotto," or "Your Majesty."

Actually, they'd never talked about whether or not she wanted their relationship to go public. Joe had just assumed she didn't, and had taken precautions to protect her.

Of course, Blue and Cowboy and Harvard knew where Joe went every night. They had to know. Without their help, it would have been too damned hard to get out from under the

FInCOM agents' eyes. But aside from the ribbing he endured when the four SEALs were alone, Joe knew his three friends would never tell a soul. They were SEALs. They knew how to keep a secret.

And as far as Joe was concerned, Veronica St. John was the best-kept secret *he'd* ever known.

She'd been upset last night. That incident in Albuquerque had really shaken her up. She'd actually *cried* because she'd been so afraid for him. For *him*. And the way she'd made love to him...as if the world were coming to an end. Oh, man. That had been powerful.

Joe had thought at first that maybe, just maybe, the impossible had happened and Veronica had fallen in love with him. Why else would she have been so upset? But even though he'd tried to bring up the subject of her concerns for his safety later in the night, she hadn't wanted to talk.

All she'd wanted was for him to hold her. And then make love to her again.

Joe smiled at the irony. He falls in love for the first time in his life, and for the first time in his life, *he's* the one who wants to talk. Yeah, it was true. He had been in bed with a gorgeous, incredibly sexy woman, and what he wanted desperately was to *talk* after they made love. But all *she* wanted was more high-energy sex.

Of course, Joe reminded himself, he sure had suffered, making Veronica happy last night. Oh, yeah. Life should *always* be so tough.

Joe closed his eyes briefly, remembering the smoothness of her skin, the softness of her breasts, the sweetness of surrounding himself in her heat, the hot pleasure in her beautiful, bluer-than-the-ocean eyes, the curve of her lips as she smiled up at him, the sound of her ragged cry as he took her with him, over the edge...

Joe opened his eyes, taking a deep breath and letting it quickly out. Oh, *yeah*. He was going out in public in about thirty seconds. Somehow he seriously doubted that old Ted would appreciate Joe pretending to be the prince with a raging and quite obvious royal hard-on for all the world to see. And he had a job to do, to boot. It was time to go.

Joe climbed from the limo and felt the sudden rush of heat. It was like opening an oven door. Welcome to Phoenix, Arizona.

As the FInCOM agents hustled him across the courtyard, Joe tried to bring himself back to the business at hand. Daydreaming about his lover was good and fine and—

Lover.

Veronica St. John was his lover.

For the past four amazing days and incredible nights, Veronica St. John had been his *lover.*

The word conjured up her mysterious smile, the devilish light in her eyes that promised pleasures the likes of which he'd never known before, the softness of her sighs, the feel of her fingers in her hair, their legs intertwined, bodies slippery with soap as they kissed in the hotel's oversize bathtub. . . .

But . . .

Did she think of him as her lover? Did she ever even consider the word *love* when she thought about him?

God, what he would give to hear her say that she loved him.

Damn, he was distracted today. He forced himself to look again at the buildings. *Pay attention,* he ordered himself. *Hell of a lot of good it'll do you to realize you're in love with this woman and then get yourself killed.*

Joe looked around him. The roofs of the office buildings were lower than the theater roof. They were the perfect height and distance from the stage—perfect, that is, for a sniper to shoot from. Of course, the office windows—if they could be opened—wouldn't be a bad choice for a shooter, either.

Joe snapped instantly alert, instantly on the job.

Damn, the Arizona Theatre and Center for the Arts dedication ceremony was the ideal setup for an assassination attempt. The crowd. The TV news cameras. The three buildings, forming a square U, with the courtyard between them. The glare from the sun. The heat making everyone tired and lazy.

"This is it," Joe murmured.

"You bet, Cat," Blue's voice came over his earphone. "If I were a tango, I'd pick this one."

"What?" Veronica asked from her seat in the surveillance truck. "What was that you said?"

The FInCOM agents were hurrying Joe to the relative safety of the theater lobby. Once inside, he couldn't answer Veronica, because the governor of Arizona was shaking his hand.

"It's a real honor, Your Majesty," the governor said with his trademark big, wide, white-toothed smile. "I can't tell you how much it means to the people of Arizona to have you here, at the dedication of this very important theater and arts center."

"Dear Lord," Joe heard Veronica say over his earphone. Then there was silence. When she spoke again, her voice was deceptively calm. Joe knew damn well that her calm was only an act. "Joe, you think that the terrorists are going to be here, don't you? Today. Right now."

Joe couldn't answer. Ronnie had to know that he couldn't answer. She could see him on her video screen. He was standing in a crowd of government officials. She could hear the governor still talking.

Joe smiled at something the lieutenant governor said, but his mind was focused on the voices of his men from the Alpha Squad—and the woman—his lover—sitting inside the surveillance van.

"Damn it, Joe," Veronica said, her voice breaking and her calm cracked. "Shake your head. Yes or no. Is there going to be an assassination attempt here this afternoon?"

Inside the surveillance van, Veronica held her breath, her eyes riveted to the video monitor in front of her. Joe looked directly into the camera, his dark eyes intense—and filled with excitement. He nodded once. Yes.

Dear God. Veronica took a deep breath, trying to steady herself. As she watched, the governor of Arizona said something, and the entire group of men and women surrounding Joe laughed—Joe included.

Dear God. She'd actually seen *excitement* in Joe's eyes. He was excited because something was finally going to happen. He was ready. And willing. Willing to risk his *life* . . .

Her mouth felt dry. She tried to moisten her lips with her tongue, but it didn't help.

Dear God, don't let him die. "Joe," she said, but then couldn't speak.

He touched his ear, the sign that he had heard her.

She could hear Blue's unmistakable accent, and the voices of Cowboy and Harvard as the three men tried to outguess the assassin.

Cowboy was on the roof of the theater with high-powered binoculars and a long-range, high-powered rifle of his own. He did a visual sweep of the two lower roofs, reporting in continuously. No one was up there. No one was *still* up there.

"Windows in the offices don't open," Kevin Laughton said, from his seat next to Veronica. "Repeat, windows do *not* open."

"I'm watching 'em anyway," Cowboy said.

"You're wasting time," Laughton said. "And manpower. We could use you down in the crowd."

"The hell I'm wasting time," Cowboy muttered. "And if you think this shooter's going to be standing in the crowd, you're dumber than the average Fink."

On-screen, Joe was still talking to the governor and his aides. "The theater and these arts buildings are very beautiful," he said. "All these windows—it's quite impressive, really. Do they open?"

"The windows?" the governor asked. "Oh, no. No, these buildings are all climate controlled, of course."

"Ah," Joe said in Tedric's funny accent. "So if someone inside absolutely needed some fresh air, they'd have to have a glass cutter, yes?"

The governor looked slightly taken aback, but then he laughed. "Well, yes," he said. "I suppose so."

"Roger that, Mr. Cat," Cowboy said. "My thoughts exactly. Court-martial me if you have to, FInCOM, but I'm watching those windows."

"Okay," Veronica heard Blue say. "They're coming out to the stage. Let's be ready. You, too, Cat."

"Shall we go to the stage?" the governor asked Joe.

Joe nodded. "I'm ready," he said with a smile.

He was so calm. He was walking out there to be a target, and he was *smiling*. Veronica could barely breathe.

Two of the FInCOM agents opened the doors that led to the courtyard. Outside, a band began to play.

"Joe," Veronica said again. Dear Lord, if she didn't tell him now, she might never get another chance. . . .

He touched his ear again. He heard her.

"Joe, I have to tell you . . . I love you."

Joe stepped outside into the sunshine, and the heat and brightness exploded around him. But it wasn't all from the sun. In fact, most of it was coming from inside him, from the center of his chest, from his very heart.

She loved him. Ronnie *loved* him.

He laughed. Ronnie loved *him*. And she'd just announced it to everyone who was working on this operation.

"Hell, Ronnie, don't go telling him that *now*," Blue's scolding voice sounded over Joe's earphone. "Cat's gotta concentrate. Come on, Joe, keep your eyes open."

"I'm sorry," Veronica said. She sounded so small, so lost.

Joe touched his ear, trying to tell her that he'd heard her, wishing there was a way he could say he loved her, too. He touched his chest, his heart, with one hand, hoping that she'd see and understand his silent message.

And then he climbed the stairs to the stage.

"Come on, Cat," Blue's voice said. "Stop grinning like a damn fool and get to work."

Work.

His training clicked in, and Joe was instantly focused. Damn, with this warm sensation in his heart, he was better than focused. Veronica loved him, and he was damn near superhuman.

He checked the stage to make sure the cover zones were where FInCOM had said they would be.

The podium was reinforced, and it would act as a shield—provided, of course, that the shooter didn't have armor-piercing bullets. Down behind the back of the stage was also shielded. There was a flimsy metal railing to keep people from falling off the platform, but that could be jumped over easily. The stage was only about eight feet from the ground.

Joe scanned the crowd. About six hundred people. Five different TV cameras, some of them rolling live for the twelve o'clock news. He knew with an uncanny certainty that the assassin wouldn't fire until he stepped up to the podium.

"Roof is *still* clear," Cowboy announced. "No movement at the windows. Shoot, FInCOM, maybe you better keep watching that crowd. I got nothing yet."

Joe sat in a folding chair as the governor approached the podium.

"We're going to make this dedication ceremony as quick as possible," the governor said, "so we can get inside that air-conditioned lobby and have some lemonade."

The crowd applauded.

Veronica's heart was in her throat. Joe was sitting there, just *sitting* there, as if there weren't any threat to his life.

"Without further ado," the governor continued, "I'd like to introduce our special guest, Crown Prince Tedric of Ustanzia."

The sound of the crowd's applause masked the continuous comments of the SEALs and the FInCOM agents. On Veronica's video screen, Joe stood, raising both hands to quiet the crowd.

"Thank you," he said into the microphone. "Thank you very much. It's an honor to be here today."

"I still got zip on either roof," Cowboy said. "No movement near the windows, either. I'm starting to think these tangos don't know a good setup when they see—"

A shot rang out.

One of the big glass windows in the front of the theater shattered into a million pieces.

The crowd screamed and scattered.

"Joe!" Veronica gripped the table in front of her, leaning closer to the screen, praying harder than she'd ever prayed in her life.

He was gone, she couldn't see him. Had he ducked behind the podium, or fallen, struck by the bullet?

On her headphones, she could hear all three SEALs reporting in, all talking at once. The roofs were still clear, no shooter visible at the windows.

Beside her, Kevin Laughton had rocketed out of his seat. "What do you mean, you don't know where that came from?" he was shouting over the chaos. "A shot was fired—it had to come from *some*where!"

"Do we need an ambulance?" another voice asked. "Repeat, is medical assistance needed?"

Another shot, another broken window.

"God damn," Laughton said. "Where the *hell* is he shooting from?"

Joe heard the second shot, felt the impact of the bullet as it hit the stage, and knew. The assassin was *behind* him. Inside the theater. And with all of the shielding facing out, away from the theater, Joe was a damn sitting duck. It was amazing he was still alive. That second shot should have killed him.

It should have, but it hadn't. The son of a bitch had missed.

Joe dove off the stage headfirst, gun drawn, shouting instructions to his men and to the FInCOM agents who were surrounding him. Cowboy was on the roof of the theater, for God's sake. They could cut the shooter off, nail the bastard.

Inside the surveillance van, the video monitors went blank. Power was gone. Lord, what was happening out there? Veronica had heard Joe's voice. He was alive, thank God. He hadn't been killed. Yet.

The gunman was inside the theater. Upper balcony, above the lobby, came the reports. The back door was surrounded, they had the assassin cornered.

Veronica stood, pushing past Kevin Laughton and opening the door of the van. She could see the theater, see the two shattered windows. She could see the FInCOM agents crouched near the front of the theater. She could see three figures, scaling the outside of the theater, climbing up to the roof.

God in heaven, it was Joe and two of his SEALs.

Veronica lowered her mouthpiece into place. She hadn't wanted to speak before this, afraid she'd only add to the confusion, but this . . .

"Joe, what are you doing?" she said into the microphone. "You're the *target!* You're supposed to get to safety!"

"We need radio silence," Blue's voice commanded. "Right now. Except for reports of tango's location."

"Joe!" Veronica cried.

One of the FInCOM agents leaned out the van door. "I can't cut this line," he said to Veronica, "so unless you're quiet, I'm going to have to take your headset."

Veronica shut her mouth, watching as a tiny figure—Cowboy—helped Joe and the rest of his team up onto the theater roof.

Up on the roof, Joe looked around. There was one door, leading to stairs that would take them down.

You all right? Cowboy hand-signaled to Joe.

Fine, he signaled back.

The gunman surely had a radio, and was probably monitoring their spoken conversation. From this point on, the SEALs would communicate only with hand signals and sign language. No use tipping the gunman off by letting him know they were coming.

Harvard had an extra HK submachine gun, and he handed it to Joe with a tight smile.

Another shot rang out.

"Agent down," came West's voice over Joe's earphone. "Oh, man, we need a medic!"

"T's location stable," said another voice. "Holding steady in the lobby balcony."

"Get that injured man out of the line of fire," Laughton commanded.

"He's dead," West reported, his normally dispassionate voice shaken. "Freeman's dead. The bastard plugged him through the eye. The sonuvabitch—"

Let's go, Joe signaled to his men. *I'm on point.*

Blue gestured to himself. He wanted to lead the way instead. But Joe shook his head.

Soundlessly he opened the door and started down the stairs.

Another shot.

More chaos. Another agent was hit with unerring accuracy.

"Stay down," Laughton ordered his men. "This guy's a sharpshooter and he's here for the long haul. Let's get our own shooters in position."

Silently, with deadly stealth, fingers on the triggers of their submachine guns, the SEALs moved down the stairs.

Veronica paced. She hadn't heard Joe's voice in many long minutes. She could no longer see any movement on the roof.

"One of the cameras is back on," someone said from inside the surveillance van, and she went back in to see.

Sure enough, the video camera that had been dropped and left on the stage had come back to life. It now showed a sideways and somewhat foggy picture of the theater lobby. Behind the reflections in the remaining glass windows, Veronica could see the shadowy shape of the assassin on the upper balcony.

It was quiet. No one was moving. No one was talking. Then . . .

"FInCOM shooters, hold your fire." It was Joe's voice, loud and clear, over the radio.

Veronica felt herself sway, and she groped for her seat. Joe and his SEALs were somewhere near the gunman—in range of the FInCOM agent's guns. Please, God, keep him safe, she prayed.

A door burst open. She heard it more than she saw it on the shadowy video screen.

The gunman turned, firing a machine gun rather than his rifle. But there was no one there.

Another door opened, on the other side of the balcony, but the gunman had already moved. Using some sort of rope, he swung himself over the edge and down to the first floor.

Veronica saw Joe before the gunman did.

He was standing in the lobby, gun aimed at the man scurrying down the rope. She knew it was Joe from his gleaming white jacket. The three other SEALs were dressed in dull brown.

"Hold it right there, pal," she heard Joe say over her headphones. "We can end this game one of two ways. We can either take you out of here in a body bag, or you can drop your weapons right now and we'll all live to see tomorrow."

The gunman was frozen, unmoving, halfway down the rope as he stared at Joe.

Then he moved. But he didn't drop his gun, he brought it up, fast, aimed directly toward Joe's head.

The sound of gunfire over the radio was deafening.

The gunman jumped to the ground—or did he fall? Who had been hit? And where was Joe . . . ?

"Joe!" Veronica couldn't keep silent another second as she leaned closer to the blurry screen.

"Do you need medical assistance?" a voice asked over the headphones.

"Alpha Squad, check in," Blue's voice ordered. "McCoy."

"Becker."

"Jones."

"Catalanotto," Joe's familiar, husky voice said. "We're all clear. No need of a medic, FInCOM."

Veronica closed her eyes and rested her head on her arms on the tabletop.

"This stupid sonuvabitch just made himself a martyr for the cause," Joe's voice said into her ear.

Joe was alive. It was all over, and Joe was alive.

This time.

Chapter 18

It was after nine o'clock in the evening—twenty-one hundred hours—before Veronica's phone rang.

She'd been busy all afternoon and evening with meetings and debriefings. She'd worked with Ambassador Freder and Senator McKinley, scheduling the remainder of Prince Tedric's tour. A report had come in from FInCOM that made them all breathe easier. The assassin had been ID'd as Salustiano Vargas—Diosdado's former right-hand man. *Former.* Apparently the two terrorists had parted ways, and Vargas was no longer connected with the Cloud of Death. He had been acting on his own. Why? No one seemed to know. At least not yet. At any rate, Vargas was dead. *He'd* be giving them no answers.

But now that the assassin was no longer a threat, the ambassador and senator wanted to get the tour back on track. Tedric was flying in from the District of Columbia. He would meet them all in Seattle in the morning, where they would board a cruise ship to Alaska. They would finish the tour with a flourish.

Security would return to near normal. Two or three FInCOM agents would remain, but everyone else, including the SEALs—including Joe—would go home.

At dinnertime, Veronica had searched for Joe, but was told he was in high-level security debriefings. She returned to her room to pack, but couldn't stop thinking. *What if he didn't get finished before morning?* Sometimes those meetings went on all night. What if she didn't see him before she had to leave...?

But then, at nine o'clock, the phone rang. Veronica closed her eyes, then picked it up. "Hello?"

"Yo, Ronnie."

"Joe." *Where are you? When will you be here?* She clamped her mouth tightly shut over those words. She didn't own him. She may have given her feelings away this morning when she'd told him—and the entire world—that she loved him, but she could stake no claim on his time or his life.

"Have you had dinner yet?" he asked.

"No, I was..." *Waiting for you.* "I wasn't hungry."

"Think you'll be hungry in about twenty minutes?" he asked.

"Hungry for what?" She tried to make her voice sound light, teasing, but her heart felt heavy. No matter how she approached this relationship, the conclusion she kept coming to was that it wasn't going to work out. Tomorrow they were both heading in different directions, and that would be it. All that was left was tonight. She'd been so worried earlier that she wasn't going to get to spend this final night with Joe. But now she couldn't help but think that it might be easier to simply say goodbye over the phone.

"Ow," he said, laughter in his voice. "You kill me, lady. But I meant are you hungry for *food.* Like, you and me—the real me, no disguises—going out somewhere for dinner." He paused. "In public. Like to a restaurant." He paused again, then laughed. "God, am I smooth, or what? I'm trying to ask you out to dinner, Ron. What do ya say?"

He didn't give her time to answer. "I'm still downtown," he continued, "but I can catch a cab and make it up to the hotel in about fifteen or twenty minutes. Wear that black dress, okay? We'll go up to Camelback Mountain. Mac says there's a great restaurant at the resort there. There's a band and dancing, and a terrific view of the city."

"But—"

"Oh, *yes*. There's a cab pulling up, right outside. Gotta run, babe. Get dressed—I'll be right there."

"But I don't want to go out. It's our last night—maybe forever—and I want to spend it alone with you," Veronica said to the dead phone line.

She slowly hung up the phone.

She had one more night with Joe. One more night to last the rest of her life. One more night to burn her imprint permanently into his memory.

Hmm.

Veronica picked up the phone and dialed room service. Joe wanted dinner and dancing and a view of the city? The view from this room wasn't too shabby. And the four-star restaurant in this hotel delivered food to the rooms. As for dancing . . .

Holding the telephone in one hand, Veronica crossed to the stereo that was attached to the entertainment center. Yes, there was a tape deck. She smiled.

For the first time, Joe actually knocked on her door rather than picking the lock and letting himself in.

With the long skirt of her black silk dress shushing about her legs, Veronica crossed to the hotel-room door and flung it open and herself into his arms. "Lord, I've waited all day to do this," she said. "You scared me to death this morning."

Having his arms around her felt so good. And when his lips met hers, she felt herself start to melt and she wrapped her own arms more tightly around his neck. Her fingers laced through his hair and—

Veronica pulled back.

His long hair was gone. Joe had cut his hair. Short. *Really* short. She looked at him, really *looked* at him for the first time since she'd opened her hotel-suite door. He was wearing a naval dress uniform. It was dark blue with rows and rows and *rows* of medals and ribbons on his left breast. He wore a white hat on his head, and he took it off, holding it almost awkwardly in his hands. His dark eyes were slightly sheepish as he watched her take in his haircut. His hair had been buzz cut around his ears and at the back. The top and front were slightly longer—just long enough so that a lock of dark hair fell forward over his forehead.

He smiled ruefully. "The barber went a little overboard," he said. "I don't usually wear it quite this short and..." He closed his eyes, shaking his head. "Damn, you hate it."

Veronica touched his arm, shaking her own head. "No," she said. "No, I don't *hate* it...." But she didn't like it, either. Not that he looked bad. In fact, he didn't. If anything, his short cut made his lean face more handsome than ever. But it also made him look harder, tougher, unforgiving—dangerous on an entirely new level. He looked like exactly what he was—a highly trained, highly competent special-forces officer. She couldn't help but be reminded that he was a man who risked his life as a matter of course. And *that* was what Veronica didn't like. "It suits you," she told him.

He searched her eyes, and whatever he saw there seemed to satisfy him. "Good."

"You look...wonderful," Veronica said honestly.

"So do you." His eyes flared with that familiar heat as he ran them down and then back up her body.

"This is the way I thought you were going to look—before we met," she said.

A brief shadow flickered across his face. "Yeah, well, I guess I oughta tell you, I can count on my fingers and toes the times I've worn this dress uniform. What you saw when we met is closer to the truth. I usually wear fatigues or jeans. And if I've been working with engines, they're usually covered with grease or dirt."

Why was he telling her this? It seemed almost like a warning. He seemed so serious, Veronica felt compelled to make things lighter. "Are you saying this because you want me to do your laundry?" she teased.

Joe gave her one of his quicksilver grins. Yes, seeing him smile that way, his teeth so very white against his lean, tanned face, Veronica could say that this new haircut definitely suited him. "You *want* to do my laundry?" he countered.

The casual question suddenly seemed to carry more meaning, as Joe watched her intently. His dark eyes were sharp, almost piercing as he waited for an answer.

Veronica laughed, trying to hide her sudden nervousness. Why were they talking about *laundry?* "I don't do my *own* laundry," she said with a shrug. "When do I have time?"

She stepped back, opening the door wider to let him in. "We're standing in the hall," she added. "Won't you come in?"

Joe hesitated. "Maybe we should just go...."

She smiled. "Think if you come inside we'll never leave?"

He touched the side of her face. "I don't just think it, baby, I *know* it."

She kissed the palm of his hand. "Would that be so terrible?" she whispered, gazing up into the midnight depths of his eyes.

"No." He stepped inside the room, closing the door behind him.

Veronica was nervous. Joe could see that she was nervous as she moved out of his grasp and into the room and—

The table was set and covered with a very grand-looking room-service dinner. And the rest of the room... Veronica had pushed all the furniture out of the center of the living room.

She'd done that before. Back in D.C. Back when he'd climbed up to the balcony and gone in her sliding-glass door and...

Joe looked up to find her watching him. She moistened her lips nervously and smiled. "Dinner and dancing," she explained. "I made room, so that we could dance."

"We?"

Veronica blushed, but she held his gaze. "So I can dance for you," she correctly herself softly. "Although, at some point you *will* dance with me, too. But maybe we should have dinner first."

The fragrant smell of gourmet food filled the air. Joe knew that he hadn't eaten since lunchtime. He also knew that dinner was the very last thing he wanted right now. Veronica was going to dance for him. She was going to dance the way he'd seen her dance when he'd climbed up to her room. Only this time, she would know right from the start that he was watching. "Maybe we should have dinner later," he said huskily.

As he watched, she crossed to the window and closed the curtains. God, his heart was pounding as if he'd just run a three-minute mile. He could feel his blood surging hotly through his veins with each pulsing beat. She was really going to do this. She knew he wanted her to—he'd asked her to dance for him. But he'd never thought she'd actually do it. He thought he'd asked for too much.

Veronica smiled at him as she crossed back to the dinner table and took a bottle of beer from a small bottle cooler. She opened it, poured it into a glass and carried it to him.

"Thanks," Joe said as she handed him both the glass and the bottle.

"Why don't you sit down?" Veronica murmured, and with a whisper of silk, she moved back to the other side of the room.

Sit down. Yeah, right. Sit down. As Joe lowered himself into a chair, Veronica crossed to the stereo and slipped a tape into the deck.

Joe knew what her dancing meant to her. She'd told him that it was private and intensely personal. It was a way to let off steam, to unwind, to really relax. And she was going to share it with him now. She was going to let her personal, private pleasure become *his* pleasure.

The fire that was shooting through his veins reached his heart and exploded. Veronica St. John had told him she loved him today. And tonight, by sharing herself with him this way, she was showing him just how much.

The music started—softly, slowly—and Ronnie stood in the middle of the room, head back, eyes closed, arms at her sides. God, she was beautiful. And she was his. All his. Forever, if he had anything to say about it. And he did. He had a lot to say about it. Hell, he could write a book on the subject.

The music changed with a sudden burst of volume, and Veronica brought her hands up sharply, into the air.

And then she began to move.

She was graceful, fluid, and her dress seemed an extension of her body, moving with her. Her eyes were still closed, but then she opened them and looked directly at Joe.

She blushed, and his heart burned even hotter. She was such a contradiction. The slightest thing could make her blush—until passion overcame her. And when that happened, she was amazingly uninhibited. Joe had never had a lover like Veronica St. John. One moment she was seemingly prim and proper, and the next she was wild, giving him pleasure in ways he'd only dreamed of, and telling him—quite specifically, in no uncertain terms—exactly what he could and should do to please her.

As Joe watched, Veronica closed her eyes again, and again the music changed, the rhythm getting stronger, faster, more insistent. Her dancing, too, became less careful, less contained. Her movements were freer, broader, more powerful.

More passionate.

She reached up with both hands and with one swift motion, removed the pins that were holding her hair. It tumbled down around her shoulders, an avalanche of red gold curls.

Joe's mouth was dry, and he took a sip of the beer she'd given him.

Veronica kicked off her high heels, and, as Joe watched, she *became* the music. She moved to the funky, bluesy instrumental piece, visually capturing every nuance, every musical phrase with her body.

Her body.

They hadn't been lovers for long, but Joe already knew every inch of Veronica's beautiful body intimately. But seeing her body in motion this way was an entirely new experience. Her dress barely restrained her breasts and they moved with and against the forces of gravity. The black silk slid across her abdomen and thighs, allowing glimpses of the firm muscles and flesh underneath when occasionally it clung for a second or two.

Veronica made a twisting, writhing motion that was pure sex, pure abandon.

The long skirt of her dress was no longer moving with her—it was getting in her way.

This time when she opened her eyes and looked at Joe, she didn't blush. She smiled—a sweet, hot, sexy smile—and reached behind her for the zipper of her dress. In less than a heartbeat, the dress pooled around her feet, and she was naked—save for a pair of black silk panties. She kicked the dress aside, still dancing, still moving and spinning.

A thong. She was wearing thong panties, black silk against her skin so creamy and white.

And still she danced.

For him.

I've died, Joe thought, *and gone to heaven.*

She moved closer to him, smiling at the look he knew damn well was on his face. He was hypnotized. Stupefied. Totally overcome. And extremely aroused.

Still moving, she held out her hands to him. "Dance with me."

It was not an invitation he needed to hear twice. He set his beer on the nearest end table and rose to his feet. And then, God, she was in his arms, moving with him and against him to that bluesy melody.

Her skin was so smooth, so silky beneath his hands. He touched her everywhere. Her softly rounded bottom, her full breasts, her flat stomach, her long, willowy arms. He was still in his uniform and she was nearly naked, and he had never, *never* been so turned on in his entire life. They were dancing so close, their legs were intertwined. He could feel the heat between her legs against his thigh. She could surely feel his arousal—she pressed against him, her slow, sexy movement driving him crazy, and the sight of her, nearly naked in his arms, making him throb with need.

"Ronnie..."

Somehow she knew that he'd had nearly all he could take. She lifted her mouth to his and kissed him. Joe heard himself groan. He couldn't get enough of her.

He felt her fingers unbuckling his belt and swiftly unfastening his pants. And then he was in her hands. It was good, but it wasn't good enough.

"Ronnie, I need—"

"I know."

She covered him with a condom she'd procured from God-knew-where, and slipped out of her panties as she kissed him again.

"Lift me up," Veronica murmured.

"Yes," he breathed. She wrapped her arms around his neck and her legs around his waist as he ensheathed himself in her wonderful, smooth heat. "Oh, baby..."

She moved on top of him, against him, with him. She was in his arms, in his heart, in his very soul. This passionate, fiery woman, who could be blazing hot one moment and gently sweet the next, this woman with the sharp sense of humor and quiet touch that hid a will of steel—a will that was ruled by the kindest heart he'd ever known—this was the one woman he'd been waiting for all his life. All the love he'd made, all the women he'd known before, had meant nothing to him. No one had moved him. No one had even come close to holding him. He'd always been able to close the door and walk away from a woman without looking back.

But there was no way he'd ever be able to walk away from Veronica. Not without leaving his heart behind—ripped from his chest.

He clung to her, holding her as tightly as she held him, plunging himself deeply into her again and again.

He loved her. He wanted to tell her, but the words—those three simple little words—didn't come easily. The truth was, saying them scared him to death. Now, wasn't that funny? He was a SEAL. He'd faced platoons of enemy soldiers, he'd looked death in the teeth without batting an eye more times than he could count, yet the thought of uttering one very simple sentence made him sweat.

Ronnie's fingers were in his hair. Her mouth was covering his face and lips with kisses.

"Joe," she breathed, "Joe. I want more—" He moved, backing her up against the wall to anchor her in place, and she tipped back her head. "Yes . . ."

Her release was incredible. She cried out as he drove himself into her, giving her all she'd asked for. Her arms tightened around his neck, her fingers clutched him.

"I love you," Veronica cried. "Oh, Joe, I love you!"

Her words pushed him over the edge. She loved him. She really did. He exploded in a blinding white burst of pleasure so exquisite, so pure that the world seem to disintegrate around him.

Baby, I love you, too.

Chapter 19

Joe slowly became aware of his surroundings.

Ronnie's head was resting on his shoulder, her breath warm against his neck. His own forehead leaned against the wall. And his knees were damned shaky.

He could feel Veronica's heart beating, hear her soft sigh.

He didn't want to move. He'd never made love quite like this in his life, and he didn't want it to end. Of course, it had ended, but as long as they stayed right here, in this same position, these remarkable feelings could linger on.

It was, needless to say, incredibly exhilarating. His future looked so much brighter, with Ronnie in the picture. For the first time in his life, Joe found himself actually considering the possibility of having children. Not for a good long time, of course. He wanted Ronnie all to himself for years and years and *years*. But down the road, making a baby, creating a new life would be exciting in a way he'd never imagined before. Fifty percent him and fifty percent her, with two hundred percent of their love...

The jeweler's box he carried in his pocket dug into his ribs and Joe had to laugh. He hadn't even asked Ronnie to marry him yet, and here he was, practically naming their kids.

"You didn't have to say that, you know," she whispered.

She lifted her head and lowered herself to the floor. The spell was broken. Or was it? Joe still felt an incredible warmth in his chest. He used to think it felt like a noose, he realized, but now it was a good feeling, a warmth surrounding his heart, giving him an amazing sense of peace and belonging.

"Didn't have to say what?" he asked.

Veronica moved away from him slightly, giving him room to adjust his clothes. She was still naked, but she seemed unaware of that as she gazed at him, concern darkening her blue eyes.

"You didn't have to say that you love me, too," she said.

Joe froze, hands stilled on the buckle of his belt. Had he actually spoken those words out loud?

"I'd rather that you be honest with me," she continued. "Don't say things you don't mean. Please?"

Veronica turned away, unable to continue looking into Joe's eyes, unable to keep up the brave front. But, bloody hell, here she'd just spoken of being honest.... "The truth is, Joe," she said, her voice shaking slightly, "I'm going to miss you terribly when you're gone, and—"

Joe drew her into his arms, moving with her so they sat on the sofa, Veronica on his lap. "Who says I'm going anywhere?" he asked softly, smoothing her hair back from her face and kissing her gently on the lips.

Veronica felt her eyes fill with tears. Damn! She blinked them back. "Tomorrow I'm flying to Seattle and you're—"

He interrupted her with another gentle kiss. "And who says when I said...what I said, that I wasn't being honest?" He ran his free hand down the curve of her hip and back up again, then cupped her breast. It was impossible not to touch her.

"You love me." Her disbelief was evident in her voice.

"Is that really so hard to believe?"

Veronica touched the side of his face. "You're so sweet," she said. At the mock flare of indignation in his eyes, she added quickly, "I know you don't think so, but you *are*. You're incredibly *kind,* Joe. And I know you have...feelings for me, but you don't have to pretend that they're more than—" She stared down in silence at the small black velvet box Joe pulled from his pocket and held out to her. "What's this?"

"Open it," he said. His face looked so serious, so hard. His eyes were so intense.

"I'm afraid to."

Joe smiled, and it softened his face. "It's not a grenade," he said. "Just open it, Ron, will ya?"

Slowly, she took it from him. It was small and square and black and furry. It looked an awful lot like a jeweler's box. What was he giving her? She couldn't even begin to imagine the possibilities. Her heart was pounding, she realized. She took a deep breath to steady herself. Then, gazing into Joe's beautiful eyes, looking for some sort of clue as to what was inside, she opened the box.

She glanced down and her heart stopped. It was a ring. It was an enormous, beautiful, glittering diamond ring.

"Marry me," Joe said huskily.

"Dear Lord!" Veronica breathed.

As she stared up into his eyes, her expression of shock made Joe smile. "I guess you weren't expecting this, huh?"

She shook her head.

"Neither was I," he told her honestly. "But that ring's not pretend, Ronnie. And neither is what I feel. I . . . you know . . . love you—" God, he'd said it and he wasn't struck by lightning. "And I want to make this thing we have permanent. You follow?"

She was silent. Her eyes were as large as dinner plates as she gazed at him. She was still naked, and he couldn't have kept from touching her, from stroking her soft skin, if his life depended on it. She was lovely, and he was already uncomfortably aroused again. God, he'd just had the best sex of his life, and already he wanted her again. He couldn't get enough of her. He never would.

But why wouldn't she answer? Why wouldn't she tell him that she wanted to marry him, too?

"Say something, baby." Joe tried to disguise his insecurity, but knew that he'd failed miserably. It showed in his eyes, in his voice. "The suspense is killing me. Tell me what you think. Good idea? Bad idea? Have I gone crazy, here?"

Veronica was dumbfounded. Joe Catalanotto—Lt. Joe Catalanotto of the U.S. Navy SEALs—wanted to *marry* her. He'd meant it when he'd said that he loved her. He loved her.

He *loved* her, and dear Lord, she should be ecstatic. She should be hearing wedding bells and picturing herself in a gorgeous white wedding dress, walking down the aisle of a church to meet this man at the altar. The one man that she truly loved.

But she couldn't picture herself at a wedding. She could only see herself at a funeral. *Joe's* funeral.

"When . . ." she started, then cleared her throat. She shivered slightly, suddenly aware of the chill of the air-conditioning against her bare skin. Joe ran his hand up and down her arm, trying to warm her. "When are you planning to retire?"

He stared at her blankly. "What?"

"From the SEALs," she explained. "When are you going to retire from active duty?"

Veronica could see that he didn't get how this pertained to his wedding proposal, but he shrugged and answered her anyway. "Not for a long time," he said. "I don't know. Not for another fifteen years. Twenty if I can manage it."

Her heart sank. Fifteen or twenty years. Two decades of watching the man she loved leave on countless high-risk missions. Two decades of not knowing whether or not he would return. Two decades of sheer *hell*. If he lived that long . . .

"I'm career navy, Ronnie," Joe said quietly. "I know I'm no prince, but I *am* an officer and—"

"You *are* a prince." Veronica kissed him swiftly on the lips. "I've never met anyone even half as princely as you are."

He was embarrassed. So of course, he tried to turn it into a joke. "Well, damn," he said. "All the naked women tell me that whenever I get them on my lap."

Veronica had to smile. "I *am* naked," she said. "Aren't I?"

"I noticed," he said, lightly touching her breast.

"Do you want me to put on some clothes?"

"I was thinking more along the lines that I should get rid of mine," Joe murmured, bringing his lips to where his hand had just been. But he only kissed her gently before lifting his head again. "Try it on."

The ring. He meant the ring.

She knew she shouldn't. She had no idea what her answer was going to be. She was so utterly, totally torn.

Still, Veronica took the ring from the box and slipped it onto her left hand. It was a little bit too large.

"Say the word, and we can get it sized," Joe said. "Or, if you want, you can pick out something different...."

Veronica looked at the ring's simple, elegant setting through a haze of tears. "This is so beautiful," she said. "I wouldn't want anything else."

"When I saw it," Joe said quietly, "I knew it belonged to you." He lifted her chin up toward him. "Hey. Hey, are you crying?"

Veronica nodded her head, yes, and he drew her even closer to him. He pulled her mouth to his and kissed her sweetly. She wanted so very much to tell him, "Yes, I'll marry you." But she wanted to go to bed every night with him beside her. And she wanted to wake up every morning knowing that he was going to be there again the next night. She didn't want a Navy SEAL, she wanted a regular, normal man.

But maybe if she asked, he'd leave the SEALs. Lord knows, he could do damn near anything, get any kind of job he wanted. He was an expert in so many different fields. He could work as a translator. Or he could work as a mechanic, she didn't care. Let him get covered with engine grease every day. She'd learn to do the bloody laundry if that's what it took. She just wanted to know that he would be safe. And alive.

But Veronica knew she couldn't ask him to leave the SEALs. And even if she *did* ask him, she knew that he wouldn't quit. Not for her. Not for anything. She'd seen him at work. He loved the risk, lived for the danger.

"Please, Joe," she whispered. "Make love to me again."

He stood, holding her in his arms, and carried her into the bedroom.

Veronica wanted desperately to marry Joe. But Joe was already married—to the Navy SEALs.

As Veronica slept, curled up next to him in the bed, Joe stared at the ceiling.

She hadn't said yes.

He'd asked her to marry him, and she'd asked him a bunch of questions in return, but she hadn't said yes.

She hadn't said no, either. But she'd taken off the ring and put it back in the box. She gave him some excuse about how she was afraid it was going to fall off. She was afraid she was going to lose it.

But if Ronnie had given *him* any kind of ring that meant that she wanted him forever, that she loved him "till death do us part," Joe would damn sure be wearing it, regardless of the size.

It was entirely possible that he was heading full steam ahead into an emotional train wreck. It was entirely possible that although Veronica had said that she loved him, she didn't love him enough to want "forever." Hell, it was entirely possible that although she had said she loved him, she didn't love him at all.

But no. He had to believe that she loved him. He'd seen it in her eyes, felt it in her touch. She *did* love him. The sixty-four-thousand-dollar question was, how much?

Across the room, from the chair where he'd thrown his clothes, his pocket pager shrilled.

Joe extracted himself from the bed, trying not to wake Veronica, but as he moved swiftly across the room, she stirred and sat up.

"What was *that?*" she asked.

"My pager," he said. "I'm sorry. I've got to make a phone call."

Veronica leaned forward and snapped on the light, squinting at him in the sudden brightness. As she watched, he sat back down on the edge of the bed, running his fingers through his short hair before he picked up the telephone. He quickly dialed—a number he had memorized.

"Yeah," he said into the phone. "Catalanotto." There was a pause. "I'm still in Phoenix." Another pause. "Yeah. Yeah, I understand." He glanced back at Veronica, his face serious. "Give me three minutes, and I'll call right back." Another pause. He smiled. "Right. Thanks."

He dropped the receiver into the cradle and faced Veronica.

"I can get a week's leave, if I want it," he said bluntly. "But I need to know right now if I should take it. And I don't want to take it if you can't spend the time with me. Do you know what I'm saying?"

Veronica glanced at the clock. "You get called at four-thirty in the morning about whether or not you want *leave?*" she asked in dismay.

Joe shook his head. "No," he replied. "I get called and ordered to report to the base at Little Creek. There's some kind of emergency. They're calling in all of SEAL Team Ten, including the Alpha Squad."

Veronica felt faint. "What kind of emergency?"

"I don't know," he said. "But even if I *did* know, I couldn't say."

"If we were married, could you tell me?"

Joe smiled ruefully. "No, baby. Not even then."

"So you just pack up and leave," Veronica said tightly, "and maybe you'll come back?"

He reached for her. "I'll always come back. You gotta believe that."

She sat up, moving out of reach, keeping her back to him so that he couldn't see the look on her face. This was her worst nightmare, coming true. This was what she didn't want to spend the next twenty years doing. This fear, this emptiness was exactly what she didn't want to spend the next two decades feeling.

"I either have to officially take leave, or go check in with the rest of the team. What do you think?" he asked again. "Can you get time off, too?"

Veronica shook her head. "No." Funny, her voice sounded so cool and in control. "No, I'm sorry, but I have to be on the cruise ship with Prince Tedric, starting tomorrow."

She could feel his eyes on the back of her head. She sensed his hesitation before he turned back to the telephone.

He picked it up and dialed. "Yeah, it's Joe Cat again. I'm in."

Veronica closed her eyes. He was in. But in for what? Something that was going to get him killed? She couldn't stand it. Not knowing where he was going, what he'd be doing, was awful. She wanted to *scream*....

"Right," he said into the phone. "I'll be ready."

He hung up the phone, and she felt the mattress shift as he stood.

"I have to take a quick shower," he said. "There's a car coming in ten minutes."

Veronica spun around to face him. "Ten *minutes!*"

"That's how it works, Ronnie. I get a call, I have to leave. Right away. Sometimes we get preparation time, but usually not. Let me take a shower—we can talk while I'm getting dressed."

Veronica felt numb. This wasn't her worst nightmare. This fear she felt deep in her stomach was beyond anything she'd ever imagined. She wanted to tell him, *beg* him to take the leave. She would quit her job if she had to. She would do anything, *any*thing to keep him from going on that unnamed, unidentified, probably deadly emergency mission.

And then what? she wondered as she heard the sound of the shower. She stood and slipped into her robe, suddenly feeling terribly chilled. She would lose her job, her reputation, her *pride,* for one measly week of Joe's company. But after that week of leave was up, he would be gone. He'd go where duty called, when duty called, no matter the danger or risk. Sooner or later it would happen. Sooner or later—and probably sooner—he was going to kiss her goodbye, leaving her with her heart in her throat. He would leave her alone, watching the clock, waiting, praying for him to return. Alive. And he wouldn't come back.

Veronica couldn't stand it. She wouldn't be able to stand it.

The water shut off, and several moments later Joe came out of the bathroom, toweling himself dry. She watched silently as he slipped on his briefs and then his pants.

"So," he said, rubbing his hair with the towel one last time, glancing over at her. "Tell me when you'll be done with the Ustanzian tour. I'll try to arrange leave."

"It won't be for another two or three weeks," Veronica said. "After the cruise, we'll be heading back to D.C., and then to Ustanzia from there. By then, Wila will have had the baby, and—" She broke off, turning away from him. Why were they having this seemingly normal-sounding conversation, when every cell in her body was screaming for her to hold him—hold him and never let go? But she couldn't hold him. A car was coming in five minutes to take him away, maybe forever.

"Okay," Joe was saying. She could hear him slipping his arms into his jacket and buttoning it closed. "What do you say I meet you in Ustanzia? Just let me know the exact dates and—"

Veronica shook her head. "I don't think that's a good idea."

"Okay," he said again, very quietly. "What *is* a good idea, Ronnie? You tell me."

He wasn't moving now. Veronica knew even without looking that he was standing there, his lean face unsmiling, his dark eyes intense as he watched her, waiting for her to move, to speak, to do something, *any*thing.

"I don't have any good ideas."

"You don't want to marry me." It wasn't a question, it was a statement.

Veronica didn't move, didn't say anything. What could she possibly say?

Joe laughed—a brief burst of air that had nothing to do with humor. "Hell, from the way it sounds, you don't even want to *see* me again."

She turned toward him, but she wasn't prepared for the chill that was in his eyes.

"Boy, did I have *you* pegged wrong," he said.

"You don't understand," Veronica tried to explain. "I can't live the way you want me to live. I can't take it, Joe."

He turned away, and she moved forward, stopping him with a hand on his arm. "We come from such different worlds," she said. His world was filled with danger and violence and the ever-present risk of death. Why couldn't he see the differences between them? "I can't just . . . pretend to fit into your world, because I know I won't. And I know you won't fit into mine. You can't change any more than *I* can, and—"

Joe pulled away. His head was spinning. Different worlds. Different classes was more like it. God, he should have known better. What was he thinking? How could he have thought a woman like Veronica St. John—a wealthy, high-class, gentrified lady—would want more from him than a short, steamy affair?

He'd been right—she'd been slumming.

That was all this was to her.

She had been slumming. She had been checking out how the lower class lived. She had been having sex with a blue-collar man. Officer or not, that was what Joe was, what he would always be. That was where he came from.

Veronica was getting her hands dirty, and Joe, he'd gone and fallen in love. God, he was a royal idiot, a horse's ass.

He took the ring box from where it still sat on the bedside table and dropped it into his pocket. Damned if he was going to let her walk away with a ring that had put a serious dent into his life savings.

"Try to understand," Veronica said, her eyes swimming with tears. She stood in front of the door, blocking his exit. "I love you, but . . . I can't marry you."

And all at once Joe *did* understand. She may have been slumming—at first. But she'd fallen in love with him, too. Still, that love wasn't enough to overcome the differences between their two "worlds" as she called it.

He should walk away. He *knew* he should walk away. But instead he touched her face and brushed his thumb across her beautiful lips. And then he did something he'd never done before. He begged.

"Please, Ronnie," Joe said softly. "This thing between us...it's pretty powerful. Please, baby, can't we try to work this out?"

Veronica stared up into Joe's eyes, and for a second, she almost believed that they could.

But then his pager beeped again, and the fear was back. Joe had to go. Now. Reality hit her hard and she felt sick to her stomach. She turned and moved away from the door.

"That's your answer, huh?" he said quietly.

Veronica kept her back to him. She couldn't speak. And she couldn't bear to watch him leave.

She heard him open the bedroom door. She heard him walk through the hotel suite. And she heard him stop, heard him hesitate before he opened the door to the corridor.

"I thought you were tougher than this, Ron," he said, a catch in his voice.

The door clicked quietly as it closed behind him.

Chapter 20

The guys in Alpha Squad were avoiding Joe. They were keeping their distance—and it was little wonder, considering the black mood he was in.

The "emergency" calling them all back to Little Creek had been no more than an exercise in preparedness—a time test by the powers that be. The top brass were checking to see exactly how long it would take SEAL Team Ten to get back to their home base in Virginia, from their scattered temporary locations around California and the Southwest.

Blue was the only man who ignored Joe's bad mood and stayed nearby as they completed the paperwork on the exercise and on the Ustanzian tour operation. Blue didn't say a word, but Joe knew his executive officer was ready to lend a sympathetic ear, or even a shoulder to cry on if he needed it.

Early that evening, before they left the administration office, there was a phone call for Joe. From Seattle.

Blue was there, and he met Joe's eyes as the call was announced. There was only one person in Seattle who could possibly be calling Joe.

Veronica St. John.

Why was she calling him?

Maybe she'd changed her mind.

Blue turned away, sympathy in his eyes. Damn it, Joe thought. Were his feelings, his hope for the impossible *that* transparent?

There was no real privacy in the office, and Joe had to take the call at an administrator's desk, with the man sitting not three feet away from him.

"Catalanotto," he said into the phone, staring out the window.

"Joe?" It *was* Veronica. And she sounded surprised to hear his voice. "Oh, Lord, I didn't think I'd actually get through to you. I thought ... I thought I'd be able to leave a message with your voice mail or ... something."

Terrific. She didn't actually want to speak to him. Then why the hell had she called? "You want me to hang up?" he asked. "You can call back and leave a message."

"Well, no," she said. "No, of course not. Don't be silly. I just ... didn't think you'd be there. I thought you'd be ... shooting bad guys ... or something."

Joe smiled despite the ache in his chest. "No," he said. *"Yesterday* I shot the bad guy. Today I'm doing the paperwork about it."

"I thought ..."

"Yes ... ?"

"Aren't you shipping out or ... something?"

"No," Joe said. "It was an exercise. The brass wanted to see how fast SEAL Team Ten could get our butts back to Little Creek. They do that sometimes. Supposedly it keeps us on our toes."

"I'm glad," she said.

"I'm not," he stated flatly. "I was hoping they were sending us down to South America. We're *still* no closer to nailing Diosdado. I was looking forward to tracking him down and having it out with him once and for all."

"Oh," she said very softly. And then she was silent.

Joe counted to five very slowly, then he said, "Veronica? You still there?"

"Yes," she replied, and he could almost see her shake her head to get herself back on track. But when she spoke, her voice was no less tentative. "I'm sorry, I ... um, I was calling to pass on some news I received this afternoon. Mrs. Kaye called from Washington, D.C. Cindy died this morning at Saint Mary's.''

Joe closed his eyes and swore.

"Mrs. Kaye wanted to thank you again," Veronica continued, her voice shaking. She was crying. Joe knew just from the way her voice sounded that she was crying. God, his arms ached to hold her. "She wanted to thank both of us, for your visit. It meant a lot to Cindy."

Joe held tightly to the phone, fighting to ignore the six pairs of curious eyes and ears in the room.

Veronica took a deep breath, and he could picture her wiping her eyes and face, adjusting her hair. "I just thought you'd want to know," she said. She took another breath. "I have to run. The cruise ship sails in less than an hour."

"Thanks for calling to tell me, Veronica," Joe said.

There was another silence. Then she said, "Joe?"

"Yeah."

"I'm sorry," she said falteringly. "About . . . you and me. About it not working out. I didn't mean to hurt you."

Joe couldn't talk about it. How could he stand here in the middle of all these people and talk about the fact that his heart had been stomped into a million tiny pieces? And even if he could, how could he admit it to her—the woman responsible for all the pain?

"Was there something else you wanted?" he asked, his voice tight and overly polite.

"You sound so . . . Are you . . . are you all right?"

"Yeah," he lied. "I'm great. I'm getting on with my life, okay? Now, if you'll excuse me, I'll get back to it, all right?"

Joe hung up the phone without waiting to see if she said goodbye. He turned and walked away, past Blue, past the guard at the front desk. He walked out of the building and down the road, heading toward the empty parade grounds. He sat in the grass at the edge of the field and held his head in his hands.

And for the second time in his adult life, Joe Catalanotto cried.

Standing at the pay phone, Veronica dissolved into tears. She hadn't expected to speak to Joe. She hadn't expected to hear his familiar voice. It was such a relief to know that he wasn't risking his life—at least not today.

But he'd sounded so stilted, so cold, so unfriendly. He'd called her Veronica, not Ronnie, as if she were some stranger he didn't know. He was getting on with his life, he'd said. He clearly wasn't going to waste any time worrying about what might have been.

That was the way she wanted it, wasn't it? So why did she feel so awful?

Did she actually *want* Joe Catalanotto carrying a torch for her? Did she *want* him to be hurt? Did she *want* his heart to be broken?

Or maybe she was afraid that by turning him down, she'd done the wrong thing, made the wrong choice.

Veronica didn't know. She honestly didn't know.

The only thing she was absolutely certain of was how terribly much she missed him.

Joe sat in the bar nursing a beer, trying not to listen to the endless parade of country songs about heartbreak playing on the jukebox.

"At ease, at ease. Stay in your seats, boys."

Joe looked into the mirror behind the bar and saw Admiral Forrest making his way across the crowded room. The admiral sat down at the bar, next to Joe, who took another sip of his beer, not even looking up, certainly not even smiling.

"Rumor has it you survived your mission," Mac said to Joe, ordering a diet cola from the bartender. "But it looks to me like you extracted without a pulse or a sense of humor. Am I right or are you still alive over there, son?"

"Well, gee whiz, Admiral," Joe said, staring morosely into his beer. "We can't all be a barrel of laughs all the time."

Mac nodded seriously. "No, no, you're right. We can't." He nodded to the bartender as the man put a tall glass of soda on the bar. "Thanks." He glanced down the bar and nodded to Blue McCoy, who was sitting on Joe's right. "Lieutenant."

Blue nodded back. "Good to see you, Admiral."

Forrest turned back to Joe. "Hear you and some of your boys had a run-in with Salustiano Vargas two days ago."

Joe nodded, glancing up at the older man. "Yes, sir."

"Also hear from the Intel grapevine that the rumor is, Vargas was disassociated from Diosdado and the Cloud of Death some time ago."

Joe shrugged, drawing wet lines with the condensation from his mug on the surface of the bar. He exchanged a look with Blue. "Vargas wasn't able to verify FInCOM's information after we had it out with him. He was too dead to talk."

Admiral Forrest nodded. "I heard that, too," he said. He took a long sip of his soda, then set it carefully back down on the bar. "What *I* can't figure out is, if Salustiano Vargas was *not* working with Diosdado, why did earlier FInCOM reports state that members of the Cloud of Death were unusually interested in Prince Tedric's tour schedule?"

"FInCOM isn't known for their flawless operations," Joe said, one eyebrow raised. "Someone made a mistake."

"I don't know, Joe." Mac scratched his head through his thick white hair. "I've got this gut feeling that the mistake is in assuming the reports are true about this rift between Vargas and Diosdado. I think there's still some connection between them. Those two were too close for too long." He shook his head again. "What I can't figure out is *why* Salustiano Vargas—Diosdado's number-one sharpshooter—would set himself up as a suicide assassin. He didn't stand a chance at getting out of there. *And* he didn't even hit his target."

Joe took another slug of his beer. "He had the opportunity," he said. "I was on that stage, with my back to the bastard when he fired his first shot. It wasn't until the second shot went into the stage next to me that I realized he was shooting from behind me and—"

Joe froze, his glass a quarter of an inch from his lips. "Jesus, Mary and Joseph." He put his beer back on the counter and looked from Blue to the admiral. "Why would a sharpshooter of Vargas's caliber miss an easy target in broad daylight?"

"Luck," Blue suggested. "You moved out of the way of the bullet at the right split second."

"I didn't," Joe said. "I didn't move at all. He *deliberately* missed me." He stood, knocking his barstool over. "I need the telephone," he said to the bartender. "Now."

The bartender moved fast and placed the phone in front of Joe. Joe pushed it in front of the admiral.

"Who am I calling?" Forrest asked dryly. "*Why* am I calling?"

"Why would Salustiano Vargas deliberately miss his assassination target?" Joe asked. He answered his own question. "Because the assassination attempt was only a diversion, set up to make FInCOM's security force relax. Which they immediately did, right? I'm out of the picture. The rest of Alpha Squad is out of the picture. Mac, how many FInCOM agents are with Prince Tedric's tour now that the alleged danger has passed?"

Mac shrugged. "Two. I think." He leaned forward. "Joe, what are you saying?"

"That the *real* terrorist attack hasn't happened yet. Damn, at least I hope it hasn't happened yet."

Mac Forrest's mouth dropped open. "Jumping Jesse," he said. "The cruise ship?"

Joe nodded. "With only two FInCOM agents onboard, that cruise ship is a terrorist's dream come true." He picked up the telephone receiver and handed it to the admiral. "Contact them, sir. Warn them."

Forrest dialed a number and waited, his blue eyes steely in his weathered face.

Joe waited, too. Waited, and prayed. Veronica was on that ship.

Blue stood. "I'm gonna page the squad," he said quietly to Joe.

Joe nodded. "Better make it all of Team Ten," he told Blue in a low voice. "If this is going down, it's going to be big. We're going to need all the manpower we've got. While you're at it, get on the horn with the commander of Team Six. Let's put in a request to put them on standby, too."

Blue nodded and vanished in the direction of the door and the outside pay phone.

Please, God, keep Veronica safe, Joe prayed. *Please, God, let him be really, really wrong about the situation. Please God...*

Forrest put his hand over the receiver. "I got through to the naval base in Washington State," he said to Joe. "They're hailing the cruise ship now." He lifted his hand from the mouthpiece. "Yes?" he said into the telephone. "They're not?" He looked up at Joe, his eyes dark with concern. "The ship's not responding. Apparently, their radio's down. The base has them on radar, and they've gone seriously off course." He shook his head, his mouth tight with anger and frustration. "I believe we've got ourselves a crisis situation."

Veronica watched a second helicopter land on the sundeck.

This couldn't be happening. Five hours ago, she'd been having lunch with Ambassador Freder and his staff. Five hours ago, everything had been perfectly normal aboard the cruise ship *Majestic*. Tedric had been sleeping in, as was his habit. She'd been forcing down a salad even though she wasn't hungry, even though her stomach hurt from missing Joe. Lord, she didn't think it was possible to miss another person that badly. She felt hollow, empty, and hopelessly devoid of life.

And then a dozen men, dressed in black and carrying automatic rifles and submachine guns, jumped out of one helicopter and swarmed across the deck of the cruise ship, declaring that the *Majestic* was now in their control, and all her passengers were their hostages.

It seemed unreal, like some sort of strange movie that she was somehow involved in making.

There were fewer than sixty people aboard the small cruise ship, including the crew. They were all on deck, watching and waiting as the second helicopter's blades slowed and then stopped.

No one made a sound as the doors opened and several men stepped out.

One of them, a man with a pronounced limp who was wearing a baseball cap and sunglasses, smiled a greeting to the silent crowd. He had a wide, friendly, white-toothed smile set off by a thick salt-and-pepper beard. Without saying a word, he gestured to one of the other terrorists, who pulled the two FInCOM agents out in front of them all.

The terrorists had cuffed the two security agents' hands behind them, and now, as they were pushed to their knees in front of the bearded man, they fought to keep their balance.

"Who are you?" one of the agents, a woman named Maggie Forte demanded. "What is this—"

"Silence," the bearded man said. And then he pulled a revolver from his belt and shot both agents in the head.

Senator McKinley's wife screamed and started to cry.

"Just so you know our guns are quite real," the bearded man said to the rest of them in his softly accented voice, "and that we mean business. My name is Diosdado." He gestured to the other terrorists around him. "These men and women all work for me. Do as they say, and you will all be fine." He smiled again. "Of course, there are no guarantees."

Veronica stared at the bright red blood pooling beneath the FInCOM agents' bodies. They were dead. Just like that, a man and a woman were dead. The man—Charlie Griswold, he'd said his name was—had just had a new baby. He'd shown Veronica pictures. He'd been so proud, so in love with his pretty young wife. And now...

God forgive her, but all she could think was *Thank God it wasn't Joe.* Thank God Joe wasn't here. Thank God that wasn't Joe's blood spreading across the deck.

Diosdado limped toward Prince Tedric, who was standing slightly apart from the rest of them.

"So we finally meet again," the terrorist said. He used his submachine gun to knock the Stetson cowboy hat Tedric was wearing off his head.

Tedric looked as if he might be ill.

"Did you really think I'd forget about the agreement we made?" Diosdado asked.

Tedric glanced toward the two dead agents lying on the deck. "No," he whispered.

"Then where are my long-range missiles?" Diosdado demanded. "I've been waiting and waiting for you to come through on your part of the deal."

Veronica couldn't believe what she was hearing. Prince Tedric, involved in arms smuggling? She wouldn't have believed he had the nerve.

"I said I'd *try,*" Tedric hissed. "I made no promises."

Diosdado made tsking sounds. "Then it was very bad form for you to keep the money," he said.

Tedric straightened in shock. "I sent the money back," he retorted. "I wouldn't have kept it. *Mon Dieu,* I wouldn't have ... dared."

Diosdado stared at him. Then he laughed. "You know, I actually believe you. It seems my good friend Salustiano intervened more than once. No wonder he wanted you dead. He'd intercepted two million of my dollars that you were returning to me." He laughed again. "Isn't this an interesting twist?" He turned to his men. "Take the other hostages below, and His Highness to the bridge. Let's see what a crown prince is worth these days. I may get my long-range missiles yet."

Navy SEAL Team Ten was airborne less than thirty minutes after Admiral Forrest contacted the naval base in Washington State. Joe sat in the air-force jet with his men, receiving nearly continuous reports from a Blackbird SR-71 spy plane that was circling at eighty-five thousand feet above the hijacked cruise ship, over the northern Pacific Ocean. The Blackbird was flying so high the terrorists and hostages on board the *Majestic* couldn't have seen it even with high-powered binoculars.

But with the Blackbird's high-tech equipment, Joe could see the cruise ship. The pictures that were coming in were very sharp and clear.

There were two bodies on the deck near two high-speed attack helicopters.

Two bodies, two pools of blood.

More detailed reports showed that one of the bodies was wearing a skirt, her legs angled awkwardly on the deck.

One man, one woman. Both dead.

Joe studied the picture, unable to see the woman's features for all the blood. Please, God, don't let it be Veronica! He glanced up to find Blue looking over his shoulder.

Blue shook his head. "I don't think it's her," he said. "I don't think it's Veronica."

Joe didn't say anything at first. "It could be," he finally said, his voice low.

"Yeah." Blue nodded. "Could be. And if it's not, it's someone that somebody else loves. It's already a no-win situation, Cat. Don't let it interfere with what we've got to do."

"I won't," he said. He smiled, but it didn't reach his eyes. "That bastard Diosdado isn't gonna know what hit him."

Veronica sat in the dining room with the other hostages, wondering what was going to come next.

Tedric sat apart from the others, staring at the walls, his jaw clenched tightly, his arms crossed in front of him.

It was funny, so many people had seen Joe and thought that he was Tedric. But to Veronica, their physical differences were so clearly obvious. Joe's eyes were bigger and darker, his lashes longer. Joe's chin was stronger, more square. Tedric's nose was narrower, and slightly pinched looking at the end.

Sure, they both had dark hair and dark eyes, but Tedric's eyes shifted as he spoke, never settling on any one thing. Veronica had worked for hours and *hours,* trying to teach the prince to look steadily into the TV cameras. Joe, on the other hand, always looked everyone straight in the eye. Tedric was in constant motion—fingers tapping, a foot jiggling, crossing and uncrossing his legs. Joe's energy was carefully contained. He could sit absolutely still, but one could feel his leashed power. He nearly throbbed with it, but it didn't distract—at least, not all the time.

Veronica closed her eyes.

Was she ever going to see Joe again? What she would give to put her arms around him, to feel his arms holding her.

But he was in Virginia. It was very likely that he hadn't even heard about the hijacking yet. And what would he think when he found out? Would he even care? He'd been so cold, so formal, so distant during their last conversation.

Diosdado had opened communications with both the U.S. and the Ustanzian governments. Ustanzia was ready to ship out the missiles the terrorists wanted, but the U.S. was against that. Now the two governments were in disagreement, with the U.S. threatening to drop all future aid if Ustanzia gave in to the terrorists' demands. But Senator McKinley was on board the *Majestic,* too. So between the senator and Crown Prince Tedric, Diosdado had hit a jackpot.

But jackpot or not, Diosdado was losing patience.

He limped into the room now, and all of the hostages tensed.

"Men on one side, and women on the other," said the leader of the Cloud of Death, drawing an imaginary line down the center of the room with his arm.

Everybody stared. No one moved.

"Now!" he commanded quite softly, lifting his gun for emphasis.

They all moved. Veronica stood on the right side of the imaginary line with the rest of the women. There were only fourteen women on board, compared to the forty men on the other side of the dining room.

Mrs. McKinley was shivering, and Veronica reached down and took the older woman's icy fingers.

"Here's how it's going to work," Diosdado said pleasantly. "We're going to start with the women. You're going to go up to the bridge, to the radio room, and talk to your government. You're going to convince them to give us what we want, *and* to keep their distance. And you're going to tell them that starting in one hour, we're going to begin eliminating our hostages, one each hour, on the hour."

There was a murmur in the crowd, and Mrs. McKinley clung more tightly to Veronica's hand.

"And," Diosdado said, "you may tell them that once again we're going to start with the women."

"No!" one of the men cried.

Diosdado turned and fired his gun, shooting the man in the head. Several people screamed, many dove for cover.

Veronica turned away, sickened. Just like that, another man was dead.

"Anyone else have any objections?" Diosdado asked pleasantly.

Except for the sound of quiet sobbing, the hostages were silent.

"You and you," the terrorist said, and it was several moments before Veronica realized he was talking to her and Mrs. McKinley. "To the radio room."

Veronica looked up into the glittering chill of Diosdado's dark eyes, and she knew. She was going to be the first. She had only one more hour to live.

One very short hour.

Even if Joe knew, even if Joe cared, there was nothing he could do to save her. He was on the other side of the country. There was no way he could reach her within an hour.

She was going to die.

Chapter 21

Joe stood in the briefing room of the USS *Watkins,* and tried to work out a plan to get SEAL Team Ten onto the *Majestic,* and the hostages off.

"Infrared surveillance shows the majority of the hostages are in the ship's dining hall," Blue reported. He pointed to the location on a cutaway schematic of the cruise ship that was spread out on the table among all the other maps and charts and photographs. "We can approach at dusk, going under their radar with inflatable boats, climb up the sides of the *Majestic,* and bring the hostages out without the terrorists even knowing."

"Once everyone's clear of the cruise ship," Harvard said with a hard smile, "we kick their butts all the way to hell."

"We'll need air support," Joe said. "At the first sign of trouble, Diosdado is going to split in one of those choppers he's got on the deck. I want to make sure we've got some fighters standing by, ready to shoot him down if necessary."

"What you *need,*" Admiral Forrest said, coming into the room, "is a go-ahead from the president. And right now, he wants to sit tight, wait and see what the terrorists do next."

The intercom from the bridge crackled on. "We have a report from the *Majestic,*" a voice said over the loudspeaker.

"Another hostage is dead. The terrorists say they'll kill one hostage every hour until they get either twenty million dollars or a shipment of long-range missiles."

Another hostage was dead. Joe couldn't breathe. God help Diosdado if he so much as *touched* Veronica. He looked around the room at the grim faces of his men. God help that bastard, anyway. SEAL Team Ten was after him now.

The telephone rang, and Cowboy picked it up. "Jones," he said. He held the receiver out to the admiral. "Sir, it's for you." He swallowed. "It's the president."

Forrest took the phone. "Yes, sir?" He nodded, listening hard, then looked up at Joe. He spoke only one word, but it was the word Joe had been waiting for.

"Go."

As the sun began to set, Mrs. McKinley was taken back to the dining room, leaving Veronica alone with Diosdado and one of his followers.

"Right about now, you're wondering how you ever got into this mess," Diosdado said to Veronica, offering her one of the cigarettes from his pack.

She shook her head.

"It's okay," he said. "You can smoke if you want." He laughed. "After all, you don't have to worry about dying from lung cancer, right?"

"Right about now," Veronica said with forced calm, "I'm wondering what your head would look like—on a pike."

Diosdado laughed, and touched her on the cheek. "You Brits are so bloodthirsty."

She pulled her head away, repulsed. He just laughed again.

"They're all going to die," he said. "All of the hostages. You should be thankful *your* death is going to be painless."

Joe met Blue's eyes in the dimness of the corridor outside the dining hall. They both wore headsets and mikes, but at this proximity to the terrorists, they were silent. Joe nodded once and Blue nodded back.

They were going in.

The door was open a crack, and they knew from looking in that both guards had their backs to them. Both guards were holding Uzis, but their stances were relaxed, unsuspecting of trouble.

Joe smiled grimly. Well, here came trouble with a capital *T.* He pointed to Blue and then to the guard on the left. Blue nodded. Joe held up three fingers, two fingers, one . . .

He pushed the door open, and he and Blue erupted into the room as if they were one body with a single controlling brain. The guard on the left spun around, bringing his Uzi up. Joe fired once, the sound of the shot muffled by his hush-puppy. He caught the Uzi as the man fell, turning to see Blue lower the other guard, his head at an unnatural angle, to the ground.

The hostages didn't make a sound. They stared, though. The entire room reeked of fear.

"Dining room secure," Blue said into his microphone. "Let's get some backup down here, boys." He turned to the hostages. "We're U.S. Navy SEALs," he told them in his gentle Southern accent as Joe searched the crowd for Veronica. "With your continued cooperation, we're here to take y'all home."

There was a babble of voices, questions, demands. Blue held up both hands. "We're not out of danger yet, folks," he said. "I'd like to ask you all to remain silent and to move quickly and quietly when we tell you to."

Veronica wasn't here. If she wasn't here, that meant . . .

"Veronica St. John," Joe said, his voice cracking with his effort to stay calm. Just because she wasn't here didn't necessarily mean she was dead, right? "Does anyone know where Veronica St. John is?"

An older woman with graying hair raised her hand. "On the bridge," she said in a shaky voice. "That man, that murderer, is going to kill her at six o'clock. They took the prince somewhere else, too."

The clock on the wall said five fifty-five.

Joe's watch said the same.

He turned to look at Blue, who was already speaking into his headset. "Harvard and Cowboy, get your fannies down here on the double. We've got to get these people off this ship, pronto, and you're the ones who're gonna do it."

With Blue only a few steps behind, Joe slipped the strap of the Uzi over his shoulder along with his HK machine gun and headed back down the corridor at a run.

"I'm sorry," Diosdado said into the radio, sounding not one bit sorry. "Your promise to deliver twenty million to my Swiss bank account isn't enough. I gave you plenty of time to get the job done. Maybe you'll do it before the *next* hostage is killed, hmm? Think about it. This communication has ended."

With a flick of his wrist, he turned the radio off. He took a sip of coffee before he faced Veronica.

"I'm so sorry," he said. "Your government has let you down. They don't think you're worth twenty million dollars."

"I thought you wanted missiles," Veronica said. "Not money."

It was 6:01 p.m. Maybe if she could keep him talking, maybe if she could stall him, something, some miracle would happen. At the very least, she'd live a few minutes longer. She'd already lived one minute more than she'd thought she would.

"Either one would be fine," Diosdado said with a shrug. He turned to his guard. "Where is our little prince? I need him in here."

The man nodded and left the room.

Veronica felt incredibly calm, remarkably poised, considering that, miracles aside, she was going to get a bullet in her head in a matter of minutes.

She wasn't going to see another sunrise. She wasn't going to see Joe's beautiful smile, hear his contagious laughter again. She wasn't going to get a chance to tell him that she'd been wrong, that she wanted him for however long he was willing to give her.

Facing her own death made her see it all so clearly. She loved Joe Catalanotto. So what if he was a Navy SEAL. It was who he was, what he did. It was quite probably the reason she'd fallen in love with him. He was the best of the best in so many different ways. If by being a SEAL, he had to live on the edge and cheat death, so be it. She would learn to cope.

But she wasn't going to have a chance to do that. Because of her own fears and weaknesses, she'd pushed Joe away. She'd given up the few moments of happiness she could have had with him. She'd given up a lingering kiss goodbye. She'd given up a phone call that could have been filled with whispered "I love you's" instead of stilted apologies and chilly regrets.

How ironic that *she* was the one who was going to die a violent and horrible death.

Four minutes past six.

"What could be taking them so long?" Diosdado mused. He smiled at Veronica. "I'm so sorry, dear. I know you must be anxious to get this over with. I'd do it myself, but when Prince Tedric comes in, we're going to play a little game. Do you want to know the rules?"

Veronica looked into the eyes of the man who was going to kill her. "Why do you do this?" she asked.

"Because I can." The eyes narrowed slightly. "You're not afraid, are you?" he asked.

She was terrified. But she was damned if she was going to let *him* know that. She replied, "I'm saddened. There's a man that I love, and he's never going to know just how much I really do love him."

Diosdado laughed. "Isn't that tragic," he said. "You're just as pathetic as the rest of them. And to think, for a moment I was actually considering sparing you."

Five minutes past six.

He'd never had any intention of sparing her. It was just another of his head games. Veronica didn't allow any expression to cross her face.

"You didn't let me tell you about this game we're going to play," the terrorist continued. "It's called 'Who's the Killer?' When Prince Tedric comes in, I'll put a gun on the table over here." He patted the tabletop. "And then, with *my* gun on him, I'll order him to pick up that gun and fire a bullet into your head." He laughed. "Do you think he'll do it?"

"You aren't afraid he'll turn and use the gun on you?"

"Prince Tedric?" Diosdado blew out a burst of disparaging air. "No. The man has no . . . backbone." He shook his head. "No, it will be *your* brains on these nice windows, not mine."

The door was pushed tentatively open, and Prince Tedric came onto the bridge. He was still wearing his cowboy hat, pulled low over his face. But his jacket was unbuttoned. That was odd—surely a sign of his despondency. Veronica had never seen him look anything but fastidious.

"Your Royalness," Diosdado said. He swooped low in a mocking bow. "I believe you are familiar with Miss Veronica St. John, yes?"

Tedric nodded. "Yes," he said. "I know Ronnie."

Ronnie?

Veronica looked up at Tedric in surprise—and met Joe's warm brown gaze.

Joe! Here?

The rush of emotions was intense. Veronica had never been so glad to see anyone in her entire life. Or so frightened. *Lord, please, don't let Joe be killed, too....*

"Get down," Joe mouthed silently.

"We're going to play a little game," Diosdado was saying.

"I've got a game for you," Joe said in Tedric's Ustanzian accent. "It's called 'Show-and-Tell.'"

He pulled the biggest machine gun Veronica had ever seen in her life out from under his open jacket and aimed it at Diosdado.

"I show you my gun," Joe finished in his regular voice, "and you freeze. Then tell your army to surrender."

Diosdado didn't freeze. He lifted his gun.

Veronica dove for the floor as Joe opened fire. The noise was incredible, and the smell of gunpowder filled the air. But just as quickly as it started, it stopped. And then Joe was next to her on the floor, pulling her into his arms.

"Ronnie! God, tell me you're all right!"

She clung to his neck. "Oh, Joe!" She pulled back. "Are *you* all right?" He seemed to be in one piece, despite all of the bullets that had been flying just moments earlier.

"He didn't hurt you, did he?"

Veronica shook her head.

He kissed her, hard, on the mouth and she closed her eyes, pulling him closer, kissing him back with as much strength and passion. She welcomed his familiar taste, giddy with relief and a sense of homecoming she'd never experienced before. He'd come to save her. Somehow he'd known, and he'd come.

"Well," Joe said, his voice husky as he drew back. "I guess this is probably the one situation where you'd be indisputably glad to see me, huh?" He smiled, but there was a flash of remorse in his eyes as he took off Tedric's jacket, revealing some kind of dark uniform and vest underneath.

He was serious. He honestly thought the only reason she was so happy to see him was because he had come to save her life. "No, Joe—" she said, but he stopped her, standing and pulling her to her feet.

"Come on, baby, we've got to get moving," Joe said. "In about thirty seconds, this place is going to be crawling with tangos who heard that gunfire. We've got to get out of here."

"Joe—"

"Tell me while we're moving," he said, not unkindly, as he pulled her toward the door. She hesitated only a second, glancing back over her shoulder at where Diosdado had stood only moments before.

"Is he . . . ?"

Joe nodded. "Yeah." Holding her hand, he led her gently down the corridor. She was shaking slightly, but otherwise seemed okay. Of course, it was entirely possible that the shock of what she'd just been through hadn't set in. Still, they had to move while they could. "Can you run?" he asked.

"Yes," she said.

They set off down the corridor at an easy trot.

She was still holding his hand, and she squeezed it slightly. "I love you," she said.

Joe glanced at her. Her eyes were bright with unshed tears, but she managed to smile as she met his gaze. "I didn't think I'd get the chance to tell you that ever again," she explained. "And I know we're not out of danger, so I wanted to make sure you knew, in case—"

Veronica was right—they *weren't* out of danger. They were at the opposite end of the ship from the extraction point, and the tangos had surely been alerted to the fact that there were intruders on board. They had surely noticed that their hostages were missing and their leader was dead. SEAL Team Ten had stirred up one hell of a hornet's nest—and Joe and Veronica were still in the middle of it.

But Joe wasn't about to tell Veronica that. They *could* pull this off. Damn it, they *would* pull this off. He was a SEAL and he was armed to the teeth. Several dozen terrorists didn't stand a chance against him. Hell, with stakes this high, with the life of the woman he loved at risk, he could take on several hundred and win.

Joe slowed, peering around a corner, making sure they weren't about to run head-on into a pack of terrorists. Veronica loved him, and even though she didn't love him enough to want to marry him, he didn't care anymore. He honestly didn't care. If he'd been five minutes later, if that evil bastard Diosdado hadn't wanted to play games with his victims, if any number of things had been different, he would have lost Veronica permanently. The thought made him crazy. She could have been killed, and he would be alone, without her forever and ever.

But she hadn't been killed. They'd both been given a second chance, and Joe wasn't going to waste it. And he wanted to make his feelings clear to her—now—before she walked away from him again.

"When this is all over," he said almost conversationally, "after you're off this ship and safely back onshore, you're going to have to get used to me coming around to visit you. You don't have to marry me, Ronnie. It doesn't have to be anything permanent. But I've got to tell you right now—I have no intention of letting this thing between us drop, do you follow?"

Silently, she nodded.

"Good," Joe said. "You don't have to go out with me in public. You don't have to acknowledge our relationship at all—not to your friends, not to your family. I'll keep sneaking in your back door, baby, if that's the way you want it. You can just go on slumming, indefinitely. I don't give a damn, because I love you." To hell with his pride. To hell with it all. He'd take her any way he could get her.

"Slumming?" Veronica echoed, surprise in her voice. "What—"

"Beg your pardon, Romeo," came Blue's voice over Joe's headset, and Joe held up his hand, cutting Veronica off, "but I thought you might want to know that I've extracted with my royal luggage. Ronnie's the last civilian on board. The tangos know something's up, so move it, Cat—fast. The USS *Watkins* is moving into position, picking up the IBS's with the hostages. I'm coming back to the *Majestic* to assist you—"

"No," Joe interrupted. Veronica was watching him, with that look on her face that meant she was dying to speak. He shook his head, touching his headset as he spoke to his XO. "No, Blue, I need you to stay with the prince," he ordered. "But make sure there's a boat waiting for me and Ronnie at the bottom of that rope at the bow of this ship."

"You got it," Blue said. "See you on the *Watkins*."

"Check," Joe replied.

Veronica watched Joe. *Slumming?* What had he meant? Then her words came back to her. *Different worlds.* She'd talked about their different worlds when she'd turned down his marriage proposal. She'd been referring to the differences between his matter-of-fact response to danger, his thrill for adventure, and her fears of letting him go. Had he somehow misunderstood her? Had he actually thought she'd been talking about their supposed class differences—assuming something as absurd as class differences even existed? Could he actually have thought she was put off by something as ridiculous as where he came from or where he grew up?

Veronica opened her mouth, about to speak, when suddenly, from somewhere on the ship, there was an enormous, swooshing noise, like a rocket being launched.

"What was *that?*" Veronica breathed.

But Joe was listening again, listening to the voices over his headset.

"Check," he said into his microphone. He turned toward Veronica. "The T's are firing artillery at the hostages. Return fire," he ordered. He listened again. "You're gonna have to," he said tersely. "We're down below, outside the game room, but that's gonna change real soon. I'll keep you informed of my position. You just use that high-tech equipment and make sure you aim when you shoot. Fire now. Do you copy? Fire *now.*"

"My Lord!" Veronica said. Joe had just given an order for the men on the USS *Watkins* to return fire at the cruise ship— while she and Joe were still on board!

A deafening explosion the likes of which Veronica had never heard before thundered around them. The missile from the USS *Watkins* rocked the entire ship, seeming to lift it out of the water and throw it back down.

Joe grabbed Veronica's hand and pulled her with him down the hallway.

"Okay, *Watkins,*" he said over his headset. "We're heading away from the game room, toward the bow of the ship." There was a flight of stairs leading up toward the deck. Joe motioned for Veronica to hang back as he crawled up and peeked over the edge. He motioned with his hand for her to follow him. "Heading toward the recreation deck," he said into his microphone as he climbed up the steps and got his bearings, hanging back in the shadows and looking around. Veronica wasn't sure what he saw, but it didn't make him happy. "We're not going to make it to the extraction point," he said. "We've got to find another way off—"

Then Joe saw it—the perfect escape vehicle—and smiled. Diosdado's helicopters were sitting there, waiting to be hijacked. But this time by the good guys.

They were twenty yards from the helicopter. Twenty yards from freedom.

"Heading for the choppers up on the deck," he said into his mike. "Keep those missiles coming in, but keep 'em clear of us."

Fifteen yards. Ten. God, they were going to make it. They were—

All hell broke loose.

It was a small squad of T's—only about five of them—but they came out of nowhere.

Joe had his gun up and firing as he stepped in front of Veronica. He felt the slap of a bullet hit him low in his gut, beneath the edge of his flak jacket, but he felt no pain, only anger.

Damn it, he wasn't going to let Ronnie die. No way in *hell* was he going to let her die. Not now. Not when he was so close to getting her to safety...

His bullets plowed through the terrorists, taking them down, or driving them away from him to cover. But the sound of gunfire drew more of them toward him.

His mind registered the first sensations of pain. *Pain?* The word didn't come close to describing the white-hot, searing agony he felt with every step, every movement. He was gutshot, and every pounding beat of his heart was pumping his blood out of his body. It wouldn't be long before he bled to death. Still firing his gun, he tried to stanch the flow. He'd been trained as a field medic—all SEALs were. He'd been trained to provide first aid to his men, and even to himself. He needed to apply pressure, but it was tough with a wound this size. The bullet had penetrated him, leaving an exit wound in his back, through which he also bled.

God, the pain.

Through it all, he kept going. If they could reach the chopper, he could still fly Ronnie out of here. If they could reach the chopper, bleeding or not, dying or not, he could get her to the *Watkins*.

The door to the bird was open—God was on his side—but Joe didn't seem to have the strength to push Veronica in. "Dear Lord, you're bleeding," he heard her say. He felt her push him up and into the cockpit. And then, damned if she didn't grab his extra gun, and turn and fire out the open door, keeping the T's at bay while, through a fog, Joe started the engine. He could fly anything, he told himself over and over, hoping that the litany would somehow make his brain respond. They didn't make a chopper he couldn't handle. But his arms felt like lead and his legs weren't working right. Still, he had to do it. He had to, or Veronica was going to die alongside him.

And then, miracle of miracles, they were up. They were in the air and moving away from the ship.

"We're clear of the *Majestic*," Joe rasped into his microphone. "Launch a full-scale attack."

The world blurred for a second, and then snapped sharply into focus.

That was smoke he saw coming from the engine. Sweet Jesus, the chopper must have sustained a direct hit. Somehow, Joe had gotten the damned thing up, but it wasn't going to stay in the air too much longer.

"Tell them you need a medic standing by," Veronica said.

"We've got bigger problems," Joe told her.

She saw the smoke, and her eyes widened, but her voice didn't falter as she told him again, "You've been shot. Make sure someone on the *Watkins* knows that, Joe."

"We're not going to make it to the *Watkins*," Joe said. He spoke into his microphone. "Blue, I need you, man."

"I'm here, and I see you," Blue's familiar Southern drawl sounded in his ears. "You're leaving a trail of smoke like a cheap cigar, Cat. I'm coming out to meet you."

"Good," Joe said. "Because I'm going to bring this bird low, and Ronnie's gonna jump out into the water, you copy?"

"I'm not going anywhere without you," Veronica said, adding loudly, loud enough for Blue to hear, "Joe's been hit, and he's bleeding badly."

"I have a medic standing by," Blue said to Joe. "Is it bad, Cat?"

Joe ignored Blue's question. "I'm right behind you, Ronnie," he said to Veronica, knowing damn well that he was telling her a lie. "But I'm not going to ditch this bird until you're clear."

He could see her indecision in her eyes. She didn't want to leave him.

God, he was getting light-headed, and this chopper was getting harder and harder to handle as he hovered ten feet above the water's surface. The combination was *not* good.

"Go," he said.

"Joe—"

"Baby, *please* . . ." He couldn't hold on much longer.

"Promise you'll be right behind me?"

He nodded, praying to God for forgiveness for his lie. "I promise."

She slid open the door. "I want us to get married right away," she said, and then she was gone.

The water was cold as ice.

It surrounded Veronica, squeezing her chest as she surfaced and tried to take in a breath of air.

But then a boat was there, and hands reached for her, pulling her up.

Veronica ignored the cold as she turned to watch the chopper, hovering above the waves, its whirling blades turning the ocean into choppy whitecaps. Someone wrapped a blanket around her— Blue, it was Blue McCoy, Joe's executive officer.

The plume of smoke from the helicopter was darker, thicker. And the chopper seemed to lurch instead of holding still.

"Why won't he jump?" she wondered aloud.

Before she finished speaking, the helicopter jerked forward and down—into the water.

She could hear shouting—it was Blue's voice—and she couldn't believe that the noise—some noise, *any* noise, wasn't coming from her own throat.

The helicopter was sinking beneath the waves, taking Joe with it, taking all her hopes and dreams for the future away from her.

"No!" she cried, the word torn from her raggedly.

"I'm going in after him." It was Blue. "Pull this boat closer."

"Sir, I can't let you do that," said a young man in a naval uniform. His face was pale. "If the chopper doesn't pull you under, the water's so cold, it'll kill you. You won't last more than five minutes before hypothermia sets in."

"Pull the damned boat closer, Ensign," Blue said, his voice as cold as the Alaskan water. "I'm a SEAL, and that's my commander down there. I'm going after him."

The water was cold as ice.

It roused Joe from his fog as it splashed him in the face.

Damn, he'd gone down. He didn't remember going down. All he remembered was Ronnie—

Ronnie telling him that she wanted to... marry him?

The last pocket of air bubbled out of the helicopter cockpit.

No way was he going to die. Ronnie wanted to *marry* him. No way was he going to *drown. Or bleed to death,* damn it.

The water was cold as hell, but it would slow his bleeding.

All he had to do was get his arms and legs to work.

But he hurt.

Every single cell in his body hurt, and it took so much god-dammed effort to lift even a finger.

This was worse than anything he'd ever experienced, worse even than Hell Week, that torturous final week of SEAL training that he'd lived through so many years ago.

He'd never wanted anything as badly as he'd wanted to be a SEAL. It had kept him going through the nonstop exertion, through the pain, through the torturous physical demands. *"You got to want it badly enough,"* one of his instructors had shouted at them, day after day, hour after hour. And Joe had. He'd wanted to be a SEAL. He'd wanted it badly enough.

He'd wanted to be a SEAL almost as much as he wanted Veronica St. John.

And she was there, up there, above the surface of that freezing water, waiting for him. All he had to do was kick his legs, push himself free and he would have her. Forever. All he had to do was want it badly enough. . . .

Veronica stared at the water, at the place where first the helicopter and then Blue had disappeared.

Please, God, if you give me this, I'll never ask for anything ever again. . . .

Seconds ticked into one minute. Two. Three . . .

Was it possible for a man to hold his breath for this long, let alone search for a wounded, drowning man . . . ?

Please, God.

And then, all at once, a body erupted from beneath the surface of the water. Veronica peered into the area lit by the searchlights. Was that one head or . . .

Two! Two heads! Blue had found Joe!

A cheer went up from the sailors on board the boat, and they quickly maneuvered closer to the two men, and pulled them out.

Dear God, it *was* Joe, and he was breathing. Veronica stood aside as the medics sliced his wet clothes from his body. Oh, Lord, he'd been shot in the abdomen, just above his hip. She watched, clutching her own blanket more tightly around her as he was wrapped in a blanket and an IV was attached to his arm.

"Cat was coming up as I was going down after him," Blue said, respect heavy in his voice. "I think he would have made it, even without me. He didn't want to die. Not today."

Joe was floating in and out of consciousness, yet he turned his head, searching for something, searching for . . .

"Ronnie." His voice was just a whisper, but he reached for her, and she took his hand.

"I'm here," she said, pressing his fingers to her lips.

"Did you mean it?" He was fighting hard to remain conscious. He was fighting, and winning. "When you said you'd marry me?"

"Yes," she said, fighting her own battle against the tears that threatened to escape.

Joe nodded. "You know, I'm not going to change," he said. "I can't pretend to be something I'm not. I'm not a prince or a duke or—"

Veronica cut him off with a kiss. "You're my prince," she said.

"Your parents are going to hate me."

"My parents are going to *love* you," she countered. "Nearly as much as I do."

He smiled then, ignoring his pain, reaching up to touch the side of her face. "You really think this could work?"

"Do you love me?" Veronica asked.

"Absolutely."

"Then it will work." The boat was pulling up alongside of the USS *Watkins,* where a doctor was waiting. From what Veronica had gathered from the medics, they believed the bullet had passed through Joe's body, narrowly missing his vital organs. He'd lost a lot of blood, and had to be stitched up and treated for infection, but it could have been worse. It could have been *far* worse.

Joe felt himself placed onto a stretcher. He had to release Ronnie's hand as he was lifted up and onto the deck of the *Watkins.*

"I love you," she called.

He was smiling as the doctor approached him, smiling as the nurse added painkiller to his intravenous tube, smiling as he gave in to the drug and let the darkness finally close in around him.

Joe stared up at the white ceiling in sick bay for a good long time before he figured out where he was and why he couldn't move. He was still strapped down to a bed. He hurt like hell. He'd been shot. He'd been stitched up.

He'd been promised a lifetime filled with happiness and Veronica St. John's beautiful smile.

Veronica Catalanotto. He smiled at the idea of her taking his name.

And then Blue was leaning over him, releasing the restraints. "Damn, Cat," he said in his familiar drawl. "The doc said you were grinning like a fool when he brought you in here, and here you are again, smiling like a fox in a henhouse.''

"Where's Ronnie?" Joe whispered. His throat was so dry, and his mouth felt gummy. He tried to moisten his dry lips with his tongue.

Blue turned away, murmuring something to the nurse before he turned back to Joe, lifting a cup of water to his friend's lips. "She's getting checked by the doctor," he told Joe.

Joe's smile disappeared, the soothing drink of water forgotten. "She okay?"

Blue nodded. "She's just getting a blood test," he said. "Apparently she needs one."

"Why?"

"Because I'm hoping to get married," Ronnie said, leaning forward to kiss him gently on the mouth. "That is, if you still have that ring. If you still want me."

Joe gazed up at her. Her hair was down, loose and curling around her shoulders. She was wearing a sailor suit that was several sizes too large, white flared pants and a white shirt, sleeves rolled up several times. She was wearing no makeup, and her freshly scrubbed face looked impossibly young—and anxious—as she waited for his answer. "Hell, yes," he somehow managed to say.

She smiled, and Joe felt his mouth curve up into an answering smile as he lost himself in the ocean color of her eyes. "Do you still want *me?*"

Blue moved quietly toward the door. "I guess I'll leave you two a—"

Ronnie turned then, looking up at Joe's XO and best friend. "Wait," she said. "Please?" She looked back at Joe. "I'll marry you, but there's one condition."

Blue shifted his weight uncomfortably.

"Anything," Joe said to Veronica. "I'd promise you anything. Just name it."

"It's not something *you* can promise me," she said. She looked up at Blue again, directly into his turquoise eyes. "I need Blue's promise—to keep Joe safe and alive."

Blue nodded slowly, taking her words seriously. "I'd die for him," he said, matter-of-factly.

Veronica had seen them in action. She'd seen Blue dive into the icy Alaskan waters after Joe, and she knew he spoke the truth. It wasn't going to make her fear for Joe's safety disappear, but it *was* going to make it easier.

"I didn't want to marry you because I was—I am—afraid that you're going to get yourself killed," she said, turning back to Joe. "I knew I couldn't ask you to leave the SEALs and..."

She saw his eyes narrow slightly as he understood her words. "Then..."

Veronica felt more than saw Blue slip from the room as she leaned forward to kiss Joe's lips. "I wasn't 'slumming.'" She mock shuddered. "Nasty expression, that."

He laced his fingers through her hair, wariness and concern in his eyes. "I can't leave the SEALs, baby—"

She silenced him with another kiss. "I know. I'm not asking you to. I'm not going to quit my job and become a career navy wife, either," Veronica told Joe. "I'll travel and work—the same as you. But whenever you can get leave time, I'll be there."

As she gazed into Joe's midnight-dark eyes, the last of his reservations drained away, leaving only love—pure and powerful. But then he frowned slightly. "Your ring's back in Little Creek," he said.

"I don't need a ring to know how much you love me," Veronica whispered.

Joe touched his chest, realized he was wearing a hospital gown, then pressed the call button for the nurse.

A young man appeared almost instantly. "Problem, sir?"

"What happened to my uniform?" Joe demanded.

"There wasn't much left of it after the medics cut it off you, sir." The nurse gestured toward a small table just out of reach of the bed. "Your personal gear is in that drawer."

"Thanks, pal," Joe said.

"Can I get you anything, sir?"

"Just some privacy," Joe told him, and the nurse left as quickly as he had come.

Joe turned to Veronica. "Check in that drawer for me, will you, baby?"

Veronica stood up and crossed to the table. She pulled open the drawer. There were three guns inside, several rounds of ammunition, something that looked decidedly like a hand grenade, a deadly-looking knife, several bills of large denominations, a handful of change...

"There should be a gold pin," Joe said. "It's called a 'Budweiser.'"

A gold pin in the shape of an eagle with both an ocean trident and a gun, it was Joe's SEAL pin, one of his most precious possessions. He'd gotten it on the day he graduated, the day he became a Navy SEAL. Veronica took it from the drawer. It felt solid and heavy in her hand as she carried it to Joe.

But he didn't take it from her. He wrapped her fingers around it. "I want you to have it."

Veronica stared at him.

"There are two things I've never given anyone," he said quietly. "One is this pin. The other is my heart." He smiled at her. "Now you got 'em both. Forever."

He pulled her head down to him and kissed her so gently, so sweetly, so perfectly.

And Veronica realized again what she'd known for quite some time.

She had found her prince.

*   *   *   *   *

▼ I N T I M A T E M O M E N T S ®
™ _Silhouette_ ®

COMING NEXT MONTH

#721 WILD BLOOD—Naomi Horton
Wild Hearts

Jett Kendrick was untamable, and Kathleen Patterson had the broken heart to prove it. She hadn't even been able to hold on to their baby before tragedy struck. So why, fifteen years later, was Jett looking at her with guilt—and longing—especially when his teenage boy was near?

#722 BORROWED BRIDE—Patricia Coughlin

One minuté Gabrielle Flanders was wedding-bound, the next she'd been abducted from the church! Connor DeWolfe claimed she was in grave danger—that he was the only man she could trust. But Gaby didn't think her "honeymoon" was the time to find out...or was it?

#723 THE ONE WHO ALMOST GOT AWAY—Alicia Scott
The Guiness Gang

She always got her man—and Jake Guiness was no exception. The infuriating playboy was Regina O'Doul's only lead in the case of her life, so she got _close_. But somehow pretending to be lovers had led to the real thing—and to very real danger for them both....

#724 UNBROKEN VOWS—Frances Williams

Ex-SEAL David Chandler had nothing left to give—but for Cara Merrill, he would certainly try. The gutsy beauty needed his soldiering skills to locate her ex-fiancé. But amid their dangerous jungle mission, David found himself wanting Cara all for himself....

#725 HERO IN HIDING—Kay David

Mercy Hamilton had one rule about Mr. Right: she had to trust him. Then dark, handsome Rio Barrigan challenged her beliefs. He was all mystery—at times warm and loving, at others almost deadly. And though he broke her cardinal rule, Mercy couldn't help but believe in him—and their love.

#726 THE BABY ASSIGNMENT—Cathryn Clare
Assignment: Romance

Agent Jack Cotter knew about guns, bad guys...but babies? On that subject he knew absolutely nothing. But single-mom-on-the-run Shelby Henderson and her bouncing baby girl taught him all he needed to know about family and fatherhood. Jack only hoped they would all survive to put what he'd learned into practice.

Take 4 bestselling love stories FREE

Plus get a FREE surprise gift!

This July, watch for the delivery of...

An exciting new miniseries that appears in a different Silhouette series each month. It's about love, marriage—and Daddy's unexpected need for a baby carriage!

Daddy Knows Last unites five of your favorite authors as they weave five connected stories about baby fever in New Hope, Texas.

- **THE BABY NOTION** by Dixie Browning
  (SD#1011, 7/96)

- **BABY IN A BASKET** by Helen R. Myers
  (SR#1169, 8/96)

- **MARRIED...WITH TWINS!**
  by Jennifer Mikels
  (SSE#1054, 9/96)

- **HOW TO HOOK A HUSBAND (AND A BABY)**
  by Carolyn Zane
  (YT#29, 10/96)

- **DISCOVERED: DADDY** by Marilyn Pappano
  (IM#746, 11/96)

Daddy Knows Last arrives in July...only from

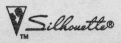

DKLT

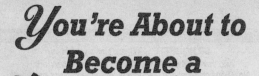

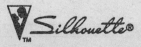